THE FOUR-PART KEY

THE ALDORAN CHRONICLES
- BOOK THREE -

written by
MICHAEL WISEHART

Copyright

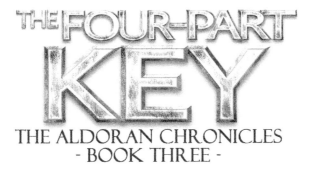

THE FOUR-PART KEY

THE ALDORAN CHRONICLES
- BOOK THREE -

Books

STREET RATS OF ARAMOOR

(First book takes place 20 years prior to The Aldoran Chronicles)

Book 1 | Banished

Book 2 | Hurricane

Book 3 | Rockslide

THE ALDORAN CHRONICLES

Prequel | Shackled

Book 1 | The White Tower

Book 2 | Plague of Shadows

Book 3 | The Four-Part Key

Map of Aldor - West

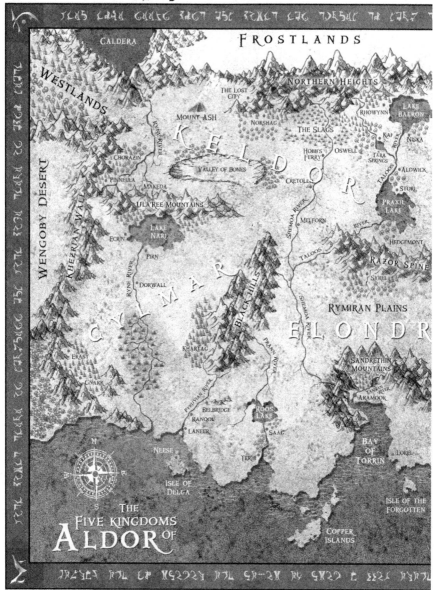

Hi-Resolution maps in the Shop:

« www.michaelwisehart.com/shop »

Map of Aldor - East

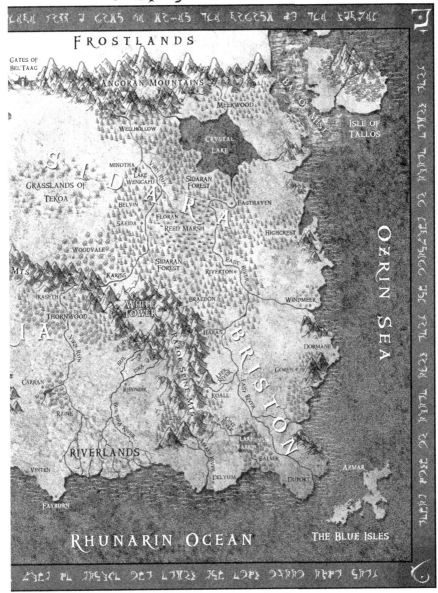

Hi-Resolution maps in the Shop:

« *www.michaelwisehart.com/shop* »

Map of Aramoor

1. LUMBER YARDS	5. WILDFIRE COMPOUND	8. BAYSIDE	12. SHIPPING YARDS	16. OLD MERCHANT DISTRICT
2. THE ROCKSLIDE COMPOUND	6. LANCER BARRACKS	9. THE TEMPLE	13. THE PIT	17. THE WARRENS
3. LANCER CORPS	7. SANDSTORM COMPOUND	10. KING'S SQUARE	14. THE ROYAL PALACE	
4. THE GUILD		11. AVALANCHE COMPOUND	15. THE GRANARY	

ARAMOOR

Hi-Resolution maps in the Shop:

« www.michaelwisehart.com/shop »

Map of Easthaven

Easthaven

1. East Bridge 2. East Inn 3. Mangora's 4. Barracks
5. Sidaran Assembly Hall 6. Overlord Barl's Estate 7. Dockworks
8. Orlyn's Apothecary 9. Harbor House 10. Reloria's Sweet Shop

Hi-Resolution maps in the Shop:

« www.michaelwisehart.com/shop »

Important Notice

NOTE: If you have not yet read the Aldoran Chronicles prequel, entitled "Shackled," or the first book in the Street Rats of Aramoor series, entitled "Banished," you need to put this book down and read those.

The characters and storyline in those books play a very important role in this third addition to The Aldoran Chronicles.

You will thank me later…

Chapter 1 | Ty

HE FIRST OF THE winter snow left a thin blanket across the alleyway behind the Easthaven Harbor House. It wasn't much more than a heavy dusting, and Ty knew its beauty would be short-lived, as the sun was sure to melt it away before the council meeting was over. Still, it did leave him with a momentary sense of peace, a feeling he was little acquainted with these days.

He stood quietly on the back step and watched his breath rise into the air. He felt different. Sure, the anger was still there, the desire to seek justice, but the rage was gone. It was as though someone had lifted an enormous weight off his shoulders, and for the first time in a long while, his thoughts were his own. With the witch's hold severed, and the last of the book's magic excised from his mind, Ty felt almost hollow, as if a piece of him were missing. He wondered how long the feeling would linger.

He hoped not too long.

"You still feel her, don't you?"

Ty cocked his head. His brother stood behind him in the doorway, taking up most of it with his broad shoulders.

"I see the way you look at that finger," Breen said, nodding at Ty's hand.

Ty hadn't noticed, but he was thumbing the empty spot where the glass ring had been. It had only been a week since Nyalis had purged him of the numori's dark tendrils, the pages of Mangora's book having done more damage than he knew. It was scary how something as innocent as a book could have nearly toppled the kingdoms of Aldor. If Mangora had gotten her way, and the Easthaven wielder council hadn't been there to stop her, she might have used Ty to kill nearly the entire Provincial Authority in one fell swoop.

The wizard had said the ring in itself wasn't dangerous. It simply put a voice to the words in the book. But Nyalis figured it was best that the artifact remained with him for safekeeping.

Ty let his hand drop to his side. "I don't know if I'll ever be rid of the feeling." He shivered as he thought about what he'd done under Mangora's control, how he'd been forced to watch as the witch used his abilities against him, against his family, his friends. If he had a way to expel those memories, he would do it. He would cut them out with a knife.

His dreams were plagued by nightmares. The worst of which involved Gilly. The look in the little man's eyes as Ty engulfed him in flame was more than he could bear. But that wasn't him, he had to keep reminding himself. It was the witch. Ty turned and looked up at his brother. He read the concern in his eyes. "Will they ever forgive me?"

Breen took a deep breath and slowly released, white mist curling above his head, forming a sort of spiral snake that widened as it rose. "The more important question is: Will you ever forgive yourself?"

Ty could feel the weight of his own guilt in his brother's eyes, and he looked away. He hated how Breen could peer inside him, and with one question, drive straight to the heart of the problem. "I don't know."

Breen waited a moment before stepping back inside. "Come on. They're waiting."

Ty nodded, expelling one last puff of mist before joining his brother.

Master Eliab stood beside the kitchen table, cradling his double-bolt crossbow like a newborn child. "Winter'th upon uth," he said, stepping over to the door and taking one last look outside before shutting it. "It'll be a cold one for thure. Mark my wordth." His mouth widened into a bright, toothless grin. He threw the door's bracer into place and started across the room, motioning for the two to follow.

They made their way down the hall to the next room, then through the open door and down the stairs to the cellar. The wielder council used the cellar as a meeting place, as well as a temporary shelter for wielders who needed a place to hide. It seemed like a lifetime since Ty's father had first brought him here and introduced him to the council. So much had happened since that night; it seemed almost a distant memory.

Ty kept to Master Eliab's heels as the former lancer captain guided them across the room to the chamber on the other side, where the council carried out its meetings. To the left and right were doors that led to rooms that had been arranged for displaced wielders. Each was barely large enough to fit a cot and small table, but those they sheltered were extremely grateful for them.

Ty balled his fists as the memory of Saleena's face flashed across his mind. She was another innocent victim who had lost her life in the White Tower's pursuit of him. She had been the last to seek shelter at the Harbor House.

Eliab stopped outside the door leading into the council's meeting chamber and knocked. Ty turned to see if his brother was watching and quickly wiped his palms down the front of his trousers, not wanting him to see how nervous he truly was. It was the first time he'd been in the same room with the other members since the Sidaran Assembly Hall, when Mangora had used him to try killing the entire council.

"Come in," Veldon's gruff voice called out from the other side. Veldon was the Easthaven dockmaster and head of the wielder council.

Ty stuffed his hands in his pockets and squeezed the material. Willing participant or not, he wasn't looking forward to this reunion. He startled when Breen placed a hand on his shoulder.

"I'm fine," he reassured his brother with a nod.

Eliab opened the door. "Mathter Breen and Mathter Ty have arrived." The Harbor House gatekeeper stepped aside to let them pass.

"We were starting to wonder if you were going to make it," Veldon said from the head of the table on the right. "Thank you, Eliab."

Eliab nodded but waited for the two to enter before stepping out and shutting the door behind them.

Nearly every seat around the long table was filled. Even Nyalis was there, sitting at the other end, quietly conversing with Ty's sister. Adarra seemed enthralled with whatever the old wizard was saying. Mistress Reloria, sitting just to the other side of Nyalis, fiddled with her hat, looking particularly on edge. In fact, most of those around the table looked anxious in one way or another: fleeting glances, nervous fidgeting, flustered adjustments of clothing and jewelry.

Strangely enough, the only person who seemed unaffected by Ty's presence was Gilly, and he was the one person who had the most to be bothered by, considering the last time Ty had seen the little man was when he had tried to burn him alive. Ty heard Gilly's screams in his mind as he lowered his head and followed Breen around the table to the two empty seats beside his father.

Breen took the chair next to Fraya, and Ty sat in the open chair on his other side, staring down at the buttons on his jacket. He tugged on each, attempting to distract himself so he wouldn't have to face the people he'd hurt.

"You're looking better," Master Orlyn's voice rang out from across the table.

When no one answered, Ty spared a fleeting glance in the old apothecary's direction. "I feel better," he said with a forced smile, then lowered his gaze back to his lap.

"Can we be sure that no one else is listening in on our conversation?" Feoldor asked, shifting uncomfortably in his seat between Reloria and Orlyn.

"The numori's magic is gone," Nyalis said, getting to the heart of what Feoldor was asking. "But the effects might be longer lasting."

"And what effects are those?" Ty's father asked.

Ty could feel the old wizard's gaze burrowing into him, and as bad as he wanted to look, he kept his head lowered.

"Nothing to fear, I assure you. A bit of rest, and he'll be back to his old chipper self in no time." The sarcasm in the wizard's voice was unmistakable.

"What aren't you telling us?" Orlyn asked. "No offense, but you tend to have a way of leaving things out. Offering half-truths and partial explanations."

Ty could almost hear the wizard smiling as he leaned back in his seat. "What our young Master Ty seems to be suffering from is a lack of confidence, brought on by an acute sense of guilt, topped with a debilitating need for reconciliation."

The room went silent.

"What in the flaming pits are you talking about?" Feoldor blurted out, the only one brave enough to do so. "I didn't understand half of what you just said."

Breen mumbled something under his breath, but all Ty could catch was *Feoldor* and *two-headed donkey*.

"Ty blames himself for what happened," Nyalis said.

Ty spared a quick peek around the table to catch the others' response, stopping before he reached Gilly's seat. He knew he needed to say something, but before he could muster the courage to do so, Feoldor cleared his throat and fluffed his side whiskers.

"Why didn't you just say so? Look here, boy," he said, grabbing Ty's attention. "There's plenty of blame to go around. I mean, sure, you might have been the one snooping through the witch's stuff and all, stealing her numori thingy—"

Reloria jabbed Feoldor in the side with her elbow. "That's hardly helpful."

"What? I was just trying to explain how—"

"What Feoldor's trying to say, dear," she said, "is that this wasn't your fault. We know it was Mangora."

Ty couldn't take the stares any longer. With a deep breath to steel his nerves, he stood. "I'd like to speak." When he had everyone's attention, he continued. "I'm sorry. Master Feoldor's right. I was the one who took the book. I was the one who listened to what it had to say. I was . . ." He stared at the faces around the table and finally lowered his head. "I was just so angry."

Ty's father laid a hand on Ty's arm, trying to coax him back to his seat. "It could have happened to any of us."

Ty shook his head. "No. It was me. I wanted Mangora dead so badly that I opened myself up to the book without question."

"But you didn't know it was her, silly," Ty's sister said. "You can't blame yourself for that."

"Adarra's right," Fraya added, releasing Breen's arm. "This isn't your fault. In fact, I'm just as much to blame as anyone. If I'd listened to Orlyn and not been so consumed with my healing, Saleena might still be alive." Her voice cracked. "She died because I wasn't paying close enough attention."

Orlyn grunted, his rune-covered staff shifting behind his seat as he scooted forward. "Now, let's don't go putting words in my mouth. What happened to Saleena could hardly be considered anyone's fault, my dear."

"Enough." Veldon scooted his seat back from the table and stood. "We are doing no one any favors, least of all ourselves, by sitting here harboring blame." He looked at Ty. "No one here holds you responsible for what happened. And if it will help to hear . . . We forgive you." He paused a moment to look around the table. "And I would like to point out that—"

Gilly stood, and everyone turned. The little man didn't come to the meetings that often, and when he did, he rarely participated beyond a friendly smile and a childlike wave at the girls, so any interaction on his part was clearly noted.

Ty tensed as the dwarfish man turned and hobbled around the back of the table, straight over to where he was standing. He wasn't sure what to expect. Suddenly, Gilly reached out and wrapped his arms around Ty's waist and hugged him.

Ty nearly started crying. In fact, the more he tried to stop it, the harder it became. Pretty soon, he was all but sobbing as he, too, reached down and wrapped his arms around Gilly's shoulders. More than one person was wiping their eyes by the time Gilly retook his seat.

Ty sat, his legs shaking to the point of nearly giving out. That one gesture had done more to heal what was broken inside him than all of the wizard's magic.

He looked around the table, warm smiles greeting him in return. Even Sheeva, on the far end beside Veldon, offered a partial grin, which looked oddly out of place for the short assassin.

Ty didn't know how he could earn back their trust, but he swore to himself he would find a way.

"Seems to me," Veldon continued, retaking his seat, "we could all use a little forgiveness. No one here's without mistake. Except perhaps our illustrious friend on the end there," he said half-jokingly as he gestured toward the wizard.

Nyalis stood, and all the light in the room dimmed, drawing everyone's attention. "Mistakes are what it means to be human," he said. "And I'm as human as they come." The room suddenly brightened. "Well, for the most part," he added with a cheeky grin. Nyalis had a strange sense of humor, one not everyone tended to get. "My point is, leave the past in the past. There are plenty of mistakes still to come, poor choices lurking around every corner. The one thing we don't have time for is to sit around wallowing in guilt over the ones we've already made." He made a point to look at Ty. "Learn from them and move on, because what is coming will be here before you know it."

"What is coming?" Orlyn asked.

Ty found himself leaning forward along with the rest of those at the table.

Nyalis scanned the room. "Uncertainty. Uncertainty is coming. And she can be a deadly adversary."

Ty shuddered. The room felt undeniably chilly, and it wasn't just the winter winds beating against the outside walls. Whatever was coming, he knew it had something to do with him. He only wished he understood more about why that was.

"Which is why it is so imperative that our young Master Ty here start his journey. The sooner he is able to find and return the Wizarding Keep of Aero'set, the better our chances will be."

"Winter is already upon us," Veldon said. "Wouldn't it be more prudent to wait until the weather has improved . . . say, spring?"

Nyalis paused. "Would it be more prudent? Yes. Is that what we should do? Absolutely not. We need Aero'set if we are to have any chance of surviving what's coming. What you've endured so far is merely a scuffle, a backyard brawl between schoolchildren. If this has done anything, it's shown us how unprepared we really are."

Ty looked at the others. Their despondent faces said it all. What they believed to have been a great victory and a justification of their skills seemed barely worth mentioning in the wizard's eyes. Then again, if Nyalis truly was as old as he claimed, Ty couldn't imagine the battles he had seen and fought.

Ty scooted to the edge of his seat. "I'm ready," he said. What better way to prove his worth than to bring back this fabled keep?

Nyalis smiled. "Then I suggest you pack."

Chapter 2 | Ty

REED MARSH! Have you lost your mind?" Ty's father struck the arm of his chair as he attempted to stare the old wizard down in the front room of their home.

Ty rarely saw his father this angry, or worried. The firelight from the hearth cast deep shadows across his father's face, accentuating his furrowed brows and the tightening around his mouth. Nyalis, on the other hand, who sat directly across from Ty's father, seemed calm.

Ty, Breen, and Adarra shared the sofa in front of the newly rebuilt bay window, quietly listening as the wizard explained Ty's upcoming journey.

"What could he possibly need to go into Reed Marsh for?" Ty's father asked. "There's razorbacks in there, not to mention quicksand, bog holes, and a hundred other deadly things. Not even the most daring of woodsmen would be foolish enough to step foot in that place."

Ty gulped, suddenly wondering if perhaps there was an easier way to earn the council's trust.

"It's where he'll find the first of the traveling mirrors," Nyalis said, his composure slipping as the first signs of frustration broke through in the form of his fingers tightening around the arm of his seat. "I have never said this task would be easy. In fact, I distinctly remember saying it would prove dangerous. But dangerous or not, it has to be done."

Ty's father was a big man, easily one of the largest in Easthaven, so when he spoke, most listened, but even he knew better than to go head-to-head with Nyalis unless there was good reason. With a heavy sigh, he turned and looked at Ty. There was a sense of defeat on his face as he slowly shook his head. "He's not ready. He still needs time to recover from that cursed book. Just look at how pale he is."

"He always looks pale," Breen said.

Ty kicked his brother in the shin.

"I find it all rather fascinating," Adarra chimed in, pen in hand and paper on her lap.

"You would," Ty countered. "If given half a chance, you'd probably volunteer to go along just to catalog the plants and animals." Ty looked at his father, his vow to earn back the trust of his family and friends urging him forward. "I can do it. I'm strong enough. You don't need to worry about me."

Ty raised his hand and drew on his fire. He could feel the warmth of the magic running down his arm. It was small at first, almost a trickle, but it gave him a sense of strength, a feeling he'd been trying to forget until now. Releasing it into his hand, the blue flames ignited and danced across his palm.

Ty's father leaned forward. "I'm your father. It's my job to worry. It's also my job to tell you when I think something is ill advised." Ty's father turned to Nyalis. "Is it really so important for him to go so soon? Would it be so terrible if he waited till spring like we discussed in the council meeting?"

Nyalis sighed and looked at Ty. "Believe me, I wish the circumstances weren't so grave, but as you've already seen, the enemy is at the door. They know where you are. Next time, they will come prepared."

Ty grimaced. "If what we faced was them *not* prepared, then I don't want to be here when they are." He scolded himself. Running and hiding and pretending everything was fine might have worked for the old Ty, but the new Ty needed to change. Apart from wanting to earn back everyone's trust, he wanted to make his mother proud, to make sure her death wasn't for nothing, to avenge it if he could. And if Nyalis was correct, bringing back the wizard's keep was the only way he could keep everyone safe.

"End of the week," Ty said as resolutely as he could while bearing up under the wizard's sharp gaze. "Give me till the end of the week, and I'll be ready."

Nyalis studied Ty's face a moment, then nodded. "Very well. I'll return on Eighthday." He stood and grabbed his staff from behind his chair and started for the front door. "Be ready at dawn."

Time had never passed so quickly for Ty as it did while preparing for his upcoming quest. He had no idea where he was going or what he would need when he got there. All Nyalis had said was there would be four tests he would have to face in order to bring back the wizards' keep, but he hadn't told him what those tests would be. The only help Ty had been given was a silver compass and the knowledge that the first leg of his journey would take him into one of the most dangerous places in Sidara: Reed Marsh.

By the time Sixthday had arrived, Ty's imagination had come up with all sorts of horrible ways he could die on this quest. He had worked himself into such a state that when his father suggested they ride into town that evening for a little diversion at the East Inn, Ty was the first one out the door. He also knew this might be his last chance to see Lyessa before he had to leave. She knew of his upcoming quest, but what he hadn't told her was how soon he was being asked to leave.

"Aren't you forgetting something?" Breen asked as he trudged across the yard toward the barn, where Ty was already waiting atop Waddle. He held up his hand. "Your cap."

Ty felt the top of his head and sighed. "Not again." He was having the hardest time remembering to keep the woolen hat on. He could have kicked himself for not remembering to ask Nyalis to change his white hair back to the ash blonde it had been before his battle with Mangora. At least with the frigid winter gusts, he had an excuse to wear the hat. He hated to think what it was going to be like during the summer.

"Everyone ready?" Ty's father asked as he swung up onto Your Highness and gave the horse a firm nudge. Your Highness raised his head with a snort and started down the lane toward the road.

Adarra was next, her thick cloak pulled tight as she guided Thistle along.

"Come on, Waddle, move your lazy backside," Ty griped, nudging his lethargic horse in the side with his boots. Waddle shook his head defiantly. "Standing here's just going to make you colder." Waddle cocked his head to look at Ty, then blew out his lips and started forward, eventually picking up speed to match the other horses' strides.

Behind Ty, Breen and Acorn patiently brought up the rear.

As predicted, the snow from earlier had all but melted, but with the sun now nearing the end of its trek across the sky, the fresh white powder was once more beginning to stick. All along the outer edge of the forest, spindly branches and evergreen needles could still be seen peeking through; however, the trees farther in that were shielded against the sun still had a full coat of white.

Ty loved the way the forest looked during the winter: the fresh snow, the long icicles, the colorful birds nesting in the lower branches. It was beautiful. The forest, like many of the creatures living within its protection, tended to sleep during the winter months, preparing for spring and its annual rebirth. Ty wished he could be so lucky. Sleep was hard to come by these days.

They passed the East Hill Orchard on their way into town. The trees here looked particularly barren, not that they looked much better during the spring and summer months, but at least then they would have had a few buds to prove they were still alive.

Ty put his hand in his jacket pocket, letting the pouch with Nyalis's compass roll between his fingers as he directed his thoughts back toward the upcoming mission. He barely paid half a glance to the icy river as they crossed the East Bridge and started through the lower part of town, his thoughts resting solely on the dangers that awaited him.

Instead of leaving the horses tied out front, they took them to the stables around back, where the guests generally paid to have their mounts fed and housed during their stay at the inn. However, because of their late arrival, they found the barn was already at capacity, so they left the horses to wander about the large pen between the barn and the main building. At least there they had a trough and plenty of hay.

Ty swung out of the saddle, and Waddle turned and gave him a doleful glance.

"What? Don't look at me like that. It's not my fault we were late." He rubbed Waddle's wet nose. "Okay, so maybe it's a little my fault." He pulled a carrot out of his jacket pocket, one of two he'd snatched from the barn as a way to entice Waddle out the door, and held it out to him. "Here you go."

Waddle grabbed hold, pulling the carrot out of Ty's hand and chomping down as though afraid Ty might change his mind and take it back.

"Let's go," Ty's father said as he led them across the yard to one of the inn's back entrances.

Ty was the last inside. He pulled the door shut and followed the others down the right corridor toward the front of the building. The thrum of a hundred conversations reverberated down the corridor, building in strength the closer they got to the main gallery.

Bue Aboloff was standing in the foyer near the front doors, greeting guests as they arrived. Generally, he would stand outside on the front steps and shake each hand and offer a quick hello, but the colder weather had clearly changed his mind. However, the one thing the snow didn't change was his cheerful disposition.

"Master Kellen," Bue said, offering his hand and a warm smile as he caught the small group coming in from the side hall. "I'm glad to see you this evening."

Ty's father smiled as he shook the innkeeper's hand.

"I wasn't sure whether to expect your family tonight," the innkeeper said solemnly, as though afraid to offend. "Again, I'd like to extend my condolences. I had the privilege of greeting your late wife last Performance Night. She always had something nice to say about my children." He released Ty's father's hand. "A very thoughtful woman, indeed."

Ty's father nodded, but the tightening around his eyes said he was having a difficult time holding his emotions in. "Thank you. I know how much she enjoyed the entertainment you and your wife provide. It meant a great deal to her. I want to thank you for that."

Master Aboloff tipped his hat. "It's our pleasure." He looked at Ty. "Will our newest celebrity be gracing us with a song this evening? The townsfolk are still abuzz about that flute of yours."

Ty smiled and shook his head. "I'm afraid I didn't bring it this time, Master Aboloff." He tried to sound regretful.

Master Aboloff pursed his lips. "That's too bad. I was rather looking forward to it." He spared a quick glance at Breen and Adarra. "Good to have you here tonight."

Both smiled and thanked him, and he quickly turned and greeted the next in line.

Ty stuck with his father as they headed into the common room, letting his father's enormous size aid them as they worked their way through the tables and those standing around them. The room was alive with chatter, everyone anxiously awaiting the evening's festivities as they caught up on the latest gossip. The way they carried on, you'd think they hadn't seen each other in years.

"Ty! Over here!"

Ty spun to see who'd called his name and eventually found Lyessa waving at him from one of the tables near the front. He tapped his father on the arm and pointed.

His father nodded, and they began making their way to the front.

Ty glanced over his shoulder to make sure his brother and sister were still with them. Even with an open book in her hands, Adarra was managing to keep up, but Breen was nowhere to be seen, no doubt searching for Fraya.

The three stopped at Lyessa's table, and Ty's father offered a small bow. "Lady Lyessa, you are looking well this evening."

She looked more than just *well*, Ty thought. She looked positively radiant. Her dark-blue velvet gown with gold trim and white lace hugged her body in all the right places, the perfect accent for her fiery hair. A matching cape hung on the back of her seat. The outfit was a stark difference from the tunic and pants she'd worn while cutting down the Northmen raiders.

Lyessa smiled. "Thank you, Master Kellen, I feel well. And your family?" She looked at Ty when she said it.

"As well as can be expected, under the circumstances."

She nodded. "Say no more. Would you care to join us?"

Across the table from Lyessa, Aiden Raycrest sat with a wide grin on his face, seemingly staring at Adarra. Surprisingly, Adarra had closed her book and was doing her fair share of staring as well. There had been quite the change in Aiden ever since his near-death experience. He'd somehow gone from a jealous adversary to someone whose company Ty wasn't completely averse to sharing.

"We wouldn't want to intrude," Ty's father said as he studied the five empty seats around the table.

"My father will be sharing a separate table with the overlords," she said, clearly noting his indecision.

"Well, if that's the case." Ty's father grabbed the chair on the end and had started to pull it out when Orlyn walked over.

"We have a seat saved for you over here, Kellen," the apothecary said, pointing to a table two or three over from where they were. Several of the council members were already seated around it. Mistress Reloria waved. "Best not to force the younger ones to put up with our dull company." Orlyn smiled and bowed in Lyessa's direction.

She chuckled. "I'm sure it can't be that dull."

"You'd be surprised, my dear."

Ty's father pushed the chair back under the table. "It appears I've already been spoken for. If you will excuse me."

Lyessa nodded, and Ty watched his father and Master Orlyn make their way over to the council's table.

"I've saved you a seat," Lyessa said to Ty with an artful grin, not giving him a chance to argue as she tapped the empty chair next to her. "And I'm sure Aiden wouldn't mind sharing your company, Adarra."

Aiden was already out of his seat and pulling out the chair next to him. "I would be honored," he said. Ty's sister walked over and quietly took her seat, smiling girlishly as she did.

Ty looked at his chair, then at Lyessa. "Aren't you going to stand and pull my seat out for me?"

"I'll pull it out from under you," she shot back.

Ty smiled but kept his hand on the chair as he sat, just in case.

"How are you feeling?" she asked.

"I'm doing better," he said, trying and failing to think of a way to bring up the topic of his leaving.

She stared at him a moment, then nodded. "Good. You had me worried."

"Had you worried?" Ty spared a quick glance across the table at Adarra and Aiden, but they were too engrossed in their own conversation to hear what he was saying. "I nearly killed you."

"But you didn't."

"Not for a lack of trying."

She laid her hand on his. "How many times are you going to apologize? It wasn't your fault."

"It feels like it was." He stared at her hand a moment, then turned his over, and they interlocked fingers. Suddenly, all thoughts of apologizing vanished. "Can I speak with you afterward? I have something I need to tell you."

"Why not tell me now?"

Ty shook his head. "It's too loud, and I don't want people to hear."

Her brows lifted. "Now I really need to know."

Before Ty could say more, loud clapping near the entrance had everyone turning as Overlord Barl and his guests crossed the foyer under the second-floor balcony and made their way to the main gallery. Ty had not yet seen the two men who walked with him, but he knew from their physical traits who they were. The first was a tall man with sharp features and a strong bearing, clearly Overlord Agnar. The second was short, round, and dressed rather garishly. His cheeks were flushed as he toted a large golden goblet in one hand. From what Breen had told him, the man with the goblet had to be Overlord Meyrose.

The crowd parted as the three men and their entourage made their way down the central aisle toward the front. It was a rare honor to have the overlords of Keldor and Briston attending Performance Night.

The clapping and cheers continued as Overlord Barl and his guests waved and finally took their places, only two tables away from where Ty and his party were seated. A detail of lancers stood close by.

"Greetings," Breen said, appearing out of nowhere with Fraya in tow. "I see you found us a good table."

Lyessa pointed at the empty chairs at the end. "Join us."

Fraya, like Ty's sister, was wearing what appeared to be her finest dress. Certainly not a gown, but it was clean and pressed. She also had another one of her brightly colored bows tied near the top of her straight raven hair.

"Thank you," she said to Breen as he held her seat. Ty noticed Fraya gritting her teeth as she attempted to sit.

"Everything all right?" Ty asked.

Fraya smiled. "It will be when Lyessa finally quits torturing us with these sparring sessions. My legs and arms have never been so sore."

Lyessa clicked her tongue and shook her head. "The more you train, the less it will hurt."

"I'll take your word on that."

Adarra giggled.

"What are you smiling at?" Lyessa asked. "You were the one requesting Gina for an extra helping of bath salts after our last session."

Adarra coughed, embarrassed by the admission, especially in front of Aiden. But before she could respond, Master Aboloff's wife, Noreen, started up the stairs to the platform and gave their ritual greeting, adding a very cordial welcome to the evening's honored guests.

The crowd once again erupted with applause, and then Mistress Aboloff raised her hands to quiet them down and announced the first performance of the evening.

As engaging as the musicians and performers were, Ty spent the majority of the evening determining how best to break the news of his leaving to Lyessa. Their relationship was just now on the cusp of flourishing into something more, the battle against the Tallosians having drawn them together in ways neither had expected. The unspoken attraction had always been there, but it wasn't until they had been faced with death that their true feelings had been brought to light.

Ty didn't like the thought of leaving her behind. He didn't like the thought of leaving any of them behind. He'd never been on his own before, and it scared him. The only thing that scared him more was how she would react when he told her.

The night continued on, and only once was the entertainment strong enough to pull him from his thoughts, and that was when Master Ethen brought out his five-string veille and delighted the crowd by playing several verses of the much-requested "Bart the Fool." As always, by the end, the entire room was out of their seats and clapping along, and those who weren't were stomping their feet and dancing in the aisles.

Ty was no exception. He joined Lyessa and the others at his table in stomping his feet along to the fast-flowing music. But once the song was over and everyone returned to their seats, Ty's thoughts were immediately drawn back to the predicament of how to let Lyessa know he was leaving.

By the time the last performer finished, and the crowd had begun to disperse, Ty was no closer to working it out than when the evening had started. Looking up from his thoughts, he noticed he and Lyessa were the last two still sitting at the table; his brother and sister, along with their escorts, were standing to leave.

"Breen, tell Father not to wait for me. I'll be along shortly."

Breen looked at Ty, then Lyessa, and smiled with a presumptuous nod. "I'll tell him." It wasn't long before his brother and the rest of their party had melted into the river of people making their way toward the back of the gallery.

"What was it you wished to talk about?" Lyessa asked, an eager expression on her face.

Ty stood and pushed his chair back under the table, taking a moment to help Lyessa with hers. The room was still far too noisy to carry on a decent conversation without raised voices, so he directed them toward the stairs at the side, which led up to the second-floor balcony. Most of its occupants had already filed down to the main floor, so they had no trouble finding seats at a table near the back.

"Your hands are shaking," she noted, taking them in her own. He hadn't noticed until she held them.

"I . . ." Ty racked his brain to figure out what to say, or at least how to begin.

"I think I know what you wish to talk about," she said, leaning in close enough to feel her breath on his face. "And if it's what I think, then just know that I reciprocate."

Now Ty really felt guilty, but he'd come tonight for a reason, and one way or the other, he had to share it.

"I'm leaving," he blurted out, unable to hold it in any longer. As soon as he said it, he regretted it. How could he have been so stupid? All this time, trying to figure out a way to let her down gently, and this was how he did it?

Lyessa didn't move for several moments, not even so much as to blink, then finally leaned back in her seat. "What?"

"The quest I told you about. I'm leaving."

"When?"

Ty gulped. "The day after tomorrow."

Lyessa released his hands. "And you're just telling me this now?"

Ty flinched. "I just found out a couple days ago. Nyalis didn't give me much of a choice. He said the longer I wait, the more dangerous it would be for everyone else."

"The day after tomorrow? That doesn't give me any time to pack. I can't be ready by then."

"Ready for what? You're not going."

Her brows lowered. "The pits, I'm not! You just try to stop me."

Ty gritted his teeth. "You don't think I'd want you there if I could? Nyalis isn't giving me a choice. The journey must be taken by the one seeking the keep, and that person alone."

"I don't care what that crazy old man says. I'm going too."

Ty almost laughed. "Lyessa, if I had a choice, I'd bring you. Blazes! For that matter, I'd bring half the Sidaran army if I could. But I trust Nyalis. If he says I have to go alone, then there must be a reason."

She stared at him a moment, her fists clenched tight in her lap. "What if something happens to you? We both know you can't swing a sword if your life depended on it. What if . . ." She took a deep breath. "What if you don't come back?"

"I will," he said and laid his hand on hers. "I promise." Of course, a promise like that was like promising a mild winter, or a good harvest the next year.

"Is anyone up there? I heard voices." It was Mistress Aboloff.

Ty stood and walked to the edge of the rail and looked down. "Sorry, we were just leaving."

Mistress Aboloff smiled and waved, then headed back toward the kitchen.

"I think she's wanting to close up," Ty said as he turned and walked back to their table. By the time he got there, Lyessa was already up and pushing their chairs back into place. "Perhaps we should—"

Lyessa grabbed the front of his coat and jerked him toward her.

Ty flinched, afraid she was going to sock him a good one for threatening to leave her behind. But before he could even start to apologize, she grabbed the back of his head and kissed him hard on the mouth.

He was stunned, completely unable to move. He'd never felt anything so wonderful in his life. Without hesitating, he wrapped his arms around her and kissed her back, all thoughts of his leaving completely forgotten. He never wanted the moment to end, and by the time it did, Ty was feeling lightheaded enough to topple over. "What . . . what was that for?"

She took a step back and straightened her cloak. "Well, after telling me there was a good chance that I may never see you again, I figured I better do it while I still could. Besides, I was growing tired of waiting on you."

Ty didn't say a word, but he quickly offered her his arm as they walked back down the stairs and out the front doors, where her driver was waiting beside her carriage. They stopped long enough for a parting hug before Ty helped her up.

With a crack of his whip, the coachman guided Lyessa's carriage down the road, but it wasn't until she had rounded the first bend and dropped from sight that Ty realized he never actually said goodbye.

Then again, her lips had said so much more.

Chapter 3 | Ty

EIGHTHDAY HAD ARRIVED, and dawn crept over the windowsill to find Ty already up and waiting. He sat on the edge of his bed, running through the long list of items he'd packed for his journey, double-checking it all to make sure nothing was overlooked.

He'd spent the night staring at the walls, the ceiling, his pillow, but was no closer to sleeping than he had been the previous couple of nights. The restlessness he'd felt earlier that week was from the apprehension of what he was about to face. Last night, it was thoughts of Lyessa that had kept him awake.

He replayed that moment in the inn over and over and over again, unable to think about anything else. The way she'd looked at him, the hunger in her eyes, the softness of her lips. Not even the discovery of his magic had given him such a rush. If there had ever been a reason to make it back alive, it was the hope of being able to experience that moment again. He would have pulled out his flute and composed a sonnet, or at least a verse or two describing the way she had made his heart soar, but that would have woken Breen.

A rooster out back crowed, and Breen shifted under his quilts in the next bed.

"That's a first," his brother said with a deep yawn.

Ty turned. "What is?"

"You up before me . . . and dressed, no less." He looked at Ty a moment, then pushed himself up to one elbow. "How are you feeling? Are you ready?"

Ty took a deep breath to calm the nervous shaking inside. "About as ready as a chicken on its way to the chopping block."

Breen grinned, but the smile quickly faded as he yanked off his covers and sat on the edge of his bed. "You don't look like you slept. Again."

Ty yawned on cue. "I didn't."

"You've got to take better care of yourself. You won't last three days if you don't get proper rest."

Ty knew his brother was right, but there was little he could do about it now, so he grabbed his rather cumbersome pack from the corner and left the room. He was too tired to properly wash, but he figured some cold water to the face might help jostle his mind awake. After a quick stop at the washroom, he made his way down the hall toward the front room, where the smell of fatback greeted him from the kitchen.

Ty's father had several pieces of meat frying in a large pan, along with half a dozen eggs and a loaf in the oven. It smelled wonderful. He couldn't remember the last time he'd seen his father cook. "I'm hungry enough to eat an arachnobe," Ty said jokingly, then wished he hadn't.

His father turned and cocked his brow.

"Sorry. Just a little on edge." Ty set his pack down and walked over to get a better look.

"It'll be done shortly," his father said, wiping his hands down the front of his apron. "Why don't you help me by setting the table? Better add an extra setting just in case."

Ty didn't need to guess who his father was referring to. Nyalis had said he would be there by dawn of Eighthday, and it was dawn. In fact, Ty had barely finished placing the last mug on the table when there was a knock at the door.

"Right on time," his father said, peeking out from the kitchen, the week-old growth on his chin covered in flour. He looked at Ty. "Don't keep him waiting. It's cold out there."

Ty walked across the room, passing Breen, who had stepped out from the hall to see who was at the door. "Adarra said she'll be out shortly," Breen announced to anyone who was listening.

Ty opened the front door. "Guess you smelled the . . . Lyessa?"

Lyessa, dressed all in leather, stood there with a smirk on her face. She looked like she was about to go on a hunt, with her bow and quiver hanging from her shoulder, her sword at her waist, and belt knife peeking out from behind her back.

Ty looked beyond her to the troop of lancers standing beside their mounts in the yard. Forget the hunt—she looked ready for battle.

"Is that bacon I smell?" Aiden asked as he strolled up the walk behind her.

There was a squeal from the front room behind Ty and what sounded like someone running back down the hall.

"Well," Lyessa said, her arms crossed, "are you going to let us in or just stand there gawking?"

"Lady Lyessa?" Ty's father walked over to the door to greet their guest. His shirt, hands, and apron were covered in flour, not to mention the spots on his face that he'd been unable to wipe. "You're up rather early. Is everything all right?" He spotted the row of lancers outside. "Has something happened?"

"They're here to join us on our quest to find this missing keep."

Ty shook his head frustratedly. "Lyessa, I told you, I can't bring anyone with me. Let alone a small army."

"Rubbish. If this fortress, or castle, or whatever it is, is as important as you say, then you'll need all the help you can get." She glanced past Ty into the front room. "Now, are you going to invite us in?"

"Whatever you're cooking, it smells divine," Aiden added, taking a couple of strong whiffs.

"I'm sure we can spare another couple of settings," Ty's father said, worriedly staring at the line of horsemen standing out front, "but I don't have enough for all of them. If your men want, there's feed in the—"

The sudden cry of one of the horses in the yard had everyone turning just as one of the lancers suddenly collapsed beside his horse. Before anyone could say anything, the rest of the entire lancer company suddenly went stiff and dropped into the snow beside their horses as well.

"What's happening?" Lyessa drew her sword and shoved Aiden behind her as she started down the walk.

Ty's father grabbed his sword from the rack behind the door and rushed out to join her. Breen did the same, leaving Ty still standing in the doorway alongside Aiden. Ty reached for his magic, and blue flames erupted from both palms.

"What's going on out here?" Adarra asked as she stepped outside wearing a new dress, her hair freshly combed.

"Someone just killed our entire escort," Aiden said, forcing her to stand behind him. Quite the difference from the last time they were all there and Aiden had tried giving Ty to the witch.

"Nothing to worry about," a voice rang out to the left as Nyalis stepped out from around the side of the cottage, staff in hand.

"Nothing to worry about?" Lyessa looked ready to swing at him. "You just killed an entire squad of Sidaran Lancers."

"I did no such thing," he said dismissively with a long stroke of his white beard. "They are merely sleeping." He sniffed the air as he headed for the front door. "My, is that bacon I smell?"

"Look here, old man," Lyessa said, her blade raised threateningly, "I've had about enough of your . . ." Before she could finish, her sword dropped from her fingers, and her eyes rolled up in the back of her head.

Ty rushed forward and caught her before she hit the ground. He looked up at the wizard. "What did you do that for?"

"I did that for her own protection, and yours." Nyalis looked down at Lyessa and tugged on his beard. "She's quite feisty, that one. I can see why you like her. Now, how about that breakfast?"

Ty tried not to think about what Lyessa's reaction would be when she woke to find he'd left without her. Even though he knew it was probably the only way to keep her from following him, he still felt bad for the subterfuge. With Breen's help, he carried her inside and laid her on the sofa. "How long till she wakes?"

"How long till they all wake?" Ty's father added, staring out at the lancers lying across the front yard.

Nyalis pursed his lips. "I imagine they'll be out long enough for us to eat and be on our way. Can't have them following us where we're going."

"Where *we* are going?" Ty asked, his hopes suddenly rising. "Are you coming with me?"

"As far as Reed Marsh," he said, leaning his staff against the back of his seat as he took the chair at the end of the table. "After that, you're on your own."

"What do we do with the lancers?" Breen asked as he stared out the window at the men in the snow. "It's too cold to just leave them on the ground like that."

"Carry them into the barn if you're that worried, but do it quickly. We don't want the food to get cold."

After dragging the men into the barn, Ty's family, plus Aiden, joined the wizard around the table for a quick meal. Not much was said that hadn't been said several times before, and with the same vague answers. Nyalis clearly either didn't know much about what Ty would be facing or didn't wish to tell. Either way, continuing to ask him was proving fruitless, so they finished their breakfast in silence.

As soon as the meal was over, Nyalis waited for Ty to collect his belongings and ushered him out the door, where he waited while Ty said his goodbyes.

"You keep your wits about you," his father said, adjusting Ty's bow on his back. "I love you, son. Fail or succeed. I'm proud to be your father."

Breen gave him a firm squeeze. "Don't do anything I wouldn't do," he said with a grin. "And don't forget what we talked about with your sleep."

Ty hugged Adarra last. She smiled and placed a small pad of paper and a charcoal pencil in one of the pouches of his carry pack. "I want to see those pages filled with the tale of your journey," she said. "In a way, I envy you."

"I'd be more than happy to let you take my place," he said with a smile, sparing a quick glance at Nyalis, who seemed too preoccupied with something in the forest to have noticed.

Ty even shook Aiden's hand, who had placed a comforting arm around Adarra's shoulders. "Tell Lyessa I said goodbye. And I'm sorry."

"We'll make sure she knows," Ty's father said.

Ty took a step back to get one last look at his family and his home. His eyes burned, and he bit his tongue to hold back the tears. He wasn't going to let his crying be the last thing they ever saw of him. He turned to Nyalis. "I'm ready."

Nyalis nodded. "Then we're off."

Ty tamped down the churning in his gut as he hefted his satchel higher on his shoulders and followed the old wizard around the side of the cottage. But one look at the small headstone where his mother's body rested under her favorite tree, and the tears broke free, soaking both cheeks as he walked across the small bridge and into the forest beyond.

Chapter 4 | Ty

HEY FOLLOWED THE trail north to the East River. Its waters were down this time of year, and they wouldn't rise until the snow from the Angoran Mountains had thawed in the spring. They stopped along the bank's edge where Ty's father kept his boat and removed the oiled canvas.

"We'll cross here," Nyalis said.

Ty knew from the map his father had given him that the northern boundary of Reed Marsh was almost directly across from Easthaven. The marsh was enormous, nearly the size of Crystal Lake. It spread from the East River all the way west to Virn Run, and just as far south.

Ty looked out at the swift-moving water. "You don't want to head west downriver first? Wouldn't that be faster?"

"It would be faster," Nyalis said, "but far more dangerous. We should skirt the marsh to the north, and you can enter from there." He turned and looked at the skiff, then at Ty. "Well, it's not going to just walk itself into the water."

"You're a wizard. Can't you just wiggle your fingers and make it do just that?"

Nyalis laughed. "Contrary to what people might think, I'm not all-powerful. I certainly can't make a boat grow a pair of legs by wiggling my fingers, or flapping my arms, or blowing my nose. Then again . . ." He turned and raised his hand, wiggling his fingers as he did, mumbling something under his breath. Suddenly the boat shifted. It rocked upright and started moving toward the water.

Ty gawked. "How are you doing that?" He bent down and looked under the hull, expecting to see it floating through the air, but instead he found dozens of small root stems poking out of the ground, carrying the boat along like a giant upside-down centipede as they moved it toward the edge of the water. As soon as the boat passed over them, the shoots in back sank into the ground while more popped up in front. Pretty soon, the skiff was resting in the water at the edge of the bank.

Nyalis chuckled as he waited for Ty to get in before climbing in himself. Once aboard, they started across. The sun was high enough for light to filter through the trees and reach their faces, its warmth fighting the cold breeze blowing across the water.

Ty didn't need to bother with the oars, as Nyalis guided the boat along with his magic, similar to how Gilly had taken them upriver to Meerwood and back.

"Brings back memories," the old man said with a hint of nostalgia as he stared off into the trees on the other side of the river. "The first time we came this way together, you were small enough to fit in the crook of my arm."

Ty had no memory of that experience. From what the wizard had said, Ty was rather thankful he couldn't remember. Apart from the hair-raising battle that had taken place between Nyalis and those the White Tower had sent after Ty, there was the death of his mother. His birth mother.

Every so often, over the years, Ty had found himself thinking about her, wondering who she had been, what she had looked like. And as always, those thoughts would eventually lead to his father. Ty had been surprised to hear from Nyalis that his father had abandoned his mother when she had needed him most. Even more surprised to discover his father wasn't even human, but one of the cursed Fae. And after coming to grips with what his father had done, he could see why they were called *cursed*.

Once they reached the far shore, Nyalis sent the boat back across. Ty watched quietly from the bank as the skiff reached the other side and two fists of water pushed it up on shore. Nyalis then raised the tarp back over the boat with a couple fists of hardened air. Ty hoped Breen or his father would check in on it before the heavier snows fell. Nyalis might have been able to get the tarp back over, but he didn't seem capable of tying it down.

Nyalis turned and took a moment to study the surrounding wood before pointing at the footpath ahead with his staff. "In we go."

The trail they took was one that led to old Dorbin's cabin, near where the enormous arachnobe had made its nest, but before they reached that lonesome valley of bones, Nyalis cut west through the trees on a deer path that seemed to follow the course of the river.

For a man of Nyalis's extremely advanced years, he did a remarkable job of keeping a steady pace, only slowing when some unexpected obstacle—like a fallen tree, or a mound of rock, or a rather dense outcropping of brush—forced them to find an alternative path. The one upside to their speed was that it kept the blood pumping to help fight against the cold.

"How long till we get to wherever it is you're taking me?" Ty asked during one of their brief periods of rest. He sat on the edge of a fallen tree and drank from his waterskin while watching Nyalis study his compass.

Nyalis looked up through the canopy of limbs overhead. "Tomorrow morning, if we can maintain this pace."

Ty was almost afraid to ask. "You're not planning on walking through the night, are you?"

Nyalis stuffed the compass back into his robe. "Of course. I certainly wouldn't want to waste all that valuable time sleeping." Before Ty had a chance to explain why that was a bad idea, the wizard turned and started back down the trail.

Ty groaned and, after taking a small swig himself, chased after the old man. Three days without sleep. He was going to collapse from exhaustion before he ever made it into the marsh. So much for his famous quest. He was doubting whether he'd survive long enough to even start.

The woods surrounding the marsh were cold, but not as cold as they should have been, given the earlier snowfall. In fact, the closer they got to the deadly waters, the warmer it became. It wasn't warm enough for Ty to take off his jacket, but it was warm enough to feel the sweat on his back, not to mention offer an explanation as to why none of the water seemed to have ice around its edges.

The farther they went, the more noticeable the changes became. It was little things that went missing first, like the fresh scent of pine, or the chirping of the birds, or the patches of green not yet covered in snow. Pretty soon the forest took on a whole new characteristic. The trees grew gnarled and gangly, the smell of rot pervasive; even the birds had slowly been replaced with the croaking of creatures more inclined to live near the water.

The wizard's pace slowed, and he stopped more often to check his bearings. More than once, he brought them to a halt as something large splashed off in the distance on their left, forcing them to divert their current path.

The hairs on Ty's arms and neck remained poised as they slowly worked their way around the outer edge of Reed Marsh. All conversation, what little there had been, had ceased, as the two focused on keeping their eyes and ears open for anything that might be out there.

Ty sent feelers out into the marsh, trying to get an idea of what might be lurking farther in. Each time left him shaken. It was similar to how it had felt when he reached out with his magic and touched the arachnobe in its lair. The marsh had a dark, deadly pulse that chilled all the way to the bone.

There were things out there that Ty had never felt before and didn't want to feel again. Creatures that made the arachnobes seem almost trivial. This was where Nyalis wanted him to go?

Darkness arrived with the speed of a jackrabbit being chased by a skulk of red foxes. It was as if the marsh were purposely keeping the sun from entering its domain.

"How are you still going?" Ty asked, out of wind trying to keep up with the thousand-year-old man.

Nyalis chuckled and gave his long white beard a stroke as he looked around. "We can stop here for a bit to catch our breath, if you feel the need."

Ty noted Nyalis's shifty sidestep of the question as the wizard directed them off the path to a mound of rock on the right. Interspersed between the moss-covered stones were thick tangled roots growing out of the ground instead of in.

Ty climbed to the top, enjoying the higher vantage, which allowed him to get a better sense of their surroundings. The ground they'd been traveling on had grown soft. It wasn't the softness of a lush grassy meadow, but a soggy unstableness, as though there was a layer of water just under the soil that made everything squish.

It felt good to have something solid under his feet once again as he took a seat on one of the uppermost boulders. "It stinks in here," he said after recorking his waterskin. He'd resorted to breathing with his mouth instead of through his nose, but it didn't seem to help. The stench of decay was too overpowering, leaving him to not only smell the rot, but taste it as well.

"Won't argue with you there." Nyalis pulled his compass out and held it up, trying to see the face in the dimming light. Finally giving up, he lowered his staff and mumbled a few words, and the stone resting snugly at the top of the staff began to glow. "Ah, much better." Once he had found whatever he was looking for, he stuffed it back into the folds of his robe.

The two sat there for some time listening to the unfamiliar sounds of the marsh. It was clear why his father had always warned them never to get too close. Only the bravest, or stupidest, of woodsmen would dare enter. Ty certainly didn't feel all that brave.

Within just a few minutes, the marsh had grown completely black.

"*Ru'kasha Kor*," Ty mumbled to himself, and the marshland suddenly lit with a pale grey light as Ty's night sight took over. "Yes!" he exclaimed giddily. "I can't believe that worked."

"Where did you learn that?" Nyalis asked, his face a mix of curiosity and concern.

"The book . . . I mean, Mangora," Ty corrected himself. "She taught it to me while she was following the wielder council upriver." Ty studied Nyalis's face. "Why? It's not going to hurt me, is it?"

Nyalis shook his head. "No. I was just surprised you knew it. It's been many years since I've seen others using magic in its proper form. I'm pleased to see you have picked it up so fast."

"I wouldn't exactly say it was fast. Took me nearly half an hour just to figure out how to pronounce it correctly."

"And I take it you learned its counterpart for shutting the spell back off?"

Ty nodded. "*Ru'kasha Sve.*" The marsh dimmed and faded into darkness once more.

Nyalis pursed his lips. "Very good. I have no doubt that will come in handy." The wizard pointed to Ty's pack. "Best you eat while you have the chance. You'll need to keep up your energy."

Ty unhooked his bow and quiver, then pulled off his pack. "Lack of food isn't my problem. I haven't slept the last few nights, and now you want me to spend another trekking through this Creator-forsaken swamp." He sighed and opened the top of his pack. "*Ru'kasha Kor.*" Everything brightened. He dug around for a moment before finding the wax paper holding the strips of dried meat his father had packed for him. He pulled one out and offered part of it to Nyalis.

Nyalis waved it off. "No, you need that more than I do." He reached into his robe and came out with a strange piece of fruit. At least, Ty thought it was fruit. It was purple with a bright-green stem. Nyalis held it up to the glow of his staff, and it looked like a miniature cantermelon, except instead of a hard outer shell, it had a soft furry one. Nyalis rubbed the fruit on his sleeve before sticking it in his mouth and biting down. The juices squirted far enough to hit Ty, and by the satisfied look on the old man's face, it must have been savory.

Ty bit off a small hunk of his meat, not wanting to fish out his biscuits and cheese, and placed the rest back in the wax paper and stuffed it into his pack. Nyalis was right about one thing: He needed to ration his provender. There was no telling how far he'd have to travel before finding fresh game. So far, he hadn't seen anything in this marsh he'd be willing to clean and cook.

Ty yawned and stretched, going so far as to pinch his arm to try keeping his eyes open. He needed to find a way to keep his mind focused, and what better way to do that than through conversation? While he had the wizard's attention, there were questions he needed answers to. Ty forced himself to turn away from the foreboding blackness ahead and look at Nyalis. "Can you at least tell me what I'm looking for in there? How far I have to go?"

Nyalis stared into the foggy marsh to the left of the trail and shook his head.

"I'm afraid I don't possess the answers you seek. I wasn't exactly on the wizard council's good side when they set this quest up. All I can tell you is that you will find the first of five traveling mirrors somewhere inside. Oh, and there is a watcher who protects this first mirror. You'll have to persuade them to let you use it."

"A watcher? Who is it?"

Nyalis shrugged.

"Can you at least tell me more about these tests I'm supposed to face?"

Nyalis smiled as he leaned on his staff. "Now that I can do. As I've mentioned before, in order to bring Aero'set back, you will need a key, but not just any key. You will need a shorlock." He raised his hand. "Before you ask, a shorlock is a type of key that can both reveal and unlock magical spells."

"And that's what I'm going in there to find? A shorlock?"

"In a manner of speaking. The shorlock was divided into four separate pieces to keep it out of the wrong hands. The pieces will need to be collected and then assembled."

"How do I assemble them?"

Nyalis started to open his mouth, then stopped, pausing a moment to think. "I believe you'll know it when the time comes."

In other words, Ty mused, he didn't know how it worked.

"The more important thing, however," Nyalis continued, "is retrieving the pieces. Each part of the shorlock will require you to pass a test. Each of the four tests is there to measure a single trait: faith, wisdom, strength, and compassion. These four combined are required to unlock the gates of Aero'set and bring back the keep."

"What are the tests like?"

Nyalis tugged on his beard. "That I don't know. Although, I have a feeling the tests will require more than simply answering a question. There is an ancient proverb that goes with these tests:

Faith in oneself is important,
but faith without wisdom can be misplaced,
and wisdom without strength can lead to complacency,
and strength without compassion can lead to tyranny."

Ty took a moment to mull over the wizard's words, almost surprised that he actually understood them. Perhaps that was the point. Guidelines simple enough for all to structure their lives by.

"Retrieving this key is all-important," Nyalis said. "And that faerie blood of yours makes you the only person alive who can do it."

Ty exhaled. "So, no pressure, then?"

Nyalis smiled, though it seemed a sad sort of smile. "Nothing worth doing is easy, I'm afraid."

"I guess not." Ty wiggled his toes, then stomped his foot a couple of times on the rock. The chill was seeping into his boots and numbing his feet, which was a blessing of sorts, since the numbness helped mask the soreness. His fingers were also growing stiff, and he found himself blowing on them more frequently. He reached over and grabbed a length of fallen limb lying between the rocks and tested its strength by giving it a couple of good whacks against the rock. It held.

The lack of sleep and constant march had left his legs feeling uncertain, but apart from helping bear the extra weight from his pack, Ty figured he could use the long stick to prod the ground and make sure his next step didn't end with him in a bog hole.

"Ready?" Nyalis asked, and before Ty could answer, the wizard was climbing back down the rock to the path below.

Ty shook his head. "Would it matter if I said no?" He took another small swig from his waterskin, just enough to wet his mouth, then followed the wizard down.

The noises within the marsh grew as the evening progressed. Nightfall had seemingly triggered the awakening of the wetlands, and what was being roused had Ty on edge. The way ahead grew more treacherous as they periodically ran out of ground to walk on, forcing them to hop from rock to rock, or root to root, in order to keep from wading through the murky waters that plagued this section of Sidara.

Ty leaped from a cypris stump back to solid ground, or as solid as the marsh allowed, then took a moment to right his pack as Nyalis once again pulled out his compass and held it up to the light from his staff. He looked up, then back down at the compass, moving it in a slow arc before finally nodding. "Not much farther now." After tucking it back in his robe, they started down another small trail.

Ty didn't know if he should be excited or terrified by the fact that they were reaching the end of their travels. Or, more accurately, the end of Nyalis's company. He followed quietly along behind the old man, making sure to step only in the other's footprints. Thoughts of traveling deeper into the marsh plagued him as he attempted to focus on anything other than the dangers he knew were coming.

First, he tried picturing Lyessa's lips, the passion and desire that had burned inside him as he held her for the first time, but a loud splash off to the right yanked that image away.

Next, he tried imagining the Keep of Aero'set: what it looked like, what secrets it held, and how it could help him better understand who he was and how he fit into the upcoming war Nyalis had been warning of. He'd barely been able to conjure a decent image of the wizarding school from the vision Nyalis had given him when his foot sank halfway into a soft piece of marsh, and he tumbled forward, barely catching himself with his walking stick.

"We're here," Nyalis said, pointing with his staff to a small break in the trees ahead.

Ty righted himself and followed him into the clearing. A narrow footpath on the left led straight into the marsh, disappearing about twenty yards in, swallowed by a dense layer of low-hanging fog. "How do you know this is the right one?"

Nyalis looked at his compass. "I just do."

Ty stared at the fog-covered pathway ahead. "You sure there isn't another way to find this keep?" His hands were shaking, and it wasn't just the cold or his lack of sleep. He tightened his grip on his walking stick, hoping the wizard would tell him he didn't have to go in after all and this had all been nothing more than a test.

"Afraid not, my boy. The only way forward is . . . forward." He finished his sentence by pointing at the entrance to the marsh with his staff. "Trust me, I wouldn't be asking such a task of you if I didn't believe it absolutely necessary." He turned and gave Ty a sympathetic smile. "I also wouldn't be asking if I didn't know you were up to the challenge. You have everything you need right here," he said, tapping the side of Ty's head. "You're a smart lad. I have no doubt you will see this through."

Ty didn't share that same level of confidence as he listened intently to the guttural calls of the creatures waiting just inside the marsh.

"You're stronger than you know." Nyalis smiled, then took a step forward and laid his hand on Ty's shoulder. He closed his eyes and mumbled something under his breath.

Ty felt a surge of energy jolt through his body, his mind clearing as the numerous aches and pains from their long hike melted away.

"What was that?" Ty hadn't felt this good since . . . Well, he couldn't remember a time when he'd felt this good. He raised his walking stick, ready to go charging into the marsh and face whatever was in there.

"That was a small gift to help you get started," Nyalis said, his face appearing more gaunt than Ty remembered. "You needn't worry about your lack of sleep—that boost of magic should have no problem overcoming it." The wizard's fingers tightened on his staff, and his legs appeared to wobble slightly.

"Did you just—"

Nyalis waved him off. "You need it more than me."

"Thank you," Ty said as he moved his legs and arms around, enjoying the unexpected limberness. "How long will it last?"

"I would say it was the equivalent of a good week's sleep. But that doesn't mean you can simply go without. It's just there to help you get started."

Ty nodded.

Nyalis gave Ty one last good looking-over. "I believe this is where I say my goodbye, my young friend. May the Creator guide your steps and protect you on your way. I will be waiting for you at journey's end."

"And where will that be?" Ty asked, surprised he hadn't thought to ask sooner. "Once I get the pieces together, where do I go to use them?"

"I thought that was obvious. Once you collect the final piece, the fifth mirror will take you to where you need to go."

"You haven't yet told me how to use these mirrors."

Nyalis's thick brows lowered, and he pursed his lips. "I haven't?" He shook his head with a sigh. "Don't ever get old. It's not for the faint of heart." He smiled. "The mirrors work in pairs. Each one has its own unique name. To activate them, you simply call out the name of the mirror you are standing in front of, then call out the name of its counterpart."

"How will I know their names?"

"It will be written on the mirror's frame." Nyalis pointed to Ty's trouser pocket. "Whatever you do, don't lose that compass. Not only will it guide you to each of the mirrors, but it will also allow you to read the inscribed names. Unless, of course, you learned to read ancient runic in your schooling?"

Ty shook his head.

"No, I didn't think so." He shook his head. "What has our education come to, I ask." Nyalis yawned and gave a firm tug on his beard. "Well, if that's all, then you'd best be on your way. The sooner you begin, the sooner it will be over." He stepped forward and gave Ty a warm hug, then turned and started north up the new path they were standing on.

"That's the wrong way," Ty said, pointing east. "We came from that direction."

Nyalis turned and smiled. "And if I were on my way to Easthaven, that is precisely where I'd be going. But, alas, my journey requires a different route." He waved once more and melted into the trees.

Ty stood staring at the empty hollow for what seemed like hours, debating whether to chase after him. However, knowing the lives of everyone he cared about depended on him accomplishing this task, and knowing he'd never be able to look his family in the eyes again if he didn't at least try, he turned back around.

With a deep breath to steel his nerves, and enough uncertainty to fill the Rhunarin Ocean, Ty shifted the pack on his shoulders and started in.

Chapter 5 | Ty

THE AIR GREW EVEN more pungent the farther into the marsh Ty went. The rot from the trees, the stagnant waters, the spongy soil beneath his feet, all seemed to release a putrefying stench that had him gasping for air. Each inhale burned his nose and left his throat aflame. Sipping from his waterskin was the only thing that seemed to help, and it didn't help much. Worse, the magic of his night sight did little to pierce the surrounding layers of fog, leaving him all but blind to what was out there. Then again, had he seen what was out there, he probably never would have set foot in the marsh in the first place.

Ty kept his eyes glued to the path ahead, what little he could see. On either side lay the murky black waters of the quag, filled with creatures who were no doubt waiting to feast on his flesh. The last thing he wanted was to accidentally step off and plunge headfirst into the marsh's unknown depths.

Deformed trees covered in damp moss loomed out of the night. Their thick roots reached out across the path like giant tentacles, forcing Ty to either climb over or crawl under. It reminded him of the great sea monsters he'd heard sailors up from Briston describe after a few too many pints at the East Inn.

Ty was surprised to find himself openly sweating. Even with the early snows of winter, the marsh seemed to maintain a sense of warmth, but not the comforting warmth of a crackling fire on a cold night, more like a pasty warmth that had Ty's clothes sticking to his back.

The insoles of Ty's boots were caked in muck as he sloshed along the center of the trail. He was thankful for the boots' longer shafts, as they rose to the tops of his calves, keeping the mud from filling the insides.

A loud croaking, followed by the high-pitched squeals of something being eaten, had Ty fumbling for his sword. There was no point in reaching for his bow. It wasn't like he could have seen what he was shooting at, and by the time he did see something, it would've been on top of him.

The weapon shook in his hand as he waited for the noises to die down. Not hearing anything further, he took a cautious step forward and sank all the way to his thigh in a bog hole. He tipped over and nearly landed on his face. "Curse this muck!"

After righting himself, he spent the next several minutes trying to pull the boot back out. By the time he did, his hands were just as filthy and smelly as his leg.

Not seeing any other choice, he yanked off the boot and proceeded to dig out as much of the bog's sludge as he could. Thankfully it had been thick enough to not get too far down his leg, most of it stopping halfway down the calf. If he'd missed his step and landed in the marsh, his entire leg would have been soaked.

Scraping out the rest of the moist dirt with his hands, he pulled the boot back on and stood. With stick in hand and sword back in its sheath, Ty felt his way along the narrow trail ahead, poking at the soil to make sure it was firm enough to walk on, not wanting to have another repeat of the previous sinkhole.

Every so often the fog would clear, allowing him to see what lay beyond the narrow corridor ahead. Unfortunately, it was more of the same: misshapen trees covered in mushrooms, moss, and vines; sporadic patches of tall grass and reeds; and a seemingly endless amount of stagnant water. He could certainly see why they had hidden the mirror here. No one in their right mind would ever come looking. The entire place was nothing but ruin and decay. Even the trees seemed to reek of death, bearing great pustules that oozed along their bark.

But it wasn't really death, Ty mused. It was life. One that he was wholly unfamiliar with—a dark, foreboding sort of life. A life that fought every day for the privilege of seeing another sunrise. Anything that could survive in this place deserved his respect. And fear.

A splash to his right had him dropping to a crouch. Ripples filled the water beside him, striking against the side of the bank. He waited.

Nothing.

He waited longer. Still nothing. Finally, he gathered his courage and struck on, keeping to the center of the path. He wondered how long it would be before the trail ended altogether and he was forced to go on without it. The thought of wading out into those murky waters had him trembling all over.

Minutes felt like hours, hours like days. The trek through the swamp seemed to follow the same pattern: a noise, a shriek, a splash, then unnerving silence. He had no idea how long he'd been on the move or how far he'd gone. It felt like miles, but with the fog as thick as it was, he wouldn't have been surprised to find that he'd traveled in a big circle.

The trail seemed to wind all over the place, crisscrossing back and forth as it meandered in and around the waterways. At one point, it widened enough that Ty felt it safe to sit for a moment and try eating a small bite while resting his legs, not to mention his frayed nerves.

Propping his sword against his leg for easy reach, and keeping his eyes peeled for any unexpected movement, he dug around in his pack and came out with the first thing his fingers managed to find—an apricot. He barely noticed its sweet taste as he hurriedly bit down and nearly chipped a tooth on the pit. He ripped the large seed out of from the center and leaned back to chuck it as hard as he could into the water, but common sense stayed his hand, and he placed the apricot's remains on the ground beside him.

Not knowing when he might get another chance, he pulled out the wrapped meat and ate the other half of the strip he'd started on earlier. Finishing quickly, he stuffed the food back in his pack, took a small swig from the waterskin, and looked up to see if he could spot any sign of the coming dawn. Having traveled half the night with Nyalis just to reach the entrance to the marsh, Ty figured the sun should be waking sometime soon. Of course, with fog this thick, it might not make a difference.

He'd barely made it back to his feet when something up ahead moved. He strained to see what it was. Had it just been the mist? The moist blanket of cloud had a way of shifting on its own, keeping Ty in a perpetual state of unease. He saw it again. This time there was no mistaking it. The creature lumbered half out of the fog ahead on his left.

Ty froze, too scared to even drop to his stomach. The animal was enormous, with scales for skin and long spikes running down the centermost part of its back, not to mention its tree trunk of a tail. He'd never seen a razorback before, but by the drawings his father had shown him, there was no mistaking it.

Ty stood perfectly still. Thankfully, its back was to him with its head stuck inside the mist. Carefully, Ty lowered himself to the ground, crawling over to the side of the trail and into a patch of long reeds near the water as he waited to see what the razorback would do.

The monstrous animal released a bone-jarring shriek, followed by several clicking sounds that had Ty holding his breath and moving even farther into the reeds. He was so close to the edge that if he shifted any farther, he'd be in the water.

He peeked out between the stalks and watched as the razorback turned.

Its front was even more terrifying than the back, with dark beady eyes as big as Ty's fist set on either side of its head and a single strip of spikes that ran up the bridge of its nose. More disturbing yet was the row of daggerlike teeth that protruded from its open maw as it sniffed the air. It wore a disturbing grin as it scanned the surrounding marsh, as though excited by the possibility of having cornered some new prey.

Ty hoped it wasn't him.

The razorback released more clicks as it continued to sniff the air, its eyes stopping on the tuft of reeds and long grass where Ty was currently hiding. Could he smell him there? With the overpowering stench of the place, Ty couldn't imagine how. The creature didn't move, its head cocked at an angle that Ty knew meant it was looking directly at him.

Ty released his sword, knowing that if the creature got close enough for him to use it, Ty was mostly likely already dead. Cautiously, he reached out with his magic and tried to connect with the enormous animal, hoping he could persuade it to move on. His magic wrapped around the razorback, and immediately it reared its head and released a loud hissing screech, then tore through the shallow water and reeds as it came for him.

That didn't work! Ty rolled to his knees and grabbed his bow, which was lying in the reeds beside him. As fast as he could, he snatched an arrow from the quiver, and with shaking hands loaded it onto the string and pulled it to his chin. He barely had time to aim when he released the shaft, and it flew from the bow with a buzz. It struck the razorback's underside, where the scales seemed the softest, and was buried to the fletching, but did little to slow the giant beast.

No!

He didn't have time to nock another. Hopping to his feet, he raised his hands, calling on his magic. The creature was nearly on top of him. Blue flames flashed to life in his palms, and he sent them like a lancer's spear straight at it. The fire hit the razorback, and the creature screamed. It was a deadly blow, but the creature was too big and coming too fast to be stopped.

A flicker of warning, and Ty leaped backward.

A monstrous shape broke the surface of the marsh beside him and grabbed the razorback in its jaws. Water and reeds rained down on top of Ty as he screamed and clawed his way back from the edge.

This new creature was like nothing Ty had ever seen or heard of before. It looked like part of the swamp had come to life and risen from the deep. Its back was shell, covered in layers of underwater grass and small brush. Out from the shell craned the neck and head of an eel.

The razorback hissed as it fought to break free from the enormous water monster. It struck at the eel's extended neck with its spiked tail, cutting deep, but not deep enough to stop something that big and powerful. The razorback's reactions were sluggish. Perhaps the water creature's bite was venomous, or perhaps Ty's arrow had done more damage than he thought. Either way, the razorback shrieked as it clawed at the dirt, but little by little the ground gave way, and it was pulled out into the deep. Blood clouded the water, and its last desperate gurgles could be heard before the giant lizard sank below the surface.

Ty lay there until the final ripples in the water had ceased. It took him several long minutes before he managed to slow the beating in his chest enough to decide what to do next. Not wanting to wait around and see if the monster came back for dessert, Ty collected his weapons and started down the trail once more.

It wasn't until he was back within the fog that he realized he'd forgotten his stick, but by then he wasn't about to go back for it. In the end, he resorted to using the tip of his boots and his sword to test the firmness of the ground as he walked. It might have slowed his pace, given he had to stop every so often to test the soggy terrain, but it was better than getting stuck in the bog, or worse, accidentally stepping off the path and into the water.

A large treefrog croaked beside him, and he dove into the mud, feeling more than a little foolish as he picked himself up and wiped off the muck before continuing.

Up ahead, the pathway was blocked by a large twisted section of root. It was low enough to climb over, so he grabbed hold of a couple of larger knots and started up. Halfway across, he decided to stop and rest his feet. Truthfully, it wasn't his feet that needed resting. His hands hadn't stop shaking since the razorback, and he was tired of jumping at every little splash of a fish or snap of a twig.

With his sword in his lap, Ty unhooked the straps of his travel bag and placed it between his legs. He took a moment to rub the soreness from his shoulders where the weight of the pack had dug into the skin and bruised the muscles, but it didn't seem to help. He could have used another dose of Nyalis's magic right about then.

Taking a moment to get his bearings, he tried to find the tree that the roots he was sitting on belonged to, but the mist was still too thick, so he opened his pack and dug around inside for another apricot. His fingers had just latched onto the fruit when the hairs on the back of his neck stiffened.

Someone, or something, was watching him.

He yanked his arm out of the satchel and grabbed his sword, spinning in all directions to find what was making him feel so unnerved. But apart from the croak of the frogs and chitter of the insects burrowing inside the thicker pieces of root bark, he saw and heard nothing. Even still, he couldn't shake the feeling that something was out there.

He grabbed his pack and climbed the rest of the way over the roots, huddling on the other side as he tried to determine if the feeling was stemming from something ahead of him or behind. He didn't want to leave the protection of the overhanging wood, but he couldn't just stand there the rest of the night either, so he forced down his nerves, tightened his pack, and started forward.

He was tempted to send another web of magic out in front of him, but he was afraid that whatever was out there might sense it. It took everything he had not to call his fire to bear. If he hadn't been so afraid that it might alert the marsh creatures to his presence, he would have. He didn't need it for warmth, but it would make him feel safer.

Pretty soon he hit a patch of fog so thick he couldn't even see his feet, let alone the path ahead. He stopped and crouched down as he waited to see if the fog would clear, or at the very least if the feeling that he was being watched would pass.

Neither did.

Whatever was out there was getting closer. The bumps down his arms had extended to his legs. He couldn't see anything.

A loud snap of a limb behind him had him spinning. At least, he thought it was behind him. The sound echoed off the surrounding trees, filling the entire swamp. Where was it? It felt as though it were right on top of him.

He didn't know what to do. He couldn't go back, but then again, he couldn't go forward either as long as he remained blinded by the cloud. *Then move it, dummy,* he could almost hear Feoldor shouting at him. *Are you some powerful half-faerie or not?*

The first time Ty had attempted to draw in the air like a vanti, he'd collapsed a Northman's chest. The second time, he sent a man flying through the air so fast that when the man hit a tree, he nearly snapped in half.

He reached out with his magic, immediately connecting with the warm moist air around him. It was sticky to the touch. The question was, though, could he control it? If he could, it might be exactly what he needed.

Ty hadn't found the time—between recovering from the battle with Mangora and her spiders and being possessed by her numori and trying to kill the wielder council—to experiment with this new form of magic. And trying to navigate through one of the deadliest places in Sidara probably wasn't the best time to start, but without it, he didn't see a way forward.

Carefully, he reached his hand out toward the fog ahead and tried imagining a small breeze, something light enough to barely whisk his hair.

Nothing happened.

He tried again, this time picturing the fog being pushed aside like a set of curtains in front of a window.

Still nothing.

Ty grew impatient. He could feel the air around him, so why wasn't it working? What was different? Before, his life had been depending on it during the battle. Then again, his life was depending on it now.

His magic tended to be like that—somewhat unpredictable.

He closed his eyes and tried again. He could feel the warmth of his magic inside as he pulled it up from somewhere deep. This time, however, instead of picturing himself creating the wind from his hands like he had the fire, he pictured himself reaching out and drawing it to him, like a ship's sail capturing the air to propel the fog away.

The air began to swirl, a slight breeze strong enough to rustle his hair. Opening his eyes, he focused on the fog ahead and raised his hand out to it. The wind hit the curtain of mist, and it parted far enough to see the next ten feet of path.

Yes! It worked! He wanted to shout and dance around at his success, but whatever was out there was drawing closer, hidden somewhere within the fog around him.

With sword in hand, he started toward the fog's edge, careful to keep to the center of the path as he prodded the dirt in front of him to make sure it was capable of holding his weight. By the time he reached the end of what his magic had cleared, the mist behind him had already closed in, and he was once again left blind.

This time, he drew in a little more of the magic, hoping to push the fog farther back, giving him more room to maneuver. Raising his hand, he once again imagined the sail as it gathered in the wind, picturing an even greater gust. With a one swift thrust, he released another fist of air, but this time instead of small breeze, the wind burst from him like a battering ram and scattered the thick cloud in all directions for at least a hundred feet.

Ty yelped, not expecting such a reaction.

Something in the marsh behind him splashed, and he turned, swinging his blade at nothing. Ty could see all the way back to the roots he'd climbed over earlier. He hadn't gone as far as he'd thought.

"Impressive," a voice behind him said.

Ty yelped again and spun. A figure stood on the path ahead. Where had she come from? His breath caught in his throat when he saw her face.

"Mangora!"

Chapter 6 | Ty

FIRE FLEW FROM TY'S HAND as he ran for the witch. Images of his mother's grave flashed in front of his eyes, all sense of reason fleeing as he desperately fought to avenge her.

Mangora gasped, not expecting the attack, and raised her staff. Ty's flames were deflected into the air, barely missing her as they scorched the limbs above.

Ty screamed, his feet digging into the soft dirt as he charged ahead, sending volley after volley of fire at the witch, hoping to put an end to her then and there. She wasn't going to hurt anyone anymore. Ty's pack bounced against his back as he sped along the trail.

Why wasn't she fighting back?

Ty's foot hit a patch of soft mire, and he sank to his knee. The momentum wrenched his leg sideways, and he landed on his face, his leg buried inside the bog. The pain was excruciating as he twisted around to unleash another round of fire. *Where'd she go?* He spun in all directions, but all he could see was the wall of mist swiftly closing in. *What just happened?* Leaning forward, he grabbed his knee and pulled as hard as he could until his foot was finally released from the freshly upturned quag with a sucking pop. Hopping to his feet, he limped forward, sword in one hand, fire in the other.

The marsh was silent. Not even the frogs dared make a sound.

The fog was nearly on top of him.

"Show yourself, witch!"

Before he could turn, something wrapped around his legs, and he went down. Ty let go of his sword and turned to incinerate whatever had grabbed him, but before he could, he was yanked into the air by a dozen snakelike vines. He screeched as he watched the pathway below him suddenly disappear to the right as the vines pulled him into the marsh and dangled him out over the dark waters below. He fought to free himself, but the creepers had wrapped him like a cocoon, and he couldn't move.

Below him, the waters began to stir as something rose to the top, something even more terrifying than the eel monster.

Ty jerked and pulled, trying to break free. He screamed as an enormous gaping mouth rose up below him. He could see nothing but rows of teeth and the back of its throat as it moved up and down, producing a deep sucking noise. He clawed at the vines, holding on for dear life.

"Are you about through?" a voice behind him called out.

Ty twisted his head around to find Mangora floating twenty feet in the air. Like a giant hand, the vines gently carried her from one place to the next. Slowly, they lowered her down beside him.

"It appears you have a choice," she said with that same gravelly voice he'd grown to hate. "Either you can behave in a civilized manner and I place you back on the trail for an honest conversation, or you can continue to fight me, and I release you right here." She cackled. "Trust me, its bite is much worse than its bark."

Ty looked down at the marsh creature below and gulped.

"Which shall it be?"

He couldn't pull his eyes away from the monstrous throat. "The conversation."

"Smart choice." She pointed toward the bank, and suddenly he was floating away from the gaping hole in the water below. The vines lowered him back to the narrow spit of land he'd been traveling on and released. They retracted a few feet but remained poised to strike.

Ty rubbed at his wrists, watching as another set of creepers lowered Mangora down onto the path a few feet in front of him. He kept his hands at his side, but his magic was right on the tip of his fingers, ready to release at any moment.

Mangora's white hair hung down over a moss-green cloak like silk drapes. Something about her seemed off, though. He couldn't quite put his finger on it, but something in the eyes felt different.

"Now that you've managed to pull yourself together," she said, giving him a good looking-over before shaking her head dismissively. "Why don't you start by telling me who you are and what in the flaming tongues of Ornak you're doing here? And, more importantly, why you just attacked an old woman without just cause."

"Without just cause?" Ty's blood flared. "You killed my mother!"

"Boy, I've never seen you or your mother before in my life!" Her eyes narrowed. "But I have a feeling I know what the problem is." She turned and looked out over the water. "You think I'm Mangora."

Now it was Ty's turn to be bewildered. "What game are you playing? You don't think I have your face forever burned in my memory, you murderer?" He raised his hands, and she turned and wagged her finger in warning.

"Ah-ah-ah. None of that, unless you want to take a swim."

Out of the corner of his eye, Ty could see the vines slowly starting to move in his direction, and he lowered his hands. He wished he'd brought Orlyn along. He could have used the apothecary's help with these plants.

"That's better," she said with a smile. "My name is Douina. Mangora is my sister. My twin sister, if you must know. And if you say she killed your mother, I believe you. There isn't much about my sister I wouldn't believe." She turned and wiggled her finger at several of the vines hanging at the edge of the water, and they hurried over and wrapped themselves up under her, forming a makeshift seat. "Much better." She laid her staff in her lap as she sat down.

"And how am I to believe what you say?" Ty asked.

"Feel me with your magic, if you doubt."

"What?"

"Don't play coy with me, boy. I've already felt your weave through the marsh. It's why I came looking." She pointed at Ty's hands. "Well, go ahead. I'm waiting."

Ty figured it couldn't hurt, so he released a thin net across the path ahead, letting it encapsulate the old woman claiming to be Mangora's sister. To his surprise, there was a noticeable difference. Mangora had always felt similar to her arachnobes—a dark sort of hatred, a deep twisted rot he had attributed to those wielders who served the Tower. But with Douina, there was a kind of peace, something he could have never ascribed to Mangora.

Ty released the weave, and like a broken cobweb, the strands came apart, evaporating one by one until they simply vanished altogether.

The old woman smiled. "Come. You look like you could use a hot meal. I can hear your stomach from here. And that leg needs tending to."

Ty limped over to his pack and slipped it on. Grabbing his weapons, he took one final look around to make sure he hadn't left anything and then quickly patted his right pocket. Good. The compass was still there. He turned and limped over to where Douina was sitting at the edge of the water. "Are you the watcher?"

Douina cocked her head. "The what?"

"Are you the one I was told would be guarding the mirror?" He didn't know if he should be talking about it, but since it was a good bet he wouldn't find anyone else living out here, he didn't see how he had much choice.

"Mirror?"

Ty gritted his teeth. "The mirror that's supposed to help me find the key?"

"Gracious, boy. Watchers, mirrors, keys?" She cackled. "Look around you. You're in the middle of a swamp." She tapped one of the thicker vines with her staff. "Up."

The long, entangled fingers lifted into the air and carried her upward into the trees. Wherever Douina went, the fog parted, giving her a clear path through the mire.

She looked down. "Well, don't dawdle. We've got a ways to go yet."

Ty shook his head. "Stupid wizards and witches. Is that part of their training? How to avoid answering questions?"

Ahead, the heavy veil of mist divided, moving to either side of the narrow footpath, just far enough for him to find his way. Not wanting to lose sight of the old woman, he took off at a pace as brisk as his injured leg would allow.

With the trail ahead cleared of fog and dawn slowly lifting the darkness throughout the marsh, Ty released his night sight. Useful as it was, night sight left the world rather colorless, everything appearing in muted shades of grey. He could still make out colors, but they were very subdued. It was a bland way to look at things, but it was better than the alternative.

He trekked through the marsh for at least another hour, limping along as he tried to keep up with Douina and her unique means of transport. Ty found it rather fascinating. He wouldn't have minded trying it himself if it didn't mean swinging out across those deadly black waters.

Douina didn't seem to mind, though, as she stepped from one set of vines to the next. Each time, there was always another group waiting on her arrival as the last branch of intertwining stems stretched to its end.

Before long, the trail ended, butting up against a wall of dense growth so tightly compacted that Ty couldn't see through it. It stretched into the distance on both sides of the pathway, long strands of vines and moss blocking the way forward. Ty stopped, waiting to see what Douina would do.

The trees lowered her down onto the path beside him, and with a point of her staff, the hanging foliage parted like curtains in front of a window, and they walked through.

Ty gasped. It was as though they'd stepped through a doorway into a new world, the darkness and stench of the marsh left behind as they crossed the threshold into a small sunlit paradise. Inside the walled-off barrier was a glen, lush with beauty and life. It reminded him in a way of Nyalis's Y'tarra, though perhaps not quite so strange.

Thick grass lay like a blanket across the soil, the dark waters of the bog nowhere to be found. It smelled of wildflowers, the way their house would when his mother had stopped to pick them on the side of Rinson's field while riding back from Easthaven.

A small angular cottage sat at the top of a hill just ahead, with a thatched roof that rose to an unnaturally sharp peak. In fact, when Ty looked at it from the side, it wasn't all that dissimilar to one of his arrowheads. But instead of steel, the cottage had the same white plaster siding as his family home, albeit in disrepair. Pieces of siding had clearly chipped away over the years, patched with what looked like globs of dark mire from the marsh. A light burned in the windows, and smoke rose from the chimney.

As strange as it was to find a home in the middle of Reed Marsh, it wasn't the house that kept his attention—it was what stood beside it. Resting at the center of the small glen was the largest tree Ty had ever seen, as wide as it was tall, with limbs the size of most tree trunks, spreading in all directions like the legs of a great spider. Some rose upward, some drooped down. All were thick with broad heart-shaped leaves as wide as both of Ty's hands.

"His name is Abinayu," Douina said, pointing at the tree with her staff. "He is the guardian of the marsh. His roots run far and wide, keeping everything in balance, caring for the life within."

"Abinayu? Strange name for a tree."

She chuckled and started for the front of the cottage. "Don't let him hear you say that."

Ty looked at the tree. Was there something there he wasn't seeing? Sure, it was monolithic, but how could a tree care for an entire marsh? Curious, he sent out a single web of magic. Couldn't hurt to see, he thought.

As soon as the web hit the base of the tree, the ground under his feet shook. In fact, the entire clearing trembled. Several of the limbs actually moved.

Douina turned. "Serves you right if he tosses you back in the marsh."

Ty gulped and chased after the old woman. "He wouldn't do that, would he?"

She shrugged. "He has a mind of his own. But let's not push him, shall we? The last time he got flustered, I was cleaning my house for a week. No telling what damage this time has done."

Ty kept a close eye on the tree as he followed Douina up the steps, imagining one of the branches reaching down and snatching him off the ground and tossing him into the marsh. Not wanting to take a chance of that happening, he released his magic, letting the heat simmer down and dissipate altogether. He didn't think he'd need it with Douina.

Douina opened the front door, tapped her boots on the entry, and stepped inside. "Come. Let's have a look at that leg, shall we?"

Ty started across the threshold, but Douina stopped him with a stern look. "Don't go tracking that in here," she said, pointing at his feet.

Ty looked down. His boots were completely covered in muck from where he'd stepped knee-deep in the bog. Quickly, he pulled them off and left them outside, placing them just to the right of the door.

"Those too," she said, pointing to his mud-caked trousers.

Feeling a little embarrassed, Ty unhooked his sword and slowly removed his pants. Thankfully, he was wearing his woolen underpants underneath as he handed her the trousers, which she took and tossed inside a nearby bucket half filled with water.

Douina nodded, then walked across the room and took a seat in one of the two rockers angled in front of the fire. She moaned softly as she leaned her staff up against the stone hearth and reclined, letting the seat tilt back to a comfortable level.

Ty stepped inside and shut the door, feeling more than a little awkward at his state of undress. He took off his bow and quiver and placed them against the wall before unhooking his pack and laying it beside them. He was glad to be rid of the extra weight. Glancing at his sword, he tried to decide whether he should lay it aside as well. Something about Douina made him feel safe, but common sense finally won out, and he strapped it over his underpants.

He turned and stretched and got his first good look at Douina's living quarters. After having suffered through Mangora's dark trinket shop and his terrifying visit up to her chambers, he had half expected to find the inside of the cottage blanketed in dust and infested with cobwebs. But, apparently, Douina couldn't have been more different than her twin sister.

The bottom floor of the cottage was a single room, cluttered, but in an organized fashion. A lifetime of living compiled into one space. There was a small rectangular table with two stools and two place settings. Shelves lined the far wall, stacked to the brim with all manner of books, loose papers and knickknacks, as well as some dishes, cooking utensils, herbs, and even a couple of gardening trowels. Directly underneath the shelves were several large trunks, a couple of barrels, and piles of stacked books.

A set of stairs at the back led up to what Ty could only guess was the bedchamber. Green vines entwined the railing as it went up. Those same roots seemed to stretch out along the walls, growing and thickening as they went up, stretching out across the rafters as they seemed to encompass most of the inside of the home. Buds with white petals and yellow centers sprouted along the bark, leaving a fresh, sweet scent in their wake. In a way, it reminded Ty of Master Orlyn's shop. He wondered if Douina possessed the same floratide gift as the apothecary.

"There are very few places you can go in this marsh where Abinayu isn't present," Douina said, noticing Ty staring at the long snakelike vines as they wove around the beams.

Ty startled for a moment. "That's all Abinayu? Can he hear us?"

She smiled. "In a manner of speaking." She nodded toward a thick growth near the fireplace. "Go ahead, he won't bite."

After Ty's last encounter with the tree, he wasn't so sure, but he walked over and carefully placed his hand on the bark, nonetheless. Ty caught the corners of Douina's mouth curl when she spotted his sword hanging from his long underwear. Not letting it bother him, he focused on the tree.

The root was surprisingly warm. Ty could feel a shallow pulsing underneath, like blood rushing under the skin. Abinayu was like nothing he'd ever heard of before. Ty was tempted to reach out once more and try communicating with it, but after being warned of getting tossed in the marsh, he reasonably decided against it, and instead, took a seat in the empty rocker in front of the fire.

He couldn't help but notice the iron skillet inside, and the mouth-watering aroma filled his nostrils. "Is someone else living here as well?" Ty asked, curious about the two rockers, and the two stools, and dual place settings at the table.

Douina closed her eyes and sighed. "A long time ago." There was a sadness in her voice that Ty figured was best left alone. She eventually opened her eyes and fixed Ty with a curious look. The kind that said she had something to ask but might have been afraid of the answer. "Tell me of my sister. I gather she's still alive?"

Ty nodded, not quite sure how to answer, afraid that whatever he said would no doubt be the wrong thing.

"You said she killed your mother?"

Ty's fingers clamped down on the arms of the rocker. He began by telling her of his first meeting with Mangora inside her shop in Easthaven, then he proceeded to describe their battle with the Tallosians and her arachnobes. He also told of being ensnared by the numori she had left behind for him to find and being forced to fight his own family.

"I'm sorry for your loss," she said sincerely, her rocker continuing to creak back and forth. "My sister lost her way a long time ago. She was lured away by a man promising her fortune and fame. She was so smitten, she would have followed him into the Pits of Aran'gal if he'd requested it. They say love is blind." Douina snorted. "I say it's flaming deadly."

"Who was he?"

"A two-bit swindler with a mountain-sized chip on his shoulder. He'd come looking for the very thing you search for."

Ty's head shot up. "Oh? How long ago was this?"

She laughed, or possibly coughed. Ty was finding it hard to tell the difference. "Many, many years ago."

"He didn't get it, did he? The shorlock." This was the first Ty was hearing about someone else going after the key.

"No. Many have tried over the decades, but none have made it through the mirror. Few have made it this far and lived to tell about it."

"Why has no one made it through the mirror?"

"Because that decision is up to the watcher, and the watcher alone."

"Why haven't you let anyone in?"

Douina frowned. "Oh child, I'm not the watcher."

Ty loosened his grip on the rocker's arm as realization sank in. When Nyalis had told him that he would have to convince the watcher to let him use the mirror, he had naturally thought it was a person. He looked at the twisted root lying across the mantel. "Abinayu's the watcher?"

She nodded with a grandmotherly sort of smile. "So, Nyalis has sent you to find the missing pieces to the shorlock of Aero'set, has he? That is quite the task for such a young boy."

Ty balked. "I'm sixteen."

"My apologies," she said. "Sixteen, you say. Such advanced years for someone with a chin as smooth as yours."

Ty bit his tongue.

"Then again," she said, her lips pursed, "I don't believe I've ever met a Fae with hair on his chin."

"You've met a faerie?"

"Well, no. Which is why I've never seen one with hair on his chin."

Ty didn't find her humor all that funny. Too much like Nyalis. Maybe that was the way it was with old people. The more advanced the years, the dryer their wit.

Douina stood and grabbed a wooden ladle from off the mantel and began to stir the pot. She dipped out a small portion and tasted. "Perfect," she said, and then dished out a generous helping to each, carrying the bowls back to the table. After offering a quick prayer of thanks to the Creator, they dug in. The stew was delicious. Ty didn't ask where the meat had come from. It wasn't like there was an overabundance of deer or rabbit around, and at that point he was too hungry to care. Whatever it was, it had a strong afterbite, but Ty found it savory enough to request a second helping. And when a third was offered, he didn't turn it down.

By the time he laid his spoon inside his empty bowl, he thought he was going to need someone to carry him back to his chair. He pushed on his stomach, and it pushed back.

Douina smiled proudly as she stood from her seat. "It's been many a year since I've had the pleasure of another's company at my table. I hope the food was satisfactory."

Ty burped, not meaning to, of course, and smiled.

"I'll take that as a yes." She walked over to one of the cabinets on the far wall and began to dig through the shelves. After a thorough search, she came back to the table with a couple of stoppered vials, a mixing bowl, and some pouches of what Ty could only guess were herbs. "Let's have a look at that leg, shall we?"

Ty raised the right leg of his woolen underpants. There was noticeable bruising around the calf as well as a nasty scrape down the front, where he'd ripped the skin trying to jerk his leg out of the hole. After a thorough examination, Douina opened both vials and poured about a quarter of each into the bowl, followed by two good pinches from one of the cloth pouches. She mixed the concoction until it was about the same color and consistency as the mire Ty had fallen into, then wiped his leg clean with a wet cloth and rubbed the pasty blend down his shin where the skin was most red.

It was cool to the touch, almost refreshing. The pain lessened immediately.

Ty felt like laughing as he sat there and stared at his mud-caked leg. He'd already done this much damage to himself, and he hadn't even made it through the first mirror yet. How was he ever going to survive the tests?

She wrapped his leg with a clean bandage, scraped what was left of the paste into a small tin, and handed it to him. "Apply this every morning and it should get you through the day."

"Thank you," he said and walked over to stick the container in his pack. He was surprised to find he was no longer limping, but he knew it wasn't because the leg had miraculously healed. Whatever she'd given him had simply taken away the pain. If he wasn't careful, he could do further damage.

"Can you tell me anything of my journey?" he asked as he retook his seat by the fire and tried not to think about how bloated he felt.

Douina shook her head. "Afraid not. This is as far as I've been."

"You've never been through the mirror?" Ty found that hard to believe.

"I'd be lying if I said I didn't think about it from time to time. Nothing more than idle curiosity, really. Curious to see where it leads. What could be waiting on the other side." She grabbed a pipe from the table beside her chair and lit it with a piece of kindling. Taking a couple of deep puffs, she slowly released, letting the rings circle her head.

It had a sweet smell that complemented the blossoms sprouting from Abinayu's roots. Ty found it relaxing, reminded of the way his father would smoke his pipe in the evenings after a long day. His eyes began to flutter as he fought to keep them from shutting, the lids weighing heavily. The gentle crackling and popping from the fire next to him made it all the more difficult. Clearly, what additional aid Nyalis had given him before entering the marsh had been spent during his escape from the razorback and his encounter with the marsh witch.

His struggle to stay awake was short-lived, and his eyes closed one last time.

Chapter 7 | Ty

TY JERKED AWAKE, turning to see where the old woman had gotten off to. Perhaps she was up in her bedchamber. He stood and stretched. His muscles no longer ached, and the weariness he'd felt during their meal seemed to have dissipated. In fact, he felt ready to take on whatever the mirror had in store for him.

Lying across the back of his chair, he found his pants, washed and dried, and he quickly put them back on. He looked out the window to see if he could spot Douina rummaging about outside, but was unable to see much of anything beyond the glass, as the sun had been replaced by the cover of night. Had he slept straight through the day? How was that possible?

"Douina?"

He marched over to the stairs at the back and called her name once more. Either she was a really heavy sleeper, or she wasn't there. He crossed the room, grabbing his bow and quiver on the way out, taking the time to string it before shutting the door behind him. "*Ru'kasha Kor.*" His night sight brightened the entire glen.

He scanned the yard around the front of the house all the way to the hanging willow barrier below surrounding the glen, but he didn't see Douina anywhere. Where was she? It wasn't like she had a great many places to hide. He made his way around the side of the house and back toward Abinayu. The tree's monstrous trunk was wider than Douina's house. He looked up, half expecting to see her flying around its branches, but instead found that the farther up the tree he looked, the denser its foliage became, leaving him unable to see past the first few layers of limbs.

"You're finally up. Good."

Ty startled and turned to find Douina stepping out from behind the other side of the trunk.

"Why didn't you wake me?"

"You needed the rest. How's the leg?"

Ty hadn't even noticed he'd been walking around on it without the slightest bit of pain. "It feels good."

She nodded.

"I can't believe I slept so long," he said, more frustrated with himself than with her for not having woken him. "I didn't want to go through the mirror at night."

"You won't have to," she said, looking out beyond the branches to the greying sky. "By the time we wash up and eat some breakfast, the sun should be up."

"What? I slept all the way through the night as well? That's impossible. I wasn't that tired."

Douina smirked. "I might have sprinkled a little something extra in your drink. I figured you'd be too stubborn to heed my warning and go running off on that injured leg without giving it a second thought."

Ty didn't know if he should be angry or grateful. In the end, he decided he couldn't do anything about it anyway, so he followed her inside for a hot bowl of porridge and a still-steaming loaf of barley that had a strong taste of ale. There was also fresh cinnamon for the porridge. All in all, it was a very satisfying meal, leaving him ready to tackle the new day. By the time he'd helped her clear the table, dawn had already begun to work its way through the side windows, spreading magnificent colors across the sky.

Ty gathered his belongings. "I'm ready," he said, fidgeting anxiously beside the door, growing rather apprehensive about his meeting with Abinayu. He had no idea if the great tree would be willing to grant him access to the mirror or not. So far, according to Douina, no one had been allowed passage, and after his not-so-warm welcome the day before, he wasn't liking his odds.

Douina gave him a quick looking-over and nodded. "I guess you are." She walked past him and out into the yard. Ty shut the door and joined her as they skirted the side of the house around to the back of Abinayu's trunk. At the back of the tree, some of the roots had knotted together to form what looked like a set of stairs leading farther up the trunk.

Ty looked around. "Where's the mirror?"

"Patience, my young friend. All in good time." Douina started up the stairs, her staff clicking on the wood as she went, coming to a stop on a small platform at the top. She turned and motioned for him to follow.

Ty didn't quite bound up the steps, but his eagerness had him taking more than one at a time. At the top, he waited for Douina to show him what to do, but after a long silence, he finally turned. "What are we waiting for?"

She kept her eyes on the tree. "Him."

Ty looked up, not understanding what she meant. Then he saw it. Above, the branches were alive with what looked like thousands of little glowworms. The entire tree sparkled. "What are they?"

"His mind. His thoughts. His words."

"Huh?"

She sighed. "Just wait. You'll see."

Ty didn't have to wait long. The lights grew in intensity the closer they came, brighter than any candle's flame. Thousands of little balls of light floated down around them, lighting on his head, his shoulders, his pack, covering Ty from head to foot. He closed his eyes as they flew around his face, and a voice somewhere in the back of his mind reached out, deep and foreboding.

"*Only those deemed worthy shall pass.*"

Deemed worthy? What did that mean? He had no idea if he was worthy or not. He doubted Nyalis would have sent him if he didn't think he was. He spared a quick peek through his lids to see what Douina was doing and if the balls of light were still there and found that not only was Douina nowhere to be seen, but the balls of light were gone as well. In fact, everything was gone: the tree, her house, the glen, even the marsh. The only thing left was darkness.

A shape in front of him slowly appeared out of the nothingness. It was a man, middle-aged, with long white hair down his back, piercing blue eyes, and skin as fair as Ty's. He wore a robe of sewn leaves and a wreath of vines around his head.

The man stopped in front of Ty.

"Who are you?" Ty asked.

"My name is Abinayu."

"You're the tree? But you look like . . ." He looked a little like Ty, or at least what Ty might look like in about twenty or thirty years.

"I wasn't always a tree. I used to appear as you see me now."

"You're a . . . a . . ."

"A faerie?" Abinayu chuckled. "Yes."

Ty had so many questions, but he didn't know where to begin—questions about who he was, how he'd come to be, if Abinayu knew his father—but before he could ask, the faerie raised his hand.

"Your questions will be answered in time, little one. Just know that there are those on both sides who'd see you destroyed if they could. You are an anathema. A product of an unholy union. There's a reason why bonding between Fae and human is outlawed. Their offspring are dangerous, to both sides. Unpredictable in nature. But for all of those that would see you exterminated, there are some that would seek to use you. Be wary of them most of all."

All of Ty's questions evaporated. His earlier excitement at finding the mirror and beginning his journey was snuffed out like a candle in the wind. He felt lightheaded, a wave of nausea rolling over him like the crashing of the tide. Ty knew the Tower wanted him, but to find out that both the humans *and* the faerie would wish to see him dead was horrifying. It was bad enough to have one race seeking his destruction, but both races?

Somewhere in the back of his mind, he'd always hoped that one day he might meet those of the other race and find a connection, a link to his heritage. But now, it appeared those dreams had been taken from him, and he was left with a hole that would never be filled. He forced the thoughts aside. They were too painful to think about. If he dwelt on them, he'd probably never leave the marsh again, content with spending the rest of his days helping Douina care for Abinayu. For a brief moment, he wondered if that would even be possible.

"No," Abinayu said emphatically. "This world needs you. And right now, it needs you to finish your quest."

How did he . . .

"Read your thoughts?" Abinayu smiled, the kind of smile reserved for children not quite old enough to understand. "Our minds are linked. There is nothing hidden from me."

Ty felt violated, and a little embarrassed. He didn't like someone being able to read his thoughts and see what was in his mind. Even he didn't like seeing what was in there half the time.

But Abinayu was right. Ty had a job to do, and he needed to get on with it.

"Am I worthy to use the mirror?"

"Do you believe you are?"

Ty thought a moment. "Probably not."

"Then you are." The faerie turned and started to walk back into the darkness.

"Wait," Ty said, desperate to keep him there. "I have so many questions."

"And those answers are out there for you to find."

"Will I ever see you again?"

Abinayu stopped and turned. "The web of life weaves as it will. Each life is a strand woven into the fabric of time." He smiled. "Perhaps our strands will cross again." With that, he disappeared back into the void, and the darkness evaporated like a cloud of smoke being driven by a harsh wind.

Ty opened his eyes, and the tiny balls of golden light lifted back into the air and disappeared in the branches above.

"He can be quite the gentleman when he wants to be," Douina said with a chuckle.

Ty turned to find her still standing beside him. "You didn't tell me he was one of the Fae."

"That was for you to discover on your own."

"What happened to him? How did he end up becoming a tree?"

Douina hmphed. "That is a long story best told by him. Right now, you have more pressing needs to worry about."

Ty was about to argue the point when something occurred to him. "He never told me how to get to the mirror."

"That's the easy part. Well, easy if you are one he considers worthy. And considering you haven't been flung back into the marsh, I'm guessing your conversation with him went well."

"You couldn't hear us?"

She shook her head. "No, that was for you and you alone." She pointed at a particularly large knot in the tree at about eye level on the right side of the platform. "Place your hand there, and he will do the rest."

Ty walked over and placed his hand over the lump of wood.

Nothing happened.

"Do I need to press—"

The platform they were on rumbled slightly as the trunk in front of the platform split, the two halves opening to form a doorway. Ty was astonished. The inside of the tree was hollow, save for a set of stairs leading downward.

"In you go, lad," Douina said with a bright smile.

"Aren't you coming?"

"I have other things to attend to. The rest is up to you. It was nice meeting you, Ty of Easthaven, and I wish you well on your journey."

Ty started to hold out his hand but found himself hugging her instead. She smelled of rich earth. After a brief moment, he released her and stepped back. "Thank you for your hospitality. And for looking after my leg."

She patted the top of his head. "It was my pleasure."

Ty watched as she hobbled down the steps and started back toward the house. He wondered how much longer she could survive here on her own. Then again, he guessed she wasn't exactly alone.

He turned back to the doorway, taking a moment to peer inside at the circular stairwell before finally getting up the nerve to go in. The doorway remained open as he stepped onto the landing and started down.

The smell of the wood was intoxicating, strong and sweet. The steps spiraled downward, and he followed it to the bottom, surprised to find the lower roots were not underwater, what with the surrounding marsh. The bottom landing opened into an empty room with walls of dark soil and intertwining roots. The same glowing balls that he'd seen earlier floated through the chamber, spreading light throughout.

Ty's eyes fixed on the far wall, where a mirror at least several feet taller than himself stood waiting. Its frame was covered in glyphs, the largest being that at the top. While the other glyphs could have been nothing more than decoration, this one was obviously important.

Ty had no idea what the glyphs said. It wasn't like he could read ancient runic. He did know that somewhere amidst the characters around the frame was the name of two mirrors, and if he were to call them out in succession, they would take him where he needed to go.

Remembering Nyalis's instructions concerning the runes, he reached into his pocket for the velvet pouch and dumped the silver compass into his palm. The arrow pointed straight at the mirror.

Even having walked in circles to reach the bottom of the tree, Ty was pretty sure that north was behind him. Testing the instrument's bearings, he turned around to see what would happen, but the needle swung to point back toward the enclosed glass.

"All right," he said, holding up the compass. "Show me what I need to do."

No surprise, the compass didn't answer him back.

Nyalis had told him the compass would help with reading the mirror's names, but what good was knowing that if he didn't know how to make it work? He held the compass up to the mirror, but other than his arm getting tired, nothing happened. He even went so far as to touch the mirror with it, first the frame, then the glass.

The runes were just as unreadable as before.

He stood on his tiptoes and touched the glyphs at the top of the mirror. The wood was surprisingly warm to the touch, and like the roots inside Douina's home, the wood pulsed beneath his fingers. Unfortunately, other than feeling the indentions carved into the wood, nothing happened, and he pulled his hand away, frustrated at not being able to figure out how to get the crazy thing to work.

With little other choice, he looked inward, closing his eyes as he reached for his magic. The familiar warmth was there to greet him. He was hesitant at first, knowing the reaction he'd received from Abinayu the first time, but necessity outweighed caution. The heat spread through him, heightening his senses, allowing him to feel his surroundings more than just see them.

Abinayu was every bit as magnificent as Douina had made him out to be. Ty could see the tree's roots delving deep into the ground and spreading out for miles in all directions. Ty wondered how long the faerie had been there. He turned his attention to the one object he'd come all this way to find. The mirror.

How did it work? He reached out with a web of magic and let it encase the wooden frame. It was old. Very old. He could feel the magic working within. It was neither light nor dark, good nor evil. It just was. The magic that held it together was more complex, and woven more tightly than anything Ty had ever seen. It must have taken a great deal of skill and time to create such a magnificent artifact.

He slid the tendrils of his magic across the frame, coming to rest on the runes themselves. He didn't need to open his eyes. He could see them spelled out in his mind as clear as if he were reading it on a sheet of paper. Each set of runes around the frame was the name of a single mirror, of which there were dozens. But which were the two he needed?

He opened his eyes to find two specific sets of runes glowing. Not only could he read their inscriptions, but he could hear their pronunciations in the back of his mind: *Ra'hanisra Tulgarin. Durkani Varool.*

Ty released his hold on the mirror and focused on the two names, speaking both as clearly as possible. "*Ra'hanisra Tulgarin. Durkani Varool.*"

The glass sprung to life so quickly that Ty jumped back to keep it from dragging him in. His reflection disappeared, replaced by a dark murky image. There were no recognizable features: no rocks, trees, or grass. It was like looking through a window in the dead of winter and watching the snow fall so thick you couldn't see through it. Except whatever he was looking at, it wasn't snow.

Was the mirror working correctly? Was he supposed to just step through? He remembered his experience with traveling through a portal such as this in Y'tarra. Only, then, he'd been able to see where the portal was leading. This time, he couldn't see anything. What would happen if the mirror on the other side wasn't working? Would he simply vanish into nothingness?

A noise above him brought him around, and he called up, "Douina, is that you?" He wondered if she was coming to see him off after all, but when no one responded, he shrugged it off. Ty could still see a sliver of light streaming partway down the circular staircase from the open doors above. Most likely a tree rat had found itself the perfect home to roost, or perhaps it was just the tree settling.

He finally turned back to the mirror, the image still unchanged. He had thought the choice to step into the marsh had been a difficult one. At least he'd known what he was walking into. This was a roll of the dice. Still, he'd come this far. Either he tried, or he packed it up and went home, dooming everyone to whatever horrible fate Nyalis had been warning them about.

Ty balled his fists. Hang defeat. He was going in.

He stuffed the compass back in its pouch and tucked it in his trouser pocket. After one last look around the room, he stepped up to the glass, took a deep breath, and stepped inside.

The glass felt like water as he passed through, leaving him with the sensation of floating. The sensation didn't end. He tried to turn around to see if he could still see the inside of the tree, and the mirror was suddenly yanked away.

No, *he'd* been yanked away!

Searing pain tore through Ty's chest as he inhaled a lungful of water. What was happening? Where was he? His eyes burned, but all he could see was sediment. The mirror had sent him to the bottom of a riverbed.

His mind screamed in panic as he tried to swim upward, but the current was too strong, his pack too heavy. He wasn't even sure which way was up. Numbing pain shot through his arm as he collided with a boulder. He raised the other to protect his face while kicking with his feet to break free from the undertow, which kept dragging him back to the bottom.

Up ahead, he could just make out the shadow of another large boulder, this one nearly the size of a vegetable cart, coming up on the right. He fought to get his feet in line so he could kick off and swim his way to the surface, but just as he was about to hit, something stopped him.

He flailed back and forth in the current as the water whipped him about. Frantically, he spun to see what had happened and found his pack had been entangled in the limbs of a fallen tree.

He was stuck.

Twisting, he reached as far back as he could to free whatever had been snagged. He couldn't find it, his hand grabbing nothing but cloth. His mind raced, desperation taking over as he reached for his magic, but there was nothing his magic could do to help. His mind was clouding over, growing as dim as the murky waters holding him under. He could feel death coming for him, and almost laughed. The powerful faeling, dying by tree limb.

The water pressed in, threatening to entomb him. He fought with everything he had to hold back the next inhale, but in the end his body won out, and he sucked in another lungful. He spasmed, unable to control his own limbs, darkness coming.

Then suddenly his pack broke free. Or did he break free from his pack? He couldn't tell. The last thing he remembered was a huge arm wrapping around his chest and pulling him upward.

Ty heaved, spewing water with every painful retch. He fought to reach that first gulp of air, but there was too much water. Pain wracked his body. His head felt like it was going to burst, his lungs on fire. Everything was spinning.

Coughing violently, he flipped over, fluid pouring from his mouth until he was able to catch his first small breath of air. It was hardly enough to fill his cheeks, let alone his lungs, but with each new attempt, he found he could draw in a little more.

"Just keep breathing."

Ty heard the words, but understanding them was beyond him. He heaved again, the vomit burning his throat.

"That's it. Let it all out."

Ty was vaguely aware that someone was there, but other than feeling a hand under his chest and the occasional beating on his back, he couldn't tell much beyond that. His chest spasmed, and for the first time, he managed a deep, gasping inhale. It wasn't until that moment that he realized he might just make it.

After two or three raspy breaths, he finally tried opening his eyes, but the blinding light from the sun and silt from the river made it difficult to see. A silhouette in front of him began to take shape.

"I was afraid I'd lost you."

Recognition hit Ty like a blacksmith's hammer, and he jerked up. "Breen?" His vision cleared, and his brother's face came into view. "Breen!" He wrapped his arms around his brother's neck, holding on for dear life, afraid to let him go in case this was all some elaborate dream.

His brother squeezed him in return.

"Is it really you?" Ty asked, releasing him long enough to get a good look. "Or am I imagining this?"

Breen smiled. "Yes, it's me. And no, it's not your imagination. At least I don't think so." He raised his hand and pinched his cheek, then smiled. "Nope. I'm here."

Ty rolled over to his knees, wincing as the rock they were sitting on aggravated the cuts and bruises along his legs from where he'd scraped and beaten them against the riverbed. Looking around, it was obvious they had left the marsh behind. They were sitting just off the bank of whatever river the mirror had sent them to. The far side was covered in trees, trees that were no longer gnarled and filled with strings of moss and weeping pustules.

The waters of the river on his left were clear and fast-moving. He could see mountains off in the distance on the right, and the air was crisp and clean. It was brisk, but not enough to warrant snow, at least not yet, which meant they were most likely somewhere to the south.

Ty turned and looked at his brother. "I still don't understand how you are here."

"How do you think? I followed you." Breen said it as if it was the most obvious thing in the world.

"But how did you get through the marsh? I nearly died . . . twice."

"I followed your trail and kept my head down. Crazy fog was so thick I thought I'd lost you a couple of times, but then somewhere along the way, I'd catch a glimpse of your footprints in the mud." His eyes narrowed, and he shivered. "Now I know why Father has always warned us to stay away from that place. I heard things out in those waters that had me thankful for the fog."

"I saw what was out there, and trust me, whatever you imagined, it's a thousand times worse. I was nearly eaten by it! Oh, did you see any razorbacks?" He didn't give Breen a chance to answer. "I did. Came at me so fast I barely got a shot off with my bow. The thing was so big the arrow didn't even slow it, and just before it landed on me, one of the marsh monsters came out of the water and grabbed it and pulled it under."

Breen shook his head.

"And that's when the marsh witch arrived."

"Witch? Is that who lives in that cottage?"

Ty nodded excitedly. He spent the next quarter hour filling Breen in on all that had happened to him, from mistaking Douina for Mangora, to his communication with Abinayu, and his near drowning. By the time he got to the part of the story that had him stepping through the mirror and ending up at the bottom of a river, Ty was completely out of breath all over again. He picked up a rock and threw it, watching as it broke the water's surface.

"Why would they put a mirror at the bottom of a river? Are they trying to kill everyone who goes through?"

Breen turned and looked out across the swift-flowing current. "Maybe it fell in by accident and was pulled downstream at some point. For all we know, there was no river here when the mirror was first set up. You said this wizard's keep has been gone for over a thousand years. Plenty of time for a river's course to change."

"I guess." Ty's head shot up. "Wait! Where is it?"

"Where's what?"

Ty spun in all directions. "Where's my pack? All my gear. Everything I need to make this journey is in it." He hopped to his feet, frantically scouring the shallow bank of rocks all the way down to the water. He couldn't believe he hadn't realized it was missing.

Breen stood and joined him at the water's edge. "I'm afraid it's gone."

"Gone?" Ty looked downriver as if expecting to see the pack floating away in the distance. "Why didn't you get it?"

"Because I had to cut the straps to get you loose. And I couldn't carry you and your pack, and mine, without risking drowning myself. So, I had a choice. Either save you or save your pack." He crossed his arms. "Are you saying I made the wrong choice?"

Ty sighed and shook his head. "No. Sorry. I wouldn't be standing here if it wasn't for you. I just . . . It was all my stuff." Ty gasped and grabbed for his pockets, releasing a loud sigh of relief. "Oh, thank the Creator!"

"What's wrong?" Breen looked down at Ty's hands.

"It's still here." Ty pulled the sodden pouch out of his trouser pocket and emptied the silver compass into his palm, squeezing the water out of the material as he did. "I thought I'd lost it. We would have been stuck here for sure. Wherever here is." He held the silver instrument up for Breen to see. "We need the compass to guide us to the missing pieces of the shorlock. Even more important, I need it to make the mirrors work."

Breen stared at the object as he thumbed his chin. "Good thing you didn't put it in your pack, then."

"Yeah, good thing." Ty angled the instrument so he could see the face without the sun's reflection and watched as the compass's needle found its bearing. He pointed away from the river toward a range of mountains rising in the distance. "That's our direction."

Breen followed his aim. "Looks like we might have a ways to go. Good thing I came along," he said, walking over to where his pack lay drying on one of the larger rocks just offshore. He had removed everything from inside and spread it out around the satchel. "I should have enough with me to last us a couple of days at least." He picked up his bow, the same unique black bow he'd found in Mangora's shop.

Ty remembered Nyalis telling them it had belonged to one of the famed Sol Ghati. Apparently, they were an elite band of rangers from out of the Westlands. It was said to have been created to fight against faeries, since its arrows had the ability to pierce magic.

Ty checked his other pockets, but other than a small pouch of coins his father had given him and a piece of leftover cheese he'd been saving for later, he didn't have much else but the clothes on his back and his sword. His own bow had been lost to the river as well. If Breen hadn't shown up, Ty would have been forced to resort to handmade traps to snare his food, and those were never very dependable.

Frustrated by his unfortunate luck, Ty turned his back on the treacherous waters and started up the bank. This trip had turned out to be quite the disaster so far. He hadn't realized how unprepared he'd been. What good was being a faeling, or having magic at all, if you didn't know how to properly use it? If there was one thing he'd learned, it was that he wasn't half the woodsman he had thought himself to be. If he wanted to survive, he was going to need to rely more on his head than his gifts.

"You coming?" Ty asked as he left the rocks and started into a field of winter grass.

Breen was stooped beside the river, refilling his waterskins. The water was clearly drinkable, as Ty had certainly gotten his fair share, and as they had learned from their father, it wasn't the moving water that tended to be the problem, it was the water that didn't.

Ty watched his brother finish and shook his head. He hadn't even given his waterskin a second thought. Just one more possession he'd managed to lose. There was no telling how far they would have to go before they reached drinkable water again. Although, at that point, water was about the last thing Ty wanted to think about.

Breen rehung both waterskins on the sides of his pack, then hooked his bow and quiver over his shoulder and started up the embankment.

"Where do you reckon we are?" Ty asked, staring at the plains ahead and the faint outline of the mountains further still.

Breen shook his head. "Somewhere to the south would be my guess."

"Yeah, that's what I thought. Only three mountain chains I know of that reach far enough south to not see snow at this time of year: the Razor Spine, the Sandrethins, and the Khezrian Wall."

Breen stared out at the peaks ahead. "Could be any of the three, not that it matters. One way or the other, we follow that compass."

Ty nodded, patting the lump in his pocket with his hand as they started into the grass, his mind wandering to Nyalis's insistence that he go alone. He hoped his brother's appearance didn't cause any unforeseen problems. Quite the opposite so far. Ty would probably still be at the bottom of the river if not for his brother's willful disregard for the wizard's instructions.

Whether he was supposed to go alone or not, Ty didn't care. He looked over at his brother and smiled. "I'm glad you're here."

Breen smiled in return. "No place I'd rather be."

Chapter 8 | Valtor

THE STEADY CLICKING OF Valtor's cane on the marble stairs flooded the spherical well at the heart of the White Tower with its 1,162 steps. If he leaned out over the rail, he could see directly from the bottom to the top. Behind him, Rowen remained uncharacteristically quiet as he followed in his master's steps. So much that Valtor would turn periodically to make sure his apprentice was still there.

Valtor paused to catch his breath somewhere between the fifty-sixth and sixtieth landing. He'd lost count. Thankfully, his mission did not require scaling them all. A few more and he would reach the scrying chamber.

There had been a time when transportation spells had allowed those living within the Tower to move about without climbing the equivalent of a mountainside. If only they could find the required spells to manage it again. Unfortunately, there were still thousands of rooms still un-searched within the vast network of towers and halls. Many of them had been sealed off, others magically hidden. The spells could be in any one of them.

"How is recruitment?" Valtor asked, casting a curious glance over his shoulder at his apprentice. Rowen had been quiet of late. More quiet than usual. Normally, Valtor would have thought that a good thing, as it meant his young student wasn't constantly beating him over the head with a barrage of questions, but for some reason, it seemed to tickle a nerve.

"Down," Rowen said, unconsciously rubbing the left side of his face. His deformity had grown to such a size that it had begun to affect his voice, leaving him sounding raspy.

"And why do you think that is?" Valtor liked to force his pupil to use his head and not rely so much on magic. The skinny youth was barely twenty and full of potential—if he could ever learn to get out of his own way. His zealous desire to use magic was a dangerous road to travel, one that led most wielders to experimentation that eventually killed them, or worse.

"Too much chaos in the world."

Valtor kept his gaze ahead as they continued to climb. "Interesting. Explain." He didn't disagree with his apprentice's assessment, but he was interested in learning what Rowen considered that chaos to be.

"Rhydan's death. Dakaran taking over. Cylmar permanently crippled. Tension between the other kingdoms."

"So how does this translate into the loss of recruitment?"

Rowen thought a moment before answering. "People don't like change." He perked up. "We did see an increase after the fall of Cylmar. People flooding over the border looking for work. Still, that was months ago."

Valtor nodded, rather surprised by his acolyte's insights. "How should we fix the problem?"

Rowen went silent once again. The silence continued long enough that Valtor finally turned to see what he was doing.

Rowen shook his head, his lips pursed. "I don't know."

Valtor sighed. The solution was a simple one. "It's the same principle that applies to any merchant starting his own business, from the grandest markets in Aramoor to the village farmer selling week-old fruit on the side of the road." He slowed, glancing over his shoulder to make sure Rowen was hearing him clearly, and was pleased to find his pupil hanging on his every word. "You must provide a product or service people want at a price they are willing to pay."

"But how do you make them want it?"

Valtor stopped on the next landing. "If you can answer that question, you will be a very rich man indeed." He leaned against the railing to catch his breath. "So, how do we get people to want the Tower?" Valtor didn't give Rowen time to answer. "We use their weaknesses."

"Their weaknesses? Like greed and fear?"

Valtor grinned. "Harness those two and you will have them eating out of your hands. True power isn't gold. It's *control*. That is why of the two, fear is the more productive. Don't get me wrong, greed can be quite valuable in its own way. The promise of something for nothing is always alluring, but I find it's not the motivator that *fear* can be.

"Can't gold bring control as well?" Rowen asked.

"It can," Valtor agreed, "but the one who can learn to control those with the gold is by far the more powerful. And for control to be truly effective, it needs to be given and not taken."

Rowen looked confused.

"I can send three or four companies of Black Watch into a village and take control, but how effective will that control be if the villagers fight me at every turn and eventually rise up against me? There are times when such measures are necessary, but there are other ways to use fear more properly. For example, imagine how effective it would be if those same villagers were being threatened by marauders and begged us to save them."

Rowen nodded, but his eyes narrowed as though not quite certain.

"We need the people of Aldor to look to the White Tower for their protection. For that to happen, we must give them something to fear, something only we can protect them from."

"Magic," Rowen said with a sudden sparkle in his eye, as though finally seeing how the pieces all fit together. The look was short-lived. "But what about places like Easthaven? If their overlord is able to sway the others away from the throne, there's nothing we could do or say to persuade them to turn their safety over to the Tower."

"As I said, there comes a time when the only option left to us is force." He grimaced. People no longer looked to the Tower as they used to. Once their fear of magic had dissipated after the Great Purge, that fear had simply been transferred to another object: the Tower itself. No longer was the White Tower considered the benevolent guardian of the Five Kingdoms.

Rowen was correct. If the Sidaran overlord managed to sway the other kingdoms against the throne and the Tower, *force* might very well be the only course left to them. And Mangora had all but seen to that with her pathological need to outwit the faeling. If the overlords had been on the fence earlier, they certainly wouldn't be after she used a numori on the boy.

Normally, Valtor would have applauded an open attack on the Provincial Authority, especially considering they had just convened a secret assembly without the king. If handled properly, it could have been used to gain another foothold for the Tower, allowing Valtor to swoop in and offer his assistance. But after Mangora's blatant attack on Barl in the name of the Tower, and worse still, her failure, Valtor was afraid there would be no coming back. The witch had unintentionally set the course, and now Valtor was going to be forced to find a way to either divert it or use it.

"We're here, Your Grace," Rowen said from the landing behind him.

Valtor, deep in his thoughts, was already on his way up to the next landing. He stopped, and with an exasperated sigh made his way back down, pausing at the bottom to rest his legs before continuing.

As he rubbed a spasm from his calf, he heard wings overhead. Moving closer to the railing, he looked up to see several dozen corax. The birds announced their arrival with dark, grating caws as they descended through the Tower's throat, circling like water flowing down a drain.

"How fares our esteemed inquisitor?" Valtor called out to them. "Does he have the smith in custody?"

The creatures began to squawk all at once. His ability to understand them had taken time, but the magic came, now, almost without thought.

"*Wielder lost. Continue tracking. Destination known.*"

"Useless!" Valtor spat. "I bring the man back from the underworld and give him only one task. One task . . . and he can't flaming do that!" Rowen took a couple of steps back as Valtor grabbed the rail and squeezed. "Tell Sylas to bring me that wielder, or he will find that his usefulness has come to a quick end!"

The corax crowed their understanding and spiraled up and out the top of the Tower.

Taking a deep breath to steady his nerves, Valtor turned from the well and headed down the corridor, conjuring a pale-green orb to guide his way to the scrying chamber. He lowered the spell at the door and stepped inside, leaving Rowen to wait in the hall. Using the orb for guidance, he passed through the outer half of the chamber and on to the white stone platform at the center of thirteen pyres.

He extinguished the orb, and the room fell into darkness. From the folds of his crimson robe, he removed a small stone, the rune engraved on it rough against his palm as it warmed in his hand.

Valtor steadied himself with his staff, concentrating on the central pyre. The rune on its pedestal brightened, and green flames burst from the top as he waited for the recipient of his summons to answer.

"Yes, Your Grace?" A bulradoer by the name of Topin appeared within the green flame and pulled back his hood.

"How goes our experiment in Belvin? How far has Argon spread his reach?" After Inquisitor Sylas's failure at capturing the swordsmith, at least Valtor could count on Aerodyne's former general and his growing vulraak army to cheer him up.

Topin didn't answer.

"Well, out with it. What's our general been up to? I want every gruesome detail."

Topin cleared his throat. "Yes, about that. How do I say this?"

"Quickly, if you want to continue living," Valtor growled.

Topin gulped. "Argon is . . . Well, he's dead."

Valtor didn't move. He felt his right eye twitch as every nerve in his body flared at once. "What do you mean he's dead?"

Topin cleared his throat. "I mean that he was killed, Your Grace."

Valtor squeezed his staff hard enough that his hand went numb. His plan had been perfect. He couldn't have chosen a more backward people had he released the vulraaks' essence on the rabid pygmies of the Barren Waste. "Killed? How is that possible? He's been alive for over a thousand years!" His face flushed.

"I'm not really sure, Your Grace. I wasn't—"

"What do you mean you're not really sure? Weren't you there?"

"I was. Well, mostly. Argon was living in the mines of Belvin. I'm fairly good at remaining hidden, but those tunnels were crawling with vulraaks. If I'd gone in there, they'd have killed me too."

"Maybe that would have been for the best," Valtor grumbled to himself.

"It seems the people of Sidara were a little more resilient than we expected. They mounted a resistance and quite literally stormed the mines. Argon's head is now on a stake in the city's square."

"Argon was one of Aerodyne's top four generals. How does a group of ignorant plow-wielding woodsfolk destroy one of the most powerful wizards to walk the face of Aldor? Who were these people? What magics did they possess?"

Topin swallowed once more. "None that I could see, Your Grace."

"Then how in the name of Aerodyne did a band of illiterate coal miners manage to fight their way into a vulraak-infested hole in the ground and kill Argon, when my own bulradoer was too frightened to even step inside?"

"You won't believe this, but they used reflectors. Flaming brilliant if you ask me."

"Reflectors?" Valtor snarled. He sent a tendril of magic through the stone and grabbed Topin's neck. The bulradoer gasped, stumbling backward as he struggled to break free of Valtor's grasp. Valtor watched as the life began to drain from the pathetic excuse of a bulradoer's eyes. He wanted to keep watching until the last spark of life had flittered away, but bulradoer were hard to come by and difficult to train. He couldn't afford to lose more than he already had, so he released his magic and let the flames vanish above the man's pyre.

"Utterly useless!" Valtor screamed. The thought of having to bear this news to his master had his hands trembling to the point he nearly dropped the scrying stone. He stumbled to a bench against the chamber wall and sat, his thoughts racing. He'd barely managed to catch his breath when the stone in his hand suddenly pulsed back to life, startling him enough that he dropped it. With a frustrated grunt, he leaned over and picked it up off the ground. Who could be trying to contact him now? He stood and walked back to the center of the platform just as the top of the central pyre burst into green flame.

The flames took shape, revealing a short, round man holding a jeweled goblet, his face full of rage. It was a face Valtor had hoped never to see again.

"Is this thing working?" The overlord spotted Valtor. "Are you mad? What in the fires of Aran'gal were you thinking, sending your bulradoer into the middle of our assembly? They nearly got me killed! If it wasn't for the help of local wielders, I'd be nothing more than a greasy spot on one of the back walls."

Valtor, already seething from today's series of failures, held his tongue as long as he could for the sake of his mission, then held it a bit longer. Evidently Overlord Meyrose wasn't aware of what had truly taken place, or of the faeling's involvement. "You were perfectly safe, Meyrose, I assure you," Valtor lied. He would have been all too happy to have wiped out every last one of the overlords if he could have, but Mangora had proven less than capable. Again. "Now, you were contacting me with news, I presume? The results of your secret convening of the Provincial Authority?"

"Yes," Meyrose said, retaking his seat. "Barl had quite a bit of news to bring to our attention, not the least of which was the recent attack on his citizens by the White Tower. I could have raised enough questionable doubt, but the man went and dropped a flaming arachnobe right down in front of us. Nearly wet myself looking at it." He held a kerchief up to his nose. "And the stench. Don't get me started." He took a gulp from his goblet and then refilled. "I'm not afraid to admit it, but after seeing that creature, I was nearly persuaded to join."

Valtor ground his teeth. "You do, and you'll lose my support." Valtor let some of his magic filter through the link and gently caress the man's throat. Meyrose's eyes bulged, and Valtor released him.

"See here! There's no need to threaten me, Chancellor. You already have my support, as long as I'm justly compensated and as long as you keep your white riders out of my kingdom."

"Then you'd better offer me something to prove your value. What else was discussed during the meeting?"

"Barl and Agnar are considering legal action against the throne for what was done to Cylmar in the aftermath of the battle with Elondria. Went so far as to have a historian read from the Aldoran Acts of Alliance." Meyrose hmphed. "Seems they have just cause."

Valtor waved his hand dismissively. Legal action against the throne hardly warranted much worry. He was more interested in Nyalis's sudden appearance after so many years. What was his old teacher up to, and why had he chosen now to finally come out of seclusion? It had to be the faeling.

He looked back up at the half-inebriated overlord. "It seems to me this arrangement is one-sided. So far, you've told me nothing I couldn't find out from any peddler riding through town."

"There is one more thing," Meyrose said, glancing around his chambers as though to make sure he wouldn't be overheard. "There is a wizard here." He shivered when he said the word.

"Yes, I know."

"Well, did you know that he's in search of a weapon?"

Valtor leaned in without even realizing. "What kind of weapon?"

"Well, it's not exactly a weapon, I guess. It's a place that he believes can stand up against the Tower. He called it, Aero—"

"Aero'set?" Valtor's heart raced at the very thought. It was the one place in Aldor that Valtor had been trying to reach since he had first heard about it as a young man, back when Nyalis had still been willing to train him. He had even gone so far as to attempt finding the hidden mirrors himself, hoping to recover the missing pieces of the shorlock. He'd only made it as far as Reed Marsh.

Memories flooded back of his time there, the weeks he'd spent with Mangora and her sister Douina, trying to persuade them to let him in. In the end, it was Abinayu who had refused him. Valtor tightened his grip on the staff, his shoulders tensing under the recovered memories. Perhaps he was being given a second chance. It must be the reason for Nyalis's return. Could his old teacher feel the weakening in the spells around Aerodyne's prison?

"Did the wizard say he was going after it?"

Meyrose nodded. "He said he was sending someone."

Valtor didn't need to ask who. Clearly, he was sending the faeling, Nyalis's newest protégé. Valtor sneered. He was surprised how much that bothered him. "Did he say when?"

"I believe they've already gone."

That didn't leave much time. If Valtor were to get his hands on Aero'set, his master was sure to forgive his failure with Argon. A small weight lifted off his chest at the thought. He looked back up at the pyre. "You have done well. Keep your eyes and ears open. And I trust you will keep our involvement secret. If word were to get out about our arrangement, I'm afraid your usefulness would come to an end."

Meyrose gulped, and for once it wasn't a mouthful of wine.

Valtor turned and dropped the stone back into his pocket, not even waiting for the pyre's fire to snuff out before turning and heading down the steps of the dais. He had a lot of work to do if he planned on claiming the lost Keep of Aero'set for the White Tower. The very thought quickened his feet, his earlier failures with Argon and the swordsmith a distant memory. Even the recovery of a true metallurgist would pale in comparison to Aero'set.

Chapter 9 | Ferrin

WE AREN'T GOING TO make it much farther without horses," Myron said, shivering beside Ferrin despite their campfire. "We can't very well cross Aldor on foot, especially not with snow already sticking to the ground."

It had taken the better part of the week for their small group to make it through the northern passes in the Razor Spine Mountains and down into the lower foothills. They had managed to escape Sylas and the Tower's white riders by taking a freezing plunge into the swift waters of the Virn Run, but it had left them destitute and forced to take shelter on the outer rim of the Sidaran Forest with little more than their clothes, a few blankets, and a fire to take the edge off the colder gusts.

"Our pursuers might have to find another way around," Myron continued, "but with us on foot, it won't take them long to catch up. Not to mention the loss of our food in the river."

There was a noticeable grunt from the other side of the fire. Rae clung to Suri, sharing her body's warmth with the little girl. Rae looked up long enough to notice Ferrin watching and turned her head. Ever since nearly drowning Ferrin in a panicked attempt to stay above water, Rae had kept to herself even more than usual. He'd told her it wasn't her fault, but her inability to meet his eyes said she didn't believe him.

Ferrin set down the long, thin strands of the green tallunicci plant he'd been peeling to dry for cordage and grabbed a rolled-up piece of vellum from his pack. He'd purchased the map in Iraseth. Thankfully, it, as well as their gold, had been packed in one of the bags Ferrin had managed to save from the river. He stared intently at the scribbles and markings along the centermost ridge depicting the mountains behind them and ran his finger northwest, stopping at a small dot.

"It looks like Woodvale is our safest bet," he said, holding the map out for Myron to see. "Kariss would be closer, but it's south of here and in the opposite direction of where we need to go."

Myron studied the area Ferrin had marked with his finger and nodded. "I haven't been there before, but it looks large enough to find horses to purchase. The question is whether we can make it that far on foot in this weather. If it were just the two of us, I'd say we stood a fair chance, but with Miss Rae and the little one . . ." He glanced across the fire and chewed his lower lip.

"Worry about yourselves," Rae shot back, her teeth chattering against the cold as she fixed the two men with a harsh glare, apparently able to hear them. "Suri and I can handle anything you can." It was the most she'd said at one time since being fished out of the river.

Myron cleared his throat. "Of course. I meant no offense. I just know how cruel this country can be without proper supplies." He turned and looked at the freshly peeled tallunicci lying across Ferrin's lap. "I wish one of us would have had the good sense to grab one of the crossbows before jumping in. Kind of hard to catch eatable game with nothing but a longsword. I don't know about you, but I can't run a rabbit to ground."

Ferrin smiled as he rolled up the map and stuffed it back in the pack. "Lucky for you, my skills as a weaponsmith go beyond simply shaping metal." He grabbed the longer strips of the fibrous inner bark and held them up. "What do you think I've been working on?"

Myron looked at the green strips, then at Ferrin, and scratched his head. "I was afraid to ask. Either you're planning on making a new type of stringy pasta or weaving some cord to hang yourself with." Myron frowned. "Not sure which is better."

There was a chuckle from the other side of the fire, but Rae kept her head lowered.

"It's bowstring," Ferrin said, giving the strands a firm tug to show their strength. "Or at least it will be once they've been dried by the fire and properly woven."

"Bowstring from butterfly plants? That's a first."

"You'll be surprised what you can make when desperate enough. I saw a hickory grove not too far back where I might be able to find some suitable staves. I'll take a look in the morning. With any luck, I can also find some straight shoots to harvest for arrows."

"Let's hope our luck holds," Myron said. "'Cause if we don't find a way to catch game, and soon, we're going to starve to death before we make it halfway to Woodvale." Myron paused a moment, then glanced across the fire toward Rae and her daughter. He turned to Ferrin and lowered his voice. "What about young Suri?"

Ferrin looked up. "What about her?"

"She seems to have a way with the animals. Couldn't she use her . . . you know, and bring the game to us?"

Ferrin spared a quick glance across the fire as well. Rae was too preoccupied with tucking her blanket around the little girl to notice. "I've already considered it," he said, "but I'm too afraid that if she were to try using her magic in that way, she could very well alert the corax to our presence."

Myron thumbed his chin. "I hadn't thought about that. You think they might notice?"

Ferrin shrugged. "I've no idea how her magic works, but if she were to try reaching out to the animals, I would assume the Tower's trackers might hear it too. Honestly, I've got no idea. Perhaps she can speak with just a single type of animal if she wants to, but as far as I can tell, she's never used her gift before, which means she's unfamiliar with it. Do you really want to take the chance she might call the wrong creatures?"

Myron frowned. "I guess not." He glanced across the fire at Suri. "We might come to the point, though, where we don't have a choice."

"Let's hope not," Ferrin said and held up several thin pieces of plant to the firelight.

Myron took one of the strands from Ferrin's leg and examined it. "Glad one of us was taught something more useful than how to dig a straight furrow. My folks were farmers. Been plowing the same fields for generations. Probably all the way back to the Great Purge." He put down the strand and shook his head, looking a little embarrassed by the admittance.

"It's an honorable trade," Ferrin said, continuing to strip the green bark.

"Suppose so. Just not for me. I wanted to see the world. The thought of getting up every morning and doing the same thing day after day . . ." He sighed.

Ferrin wanted to laugh. "I've seen more of the world in the last year than I care to in a lifetime. Give me the warmth and routine of my smithy any day."

Myron's belly grumbled loud enough for Ferrin to hear, and he patted it with a slight smirk. "Then again, I suppose there's something to be said for stability and setting down roots as well."

Ferrin spread another batch of peeled strands on some rocks in front of the fire.

"You think they'll work?" Myron asked.

"Should. Sinew would have been better, but since the whole point in making this is we can't catch game, then that's out of the question. Besides, sinew tends to stretch in wetter conditions. If we could have found some milkweed or nettle, those would work as well, but for now, we use what's available."

"Can I help? The sooner we get finished, the sooner we can get some meat. I don't know about you, but I'm tired of burdock and pine nuts."

Ferrin handed Myron a couple of the larger pieces. "If you can start splitting them, it'll make it easier for me to braid. Make sure to peel thin, even strips."

"Give me some," Rae said.

Ferrin, happy to see her participate, handed her a couple of the smaller ones. If she messed them up, it wouldn't be much of a setback. He gave her a quick demonstration by splitting the ends and peeling back the soft, fibrous tissue.

She took the plants and got to work, her smaller hands seemingly a benefit. She'd finished all three pieces before Myron had made it through half of his first, so Ferrin gave her some of the longer ones, even taking a few from Myron's stack.

They continued in silence, peeling the green bark into long fibrous strands before laying them out in front of the fire to dry, using tree bark as weights to keep them from blowing away. At the very least, the work gave them something besides their hunger to think about.

Another stiff wind billowed down across the mountainside and into the trees, setting Ferrin's teeth to chattering. He hadn't realized how much the mountain had protected them until they left the lower passes. They'd always been able to find a small cave or large cleft for the four of them to squeeze into at night, but now they were left to the animosity of the wind with little but the outer trees and a fire to keep them warm. They were going to have to huddle close tonight to keep from freezing to death.

Rae wasn't going to like that.

"I'm hungry, Mama," Suri said as she watched Rae strip the tallunicci.

Rae stopped long enough to pat down the loose strands of hair on her daughter's head. "I'm hungry too. We'll get something tomorrow. You'll see." She spared a quick glance across the fire at Ferrin, as if looking for some small hint that what she was promising the little girl was true. "Here, help me with these plants."

Suri grabbed one end and started jerking, grunting as she did. The little girl was offering little help, but Rae was clearly just concerned with keeping her occupied.

By the time the tallunicci had been peeled, stripped, and the strands set to dry, the small band of runaways were more than ready to crawl into their bedding and dream of better days. Reluctantly, Rae moved her and Suri's blankets over between Ferrin and Myron for warmth.

Ferrin pulled his blankets up over his head, trying and failing to ignore the knotting in his stomach as the pangs of hunger set in. The roots, wild onions, nuts, and occasional chickweed were hardly enough to keep them going. If they didn't manage to find game soon, they weren't going to make it. Starvation would be a painful way to go.

Ferrin and Myron took turns at watch, more to keep the fire stoked than from worry about unexpected visitors. At one point, Ferrin woke to the howls of timber wolves. He lay there for some time, listening as he clutched the hilt of his sword under his blankets. He remembered their last encounter with a pack of wolves, and the fear he'd felt as the wolves cornered them against the mountainside. If it hadn't been for Suri and her strange ability to communicate with them, who knew what would have happened.

A heavy thud jerked Ferrin awake with a start, and he fumbled for his sword, but it turned out to be nothing more than Myron tossing a chunk of log on the dwindling fire. Sparks rained upward, quickly disappearing into the spindly branches above.

"Sorry about that," Myron said with an apologetic glance over his shoulder. "Didn't mean to wake you."

Ferrin yawned and stretched, sore from the cramped position he'd slept in so as to not accidentally roll over on Rae and Suri during the night.

Myron had a pot of something already sitting over the fire. Smelled like another one of his morning concoctions. Recently, he'd been using spruce needles. Myron's family had been steeping them in teas for decades. Good for the sneezes and even common stomachaches, Myron said. The strong taste, however, was enough to make Ferrin's stomach ache all on its own, but he did find that drinking the brewed tea eased his breathing.

As bad as it tasted, he was grateful for the heat as it warmed his insides on the way down. Holding the hot tin in his hands to loosen the joints of his fingers, he eagerly walked around to check on the long strands of tallunicci spread by the fire. They were no longer green, but an earthy grey, which meant they had dried enough for him to start weaving. He gave a few a good tug, and they held fast. At least, most did. There were a couple that had overdried and were now too brittle to use.

With a satisfied nod, Ferrin drank the last of his needle tea and handed Myron the cup.

Myron smiled. "More?"

Ferrin shook his head adamantly.

Myron frowned and set the cup down. "I know it doesn't taste the best. Could use a spoon of honey."

"It could use a cup of honey," Ferrin said, dragging over a log to sit on as he gathered a handful of the dried tallunicci. "However, taste is the least of our concerns. Pull up a seat. I want you to watch how I weave this, that way you can take over while I go find us some staves and arrow shoots. When Rae wakes, show her as well."

Myron anxiously sat down on the log beside Ferrin and watched as Ferrin took the fibrous strands and dipped them in water until they were good and pliable. He then twisted them together into a strong, tight cord. As some of the shorter strands ran out, he showed Myron how to weave in newer pieces, continuing the same twist-and-spin maneuver that he'd been doing all along. Pretty soon, Myron was handling his own batch. It was slow at first, until his hands found their groove, but soon enough he was intertwining the strands like a weaver.

"I'm going to go look for those staves," Ferrin said, walking over to his bedding to retrieve his sword. "You fine here?"

Myron never even looked up. "Don't worry about me. I'll have this done before you get back."

Ferrin pulled his sword from under his blankets, and Rae stirred in the bedding next to his, peeking out to see what was going on. Her pale-green eyes were as bright as ever, such a contrast to her caramel skin and dark hair.

"Where're you going?" she asked, barely managing to drop her blanket far enough below her mouth to speak.

"I'm going to look for some wood I can use to shape a couple of bows with."

"I want to come."

Suri peeked out from under her mother and smiled, yawned, then smacked her lips. "I'm hungry, Mama."

"I won't be gone long," Ferrin said, easing away from the bedding, not really relishing the idea of them tagging along, especially Suri. If they came, instead of looking for staves, he'd be spending his time answering the little girl's unending questions. "Perhaps you can help Myron with the string. You were faster than all of us last night."

Rae climbed out of her bedding and headed straight for the tea kettle. By the time Ferrin had eased his way toward the outer edge of the camp, both she and Suri were sipping slowly on the spruce tea as they watched Myron work. Rae seemed enthralled with the way Myron's fingers twisted and spun the tallunicci into place.

It didn't take Ferrin long to find the small hickory grove he'd seen the day before, and as luck would have it, he also found several mature bushes of ringwood as well. He knew from his time hunting with Pinon that the shoots from the ringwood shrub were more durable than most hardwood. Pinon, the former Rhowynn captain turned peddler who had raised him and his sister, had taught him how to not only choose the right shoots but to shape them as well.

Sadly, Ferrin didn't have an axe or even a good hatchet to fell them with. All he had was his sword. If he'd had the time, he could have reshaped the blade to add more girth to the end, but then the handle would have been too short to offer any kind of real power. In the end, he managed to bring down what he needed without it.

With two thick staves—at least three inches in diameter—and close to a dozen young sapling shoots for arrows, he marched back to their campsite to begin the arduous task of shaping the wood. The sooner he could get these weapons made, the sooner they could start looking for game.

Myron and Rae were just finishing up the two bowstrings as Ferrin laid the wood he'd collected down beside his seat. "Fine work," Ferrin said as he stopped to take a look. "I don't believe I could have done better myself." He tested the strength of the cords and smiled. "Yes, this will do nicely."

Both Myron and Rae smiled proudly, basking in the rays of a job well done.

Shaping the bows took Ferrin the rest of the morning and most of the afternoon, but with the help of a sharp belt knife and a stout piece of wood he used as a makeshift hammer, he managed to whittle down the belly of each bow, marking the center where he wanted the handle set and letting it taper toward the ends. He tamped down his frustration at not having his smithy available and the proper tools to make the process go more smoothly and quickly. They couldn't afford to lose another day without food.

He decided to keep the design of the bows flat instead of round, which would give them more power, allowing for a stronger pull. It was also safer when dealing with green wood that didn't have the benefit of spending five or six months drying.

He was careful not to dig too deep and splinter the wood. He also left a thin layer of bark in place on the back of the bows to help stabilize the wood and keep them from snapping under pressure. He stuck the tip of one side in the ground, and while holding the other firm, he pushed on the handle at the center, watching how the wood bent, then did the same to the other side. He continued to shape the belly of each, carefully tapering the upper and lower limbs from the handles all the way to within three or four inches of the tips, where he left a little more thickness for support.

By the time he finished, the bellies were smooth, and the bows had an even bend.

Once satisfied with the weight and balance of the give, he tapered the sides of the handles, leaving the backs as untouched as possible. Thinner sides would allow for better placement of the arrows against the fist, as well as a more comfortable grip.

"I think we're ready to string these," he said, eagerly looking over at Myron and Rae as he finished carving the grooves into the upper and lower tips.

Rae was the first to grab one of the tallunicci cords they'd braided and offer it to Ferrin. He wrapped his leg around the bottom of the first bow to hold it in place as he strung it. The cord fit perfectly inside the nocks. It might not have been the prettiest bow to look at, but it had a strong draw weight. Pulling the string allowed him to see that one side bent slower than the other, so he shaped it a little more until he had an even draw.

Ferrin looked up at the others with a smile. "Now for the arrows. While I work on them, see if you can find something to use for fletching. Crow feathers will work if you can find them. If you can't, we might have to try making some spruce-needle fletching."

"I'll see what I can find," Myron said, strapping on his sword. He turned to Rae and Suri. "I could use some sharp eyes to help me look."

Suri bounced up and down. "I want to go. I want to go." The little girl had been able to sense when the corax were nearby, and Ferrin wondered if she could do the same with normal birds.

Rae looked at Ferrin as if wondering if she should stay and help him instead.

"I've got plenty to keep me occupied," Ferrin said. "I'm sure Myron could use an extra set of eyes."

Rae wrapped Suri's cloak tight around the little girl's shoulders and, after grabbing a belt knife, headed into the forest with Myron.

By the time they made it back to camp, Ferrin had managed to skin the bark from the arrows, carve the points, and nock the ends. "How did you do?" he asked, laying the final arrow down on the pile beside him.

"Better than expected," Myron said.

"Look!" Suri exclaimed, holding them out. "Feathers!"

Ferrin couldn't help but laugh at the little girl's untold delight.

"Wild turkey," Myron said. "And where there's one, there's bound to be more." He licked his lips hungrily and looked at the feathers in his hand. "Don't think we have enough for a dozen arrows, but maybe four or five." He laid the feathers down on the log next to Ferrin. Suri followed suit, waving hers in Ferrin's face before carefully placing them on top of the pile.

"Very nice," Ferrin said, patting the little girl's head. She laughed and spun, then went to see if there was any of the needle tea remaining.

Myron took a seat next to Ferrin and examined one of the ringwood shoots. "How's it coming? What can I do?"

"Collect as much pine resin as you can in one of those mugs."

"Smart," Myron said. "That'll be strong enough to hold the fletching and whatever tips you're planning on using." He looked over at Ferrin. "What are you going to use for the heads?"

"I'll fire-burn them to harden the ends, then probably use one of our tins for tips."

"How do you plan on cutting the . . ." Myron looked at Ferrin. "Oh, never mind," he said with a smile as he realized who he was talking to. "I hate losing one of our cups, though."

"Either that or I use some of our coin?"

Myron's eyes widened. "I reckon we can spare a cup if it comes down to it."

Ferrin chuckled. "I had a feeling you'd agree."

While Myron and Suri went to collect the resin, Rae helped Ferrin by hardening the tips of the arrows in the fire while he split the turkey feathers and cut them to size, three for each arrow. He ended up with enough pieces of proper length to fletch four. Wasn't much, but it only took one well-placed shot to bring down some game. He just needed to get enough food to keep them going till they reached Woodvale.

"I'm done," Rae said, pulling the final arrow out of the fire and blowing on it before laying it with the others.

"Good. And as soon as they get—"

"We've got it!" Suri exclaimed, running into camp. She flew to her mother and hopped up in her lap. "The resin is sticky. See?" She stuck her finger on Rae's cheek just to show her.

"Eww. What are you doing?" Rae said, prying Suri's finger from her face. When she did, it left a dark amber stain.

Ferrin chuckled.

Rae's eyes narrowed. "What are you laughing at?" She turned and looked at Suri. "Go show him how sticky it is. Start with his beard."

Ferrin hopped to his feet, raising his hands to stop the little girl, who was already halfway to his log with her arms stretched out. "No need, Suri. I already know it's sticky."

She looked disappointed as she turned back to her mother.

"That's why we collected it," Ferrin said, waiting until he felt it safe to sit back down. "We're going to make glue to stick the feathers on our arrows."

"Didn't make as many as I thought," Myron said as he looked at the four arrows beside the pit where Rae had left them. "Hope it's enough."

"Don't forget the charcoal to temper the resin," Ferrin said as Myron laid the tin of resin over a small flame to soften.

Myron wagged his hand over his shoulder, not turning around. "I might not know how to make a bow from tree limbs and plant guts, but I do know how to make a strong pine pitch glue."

Ferrin left him to it as he searched through the arrows, picking out the four straightest. He laid the cut feathers out beside each, getting them ready for when Myron was finished with the resin.

"That should do it," Myron said, stirring the inside of the tin around with a small stick. The color had changed from a burnt amber to as black as a starless night.

Ferrin took the stick and collected some on the end, applying a generous amount along the back of the arrow, careful not to get any in the notch where the string would eventually go. He then placed each of the three feathers on top of the pitch, pressing down firmly once they were lined the way he wanted.

Ferrin's fingers were black and sticky by the time he finished with the first. He wrapped a very thin strand of the tallunicci around the three feathers, tying them firmly to the wood. "That should do it," he said, then moved on to the next.

Myron was forced to reheat the resin after each arrow, just to make sure the pitch was soft enough to apply, but by the time they finished, there was still plenty of glue in the tin.

"We can use the rest for the tips," Ferrin said, eyeing the cup in Myron's hand. "And if you'll collect the pitch on your stick, I'll use that mug to shape some heads for our arrows."

Suri found a larger stick for Myron to use, and he worked it around in the tin, collecting what was left of the resin and letting it harden into place, forming a rather useful glue stick. He left the stick on a rock to keep from getting black residue on everything it touched and handed the empty mug to Ferrin.

Ferrin pulled on his magic, letting its warmth fill him as he focused on the metal. He softened it to where he could divide the tin into several pieces, and while Myron dabbed a good thick paste onto the tips of the arrows, Ferrin used his magic to mold the metal around each tip. It certainly wasn't his best work, but at this point, it was usability over embellishment.

Once the heads had been fitted, they took the arrows and heated them over the fire once more, softening the resin so that it molded into every crack and crevice, securing the tips for use.

By the time the last arrow was finished, the sun was already beginning to lower in the sky. "Looks like we'll have to wait one more day to fill our bellies," Myron said half-heartedly. "And I was so looking forward to a thick, juicy turkey leg."

"Whatever we do, it will have to be quick," Ferrin said. "The longer we wait, the more time Sylas has to catch up."

Myron grimaced. "Don't remind me." He turned and looked at the surrounding trees. "We'll hunt at first light. Let's pray our luck holds out."

Chapter 10 | Ferrin

MORNING CAME EARLY. With all the excitement of using the new bows, and Suri's continual tossing and turning next to him, Ferrin hardly slept a wink. He crawled out of bed to sit in front of the fire, feeling very grateful for Myron's needle tea, even taking a second cup when offered. He needed all the help he could muster.

A light snow had begun to fall sometime in the night, forcing them to stack additional wood to keep the blaze going. Ferrin hoped it didn't turn into sleet or worse. Without proper shelter or food, weather like this could kill. If the snow continued, it would slow their travels all the more. Not only would it make it more difficult to trek through, but it would force them to build shelters every night, which would mean stopping earlier in the evenings, giving Sylas and his Black Watch guards more time to catch up.

"You ready?" Myron asked, his bow wrapped around his shoulders.

Ferrin nodded, finishing off the rest of his mug and enjoying the warmth while it lasted. Waking was getting harder. He could feel his energy slipping, his movements more sluggish. They were all showing signs of weakening. With nothing but a few foraged roots, nuts, and inner tree bark to eat, they were soon going to be too weak to travel. They had to catch some game, and soon.

Ferrin strung his bow and tested the pull. "I found a couple of trails yesterday while searching for staves. I'll hunt there. I suggest you take the area where you found those feathers. Hopefully, one of us will get lucky."

Myron nodded, grabbing his bow and nocking one of the arrows.

"Don't forget, yours tends to shoot low and to the left," Ferrin said.

"Got it."

Ferrin looked up through the branches. The stars were gone, but the sky was just as black as ever, and by the sound of it, the forest was still asleep. "We better get going. If we haven't seen anything by the time the sun peaks, we break camp. We can't lose another day. We have to push for Woodvale."

Myron held out his gloved hand and watched a couple of flakes land on the leather and melt. "If this gets any heavier, we won't be traveling far."

"Another reason to hurry." With a brisk nod, Ferrin headed across camp. He passed Rae and Suri's bedding on the way; neither moved. If they were awake, they weren't showing any signs of it.

Quickly, he slipped into the woods, making his way toward a spot where a couple of trails converged, and where he'd spotted several types of tracks the day before. He hoped to at least find some coneys. At this point, he'd even settle for a tree rat, but they would be even harder to hit by bow than a coney, and they'd have less meat.

It didn't take Ferrin long to reach the spot he was looking for and find a tree with a limb large enough to perch on. The sky was already beginning to lighten, but not enough to see color. Now for the difficult part. Sit and wait.

By the time the sun broke through the trees and its rays permeated the forest, Ferrin was numb all over. His teeth were chattering hard enough that he was worried he'd scare the game away. His hands were shaking so bad that a twelve-point buck could have walked under his tree and he'd probably have missed it.

He waited what seemed like hours with no sign of anything coming. He guessed the animals had better sense than he did, sitting out in weather like this. Resigning himself that he wasn't going to have any luck, he turned to try climbing down. Just as he did, he caught movement out of the corner of his eye. Slowly, he turned his head, but there was nothing there. His eyes scanned every inch of the snow-covered terrain but came up empty.

Then the snow moved. Except, it wasn't snow. It was a white rabbit. His mouth was already salivating at the thought of hot coney stew as he slowly raised his bow. His fingers were so stiff he wanted to blow some warm air on them to loosen them up, but he was afraid the movement would frighten the rabbit off.

The rabbit stopped moving, and for one frightening moment, Ferrin lost sight of it. His eyes darted back and forth across the snow where he thought he'd last seen it, the rabbit's white fur making it hard to spot, as it blended so perfectly with its surroundings. Then it moved, and Ferrin nearly shouted for joy. The rabbit's black eyes and the periodic twitch of its long ears helped him aim as he pulled the string to his chin and sighted down the semi-straight shaft, making sure to adjust for the bow's naturally high pull. He took a deep breath.

"Ferrin!"

Ferrin startled at the unexpected shout, and the arrow released high over its intended target.

The rabbit bounded away.

"Son of a faerie!" He flung his bow so hard he toppled backward out of the tree and landed with a jarring *thud* on the snow below.

"There you are," Suri said, running over to look down at him. "Look what I have." She held up an enormous pinecone. "It's the biggest one yet," she said, a proud grin spreading across her face as though she'd just won first prize at the harvest festival.

Anger seething through every pore, Ferrin crawled to his knees and nearly snatched the cone from the little girl's hands and threw it. "Do you have any idea what you just did?" He shook the snow from his cloak as he stood.

She looked up at him, fear in her eyes. It was the first time she'd ever looked at him like that, and it broke his heart. "I'm sorry. I didn't mean to get so upset. It's not your fault," he lied as he hooked his bow back over his shoulder and grabbed the little girl's hand. "Come on. Let's see if we can find my arrow."

Thankfully, by the time they managed to find it and return to camp, Suri seemed back to her formerly chipper self, tossing her large cone in the air and catching it. Ferrin, on the other hand, was practically shaking, the fear of not finding food overwhelming everything else. They'd been depending on him, and he'd let them down. If only he hadn't lost sight of the stupid animal when he did. He could have made the shot before Suri had shown up.

Myron had already returned to camp as well, and not too long before them, judging by the way he was warming his hands over the fire.

"Well?" the former captain asked, turning as he heard them approach. He looked at Suri, then at Ferrin's empty hands. "I take it your hunt went about as well as mine."

Ferrin frowned. He'd been hoping Myron would have made up for his own bad luck. "We would have had coney stew tonight," Ferrin said, "but someone paid me an unexpected visit and frightened it off."

Suri didn't seem to notice as she skipped over to where her mother was shaking the snow from their blankets.

Myron shook his head with a sigh. "That's unfortunate."

Ferrin agreed. "I say we break camp and try to make it as far as we can while we have daylight. Perhaps we can hunt on the way, or maybe we'll find a stream with trout. Whatever we do, we can't stay here."

"True. The sooner we get moving, the sooner we reach Woodvale and the sooner we get provisions."

"We're leaving?" Rae asked.

"Yes," Ferrin said, walking over to his own bedding. "We need to get as far as we can before nightfall. With the snow setting in, we'll need to find a good place to shelter for the night."

"My stomach hurts, Mama," Suri said, still holding on to her pinecone. "I'm hungry."

Rae put her arm around her daughter. "I know. I'm sure we'll find something soon." She looked at Ferrin, her face saying that he needed to find a way to reiterate her statement or else, so he attempted an encouraging smile.

"Yes, I'm sure we'll have something very nice to eat this evening," he said. "But right now, you need to help your mother by packing up your blankets."

Suri held up her pinecone. "Can Tippi come too?"

"You named your pinecone Tippi?"

Suri nodded, hugging her cone protectively to her chest.

Ferrin blew out through his lips. "Yes, I suppose Tippi can come along, as long as he behaves himself and doesn't talk too much."

Suri giggled. Even Rae smiled, but she quickly hid it by turning around and folding the rest of her blankets.

It took them a good hour to get everything packed and the fire put out. They covered the entire pit with snow and fallen limbs to hide their passing as best they could. With nothing left but to keep moving, the small band of half-frozen travelers left camp and headed into the woods. They maintained a northwesterly route with the help of a compass Myron had purchased back in Iraseth.

The flurries continued throughout the day, slowing their pace considerably. They weren't equipped for these types of conditions, and the snow was deep enough in places that Ferrin was forced to carry Suri.

Everyone kept their eyes peeled for game. Unfortunately, the animals had better sense than they did and were remaining tucked away in their nests and holes.

By late afternoon, the sky was darkening even further.

"We need to find shelter, and fast," Myron said. "Food or not, if we don't find a way to keep this snow off our backs, we're likely to freeze to death long before we starve."

Ferrin nodded. "There," he said and pointed toward a fallen oak, whose entire root system had been ripped out of the ground, leaving a large bowl behind.

Quickly, they made their way over to the back of the fallen tree and dug around the roots, using one of the cooking pans as a shovel. Once they had dug down deep enough, they used the snow to build barriers on the sides of their shelter to protect against the freezing gusts, and while Rae and Suri were left in charge of gathering spruce boughs to pad the walls and floor, Ferrin and Myron hunted for saplings large enough to frame a sturdy lean-to.

It only took a couple hours to get the frame in place and its backing set with long strips of tree bark, topped with several layers of boughs, leaves, dirt, and snow to hold the bark in place and to keep them as dry as possible. Once the shelter was up, the two men carried over logs large enough to last the night, some so heavy it required both of them to carry.

The temperature was cold enough to keep the snow from turning any wetter, but it also had stiffened their joints to the point of making it difficult to move. Ferrin worried about catching the chill in their feet, especially the toes.

Their empty stomachs were soon forgotten as the four sat around the flames, greedily soaking in the warmth. They went so far as to remove their boots and stockings in order to get the heat directly to the skin, and Rae even used some of the little strength she had to try healing where needed. Unfortunately for her, she couldn't use any of it on herself, so Ferrin found himself rubbing some life back into her feet on his own. He was surprised she allowed him to do it, but necessity won out.

"I don't know how much longer we can keep going," Myron said to Ferrin, trying to keep his voice low so the other two wouldn't hear. "My legs are stiff as boards, and I can hardly put one foot in front of the other. Without food, I give us one more day, maybe two, before we end up becoming food ourselves for some hungry scavengers."

No sooner had the words escaped his lips when a howl rose in the distance, the call driven in on the back of the wind. It was too far away to need to worry, but it was still a sharp reminder that they weren't the only ones looking for food.

With their bedding out and another pot of spruce tea having been quickly consumed, the four turned in for the night. It was Ferrin's time at watch, which at this point meant while the others lay there, he'd do his best to stay awake. That was about all he could manage, along with stoking the fire so they didn't lose the coals. Guarding against intruders came a distant second, as they were all too weak to have fended anyone off had the need arisen.

The snow continued to fall, but their lean-to shelter did a surprisingly good job of keeping them dry, and the logs were of such size that they didn't need to worry about the fire being choked out. Ferrin sat quietly and listened to the lulling sounds of the crackling blaze, mesmerized by the little red and yellow sparks as they shot out of the wood and intermingled with the falling snow above.

It was a peaceful stillness that he would have enjoyed much more if his stomach didn't ache so. It growled and gurgled constantly, begging him to put something in it, but apart from their spruce tea, and a few grub worms Myron had found under some bark they'd peeled for their shelter, food was a distant memory. Ferrin's eyes grew heavy, and more than once, he had to jerk himself back awake. Apart from the occasional howl of the wolves or hoot of the owls, the forest remained silent.

". . . Ferrin. Wake up."

Ferrin jerked awake at the touch of someone's hand on his arm. "What time is it?" Had he fallen asleep? Was it his turn at watch again? He shook his head and sat up. The sky was already lightening, the stars gone.

"You must have fallen asleep," Myron whispered, crouched beside him. "You never woke me."

Ferrin yawned, too tired to do much else. He tried to stretch, but every muscle in his body ached, and he gave up the attempt. Myron had said he didn't believe they'd make it two more days, but the way Ferrin felt, he didn't think they'd last the morning.

"Come," Myron said, motioning with his hand. "You need to see this."

Ferrin's head cleared rather quickly at Myron's eagerness. What had the man found? Pushing back his blankets from his legs, he stood and followed Myron out of the shelter, sparing only a quick glance at the two lumps where Rae and Suri still slept.

"You won't believe this," Myron said, leading Ferrin a little way beyond the fire. "I found them while coming out to relieve myself."

"Found what?" Ferrin asked. "I don't see anything."

Myron reached behind one of the large pines and pulled out two long-eared coneys and held them up with a broad grin.

Ferrin stood there in shock.

"Yeah, that was my exact reaction too. Even holding them, I still can't believe it."

"How did you manage to shoot them in the dark?" Ferrin asked.

"I didn't. I just found them lying here."

"You found them?" Ferrin scanned the surrounding woods. Was someone out there watching them?

"I don't care how it happened," Myron said, leaving Ferrin standing there in the snow as he headed back to the fire. "All I know is that we will be eating well this morning."

Ferrin stood there a moment longer, looking for any sign of who could have provided the two animals. Not seeing anyone, he finally gave up and joined Myron as they cleaned and prepared the much-needed meal.

Both Rae and Suri poked their heads out of their blankets at the first whiff of roasted meat. Without the proper ingredients—or any ingredients at all—for a stew, they opted instead to cook the two rabbits on a spit, pouring a little melted snow seasoned with wild onions over them.

"You hunted this morning?" Rae asked as she and Suri scooted closer to the fire to inspect the welcomed meal.

"Not exactly," Ferrin said, passing Myron a keen look.

Rae looked confused but was apparently too eager to eat to press the issue.

"I want some," Suri said, reaching out to touch the first rabbit.

"No," Rae said, pulling Suri's arm back. "You'll burn your hand."

The four barely waited long enough for the meat to cook through before grabbing it off the spit and stuffing it in their mouths, all thoughts of how they had gotten the meal vanishing into the cold morning air as the meat practically melted in their mouths. Two coneys, even large ones as those were, were hardly enough to overcome the pangs of hunger they were feeling, but they certainly went a long way toward it.

Too tired to move, they decided to wait out the snow for one more day, resting as much as possible so they could gather their strength to press on the following morning.

Ferrin was the last at watch that night, and after checking the surrounding campsite for leftover surprises and finding none, he trudged back into camp and woke the others, hoping to make an earlier start of it.

Even with the storm having passed, the snow on the ground was deep enough in places to hinder a faster pace, and by the time the sun had begun to wane in the sky and they had found a new place to shelter for the night, it felt like they had not covered much ground in their travels. Their meal that evening consisted of more of the same: spruce tea, a couple of leftover roots they'd foraged a few days ago, and some grub worms they cooked over the fire. It did little more than set their stomachs to gurgling.

Ferrin felt as though he'd just nodded off when he was being shaken awake once again.

"You won't believe it," Myron stated, "but someone has gifted us another meal." He moved to the side to reveal what appeared to be a mountain goat. "I found it just over there by those bushes. But no sign of who left it. I even tried to find some tracks, but the couple hours of snowfall we had earlier covered them up—if there were any in the first place."

Ferrin looked at Myron. "What do you mean *if?*"

Myron stared skyward. "What if the Creator left them for us?"

Ferrin shook his head. "Don't think He works like that, if He even exists."

Nonetheless, Ferrin spared an uneasy glance around the campsite as if expecting someone to suddenly step out from behind a tree and claim responsibility. It might not have been the Creator, but clearly someone out there was watching them. He wished he knew who it was, and why.

"You never know," Myron said reverently.

"What I *do* know," Ferrin said, pulling his knife out of his pack, "is that the meat from this should last us to Woodvale."

"What's that?" a muffled voice behind them called out, causing the two men to turn. The top half of Suri's head was poking out of her blankets, her question waking her mother as well.

"What's going on?" Rae asked, then spotted the goat. "What is that?"

"Food," Myron said with a bright smile. "Or it soon will be after we dress it. Don't you worry, Miss Rae, we will have you and Suri back to health in no time."

It took a few hours to clean and dress the meat. They cooked every piece they could, sparing nothing. After letting it sit, they packed most of it away for their journey, sparing a good portion to fill their bellies with before pressing on.

Even without the luxury of herbs to season the meat, it was the best-tasting food Ferrin had eaten since their time at the Smelly Trout. The bitter memory of the gruesome deaths of the old innkeeper, Tibble, and his wife, Kyleen, threatened to curb his appetite, but not enough to stop him from eating a second helping. The meat left him a little nauseous at first, having not eaten much in the way of solid food for the last several days, but it soon passed.

Feeling somewhat revived, the small group broke down their shelter and once again went about the arduous task of covering their tracks, relying mostly on the fallen snow to help conceal their passing.

With bellies full and the hope of reaching Woodvale once again restored, the travelers continued their journey. Ferrin made a point of keeping his eyes and ears open for who it was that was tailing them. Whoever they were, they had managed to make it all the way into their camp without being spotted and without leaving a single trail worth following.

The question was . . . Why?

Chapter 11 | Ferrin

BEFORE THE SUN HAD peaked in the sky, the band of weary travelers came across their first sign of civilization: a road. Ferrin studied the clearing. It was wide enough to fit two wagons comfortably, and even covered in snow, the ruts were clearly seen.

"Been wondering how long it would take before we hit one," Myron said, walking out to the middle and looking both ways. His footprints were the only marks on the open stretch of track. They appeared to be the only ones to have used it that day. "Must run from Woodvale to Kariss."

"The question is," Ferrin said, "how close are we? And do we dare follow the road and take the chance of running into someone, or do we stick to the forest and delay our journey?"

"We take the road," Rae said without the faintest hesitation.

Myron looked at Ferrin and shrugged. "The sooner we get to Woodvale, the sooner we get some horses. The longer we wait, the more likely our pursuers will catch up. From what we saw of that map, it looked like the closest pass through the mountains lies to the west between Iraseth and Syrel. We've been traveling a week, which I'm sure has given our pursuers time to at least reach the pass, if not make it out the other side." He looked at Rae and Suri, then back at Ferrin. "I say we risk it."

Ferrin looked at Rae, who promptly nodded in agreement. Suri, clinging to her mother's hand, held up Tippi and waved him in the air, which Ferrin guessed was the pinecone's way of saying that he wanted to take the road as well.

"Fine," Ferrin said, slinging his pack higher on his shoulder. "The road it is."

Rae and Suri followed him out to join Myron, and the four made their way west. The snow wasn't as deep on the road as it had been in the forest, and with the lack of undergrowth and trees blocking their way, their pace greatly increased. Ferrin caught himself glancing back over his shoulder every now and then, hoping to catch sight of whoever it was that was providing them food, but each time he came up empty.

"We have to be close," Myron said, glancing at his compass. "With the direction we've been traveling since leaving the Razor Spine—if this road does indeed stretch between Woodvale and Kariss—I'd say maybe a day, two at most."

"I like the sound of that," Ferrin said, looking over at Suri, who was walking between him and her mother. "You hear that? We could be in Woodvale by tomorrow, which means a warm bed, a hot meal."

"And a good scrubbing," Rae added, making a point to turn up her nose at Ferrin.

"Ah, yes," Myron said. "A long soak would set me up for sure."

The thought of a hot bath, a warm meal, and a soft bed had their strides increasing. By midafternoon, they came across another road, this one every bit as wide as the one they were traveling but heading due north. They stopped to rest their legs and eat some of the meat they had cooked the night before while Ferrin took the opportunity to open his map.

"If this is the road we're standing on," he said, pointing at the map, just east of Woodvale, "then we're closer than I thought."

"Looks that way," Myron said anxiously.

Ferrin traced the road north with his finger. "It appears to run all the way to Wellhollow, which is almost straight across from where we're heading. See here? Rhowynn." He pointed almost directly across from Wellhollow to the northwestern side of Lake Baeron.

"Aye," Myron said, Rae and Suri leaning in to take a look as well, "I'd say the toughest leg of our journey is nearly complete. Making it up and through the Razor Spine turned out to be more treacherous than we could have expected, but it looks to be a fairly straight ride from Woodvale."

Ferrin rolled the map back up and tucked it in his satchel. "Let's just hope they have horses to spare."

By late afternoon, they were walking into Woodvale's outer limits, which was primarily residential. They hadn't yet made it into the town proper or seen any of the shops, but from the number of well-kept homes they had passed, Ferrin hoped the town to be large enough to support their needs.

They received wary glances from the locals, most stopping whatever they were doing just to stare as Ferrin and the others walked by. "We need to find supplies before the shops close," he said, doing his best not to pay too much attention to the strange looks. He even attempted a smile or two, but those he smiled at scowled even deeper.

"I agree," Myron said, "but it might be prudent to find a room first to drop off our bags." He nodded at a man mending the front of his fence and received a growl in return. The way the man held his hammer didn't look too inviting either. "Friendly lot, these."

"You noticed that too, huh?"

Myron pointed at a sign that had been nailed to a tree on the right. "Looks to be where we might find some lodging." The sign stood beside a single dirt lane off the main road, leading back into the woods. It read: *THE SMOK'N PIG.*

Ferrin took a deep whiff, his mouth watering from the aroma of freshly cooked meat coming from the open drive. "Smells like a place I want to visit."

Myron smiled and took the lead. "My thoughts exactly."

Rae and Suri stayed close to Ferrin as they headed down the drive. Rae had a nervous look in her eyes as she kept a close watch ahead. Even Suri didn't seem her jovial self. She clutched Tippi to her chest as though afraid some ruffian would leap out of the trees and steal her precious pinecone.

The trees parted soon enough, giving them their first look at the inn. It was pleasantly situated, with the main building straight ahead, backed up against the forest. It had three stories, the upper two looking to be lodging, as many of the windows had lights on inside.

In front of the inn, on the right, was a stable. A young man no more than sixteen stood out front rubbing down one of the horses. "We're full tonight. You'll have to stable your . . ." He stopped when he finally looked up long enough to notice they were on foot. He stiffened as they drew closer, even going so far as to place his hand on the hilt of his belt knife. "Who are you? I mean, what's your business here?"

Myron stopped about ten feet from the lad, giving him plenty of room. "We are but weary travelers looking for lodging." He pointed toward the inn. "Would you know if they have room for the night?"

The teen shook his head adamantly. "They're full. No room. Need to find somewhere else."

Myron passed a curious glance to Ferrin.

"You're saying they don't have a single room to spare for the night?" Ferrin asked, dropping the carry bags he'd been toting onto the hard-packed snow.

The boy gulped, then looked at the inn, then looked back at the four of them and shook his head. "No. No room."

"Rather strange to be filled this time of year," Myron said. "Is there a special holiday or town festival taking place?"

The boy cast about, either looking for an excuse to leave or for the protection of a familiar face.

"They do at least have food, do they not?" Myron asked.

"I don't know," the boy said with a nervous shrug, then quickly pulled his horse into the stable and shut the door.

Myron turned. "What do you make of that? We don't smell that bad, do we?"

Rae shook her head, not quite catching Myron's sarcasm.

"Doesn't bode well for us," Ferrin said.

"What do you think?" Myron asked. "Look for another inn?"

"From what we've seen so far, I doubt they have another," Ferrin said, leaning over to pick up his bags. "I say, if they have no rooms, we hear it from the proprietor's own mouth. That boy looked frightened enough to soil himself."

"And then some," Myron added, taking a moment to look down at their state of dress. "Guess I can't blame the youngster too much. We look a sight worse for wear."

"What are we doing?" Rae asked. "You promised us a bath and food."

Ferrin sighed. "I guess we go inside and talk to the innkeeper. If the stable boy was right and they don't have rooms, at least we can get a decent meal." He led them toward the main building. Most of the hitching posts out front were filled, and the noise from inside spoke of a full room, which wasn't surprising for a cold late afternoon such as this one, even if the sun hadn't yet set.

"Might be best if I went in alone," Ferrin said.

"Why?" Rae asked. "I want to go in where it's warm."

"Because if that boy's reaction was any indication, it would be in our best interest not to have us all trudging in like a horde of vagabonds, carrying our life's belongings over our backs."

"Ferrin's right," Myron said. "Best not to draw attention until we get the lay of the land, so to speak."

Rae walked Suri over to a bench on the far end of the porch and took a seat, not bothering to even look in the men's direction.

Ferrin laid his bags down on the porch beside Myron. "Oh, and let's not forget this," he said, handing over his rather ugly makeshift bow. "One look at these and the innkeeper will be throwing us out on our heads for sure." Ferrin sighed as he looked at the bow. All the work that had gone into their making, and they never even got the chance to use them.

Myron gave Ferrin a sympathetic smile as he took the bow and the bags. "Good luck in there," he said, then took a seat beside Rae and Suri, placing their belongings on the floor.

Before walking inside, Ferrin patted his trouser pocket where he kept a pouch with some of their gold, then adjusted his sword. Taking a deep breath, he opened the door and stepped inside.

The common room was filled with pipe smoke, rowdy conversations, and hungry patrons. There was a nervous sort of energy to the place, mostly written on the hardened faces of those seated around the tables.

He shut the door behind him, and heads turned. Hushed whispers and wary glances were passed his way, but soon enough the volume lifted once again as the patrons returned to their conversations, managing to keep a close eye on him as they did.

Taking a quick look around the room to get his bearings, he could see that most of the tables were filled. There was even a balcony that ran around the sides and back, no doubt leading up to the inn's lodging. In the back, a stone hearth rested against the wall, spreading its light and warmth across the room. Inside the hearth was a spit holding the inn's namesake—a large pig.

Ferrin's mouth watered at the sight of it.

An older gentleman in the back-right corner sat on a makeshift stage, attempting to entertain the patrons with a very poor rendition of "The Woodcutter's Daughter." Those at the tables were either too drunk or too enthralled in their own conversations to pay the old man any mind, which was probably for the best since his voice was about as unstable as his fingering on his worn langeleik.

The front corner of the room on the right was taken up by the bar. It was flanked on either side with stacked casks, some four high. Hanging on the wall behind the bar were rows of shelving, each holding an assortment of bottles with varying colors, along with a random mixture of clay jugs. The long bar in front was filled with thirsty customers tipping wooden tankards and making merry with frivolous conversations and laughter.

Across the common room, serving girls wove through the maze of tables with incredible accuracy, toting fresh drinks and platters of food that smelled so good Ferrin nearly grabbed a plate on its way by.

He did stop one of the girls to ask where he might find the innkeeper. She gave him a curious look, not quite as frightful as the stable boy, but enough to let him know she felt uncomfortable, then pointed back over her shoulder. "Blithe's in the kitchen." With that, she scooted past and headed for the next table over.

Ferrin spotted a large bear of a man behind the counter on the left, standing in front of a stone oven and shouting out orders as he flung food onto plates. Blithe wore a long white apron over his white shirt, with his sleeves rolled to the elbows. His face was flush and his forehead slick from standing so near the open flames. Ferrin was considered a big man by most, but Blithe would have given him pause had he come across him in a dark alley. He didn't look like the type of man you wanted to cross.

Keeping to the outside wall and as far from the tables as possible, Ferrin worked his way over to the open kitchen and stood to the left of the entrance, doing his best to keep out of the way of the steady stream of servers rushing in and out with their orders. After waiting for several minutes for the innkeeper to turn around, he finally cleared his throat. "Master Blithe."

The innkeeper didn't so much as flinch, let alone look up. He was too busy slinging slices of cheese around three half-filled platters to notice, or perhaps he never heard over the servers shouting out their orders and demanding those in the kitchen get them their salvers.

Ferrin tried again, this time with a little more force. "Master Blithe."

"For the love of Aldor! I heard you the first time! Can't you see my hands are full? I'll be with you in a moment." He shook his head, mumbling something as he did.

Ferrin waited patiently, none too happy about having angered the innkeeper before he'd even gotten the chance to speak with him. The odds of him getting the rooms were looking slimmer by the moment.

The huge innkeeper finished up with the cheese, filled five bowls with stew, and cut several loaves, placing individual pieces on each plate before it went out. Wiping his hands on his apron, he finally turned his attention to Ferrin, walking over to the other side of the counter and giving him a good looking-over.

"Can't say as I've seen you 'round these parts before. Who are you and what's your business here?"

Ferrin was surprised by the cold greeting, especially to a possible customer, but after the reactions they'd received so far from the townsfolk, he wasn't completely taken aback.

"My name is Ferrin, and myself and three others are passing through town, hoping to stock up on some provisions. We're on our way to Rhowynn."

"Rhowynn, you say. That's quite the journey. And how is it you'd be coming through Woodvale to get to Rhowynn? Seems a mite out of the way, don't you think?" Blithe gave him a questioning look.

"Aye," Ferrin lied. "We're on our way back from trading along the eastern sea line. The work took longer than expected. We were hoping to have made it back before the first snow. Unfortunately, we were happened upon by bandits, who stole our horses and most of our supplies. We've been on foot for nearly a week."

"On foot, in the snow, for a week? Seems a highly unlikely tale."

"Unlikely or not, sir, it's the truth."

"And where are the rest of these unlucky travelers?"

"They're waiting on a bench outside. With the looks we've been receiving, they were a little wary of coming inside. We're looking for lodging for a single night, no more. Our hope is to replenish our stores before moving on."

Blithe stared down at him without saying anything, as if weighing Ferrin's words.

"If you don't believe me, please step outside and take a look for yourself. I promise you, one look at the others and you'll see the need."

Blithe turned to a short, petite lady on the far side of the kitchen. "Molly, I'm going to step outside a moment. Can you handle things here?"

She glanced over her shoulder long enough for Ferrin to notice the flush of her cheeks as she pounded away on a pile of dough, kneading it to the right consistency. Her hands worked methodically with a continual press, fold, and turn. She sighed gruffly, but nodded regardless. "Don't be long, my love, things are piling up quick."

Blithe waved his understanding, then moved around the counter and followed Ferrin to the front door and out onto the porch. The sunlight was dissipating through the trees as it slowly lowered in the sky.

One look at the enormous innkeeper, and Myron was on his feet with Rae and Suri hopping up beside him. To Ferrin's relief, the former captain didn't reach for his sword.

Blithe took one look at Rae and little Suri and rubbed his hands down his apron, an almost automatic response, it seemed. "I reckon you tell the truth. You lot look near skin and bone."

Before he could say more, Suri took a step forward and held out her pinecone. "Tippi's freezing. Can he go inside where it's warm?"

Ferrin smiled. He could have kissed the little girl. She couldn't have been more convincing had they planned it. The corners of Blithe's mouth lifted wide enough to be seen through his dark beard. "Of course you can come inside. You and . . ." He stared at the large pinecone. "Tippi?"

Rae put her arm around Suri and smiled, a reaction Ferrin wasn't used to seeing all that much, especially when it came to strangers.

"I reckon we can find you a couple of rooms. Won't be the best, mind you—most of those have already been spoken for—but I have a couple in the back I'm sure I can spare."

"We can pay," Myron said, wanting to make sure the innkeeper understood they weren't asking for charity.

Blithe turned and gave Ferrin a curious look. "I thought you said you was robbed by bandits."

"We were. They took our horses, along with what was in the saddlebags. Thankfully, though, we don't keep our coin in the saddlebags."

"Well, that's good, I guess." Blithe opened the door. "Follow me, and we'll get you sorted."

They followed the innkeeper inside.

One look at those inside and Suri grabbed hold of Ferrin's hand. Most of those seated near the front quieted as they watched the small group keeping close file behind Blithe. They gave Ferrin and Myron a mindful glance, but it seemed most of their attention was on Rae. Ferrin wondered if perhaps they'd never seen an islander this far north before. Her caramel skin might have been a curiosity.

They passed by the kitchen, and Blithe stopped only long enough to grab a set of keys off the wall before heading up the stairs just beyond.

The stairs ended at a corridor leading back to a set of rooms. The walls were lined with burgundy and gold material, something Ferrin wouldn't have expected to find in a simple country inn. Bronze sconces lit the way as they passed by several doors before finally coming to a stop at the last two.

"Here we are." Blithe opened the first and turned to Ferrin. "You and the . . . missus," he said, seemingly noting Suri's hand in Ferrin's and the way Rae tended to look in his direction, "can take this room. And you, sir," he said, looking to Myron, "can take the last."

Rae puffed out her chest. "I'm not his—"

"That'll be just fine," Ferrin said, not letting her finish. He could almost hear her frustration in the stiffening of her shoulders. He didn't dare look her in the eyes, too afraid he might get singed. "How much for the rooms?"

"And food for tonight and in the morning," Myron was quick to add.

Blithe thumbed his chin a moment, looking at each in turn before stopping at Ferrin. "Since you don't have horses to stable and feed, and you're only wanting the one night, I reckon I can let you have the lodging and meals for . . . one silver and two. But," he said, raising a finger, "anything beyond a single serving of ale will be extra."

Ferrin looked at Myron and pursed his lips, wanting to make it appear they were desperate but were at least considering the price. As it stood, Ferrin would have gladly paid ten times that amount just for the bed, but he also didn't want the innkeeper to know of their well-lined pockets.

With a nod from Myron, Ferrin turned to Blithe. "It appears we have a deal." He dug around in his pockets, opening the purse with his fingers and grabbing what he guessed was, by their size, one silver coin and two coppers. He lifted them out, took a look, and then handed them over to the innkeeper. He then passed Blithe three additional coppers. "And this is if you can manage to find us a table away from the main crowd."

Blithe wiped his hands greedily down his apron. "That I can do. I have a couple of private seating areas for special guests and town meetings. They aren't being used at present." Blithe accepted the coins, turning them over in his hand before pinching the silver between his teeth. "You can't be too careful nowadays," he said, then handed them two keys from the ring. "Meals will be served until eighth hour, drinks until closing, which, during these colder nights, could be around midnight."

"We certainly don't want to miss what smells like a mighty fine meal," Myron said.

"I'm hungry," Suri announced, no longer clinging to Ferrin's hand, opting instead to toss Tippi in the air and catch him on the way down.

Blithe smiled. "You won't be for long, little one. I can say, without a doubt, that you won't find a better-tasting stew this side of the Razor Spine than what my Molly makes."

"I'm looking to put that challenge to the test," Myron said with a twinkle in his eye as he licked his lips.

"Once you get your gear stowed, I'll be sure to have your table ready." Blithe half turned to leave. "But if I don't get back to the kitchen, I might be sleeping in the barn tonight." With a brisk nod, he left them to their unpacking.

Ferrin was about to stop him and ask about purchasing supplies and horses, but Suri wasn't the only one whose stomach was rumbling. "Let's get our gear in the rooms and get a bowl of that stew before looking for supplies."

Myron rubbed his thinning waistline. "Took the words right out of my mouth. Besides, I think better on a full stomach."

"Why did you make him believe we were bonded?" Rae asked, snatching the key to her room out of Ferrin's hand.

"Didn't you notice the way the men downstairs were staring at you? Hopefully, if they believe you are already spoken for, they might be less inclined to act rashly. I don't want them thinking that a beautiful woman like yourself was alone in her room for the night.

"I can handle myself," she said, and with a flip of her wrist, a dagger appeared in her hand.

Ferrin gulped. "I suppose you can."

"And don't go getting ideas about sleeping with us tonight."

Ferrin grimaced, especially with her waving that blade under his nose.

"Wouldn't dream of it. Besides, I have every intention of keeping Myron up with my snoring."

"Lucky me," Myron said wryly. "Maybe you should join Master Blithe in the barn tonight."

Rae grabbed Suri's hand and pulled her into the first room and shut the door.

The two men stood in the hall for a moment staring after them.

"I'd hate to be any man that tries to break into their room," Myron said.

Ferrin nodded. "Perish the thought." With that, they picked up their bags and opened the door to their own room and stepped inside.

Chapter 12 | Ferrin

THE ROOM WAS SMALL, not much more than a wooden box with a single bed and a table with one candle on top. A small fireplace rested on the left side of the room with a couple of logs and unlit tinder waiting for the next occupant's use. The one bed, on the opposite wall, was going to be a tight fit for the two men, but it certainly beat sleeping on pine roots and slush. There was a window at the back that stared out over the woods behind the inn, but they weren't there to admire the trees. All in all, it wasn't the elaborate stay Ferrin had envisioned, but the mattress wasn't lumpy, and there were two pillows.

Ferrin tossed the satchels up on the spread, the ropes under the mattress tightening against the added weight. He tried to think whether there was anything they would need out of the bags before heading into town. They couldn't take the chance of leaving their gold behind, so he divided it between himself and Myron.

Unable to spare the time for a much-needed bath, they left the rest of their belongings in the room and locked the door on the way out. Rae must have heard their door opening and closing, because by the time Ferrin had stuffed the key back in his pocket, she and Suri were already in the hall waiting for them.

Testing the two doors to make sure they were secure, Ferrin led the small group up the hall and down the stairs. Blithe spotted them as they reached the main floor. He slipped around the counter and motioned for them to follow. "I have a place waiting for you in the back."

The common room was just as filled as before, if not more so. The old man on stage was taking a break, enjoying a tankard of something that had a smile on his face, or perhaps he was just happy not to be performing. Ferrin was happy as well, considering the squawking he'd heard earlier.

They kept well clear of the tables as they followed Blithe around the left side of the room, stopping outside a burgundy curtain that separated the common room from a much smaller private seating area. As promised, there was no one there, allowing them the comfort of eating in peace without the unrest of having all those suspicious eyes weighing on them.

On Blithe's recommendation, they ordered Molly's stew, and Ferrin even placed a couple of extra coppers down if Blithe was willing to keep their platters and glasses filled. The extra coin put a smile on the big innkeeper's face and speed in his step as he rushed to fill their orders.

It was worth every coin.

The stew was spicier than most, but it had a fair amount of meat, which was nice. The chunks of potato and carrot only added to the stew's thickness, encouraging Ferrin to continue stuffing his mouth as fast as he could manage.

They each had at least three bowls of the stew and just as many mugs of the hot spiced cider, which had a stronger taste of spice than cider, but there were certainly no complaints. Ferrin and Myron decided to wait on the ale until after their business in town, a way to settle themselves down to what would hopefully be a much-needed night's rest.

Blithe personally refilled their glasses and collected their plates once they had signaled their inability to put another spoonful in their mouths.

"What are the chances of us replenishing our lost supplies?" Ferrin asked the innkeeper before he rushed back out to the main room. "More importantly, is there a stable in Woodvale where we can purchase horses?"

Blithe pursed his lips, still holding a couple of dishes he hadn't yet cleared. The innkeeper's hesitancy had Ferrin wringing his hands. "There's a stable," Blithe finally said, "but I can't say as to how easy it will be to purchase the horses, or even supplies for that matter."

"Oh?" Ferrin passed a concerned look at Myron, who appeared to be sharing the same sentiment. "And why is that? Are they running low on stock?"

Blithe shook his head. "No. But they might not be willing to sell to strangers."

"We noticed the rather cold greeting when we arrived," Myron said. "And I don't think it had anything to do with the weather."

"And *cold* is being generous," Ferrin added. "I've seen snow caps with warmer dispositions."

Blithe set the platters back on the table and rubbed his paw-like hands down the front of his apron. "Yes, well, Woodvale's had its fair share of troubles lately. People on edge, especially with the type of rumors we've heard coming down from the north."

"Oh?" Myron asked, joining everyone else around the table as they leaned forward in anxious anticipation.

Blithe glanced over his shoulder at the curtain behind him, as if to make sure it was closed, then leaned in himself and lowered his voice. "There's talk of entire cities going mad, people killing . . ." He gulped and looked at little Suri as if wondering whether he should continue. ". . . and eating each other. There's talk of white-skinned faeries, creatures from out of the Pit, and the Defiler himself rising." The innkeeper wiped his forehead with the rolled sleeve of his forearm. "People are scared, and certainly suspicious of any new faces in town. There was even a battle fought right here, outside the Smok'n Pig, not two months ago."

"A battle?" Ferrin asked, the hairs rising on his arms. He didn't like the direction this was heading. Perhaps spending the night wasn't such a good idea after all. Maybe they should find some horses and get back on the trail.

"Aye," Blithe said. "An entire company of Black Watch was here."

Myron shifted in his seat. Ferrin could feel his eyes on the back of his neck. Rae grabbed Suri, and for a moment, Ferrin thought they were going to bolt, but instead she scooted her seat closer to Ferrin's.

"I take it you don't harbor much love for the Tower?" Blithe said, noticing their reactions. "Don't you worry none. You won't find much love for 'em around these parts either. Take it from me, I'd house a wagonload of wielders over that dark lot any day." He wiped his forehead. "I tell you. I've never seen the like of it before."

"The like of what?" Ferrin asked, almost afraid to find out. "Who were they fighting?"

Blithe pulled out the empty seat on the end and sat down. "It wasn't just the white riders that was there. For the most part, I can handle the Watch, as long as they don't go tearing up my place or mishandling my girls." Ferrin felt sorry for anyone who rose Blithe's ire. The man had arms the size of olive wood trunks. "No. It wasn't the Tower's guards that had me quaking in my boots, it was the creature they carried with them."

"A sniffer?" Myron asked before Blithe could finish.

Blithe gulped. "You know of it, then?"

Myron nodded. "I may have come across one before."

"Then you know what I'm talking about. It was like something out of your worst nightmare. Actually," he added, "I don't think I could have ever dreamed up something so horrific had I tried."

"You mentioned a battle," Ferrin said.

"Most incredible feat of swordsmanship I've ever seen. And those black blades. I've never seen their like."

Blithe had Ferrin's full attention. "Black blades, you say? Rather unusual weapons."

"Most unusual." He leaned forward and lowered his voice. "And those dragon hilts . . ." He shook his head. "I've never seen craftsmanship like that before."

Ferrin's eyes widened further. "Dragon hilts? Can you describe them?"

Blithe scratched his head. "I don't know what more to say than they were dragons. Wings that rose out over the hand, like so, and scales fully across the grip." He shook his head once more. "No, I've never seen their like, or the man who wielded them." The innkeeper looked down at his flour-coated hands and wiped them on his apron before standing. "Reckon I've said too much."

Ferrin started to grab the innkeeper but thought better of it. "Who was this man?"

"Afraid I can't say," Blithe said, almost regretfully. There was something in the man's eyes that said he knew more but wasn't willing to say. "He rode with a pair of tinkers."

"Tinkers?" Ferrin was astounded. He'd created those swords for the king. How could they have come into the hands of tinkers?

"Don't believe I should have shared what I did," Blithe said. "But you lot look honest enough. I trust you'll keep that last bit to yourselves." It was more of a declaration than a question.

"Blithe!" a woman shouted from somewhere out in the common room.

By the fear on the innkeeper's face as he rushed through the curtain divider, it had to have been his wife.

"Black Watch?" Ferrin looked at the others. "Perhaps us staying here wasn't such a good idea after all."

"He said it had been several months since the incident," Myron said.

"Yes, but he also said that appearances by the Tower's guards isn't an uncommon thing. For all we know, they might have some in town this very night."

Myron shook his head. "I think the innkeeper would have mentioned it if there were." He clearly didn't want to give up his opportunity to sleep in a warm bed. "I say we keep to the plan. Get some horses, restock our supplies, and make a quick departure in the morning."

"I guess." Ferrin smiled. "But not too quick. I'd like to have one night's sleep where we aren't up taking turns at watch."

"I couldn't agree more."

"What's a sniffer?" Rae asked.

Myron explained as best he could about the Tower's use of sniffers, making sure to keep his voice lowered and a careful eye on the curtain. Shadows on the floor under the material would have given away anyone's presence.

By the time Myron had finished, the frightened look on Rae's and Suri's faces gave Ferrin the impression that Rae was wishing she hadn't asked. Ferrin had never heard of the creatures before either, and after listening to Myron's explanation, he hoped they didn't have the misfortune of coming across one.

Ferrin stood, pushing his seat back from the table. "We need to get going before the shops close for the evening."

The others followed him out and back into the main room, which was now at full capacity, the smoke thick enough to burn the eyes. Ferrin waved at the innkeeper on their way past the kitchen, letting him know they were done with the room.

Outside, the wind was colder than it had been earlier, and the sky was bright with color, signaling the slow ending of another day.

"We best be quick," Ferrin said as he stepped off the porch and into the packed snow.

They headed up the narrow path to the main road beyond, then took it west toward town. Smoke could be seen rising above the trees ahead, signaling they wouldn't have to walk far.

Sure enough, they rounded the next bend, and the forest opened up. Like a casement around a small gem, the trees formed a perfect placement for the town. It certainly wasn't Iraseth, but it also wasn't as backwoods as that first village they had sheltered at, where they had been attacked by the innkeeper and her cutthroat patrons. At least, Ferrin hoped that wouldn't be the case.

Woodvale seemed a quiet sort of place. The buildings, even though not grand, were well kept. The signs out front were freshly painted and readable, fences well mended, whitewash neatly applied. Seemed to Ferrin to be the kind of place you'd want to plant roots and raise a family, where everyone knew and watched out for each other in turn. It certainly wasn't like that in Rhowynn, where he'd spent his later years. Then again, it was harder to find substantive work in these smaller communities. A town this size wouldn't be able to support two smithies.

If only the people looked as inviting as the buildings.

All along the main stretch through town, those outside stopped to stare, and not in the friendly wave-at-the-newcomers sort of way. Women gathered the children, whether theirs or not, and pulled them inside; men reached for the closest possible weapon, typically a broom or shovel. Even the horses nickered nervously as they passed.

"I don't like the look of this place," Rae whispered, moving closer to Ferrin.

Suri was the only one who didn't seem to notice, as she was too enthralled with picking at Tippi's scales.

"I agree," Myron said. "This doesn't bode well for us. We might find it harder to purchase supplies than we thought. See?" he said, pointing to one of the shops on the left that looked to be the town cooper. "The people are so frightened of us they're actually locking their doors." A woman inside the shop quickly closed the curtain in the window.

Ferrin sighed as they stopped a moment to look around. He spotted what looked like the stables up ahead at the edge of town and nodded toward it. "Let's see about the horses first. They're the most important item on the list. Without them, we won't be going anywhere. It's not like we can just walk to Rhowynn."

They reached the end of town and stopped in front of a wide two-story barn with an overhang on the front, holding shelves with varying sizes of horseshoes, tools, and other strips of metal. Beside the barn was a pen with at least half a dozen horses milling around inside, any of which Ferrin would have paid handsomely for. One of the barn doors was open with three men standing just inside the entrance, chatting quietly. Whatever they had been discussing was cut short as they turned to give Ferrin's group a scrutinizing glare.

Just to the right of the barn was a covered walkway that connected to a smaller stone building with a strong funnel of smoke billowing up from the stack on the back. Ferrin recognized the strong metallic smell wafting from the chimney, not to mention the repetition of the hammer as it sang its siren song, calling to him, drawing him in. He headed down the covered walkway to the front door, wanting to sprint the entire way but forcing himself not to, as those with shorter legs were having a difficult time keeping up.

The three men stepped outside the barn, slowly making their way toward the smithy. They weren't armed, but they did grab some tools from the front on their way by: a mallet, a short-handled axe, and a pitchfork.

Ferrin tried not to make it look like he was overly worried about the men, but he didn't let them fall out of his line of sight either. Stopping at the door, he knocked three times with firm strokes, knowing it would be hard for the smith inside to hear much above the echo of his hammer on the anvil.

The hammer continued its tuneful cadence, so Ferrin knocked once more, this time with enough force to shake the door. The hammer inside stopped, and a voice called out: "Leflin, is that you? It's open! Quit your pounding!"

Ferrin spared another quick glance back at the three men, who were just making their way under the overhang where they were standing, then opened the door. Myron moved to the back of the group to keep Rae and Suri between him and Ferrin.

Stepping inside, fond memories flooded back, memories of Rhowynn and his own smithy. The smell was intoxicating. The heat inviting. Even without the crystal, which Rae happened to be wearing in case they needed a healer, Ferrin could feel every inch of metal surrounding him. He could feel the weight, the type, the strength. They each had their own unique touch.

He remembered the game he and his sister would play as she tested him with a blindfold. She'd tie it tight to make sure he couldn't peek, then hold out a certain piece of metal for him to wave his hand over, and without looking or touching, he could tell her what she was holding.

It was almost like a second sight. He never could quite explain what he was feeling to Myriah. It was more innate than anything, almost second nature. It was like breathing. In the same way you didn't have to teach a child to eat or cry or sleep, Ferrin never had to be taught to feel the ore.

"Who are you?" the blacksmith demanded, taking a step back from his anvil and raising his hammer. "And what's your business here?" He was a short man, but he was stout with forearms that showed his trade. A dirty leather apron hung over an even dirtier white tunic. His beard, like his hair, was streaked with grey, and he wore a leather cord around his forehead to keep the longer strands from covering his face as he leaned over the anvil. He had a hard face and even harder eyes as he looked them over, waiting for an answer. "Well? You gonna say something, or just stand there a-starin'?"

Ferrin took a step forward. Just as he did, the door behind them opened, and the three men stepped inside, spreading out cautiously as if to surround the small group. From closer inspection, Ferrin would have guessed the three men were the smith's sons. Although not sharing their father's shorter stature, they did have the same squared-off jaw and wide nose, nothing compared to Myron's grand pointer, but certainly noticeable.

"My apologies for the interruption, Master Smith," Ferrin said, turning back to the older man with the hammer. From the cluttered look of his shop and the quality of the pieces he'd seen outside, not to mention what hung on the walls, the man was anything but a master. More like a second-rate apprentice. But they were there to make a deal, and insulting the owner of what they were hoping to purchase would not have been the wisest course.

"I'm a smith myself. Have a place in Rhowynn. In fact, we are on our way back there now. We've been traveling west on the road from Kariss for the last week, and found ourselves at the mercy of highwaymen. Made off with our horses, I'm afraid. We were hoping to purchase three from your stables. We'll pay fair value, of course."

"They ain't for sale," the smith said.

"Sir, we aren't asking for charity. We'll pay you fairly for them."

"You heard me, they ain't for sale."

"The sign on your corral out front begs to differ," Myron added, an edge to his voice that Ferrin hoped didn't worsen their chances. Not that it seemed they had much to begin with.

The smith took a step forward and pointed at them with his mallet. "Let me be more clear, then: They ain't for sale to the likes of you." The three younger men behind Ferrin's group took a slight step forward. "Now be gone from my smithy, the lot of ya."

Myron reached for his sword, but Ferrin shook his head and nodded toward Rae and Suri. They could have taken the smith and his sons without a problem, but Ferrin didn't want to risk Rae and Suri getting hurt in the process. And what chance did they have of finding food and supplies if they injured the town's only smith?

Ferrin turned back to the short man and raised his hands submissively. "We don't want trouble. We're just looking for a fair trade. It seems to me that if you wanted us out of your town so badly, then allowing us to purchase some transportation would definitely help speed up that request." He slowly started backing them toward the door, keeping a close eye on the three men as they did.

"You'll be out of our town by tomorrow if you know what's good for you," the older man said.

"You gonna just let them go, Pa?" one of the men on the left asked, causing Myron's hand to slowly reach for his sword once again. "What if they's infected with the madness? What if they spread it around?"

"He's right," the one on the right said, the tallest of the three. "Best be done with them here and now."

Ferrin was now reaching for his sword as he and Myron scooted in closer to protect the women. He stared down the two men on the right as he called back over his shoulder to the smith. "I told you we don't want any trouble, but if you don't get control of your men, I promise you, you won't have any left by the time we leave here."

The tallest bared his teeth and rushed Ferrin, his short-handled axe up over his head. Ferrin didn't even bother drawing his sword. He leaped forward into the man's path and punched him so hard he nearly flipped over backward. Two of his teeth hit the shelf on the left.

No one moved, the others too shocked to respond.

Ferrin motioned with his head for Myron to start moving. With their hands on their swords, they backed toward the door, keeping an eye on the smith and his remaining sons. Before they made it all the way out, the others raced across the room to see about the one lying unconscious on the floor.

Ferrin was the last one through, shutting the door behind them.

"Well, that could have gone better," Myron said as they hurried back to the main road and as far from the smithy as possible. "Don't reckon we'll be getting any supplies in this town."

"What gave you that idea?" Ferrin huffed. He hoped the smith had enough common sense not to press the issue by charging out after them. These people were clearly spooked by whatever was going on in the northern communities, and he hoped they didn't find themselves stumbling across it. They couldn't afford any more setbacks than what they'd already been dealt. Going mad and eating each other didn't seem like something he wanted to find himself in the middle of.

"He has an ouchy, Mama," Suri said, pointing at Ferrin's hand.

Ferrin stopped long enough to take a look. Blood was running down two of his fingers. In all the excitement, he hadn't even noticed.

"Is that . . . ?" Myron looked at the white protrusion between Ferrin's second and third knuckle and laughed.

"Yes," Ferrin said. "It's his tooth." He pulled it out and dropped it in the dirt.

Rae shook her head, then put her hand over his.

"Not here," Ferrin said, looking around cautiously. Even though he couldn't see the people, he could feel their eyes on them. "Wait till we're out of town."

They left Woodvale much quicker than they entered. Behind them, the sun had nearly set, and the bright colors that had covered the sky were gone, leaving behind a blanket of ash grey that brought with it a sense of urgency, as it signaled the ending of another day and the soon closing of the shops.

They stopped only long enough for Rae to use her magic on Ferrin's injured hand. A deep-seated chill ran up Ferrin's arm as the glow from her palm faded. As many times as she had used her ability on him in the Tower, he didn't think he'd ever get used to the tingling sensation her magic brought as it coursed through his body.

"What are we going to do about supplies?" Myron asked as they made it back to the Smok'n Pig and started up the front steps. "We aren't going to get far without them."

Ferrin grabbed the handle to the door and turned. "I might have an idea."

Chapter 13 | Ferrin

HE INN WAS PACKED. The tables had been filled to overflowing when they left to walk into town. Now, Ferrin could barely see them. The crowd stretched across the common room and even up the stairs, where Blithe had apparently placed more chairs around the walkway to provide additional seating. Ferrin couldn't imagine how they managed to keep enough food in the kitchen to feed a mob like this. Was it like this every night?

The one positive aspect to having standing room only was that they were able to blend into the crowd. Ferrin took them left around the outer wall, trying his best to reach the kitchen. Even though he couldn't see the musician through all the people, Ferrin could hear the old man plucking away on his instrument, squawking out another tune, giving it everything he had as he tried to sing loud enough to be heard above the din of laughter, the thump of tankards, and the shouts for more ale.

It seemed half the town was in attendance.

Ferrin put his arm around Rae to keep her close as they pushed through the bodies, and for once she let him, keeping a tight grip on Suri as they went. Myron was only a step behind. What should only have taken a few seconds to get from the door to the kitchen took several minutes.

Servers, both young and old, rushed in and out through the single opening, doing their best not to upend their trays of food and drink. Ferrin had to marvel at the remarkable skill it took to move through a crowd such as this without bathing half its patrons in strong ale and even stronger stew.

He tucked Rae and Suri against the corner and out of the way of the servers. Both of them looked like frightened jackrabbits as their eyes darted from one person to the next, Rae's arms trembling as she held Suri close. They'd never been in a crowd this size before. They looked ready to bolt.

"Watch them," Ferrin said to Myron. "I'll be right back."

"We'll be fine," Myron said, moving protectively in front of his charges.

Ferrin pushed his way to the opposite end of the counter, between the kitchen and the stairs. If he leaned far enough over the counter, he could just make out Blithe in the back, slinging food as fast as he could with hands that seemed to be working on their own. Ferrin tried calling out the innkeeper's name, but with the shouts of orders coming from the innkeeper's wife and the servers rushing in from the common room, Ferrin could see there was no way he was going to be able to get the man's attention. He needed to try something else.

Looking around, he spotted a spare apron hanging on a peg on the wall and an empty tray lying on the counter. Quickly, he grabbed the apron and tied it on, then held up the tray to cover his face as he made a dash for the opening, sparing a quick wink at Rae and Myron on his way by.

Rae looked startled. Myron shook his head.

Slouching to hide his height, he hollered out a fake order on his way in and continued his way through the kitchen, making sure to steer clear of Molly as he headed for the back, where Blithe was slicing up a loaf of bread as fast as you would a stalk of celery, each slice a perfect replica of the last. If Ferrin hadn't been so preoccupied with getting the man's help, he would have pulled up a stool just to watch him work.

Ferrin moved up alongside the big innkeeper and lowered his tray. "Master Blithe."

Blithe's hand slipped, and he cut the next slice twice as thick. "Flaming Pits!" He spun on Ferrin, his knife raised. For a moment, Ferrin thought he was about to attack him, but Blithe just stood there staring, a confused look on his face.

"It's me, Ferrin. You checked us in earl—"

Recognition set in. "Yes, yes, I remember." He looked at the apron around Ferrin's front and cocked a brow. "You shouldn't be back here." With that, he turned and finished the loaf, tossing the warm slices on several plates waiting to be taken out. "Bread is on!" he shouted, and one of the cooks grabbed the tray, sliding it down the counter to the next set of hands, which were busy scooping out stew and shuffling slices of cheese around each plate.

Blithe grabbed the next loaf from off the pile in front of him and started cutting once more, seemingly forgetting Ferrin was still standing there.

Feeling a bit awkward, Ferrin cleared his throat. "Master Blithe, may I beg a favor?"

"Make it quick," the man said, having to shout to be heard over the kitchen staff. He never turned, his knife working repetitiously through the bread.

"We attempted to purchase horses from the stable, but we were told in no uncertain terms they would not be selling to us."

"I told you as much," Blithe said, grabbing the next loaf and continuing his work. "Waste of time."

"I agree. Which is why I'd like to hire you to purchase them for us."

Blithe bellowed out a roar of laughter. "Are you mad? Look at this place. I can't stop long enough to relieve myself. How am I going to go into town and do your shopping for you?" He continued laughing up until Ferrin slapped down three silver pieces on the counter in front of him.

"And there'll be another waiting for you just as soon as you finish." Ferrin placed a folded piece of parchment down beside the coin, the list of items they had drawn up before heading into town. "This is what we need." Four pieces of silver to make a purchase run was absurd, but getting those supplies was everything. He laid a small pouch of coins down beside the note.

Blithe's eyes bulged as he snatched the silver off the counter. He grabbed the list and pouch as well. "Molly! Take over!" The big innkeeper didn't even bother taking off his apron as he rushed for the door at the back of the kitchen and ran out.

Ferrin turned to leave but found Molly blocking his path with a stout ladle in her hand. "Where does he think he's going?"

Ferrin shrugged, but before he could try squeezing by, the short innkeeper's wife grabbed him by the arm and turned him back toward the counter. "Fine! Then you can take his place." She looked down at his disguise. "Appears you're already dressed for it anyhow." With that, she turned back around and started shouting orders, waving her ladle at anyone who looked in her direction.

Ferrin spared a glance back to the front and found Myron laughing. Myron shouted out over the staff. "Bring us a couple of ales as soon as you finish! We'll be in the back." Still laughing, Myron directed Rae and Suri toward the private sitting room they'd shared earlier.

"Figures," Ferrin grumbled.

"What are you waiting for?" Molly shouted, giving him a harsh glare and waving her ladle.

What else could he do? With an exasperated shrug, he picked up Blithe's knife and began cutting. It wasn't as easy as the innkeeper made it appear, but by his third loaf, he had at least managed to keep the slices from looking completely mangled.

By the time Blithe returned, the dinner orders had slowed to something more manageable. Ferrin's cutting arm, however, felt like it would fall off if he shook it hard enough. His knuckles were white from having gripped the blade for so long.

"I see my Molly has put you to work," Blithe said with a forced smile. Something was bothering the man. He cleared his throat. "There was talk of another silver piece?"

Ferrin eagerly handed the man back his knife before rubbing at the knots in his forearm. "Did you get our supplies?"

Blithe fished Ferrin's purse out of his pocket and handed it back to him. It was heavier than expected, which didn't bode well for Ferrin. "Had to rouse a couple of them from their dinner tables to open the shops, but I got what I could. They didn't have everything." He pulled out the list and pointed to one of the items. "Fowlin didn't have any crossbows."

Ferrin nodded with a polite smile, but what he wanted to do was throw the bread knife at the wall. They needed those weapons almost as badly as they needed the horses.

"He did, however, have a pair of long bows, so I purchased them, along with two full quivers. Can't say as they're the best I've ever seen, but they'll hit the mark at thirty paces."

The tension in Ferrin's back eased. He supposed it was better than nothing, certainly better than the poor tallunicci bows they'd been using. "How about the horses?"

Blithe's shoulders lowered, and he cast his gaze about the room one more time. "Afraid there's no helping with those." His face grew pensive. "You didn't tell me you attacked one of Tomos's sons. Looks like half his front teeth are missing." He shook his head. "You shouldn't have done that."

"He didn't leave me much choice. They threatened to kill us to keep from spreading some sort of plague, and when I told them we didn't want any trouble, they attacked."

Blithe rubbed his hands nervously down his apron. "Still, if there's one person in town you don't want to go riling up, it's Tomos. He's head of the town council, and there's nothing he values more than his sons, except perhaps his smithy, and it would be a close tossup. If I was you, I'd be thinking about packing up and hitting the road tonight."

"We can't leave without those horses. How far would we get?"

"Farther than sittin' around here, I reckon." Blithe ran his hands through his hair. "I've got an older mare I can sell you, but that won't be enough to carry four.

Whatever you're gonna do, do it quickly. By the look in Tomos's eyes, I'd say you don't have much time."

Ferrin glanced out at the common room, clutching his apron between his hands. This wasn't working out as he had hoped. "Where's the supplies?"

Blithe thumbed back over his shoulder toward the side door. "I've got them locked in the shed out back."

Ferrin nodded and slipped the fourth silver coin he'd promised from his pocket and handed it to Blithe. "We'll start packing now," he said, and quickly shuffled through the kitchen and out into the common room, leaving his apron on the counter as he headed for the private dining area. He opened the curtain to find an empty room. Where'd they go? Spinning on his heels, he headed for the stairs and up to their rooms.

He stopped first at Rae and Suri's door and knocked lightly. "Rae," he said softly, sticking his head up to the door. "You in there? It's Ferrin."

No answer.

He knocked a little louder.

Still nothing.

The hairs on his arms were beginning to stand. He tried the handle and found it unlocked, so he pushed open the door and peeked inside. The room was empty. There was a candle burning on the table beside the bed, and their bags were laid neatly to the side, but no sign of them. Before he managed to get the door shut, another one behind him opened.

"We're in here," Myron said.

Ferrin released a heavy sigh as he crossed the hall. "I thought something had happened."

"Like what?"

Ferrin stepped in the room, and Myron shut the door. Rae and Suri were both sitting on the bed. "Blithe said it might be in our best interest to leave now."

"What? Right now?" Myron looked stunned. "We just got here."

"Apparently, the blacksmith, Tomos, is the head of the town council, and from the look of his son, he's not about to let us leave without repercussions."

Myron released a deep frustrated groan. "Why does this keep happening to us? We are truly cursed."

"You mean we can't sleep here tonight?" Rae asked, confused. "I want to take a bath."

Ferrin shook his head. "Afraid we're going to have to find other accommodations."

"What about the supplies?" Myron asked. "What about the horses?"

"Blithe managed to get the supplies, but other than an old mare he said he could sell us, it looks like we'll be on foot." Ferrin grabbed one of the satchels from beside the bed. "But if we leave now, maybe we can get out of town before they come looking for us. From the way Blithe was talking, it doesn't sound like we'll have much time." He looked at Myron. "Grab Rae and Suri's bags while I pack ours."

Myron slipped out the door, and Ferrin turned to Rae, whose pale-green eyes seemed less bright at the moment. "I'm sorry. I know you were looking forward to that bath, and we could have all used a good night's sleep."

Before Rae had a chance to say anything, the door opened and Myron rushed in, carrying two satchels while trying to stuff a blanket in one. "I can hear something down in the common room, and it ain't the entertainment. Raised voices. Don't know what they're saying, but by the sound of it, I'd say we don't want to stick around to find out."

Ferrin quickly tied off the satchel he'd been digging around in and hefted both over his shoulder on his way to the door. He opened it and stuck his head out. Myron was right. Something was happening, but the voices were muffled, although he could hear Blithe's booming voice over the rest. Ferrin glanced over his shoulder at the others. "We've got to go."

"What about the supplies?" Myron asked.

"They're locked in the shed behind the kitchen." Thankfully, there was a door at the end of the corridor that led out back. It was pretty obvious they weren't going to make it down to the common room and out through the front. "Stay here," Ferrin said. "I want to see what's going on." He set his satchel down beside the door and carefully made his way to the front of the hall.

"This is my establishment!" Blithe shouted. "You have no right coming in here and demanding anything." He was standing in front of the staircase, holding a large cudgel, blocking others from going up.

"I have every right." Ferrin recognized Tomos's voice immediately. The blacksmith walked over from the kitchen area to stand in front of the large innkeeper. Several other men moved to stand with him. "I'm the head of the council and I say we rid our town of them. They attacked my sons like rabid animals. You saw what they did to Leflin's face. I tell you, they had the look of plague on them. You want our town going mad like Belvin?"

The growing crowd behind the smith shouted, "No!"

"You want them infecting our town?"

Chairs scraped the floor as more people made their way over to put in their two coppers' worth.

Tomos raised his mallet and pointed it at Blithe. "Step aside, Blithe, 'cause one way or the other, we're going up."

Ferrin didn't wait to see if Blithe would move or not. As fast as he could, he raced back down the hall, waving his hands in the air. "Go, go!"

Chapter 14 | Ferrin

EFORE FERRIN HAD REACHED their rooms, Myron was already ushering the girls out the back door and down the steps. Ferrin tore through behind them, but not before he heard Tomos shout and what sounded like a stampede coming up the stairs behind him. Ferrin shut the door as fast as he could, hoping no one had seen him, and flew down the back stairs, taking three at a time.

At the bottom, he ran past the others. "Hurry, this way."

Swiftly, they ran down the side of the building toward the kitchen. They might not have had horses, but they certainly couldn't leave without their supplies. He just hoped they had time to get them and disappear into the woods before Tomos and the rest of the town figured out where they'd gone.

Stopping at the side of the inn, Ferrin peeked around the corner to see if the kitchen door was open or if anyone was outside waiting. The moon, and a single torch mounted just outside the kitchen door, bathed the small yard with enough light to see that it was empty—nothing but a covered well, several hang lines for drying sheets and clothing, a well-stocked woodpile, and the shed. He motioned them forward, and they sped across the yard, ducking under the empty lines on their way to the wooden outbuilding.

Ferrin tried the handle. It was locked just as Blithe said it would be. Taking a step back, he kicked the door as hard as he could. The handle splintered, and the door flew open. He hated damaging Blithe's storeroom like that, especially after all the help the man had given them, but he didn't have a choice.

The inside was dark. "We need light." He ran over to the back door leading into the kitchen to grab the torch resting just to the side. He could hear raised voices inside. Clearly, they were still looking. It wouldn't take long before they started searching the grounds. He grabbed the torch, and the kitchen door flung open.

Ferrin almost yelped.

The big man standing inside did, and then quickly shut the door behind him. "I thought you'd be gone by now," Blithe said. "It's not going to take them long to figure out you aren't inside. I didn't tell them which rooms you was in, so they're searching them all. You need to be gone."

"We can't leave without those supplies."

Blithe nodded. "Well, hurry. I'll try to distract them as long as I can." The innkeeper turned and slipped back inside.

Ferrin ran back to the shed with the torch. With its help, they were able to find the bags of supplies Blithe had purchased, including the two bows and arrow-filled quivers on the side. They didn't even take the time to consolidate as they snatched up everything they could carry and turned to leave.

"Wait," Ferrin said, holding up a hand. "Someone's coming." He closed the shed door just as a couple of men ran around the front side of the inn. Ferrin couldn't see who they were, but he could hear them through the door.

"There's no one back here. I'll check the shed. You check the stables."

Ferrin ground his teeth. There was no stopping it now. They were cornered with nowhere to run. The shed didn't even have a window to try crawling out of. Worse, they were holding a torch with no way to put it out. Anyone who opened the door would spot them immediately.

Ferrin could hear Rae panting behind him. "Hide behind the door," he whispered to the others, and handed Myron the torch. Myron, Rae, and Suri shuffled to the far side of the shed, and Ferrin took up a spot on the side, closest to the opening. If he couldn't stop this man before he gave away their position, they wouldn't be leaving this crazy town alive.

The door swung open and a head peeked in, but before the man could turn, Ferrin yanked him inside, covering his mouth as he did. He hoped there hadn't been anyone outside watching as the man suddenly disappeared into the building. Whoever he was, he didn't even have time to scream as Ferrin's fist met the man's jaw. Once, twice, three times. In fact, he didn't stop till the man was no longer moving.

Ferrin felt someone grab his shoulder, and he spun.

"Hey, it's me," Myron said, then looked down at the crumpled body. "I think you got him."

Ferrin's blood was pumping so hard he could almost hear it. He looked down at the man and finally nodded, then dragged the body farther in and stuffed him behind some barrels in case anyone came looking. "We need to go. These people have lost their minds." He cracked the door and peeked outside. The yard was empty. He grabbed the torch from Myron and doused it in the snow just outside and stuffed it in his pack. "Run for the trees." He held the door for the others, then shut it as best he could with a shattered handle and lock.

With two bags over one shoulder and a bow and quiver over the other, he raced behind the shed and headed straight for the tree line. Behind him, he could hear raised voices from around the side of the inn. He broke through the tree line and ducked behind one just in time to see several of the townsfolk charging around the side of the building. He stood there for a moment trying to calm his nerves, waiting to see what the group would do. It didn't take him long to realize it didn't matter what they did, they needed to get out of there.

Cautiously, he slid backward into the woods, letting the shadows swallow him up.

The others were waiting a little farther in. Without a word, he waved them forward and took the lead. He didn't exactly have a plan. It wasn't like they could take the main road out of town. Without horses, their only hope was cutting through the woods and hoping the townsfolk wouldn't be able to figure out where they'd gone. Although, with the snow on the ground, Ferrin didn't know how feasible that would be, as they were no doubt leaving a rather noticeable trail. But that couldn't be helped.

When being chased by townsfolk who think you are there to infect them with some unmentionable disease, you don't take the time to cover your tracks. You run—as fast and as hard as you can.

The Smok'n Pig and its promise of a warm bed and a hot meal was a distant memory. At least they had gotten the hot meal, and even most of the supplies, but without the horses, Ferrin knew they'd never be able to reach Rhowynn ahead of Cheeks and his merry band of White Tower cutthroats.

"Which way are we going?" Myron asked as they fought through the snow, beating back against the low-hanging limbs and thick underbrush. Rae was having a difficult time helping Suri through the deeper drifts.

"I have no idea," Ferrin said, his breath misting in front of him. "Just so long as it's far away from Woodvale, and in a northernly direction. I think these trees open up a few miles out of town, from what I remember on the map." Ferrin was growing winded. They were all in dire need of sleep, and even with the help of a full stomach, his strength was nearly depleted.

The trees helped hide them from those who might be giving chase, but they also hid them from the only source of light they had. And using a torch was out of the question. Too easy to be seen. Several times, roots or fallen limbs snagged their feet and they landed on their hands and knees in the snow. Their only choice was to stumble about in the dark, hoping they were going in the right direction.

"We need to stop," Myron said, out of breath as he grabbed Ferrin's arm and pulled him up short. "We have no idea which direction we're heading. For all we know, we could be going in circles and end up right back in Woodvale."

Up until that point, Ferrin hadn't noticed the cold, too preoccupied with staying ahead of their pursuers, but now that they'd begun to slow, it was catching up with him. He could feel it in the trembling of his hands and the slight chatter of his teeth. "What do you suggest?" he asked, taking a moment to blow on his fingers. They were all huddled together to keep from speaking too loudly. He looked at Rae and Suri. He couldn't tell much in the dark, but he could feel their shivering through his thick cloak.

"I say we risk a small flame to check the compass. I haven't heard anything but the wind for some time. They've probably given up on us, gone back to their fires and ale now that we're no longer around to infect them."

Ferrin cocked his head, but the only sounds he heard were the wind whipping through the trees and clumps of snow falling from the upper boughs. He nodded, not that the others could have seen. "Fine." He lowered his packs and grabbed the torch he'd taken from the Smok'n Pig and held the pitch-covered tip out to Myron.

It took a while, what with having doused it earlier in the snow, but with a little bit of patience and a lot of determination, Myron was finally able to bring the torch back to life. Everyone huddled close to enjoy the warmth as Myron shuffled around in his cloak for the compass. He pulled it out and held it up face first toward the flame. "Northeast."

"We need to be heading more west," Ferrin said, like Myron didn't know how to read a compass. "At least we know we're still heading away from Woodvale and haven't doubled back."

"Right," Myron said, tucking the compass back in his pocket. "We head—"

"Someone's coming," Suri said.

Ferrin turned. "What?"

"They don't like deep snow," she said, stomping her foot down into the thick powder as far as it would go.

"Who doesn't?" Ferrin asked.

"The horsies."

Ferrin grabbed the torch and thrust it into the snow, then stuffed it in his bag and threw the rest over his shoulders. He'd learned not to question Suri when it came to animals.

By the time they'd gathered their bags and started running once again, Ferrin could hear baying behind him and the faint sound of men shouting. Why hadn't they given up? The supposed threat was gone. He pushed them faster, practically carrying Suri along with the bags since her little legs couldn't keep up and Rae didn't have the strength to carry her.

Myron took one of Ferrin's sacks, but at this point nothing was going to make much of a difference. Ferrin's legs were shaking, and it wasn't just the cold. The horns and shouts behind were growing louder. They might have stood a chance if it had just been the townsfolk, but there was no way they were going to hide from hounds or outrun horses. They needed to find somewhere to make a stand before they dropped from exhaustion.

"There!" Ferrin called out, pointing at what looked like an opening in the trees. The moonlight filtered through, lighting a small patch of a glen. At least from there they could see what they were shooting at. They raced out of the woods and bounded across the open grass and rock, struggling to reach the other side.

Ferrin's feet broke through a patch of snow and sank to the ankles in water. "Blazes!" He hopped forward out of the stream and stopped the others before they did the same. One by one, they jumped over the hole in the ice, making it to the other side without soaking their boots as well. Ferrin's feet were already too numb to tell if any of the water had permeated the leather. Quickly, he led them into the trees on the other side.

"We can't outrun them. We have to make a stand here. Pick as many off as we can with our bows just as soon as they clear the woods."

Rae pulled Suri behind a large tree just behind Ferrin and Myron. In her hand, she held a long dagger. Ferrin had already seen how far she'd go if it came down to it. He only hoped it didn't.

"I can't understand why they are still pursuing us," Myron said, barely able to catch his breath. "It's not like we can still infect anyone."

No sooner had he said it when a familiar voice rose out of the darkness on the other side of the glen. "This way! They can't be far!"

Ferrin recognized Tomos immediately, the same grating voice he'd heard inside the smithy. Ferrin strung his bow, and just as he nocked the first arrow, three dogs plowed through the trees, all stopping at the edge of the woods to sniff. They moved slowly along the outer rim, noses down, before one of their heads suddenly jerked upward and released a deep-throated bay, the other two joining in. Surprisingly, the dogs remained on the other side of the clearing. Much like a good pointer ushering the hunters to their game, the hounds held their ground as they bayed in the direction of the trees and undergrowth where Ferrin and the others were hiding.

"Where are they?" Tomos shouted at the dogs as he rode out of the darkness behind them, a torch in one hand and a sword in the other. "Where are they, Bella? You smell them out there?" Tomos was joined by five others, all remaining on the far side of the glen. Three of them Ferrin recognized as Tomos's sons. The tallest had a wad of something white in his mouth. Either cloth or packed snow, Ferrin couldn't tell.

"That's why they're still coming after us."

Myron nodded. "At least it's not the whole town."

"Still outnumber us three to one."

"Four to one," Myron corrected, "if you count the fact that I can barely keep my legs under me."

Ferrin almost chuckled, but his teeth were shaking too hard to manage it. He had to look down just to make sure the groove of his arrow was still holding. He could barely feel his fingers, let alone the bowstring.

"I know you're out there!" Tomos shouted from across the clearing. "No one attacks my boys and walks away. Step out, and I promise to make it quick. You won't be spreading your vile disease around these parts anymore."

Ferrin took a deep breath, but all he managed to do was cough, which was sure to make Tomos even more certain of their supposed sickness.

Before Myron could stop him, Ferrin placed his bow and arrow against the back of the tree and stepped out, wanting Tomos and the others to believe they were unarmed, while hopefully drawing them into the open so Myron could get a clean shot.

"I told you, we don't want any trouble," Ferrin said. "We don't have any sickness. We came from Kariss. In case you've forgotten, that's to the south, not the north. We aren't a threat to anyone. Just let us go and you'll never hear from us again." Ferrin clenched his gloved fists. Yes, he had stooped to begging. He would have gotten down on his hands and knees if he thought it would help, especially with Rae and little Suri there.

But it was clear that Tomos wasn't after them because he was worried about some disease. If he had been, he would have given up like the others just as soon as they realized the infection had left their town. Tomos was there because of his pride, and pride was a dangerous thing to take from someone, especially someone in authority, even if that authority was just the head of a council to some backwoods community.

Leflin hollered as best he could with a mouthful of bloodstained wrapping. The words were muffled, but the sentiment was clear. "I want them to pay!" He pointed straight at Ferrin. "He's mine!" Before his father could stop him, the young man raised his sword and dug in his heels, and his horse sped across the glen.

"No! Leflin! Wait!" Tomos yelled, but his son wasn't to be stopped.

"You ready?" Ferrin called over to Myron, who was leaning against the next tree with a nocked arrow pulled to his cheek.

"Tell me when," Myron said.

"Now!" Ferrin jumped back behind his own tree and grabbed his bow just as Myron stepped out, aimed, and released.

Ferrin heard a garbled scream, a soft thump, and the whinny of a panicked horse who'd just lost its rider.

"Kill them!" Tomos shouted. "Kill them all!"

Ferrin spun out from behind the tree, but before he could get a shot off, Tomos and the four remaining men had darted back into the forest and were riding hard to circle them, using the woods as a barrier. He couldn't see them, other than the faint glow of their torches against the black backdrop, appearing and disappearing as they galloped through the trees. All Ferrin and Myron could go on was the sound of the horses' hooves as they punched through the snow and struck solid ground.

"Blazes!" Myron shouted. "We shoot now, and all we'll do is lose arrows."

Ferrin pulled his sword. "Fine, then we—"

A muffled scream behind them brought both men around as a large shadow detached itself from behind one of the trees. Ferrin didn't recognize the man, but he had his arm over Rae's mouth and a blade to her neck. The moonlight, what little there was at the edge of the forest, reflected off the steel as it pressed tight against her caramel skin.

Ferrin froze. Where had he come from? He looked at Myron, but Myron was just as stunned as he was. What could they do? Behind them, Tomos and his men were going to be riding in at any moment, and one of his men had Rae by the throat.

Ferrin lowered his sword and took a step forward. "Please, you don't need to do this."

Tomos and the other four rode out of the forest behind Ferrin and Myron, and when they saw the two of them standing there, Tomos reined in his horse. "Kill them!" he shouted at the man with the knife.

"Stop!" Suri cried as she swung her little fists at the big man holding her mother. "Let go of my mommy! Let go!" She grabbed hold of his pants and tried jerking him away, but the man backhanded the little girl and sent her cartwheeling.

Tomos raised his sword. "What are you waiting for? Slit her throat and—"

A shadow flew out of the trees and grabbed the man holding Rae, knocking her from his arms and into the snow. The man screamed and was yanked into the woods before anyone could see what had happened. Two more screams pierced the night, and then everything went silent. Every hair on Ferrin's body stood on end as he and Myron ran to grab Rae and Suri and pull them back toward the edge of the glen.

Tomos and the other four spun in their saddles, searching the surrounding trees, torches held high, hoping to see what had happened to their comrade.

Ferrin had barely made it out of the trees when another shadow flew out of the darkness and grabbed a second man, this time one of the men on horseback. The horse reared and screamed, causing the other horses to react. One of Tomos's sons was thrown, and his mount galloped into the woods, leaving him to crawl back to his feet, sword up and shaking as he spun in all directions.

"What was that, Pa?" the first son called out from his mount behind his father. "What's happening?"

"I ain't gettin' paid enough for this," the last man shouted, and he spun his horse around and sped into the woods, leaving Tomos and his two remaining sons on their own.

A faint shrill sounded from somewhere deeper in the trees where the shadow had just taken the last man. It was the sound of someone dying. Tomos whipped his horse around. "Let the woods have 'em!" he shouted and dug in his heels. The young man on the ground mounted behind his brother, and all three took off as though the Dark One was on their tail.

Ferrin huddled next to the others as they formed a tight circle, blades up, waiting for whatever was out there.

"Into the glen," Myron said, and they stumbled out into the moonlit clearing, just in front of the stream. "We can't fight what we can't see. At least from here we have some light."

In all the rush, Ferrin had left his bow behind the tree. He raised his sword, one of the two he'd forged with magic, and waited. Myron had his bow up and the string pulled as they strained their eyes to see what was out there. Every snap of a twig or fallen clump of snow had them spinning.

"Where is it?" Ferrin asked, more to himself, but loud enough for everyone else to hear.

"*What* is it?" Myron countered.

As if to answer their questions, a grating howl rose out of the darkness, and a set of yellow eyes flashed at the edge of the woods. Ferrin gulped as an enormous wolf stepped out of the shadows, fur as white as the fallen snow and thick as a lion's mane. The animal was much larger than any wolf Ferrin had ever seen, as tall as a horse. The fur around its neck was bristled, ears erect as it bared its fangs and growled. Wolves very rarely ever attacked humans. Then again, Ferrin had never seen a wolf quite like this before.

"What's it waiting for?" Myron whispered, his string still drawn.

"Wait till it gets closer," Ferrin whispered back. "You'll only get one shot."

Suddenly, the wolf's ears lowered, its fur doing the same as it slowly made its way through the snow toward them, paying no attention to a dead Leflin, who lay face up in a patch of red snow with one of Myron's shafts sticking out of his chest.

The wolf's teeth were no longer bared, and the deep growling they'd heard before was gone. In fact, it looked more curious than anything. About halfway out, it turned and loped back into the trees and disappeared.

Ferrin turned and looked at Myron. "What was that about?"

Myron lowered his bow with a shrug, but before he could say anything, the wolf reappeared, this time with something in its mouth.

Ferrin started to raise his sword once again, and the wolf stopped.

"Maybe we shouldn't provoke it," Myron whispered, motioning for Ferrin to lower his blade.

Ferrin nodded and dropped the tip back to the snow.

The wolf slowly sauntered out of the trees and made its way into the clearing, stopping just out of reach of Ferrin's sword. Ferrin's arms tensed, his muscles taut as he waited for the attack.

But it never came. Instead, the enormous animal opened its jaws and dropped a pair of coneys in front of them, then took a step back and watched to see what they would do.

"I'll be a horse's . . ." Myron paused and looked down at Suri. ". . . tail. That's what's been feeding us for the last week?"

The wolf cocked its head, its attention clearly on Suri, who held out her pinecone as if wanting to show it to their new friend. At least, Ferrin hoped it was a friend. After seeing the way it had disposed of Tomos's men, he would have hated it to be anything else. The last batch of wolves they'd come across hadn't been quite so obliging.

"I'm Suri," the little girl suddenly called out, then raised her pinecone once more. "This is Tippi."

The wolf looked confused, but it opened its mouth and released a half growl, half bark that had Rae snatching her daughter up in her arms.

Suri giggled. "She said her name is Nola. It means Moon Dancer." The little girl turned and looked at her mother. "She's very pretty, Mama."

Rae looked at the wolf, clearly unsure how to respond other than to nod.

The enormous animal growled again, barked, and growled once more, shaking her head as she did, even added in some pawing at the snow with her front foot.

Everyone looked at Suri.

"She said she's been following us since we left the big rock."

Myron exchanged a curious look with Ferrin. "You think she means the Razor Spine Mountains?"

Ferrin shrugged. "Could be." He looked back at Nola. "Most wolves are territorial. I can't believe she's followed us this far." Ferrin looked at Suri. "Can you ask her if she is alone?"

Suri smiled as she turned to look at the wolf. "Where's your family?"

The great wolf raised her head and howled. It was a mournful cry that had both Ferrin and Myron suddenly scanning the tree line, waiting for others to come barreling out of the shadows.

"She says the others don't want her. She's not like them. Too big."

"You got that right," Myron remarked. "She's enormous. Scariest thing I've ever seen in the woods. And trust me, I've seen some frightening things."

Suri crossed her arms. "She's not scary. She's pretty."

Ferrin smiled at the little girl's innocence. "She is that." Coming down off the rush of nearly dying, Ferrin's hands were beginning to shake once more, and this time from the cold and not just the excitement of coming face-to-face with a wolf that was big enough to put a saddle on. "Do you think she will mind if we build a fire and set up camp? If we don't get some warmth, and soon, we're going to freeze to death. Unlike our furry friend, we don't have a thick pelt to keep us warm."

Suri turned back to the wolf. "We are going to cook those," she said, pointing at the two large rabbits. "Do you want to eat with us?"

"I don't know if asking her to dinner is the best thing," Myron said, still maintaining a tight grip on his bow.

The wolf turned and slowly sauntered back toward the trees.

Myron looked at Ferrin and shrugged. "Guess that means no."

As soon as the wolf melted back into the forest, they went about setting up camp. It took them a while, but they did manage to dig out a pit and gather enough wood and dry bark to start a fire. The nearly frozen group gathered round, anxiously holding their hands and feet out to warm. Ferrin was so cold he could have walked through the flames and never known it. Eventually, his fingers and toes began to tingle and burn as feeling returned. It took a while before he could open and close his hands without stiffness, but as soon as he could manage it, he set out to clean the coneys for cooking.

He kept his eyes peeled to the surrounding woods, wondering where Nola had gotten off to, and if she was nearby watching. The rigid hairs on the back of his neck said she was. By the time he'd finished skinning the two rabbits and had them on a spit over the fire, Myron had a pot of tea brewing. This time, unlike his homemade remedies, it was a fresh store-bought blend. There was even a little sugar to go with it. It smelled wonderful.

They devoured the meal quickly, leaving nothing behind. The warmth of the tea was exactly what Ferrin needed. Now if only they could manage a single night's rest. With a few extra blankets that Blithe had managed to procure for them, they were able to sleep a little more soundly. Although, having a horse-size wolf traipsing around didn't help.

After taking first watch, Ferrin closed his eyes and didn't open them again until he felt someone shaking his shoulder.

"Ferrin. Ferrin. Get up."

Ferrin turned over and yawned. He was so stiff he could hardly raise his hand to cover his mouth. "What is it?"

Myron pointed at something behind him. "You'll never believe who came back."

Ferrin's eyes jerked open. His first thought, groggy as it was, was that Tomos had gone back to town for reinforcements and had returned to finish the job. Reaching for his sword, he spun in his bedding, but instead of finding a posse of angry townsfolk, he saw three saddled horses warming themselves beside the fire, with Suri standing between them, nuzzling their noses.

"Are those . . . ?"

Myron laughed. "Looks like our luck just turned. We got Tomos's horses and didn't even have to pay for them." He clapped Ferrin on the back. "We won't have to walk to Rhowynn after all."

Chapter 15 | Lenara

’M LOSING MYSELF, LENARA,” Joren said. “I can feel it. Every day I grow weaker while he gets a little stronger.”

Joren’s appearances had grown less frequent over the last several weeks, ever since the Tower’s run-in with the swordsmith in Iraseth, who had narrowly escaped into the icy waters of Virn Run. Lenara had chalked Joren’s inability to manifest up to Sylas and his lack of sleep while pushing them to find the smith. It seemed the only time Joren was able to take back control of his own body was when Sylas had reached a deep enough measure of unconsciousness. She hadn’t said anything, to keep from adding to the young guard’s already frayed nerves, but she, too, was worried.

After the smith and his cohorts had escaped them inside the passes of the Razor Spine, Lenara and the rest of the Tower’s company had spent the last several weeks heading north along the mountains, looking for a way through and not finding one until they had nearly reached Syrel. The smith and his friends certainly had a good lead on them, but they were on foot, and unless they found some horses, traveling through the lower mountains at this time of year was going to be arduous at best.

Lenara sat with Joren in front of their fire, a couple of feet apart, with their backs to the trees at the edge of camp, making sure to keep a safe distance from the remaining members of the Black Watch, those that Sylas hadn’t killed during their attempted coup. The sight of those men being torn limb from limb by forest animals haunted her dreams for several nights afterward. It wasn't like she wasn't used to seeing death. It was more the disturbing pleasure she saw in Joren's eyes as Sylas did it, the same spark Sylas would get when performing one of his inquisitions.

"It just means Sylas isn't sleeping well," she said, hoping to allay the young guard's fears. The crooked smile and half nod Joren offered in turn told her it hadn't worked. "None of us are sleeping well. And who would," she added, poking at her blanket roll, "when forced to spend every night sleeping on roots and rocks and packed snow?"

"I suppose." Joren held his hands back up to the fire. "Still, it would be nice to be around more often. I don't like it when I'm gone."

Lenara didn't like it either. She'd grown rather fond of the young man's company, more so than she cared to admit. Ever since being brought to the White Tower as a young teen, she had spent all her time learning and training and serving the Tower's needs. There'd been no time for anything personal. This newfound attraction couldn't have come at a worse time.

"At first, I didn't notice being gone," Joren said. "It was like sleeping, you go to sleep and hours later you wake, and it feels as though no time has passed, other than the fact that I seem to wake at different locations each time . . . but that's changing."

"Changing?" Lenara scooted to the head of her blanket, which butted up against the head of his. "How?"

"I'm starting to feel time pass." He looked at the fire a moment. "I don't really know how to explain it. When Sylas first started taking over and I was forced to leave, it was as though I didn't exist. One moment I'm lying there watching you sleep, and the next I'm waking up."

Lenara blushed. "You watch me sleep?"

"I, uh . . ." Joren wrung his hands. "I hope you don't mind. You always look so . . . peaceful. Not exactly something I get to experience all that often." He chuckled. "You have a cute way of wiggling your nose when you sleep." He lifted his hand and flicked the tip of his nose with a flirtatious smile.

She found herself wanting to hide in that smile and never leave. Her cheeks reddened. She wasn't going to sleep tonight at all, knowing he was lying there watching her. She cleared her throat. "So, what does this time passing feel like?"

The intoxicating smile vanished, replaced with a tightening around his eyes as he turned back to the open flames. He shivered, then pulled his blanket tighter over his shoulders. "It's as though I'm dreaming. I can see things and hear things, but I'm not quite sure how to explain them. At first, I couldn't remember what I'd seen, much like when you wake, not being able to remember what you've dreamed, although the emotions are sometimes still there. But now, I seem to be remembering things from those dreams. Random things." He lifted his head and looked her in the eyes. "Things I wish I could forget."

Lenara stared into his soft brown eyes. The shame and horror she saw there sent bumps running up and down her arms. Had he seen what Sylas had done with the Tower's guards? Worse, had he borne witness to Sylas's questioning techniques? She shuddered at the thought.

Draping her blanket around her dark robes, she stood and walked over to where he was seated and sat down beside him, taking one of his hands in hers. "I want you to remember something," she said softly, putting to memory every feature of his face. "Whatever you saw, it had nothing to do with you. It was Sylas."

He looked her in the eyes, tears staining his cheeks. "It feels like me."

She squeezed his hand even tighter. This was what she had feared. Joren's consciousness was beginning to wake while Sylas had control of his body. That meant he might have also seen things she had done. She chewed her lower lip, suddenly wondering what Joren must think of her as she stared deep into his eyes. Those soft, beautiful eyes. What she found staring back wasn't anger or disgust, or even loathing. She saw something else, something that had her grabbing the back of his head and pulling him to her, their lips connecting so hard it nearly took her breath.

She'd never felt anything like it before. The heat of her magic didn't hold a candle to what flooded through her body at that moment, enveloping her very soul. *So this is what love feels like.* Why hadn't she done this before?

By the time she finally pulled away, she was panting and slightly dizzy, and suddenly embarrassed, but not too embarrassed to continue holding his hand. It was larger than hers and quite strong, rough from years of hard labor. She did, however, keep her attention on the flames, too nervous to look him in the eyes again.

They sat listening to the wood crackle for some time. The silence was unnerving. Why wasn't he saying anything? Was he upset by her forwardness?

Joren cleared his throat. "So, where are we heading now?"

Where are we heading now? What kind of question was that to ask? She fought back the urge to strangle him, the realization slowly dawning on her that he was giving her a way out in case she was too embarrassed to talk about what had just happened—which, of course, she was. "We just crossed through the Razor Spine into Sidara yesterday."

"I take it we haven't found this swordsmith yet?"

She shook her head slowly, watching her breath mist in front of her face and intermingle with the smoke from the fire. "Not since we lost him and his companions in the passes outside of Iraseth."

Joren nodded, then sat quietly for a moment staring at the dancing of the flames as the tongues licked at the wood. "Why exactly are we after them?"

She looked at him for a brief moment, suddenly wondering if he was losing his memories. "They are escaped prisoners. Well, the swordsmith is at least, the others helped break him out. He also killed . . ." She gestured in his direction. "Well, you know."

He didn't nod, but she could see from the stiffness in his neck as he turned back to the fire that he knew who she was referring to. "After seeing the things I've seen, I'm not sure that was such a bad thing," he said, his tone hardening. "I don't know who this Sylas is, but he doesn't seem to be a very good man. Certainly not the kind of person I would want working for me."

"No," she admitted offhandedly as she stared at the fire, "I suppose not."

"Why do you do it?"

"Why do I do what?"

"Why do you keep following him?"

She started to open her mouth, then stopped, not quite sure how to answer. "It's my duty," she finally said, suddenly feeling the need to defend herself. She released his hand and laid hers in her lap, tucking them up inside the black robes of her office.

"I didn't mean to offend you," he said somewhat cautiously.

It wasn't that she was offended as much as it was the truth behind his words. They stung. Unlike Joren, she'd never thought to ask questions. She had always been the perfect pupil. The Tower had promised to fight back against wielders, had promised her the chance to protect those, like her sister, who had fallen victim to magic. She'd been told, just like Joren, that the only way to defeat magic was with magic. Fight fire with fire. Looking back, sometimes she wondered how she could have been so naïve herself.

"The Tower works with those it must to see the job completed."

Joren sighed. "If I had known what I do now of the Tower, I would have never left Ecrin." His face darkened. "I would have stayed and worked in the mill till I was old and grey and been thankful for it."

Lenara watched the logs shift and drop as they continued to burn. Joren, unlike many of the recruits, had had his eyes opened to the innermost workings of the Tower in the worst way possible. Any early preconceptions he had borne for the White Tower had been expelled after what had been done to him.

"Why do you stay?" he asked. "Why don't you just leave?"

Lenara sighed. "It's not that simple." How could she explain to him that the

Tower was her home? Being a bulradoer was all she'd ever known. Sure, there'd been times when things had gotten hard enough that she wanted to give up, but she'd never considered the option of giving up on the Tower itself, giving up on her life, on everything she had trained for. If she turned her back on what she had been raised to believe, then all of the things she herself had done in the Tower's name would have come into question. And that was something she couldn't bring herself to face.

"Seems simple enough," he said, glancing her way. "You just leave."

She turned on him, angered at having her life questioned. "And do what? Go where?" "I'm a bulradoer, a wielder, one of the very people you joined the Tower to get rid of. What do you suggest I do?"

Joren was stunned into silence. The way he was looking at her, as if he didn't recognize her, stoked the fires roiling inside her gut. It was the same way all the other members of the Tower looked at her, the way they did their best to stay clear. It was a look of fear. Normally, that was a good thing, but for some reason having this young guard look at her the same way turned her stomach. She stood and marched into the woods, leaving him and the fire behind.

She barely felt the cold, her anger seething as she trudged through the snow. She finally stopped and leaned against one of the larger pines, no longer able to see the campfires behind her. Who was he to question her choices? He had come to the Tower same as her. She took a few slow breaths, trying to calm the heat inside. It was working. The winter chill seeped down through her robes and sent her quivering. Her hands tingled and her fingers stiffened against the cold as the occasional gust moved through the trees.

Having had time to let the initial anger quiet, she tried thinking back on what had been said, and why she felt storming off into the snow-covered woods in the middle of the night was a good thing. What was it about his question that had gotten her so worked up? It was an honest question. *Why stay?*

In truth, she was afraid. She didn't have anywhere else to go. She'd known nothing but her duty to the Tower. It was her life. Even if she decided to go looking for her family, she'd doubted she'd find them, and if she did, they'd probably reject her for being what she was, which was why she had stayed at the Tower in the first place. Whether she liked who she had become or not, it was safe.

Now that she felt she had a better answer, she returned to continue their conversation, but Joren was asleep. She looked down and shook her head. If she tried waking him, there was no telling who she would actually awaken, so she dragged her bedding farther away from his before crawling inside. Sleep was a long time in coming as she lay awake contemplating everything that had been said. How could they have gone from something so wonderful as that kiss to being so angry that she had to take a stroll through the freezing snow to cool off? Why was liking a man so difficult?

Dawn came sooner than she would have liked, and by the time she opened her eyes and rolled over, she found Joren up and packing his bedding. One look into those eyes let her know Joren was no longer there.

"Thought you'd never wake," Sylas said with a wry grin that made him look like he had something to hide. "We ride east."

"East?" She was confused. "Rhowynn is north."

"Yes, but if I can catch them sooner, all the better. They are on foot, which means they'll be looking to purchase horses, and the only decent-sized town around these parts is Woodvale. My guess is they'll be heading there first." He poured a cup of tea from the pot sitting on the coals at the edge of their fire and began to sip, his crooked smile never fading from his lips. The way he looked at her had Lenara pulling her black robes tighter around her neck.

If they did manage to capture them at Woodvale, that would mean they wouldn't have to ride all the way to Rhowynn, which meant fewer days having to sleep in the wild, but it also meant fewer days to be with Joren. She still hadn't figured out a way to free him from Sylas yet. She was afraid that if there was an answer, it probably lay somewhere back in the Tower.

After a quick breakfast of cold cheese, an apple, and some very strong tea, Lenara packed her bedding and joined the others in breaking camp. They were back on the trail and heading east before the first rays of the sun had broken through the treetops.

They rode hard that day, slept hard that night—Joren once again not making an appearance—then rode hard the next day as well, reaching Woodvale just as the sun was setting behind them.

Chapter 16 | Lenara

OODVALE SEEMED TO LIVE up to its name—a small vale made up of simple woodsfolk. They passed a smithy and stables on their way into town as well as a few sporadic shops that lined the main street. The town itself was clean, simple wood-and-plaster buildings with stone foundations. The buildings were mostly two or three stories right around the center of town. Whitewashed picket fences quartered off the homes that flanked the perimeter of town, while empty clotheslines and snow-covered flower beds fronted most of the residences.

The streets were empty. If it wasn't for the cracked doors or faint rustling of the curtains in the windows, Lenara would have thought the town abandoned. It wasn't anything surprising, though. Most of the smaller communities reacted the same when the Black Watch showed up. Of course, the ending of another day, and a snowy one at that, also hurried residents to their homes, or the local tavern, where they'd find a hot meal and a warm fire. Lenara longed for a comfortable seat in front of a fire with a steaming glass of spiced wine—the stronger the better.

Still, Woodvale seemed to be more withdrawn than most. Townsfolk were never friendly, but they'd at least share the road with you. The main thoroughfare was completely deserted, apart from a few mutts that had taken the absence to their advantage and were working their way through some of the garbage between the buildings.

"Quiet little community, don't you think?" Sylas said as his head swiveled back and forth, no doubt looking for someone to question.

"Too quiet," she replied, feeling a slight tingling down her back. Something about this place just didn't feel right.

Lenara rode side by side with Sylas, the thick black robes of her office shielding her against the harshest of the icy gusts. They were escorted in front and back by the Tower's guards, their white mantles slapping the sides of their legs as the wind whipped through the center of town. The men were looking the worse for wear, hair and beards long and shaggy, eyes dark-rimmed, clothes dirt-stained. She hadn't seen herself in a mirror in some time and was thankful for it. She'd been in the saddle nearly every day since leaving the White Tower. Iraseth was the first place she'd been able to take a bath and rest on an actual mattress and pillow, even if it was for just a few hours.

Sylas drove them like a man possessed. It was understandable why some of the guards had tried to get rid of him. He didn't treat them much better than . . . Well, than he did anyone else, she supposed.

Joren's words continued to play over in her mind. *Why don't you leave?*

"Where is everyone?" Sylas held up his hand for the men to stop. He pointed at what looked like a cobbler's shop on the left, with a sign out front displaying a pair of boots on one side and some daintier women's shoes on the other. "Go knock on that door," he said to one of the guards.

The man nodded and directed his horse over to the front of the building. He hopped down and walked over to the door and tried the handle, but it wouldn't give. He turned and shrugged.

"Well, don't look at me," Sylas said. "Bang on it until someone answers. And if they don't, kick it down." He made sure to say it loud enough for anyone inside to hear.

Before the guard had managed three hard knocks on the wood panel, the door swung open, and a short, older gentleman with a white beard and a bald head stood in the doorway. He wore a red shirt and wool vest with an apron that hung from the waist down to the middle of his boots. A small hammer rested in his right hand, probably still in the middle of his work. He looked out across the line of guards.

"How . . . how can I help you?"

Sylas rode his horse over to the front of the building, forcing Lenara and the others to follow. "Why have all the shops closed so early?" he asked, staring down at the man with a fake smile. "Sun's barely below the trees." Actually, it was low enough that the colors had already faded to a dull grey and the first of the stars could be seen shining through.

The cobbler's hands were shaking so hard the head of the hammer bounced against the side of his leg. "We close early during the winter. Even more so with the plague. Town council says—"

"Plague? What plague?" Sylas took a moment to scan the street behind him.

The cobbler looked at him funny. "What do you mean, *what plague*? Everyone knows about the plague. Up north. People going stark mad. Killing each other. Eating each other, from what we've heard." He shook his head in disgust. "We don't want no strangers coming through here."

"Have you seen strangers?" Sylas asked, his attention perking up.

The cobbler nodded. "'Bout three days back a group came wandering into town. Had a run-in with Tomos and his sons. Killed one from what I heard."

Sylas leaned forward, the cold leather creaking under the sudden change in position as his hand tightened on the reins. "Killed one of them? You killed one of the strangers? Which one?" he demanded, his voice harsh enough that the man took a step back.

"No. You mistake me, sir. We didn't kill the strangers. The strangers killed one of Tomos's sons. Also killed a couple of trappers that worked for Tomos. Used dark magic on them, they did." The old man spared a hesitant look at Lenara, not that he could have seen much of her with her hood raised. "Called up some faerie-lovin' monster out of the woods to devour them."

Sylas gave Lenara a questioning look, and she shook her head. She didn't have any more insight into what the cobbler was saying than he did.

Sylas turned back around. "Where is this Tomos?"

The cobbler pointed back toward the large stable they had passed. "He's the town blacksmith. But if you don't find him there, he'll most likely be at the Smok'n Pig. Just follow the main road east and you'll see the sign on the left just outside of town." The little man watched nervously as Sylas finally nodded and spun his horse around. Before Lenara had caught up, the cobbler was back inside and bolting the door.

The company rode back to where the stable and smithy were located. The chimney on the stone building was void of smoke, but Sylas sent someone to check it anyway. He also sent someone to check the main residence, which was a quaint two-story log home tacked onto the back of the stables and connected by a covered walkway, much the same way the smithy was. Both guards returned, shaking their heads.

Sylas ground his teeth and turned to Lenara. "I guess we find this Smok'n Pig." He turned his horse about, and they rode back through town, this time not stopping until they saw the sign for the inn.

Halfway down the narrow lane, Lenara spotted a young stablehand rushing into the barn on the right and shutting the door. If she were to guess, he was probably halfway to the loft and about to dive under a pile of hay, which was the normal reaction the Tower's guards received out in the more rural districts. One look at the white mantles and most ran.

Sylas didn't seem to have noticed, or cared—his focus was on the three-story building in front of them. She didn't much care for the all-too-familiar grin on his face, which tended to appear when he thought he was about to get the chance to apply his tradecraft.

The Black Watch pulled to a stop in front of the inn, but every hitching post was completely filled. Even the trees around the front of the inn were in use. Half the town must have been inside, which would work to their advantage. What better way to gather information than to address everyone at once? Lenara just hoped this didn't turn into another incident like the one they'd had prior to Iraseth, especially now that she knew Joren might be watching.

She swung down and took a moment to rub her tender backside while several of the Tower's guards walked the line of hitching posts, releasing all the horses to make room for theirs. She joined Sylas up on the front porch as they waited for the guards to finish. He cradled a small pouch under his left arm, the same pouch he had taken with him before his last round of questioning, a bound leather satchel filled with various tools.

"No bloodshed," she told Sylas, who was shifting anxiously from one foot to the next, like a child about to walk into a confectionery. She didn't bother looking at him. She could feel his smile from there.

"Bring the box," he said, glancing over his shoulder as two of the guards untied a chest from the back of one of the pack horses.

Lenara watched them carry it up onto the porch. It held the durma collars each team from the White Tower was sent with in case they ran into wielders that needed to be dealt with.

As soon as the men had assembled behind them on the porch, Sylas opened the door, and they walked inside. The common room was filled to the brim, every seat and table taken. Even the upper floor with its additional seating was filled to overflowing. Smoke lay across the room like a morning fog, strong enough to burn the eyes. In the corner, an old man holding some form of stringed instrument Lenara wasn't acquainted with stopped his croaking and stared at them from over the heads of the crowd. Those few who were actually listening to the man's sad talents shouted at him to continue, wondering why he'd stopped.

It wasn't long before the roar of laughter and clanging of mugs faded, then died as everyone turned in their seats to get a look at the newcomers. Those standing near the door quickly moved, forcing those around the outside wall to shift to make room, backing people all the way up to the long counter in front of the open kitchen on the left.

A man wearing a white apron pushed his way through the kitchen staff. He was one of the biggest men Lenara had ever seen. A white shirt rolled to the elbows revealed forearms the size of her calves, and with his chin-length black hair and full beard, he looked more bear than man. His hands were empty, but he carried a paring knife in the waistline of his apron. The people in front of the kitchen parted as he made his way toward them.

Lenara reached into her robes, her fingers wrapping around the silver handle of one of her ter'aks, easing her worry, if only slightly. She didn't think the man would openly attack them, but she was never one to take anything for granted, especially in a town as on edge as this one seemed to be. The way the people were staring gave her the same unease she'd felt riding through the deserted streets outside.

"Evening," the big man said, stopping several cautious feet away. "The name's Blithe. I'm the owner. Is there something I can help you with? We have a private room at the back for guests if you're so inclined."

Sylas took a small step forward from the rest. He scanned the room, his smile never wavering. "Yes. Yes, I do believe you could help me with something." His hand involuntarily stroked the edge of his bundle. "We are looking for information."

When he didn't say more, the big innkeeper gave a tug on his beard, staring down the row of white-cloaked men. "Information, you say. And, uh, what sort of information is it you're looking for?"

Sylas looked out across the common room. No one moved. No one spoke. It was silent enough to believe that no one was breathing either. "I am looking for Tomos, the blacksmith."

Heads began to swivel toward a couple of tables at the back near the open hearth.

"And what is it you want from him?" a raspy voice called out near the fire.

"To talk. Just to talk." The spark of excitement was building in Sylas's eyes. Lenara didn't like where this was going, not in a room filled with what looked like most of the town. The town was already on the verge of paranoia from some unknown plague she had never heard of. If they weren't careful, it would be them who'd be leaving toes up.

A short, stocky man stood from a table just left of the fireplace. He had grey hair and arms that spoke of swinging a hammer every day for the last forty years. His clothes were not extravagant, but for the likes of Woodvale, they seemed newer than most. The blue had not faded on the shirt, and his tan overcoat had no patches. There was even a bit of fur around the collar.

"I'm Tomos. What is it you wish to address me about?"

Sylas held his smile. "It's of a sensitive nature. I'd prefer to discuss the matter somewhere a little more private."

Tomos took a moment to look out across the room. "Whatever you wish to say, you can say it here." The man clearly had enough sense to stay where he was, surrounded by friends.

Sylas's smile slipped, if only for a moment, then it was back in place and as strong as ever. Lenara only hoped he had enough sense not to poke a nest they couldn't run from.

"As you wish," Sylas said, holding Tomos's gaze. "I have been informed that you had a run-in with some strangers a few days back. I'd like to know more about them. How many were there? Where were they going? Did they have anything of interest to say?"

"A pack of magic-wielding murderers, they were!" the man shot back, waving his arms. "Bringing their dark plague down on us! Calling forth creatures from the Pit!" If Tomos had been holding a tankard, those sitting next to him would have been thoroughly doused. "Killed my son, they did! We tried to fight them off, but there were too many of them."

Too many? Lenara was confused. *Had the smith hired some armsmen?*

"How many?" Sylas asked, looking a bit muddled himself.

"At least a dozen," Tomos said. "Maybe more."

A dozen? Now Lenara really was confused. Were they on the wrong trail, chasing the wrong group? Had the metallurgist and his companions given them the slip once again?

The huge innkeeper to Lenara's left shifted uncomfortably. "There weren't a dozen men. There was only four of them. Two men, a woman, and a child."

Tomos glared at the innkeeper like he was ready to beat him to death with his hammer.

Sylas looked at Tomos. "Apparently, you seem confused. The innkeeper has accurately described those we are seeking. Are you saying you saw more?"

"Are you questioning my eyesight?"

The room went deadly silent. Lenara could hear the fire crackling in the hearth on the other side, and if she listened close enough, she probably could have heard snow falling on the roof overhead.

Slowly, she lifted her ter'ak out from its holder under her robes, still keeping it hidden. She hoped she wasn't forced to use it.

Sylas took a slow breath, adjusting his bundle under his arm. "I have found that people, when placed under extreme emotions like rage or fear or pain, can sometimes embellish." He turned his attention back to the innkeeper. "Which way were they heading?"

"They were heading north!" Tomos shouted from across the room.

Sylas ignored Tomos and kept his eyes on the innkeeper.

The man licked his lips and passed a quick glance at Tomos. "East. They said something about reaching Riverton and finding a boat to take them south into Briston."

Lenara didn't need to be an inquisitor to know the innkeeper was lying, but why would he admit to who was there and then turn around and try misleading them as to where they were going? There was something really wrong with this town.

"It seems we have quite the predicament here," Sylas said, looking at the two men. "One says there were a dozen traveling together, the other says four. One says they are heading north, the other east. Either one of you is lying, or both."

"Are you calling me a liar?" Tomos said, reaching for his sword. All those standing nearest the Black Watch moved to the sides, chairs scooting back from the tables.

Lenara tightened her grip, the name of her ter'ak on the tip of her tongue, ready to call if needed. She hoped Joren wouldn't see her like this, a viper balled and waiting to strike.

The Tower's guards stood where they were, waiting for orders. To their credit, they hadn't reached for their weapons—yet. Of course, as heavily outnumbered as they were, they probably had enough sense not to press too hard. If only Sylas could show such wisdom.

The inquisitor held his smile as if it had been painted on his face. "I'm simply stating the obvious. We have two conflicting statements here. You can't both be right. And the only way to find out which one is telling the truth would be further questioning." He stared at the two men a moment longer, then finally turned to two of the guards behind him. "Take the innkeeper. We'll soon have the truth."

The two guards pulled their swords and started for Blithe. Just as they did, every man and woman inside the inn came to their feet. Swords, daggers, mallets, and hatchets were ripped from leather sheaths and waist belts. Bows came off the back of chairs, and nocked arrows were aimed down at them from the balcony above.

The guards stopped where they were.

Lenara drew her ter'ak and held the silver rune-covered rod out in front of her, while at the same time conjuring a shield of air to protect her and Sylas from any immediate attack. She didn't care one bit if Sylas took an arrow to the neck, but she had to protect Joren. She leaned in, keeping her voice low enough to not be heard by those standing nearby. "This is not the time to pick a fight. I can't protect us from a number this large. We need to leave."

"It seems you've grossly misjudged your situation," Tomos said from the back. "You're strangers and can't be trusted." He looked at the townsfolk. "They're probably carrying the plague, sent to spread it to our town."

Heads turned, feet shifted, hands tightened on their weapons. If they didn't get out of there now, they never would.

Lenara grabbed Sylas by the arm and pulled him bodily toward the door. The other guards took the hint and started backing away as well. Sylas jerked out of her grip. "The White Tower doesn't cower from anyone." He glared at Lenara. "You're one of the chancellor's bulradoer. Kill them!"

Lenara's face was sure to have matched her hair. They weren't going to get out of this alive. She turned to the guards behind her. "Get that fool out of here!"

The two guards carrying the chest of durma collars were the first out the door. Several others grabbed Sylas, who kicked and screamed as they pulled him with them, threatening them all with dire consequences. Thankfully, the Watch knew enough to be more frightened of her than of Sylas.

Holding her shield in place, she drew on the wind. The townsfolk seemed to have no idea what a bulradoer was, which was to her advantage. They still believed, like Joren, that the White Tower was there to protect them from magic. The very thought that the Tower would be using magic was not something most could imagine.

She raised her hand submissively out to the side, letting the heavily armed townsfolk believe she was surrendering as she drew the wind to her. Once she'd gathered what she needed, she sent a strong gust across the entire room, blowing out every candle, extinguishing every flame, even snuffing out the fire from the hearth.

They were in complete darkness.

The snap of bowstrings filled the common room, and her shield was assaulted with arrows. She kept it up long enough to protect those Watch still trying to get through the door behind her. She raised her ter'ak. If this didn't get their attention, nothing would.

"*Cryora!*"

A flaming red lash spread out from the tip of her rod and stretched across the ground, causing the wooden planks to hiss under its heat. The room glowed a dark red around her.

"What sorcery is this?" She recognized Tomos's voice from somewhere in the back. "Since when does the Tower consort with the ven'ae? She's a dark witch! Kill her!"

Lenara swung the whip over her head and let it crack in the air, releasing an ear-piercing snap, like the clap of a thunderbolt, momentarily disorienting their senses. A few more arrows bounced off her shield as she turned and ran through the door. She swung at the nearest posts holding up the roof over the porch, slicing straight through. The wood cracked, and the snow on top poured down as the entire overhang collapsed in a heap in front of the building, blocking those inside from getting out.

She released the magic to her whip, letting the flames disappear as she grabbed the reins from one of the guards who had stayed behind to hold her horse. Swinging into the saddle, she stuffed the ter'ak back within her robes and dug in her heels. The two of them rode up the lane toward the main road. Even if she hadn't taken the time to slow the angry mob by bringing down the front porch, the Tower's guards had already scattered the other horses to keep the townsfolk from giving immediate chase.

It didn't take long to catch up with the others, and the entire company rode hard back through town, not even stopping to get their bearings. A mile out of Woodvale, Lenara finally began to breathe a little easier. Sylas rode in silence, his smile no longer visible. She was going to have to have a strong word with him as soon as they made camp. She didn't care if he'd been put in charge of the expedition or not. She wasn't about to let him put her and Joren's life in danger like that again.

Chapter 17 | Ayrion

ARE YOU SURE WE can't talk you into staying?" Abiah asked, hooking his thumbs into the front of his pants. The former Saeida taverner looked quite the worse for wear, but after what they'd been through defending Belvin against Argon, it was no wonder.

Ayrion smiled, pulling his long black leather coat tighter around his shoulders. The snow had begun to settle in, leaving a white blanket across the roads and rooftops, almost hiding the devastation that had been left from the vulraaks.

"Belvin could use a man like you." Abiah looked at Tameel and Zynora, who were back in their typical baggy clothing, colorful enough to make even the flowers jealous. "All of you. The people already consider you something out of legend, and it's gonna take a firm hand to rebuild what was lost around here."

Ayrion took a moment to look out across the battleground that had at one time been Belvin's central square. The people were just now working to move the burnt remains of the rover wagons from the front of the Justice House.

Abiah released a heavy sigh and shook his head. "There's not much left of my precious Saeida, and those displaced don't have any desire to be going back. We've decided to rebuild here in Belvin."

Ayrion shook his head. "I'm sorry, my friend, but I'm afraid our path is taking us elsewhere."

"Look here," Abiah said, leaning in. "They're trying to make me the city's magistrate." He flung his arms out to his sides. "What do I know about being a magistrate? I'm a barkeep, and not a very good one at that."

"Nonsense," Zynora said, the charms around the hem of her headband jangling as she spoke. "When Saeida came under attack, it was you the townsfolk all looked to when they needed someone to take charge."

"Aye," Tameel agreed, scratching at the tuft of white hair exploding out of his burgundy headband. "The wife's correct. Even here, you seemed more a leader than anyone."

Ayrion smiled at the taverner. "Seems the people have made the right choice. I can't think of a better person to help organize the rebuilding of this city than you." Ayrion was going to miss Abiah, loud opinionated mouth and all. He was a good man and would probably make a fine magistrate—if he could keep his temper in check.

Abiah rubbed the balding spot on the top of his head with his hankie. "Well, truth be told, they actually offered the position to the big man there first," he said, nodding toward Bek, "but he wisely turned them down."

Bek grunted and folded his arms, but Ayrion noted the slight smile around the corners of his mouth. "I've no desire to be the head of anything." Bek was decked from head to toe in fur, apart from his zabatas. He must have had more than one pair of the soft leather shoes, since this set didn't seem to be covered in vulraak blood. "Just leave me to my trappings and I'll be a happy man. Never liked going into the city all that much anyway. Too many people." He turned to Ayrion. "If it wasn't for Nell here," he said, placing an arm around her shoulders, "I'd have half a mind to go with you."

Ayrion wasn't sure if the big man was saying that to tease his wife, or because he meant it.

Nell placed her arm around her husband's waist and squeezed. She seemed to be back to her normal self, for the most part, though there were times when her eyes would drift off, tears forming at the corners. He knew what it felt like to be under Argon's control, the way it felt to have the wizard's essence inside of him, manipulating his body without any way to stop it. It might not have been to the extent Nell's experience had been, but it was certainly enough to understand it was going to take a while before she—or the town—fully recovered.

Belvin had more to rebuild than its buildings.

Behind Nell, Taylis played with Marissa. The two rover children, like many of the others in town, had found themselves without a home or family. Bek and Nell said they would take responsibility for the two. The couple had been unable to have children of their own, so Nell seemed especially delighted.

"Well, I can see your mind is made up," Abiah said as he put his arm around his son, Willem. The lad was hard-pressed to be too far away from his father's apron strings of late, after what he'd survived. Many who experienced such horror were never right in the head again. Willem was a tough boy, though. He got it honestly.

"I guess there's not much left but to wish you safe journeys. And if you find yourselves back in these parts again," Abiah said with a wink, "you be sure to pay us a visit. You'll always have a home here in Belvin. This city thanks you for what you've done."

Ayrion smiled. The man was already sounding like a magistrate. "And we wish you luck in restoring this city to its former glory." He put a hand on Abiah's shoulder. "I meant what I said, they got the right man for the job."

Abiah straightened with a nod, then took a step back and actually saluted, fist thumping his chest hard. "Yes, sir, Commander." He smirked.

Ayrion shook his head, and before he could take a step back, the taverner had wrapped his arms around him. Willem, too, gave Ayrion and the others a hug, thanking them for not letting him get eaten.

Ayrion hugged Nell as well. "Take care of this big oaf for me, will you?" He nodded to the big man beside her. "Not sure he can handle it on his own."

She smiled. "I'll do my best, but you know how he gets." She gave Bek a playful nudge.

Ayrion looked at Bek. "Well, it's been quite the journey, my friend."

Bek nodded, his hands resting comfortably on the hatchets at his sides. "One I wish we had never undergone, apart from the meeting of you, of course, and Tameel and Zynora." The older couple were too busy saying their goodbyes to Abiah and Willem to hear. "I don't make friends easily."

Nell agreed with an adamant nod of her head.

"But you are one of the best I reckon I ever will." The big trapper cleared his throat. "Look at me, getting all emotional. I understand now what they mean by a brother in arms."

Ayrion could feel his eyes beginning to sting, tears forming at the corners. "I can't think of anyone I'd rather have at my side than you." He took a step forward, and Bek swallowed him in his arms, nearly squeezing the air out of him before releasing.

"We'll take good care of Taylis and Marissa," Bek said. "Don't you worry none."

At the sound of their names, the two rover children stopped what they were doing and walked over. Marissa wrapped her little arms around Ayrion's leg until he finally picked her up so she could give him a kiss on his cheek. She smiled, and he gave her a warm hug in return, holding her longer than he needed to. She always made him feel like he was home, in a way. "I'm going to miss you two," he said. "You'll behave for Master Bek and Mistress Nell, won't you?"

Marissa nodded with a smile, and Ayrion placed her down beside Taylis, who was busy examining bugs with his crawly killer. He stopped long enough to nod as well.

"Here, these are for you, Marissa," Zynora said, handing the little girl a new dress in the rovers' colorful style, along with several very colorful ribbons for her hair. Marissa beamed as she took them.

"And this is for you, Taylis," Ayrion said, turning to signal Tameel, who was standing behind Ol' Lerra. The old green-and-gold wagon had surprisingly come out mostly unscathed, a miracle considering the battles it had been through. "He can't make up for Ol' Bleu, but every boy needs a horse."

Tameel stepped out from behind the wagon, leading a hazel-colored stallion with white markings on the sides. Taylis squealed and ran for the horse. Even Marissa ran over to pet the big animal. Taylis gave Tameel a hug, then Zynora, and finally Ayrion. "He's perfect. I miss Ol' Bleu, though."

"I know," Ayrion said as he knelt down and placed his hands on the boy's shoulders. "He'll never be able to replace Bleu, but give him time, and I'm sure you'll grow to love him as well."

Taylis smiled, then ran over to take the horse's reins. "You hungry, boy? I know where I can get some apples." Taylis and Marissa took off through the snow, leading the horse toward a couple of the other rover wagons that had survived the battle.

Ayrion turned to the others. "I believe it's that time."

Tameel was already opening the back of the tinker wagon and letting down the steps for Zynora to climb in. Once in, he raised the steps and locked them into place with a short rope, then headed around to the front and climbed up onto the seat.

Ayrion stroked the long white mark running down the front of Shade's forehead. The powerful warhorse blew out his lips, shook his mane, then nuzzled Ayrion's hand. He'd saved Ayrion's life more than once, coming to his aid when things were most dire. Ayrion wished he better understood the bond they shared, but for now, just having someone there from his past helped. He swung up into the saddle and turned to those they were leaving behind. "If we're ever in these parts, we'll be sure to stop."

"I'll hold you to that, Commander," Abiah said, still getting a kick out of the label.

"Safe travels," Bek said with a wave. "I hope you find whatever it is you're searching for."

Directing Shade alongside the front of the wagon where Tameel was seated, he turned in the saddle and waved back at those behind as the old tinker snapped the reins and the wagon lurched forward, slowly heading on to what was sure to be their next adventure. Ayrion hoped it wasn't as treacherous as the one they'd just survived, though with the direction his luck seemed to be taking him, that seemed unlikely.

Wellhollow was still a good ways off. There was no telling what could happen between now and then.

Chapter 18 | Ayrion

RAVELING BY TINKER WAGON was a test of patience, as you didn't seem to get anywhere very quickly. They sluggishly plodded along at a reasonable pace, which generally meant slow to meandering when it came to Tameel. He said he didn't want to overburden the horses, but Ayrion knew it had more to do with not wanting to overburden his backside on the wooden seat.

The two horses pulling the wagon had been well trained. They'd been hauling Ol' Lerra around the Five Kingdoms for most of their lives. Half the time, Ayrion would find the old man asleep on the seat, and yet, somehow, the horses kept plugging along, stopping occasionally to gnaw on some of the patches of dried grass tall enough to poke through the snow.

The flat plains to the north and west were covered in snow as far as the eye could see, a vast emptiness of white. Ayrion squinted against the sun's blinding reflection. Even with his hand up to help shield his eyes, he could barely see three feet in front of his face, and his head was beginning to pound.

He twisted in his saddle and grabbed his leather shaders from one of the panniers strapped to the back of his horse and pulled them down over his eyes.

He looked over at Tameel and Zynora, who had come out to sit in the front with her husband for a spell. "These things look ridiculous."

"Nonsense," Zynora said. "They make you look fierce, especially with that long black leather coat, and those swords."

"Besides," Tameel added, "your eyes are more sensitive than most. You could permanently damage them out here if you aren't careful."

"I know. Still, they feel awkward on my face."

After the first week with nothing changing other than the distance of the tree line from the road and the depth of the snow, Ayrion was beginning to feel weary. The journey was growing tedious, forcing him to come up with new and inventive ways to pass the time. He would spend the first part of the day in the saddle, riding alongside the wagon, conversing with Tameel and sometimes Zynora, when she stuck her head out.

Then he'd spend the second part walking alongside Shade, discussing anything from the proper way to clean his swords to the various owls he had heard over the last several nights while lying in his bed, staring at the ceiling. He hoped his conversations would somehow spark a new memory from his past life. They never did. Thankfully, Shade was a great listener. Never argued, at least not often, but there was the occasional flick of the neck or disagreeing neigh when the giant warhorse felt Ayrion was talking nonsense.

Finally, Ayrion would spend the remainder of the day in the front seat, listening to Tameel drone on for the third or fifteenth time about some interesting sight they'd seen or grand adventure they'd taken part in during his and Zynora's illustrious travels throughout the Five Kingdoms. There never seemed to be an end to the amount of stories Tameel could produce on any given subject.

When the wagon hit a particularly rough patch of snow, forcing them to climb down and dig it out, Tameel spent the entire time relaying his and Zynora's harrowing experience of being snowed in one year in the northern regions of the Angoran Mountains, and how they had been forced to spend the entire winter there until the passes had melted far enough for them to make it back down. Of course, the recounting took just long enough for Ayrion to finish shoveling the snow while Tameel leaned against the wagon wheel and looked on.

After supper, the three would sit around the small potbelly stove inside the wagon as Zynora read to them out of one of her histories, relaying stories of times long past, some even of times when magic was freely used throughout Aldor, before the Wizard Wars and the Great Purge that had come as a result. Ayrion always enjoyed hearing about those times. He wondered what it had been like to live freely in the world without having to worry about people discovering his abilities, to not have to hide who he was.

They passed through several small villages with sharp, snow-covered roofs and wood-plank siding. The houses didn't have the same picket fencing that they had seen in Belvin or Woodvale. The yards were separated mostly with long thin poles that rested atop unevenly spaced bracers. Stacks of firewood and bales of hay could be seen under makeshift overhangs against the houses, along with cords of firewood, clotheslines, and the occasionally privy.

The villages were too small to have an inn or shops to purchase from. According to Tameel, these more remote communities would make trips once a month to the closest township large enough to buy goods, content with remaining to themselves and working the land. The closest town large enough to support trade was Minotha, which had been built off one of the western branches of Virn Run. It was also about halfway between Belvin and Wellhollow, a good stopping point to sell more of their own goods in exchange for items they were running low on, such as flour and cheese.

"It's a fine town, Minotha," Tameel said from his chair in front of the stove, having finished the last of Zynora's biscuits. He pulled out his pipe, stuffed it, and lit. The tobac inside caused his face to glow a deep orange as he sat back with a satisfied grin, took a deep breath, and released. "Plenty of good people willing to work with the Rhivanni there."

"It's a fair size, then?" Ayrion asked, sitting at the table, sharpening some of the blades that Tameel and Zynora had salvaged after the Belbridge Battle. It gave him something to occupy his mind while still keeping his hands busy. He found the repetitive movement of running the blades over the whetstone calming, the soft wet scraping relaxing him for sleep.

"Sizable enough for these parts," Tameel said. "Larger than Woodvale, I reckon. What do you think, dear?" Tameel cocked his head toward Zynora, who was entertaining herself with a thick-spined book in the rocker next to his.

"Hmm? What's that?" she asked, not bothering to lower the tome an inch.

"Minotha," Tameel repeated. "Comparable to Woodvale, wouldn't you say?"

"Woodvale? Yes, yes, very comparable." She went back to her reading, chuckling every now and then at whatever it was that had managed to capture her attention.

Tameel shook his head and sent a puff of smoke up to join the others. "We have a couple of good friends living there, Aylin and Misha. Stop to see them any time we have the opportunity. They own the chandlery, which is convenient, since we're usually running low on supplies by the time we get there. Honest barterers, too, always willing to give a fair trade for our own provisions. I have a feeling we should do very well in Minotha with our newly acquired stock." He pointed to the longsword in Ayrion's hands. "Those'll fetch a fine price, I'm sure."

"How much farther?" Ayrion asked, anxious to see something more than snow-covered grasslands. The terrain had begun to take on a wavelike pattern as larger hills were introduced the closer they got to the Angoran Mountains.

"One, maybe two days." Tameel looked over at Zynora. "What you say,

Mother? One, two days to Minotha?"

Zynora grunted, which could have been interpreted as an agreement, or not, but was certainly hinting that she didn't want to be disturbed.

Tameel nodded. "One to two days, depending on the weather." He pulled the pipe from between his lips and released another ring that floated up over his head and broke apart against the ceiling.

Ayrion finished the longsword and then a short belt dagger before walking outside to make sure the horses were tucked in for the night. They had attached a canvas tarp from the side of the wagon to a couple of poles to give the animals shelter against the snow. All three were busy chewing on the bale of hay he'd left. Once satisfied they had plenty to eat, he walked back inside and crawled into bed.

His dreams seemed plagued with violence of late. If he wasn't fighting off white-skinned vulraaks, he was battling some sort of enormous wolflike creatures. Faces of men he put to the sword came and went. Faces of those he fought alongside lingered. Recognition was right in front of him but somehow just out of reach, and by the time he would awaken, it was all forgotten, leaving him irritable.

Ayrion could smell Zynora cooking over the stove in the corner. He yawned and crawled out of bed, eager to get underway. He was ready at the table before she'd managed to get it set or rouse Tameel from his snoring.

After a meager breakfast—they were running low on supplies—Ayrion was out the door and saddling the horses. By the time he finished folding and stowing the tarp and poles and tying off what was left of the hay bale to the side of the wagon, Tameel was up on the front seat and ready to go. Ayrion tossed him the reins and swung up onto Shade, who shook his head and pranced around, clearly feeling Ayrion's excitement.

Unfortunately, the snow was falling even harder than it had the previous day, which Ayrion knew was going to slow their travel and force them to make camp at least one more night. As luck would have it, that snow continued on most of the day, only letting up by the time they had decided to finally stop for the night. Ayrion went about his routine of making sure the horses had a tarp to keep the snow off their heads and hay to fill their bellies.

After dinner, the three took to their beds, forgoing Tameel's evening ritual of smoking his pipe and Zynora's ritual of spending an hour or two pondering over one of her books. Everyone was eager for morning to arrive.

"One good thing," Tameel said from his and Zynora's bunk on the other side of the wagon. "We're close enough to Minotha now to reach it by late morning, which will give us plenty of time to get set up and possibly begin selling our wares."

"Wonderful," Ayrion said, turning over in his bunk. The last thing he wanted to do was peddle more goods.

As they had hoped, the snow did indeed let up the next day, and by the time the first rays had crested over the horizon to the east, they were packed and heading for Minotha. The road veered east toward the tree line, and soon enough they were completely swallowed by forest. The change in scenery was welcome, even though the exchange cost them the sun's warmth.

The road meandered along, but for the most part it maintained a steady northeasterly direction. Even with the heavier snow the previous evening, it was clear theirs wasn't the only wagon to have traveled through that morning. By the number of hoof prints and evenly spaced rows, there had been several. The houses on either side of the road grew in number the closer they got to their destination. Unlike Woodvale, the citizens of Minotha didn't appear frightened or nervous of strangers. In fact, several even stopped their chores long enough to wave at the tinker wagon as it passed.

"Apparently, the plague hasn't spread this far north," Ayrion said, keeping Shade abreast of Ol' Lerra's front seat.

Tameel rubbed the top of his white head and shifted his pipe to the side of his mouth. "Aye, I don't mind admitting I was a bit worried, what with it having reached as far south as Saeida." He smiled. "Perhaps Argon doesn't much like the colder weather."

"Whatever the case," Ayrion said, shifting in the saddle to find a more comfortable position, "I'm looking forward to a hot bath I can stretch out in."

Tameel chuckled. "That tub of ours wasn't exactly made for someone of your stature."

The wash basin, snugly tied to the left side of the wagon, wasn't much larger than the one they used to clean the dishes in. The only way Ayrion could make it work was if he tucked his legs in far enough that his knees rested under his chin.

Before long, the trees opened up, and they found themselves at the edge of a ravine looking down at a small lake. Tameel pulled back on the reins. "Now that's a sight for sore eyes."

The snow and ice settling around the outer banks of the dark-blue water seemed almost like a casing for a precious gem. The forest stretched along the right side as far as the eye could see, like the bushy whiskers of a giant, covering the lower chin, with the lake for the mouth. On the left, the trees ended a mere few hundred feet away, leaving the lake and the town visible. From his vantage point, Ayrion could see where the river funneled out of the trees and fed into the lake on the far side.

The front window of the wagon opened and Zynora stuck her head out and smiled as she took in a deep breath of fresh air. "Lake Wenigapu." She turned and looked at Ayrion. "In the old tongue it means *hidden beauty*. At least, that's as close as I can interpret it to mean."

"Fitting," Ayrion said as he stared out across the placid waters. It was certainly a beautiful place to build a town. The people of Minotha were lucky to have found it.

"We don't have all day, husband. Let's get a move on. These goods aren't going to sell themselves."

"Wouldn't that be nice," Tameel said with a quick wink Ayrion's way. Zynora shut the front hatch, and Tameel picked up the reins and gave them a gentle pop. The old wagon wheels creaked along as they followed the road left and down a gentle sloping ravine toward town.

Smoke could be seen rising from every chimney in Minotha, producing a rather thick haze above the town, but with the forest having been cut back to give the town a wide berth, it wouldn't take the sun long to break through. In fact, by the time they reached the bottom of the gorge, the rays were already melting through the barrier, brightening the buildings and giving Minotha a rather welcoming appeal.

Tameel had been right. Minotha was definitely larger than Woodvale, but that could have been because, unlike Woodvale, there was plenty of open space between the forest and the lake's shore for the town to spread out naturally. Instead of just one road in and out of town, there were several roads, all crisscrossing like a giant batmyth board, with the buildings for pieces.

Docks lined the backs of buildings closest to the water, each with at least one good skiff, some two or three. The wooden piers looked like giant fingers reaching up out of the lake, as if to hold the town in place and keep it from slipping into the deep. Several of the docks bustled with activity as fishermen stowed their gear for what looked like a day out on the water. By the spread of the ice, it didn't appear that they had too many days left. A couple of the boats closer to shore that hadn't seen regular use were already locked in the ice, and no doubt would remain that way till spring.

Also distinct from Woodvale, Minotha's residents seemed to prefer living as close to the heart of town as possible. Who could blame them with a view like Wenigapu to enjoy every time you looked out your window?

"The town seems to have grown since last we were here, Mother," Tameel said as Zynora crawled out the front opening to join him on the seat.

Zynora studied the buildings ahead as they reached what looked like the main road into Minotha. "Aye, Father, it has. I'd have to say they've exceeded Woodvale by a fair bit. Give them a few years and they might overtake Belvin."

Both Zynora and Tameel were wearing their brightest outfits: Zynora in a patchwork dress of gold and maroon and teal, charms dangling from her headdress, and a sash around her waist, and Tameel in his blue, orange, and gold cloak with a pale-green sash wide enough to hide his coin purse. On their arms, they wore their sidrix, the bronze cuffs of the Dar'Rhivanni that bonded the wearers in a way that allowed them to sense the other's feeling. When Tameel had first explained what they were after Ayrion's first confrontation with Argon outside Bek's cabin, all he would say was that it was impossible to describe, and neither would go long without them. Tameel said that not wearing them was like sleeping next to the same woman for the last forty years and then suddenly finding the bed empty.

Like the old tinker couple, Ayrion's garb stood out from the common work dress of the Minothans as well. Ever since his battle with Argon, he'd taken to wearing his dark leathers once more. It had taken Zynora most of the trip to mend the numerous lacerations his black coat had received from the vulraaks' claws, and even though she claimed not to possess the talent of a true tailor, Ayrion was hard-pressed to find the stitchwork once she was finished. It looked as good as new, apart from some bloodstains that wouldn't come out, but even those left an interesting texture to the leather that he found quite complimentary.

Ayrion kept Shade close to the wagon. Riding into a new place filled with people he didn't know made him nervous, but he also wanted to let the townsfolk know that he was with the tinkers. Those who stopped to acknowledge their presence tended to eye Ayrion with a little more scrutiny. Perhaps they thought he was a paid escort, hired by the tinkers to protect their wares.

He felt uncomfortable not wearing at least one of his swords, especially after what had taken place at the last town they'd stopped in. From what Ayrion could see of Minotha, it seemed he would have fit right in. Everyone they passed appeared to be armed, even the women, which made it look all the stranger as they bustled down the street in their dresses and cloaks with a belted sword or dagger at the waist.

Tameel and Zynora had noticed it as well. Zynora pointed out a group of ladies gathered around the front of an embroiderer shop, half of whom carried swords. One lady, who wasn't wearing an outer cloak, had a dagger tucked in the back of her skirt. Ayrion wondered how she managed not to slice through the delicate waistline and drop the skirt to her ankles.

Even with an entire town of armed citizens, Ayrion's twin dragon blades would have probably drawn too much attention—the kind a couple of tinkers couldn't afford when trying to sell their goods. As it was, he did receive a few lingering glances. Zynora had tried talking him into wearing some of their more colorful, baggy clothing he used to wear before Woodvale, but he wouldn't budge. With a few scattered memories returned, he found himself clinging more and more to the familiar in hopes of retrieving what had been lost.

So far, apart from his dreams, the only times he'd managed to spark any form of remembrance of his old life was during a time of heightened emotion. But if it took another fight to the death with the vulraak and Argon to release those memories, he'd be more than willing to live out the rest of his days in happy ignorance.

The horses' hooves went from a soft pad to a distinct clop as the road leading into town changed from packed mud to laid cobble. The road was wide enough to fit three or four wagons and still have room for pedestrians. They passed a couple of carts heading in the opposite direction; those in the seats smiled and waved, some calling out in greeting. Tameel and Zynora offered their *good mornings* in return, while Ayrion simply nodded.

The buildings in town were three and four stories, each constructed from quarry rock, plaster, and cedar, with wood shingles and stone chimneys. A few trees dotted the landscape, mostly for decoration. They would have added a nice pop of color to the otherwise brown and white backdrop, but, as it was the beginning of winter, they were just as brown and bare as the buildings around them.

The streets of Minotha were abuzz with activity as the citizens went about their daily lives. Shops were already beginning to open: curtains parted, signs hung, windows dressed. Many of the shopkeepers were outside clearing off the walkways from the previous night's snowfall to not only encourage visitors but to also keep them from tracking the snow inside their establishments. There wasn't much in the way of displays out front, but with a tight-knit community such as this, everyone would already know what the shops were selling. For those passing through, the signs above the doors were clearly posted.

Ayrion spotted the lake between the buildings on the right, the sun's rays causing the blue waters to flare to life, sending millions of sparkles shimmering across the surface. Thankfully, he hadn't found a need to wear his shaders in town, since the trees and buildings had been enough to dampen the reflection off the snow.

Passing through what Ayrion would have deemed the center of town, Tameel slowed the wagon to a stop in front of a three-story building on the right with a large sign out front that read in gold letters: THE CHANDLERY. It also had a couple of candlesticks with flaming wicks painted on either side.

A plump man with red cheeks and a thin mustache, which Ayrion thought was too thin for the size of his upper lip, looked up from his shoveling and, upon seeing the wagon, smiled. "Tameel! Zynora! It's been an age." The man was dressed nearly as colorfully as a tinker, with a blue-and-gold surcoat that hung below the knees, offset by a deep-orange outer robe with gold triangular patterns that ran along the outer rim. He certainly stuck out from the rest of the townsfolk, with their dull wood-tone colors and brown woolen jackets. He also differed in another way: He wore no weapons, at least none that Ayrion could see. As baggy as his trousers were, there was no telling what all might have been hidden away.

"I see Misha has taken good care of you, Aylin," Zynora said, pointing at the man's midriff. "Every time we see you, you seem to have grown."

The man bellowed out a hearty laugh, nearly dropping his shovel. "And I see you are as lovely as ever."

Zynora hmphed. "Save that smooth tongue for your customers, you old charmer, before I tell your wife."

Aylin laughed once more, then motioned with his shovel to the side of his shop. "Pull around back, and I'll see to your horses."

Tameel flicked the reins and directed Ol' Lerra off the road, pulling to a stop just in front of a small stable alongside the chandlery. By the time he and Zynora had made it out of their seats, Aylin was there to greet them. He hugged each in turn, the sleeves of his surcoat rising high enough for Ayrion to notice he was wearing a similar pair of sidrix cuffs to that of Tameel and Zynora. Had he been part of the Rhivanni as well?

"It has been several winters since you've passed this way, my friends," Aylin said, stepping back to get a good look at the two of them. He hadn't yet noticed Ayrion atop Shade on the other side of the wagon. "Even still, you are early, are you not?"

"We ran into a little trouble in Woodvale and decided it might be in our best interest to winter in Wellhollow this year."

"Wellhollow?" Aylin tipped his fur cap to wipe his forehead, revealing a thinning head of grey hair. "Tough folk, those that live up there. We get a few this way every so often. Usually have to replace a table or two in the tavern when they do."

Tameel smiled. "We've been trading with them for years. I'm sure we'll be fine."

"If you say so." Aylin spotted Ayrion from the other side of the wagon and stiffened. "Is he with you? Since when did you start hiring armsmen for your travels?"

Zynora took Aylin's arm and directed him toward a door on the side of the shop. "A story best told inside and out of the cold."

Aylin tried to turn back around. "But what about the—"

"They will handle the horses," Zynora said as she yanked the chandler back around and marched him over to the door. "You take me to that poor woman who's managed to put up with you for all these years. I'm sure she can use some comforting." The two of them disappeared inside, and the door shut firmly behind them.

Getting out of the cold sounded wonderful. Ayrion swung down out of the saddle and walked Shade into the barn. The window at the back pointed due east, letting plenty of the light in from off the lake. The stable consisted of four stalls, an overhead loft where they stored the hay, and some space at the back where Aylin kept his tools, all neatly hanging from racks or sticking up out of empty barrels. The floor of each stall was lined with straw, giving the animals something dry to sleep on, and from the lack of smell, they'd been recently mucked.

By the time Ayrion got Shade into the last stall, Tameel had managed to unhitch the other two horses. Ayrion helped him bring them in out of the cold, taking time to rub each down and toss in some grain from the half-filled barrel at the back under the window.

"Don't eat too much," Ayrion said with a wink at Shade. Ayrion could have sworn the horse winked back. Shaking his head, he turned and followed Tameel inside, stopping only long enough to make sure the doors to the wagon had been secured. Tameel had told him early on that if you left your possessions where people could get to them, you shouldn't be surprised when they do.

"Who are Aylin and Misha?" Ayrion asked Tameel as he lifted one of the harnesses and carried it to the barn. "I noticed he was wearing cuffs that looked similar to yours."

Tameel started to pick up the other harness, but quickly opted to carry some of the loose cord instead. "Aylin and Misha are Rhivanni, at least, at their core. They were members of the Sil, a stricter clan. Similar in many ways to the rovers in that they hold to a stronger isolationist viewpoint. They don't believe in mixing with other societies. They consider the rest of the world to be tainted."

"By magic?" Ayrion hung the harness on one of the racks in the back and started for the second.

Tameel stopped and rested against the barn door, pulling his pipe from his pocket and nibbling on the end. "No, the Sil'Rhivanni tend to use more magic than the rest of the clans. They just perceive the rest of the world to be under the control of the Dark Wizard. Greed, power, corruption, wars, slavery . . ." Tameel scratched the top of his head where his white hair stuck out over the headband. "Basically, the human condition. We don't need the Defiler's help to do the wrong thing, we can flaming do that all on our own." He moved out of the way as Ayrion carried the harness inside and hung it beside the other. "Anyway, Aylin and Misha never held all that strongly to their clan's ways and ended up breaking from them over a decade ago. After wandering around Sidara for a couple of years, they ended up here."

"And never looked back," a voice said behind them.

Tameel startled and spun around.

Aylin stood in the doorway with a smile.

"Didn't your mother teach you right?" Tameel said, bending over to retrieve his pipe where it had popped out of his mouth and landed in the straw. "Never sneak up on a man in the middle of his story."

"Well, I figure since your story was about me, I might as well get in my two coins' worth." Aylin motioned them out of the barn and shut the doors behind him. "Come. Misha has a hot kettle of clover tea on the stove. Take some of the stiffness out of those bones." He looked at Tameel and grinned. "At least what old age hasn't already claimed."

"Watch yourself," Tameel said, pointing at the chandler with the stem of his pipe. "I'm still young enough to thrash you. And I've had plenty of practice of late."

"Oh?" Aylin said, directing them toward the side of the chandlery. "Sounds like a story worth hearing."

Chapter 19 | Ayrion

AYRION STOMPED HIS FEET to shake off the loose snow before stepping inside. Aylin followed, and he shut the door behind them, shivering slightly as he did.

"Getting colder by the day." The chandler glanced out one of the three windows at the back of the room, where they could just make out the lake through a small patch of trees behind his shop. There were a couple of boats already out in the deeper water, with several more just breaking shore. "Wenigapu will be frozen by this time next week. Soon enough, they'll be digging holes in the ice to bring up the fish." Aylin shook his head. "Nope. You won't catch me out there, tempting fate." He grabbed the front of his belly and jostled it around. "I'd go through for sure."

Ayrion wasn't all that fond of the cold either. He took a moment to get a better look at the workshop they appeared to be in. The walls were lined with shelves, stocked full of assorted goods. Several of the shelves in front were filled with candles of all shapes and sizes and even colors. The whole room smelled of cinnamon and honey and something else that Ayrion couldn't quite put his finger on. Perhaps some type of fruit.

A workplace was set along the back wall just in front of the windows, with several large wheels hanging from the rafters. From each wheel hung dozens of strings, which Ayrion could only guess were wicks getting ready to be covered in wax. Underneath the wheels were several tables and a flattop stove.

The first table was lined with rows of pewter urns, along with bolts of wrapped wicking and the necessary measuring and cutting tools. The second table held a selection of wooden molds of varying widths and heights for the shaping of larger candles. There was also a trough on the floor with a rack hanging over it, clearly being used to dip multiple wicks at once.

Between the two tables was the stove with a cauldron resting on top, steam rising above the rim. The tallow and wax inside had drizzled down the front and pooled around the base.

Aylin spotted him staring and started toward the tables. "Come, come. You must see my latest creation." All three walked over to the table on the right, and Aylin picked up one of the taller molds on the end. After a couple of good squeezes around the sides to loosen the contents, he tapped it gently on the back with his hand, and out slid a pale-violet candle. Ayrion had never seen colored candles before.

"Here," Aylin said, holding it out. "Smell."

Tameel leaned over and cautiously took a sniff of the purple candle, his thick brows rising in surprise. Ayrion wasn't sure whether it was a good surprise or a bad one, but before he could ask, Aylin was holding the candle out for him to smell. He took a quick whiff, and his brows mirrored Tameel's. He'd never smelled a candle so sweet. Most of the time one would hope to find some decent beeswax that left an after hint of honey as opposed to the stronger tallow, which smelled like whatever animal the fat was being harvested from, but this was something altogether different.

"That's what I've been smelling since I stepped in here," Ayrion said, taking a second whiff. "What is it?"

Aylin grinned, clutching his candle affectionately, much like Ayrion was known to do with his swords. He took a long deep whiff himself and slowly released with a heavy sigh. "I call it ashim berry."

"Never heard of it," Tameel said, "but it sure smells sweet. Sweet enough to eat."

"No one's heard of it," Aylin said, his face beaming with pride. "I found the berries this summer while harvesting my hives. And since they are a new variety, I was given the privilege of naming them."

Tameel nodded. "Why ashim?"

There was a twinkle in Aylin's eyes as if he'd been waiting for someone to finally ask. "What does it spell backwards?"

Ayrion tried picturing the word spelled out in his head and then attempted to reverse it. He chuckled about the same time Tameel figured it out.

"Only you would be so presumptuous," Tameel said with a sly wink.

"Took Misha three days to figure it out," Aylin said with a hearty laugh as he laid the candle back on the table. "You can't imagine how many of these I've sold. Have you ever seen such a thing in your journeys?"

Tameel tucked his pipe back in his pocket and shook his head. "Can't say that I have. Best we sell is beeswax with a hint of cinnamon, which we purchased from you the last time we were through here. They're one of our top sellers. Was hoping to trade for some more before we head further north, but after smelling something as divine as that ashim berry, I can see we're going to have some heavy dealings later on."

"Yes, but before we get into any haggling, I want to hear what you've been up to of late. What's happening in the world? Misha and I don't get out much ourselves, and those that pass through don't travel as extensively as you and Zynora." Aylin turned and started for a door on the opposite side of the workroom from the one leading out to their wagon. "Besides, Misha will be wondering what's happened to us, and after clearing those walkways, I'm ready for some of that clover tea."

"Yes," Tameel said. "I wouldn't mind a cup or two myself."

Ayrion followed them into the next room, which looked like a mirror copy to the room they were just in, at least in size, but this room seemed more of a sitting room. There were a couple of couches, a small table just large enough for two, and a fireplace with a rug in front. The walls were draped with colored linen, adding a splash of vibrance to the plaster and wood.

Zynora and Misha were already enjoying the fire from one of the cushioned sofas, sipping from a couple of brightly decorated cups. Misha was a heavyset woman, not quite as solidly built as her husband, but not too far behind. She had a kind face and a welcoming smile that lifted her rosy cheeks up under her green eyes, causing them to pinch. Like her husband, her hair was the color of ash, but unlike Aylin, hers was thick, hanging halfway down her back.

The women looked up, and Misha started when she caught sight of Ayrion, nearly spilling her tea. She gaped as she stared at his eyes. Apparently catching herself, she quickly turned her attention to her husband. "We were wondering where you had gotten off to. Figured you had taken them down to the lake."

"No," Aylin said, directing Ayrion and Tameel to the sofa opposite the ladies, "I was showing them the new candles."

"Oh." She looked at Tameel. "And what did you think of our new *ashim* berry?" She giggled slightly at the mention of its name.

Tameel accepted a cup of tea from Aylin and leaned back in his seat. "Sweet as honey and succulent as a spring rose." He took a sip and yipped. "Ooo, that's good and hot."

Ayrion accepted his cup as well, thanking Aylin for it. He let the warmth seep into his hands while Aylin poured one for himself and took a seat on the end, blowing across the top before slowly testing the temperature with the tip of his tongue. Ayrion held his cup up to his lips, but instead of sipping he simply inhaled, letting the aroma fill his nostrils. He could almost sense the chill in his bones lessening as he released a slow sigh and lowered the cup back to his lap.

He was familiar with clover tea, as it was one of Tameel's favorites, but Zynora preferred her tea to have a bit more bite, and since she was the one usually doing the brewing, Ayrion and Tameel simply had to make do.

Misha stared at Ayrion over her cup whenever she thought he wasn't looking. He tried not to notice but was finding it more and more difficult to accomplish, since she was seated directly across from him. He kept his focus on the fire, letting himself be mesmerized by the dance of the flames. He did finally take a few sips from his cup. It was sweeter than Zynora's, which was a nice change.

"So," Aylin said, turning to refill his cup, "who would like some more?" He held out the kettle for anyone else who required another helping. Tameel held out his cup, but the two ladies were only halfway through theirs as they did their best to maintain a sense of proper decorum by sipping small quantities very slowly. Aylin and Tameel didn't seem to care all that much for decorum. The tea was good, so they finished it with relish.

On Aylin's third helping, Misha cleared her throat with a stern look in his direction. Properly admonished, he poured part of what was in his cup back in the kettle and sat down. Gulping down what little was left in his cup, he turned to Tameel. "Give us the latest news. Anything of interest to speak of since last you were here? We've been hearing rumors about strange things happening further south. The touch of the Defiler, some are saying."

Misha grunted. "Don't hold much stock in rumor. By the time news reaches us, it's embellished to the point that you'd believe the Dark One had returned and crowned himself king." She shook her head and took another sip, frowning as she looked in her cup. "Gone cold. I believe I'll get a refill." She looked at Zynora, and Zynora nodded, handing Misha her cup.

"I'm afraid that for once," Tameel said, "the rumors are true."

"True?" Misha nearly spilled tea down the front of her blouse, righting her cup as quickly as possible.

"The Dark Wizard has returned?" Aylin asked, making the sign of an X on his chest then kissing two fingers and planting them on his forehead. Misha followed suit as best she could while still holding the teapot.

"No, the Defiler hasn't returned, thank the Creator," Zynora added, "but nigh on close to it."

Misha refilled their glasses and handed Zynora hers as she eagerly made her way back to her seat. "What do you mean by close?"

Tameel and Zynora did their best to relay the events of the previous months, starting from their discovery of Ayrion—which had both Misha and Aylin staring at him all the more—to their arrival in Woodvale and the fight with the Tower's guards and the sniffer, leaving out, of course, Ayrion's discovery of being the former Guardian Protector to the king. They then told of the slaughter of the rovers by the half-human creatures called the vulraak. Both Misha and Aylin were familiar with the name *vulraak*, having grown up as Rhivanni, where they placed a good deal more emphasis on history than most. But neither had ever pictured what the creatures looked like or where they came from, or in this case, how they were made. In truth, no one had.

The two were on the edge of their seats as they listened to the harrowing tale of how Ayrion had rallied together a small army of locals, and how they had marched against Argon and his creatures, armed with nothing more than their swords and a wagon full of mirrors. They told of their fight at the Justice House and their battle deep within the Belvin mines, of Argon trying to steal Ayrion's body and of the former wizard's eventual defeat. Misha's hands were shaking so hard the clanging of her cup and saucer distracted Tameel on more than one occasion during the telling.

By the end, the two former Sil'Rhivanni were wiping sweat from their foreheads as they leaned back in their seats, their clover tea completely forgotten. Aylin stared at the fire in silence for a moment, gathering his thoughts. "I'm without words."

"And that's no little thing, for anyone who knows my husband," Misha said, squirming uncomfortably in her seat, as though the fire had suddenly gotten too warm. She remained in her place, though, the plump toes on her bare feet wiggling out from under her long colorful dress. "If it had been anyone else, we would never have believed such a story," she said, looking at Zynora. "Sounds more like something Elder Herrin might have read to us as children, talking about the end of the Third Age and what took place during the times of the Wizard Wars." She glanced at Aylin, and he nodded. "And to think it happened here in Sidara, right in our own backyard. We might have been next." Her cup and saucer went rattling again, and Zynora took it from her and placed it on the table alongside her own.

Tameel stared into his empty cup and shook his head. "But what's to say that what comes next might not be worse?" He looked up long enough to spot Zynora glaring at him from the other sofa and cleared his throat. "Then again, what's to say anything comes next at all? Perhaps this was it."

Aylin sat forward far enough to get a proper look at Ayrion. "I don't know who you are, but I'm thankful you're here to watch over these two," he said with a subtle pat on Tameel's leg. "They mean more to us than you know."

Ayrion nodded. "It is they who deserve *my* gratitude. If not for them, I would not be alive today."

"Still," Aylin said, "having someone like you there eases my conscience."

Ayrion smiled and nodded once more, suddenly wishing he had some tea left in his cup. The awkwardness only increased, as no one seemed to know what to say.

Tameel was the first to break the silence. "And what's the latest news from Minotha? Everyone seems to be carrying weapons?"

Aylin and Misha shared a concerned look.

Zynora spotted it too. "What's going on?"

Before either of them could say anything, they were interrupted by a loud knocking on the door out front. Both Aylin and Misha hopped to their feet like the building was on fire.

"Sounds like Misses Cantanil," Misha said, heading across the room. "Delise is always the first one here on Fifthday. She likes to be the first in after the shelves are stocked to make sure she gets the best selection before they get picked through." The knock sounded once more, this time louder and more persistent. "I'm coming! I'm coming!" she said and rushed out the door of the sitting room and into the main shop to let the woman in.

"How long do you plan on sticking around?" Aylin asked as he poured himself one more cup from the now-lukewarm pot and gulped it down.

"Long enough to sell or trade as many wares as we can," Zynora said, giving Tameel a strange look of her own as they all started for the side door leading back into the chandlery workshop. "Which means we better get a move on. Sunlight's a wastin'."

Ayrion wondered why Zynora or Tameel didn't re-address the question as to why so many people around town were armed. Perhaps they didn't want to seem pushy.

"You'll be staying here with us, of course," Aylin said, almost more a question than a statement.

Tameel smiled. "If you don't think we'll be any bother."

Aylin shook his head, but it took him a moment to respond. "Of course not. Always happy to have you. You know that. I'll have Misha get your rooms prepared while I see to the shop. You'll join us for dinner this evening. I insist."

"You won't have to twist my arm," Tameel said with a smile as he stepped out the side door and made his way to the wagon.

Ayrion beat him there and unlocked the back door and lowered the steps, waiting for Tameel and Zynora to climb in before he made it up. He shut the door behind them. "Was I the only one who found their behavior a little strange?"

"No," Zynora said, fingering the charms on her headdress. "Something is clearly bothering them. Perhaps we'll find out more at supper this evening."

Tameel nodded in agreement as he pulled out his pipe and began nibbling on the end. "All the same, keep your eyes open today. If something is amiss, we don't want it sneaking up behind us and grabbing us by our throats. But for now, let's focus on selling some of this stuff, shall we?"

Ayrion looked around the wagon. "So, what do you want to start with?" His eyes naturally drifted toward their stash of weapons. They were the most profitable items they had, and clearly this seemed an opportune time to be selling them. A good sword was worth its weight in gold, and having collected quite the selection from the battlefield, they were never short of supplies. And no one could sell better than Tameel.

"We'll start there," Tameel said, noticing what Ayrion was looking at. "We can try the local swordsmith, and perhaps the bowyer and fletcher, then maybe even the haberdasher. If all else fails, we might just go door to door."

Ayrion nodded but secretly hoped it didn't come to that. He detested selling door to door. Folks just didn't like you pawning off your wares at their doorsteps. If they wanted something, they'd walk into town.

"While you do that," Zynora said, "I'll begin gathering supplies, at least those we have enough coin for. We still have a surplus from the last set of blades we sold between Hedgemont and Woodvale. I should be able to get a fair amount of what we need with that. The rest we can purchase depending on our sales here. So be extra charming, my dear husband."

Tameel donned his brightest smile. "Always, Mother. Always."

The morning and afternoon flew by at an incredible speed. They bundled together a goodly selection of the blades, tied them off to one of the horses, and headed across town on foot. Surprisingly, it didn't take much finagling on Tameel's part to encourage the swordsmith to purchase, although it did take a while to coax the man out from behind his desk after he spotted Ayrion. The man's eyes kept drifting to Ayrion's waist as if surprised by the fact Ayrion wasn't armed. But since Tameel did all the talking while Ayrion hefted the bundle of goods, the man soon gathered enough courage to step out and inspect the merchandise.

He did more than just inspect it. He purchased the entire lot, then asked if they had more. Tameel was so elated that he failed to notice the almost desperate look in the shopkeeper's eyes.

Ayrion didn't miss it, though. It was a look that said trouble was coming, and the merchant was trying to ready himself for it. "Why the sudden need for so many swords, if you don't mind me asking?"

"What does it matter why the man needs a few swords?" Tameel said with a nervous chuckle. "If he wants swords, then swords he will get. We'll be back to fulfill your order, good sir." If Tameel had been wearing a hat, he would have tipped it. As it was, he offered a fine flourish and bow, then quickly headed for the door, pulling Ayrion along with him.

Ayrion sighed and followed him out. "Don't you want to know why he's suddenly wanting so many blades?"

"No, not really," Tameel said, practically jogging down the sidewalk, all but forgetting their horse. "I reckon it's because his shop was nigh on empty, if you didn't happen to notice."

Ayrion grabbed the brown mare by the reins and dragged her along, trying to catch up. "My point exactly. Why would a swordsmith in the middle of nowhere suddenly have an empty shop? Why are so many people around here armed?"

"Fine," Tameel said, "I admit, it's a little strange. But what town nowadays isn't?" He glanced at those they passed with a wary look. "We'll just be sure to keep our eyes open."

Ayrion bit his tongue. "I thought you said this was a town full of friendly people willing to trade with tinkers?"

"It is. They are." He pulled out the heavy purse from his pocket and bounced it in his hand. "Just look at this haul. So heavy I can barely hold up my breeches."

Ayrion took the purse and placed it in one of his inner jacket pockets, offsetting a couple of knives tucked away on the other side. "I'm just saying, I don't like the feeling I'm getting from this town. Something feels—"

"Off," Tameel said. "Yes, the people are nervous about something." He spared a glance at several men standing around the front of the Red Fox tavern. They watched Tameel and Ayrion like hawks to a field mouse. It was an uneasy look, people unsure as to whether they should reach for their swords or scurry back inside. "Yes, we'll keep our eyes open."

They made it back across town in good time and loaded up another bundle of blades, along with a choice selection of bows, arrows, and quivers to put them in. Tameel said there was no point in waiting around; they might as well take the lot. Ayrion thought for a moment that Tameel was going to have him hitch up the team and start parading Ol' Lerra through town, hawking goods off the back like a peddler, but fortunately for Ayrion, he didn't. Instead, they loaded everything on Shade, since he was by far the biggest and strongest of their horses.

Ayrion rubbed Shade's forehead, even taking a moment to scratch the whiskers under his chin. "Sorry, boy. I know it's demeaning, but desperate times and all."

"What's that?" Tameel asked, making one last trip inside the wagon to see if they'd forgotten anything. He climbed down and locked the door, stuffing the key in his pocket. "Did you say something?"

Ayrion shook his head and pulled out a carrot from one of his pockets and held it out to Shade. "Just visiting with my horse."

Tameel chuckled. "You spend more time talking with that animal than you do us. Keep that up and people will think you've been sun struck."

Ayrion patted Shade's neck and led him out onto the snow-covered street. The sun had warmed enough to melt through partway, revealing the cobbles buried within the deepest of the wagon grooves, but the snow was still deep enough in places to reach halfway up their boots and slow their trek.

They did manage to sell several more blades to the swordsmith, but even he didn't have the funds to buy the lot, so they proceeded on to the bowyer and the fletcher. In both cases, they received nearly the same response as the smith, both shops eager to purchase whatever Tameel and Ayrion could provide, leaving them with two more full purses.

In each case, the merchants asked how long they planned on remaining in town. Said that if they were able to sell off what they had purchased, they would be willing to buy more. Ayrion wasn't sure what Tameel's plans had been for staying in Minotha, how long they had intended to hang around, but from the gleam in the man's eyes and the stout purse in his hands, it would have taken a horde of vulraaks to pull him away.

Tameel was so enraptured by the haul, he insisted they go back to the wagon immediately and bundle up some more. "With sales like this, we'll be set for a year. Blazes! What am I saying? With sales like this, we'll be set for several years, maybe even look at retiring."

They made it back across town and found Zynora waiting at the wagon, holding an armful of goods, not to mention overstuffed sacks lying in the snow at her feet. She frowned when she saw them coming across the street. "Where've you been? I've been standing here in the snow like a beggar."

"Why didn't you go inside, crazy woman?" Tameel said.

She hmphed. "'Cause you got the keys, you silly old man."

"What?"

Ayrion felt around inside his jacket pocket and blushed as he pulled out one of the keys to the back door. "Actually, it's my fault. I'd used the spare key to lock up on our first trip and forgot to leave it on the hook."

Zynora chuckled, then shook her head with a sigh. "Well, no use crying over spilt ale. Help me get these inside and we'll discuss how productive your smiling was this morning."

Tameel grinned on cue. "Just wait till I show you how good your husband was."

She grunted as she started up the back steps. "I'll believe it when I see it."

Chapter 20 | Ayrion

HE REST OF THE AFTERNOON carried on about as well as the morning had. Tameel and Ayrion managed to sell off several more blades, a few well-used bows and arrows, and even a couple of Elondrian shields with the royal crest painted on the front. They didn't fetch as high a price as Tameel would have been able to get if they had been selling them in Elondria, but for a backwoods town in the middle of Sidara, it was certainly fair. Ayrion was just glad to be rid of their bulk. They had been taking up quite a lot of room behind his cot.

The man who had purchased the shields was the town lampwright. He didn't much care about the crest—something he intended to paint over—but he did rather like the shape of the shields and thought they would make for unique-looking signs in front of his shop. His wife had been after him for months to replace the one they had. Weather had faded the paint and termites had eaten the wood, and this would keep him from having to spend more by commissioning Garmon, the town carpenter, to drum up a new one.

So, for about the price of a good sword and a sturdy dagger, he was able to acquire not one but two signs for his shop, and by the look on his face after making his purchase, the man was clearly expecting high praise from his wife that evening.

After selling off a few more of their less-dangerous goods like Sidaran tobac, bottles of Bristonian wine, and a collection of tin plates, cups, and eating utensils, which were generally considered some of their better-selling items, Tameel managed to entice one of the tailors into purchasing several lengths of Cylmaran lace, some rolls of Blue Isles silk, and a couple baskets of ribbons of varying sizes and color, which had no origin of note, but by the time Tameel had finished singing their praises, they might as well have been used by Queen Ellise herself.

By the end of the afternoon, Tameel was practically floating on air as the two made their way back across town, having wrapped up their sales for the day. Ayrion was starting to worry they'd need to post a guard on the wagon if Tameel kept yammering on about the size of their purse or, in this case, *purses*. They had indeed sold enough that morning to last them the next several years.

"Are you trying to get us robbed?" Ayrion asked, keeping his voice lowered as they passed other pedestrians along the way. "You might as well start tossing coins to people in the street the way you're carrying on."

"Hey, that's not a bad idea," Tameel said, suddenly turning them down the next street in the opposite direction of the chandlery.

"What? I was joking. Where are you going?"

"You'll see."

Up ahead, the Red Fox tavern came into view, and Tameel headed straight for it.

"Probably not the time to be stopping," Ayrion said. "Not with two full purses in my coat."

Tameel just smiled and walked inside.

Ayrion tied Shade up to one of the posts in front of the tavern, not worrying too much about keeping an eye on their goods, seeing as how they'd sold most of it already. Ayrion's coat kept wanting to slide forward from the weight of the purses.

"Now you behave," Ayrion said to Shade with firm look. "Play nice with the other horses and there will be an apple in it for you when I get back."

Shade shook his mane and blew out his lips.

"Right," Ayrion said with a faint grin. "Just so long as we understand each other." With that, he followed Tameel inside.

The tavern wasn't much larger than Aylin and Misha's chandlery. If you took out the walls to the back rooms and made them into one large sitting area, then turned the building sideways, you'd just about have it. The inside of the Red Fox was rather dimly lit, considering the sun was still a good hour or two away from setting. It gave Ayrion's eyes a rest from the reflective sparkle of the snow-covered streets outside.

The common room was thick with smoke, both from the strong tobac being piped by the patrons and the hog that was turning on a spit in the hearth on the left. The smell of the meat had Ayrion's stomach rumbling. Lunch had been little more than some biscuits and cheese with a strip of dried meat. Tameel had been so anxious to get back to selling that Ayrion had barely had time to swallow before they were running back out the door.

Those inside turned to get a look at the two newcomers, their eyes skimming over Tameel and his colorful clothing—most likely used to seeing similar worn by Aylin and Misha—and coming to rest on Ayrion. Their gaze drifted to his waistline, and after realizing he wasn't wearing a sword, they eased in their seats. Most were too far away to notice his eyes. Still, they followed the two as he and Tameel made their way over to the bar on the left, where a tall, slender middle-aged woman stood waiting behind the polished wood to take their orders. She had carrot-colored hair, freckles, and a patch over her left eye. She was busy wiping out a couple of tankards with her apron as they approached.

"What'll it be, gentlemen?" she asked as Tameel and Ayrion took the two empty stools on the end. She hardly took the time to look up from her scrubbing. When she did, her eye caught Ayrion's, and she gasped, dropping the tankard in her hand and causing those seated down the row to turn. She took a step closer. "What happened to your eyes?"

"What happened to yours?" he shot back, studying the socket-shaped piece of black leather strapped over her left eye.

She leaned back and bellowed out a hearty laugh. "You got me there." She took a moment to look him over. "Aren't you the pretty one? Tell ya what. How about the two of us get better acquainted in the back. We can exchange stories, aye?" She batted her one good eye at him, and he blushed, causing those seated nearby to burst out laughing, including Tameel.

This was about the last reaction he would have expected from a group of strangers, but he figured it was better than others he'd had. Thoughts of his first meeting with Abiah back in Saeida came to mind, almost causing him to laugh as well. "No offense, but I think I'll stick with the ale."

The woman shrugged and flicked a lock of her curly red hair back behind her shoulder. "Have it your way. Don't know what you'd be missin', though."

He smiled in return, not willing to respond, knowing that whatever he said would most likely land him in hot water, or worse, the back room she had been teasing him with.

"The name's Marzell," she said, "but everyone just calls me Marz."

Tameel leaned back on his stool. "Tameel's my name," he offered with a bow of his head. "And the bashful one on my left is Ayrion."

Ayrion nodded, this time forgoing the smile.

"Well, Tameel, Ayrion, what brings two fine strapping men like yourselves to

Minotha? And more importantly, what'll ya be drinking?"

"An ale for myself and my young friend here. Mind you, I want the best, now. None of that watered-down dribble being fleeced on those you think don't know no better." Tameel turned and looked around the room. "In fact, drinks for everyone!"

Ayrion choked, nearly swallowing his tongue. What was Tameel thinking? He might as well tell the town they had something worth stealing. Next thing he knew, Tameel was going to be dancing on a table, claiming he could sell anything to anyone.

Marz's face lit up like a beacon. "Aye! Drinks on the tinkers!" She started pulling out tankards and lining them all down the bar. "What's the occasion?"

"Just a bit of good luck, that's all," Tameel said with a wide grin. "Figured we'd spread it around."

Behind them, seats were scooting back from tables as men and women made their way across the room to get in on the free drinks. Ayrion quickly pulled one of the purses from the inside of his coat and grabbed a handful of coins to put in his pocket, so he wouldn't have to reveal the full purse when he was forced to pay later.

"We could certainly use a bit of good luck 'round these parts," Marz said as she quickly went about pouring drinks and passing them down the polished bar. "In short demand lately." Quite a few patrons echoed her sentiments with a round of "ayes" as they tipped their glasses in salute. Tameel even received a few warm pats on the back, the patrons too afraid to get close enough to Ayrion to do the same.

"So why the long faces?" Tameel asked Marz as she swiftly refilled his mug on the way to the next one down. "Been coming to Minotha for years, but I've never seen the place so uneasy before. Couldn't help but notice the number of townsfolk toting weapons." Tameel turned and winked at Ayrion.

Ayrion smiled. Tameel was a genius. What better place to loosen tight lips than a tavern full of people receiving a free round?

"Nothin' wrong with want'n to protect ourselves," she said, wiping the foam off the top of a new glass before placing it down in front of another pair of anxious hands. Her smile was wide, but her eyes cast about like a cornered animal looking for somewhere to run.

"Aye, nothing wrong with that," Tameel said offhandedly before taking a long pull from his mug and wiping the foam from his mouth. "But what might you need protection from in a place like this?"

A short man down the bar drained the rest of his tankard and raised it to Tameel. "From the young lord En—"

Marz slammed a tankard on the table, interrupting the man, who was already several sheets to the wind. "From just about anything, I suppose," Marz said. "Nowadays, you just can't be too sure about folk." She turned and gave Ayrion a sharp look.

Those seated closest began to shift uncomfortably on their stools; others left the bar altogether and walked backed to their tables. What was everyone so worried about? Ayrion watched their faces go from festive to frightened in the blink of an eye. And who was this young lord the man was referring to?

It was pretty clear they weren't going to squeeze any further information out of this lot no matter how many drinks they divvied out, so they finished their tankards while idly chatting about the weather and what was certainly the last few days of fishing on Wenigapu. Once their tankards had been drained, they promptly left.

Marz invited them back, making sure to offer Ayrion one last chance to spend some quality time with her "swapping stories." He thanked her for the drinks, paid their tab, and joined Tameel outside, taking a moment just to breathe in the fresh air. Cold or not, it was a far sight more enjoyable than the pall of smoke inside.

"Well, that was a waste of good coin," Tameel griped. "Other than something about a young lord, we learned practically nothing. The only lord I know of around here is Talmanes, and he ain't young."

"Got the feeling they didn't trust us much," Ayrion said as he untied Shade from the rail.

"Oh, you got that feeling, did you?" Tameel shook his head. "Something around here's got them all worked up." He cast a shrewd look in Ayrion's direction. "Perhaps you should've taken Marz up on her offer after all."

"Keep walking, you dirty old man," Ayrion said with a smile.

Tameel's smile slipped, replaced by one of determination. "We're gonna get to the bottom of this once and for all," he said, storming off in the direction of the chandlery. "Come on."

They turned right on the next street, and Ayrion caught a glimpse of the town square just ahead, which wasn't much more than a widening of the main road for a small fountain and a couple of leafless trees to give it shade during the spring and summer months. The butcher's shop was just coming into view when Ayrion picked up speed, anxious to get back himself. Lunch, what little he'd gotten, had come and gone hours ago.

They were three shops down from where the street they were on merged into the square when a group of horsemen rode out from the left, not bothering to slow, even for pedestrians. A sudden flash of memory struck Ayrion, and he saw a large white carriage barreling straight for him. His heart skipped a beat as he jumped out of its way. No, he was jumping in front of it. To save someone. A boy. A boy with a . . . a frog? Ayrion shook his head, and the memory faded.

Ahead, the square emptied as the townsfolk scattered in every direction to keep out of the way of the riders—men grabbing women, women grabbing children. Several people carrying packages were forced to rush up onto the sidewalks to keep from getting hit. It was pandemonium. The horsemen, whoever they were, encircled the fountain and came to a stop on the far side.

Ayrion counted at least a dozen men. Quickly, he pulled Shade and Tameel off the road and up against the corner of a tannery on their left. "Who are they?"

Tameel shook his head as he leaned out to get a better look. "Don't reckon I've seen them before. Look to be flying the colors of Lord Talmanes, though."

"Lord Talmanes?"

"He's a minor lord in the Sidaran Assembly. You can see his estate on the other side of the lake from the back of the chandlery. Hard to miss. His family owns most of these lands. Most of the town as well." He leaned out a little farther. "But I don't see Talmanes anywhere in this lot. Of course, I've never met the man, but from what I've heard, he's not one for running people over in the streets."

Ayrion hovered over Tameel's shoulder, studying the newcomers. The rider in front carried a dark-green banner with what looked like a golden stag at the center. Ayrion was having a difficult time judging the emblem, as the wind continued to whip the material around from the top of the lance.

All but three of the riders wore livery of the same dark green and gold as the banner, and every one of them was armed, which wasn't surprising, considering how everyone else in town was. The one man who stood out from the rest rode about three horses back from the front and was flanked on all sides. He looked no older than Ayrion. Was this the young lord they were speaking of in the tavern?

Whoever he was, he was a man of some worth. If his demeanor didn't give it away, then the cut of his clothes would have. He wore a midnight-blue formal riding coat with silver designs embroidered into the material. Underneath was a brown leather vest with silver buttons, and breeches to match. His face was harder to make out in the shadow of his brown leather hat, but Ayrion was sure it wasn't a friendly one, not by the way he could feel the pit in his stomach churning. It was a gut instinct that seemed to appear whenever something was about to go horribly wrong, which for him was quite often.

As elegant as the man's outfit was, it was also tailored for more than just manor life. He certainly had no difficulty twisting about in his saddle or dismounting to stand on the top edge of the fountain as he turned about the square.

"What are you waiting for?" the newcomer said to the riders. "Start collecting."

Two men stayed with the well-dressed gentleman, while the other horsemen dug in their heels and rode off in different directions. Something about the remaining two gave Ayrion pause. He couldn't see much more than their sides from where he was standing, but something in the way they dressed, something in the way they carried themselves, seemed to want to spark a memory. It just couldn't quite come to the surface.

He started to move farther out into the street to get a better look when the growing sound of horses' hooves had Tameel grabbing Ayrion's coat and dragging him into the alleyway. "This way," he said. "I think we better find a different route home."

"I think you could be right." Ayrion guided Shade around a couple of barrels at the entrance. He reached for his swords and groaned. He was regretting having listened to Tameel about not wanting to scare the customers.

"What's wrong?" Tameel asked over his shoulder as they scrambled down the side street between the two shops.

"This is a terrible time for me not to have my swords."

Tameel sighed. "For once, I agree."

Ayrion patted the left side of his coat. At least he still had his knives.

They reached the far end of the alley and peeked around the corner to see if the street was clear. With a quick nod, they rushed across the street for the next alley up. Just two more and they'd be able to see the chandlery.

At the end of the next passageway, they stopped once more and peeked around the corner. Shade nuzzled Ayrion's left pocket, and Ayrion pushed him away. "Not now. I'll get you an apple when we get back."

"Looks clear," Tameel said and took a step out. Before he could take his second, a door two shops down on the same side of the street opened, and one of the green-and-gold armsmen stepped out, fending off an older woman whose elderly husband was doing his best to hold her back. She carried a broom, which she used to swat at the collector, not close enough to reach.

"It's robbery, I tell you. Robbery. We can't afford such taxes on top of what's already being taken. How will we feed ourselves?"

The guard laughed. "Not my concern. Now get your wife under control." He reached for his sword, and the old man grabbed his wife by the shoulders and forcefully dragged her back toward the front door, his wife waving her broom the entire way and calling the man every name in the book and a few Ayrion had certainly never heard before, but thought appropriate.

"You tell Endric that his father should be ashamed for raising such a spoiled, thieving young whelp!" The woman was quickly pulled inside by her husband, and the guard started for the next shop.

"I don't like the look of this," Tameel said. "We need to get back, and fast."

They ducked farther into the alley as the guard opened the door of the very shop they were standing beside and walked in. They waited for the door to shut before making a run for it, but it never did.

"What do we do?" Tameel said, chomping on his lower lip.

"We can't wait here. He's going to walk right by. We need to risk it." Ayrion peeked around the corner. The guard was still inside. "Now."

They broke from their hiding spot and dashed across the street, leaving nothing but tracks in the snow behind them. The alleyway was just ahead. They were going to make it.

"Hey, you! Where do you think you're going?"

Ayrion and Tameel kept going, pretending they hadn't heard.

"Hey, I was talking to you. Stop!" Ayrion could hear the clanging of the man's sword on his side as he ran after them.

Ayrion waited until they were farther into the alley's shadows before stopping and turning, his hand sliding inside his coat. "Were you talking to us?"

The armsman stuffed a small satchel into his shoulder bag, no doubt the money he'd just collected from the last shop. "Yes, I was talking to you." He came to a stop a few feet away, his hand resting on the hilt of his sword as he tried to get a better look at the two of them.

The man looked to have at least ten years on Ayrion. He was taller, with an average build. His brown hair was cut shorter than most, and he had a thinly groomed beard that was thickest around the mouth. His eyes, though narrow set, were sharp and hard, made to look all the more so by his pockmarked cheeks.

"Is there something we can help you with, sir?" Tameel asked.

The man's eyes must have begun to adjust to the darkness, because he took a step forward and released his sword. "Don't reckon I've seen you around these parts before. Who are you?"

He stared at Tameel a moment, then looked at Ayrion, his eyes hardening. Thankfully, Ayrion was far enough in the shadows that the man couldn't make out that his eyes weren't quite like everyone else's.

"Travelers," Tameel answered with a friendly smile, one that he generally saved for difficult clients. "Just simple travelers." Tameel scratched the top of his white head. "It's been many a season since we've been this way."

"What's your business here?"

"No business. Just passing through on our way to Wellhollow. Hoping to make it before the deeper snows set in."

"Where are you staying? The Hook and Line?"

"No, sir. We are staying with friends."

Ayrion wondered if perhaps it would have been better to have lied and told him they were staying at the inn. Then again, it would have been difficult to keep something as large and obvious as their tinker wagon hidden if they had.

The man looked at Shade. "Where'd you get the horse?" He walked over for a closer inspection, petting Shade's back as he did. "Fine animal." He ran his hand along Shade's coat, peering at the two of them over the horse's back. "Too fine for a couple of tinkers. No doubt stolen."

"The horse is mine," Ayrion said, not liking the greedy look in the man's eyes. Shade blew out his lips and shook his head.

The man walked around to the front, keeping one eye on the horse and the other on them. "That horse was bred for nobility. Something that neither of you are." The man's hand slid back to his sword. "And unless you can produce a legal writ of sale, then I'm hereby confiscating this animal in the name of Lord Talmanes."

"The horse was a gift," Ayrion said, his hand wrapping around one of his knives. It would have been easy to kill the man, but what kind of trouble would that bring on everyone if he did? "I don't have a writ of sale." Honestly, he had no real idea whether Shade was his or not, other than the strange connection the two seemed to share, and the few flashes of memory he'd recovered, which showed the two of them together.

The man smiled, stretching the pockmarks on his upper cheek, making his face even more menacing. "No writ of sale, then no horse." He reached for the reins, and Ayrion took a step forward, forcing the man to draw his sword partway in warning. "Don't be foolish. Just be thankful I don't arrest you for horse theft. Now hand him over."

Tameel started to reach for Ayrion's arm, but one look in Ayrion's eyes, and he quickly moved back.

Ayrion's hands tightened on the straps. "Shade is as close to me as any brother." He could feel the warmth building inside him. A warmth he had grown very accustomed to over the last several months. An all-consuming heat that he both longed for and feared. He looked the man in the eyes. "And no one messes with my family."

The man paused for just a moment, then his eyes slid once more to Ayrion's swordless waist, and he smiled and drew his blade the rest of the way. "And how do you plan on—"

Before he could finish, Shade reared and kicked the man so hard it sent him flying into a pile of crates against the wall. He hit the wall and bounced off, the crates toppling overtop, covering the body. The only piece of the man Ayrion could see was his right hand, which, miraculously, was still gripping his sword.

Ayrion grabbed Shade's reins. "It's all right, boy, calm down." He glanced over his shoulder. "Is he dead?"

Tameel pushed a couple of crates aside and knelt over the body.

"Well?" Ayrion asked. "Is he?"

"He is now," Tameel said, standing and wiping the blood from his belt knife.

Ayrion was too stunned to speak.

"I did what had to be done. He'd seen our faces, and he would have known me by my cloak. And from the way the people in this town are behaving, I don't want to find out what this young Talmanes would do to us or Aylin and Misha if he were to find out." He stuck his knife back in his belt. "Here. Help me hide the body."

Ayrion helped throw a couple more crates on top, pushing the dead man's arm back underneath, along with his sword. He was still a bit in shock at the calm manner in which Tameel seemed to be handling the situation. Tameel was right, it had to be done, and Ayrion had been ready to do it if not for Shade's interference. But it was the way Tameel didn't even think twice about it that had Ayrion a little unnerved. It was a side of the old tinker he'd never seen before.

Tameel cast a quick glance back up the alley. "We need to get out of here."

Ayrion grabbed Shade's reins. "Don't look at me like that. I wasn't going to give you away." He scratched the whiskers up under the horse's chin. "Not that I wouldn't think about it if you keep eating all the apples."

They made it back to the chandlery without further incident and had barely managed to stable Shade when Zynora met them with folded arms and a cross look.

"And where have the two of you been, might I ask?"

Ayrion and Tameel shared a nervous glance. Did Zynora know something?

Zynora stood in the barn doorway wearing a long apron over her purple-and-gold skirt. The apron had floral designs across the front with finely woven stitching. "Do you know what time it is? Misha and I have been slaving away all afternoon, preparing a special meal for tonight. You could have at least had the decency to show up to eat it before it got cold." She walked over to Tameel and took a whiff. "You were at the Red Fox, weren't you? No need to deny it." She took a step back to give her husband time to answer for himself.

Tameel cleared his throat and straightened his colorful cloak. "Now see here. If I want to wet my throat after a long day of selling, that's just what I'm going to do." He pointed at Ayrion. "Show her." Apparently, Tameel was going to carry on like they hadn't just killed a man and stuffed his body in some back alley garbage.

Ayrion reached into his coat and pulled out the two hefty purses and tossed one of them to Zynora. As soon as it hit her hands, her eyes lit up. "Bless my soul."

Tameel smiled. "Thought that'd change your tune."

Zynora hmphed, but there was an unmistakable grin on her face as she opened the top and peered inside. Her breath caught in her throat. After a long pause, she eventually tightened the strings and walked over and kissed her husband full on the mouth. "I guess I can forgive you this once." Handing the purse back to Ayrion, she took her husband's arm and led them back toward the chandlery. "But don't let it happen again."

Ayrion stuffed the coin pouches back into his coat and followed the two toward the side entrance.

"Actually, there's more to our delay than just stopping off at the Red Fox," Tameel said. "Is Aylin inside? I need to talk with him. Now."

Chapter 21 | Ayrion

HEY'RE EARLY," AYLIN SAID, not bothering to hide the tremor in his voice or the shudder in his hands as he set his glass down beside his plate. He never even took a swallow of the strongly spiced wine, instead scooting his seat back from the table.

Tameel kept his gaze at the front of the table where their host sat. "Then you know who these men are?" Tameel had just finished divulging their run-in with the armsman in the alley, and the large group of armsmen they'd seen riding into town, bearing the crest of House Talmanes. He even told them of their encounter with the guard who'd attempted to steal Shade and what Tameel had done to make sure the man was unable to identify them.

"Unfortunately, we do," Aylin said, then looked at Misha. "Get the box."

She nodded and started for the door at the back, which led up to their living quarters.

"What's going on, Aylin?" Zynora asked, laying her fork down on her mostly untouched food.

"They work for Endric Talmanes," Aylin said, his mouth twisting into a snarl. "Endric is Lord Talmanes's only living heir. Nothing more than a spoiled, good-for-nothing whelp that could have used a few sound paddlings over his father's knee, but ever since the lord's wife passed during childbirth, he turned over all care of the boy to his family's steward. Some say Talmanes didn't want to see the boy because it reminded him too much of his wife." Aylin shook his head. "Come to think of it, perhaps someone should have put a switch to the old man as well."

The conversation was interrupted as Misha stepped back into the room from the landing behind the door. She had a box no bigger than a loaf of bread tucked under one arm.

"Do we have enough?" Aylin asked, rising from his seat as Misha brought the box over and set it on the table in front of them. It was made from a soft white wood, probably sapwood, and each side bore a single carved image of a flower Ayrion didn't recognize.

"There are only three left."

Aylin sighed as he lifted the lid and looked inside.

The smell hit Ayrion immediately, leaving him almost lightheaded with euphoria. He thought he'd never smell anything as wonderful as those ashim berry candles, but the three pale-green candles in this box were bordering on the divine. He had nothing to even compare them to. He could smell a dozen different odors with each whiff. It was clear by the blissful expressions on Tameel's and Zynora's faces that they were just as enraptured as he was.

"What are they?" Zynora asked hungrily as she leaned her face closer to the box. "I've never smelled anything so . . . so . . . ."

"So glorious," Tameel said.

Misha placed her hand fondly on her husband's arm. "My husband's a wizard when it comes to creating new and wondrous fragrances for our candles. We call this scent *Desire*. It tends to bring on strong urges."

Tameel coughed embarrassingly as his thick brows lifted well over his eyes.

"As much as I'd love to spend the rest of the day smelling them," Ayrion said. "Why do I get the feeling they're used for more than just selling in the shop?"

Aylin closed the lid on the box. "Which way were the men heading?"

"Which men?" Tameel asked.

"The collectors. Where did you see them?"

Tameel scratched the top of his head, taking a moment to adjust his headscarf. "Well, we had just left the Red Fox and were heading back toward the square when they first rode in. They seemed to scatter after that."

"Which direction? How far north did they go?"

"The only one we saw this side of the square was the one we had the altercation with, but that doesn't mean there couldn't be more."

Aylin nodded, his lips pursed as he thumbed the bottom of his chin. "Good. Then perhaps they won't make it to us today."

"Why?" Zynora asked. "What is going on, Aylin? What is this *collecting* you keep talking about?"

The small group retook their seats around the dinner table, although none of them were hungry enough to eat. Aylin did manage a small sip of his wine before beginning. "Lord Talmanes left some months back after Overlord Barl called for the Sidaran Assembly to reassemble. Apparently, there's been word of some big goings-on in Easthaven, something important enough for Talmanes to send a communiqué that he would be wintering in Easthaven. To our misfortune, that left Endric in charge, and the pathetic excuse for a human being has since seen fit to force a levy on the citizens of Minotha, just because he can."

Misha laid her hand on Aylin's quivering arm, and he took a deep breath.

"What's the purpose of this new tax?" Tameel asked.

Aylin shrugged. "Purpose? Does there need to be a purpose for someone to abuse their authority? All you need is a single lord, or lord's son, with a lust for something that doesn't belong to him."

"What does the town council have to say about it?" Zynora asked.

"Town council? Ha! Who do you think pays the council's salaries? They've been in Talmanes's pockets longer than his lint. At least, until now, old man Talmanes has been a decent enough sort of fellow. But his son is as rotten as the day is long. Some of the shopkeepers got together and approached the situation with Endric, thinking . . . well, hoping, he would at least listen to reason."

After a moment's pause, long enough to put everyone on the edge of their seats, Aylin continued. "Instead of coming to some kind of negotiation, he used the money to hire mercenaries to ensure his monthly collections continued. It started with just a few men, but those numbers quickly grew after several of them were accosted by shopkeepers who had no intention of giving up their hard-earned coin. Then, last month, two men showed up as his personal guard. No one knows who they are or have gotten a good look at them. They stay at Endric's side at all times."

"We saw them earlier," Ayrion said.

Aylin nodded. "Not anyone you want to bump into in a dark alley on the way home, or a sunlit alley on the way to work. Come to think of it, best not to run into them at all. We heard they'd been hired to train Endric and his men."

"If the man we ran into was any proof of their capabilities," Ayrion said with a grunt, "I'd say Endric isn't getting his money's worth."

"Well, I don't plan on finding out one way or the other."

"Not to be overly blunt," Ayrion said, "but what's all the fuss with the box?"

Aylin looked down at the box and tapped the top of the lid. "Apparently, Endric's latest conquest has a love for unique smells, and once she found out about our store, Endric has demanded that part of our payment is to supply him with the most expensive of our stock. But with winter here, I won't be able to harvest enough ingredients to make more. These three are the last anyone will see till spring." He looked at his wife and shuddered. "I'm afraid of what he'll do when he finds out that there are no more to be had."

The table was silent for some time. Ayrion continued to study the floral designs on the box, and by the time he looked up, Tameel and Zynora were both staring at him. "No." Ayrion shook his head. "Don't look at me like that. I know exactly what you're thinking, and you can get it out of your heads right now. This is not our fight. We are on our way to Wellhollow, remember? We are trying *not* to attract attention. The last thing we need is to—"

A loud knock on the door out front cut him short.

"You did hang the sign, didn't you, dear?" Aylin asked.

Misha nodded. "Yes, just before pulling the curtains." She looked at Aylin, fear in her eyes. "You don't think . . . ?"

Aylin stood from his seat and started for the door leading into the shop. "Stay here. I'll see who it is."

The prickle down the back of Ayrion's neck told him he already knew. Aylin shut the door behind him, so Ayrion couldn't exactly hear what was going on in the next room, and he didn't feel comfortable enough with Misha sitting there to get up and crack the door to eavesdrop. However, when he heard raised voices, he left his comfort sitting on his plate and quickly made his way to the door and slid it partway open. Was Endric upset about the candles? Ayrion wondered how much the shopkeepers were being forced to pay.

". . . don't know any tinkers," Aylin said.

Ayrion's heart thumped.

"What kind of fool do you take me for? Their wagon is parked right there in front of your stable."

Ayrion's breath caught in his throat. Why were they asking about tinkers? He cracked the door a little farther, just enough to get a look at the front. Ayrion was expecting to see Endric standing there in his fine suit, but instead it appeared to be a couple of his guards. The curtains in the windows were drawn, so he couldn't see if there were others standing outside.

"I know they're in there," the uniformed guard at the front stated. "Now bring them out!"

Ayrion raised his hand and stopped halfway to his back. *Blood and ash!* He was going to have to quit listening to Tameel about not carrying a weapon. His swords were in the wagon, the one place he couldn't get to. He shut the door. "They're looking for us." He looked at Tameel. "I thought you said you killed the man."

"I did. He was as dead as they get."

"Then why are they looking for tinkers?"

Zynora stood. "Are they expecting us to pay tribute as well? Perhaps they saw our wagon riding through town?"

Tameel balled his fists. "I'll be hanged if they think they're gonna take our hard-earned money."

Ayrion patted the front of his coat, realizing he was still carrying their purses. He pulled them out of his jacket and looked at Misha. "Do you have somewhere I can put these?" He pulled out a few coins in case they needed to pay part of this collection Aylin and Misha were talking about.

Misha scurried over to the rug in front of the fireplace and pulled back one corner. "There," she said, pointing at one of the boards.

Ayrion pulled the board and it gave way. Lifting it, he found a box tucked underneath. He stuffed the coins beside the box and lowered the board back into place and slid the rolled carpet overtop with his boot. As soon as he did, he was struck with another vision.

It was dark. There were long strands of light above him, dust falling on his face. He could hear raised voices. One man's voice was older, somehow recognizable. "Boys, you say? No boys here. My boys are all grown up."

"Not you, you old fool! Two street kids who came through here . . ."

Suddenly Ayrion felt someone move beside him. There was someone hiding with him. He turned to see who it was in hopes of sparking further memories, but suddenly everything vanished, and he was back inside the chandlery, staring at the rug on the floor.

Misha took a step closer and looked down at where Ayrion had been staring. "What's wrong?"

"Another vision?" Zynora asked.

Ayrion took a deep breath and nodded. The visions were so strong, it was like he was reliving them. He finally pulled his attention away from the floor when the door leading into the shop opened and Aylin stepped inside. He gulped and looked at Tameel and Zynora. "Lord Talmanes wants to see you."

Ayrion wondered why Aylin was trying to sound all official, but then he saw that one of the guards was standing just off the doorway behind him.

Tameel looked at Zynora. "Come, Mother, let's make ourselves presentable." Tameel made a show of straightening his head scarf, then grabbed his long, baggy, colorful cloak from off the back of his chair and flung it over his shoulders.

Zynora wrapped her teal-and-gold shawl over her shoulders and joined him. "Lead the way, Father."

Misha grabbed the box of candles off the table.

Ayrion was the last one out, closing the door behind him. He kept his head lowered, as the armsman had his hand on the hilt of his sword. The guard moved in behind them as he ushered them across the shop. Ayrion could have dispensed with the man right there, but that would have just put Aylin and Misha in even more trouble. Best to see what the fuss was about. If it was just the collectors there to get their pay, then they could give it to them and move on.

Ayrion stepped outside with the others, the cold wind hitting him in the face and sending a slight shiver down his back. He had no need to squint, since the sun had already set and the last of the colors in the sky were fading to grey.

"That's them, Your Lordship!" someone shouted. "That's the killers, there! The one in the colored cloak, and the black one!" A man dressed in regular woolen townsmen garb was standing to the side of the young lord's horse, pointing directly at Ayrion and Tameel.

Ayrion was in shock. He'd never seen the man in his life. How could he possibly—

"Are you sure?" the nobleman asked.

"As sure as I'm standing here. I saw it all from my bedroom window. They trapped your man and then killed him. Stuffed his body up under some crates. When they left, I dug him out, then ran to get one of your men." The man held out his hand. "You mentioned something about a reward?"

The lord nodded to one of his men, and they tossed the man a small bag of coins, and he ran off down the street.

Ayrion couldn't believe his luck. He raised his head to get a better look at what they were facing, but it wasn't the armsman who captured Ayrion's attention. It wasn't even Endric with his fine clothes and fancy hat. It was the two mercenary guards who flanked him, the ones who had given Ayrion a strange feeling when they'd first rode into town.

Endric didn't even get a word out before the two men were off their horses and starting across the street for him. They moved with precision, as though everything they did had been planned, every action made with purpose. He could see they were dangerous, and it wasn't just the way they carried themselves. It wasn't even the weapons they carried.

It was their eyes.

They were just like his.

Zynora gasped, and Tameel mumbled "Upakans" under his breath.

"What clan are you?" one of the grey-eyed men asked as they approached. Their hands held no weapons, but Ayrion had no doubt that if the need arose, they'd be out and ready to use before he could blink. "Are you under contract?"

Contract? Something about that felt familiar. If they were Upakan, then perhaps they could tell him something more about who he was. They might even recognize him. He wasn't sure if that would be a good thing or a bad thing. He had no idea what clan he was from, if he was from any clan at all. The only clan he'd ever heard of was Tameel and Zynora's. "I'm Dar'Rhivanni." Someone on his left groaned. It sounded like Tameel.

The two men stopped a few feet away and looked at him like he'd lost his mind. Each of the two had strong faces, lean, hard, and covered with scars from what looked like years of armed combat. They both had dark hair similar to Ayrion's, and when the fading light caught their eyes in the right way, they seemed to glow, much like an animal's. Was that how his looked? He could finally see why he made people feel so uncomfortable.

The man on the right was a little taller than the other, with a broad nose and inset eyes that made his cheeks stand out. He wasn't as thick in the chest as the second man, but that would only make him more nimble with his movements, probably favoring lighter weapons. Ayrion had already spotted the two bulges beneath his coat, where he no doubt kept a brace of knives.

The shorter but stronger-looking man on the left had a wide face covered with week-old stubble. He had a short sword with a curved leather grip on the left side and a long-handled kama on the right, reminding Ayrion of Bek's hatchets.

"Are you under contract?" the taller man on the right asked once again. He glanced momentarily at Tameel and Zynora almost with disdain, no doubt wondering why an Upakan would be traveling with a pair of tinkers.

From what Ayrion had gathered, his people were paid mercenaries, renowned for their skills in combat. Perhaps they thought he'd been hired by Tameel and Zynora to protect them on their travels. Ayrion dismissed that idea as soon as it arrived. He doubted any self-respecting Upakan would take a job as the protector of a tinker wagon. Besides, from what Tameel and Zynora had said, he got the impression that when you hired an Upakan, it was because you wanted someone, or a bunch of someones, dead.

"Yes, I'm under contract," he said, keeping his voice lowered. For all they knew, he could have been there to kill Endric. That thought suddenly sent a chill down his spine. What if that was *exactly* what they thought? They might try killing him right there, and all he had on him were a couple knives and some coins. "And before you think otherwise, no, my contract will not interfere with yours."

The two men stared at him a moment, then seemingly relaxed—that is, one of them blinked—but it was enough that Ayrion could see that his initial assessment had been correct in that they were indeed wondering if they'd been given opposing contracts.

Ayrion had so many questions, but he doubted he was going to get much in the way of answers from either of these two. They had a job to do, and at present that job seemed to clash with his.

"Well?" Endric demanded after having sat in silence for this long. "Who is he?"

The two Upakans took several steps back from Ayrion before turning, clearly wanting to keep out of weapon's reach before showing him their backs. They remounted, and the taller one bent in and whispered something to Endric, which had the lord's son looking more than a little displeased. Then again, Ayrion couldn't remember seeing Endric looking anything but unpleasant. Ayrion glanced at Tameel, and Tameel shook his head as though to tell him not to do anything stupid.

Ayrion smiled, which made the old tinker look even more distraught, and before Ayrion could say anything to reassure Tameel, he was struck with an overwhelming sense of anger. Before he realized what was happening, he heard Shade's cry.

Several armed men pulled the black warhorse out from behind the chandlery. Two had hold of his reins and the third was cracking a whip over his head. He fought them the whole way.

Ayrion broke from the group at the front of the shop and started for the men, his hand sliding into his coat for his knives. Tameel and Zynora both tried grabbing him, but they weren't fast enough.

"I wouldn't do that if I were you," someone across the street said.

Ayrion turned. The two Upakans had their bows up and arrows nocked, but not at him. The arrows were pointed directly at Tameel and Zynora.

Ayrion stopped. He looked at the old couple, then back at Shade. His blood was pulsing through his skin, every nerve on fire. He wanted to kill them all, but instead he turned to Endric. "What are you doing with my horse?"

Endric smiled as he studied the enormous stallion. "I'm confiscating this animal in the name of Lord Talmanes. That horse clearly does not belong to any commoner, so I—"

"The horse was a gift."

"And who would give such a gift to someone like you?"

Ayrion knew Shade belonged with him, the same way he knew there was a special bond between him and the horse, but he didn't know how or why. Worse, he didn't know who had given him the horse. If he had been the king's protector, the horse was likely a gift from him, but that was something he could never admit to.

"I don't know," he mumbled, the words all but dragged out of him.

"What was that?" Endric said with a smirk.

Ayrion bit his tongue and balled his fists. "I said, I don't know who gave me the horse."

One of the two Upakans turned to Endric and whispered something in his ear.

Endric shook his head. "I don't care who he is. No one is going to come into my town and kill one of my men without consequence." He looked at the two Upakans with almost as much disdain as he had Ayrion. "You're not being paid to think. You're being paid to protect me."

The Upakan didn't appear very happy with Endric's decision, but he kept his mouth shut all the same.

Shade reared and kicked out at the men trying to hold him, but they managed to keep clear of his hooves as they grabbed his reins and yanked him back to the ground. He whinnied, but this time it was a sad, sort of forlorn sound, not the same confident spirit he'd shown earlier. It was as though he could feel Ayrion's resignation. He knew Ayrion wasn't going to stop these men from taking him.

Ayrion could taste blood in his mouth from where he'd bitten his tongue a little too hard. His knuckles were white, but he managed to maintain an outward calm, not giving Endric the satisfaction of knowing how deep his rage went. "What do you want?"

By now, most of the windows in the surrounding buildings had curious faces peering through as they watched the scene below, too frightened to do anything about the situation themselves.

"I want to keep the peace," Endric said, rather loudly. Endric had spotted the audience as well, and he was clearly pandering to them. "Having outsiders come into my city and disrupt our tranquility by publicly ignoring the collectors, and then attacking them in the streets while they simply carry out their duties, will not go unpunished. The good people of Minotha deserve better." By this point, he was no longer addressing Ayrion or even those standing in front of the chandlery. His head shifted from left to right as he looked up at the faces in the windows. He even twisted in his saddle to look at the buildings behind him.

This guy really likes to hear himself speak, Ayrion mused. He wondered if he'd be half so chatty if he didn't have those two sitting beside him, or the dozen or more guards lining the street.

"Let this be a lesson to any who would dare disturb the good people of Minotha or interfere in its business. We do not stand for thievery here."

Zynora mumbled something under her breath, loud enough to give Endric pause. He sneered. "I want you out of our town. If you haven't left by sunrise, I will be forced to confiscate that hideous wagon and have the lot of you thrown in the cells." With that, he turned and motioned his riders to move out, not even stopping long enough to collect his candles.

Ayrion stood in the road, the cold wind whipping his coat around his legs, as he watched Endric and his men disappear into the distance. A hand on his shoulder had him turning.

"I'm sorry, Grey Eyes," Zynora said comfortingly. "I know how much he means to you."

"I wonder why he didn't just go ahead and order them to arrest us?" Aylin asked, his arm around Misha.

Tameel snorted. "'Cause he was afraid of what Ayrion might do."

"I highly doubt that," Ayrion said. "He had two of my people there to protect him."

Tameel walked out to join them in the street, staring off in the same direction the men had taken. "It sounds like we had better pack up, then."

Ayrion squeezed his fists. "I'm not going anywhere."

Chapter 22 | Ayrion

"WHAT ARE YOU GOING TO DO?" Zynora asked.

"I'm going to do whatever ever it takes," he said, as he pushed his food around on his plate. By the time they'd made it back inside, their food had gone cold, and since no one was in the mood to eat, they left it where it was. "I'm not leaving here without him. Shade has saved my life more times than I know. There's no way in Aldor I'd leave him behind."

"But they have others like you," Aylin said. He looked like he was regretting having ever invited them into his house. Not that Ayrion could blame him. It seemed wherever he went, trouble followed him like flies on a dunghill. Aylin couldn't take his eyes off the twin dragon blades resting against the table's edge. Ayrion had grabbed them from the wagon before coming back inside. He wasn't going anywhere without them now.

"I don't care if he hired an entire Upakan clan, I'm not leaving without my horse."

Aylin wrung his hands and looked at his wife, who seemed to be sharing his concern. "Look, we can't afford to get mixed up in any of this. This chandlery is all we have."

Zynora frowned. "I can remember a time, Aylin, when you would have been the first one out the door with a sword in hand, looking to put things right. When the Cylmaran brigades were determined to drive the Rhivanni out of Aldor for good, to put an end to us, you were one of those at the forefront who fought them back. They still sing songs of that final charge. *Torshuga*, isn't that what they called you? *The man who wouldn't stop.* Now, here you are, cowering in your home, handing out perfume candles." She sneered. "What's happened to you?"

"I got old," he said, waving his hand. "I was a younger man then."

"Braver too, apparently."

Aylin hmphed and crossed his arms. "No. Just too stupid to see the difference."

"Better too stupid than too cowardly."

"Zynora." Tameel reached for her arm. "That wasn't called for."

Aylin scooted his seat back from the table, the wood scraping against the floorboards as it slid backward. The man looked on the verge of grabbing one of Ayrion's swords and proving her wrong by taking a swing at her. Instead, he just sat there scowling, staring her down, neither willing to flinch. "How dare you come in here and question my resolve, you . . . you old troublemaker."

"How dare *you* sit on your fat backside and let this town be squeezed by the likes of that whelp and his paid ruffians."

"Easy for you to say. The only place you've ever given a flaming care for, you walked out on and never looked back."

Zynora's eyes sparked with anger. Now Ayrion was worried she might be the one to go for the blades.

"That's enough!" Tameel said, hitting the top of the table with his fist, just missing his platter but catching the side of his spoon and sending it careening across the table, where it landed against a loaf of barley. He groaned and rubbed the side of his hand. "You two are acting like a pair of siblings."

"Always have," Misha said with an embarrassed shake of her head. "Both as stubborn as mules. Always thought the two of them would have ended up together."

Aylin choked, and Zynora patted her brow. They turned and looked at Misha, both red in the cheeks.

"Well, I did," she continued, "but I can see the Great Father in His infinite wisdom had enough common sense to keep you two separated. You wouldn't have made it to your bonding ceremony before one, or both of you, had killed the other."

Zynora and Aylin turned and looked at each other, both trying not to smile, neither succeeding.

Aylin reclined in his seat with a long sigh before nodding to his wife. "Aye, He knew what he was doing when He brought you into my life."

Misha smiled, and the two shared a lingering look.

"The council had thought to write to Lord Talmanes to let him know about what was going on," Aylin said, "but by the time such communication ever made it to Easthaven and back, we'd have lost our business anyway. As we said before, there are those on the council who've been paid, or threatened, to vote the way Endric wishes. Not that it matters what the town council votes on. With Endric hiring his own personal militia, there's not much more we can do. Besides, I'm not about to go dusting off my sword for a horse."

"What about for your town?" Zynora said. "Or do you plan on letting this thug bleed you dry? That is a slow, painful death. Starvation over a longer period of time."

"You don't understand. Those with him today were just his personal guard. There's an entire barracks of mercenaries living on his estate." Aylin blew out his lips. "I'm sorry. It's just not worth it. You have the freedom to leave, but this is our home. We can't afford to lose it. If we went up against them, Endric would just as soon burn this town to the ground as admit defeat." Aylin rose from the table and grabbed his candle box. "You are welcome to share our fire this evening, but it might be best if you go by morning." He looked across the table. "Misha, you coming?"

Misha stood, looking embarrassed. "Take the food with you," she said, motioning to what was left on the table, before following her husband to the back, where they took the stairs up to their living quarters.

Ayrion stared at his plate as he listened to the creaking steps.

Zynora let out a long, slow exhale and shook her head. "I never thought I'd see the day when Torshuga would back down from a fight."

"Time changes people, Mother, as you well know. Look at us. Once part of a proud clan, now nothing more than glorified scavengers, pilfering the dead and profiting off their misfortune."

Zynora's eyes were hard. "It's not the same and you know it."

"What I know is that we better turn in so we can be back on the road before dawn. I don't want to test the young lord's resolve. He strikes me as the sort who would have men here by first crack of light in hopes of making good on his promise." He stood from the table. "I don't plan on giving him the satisfaction. In fact, I mean to be away from Minotha this very night."

Ayrion grabbed his swords and swung them on his back. "I'm not leaving without Shade."

Tameel procured a piece of meat from his plate, wrapped it in a napkin, and stuffed it in his trouser pocket. "Nor would I expect you to. But those men will be looking for us, and Ol' Lerra sticks out like a sore thumb. Best we get a fair piece down the road and out of their line of sight before doing anything rash. And by the look on your face, I'm sure *rash* doesn't quite do it justice."

Ayrion didn't respond. He did, however, follow Tameel's example and abscond with the meat from his plate, along with two cold biscuits and an apple, and stuffed them in a napkin, which he tucked away safely in a jacket pocket for later. Leaving the table, he walked over to the rug in front of the fire and rolled back the right corner, lifting the loose floorboard and collecting their sacks of earnings before replacing the board and rug and following the others through Aylin's workshop and out the side door to the wagon.

Without thinking, Ayrion started for the stables, forgetting momentarily that Shade wasn't there. He had planned on giving him his apple, but once the realization set in, he just wanted to throw it. Who did this Endric think he was? How could he just take something that belonged to someone else like it was nothing and expect to get away with it?

Argon had been a ruthless son of a faerie, and about as psychotic as they came, but Ayrion found himself more angered by this pathetic upstart than he did the former Aerodyne general. Argon had slain hundreds and had planned on conquering the world for the Dark Wizard, and yet Ayrion had never wanted to get revenge on anyone as much as he wanted to on Endric.

He wasn't sure why, but he seemed to bear a deep hatred for people who used their position to prey on others. Had he always felt like this? Was there something in his past that triggered this hatred? He wished he could remember. Turning, he set his jaw and started for the wagon, but Tameel stopped him.

"Let's get the team harnessed, shall we?" Tameel said, a cut of meat gripped between his teeth. He bit down, then raised his hand to examine the other half in the light of a lantern Zynora had just placed on the side of the wagon. He pursed his lips. "Not bad, if a bit chewy." He smiled and stuffed the rest in his mouth as he opened the barn doors. His lips were too full to speak, so he simply pointed toward the back.

Ayrion didn't need to hear the words; they'd been going through the same routine for months. He knew how to get Ol' Lerra ready in his sleep. As fast as he could, he harnessed the team, stopping only long enough to feed and water the animals before sending them out into the cold, something they seemed grateful for. At least Ayrion thought they were grateful. He couldn't feel the other horses like he could Shade. Even now, he thought he could vaguely sense the warhorse's anger, or perhaps it was his own emotions.

He'd find out soon enough.

Once the team was hitched and the wagon loaded, Ayrion helped Tameel back the wagon out into the road in front of the chandlery. He hopped into the front seat alongside Tameel and looked up at the windows. Two on the second floor were lit, but the shutters were closed. Ayrion thought he saw a shadow pass in front of one, as if someone had been watching them leave, but as soon as it was there, it was gone again.

Unlike Saeida, the people of Minotha didn't seem all that interested in defending their rights. Of course, they also didn't have white bloodsucking vulraaks running around trying to eat them either. Apparently, things weren't bad enough yet for the people to be willing to risk anything themselves. He wondered how long that would last. If they weren't willing to fight for their own rights, then they didn't deserve them.

Tameel snapped the reins, and the old green-and-gold wagon started forward, creaking as it went. The streets were near empty this time of evening; a few lights in the windows let them know that not everyone had retired yet, but most were well on their way. One or two passersby tipped their hats as they hurried along, some turning to look, curious as to where they'd be going in the middle of the night.

The half-moon was resting low over the trees on the other side of the lake as they exited the north side of town, its light reflecting off the water's surface like a million stars resting just beneath the glassy top. It was a beautiful sight to behold. One quickly forgotten as another frosty gust swept across the lake and struck his face. He shivered, then raised the collar of his black leather jacket and lowered his stocking cap even farther over his ears.

The road leading out of town was similar to the one leading in—easily passable and wide enough for two wagons with ample room to spare. They soon hit a fork in the road, and Tameel pulled back on the reins and slowed the wagon to a complete stop. The main part of the road continued north through the trees, but a branch cut to the right, heading east around the lake. It no doubt led to the residences on the other side, including Lord Talmanes's estate.

The front window opened, and Zynora stuck her head out. "Why've we stopped?" She shivered and wrapped her shawl tighter around her shoulders.

"This is where we part ways," Ayrion said and climbed down from the seat. His swords pressed firmly against his back, a comforting feeling after their absence over the last couple of days. He slid them partway free, then snapped them back into place.

"You be careful, Grey Eyes," Zynora said, her tone letting him know she expected him to listen. The light from the two lanterns hanging to either side of the front opening revealed the concern on her face.

Ayrion smiled. "I'll be back soon enough. Might take me most the night, depending on the layout of the property and the number of guardsmen on duty, but I'll be back."

Tameel nodded. "We'll travel a few miles out of town and find somewhere to wait for you. I'll keep a warm kettle on for when you return. I'm sure you'll need it." Tameel made a show of rubbing his arms and blowing some warm air into each of his gloves. "Getting right chilly this evening."

"Hopefully, you won't have to wait long." With nothing left to be said, he started down the road at a medium pace, wanting to warm the blood in his legs. He glanced over his shoulder and watched as the wagon slowly disappeared, leaving nothing more than the hazy glow of the two lanterns in its wake. Soon enough, they had disappeared as well.

The road had patches of snow along the outer edges, most having melted earlier in the day, but some were still deep enough to snare the unwary foot, so Ayrion kept to the center as he jogged down one of the deeper ruts. He figured the estate couldn't be much more than a couple miles from this side of the lake.

The moon still hadn't yet risen high enough to be seen on this side of the lake, what with the surrounding trees, not that Ayrion was too worried. He wondered to what extent the other two Upakans could see. Were their eyes as capable as his? That had been the first time he'd come face-to-face with one of his own kind—at least the first time since losing his memories. Why did it have to be under such circumstances? He would have much rather sat down in front of a cozy fire with a nice glass of Misha's clover tea and discussed his heritage in a civilized manner than be forced to face off in a possible skirmish.

He hoped it didn't come to that.

Mist steamed in front of his face with every breath. He kept a slow but steady pace, not wanting to wind himself, but also so he could keep an ear and eye out for any possible scouts that might be planted along the roadway. He passed a couple of smaller homesteads, each with narrow drives leading back to quaint wooden homes.

The houses seemed to grow in frequency the farther around he went, which meant he was probably getting close to Lord Talmanes's estate. Moving to the side of the road, he started down the tree line, keeping close to the shadows, letting his black leather blend in with the forest.

It didn't take long before he reached the front of the estate. A clearing in the trees opened to reveal a large stone portico and gate erected at the entrance to a long drive that led somewhere back into the woods. On either side of the archway was a stone wall that ran only so far as the forest would allow, stopping at the tree line. Clearly, Lord Talmanes had never had cause to fortify his estate, leaving the forest and the waterfront to act as natural boundaries.

There was movement around the gate, letting Ayrion know that guards had been posted, though how many, he wasn't sure. There wasn't much in the way of a guard house, just a lean-to with a small fire. He could make out at least three around the fire, possibly more on the inside of the gate. He wasn't sticking around to find out.

Abandoning the road, Ayrion melted into the surrounding trees and made his way quietly in the direction of the lake, following the property line. His sense of Shade's presence was growing stronger. The forest was thick with undergrowth, and it took a while to work his way around impassable sections. Several times, he was forced to backtrack and detour around an area where the brush had thinned enough to see the estate.

Talmanes's property was extensive, partly on a cliffside overlooking Wenigapu. Ayrion hadn't realized how much of an incline he'd traveled up on his way around. The climb wasn't nearly as steep as the south side they had passed when first arriving in Minotha, but the cliff was certainly high enough to kill anyone who fell over the side. It was a breathtaking view, which was probably why the lord had chosen that piece of land to build on.

On the left, Ayrion could see the carriage-size lane leading out of the woods and around the gardens to the front of the house. The house itself backed nearly all the way to the cliff. It wasn't close enough to worry about the inevitable erosion, but enough so that they could see over the face from any of the upper-story balconies. Ayrion had no doubt the family rooms had a waterside view.

There was a courtyard in the back that led from the house down to a stone wall that ran along the cliff face. There were also several outbuildings dotting the grounds, but only one resembled a stable. Unfortunately, it happened to be on the other side of the property. Just his luck. He stood there for some time, studying the estate, counting the number of men on guard and marking their rotations.

The place, even though seemingly quiet, appeared to be well guarded, with a roaming patrol that circled not only the main house but the surrounding wood as well. Say this for the Upakans: They certainly knew how to stagger a proper watch. His best chance of getting to the stables without being seen would be to circle back around and cut through the woods.

If he had been dealing with regular guards, he wouldn't have hesitated, but with two Upakans that could possibly see in the dark, he couldn't take any chances. Knowing Endric, he probably demanded they stay close to him.

A twig snapped behind him, and he froze. It had been somewhere off to the right, over near the cliff. He turned his head slowly and scanned the area where he thought it had come from. He was about to step back when a shape moved out from behind a tree about twenty feet away. Whoever it was hadn't spotted him, but they appeared to be coming his way.

Slowly, Ayrion lowered himself back against a tall pine just behind him, keeping it between him and the patrol. The Upakans might have designed a well-organized watch, but they clearly hadn't trained the men in the art of moving through the woods without being noticed. Whoever the patroller was, they'd never done any sort of hunting before, judging by the heavy, careless footfalls coming Ayrion's way.

Ayrion didn't need to peek out from around the tree to know exactly where the man was. His passage was so loud, Ayrion would have been surprised if those at the house couldn't hear him. He was almost at the tree. Ayrion didn't bother with his swords as he counted down the man's steps.

Three . . . two . . . one.

Ayrion stepped out from behind the tree just as the guard passed. He wrapped his arm around the man's neck and squeezed. The guard tried to shout for help, but Ayrion muffled his cries with a gloved hand. The patroller jumped, fighting to break free, nearly taking Ayrion with him, but Ayrion managed to keep his footing.

The mercenary clawed at Ayrion's arm, but it was locked in place, and by the time the man realized it, his body was shuddering. He gasped and jerked and then went limp, and Ayrion lowered him to the ground. He was dressed in the same dark-green-and-gold livery as the rest of Endric's mercenaries, which gave Ayrion an idea.

Thankfully, the watchman was quite a bit heftier than Ayrion, so his uniform fit overtop Ayrion's leathers, if a bit snugly. Ayrion shook his arm to get the tunic sleeve to slide down over his coat. The hunter-green cloak was long enough for him to conceal his swords once he strapped them to his sides. In the dark, with his hood up, he doubted anyone would take notice.

Standing just inside the tree line, he glanced across the yard to the stables on the other side. It was a long way off, and there was a lot of open ground between. The moon moved behind a wisp of cloud, giving Ayrion the perfect opportunity to make his move. With a deep breath to steady his resolve, he stepped out of the trees and started across.

Chapter 23 | Ayrion

YRION HAD BARELY MADE it to the back of the first stone block building on the near side of the property when the clouds parted, and the half-moon relit the yard once more. He could hear conversations coming from inside and around the front. Creeping up the side, he peeked through one of the windows to find men moving about, some still wearing their uniforms, others half dressed, some in their undergarments. The building was evidently being used as some sort of barracks for the mercenaries.

Adjusting his cloak once more to make sure it covered his swords, Ayrion stepped out from around the front of the building and made as though he were heading for the main house.

"You coming in from perimeter watch?" someone called out, loudly enough that it was obviously meant for him.

Ayrion stopped and turned, keeping his head lowered but letting the hood hide his face from any direct light. There were three men standing in front around a small fire, smoking their pipes.

"Needed to warm up a bit before going back out," he said, making a conscious effort to mask his voice in case any of these men had taken part in Endric's collection earlier in town. He made a show of pulling his cloak tighter around his shoulders, pinching it off at the front. "Getting colder every night."

"You got that right," the first man on the left said, pulling his pipe from his mouth and pointing it at Ayrion.

The second tapped the ashes from his pipe's bowl into the open flames. "Was on outer watch duty last week. Almost had me reconsidering my position here." He chuckled, as did the other two.

"Waste of time if you ask me," the third man said, warming his hands over the fire. "What's Endric so afraid of, a couple of jackrabbits wandering onto the property without permission?" All the men laughed at that.

"He's about as paranoid as a three-legged cat being chased by a starving mongrel," the first man said. "But if he wants to pay me good coin to watch his backside all day, that's fine with me." The others nodded and continued puffing on their pipes.

Ayrion nodded. "The scariest thing I've spotted so far is an old hoot owl."

A couple of the men chuckled.

"If you ask me," the man on the left said, waving his pipe around like he was conducting a small chorus, "we were a whole lot better off before those two white eyes showed up. Now it's watch duty nearly every night, and arms practice every morning and evening. Who do they think we are, the flaming Sidaran Lancer corps?"

More grumbles from the other men let Ayrion know they were clearly unhappy with the arrival of his fellow Upakans. He wondered if there was a way he could use that to his advantage. "Yeah, I'm getting sick of those faerie-lovin' freaks telling us all what to do as if we were their personal slaves." He received more than a few hearty grunts over that. "Someone ought to tell them we've had enough. There's only two of them. If an accident were to befall them, that wouldn't be too surprising, right?"

The others weren't so quick to respond this time, sharing furtive glances and taking a few extra puffs on their pipes.

The man on the left was the first to speak up. "That kind of talk might get you a quick trip over the wall," he said, nodding toward the cliffside. "You remember what happened to the last group that tried to take matters into their own hands."

Ayrion nodded, but of course he had no idea. But by the way the men were staring out at the edge of the cliff, he could probably guess.

"Best keep those thoughts to yourself," the man said, looking a bit nervous having Ayrion there. "Even the trees around here seem to have eyes."

"Good advice," Ayrion said. "I think I'll get a horse and ride up to the front gate and see about relieving one of the guards up there."

"Yes, you do that," the man said.

Ayrion took the hint and left the men to their pipes. Clearly, the two Upakans had all the mercenaries on edge. It sounded like they had given a demonstration early on, leaving the others with little doubt of why it would be in their best interest not to challenge them. Ayrion wondered how many had died in that demonstration. The way the men had looked almost reverently toward the stone wall led him to believe quite a few.

He was beginning to wonder what would happen if he was forced to face off against two of his own kind. From what Tameel and Zynora had told him, Upakans trained to fight from birth, and Ayrion was at a bit of a disadvantage right now with his loss of memory. How much of his own training had he lost? He hadn't seemed to have too much problem recalling how to use his blades against the vulraak. But that had felt like instinct.

He tightened his jaw as he neared the front of the house. He needed to focus on where he was going, not on whether he could take two Upakans at once. The goal was to slip in and out without confronting anyone.

Lanterns and torches lined the crushed rock drive leading between the front of the house and the gardens on the other side. Several guards stood at the bottom of the steps in front of the house, but they were in too heavy a discussion to notice Ayrion as he kept to the other side, not wanting to appear interested in the home at all. He didn't even bother looking at the upper floors to see if any of the windows were lit. With his luck, as soon as he did, one or both of the Upakans would be looking down at that exact moment. So, keeping his head lowered and cloak pulled tight, he continued on, counting down the steps till he reached the other side.

Once past the main house, he breathed a little easier. There was still some distance between the house and the stables, but other than what appeared to be a carriage house where the crushed rock drive ended, there wasn't much standing in his way. It was a pretty straight shot with no other guards moving about. Most of the outbuildings, including the barracks, were located on the other side of the property.

He continued down the graveled path, stepping off just before the carriage house. There was a single guard sitting out front, looking more preoccupied with warming his hands than with where Ayrion was going. And with Ayrion's new uniform, there wasn't much need to worry, as he blended right in with the others, even going so far as to change his walk, giving a more unconcerned sense as to what he was doing and where he was going.

The stables were quite large, running at least three times the length of the carriage house, stopping twenty or thirty feet from the stone wall at the back of the property. The wall appeared to end just to the other side of the stable, up against the tree line. The horse pen, which ran the length of the stables, took up most of the space between the carriage house and the barn, but at this time of night it lay empty, the horses having no doubt been brought in out of the cold.

The stable was closed, two guards standing off to one side, warming themselves over a fire. Even the window on the second floor just above had been shuttered. A faint light from inside traced the edges of the doors, indicating there was probably a groomsman or two tending to the horses.

"Cold night to be on watch," Ayrion said in greeting as he approached.

The two men looked up from their conversation. The heftier man on the right was the first to answer. "Cold night to be doing anything but curling up beside a woman." He chuckled. "Even one as ugly as Hussen's."

The shorter man spun on the first. "I've killed men for less." He paused. "And if it weren't true, or so flaming cold, I'd do something about it."

They both laughed, almost forgetting Ayrion was standing there.

"I'm here for a horse," Ayrion said. "My night to be on watch at the front gate."

The first man, a stalwart fellow, rubbed the stubble growing in patches along his jawline. "Bit late, aren't you?"

"Yes," Ayrion said with chagrin, trying to think of an excuse to offer. "One of those faerie-lovin' cave dwellers had me fetching water for our lord's bath. What do I look like, a handmaid?" The other two grunted. "I thought they were going to have me scrubbing Endric's back by the time it was over with. As if the miserable little twit couldn't wash it himself. Useless if you ask me."

"As long as his gold is good," the larger man on the right said, "I'll wash any part of him he wants."

The two guards burst out laughing once more. Ayrion joined them, just long enough to appear sociable before heading for a small door on the right. "Anyone up inside to saddle me a horse?"

Hussen nodded. "Aaban should be. You might have to wake him, though. He has a tendency to nod off if someone ain't there to keep him company."

Ayrion nodded. "Much appreciated." He turned the handle and stepped inside, thankful to be out of the cold, the horses producing enough heat to actually make it comfortable.

He didn't need to wait for his eyes to adjust. Along with the moonlight coming in from the upper windows on the right side of the barn, there were lanterns lighting the central walkway down the middle aisle between the individual stalls.

A man was propped on a stool near the back, reclining against one of the doors. His arms were crossed, his hat pulled low over his face. There didn't seem to be anyone else inside, no movement apart from the occasional head sticking out of one of the stalls from a curious horse that hadn't yet decided to bed down for the evening.

Ayrion could sense Shade's presence. The horse could apparently sense him as well, as a black head poked out from what looked like the last stall on the left. *I'm coming.*

Slowly, Ayrion made his way down the aisle, keeping his eyes and ears open, his hands on his swords. The stableman was snoring peacefully on his stool, his chest rising and lowering in time. If Ayrion had been a proper Upakan, he would have just slit the man's throat and left him there, but lucky for the man, he wasn't. Quietly, Ayrion knelt down beside the sleeping guard and, like the guard in the woods, he grabbed him around the neck.

It didn't take long for the man to tip off his stool and go still.

Ayrion pulled him around the back of the last stall and then turned to see if anyone had heard. Everything was silent, apart from the odd creak in the rafters on the second floor where they stored the hay. Shade whinnied, urging Ayrion to hurry up and release him.

"Hold your horses," Ayrion said with a wry grin. "I'm coming." Apparently, Shade didn't appreciate that, as he whinnied once again. Ayrion shook his head as he walked over to the stall. "What's your prob—"

"We've been waiting on you."

Ayrion jerked one of his swords free as Shade's stall door suddenly opened and a man stepped out, sword in one hand, long dagger in the other. Ayrion couldn't say he was too surprised, not if the stories about his people were even half true. Even with his hood pulled, Ayrion could see the glow in the man's eyes as he passed the lantern hanging just to the right of the stall.

Ayrion tightened his grip. At least there was only the one. Problem was, though, the first strike of steel on steel and those outside would be rushing in and sounding the alarm, which meant Ayrion was going to have to be quick about disarming the man. If he could overpower him quickly enough, he still might be able to make a run for it before the rest of the mercenaries were the wiser.

The Upakan slowly circled out toward the center of the aisle, giving them the most open space for a fight. He didn't appear all that worried, his arms relaxed, posture the same. He did keep his shoulder turned, not presenting his chest as an open target.

"What clan do you belong to?" he asked once more.

A flash overtook Ayrion and suddenly he was standing in a small circular arena, sand under his feet, reams of people encircling the ring, each with the same light-grey eyes. There was a boy standing in front of him, Upakan as well. *Flon.* The name sounded so familiar. Suddenly, the vision shifted, and the boy was lying at his feet, his neck twisted at an awkward angle, one Ayrion instinctively knew could only mean one thing. *Did I kill him?*

"Why don't you answer?"

The question brought him out of his trance. He noticed the Upakan eyeing his sword.

"That's a unique weapon," the Upakan said. "Don't believe I've seen its like before." He waited a moment longer, then raised the tip of his sword in Ayrion's direction. "I'll only ask this once more, who is your clan?"

Ayrion dug deep, trying to find a name, something that was familiar. What was his clan's name? What if this Upakan belonged to the same clan? Wouldn't he have recognized him? The answer just wouldn't come. "What is your clan?" he asked, unable to think of anything else to say.

The man continued to circle. "I'm Paran of Clan Kovaa."

Kovaa? The name sparked a memory. *Orpa.* Ayrion didn't know where the name had come from or if it was relevant, but at this point, how could it hurt? "Orpa."

The man's face twisted. "Figures," he said. "Brim's all but run that clan into the ground. After the death of his son, he's never been the same."

Suddenly, Ayrion was standing in front of some sort of tribunal. Three chairs sat on a dais in front of him, two men and one woman. The man in the middle was clearly the leader, dwarfing the other two. There was anger in his eyes, deep and personal. Ayrion didn't have to guess whether it was this Brim Paran spoke of. He could feel it inside, a pit rolling around in the center of his gut. Before the man in the central seat could speak, the vision vanished, and Ayrion was back in the stable, facing Paran.

"What is your name?"

Ayrion almost told him, but thought better of it, and instead used the name Zynora had given him before his fight in Woodvale. "Jair."

"What is your contract?"

"I told you already, my contract won't interfere with yours."

"You expect me to believe that an Upakan from Clan Orpa just happens to wander into this remote backwoods town at the same time two from Clan Kovaa are here?"

"I don't care what you think," Ayrion said, getting tired of standing there. The longer he waited, the greater the chance of his discovery. "I'm just here for my horse."

As much as he would have liked to learn about his people, he needed to be out of there before the rest of the barracks were notified and the place went on alert. Perhaps, if he was quick enough, he could subdue the man and take him with him. He could question him later.

As soon as the thought surfaced, he pushed it aside. Kidnapping the man would all but guarantee the other Upakan would try chasing them down, and their green-and-gold tinker wagon was hardly capable of outrunning, or hiding from, pursuers.

"This doesn't need to get ugly," Ayrion said, keeping his eyes on the man's weapons, ready to defend if the need arose. He wished Tameel were there. Tameel could talk a snake out of its hole. "Just let me take my horse, and I'll be on my way." Ayrion took a step toward Shade's stable door, and the Upakan matched it, keeping himself between them.

"We can't take that kind of chance," Paran said. "We have a contract to fulfill, and we can't allow another contract, especially one from Clan *Orpa*, to get in the way."

"Then it appears you leave me with little choice, because I'm not leaving here without my horse." Something inside Shade's stall clanged against the wood, and Ayrion turned for a split second, wondering if the other Upakan had been hiding there all along. As soon as he looked back, he noticed the man in front of him had somehow shifted stances. Paran was now leaning forward with one of his arms extended. It was the arm holding the dagger.

The dagger was no longer in his hand.

Sharp pain burned through Ayrion's shoulder as the Upakan's blade plunged straight through and out the back. His hand went numb, and the dragon blade slipped from his fingers. But before it hit the ground, everything shifted. The dagger was no longer in his shoulder, and he was once again in the process of turning to look at Shade.

Without even thinking, he sidestepped to the left and batted the knife away with his blade, where it struck one of the stalls behind him.

Paran pulled another weapon out from behind his back to replace the dagger. It was a short wooden handle with a chain connecting it to a spiked ball at the end. Very similar to a common flail, but with an extended reach.

Ayrion drew his second blade, not willing to take any chances. Paran was every bit as trained as he was, and not suffering from lost memories. The two circled each other. Paran didn't seem as willing to jump in headfirst this time.

"Our laws might not allow me to kill you," the Upakan said, "but that doesn't mean I won't drag you all the way to death's door and leave you on the threshold. Give up now and save yourself the embarrassment."

Upakan laws wouldn't allow Paran to kill him? That was new. Strange law to have for a society of mercenaries. Before he had a chance to ponder it further, Paran attacked. His movements were catlike: fast, agile, precise.

Ayrion dodged the flail, and the ball struck the ground, sending dirt flying around his ankles. No sooner had the ball struck than Paran's sword was already on the move, and Ayrion moved with it. The man moved with incredible speed, whirling his weapons like a windmill, but never quite landing, growing more frustrated by the moment.

Ayrion swept from one side of the stalls to the other, deflecting, dodging, spinning, leaping, never actually attacking himself. Paran was good, very good, better than any other Ayrion had faced, with the exception of Argon, and it was taking all his concentration to keep up with him. But Ayrion was patient, waiting for the right opportunity.

Paran thrust his sword, forcing Ayrion to deflect, then swung with the flail, hoping to catch Ayrion in the middle of a retreat. Ayrion dove into the dirt and rolled, resulting in the spiked ball being buried in the stall door behind him. He rolled to his feet and swung, cutting the chain before Paran was able to pull it from the wood.

Paran jumped back and pulled a second, smaller blade from inside his coat and attacked once more. Ayrion parried each strike, swatting them just out of reach, never exerting himself more than necessary. Paran was beginning to slow, his frustration causing his movements to slip. Ayrion could see uncertainty in his eyes. He was leaving a small opening on his left.

Ayrion didn't let the opportunity pass.

He swung for the right, drawing Paran's attention, then kicked his left leg out from under him. Paran tried to roll to his feet, but Ayrion was already there with his sword pressed to Paran's neck. "Release . . . your blade."

Paran reluctantly dropped his sword, but there was a smile on his face that had Ayrion frowning. *Why—*

"Very good," someone behind him said.

Ayrion yanked Paran to his feet and spun to face the newcomer, keeping his sword planted against Paran's throat.

It was the second Upakan.

Unlike Paran, this man had his hood lowered, not bothering with trying to hide his face or his eyes. Ayrion looked behind him and into the stall. If both of them were here, where was Endric? The second man didn't leave the stall, standing in the doorway with his hand gripped tight around the rope on Shade's neck. "I'm Siranu of Clan Kovaa." He took a moment to look Ayrion over, pausing on the sword resting in Ayrion's hand. "You would do well in the games. Why haven't we seen you before? Talent like that, and Brim would have had you signed up for every competition between now and Dark Winter's Eve."

"I'm too busy running contracts to worry about competitions," Ayrion lied.

The second guard looked puzzled. "With Orpa's reputation, I doubt that. Brim would have wanted to show you off, to option for better contracts for his clan." The second Upakan shrugged. "Regardless, I think it's time you released Paran and surrendered your weapon."

Ayrion didn't like the calm demeanor on the man's face. It was the same expression Paran had been wearing just before Siranu had shown himself. Ayrion looked at the other stalls, wondering what he was missing. "I think I'll keep my weapon if it's all the same to you," he said, shifting the blade a little higher against Paran's neck, forcing the Upakan to lift his head.

"You mistake me as someone who is giving you an option," Siranu said. "We let it go on this long to see what you were made of, and now that we have, I'm afraid our fun is over."

Something was very wrong. Ayrion tightened his grip. "Move away from that horse or I'll slit his throat."

Siranu looked puzzled. "We both know that isn't true, so why argue the point? Talent or not, you'd be banished from all Upakan society, if not sentenced to death on the spot. It's a hollow threat. This, however, is not." He whipped out a dagger and held it up to Shade's neck. "If you don't release Paran by the time I count to three, then we'll be feasting on horse for the next week."

Shade tried jerking away, even cried out in frustration, but Siranu dealt one punch to Shade's nose, and Siranu managed to get the stallion under control. He placed the dagger's blade back against Shade's neck.

There was nothing Ayrion could do, not while Shade's life was the consequence. And this Upakan law that both men referred to had Ayrion even more hesitant.

"One."

Ayrion glanced around at the other stalls, looking for any kind of leverage.

"Two."

He bit down on his lip. Unless he planned on letting them kill Shade, he didn't have a way out of this. Sure, he could have let the animal die and then killed both the Upakans, but Shade was more than just an animal. There was a bond between them that went deeper than anything he understood. At least for the moment, he didn't believe the Upakans would kill him, so perhaps there was still a chance to find a way out of this. "Fine," he said, lowering his sword and releasing Paran, who quickly moved back out of the way.

"Your weapons. Toss them over."

Ayrion reluctantly tossed his swords into the straw. He also unhooked the set of knives he had inside his jacket and dropped them on the pile. Paran patted him down, even going so far as to have Ayrion remove his boots long enough to check for hidden blades. "All this over a horse? No wonder Brim has kept you hidden. You might be able to fight, but you have about as much sense as a scalenbat in heat."

"Take him up to the house and lock him in the lower cellar," Siranu said to Paran, who was in the process of collecting his weapons. "And post a guard." He looked at Ayrion. "Post several guards." Siranu never moved from his place beside Shade, his blade never dipping. It was clear he had every intention of staying right where he was until assured that Ayrion was safely locked away.

"And how do I know that you won't kill my horse as soon as I leave here?"

"Because it won't be in our best interest to take away your incentive to play nice," Siranu said with a smile. "Who knows, once our contract is completed, perhaps his lordship will see fit to let you and your horse go."

"And how long will that be?"

Siranu looked at Paran, who simply shrugged. "At least until Lord Talmanes returns in the spring, I suppose."

Ayrion was marched at the end of Paran's sword back toward the side door at the front where he'd entered. Ayrion glanced over his shoulder at Shade. "Don't worry, boy. I'll be back soon enough." With that, he turned and let Paran lead him out into the cold blistering wind. He seemed destined to be driven on the wind from one unfortunate event to the next. *Spring?* He couldn't wait till spring. What would Tameel and Zynora do if he didn't return? It wasn't like they could storm the estate with Ol' Lerra, and it was clear the townsfolk had no intention of getting involved.

With a heavy sigh, he followed Paran back toward the main house.

Chapter 24 | Ayrion

THREE DAYS HAD PASSED, and Ayrion wasn't any closer to figuring out how to escape than the day they'd locked him in. The underground windowless room was well stocked with casks of wine, and the walls were lined with racks of even rarer vintages, mostly from Briston. He even managed to come across a couple smaller casks of Black Briar, something he was sure Abiah wouldn't have minded being locked in a room with. The cellar had only one door. In addition to being cold, the room had a strong damp smell—a mixture of wet soil, wooden shelves, and sweet vinegar—which left his stomach unsettled.

The only interaction he'd had with those keeping him hostage was the brief exchange with the guards bringing him his meals. The biscuits, hard as they were, had softened quite nicely after being dipped in some of Lord Talmanes's finest wine. Ayrion had hid the bottles he'd used in one of the larger barrels near the back. He found the wine helped him make it through the cold nights, as no one had seen fit to provide him with even the barest of essentials, like a blanket. He was thankful for the extra uniform he'd stolen from the mercenary in the woods, but even that was soon taken when a couple of the guards demanded its return. Apparently, the mercenary who it had belonged to had stumbled out of the woods half frozen, swearing to gut the man who'd done it.

At one point, Ayrion had considered setting a fuse to one of the casks in an attempt to blow off the door; however, it would have probably ended with him bringing the house down on his head. Some of these vintages could be quite volatile, as he remembered during his time in Belvin at the Justice House.

Even if he did manage to escape, what good would it do while they were holding Shade hostage? Breaking out of the room, he could handle. Fighting his way to the stables, he could handle. Getting there before they killed Shade . . . that was something he couldn't manage.

The lock on the door snapped, and Ayrion got to his feet. The door opened, and several guards stepped inside, holding lanterns. Warm light filled the room, sending shadows across the shelves and momentarily blinding Ayrion.

"Ah, there he is," Endric said with an overly enthusiastic grin as he and Siranu walked into the room. "The man who'd risk it all for a horse."

Paran didn't seem to be in attendance. Knowing the Upakans, he was probably standing guard over Shade in order to keep Ayrion in line. Endric stopped several feet away from Ayrion. "How much will it take?"

Ayrion was puzzled as to why they didn't just kill him and be done with it. "How much will it take for what?" he asked.

Endric pulled out a hefty purse from his trouser pocket and jostled it in front of Ayrion. "How much will it take for you to break your contract? I'll double it if you tell me who it was who hired you."

All Ayrion could do was shake his head. Was there nothing this lordling didn't feel he could do just because he had gold?

On his left, Siranu studied Ayrion's face. "He won't break the contract. No Upakan would. Our reputation would be ruined. Who would want to hire us if they couldn't trust we'd stick with it?"

Ayrion didn't respond, though he had to admit he felt a sense of pride at such loyalty to one's task. Surely, the Upakans couldn't be all bad, with such a high sense of duty. Then again, that duty most often seemed to be murder for hire.

"Well, I seem to be in a bit of a predicament, then," Endric said as he replaced his purse and crossed his arms. "The question is what to do with you. The easiest answer would be to toss you over the back wall and see if you hit the water or the rocks, but my personal guard," he said, sparing a frustrated glance at Siranu, "tells me that they cannot be held accountable for the death of another Upakan. In fact, it would be in their right to do whatever it takes to stop such an incident."

Ayrion looked at Siranu, who held a straight face, no hint of what he might be thinking. "Then might I suggest you let me go. I promise I will leave your fine city, and you won't see me again."

Endric grinned. "I can't really take that chance, now can I?" He took a couple of steps forward, holding out his hand to warn Siranu off as he leaned in to Ayrion, so that the others couldn't overhear their conversation. "Your fellow Upakans might not be willing to lay hands on you, but what's to stop something from accidentally happening the next time we head into town? If we were to return and find you missing, they would have no one to blame. Perhaps I will tell them you simply escaped." Endric chuckled and stepped back with the others. "Think about my offer."

For the first time since stepping into the room, Siranu had an uncertain look on his face.

Endric turned and headed for the door, the guards behind him quickly moving out of the way. He stopped and glanced back over his shoulder. "Oh, I believe I have a meeting in town tomorrow." He smiled, and the guards shut the door. Ayrion could hear Endric laughing all the way down the hall.

Endric obviously thought he had Ayrion concerned. Still, this presented him with a possibility. With Siranu and Paran gone, it would at least give him a chance to make a run for it. And from what he'd seen of the mercenaries guarding the property, they hardly measured up to the Upakans. He was all but certain that Siranu would have set a watch on Shade, but unlike Siranu and Paran, Ayrion doubted that whoever they put on watch would be standing over Shade with a knife in their hand, ready to slit his horse's throat at the first sign of danger. The last person they had watching over the horses had been asleep on a stool.

No. The men he'd seen so far were there for the coin, mostly thugs paid to frighten poor workers into turning over their hard-earned money. If he were to escape, it would have to be when they came to execute him in the morning, which didn't give him long to plan, not that there was much to plan for: subdue the guards, recover his weapons, free Shade, then ride as fast and as far from Minotha as possible.

Ayrion didn't have much notion as to whether it was day or night, apart from the guards bringing him his meals, or by the heaviness of his eyes. The night passed swiftly, as swiftly as it could with Ayrion knowing that in a few hours armed men would be coming to collect him and toss him over a cliff. By the time he heard the boots and the clanging of keys, he was ready.

Muffled voices grew in number as a light appeared under the door. Ayrion stood behind the barrels he'd spent most of the night stacking, waiting for the right moment. He kept his shoulder pressed against the wood, listening for the lock to click and the hinges to squeal. A blade left its scabbard.

The lock snapped, and Ayrion tensed, tilting the barrels slightly as his back foot pressed against the stone floor for leverage. He waited. Rusty hinges squealed.

Now! He shoved with all his might, and the barrels tipped, crashing through the door and into the hall, dousing everyone in a strong rum. The barrels took down the first four guards who were standing in the doorway. One of the guards happened to be carrying a lantern, and when he went down, the glass shattered on the floor and the open flame was released, licking up the contents of the barrels and lighting those standing nearby like tar-pitched torches.

Ayrion flew out of the doorway, leaping onto the downed barrels and diving through the flames before they completely blocked the hallway. He hit the ground and rolled, stamping out a couple flames that had reached his pants legs. The four guards' screams were short-lived, as they barely made it halfway down the hall before collapsing under the heat and smoke. Their burnt flesh lit the hallway and left behind a sickly sweet smell, vaguely similar to that of the wine cellar.

Ahead of him, three remaining guards made a break for the stairs. He had to stop them before they reached the top and sounded the alarm.

Racing down the hall, he leaped over a couple of burning corpses, one still jerking. The three men saw him coming and ran all the faster, but desperation poured through Ayrion and sent him careening into the three about halfway up.

He knocked the first unconscious with a fist to the jaw and threw him back down the stairs. The second spun with his dagger, slashing wildly to give his friend a chance to escape and warn the others. Ayrion dodged left, grabbing the man's arm and breaking it. He then sent the dagger flying up the stairs, catching the third man in the back. The mercenary stiffened and slumped forward onto the steps.

Ayrion grabbed the man whose arm he just broke and pulled him to his feet, relieving him of his sword. "Don't say a word," Ayrion threatened. There were tears in the man's eyes as he cradled his arm close to his chest. "If I hear even a peep, you'll join the others, you hear me?"

The man nodded with a hesitant whimper.

Smoke was already filling the hallway below and rising up the stairs, looking for a way to escape. Ayrion's eyes were beginning to burn as he dragged the helpless man up the rest of the flight, stopping long enough to pull the dagger from the other mercenary's back and free him of his outer mantle. With the robe pulled tight and hood raised, Ayrion cracked the door and peeked out. The hallway was empty. Quickly, he pulled the guard out and shut the door behind them. Smoke was already seeping around the edges and under the door. They needed to hurry, before someone else spotted it as well.

Ayrion looked at the man and was momentarily startled that he recognized his face. It was the same man he'd assaulted in the woods days before. The rage in the man's eyes was nearly as hot as the fire in the cellars below.

"Where are my swords?" Ayrion asked.

The man's mouth tightened.

Ayrion grabbed the man's broken arm.

"Endric's chambers," he hissed.

"Take me there. Now." Ayrion punctuated the urgency by pressing the dagger's tip into the small of his back. The mercenary winced but nodded, and they headed down the hall.

They reached another landing and took the stairs up two floors, where they started down another corridor leading to several doors on the right and double doors at the end of the hall. That particular set of doors had an armed guard out front, who watched with curiosity as they approached. He looked at the guard in front, noticing the injured arm.

"What happened to you?"

Before the man could answer, Ayrion pulled the knife from where he had it leveled against the first guard's back and quickly stuck it up under the second guard's chin.

"What's going—" The second armsman saw Ayrion's eyes and gasped but was careful not to move.

Ayrion turned the man around to face the door. "Open it."

The mercenary grabbed the handles and shoved the two doors open, slowly stepping inside. Ayrion quickly shut the doors, scanning the room. He spotted his swords over on the bed and guided the two men over to them. He had them undress down to their skivvies and, using their tunics, tied them each to one of the corner posts of the bed, gagging them with a strip of cloth.

Quickly, he strapped his blades around his waist and put on the uniform of the man whose arm he'd broken. "We keep meeting like this."

The guard mumbled angrily behind his gag.

Taking a brief moment to look out the bedroom's windows, Ayrion noticed that the grounds stood fairly empty. Endric must have taken a good number of the mercenaries with him when he went into town. Probably another day of collecting.

One thing was for sure, he didn't have time to waste. It wouldn't take them long to notice the—

"Fire! Fire!"

He turned and ran for the door. Before he made it halfway down the hall, the entire corridor suddenly lurched as the booming sound of muffled thunder echoed in his ears. He didn't need to guess what had just happened.

The Black Briar.

Quickly, he raced down the steps, looking for the closest way out. Smoke was already filling the home, and men in uniforms were scampering about, not knowing what to do. He held part of his robe to his mouth as he made his way through the fog. The smoke burned his lungs. His eyes were watering so much, he could hardly see where he was going, bumping into walls and furniture as he went. Finding an empty room on the first floor, he threw a chair through the window and climbed out, smoke billowing out behind him.

He stumbled into the courtyard at the front of the house, coughing and wheezing, fighting for breath. He felt a twinge of regret, having tied those men to Endric's bedpost; however, he hadn't tied them very tight, since all he had to work with was the sleeves from their tunics. Hopefully, they had managed to free themselves by now. It was definitely not something he needed to worry about at present. It wasn't like they hadn't just tried executing him moments before.

He raced down the crushed rock drive toward the stables, passing men on the way who were running toward the main house and the flames issuing from it. Ayrion couldn't have asked for a better distraction. The outside of the main barn stood empty of guards, and while there were several horses roaming around the pen at the side, Ayrion didn't see Shade among them. The two doors at the front stood ajar, and he dashed through, only to be met by a dozen armed men.

Ayrion slid to a stop, his swords in his hands before his boots had stopped skidding across the loose dirt. He quickly removed the outer robe of his borrowed uniform, knowing it would do him little good here. His fingers tightened around the familiar grip of the dragon's scales.

Shade whinnied from the back. Ayrion could feel his fear.

"Lord Endric warned us you might try something like this," a man near the front said as he raised his sword. He was a giant of a man, standing head and shoulders above the others, with a jaw as square as Endric's bed posts. His doublehanded sword was nearly two-thirds the size of Ayrion, and those standing closest gave him a wide berth. "He also said that if you were to attempt an escape that we were to slit your horse's throat and toss you both over the wall."

Ayrion had no doubt he could cut through these men to reach Shade, but not before they had made good on their word. The warhorse thrashed around in his stall as three men fought to hold him down. Ayrion bit his lower lip. Once again, he was left without options, and at this point, he'd already committed himself. There was no turning back now. "You harm a single hair on that horse's head, and I'll feed you your intestines."

A couple of the guards took a step back, leaving their leader out front. The big man smiled, making his cleft chin protrude even further. "We'll see about that." He glanced over his shoulder. "Do it!"

Ayrion's breath caught in his throat, and he raised his swords, but before he could even muster an attack, two of the three men holding Shade flew out the stall door, one with a gaping hole on the top of his head. Before the second had time to even turn around, a third man shot out after them, swinging two very familiar hatchets as he tore into the back of their gathering.

It can't be.

Ayrion leaped to the side as the doublehanded sword buried itself in the dirt beside him. He spun, and with a single swing took both the man's hands at the wrists, then took his head as well and quickly moved to the next. Uniformed guards ran in circles like headless chickens, so confused by the fact that Ayrion was wearing one of their uniforms that they started swinging on each other.

By the time it was over, the barn floor was covered in death. Blood streaked the stalls, the floors, even some of the horses, filling the stable with its strong metallic odor, one just as wrenching as the burnt corpses in the cellars.

"Can't leave you alone for a minute," Bek said with a bright smile. "Trouble follows you like the Defiler's curse."

The two men embraced.

Ayrion was all but laughing at the sight of the big trapper. He'd never been so happy to see anyone as he was at that moment. "What are you doing here? Where are Nell and the children? How'd you find me?"

"All in good time," Bek said, wiping the blood from his hatchets and stowing them back in the hooks at his waist. "We need to get out of here, and fast. There was a heavy rumble earlier. I'm guessing that was you?"

Ayrion smiled as he leaped over bodies to reach Shade, who had already left his stall and was quietly waiting for Ayrion. Ayrion rubbed the black warhorse's nose. "I told you I'd be back." He turned to Bek. "Did you bring a horse?"

"I brought one of the wagon's horses. It's just outside."

"Then grab it and let's get out of here." Before mounting, Ayrion procured one of the outer robes with the Talmanes crest on the back and flung it over his shoulders. "Here," he said, tossing Bek another. "Put this on first. Best not to draw attention to ourselves if we don't have to."

Bek covered his furs with the robe and raised the hood, then walked outside and around the side of the barn, returning momentarily with a brown mare. "Ready?"

Ayrion hopped up on Shade and nodded. "We ride hard and fast. Straight for the gate. They might have four or five guards on duty. Nothing we can't handle." Ayrion nudged Shade with the back of his boot, and the warhorse trotted over to the now-open barn doors.

The grounds were in chaos as uniformed men rushed to gather buckets of water from the well and even from the garden fountain, to help put out the fires. By the time Ayrion and Bek rode past, over half of the house was engulfed in flames. Most of Endric's wealth was no doubt buried inside. Ayrion chuckled to himself. The arrogant prig was going to need the townsfolk now more than ever, which would give them the leverage they needed to negotiate. If Endric and what was left of his mercenaries wanted to survive the winter, they were going to need the town's help. Hopefully he was wise enough to see that.

They galloped up the crushed rock drive and into the woods, heading directly for the gate. Ayrion wondered if the explosion from the wine casks in the cellar could have been heard or felt all the way back in town. He doubted it, but there was a good chance they could see the smoke from across the lake. The trees finally parted, and the gate came into view. A small fire was lit on this side with three uniformed guards standing around. The guards turned when they saw them approaching.

"Can't you see the smoke?" Ayrion shouted as he pulled Shade to a halt. "Lord Talmanes's house is on fire! They sent us to get you. They need every able body to help put it out!"

The men on both sides of the gate looked confused.

"Did you not hear me? Talmanes's house is on fire!"

"The gold, you fools!" Bek said. "All of Talmanes's gold is inside. You want to get paid? Then get a move on!"

The men rushed to open the gate. They jumped on their horses and took off down the drive. Ayrion and Bek didn't wait for them to reach the tree line before they raced off in the opposite direction, riding the horses at a full gallop back around the side of Lake Wenigapu. With every new bend they crossed, Ayrion was half expecting to find Endric and his men waiting for them.

They reached the fork in the road, stopping only long enough to see if anyone was coming from the direction of town, but it appeared to be empty. Luck was for once on his side. They turned the horses north and away from Minotha. It was several miles before they came across a small opening in the trees and found two covered wagons parked around a cooking fire. Alongside Ol' Lerra was the dingy red wagon that Bek and Nell had borrowed from the rovers after they had been all but wiped out by the vulraak.

"We were getting worried," Tameel called out as he and the others stood from their places around the fire.

Ayrion barely had time to dismount before something had latched onto his leg, causing him to lose his balance and almost land on his face in the snow. He looked down to find a bright set of eyes and a beaming smile shining back up at him. "Marissa." He unhooked the little girl's arms and lifted her up into his, not thinking about the fact that he was covered in mercenary blood.

She wrapped her arms around his neck and looked ready to kiss him, but whatever she saw gave her pause. "Ick! You need a bath."

He laughed and put her back down.

"You like my ribbon?" she asked, pointing to the top of her head.

"I don't know, it's covered by your hat."

She pursed her lips. "Oh." Gleefully, she yanked off the blue stocking cap to reveal a soft orange bow tangled amidst a wad of dark curls.

He patted the top of her head, making sure not to squish the bow any more than it already was. "It's lovely." He smiled and started for the fire, but only made it a few feet, as Taylis blocked his way. He held up a circular object with a short handle attached. At the center was a thick piece of glass. "You like it?" he asked, holding it for Ayrion to inspect.

"It's, uh . . . It's very nice." Ayrion looked over at Zynora for help, but she just stood there chuckling.

"It's my new crawly killer."

"Ah, I see." Ayrion took the glass and held it up to look through. Everything was distorted to the point of making him nauseous. He lowered it before he became any more dizzy and handed it back to Taylis. "That is quite the powerful weapon you have there. I hope you wield it well. I almost feel sorry for those crawlies."

Taylis smiled. "They don't stand a chance."

Ayrion left Taylis to his newfound tool and followed Bek over to the fire and joined the others. He stopped first to grip Nell's hand before taking a seat between Bek and Tameel.

"It's good to see you again," Ayrion said. "How are you doing?"

Nell's hair was just beginning to grow once more; Ayrion could see the stubble coming in around the bottom of her cap. Her eyebrows weren't much longer.

"I'm doing better," she said with a brave face. "Some days are harder than others."

"Nights are the worst," Bek said, placing a comforting hand over hers. "Nightmares. Wakes up screaming."

"Can't ruddy blame her," Zynora said. "When I wake up and turn over and see him," she said, nodding toward Tameel, "I want to scream as well."

Nell smiled, and the others chuckled, even Tameel. Normally, he'd been the first to have a witty comeback, but this time he held his peace. The man was smarter than most gave him credit for.

Ayrion looked at Bek and Nell. "Why are you here?"

Bek accepted a cup from Zynora, the contents warm enough to set steam rising above the rim. He took a sip and relaxed on one of the stools. "We tried hanging around Belvin, but everywhere we went was just another reminder of what we'd been through. Our cabin is destroyed. Even if the front wall was still there, the place was littered with bodies and painted with blood. Too many unpleasant memories." He took another sip from the cup. "Abiah, Creator bless him, offered us a place in town. He did whatever he could to get us to stay, but . . ." He shook his head. "I need space to breathe. Don't want to be cramped inside a city where you can open your window and shake hands with your neighbor, where everyone knows everyone else's business. Just not for me.

"So, the wife and I decided we'd pack up and follow you lot north, try to catch up if we could. Didn't think we was going to find you, until someone in Minotha mentioned seeing your wagon a few days back." He looked at Ayrion. "We just arrived yesterday. Tameel and Zynora said you'd been missing for three days, and they filled us in on what was going on." He looked at Shade. "That must be some kind of horse."

Ayrion smiled. "He is."

"So?" Tameel said, anxiously rocking on his stool. "What happened?"

Ayrion took the next half hour walking them through his arrival at Lord Talmanes's and his subsequent kidnapping and escape. He told them about his discussion with the Upakans and how Endric had threatened to kill him that morning. He finished with Bek's unexpected arrival and their quick departure.

"I still can't believe you're here," Ayrion said, accepting another refill from Zynora and taking a small sip. "Bek has never had such impeccable timing."

"The Great Father sees all," Zynora said as she kissed the tips of her fingers and touched some of the charms dangling from her headdress. "And apparently, He isn't through with you yet."

Ayrion grimaced. "I don't know if that's a good thing or a bad thing."

Zynora smiled. "Time will tell."

Ayrion took another long sip from the hot cider. It warmed his insides, leaving a wonderful tingly sort of feeling in his arms. "We should be on our way."

Tameel paused in the middle of scratching the top of his white head. "Leave? We just got the fire going. I was about to make us a nice lunch."

"It'll have to be a fast one," Ayrion said. "Best we get as far from this place as possible. When Endric returns to what is left of his home, I don't want to be around to see what he does."

Tameel's eyes widened. "True enough." He rose and carried his seat back to the wagon, Ayrion and the others following suit.

It wasn't long before they'd managed to get everything repacked. They ate a quick meal of cold meat, fresh fruit, and some cheese, washed down with more of Zynora's spiced cider, and climbed back aboard the two wagons. Bek had to reharness the mare he'd ridden over to Talmanes's before they were ready. Apparently, young Taylis hadn't wanted his new horse to be used in case it got taken as well.

"Where to?" Bek asked, climbing up onto the front seat of the red wagon and looking excited about the prospect of getting back on the open road. As a trapper, Bek had a love for roaming about, adventuring in new places, taking in the sights.

And with his wife actually in the position to want to join him—for the first time—
Bek looked as giddy as a young schoolboy skipping classes to catch frogs.

"We head north to Wellhollow," Tameel said from the front seat of Ol' Lerra.
"As long as the passes remain clear."

Bek nodded and snapped the reins, and the two wagons slowly pulled out and
started back up the road.

Chapter 25 | Kira

"QUIET," KIRA SAID as she sat down at the table inside the meeting room for the heads of the Warren clans. "I can hardly hear myself think."

She looked around the table at the hardened faces staring back at her. All four heads of the Warren clans were in attendance. The meeting room was near the main assembly hall and was used as a way to work out differences in a more civilized—less violent—fashion. If every argument was settled at the edge of a blade, there wouldn't be anyone left to lead.

It had been a long night. She'd spent most of it sitting in front of the fireplace in her chambers, still pondering over the meeting she'd had with Amarysia and Commander Tolin. She couldn't believe that the high queen had been there. It had been a few weeks, but she had thought of little since. Learning how Ayri had died and Dakaran's betrayal was something that had stuck with her.

The round table they used for their meetings had been created specifically by Kira shortly after taking her place as chief. It was something she had picked up from her time spent running with the street tribes and the tribal guild, a way of forcing everyone to face each other on equal footing, no one feeling like they were receiving preferential treatment.

There were five seats around the table, one for each of the four clans and a fifth for their chief. Engraved into the wood were four names: Tabesh, Azdak, Bedar, Kaiwin. Each named represented one of the four founding members of the

Warren underground.

"I skipped breakfast for this?" Shilvin grumbled on her right, picking at the pointed nails on his left hand with his dagger. He was the head of Clan Tabesh. "This better be worth it." He had a fondness for cutting faces with those nails. You could always tell who the newest members of his clan were by the smoothness of their skin. He had attempted to use them on Kira a few years back when she'd been working her way up the ranks of Clan Kaiwin. He was missing the smallest finger on his left hand for his troubles.

"Got somewhere better to be, Shilvin?" she responded with a glare, daring him to argue.

Wisely, he didn't. He simply flicked the tip of one nail with his finger and grinned up at Kerson, whose shadow was looming over the back of Kira's seat. Kerson had been the former head of Clan Tabesh, at least until Ayrion had defeated him during the Rite of Oktar. Shilvin had been quick to lay his claim to the position. A clan seat was won by combat. He had killed two men and one woman who had laid their swords in the ring for a right at the seat.

"What is it you wish to discuss, Chief?" Yorik asked from Kira's left. Yorik was the head of Clan Azdak. He wasn't as big as the others, but he was twice as devious. He wasn't much taller than Kira, with a strong chin, piercing green eyes, and light-brown hair cut unfashionably short to keep from having it used against him. He had fought his brother in the ring for their clan's seat. His brother had prided himself on his long wavy locks, and Yorik used them to his advantage by grabbing a handful and yanking him into his knife.

Yorik was now the head of their clan . . . and an only child.

"We need to discuss these kidnappings," she said. "More importantly, how we plan to deal with them."

"Why deal with them at all?" Tolferd asked, seated next to Yorik. He was the head of Bedar. "If what you say is true about what you found in the dungeons, I vote not to get involved. Best we don't stick our necks out for them to get chopped off," he said, laying his axe in front of him on the table.

Tolferd had always preferred the axe to the sword. He had a strong upper body, well built for swinging a top-heavy weapon. He was also the Warrens' executioner. He had a gift for taking a hand or arm, and in some cases a head, with a single blow. The executioner they had used prior to Tolferd would take two or three swings to get a complete cut. Even for the hardened criminals who lived down there, the screaming was more than what they could handle. Plus, it made cleaning up the mess that much harder.

Ren, who was sitting quietly on the other side of Shilvin to Kira's right, fidgeted as she watched the other three press Kira for more information. She was the head of Kaiwin, the clan Kira had led before taking her place as chief. Ren was tall for a woman, with dark-brown hair that hung to her shoulders, curling inward at the bottom. Her brown eyes were constantly on the move.

Kira had been surprised when Ren stuck her weapons in the ring for a chance at her clan's seat. She had been even more surprised when Ren won. The woman was nimble and quick, much faster than Kira would have given her credit for, something she had clearly kept hidden from the others, including her opponent. Her weapons of choice were her kamas, and she was very good with them. In fact, her challenger relinquished his claim before the fight had barely gotten started. She took his hand on her first swing, and he took off running before the second.

No one had seen him since.

"What do you have to say, Ren?" Kira asked, staring down the table at the woman. "You've been uncommonly quiet."

Ren leaned forward, resting her arms on the textured wood. "I agree with you. These kidnappings affect us all—"

"You agree with Kira?" Tolferd said with a laugh. "No surprise there."

Ren hissed and reached for her weapons.

"Enough," Kira said, pressing her thumbs to her temples. "You're giving me a headache. You two bicker like an old married couple."

Both Ren and Tolferd quieted at that, neither daring to look the other in the eye.

"The fact is, Ren's correct—this does affect us all. Aramoor is still our home. And these kidnappers have not only walked through the front door, they've gone from room to room looking for valuables to steal, and then had the gall to walk out with our children."

"How did your meeting go with Tolin?" Yorik asked, spinning his dagger on the table in front of him. "Will there be any help from the lancers?"

"Hardly," she said. "Tolin is no longer commander of anything. In fact, it seems those who were in a position to help are packing up and leaving Aramoor."

"Cowards," Yorik said with a sneer, stopping the knife's spin with his finger. "And they say we're the ones who are weak."

"This city's gone to the faeries," Tolferd said, his hand resting on the butt of his battle-axe. "And as much as I hate to admit it, we could have done a whole lot worse than old Rhydan. Too bad he had to go and get himself killed fighting Cylmarans."

Kira could feel Kerson staring a hole in the top of her head. But she wasn't about to mention the circumstances of their meeting with Tolin, and the possibility of treason on the part of Dakaran, at least not until she had had more time to consider the ramifications. Until then, she'd keep the clans in the dark. It wasn't a necessary piece of information to keep the Warrens running anyway.

"As it stands," she said, "we're on our own."

"How's that any different than it's always been?" Ren asked. "When have those up there given a bent copper about those of us down here? We've always handled our own business."

Ren was right. The Warrens had always preferred to deal with their own affairs. Although, Kira had to admit, she had been looking forward to Ayrion's help. Working with him again had given her hope. Now there was none. She tightened her grip on the arm of her chair as the feeling of loss overpowered her. She shoved it aside. She couldn't afford to be emotional. She'd already had her cry in the privacy of her chambers. Now it was time to get down to business.

"Here's my thoughts on—"

A knock on the door had her looking up from her seat. "Come!"

The door opened partway, and Po stuck his head in. "Sorry. Thought you might want to come see this. Gwen, Griff, and Preece captured three of the kidnappers last night, and they're just bringing them down now."

Perfect timing, she thought as she stood from her seat. "It appears our meeting will be moving to a different location."

The others stood eagerly and followed her out the door and down the hall to the main assembly room. All five took their seats on the platform. Kira sat at the top, watching the room begin to fill, everyone waiting anxiously for the metal door on the left to open.

Evidently, word had spread about who they were bringing in, and by the throng near the door and the shouts for "death" and raised weapons, Kira was afraid they might kill the prisoners before they made it to the front.

"Stand back!" she shouted, rising from her seat to get the people's attention. "Give them room! Anyone who lays a hand on the prisoners before we get a chance to question them will take their place in the barrel."

The very mention of the barrel was enough to get the crowd moving. They parted down the middle, leaving a wide-open walkway from the door to the front of the platform.

Kira retook her seat as soon as the circular door swung open on grating hinges and a set of armed guards stepped through, including Gwen, Griff, and Preece. Griff was still healing from the burns he'd received during their battle in the palace dungeons. Reevie and Sapphire had done a remarkable job not only of saving his life but also getting him back on his feet in such a short time.

Po met them at the entrance and escorted their prisoners to the front of the room. The prisoners wore the same black robes Kira had seen the others in before, but this time their hoods were not up to conceal their faces.

All three looked like they'd suffered numerous punches to the face before arriving. The bruises had already begun to darken. One had a nose that was bent awkwardly to the side, blood still seeping from the right nostril.

The men dragged them in and kicked all three in the back of their legs. The prisoners collapsed to their knees in front of the stage. Whoever they were, they seemed more angry than frightened. Belligerent even. The man with the broken nose spit up at the platform, receiving a boot in the face for his effort. He screamed and tried covering his nose.

Surprisingly the kick had somehow popped it back into place. Kira hid a smile, noting it didn't look quite so crooked now. She leaned forward and looked at the crowd. "You would have thought that after our last raid, these imbeciles"—she pointed at the three prisoners—"would have had enough common sense to at least wait a few weeks before jumping right back into their kidnappings." She shook her head as she stared down at the three men. "Who sent you?"

The prisoners didn't open their mouths. In fact, they shut them, tightening their lips in defiance.

She nodded. "How many of you are there?"

Nothing.

"I see you have forgotten how to speak." She scooted to the edge of her seat and smiled. "We have ways to help with that." She looked at Po. "Take them to the barrel."

The excitement in the room grew as the prisoners were hauled to their feet and dragged up the center tunnel, passing the clan heads' meeting room on the way. The crowd pressed in tight as they followed the prisoners down the stone corridor.

They passed rooms of all shapes and sizes, most used for storage: food, clothing, materials, even the vault, where those in the clans kept their most prized possessions that they didn't want to simply leave lying around for someone else to steal.

The processional stopped a few doors down from the end of the hall. Po opened a door on the left and waited for Kira and the other heads to make their way to the front. Kira was the first through, followed by Shilvin, Tolferd, Ren, and Yorik.

The room smelled strongly of sage, covering most of the faint metallic smell that lingered from the last time it was used. No matter how many times they scrubbed the floor or burned incense after each session, the stench never quite seemed to leave.

Like the floor, the walls were lined with grey stone. Torches flickered in their brackets around the outer edge and on either side of the door, casting harsh shadows across those that were gathered inside. The room was no bigger than the storage rooms they had passed, and only slightly smaller than her chambers. However, unlike the others, this room was empty, save for an enormous barrel that had been turned over on its side.

"Bring the prisoners forward," she said, taking her place on the opposite side of the barrel from the rest of those who had pressed in to watch. The four heads stood to either side of her.

Po motioned for the guards to bring the three robed men forward.

The indignant expressions they bore inside the main hall were still present, as though engraved in stone. Their feet dragged on the floor, forcing the guards to shove them the rest of the way. All three took a moment to study the gigantic container, noticing the dark stain that smeared most of the outside. A hint of fear sparked in two of the men's eyes. The one with the broken nose was too enraged, and no doubt in too much pain, to show anything but hatred. Kira figured he must be the leader. He was also the one she'd use for an example.

She found it was always more efficient to question more than one person at a time when possible. Find the weakest and let them watch, and by the time it was their turn, the answers would pour from their mouth like water from a fountain. And she needed them to talk. The more information they got about what was happening up top, the better her chances of solidifying the clans' vote.

"Last chance," she said, holding her smile, hoping it was unsettling enough to encourage them to indulge her questions. She stepped forward and pointed to the man in the middle with the broken nose. "Him."

The guards on either side grabbed the man by the arms and dragged him forward. He cursed and spat the entire way, prophesying their coming demise. They walked him up a set of stairs to a small platform beside the barrel, while two other men moved around to a wheel at the back, connected to a contraption that both raised and lowered the enormous cask. The barrel was far too big to try maneuvering by hand. There was a large metal ring around the center of the barrel. The ring was connected to an arm that in turn was connected to a set of gears, which spun when the wheel was turned, raising the container into place.

The two men turned the wheel, and the barrel was lifted to a standing position, its rim rising just a few inches above the platform where the prisoner was being held. The lid was lying off to the side, which allowed the prisoner a chance to see what was inside.

At present, it was empty.

"I'll ask you again," Kira said, looking up at the man on the platform. "Who sent you?"

The man spat into the barrel. "Burn in Aran'gal."

Kira held her smile. She'd known the man wasn't going to speak. She was counting on it. "Bring them."

Po motioned to a couple of men near the back, and they hefted a large wicker basket through the crowd.

Kira had found the idea of the barrel repugnant at first, but over the years she had grown accustomed to its purpose. Both the inside and outside of the barrel had been made use of. Men and women had been tied to it and lashed, or cut, or simply rolled over as the barrel's immense weight crushed them. Others were stuck inside before they filled the barrel with a variety of things like water, boiling oil, or broken glass. Once inside, the lid would be sealed and the wheel turned, rotating the barrel over and over and over again, until the one inside was dead.

Before Kira had risen in rank to head of the clans, they had gone so far as to use rats in the barrel, heating the outside to the point that the rats nearly went crazy, clawing and eating their way through whoever was inside.

Kira hated rats. It was one of the first things to go when she took her seat.

Needless to say, no one had ever survived the barrel without spilling their guts, either figuratively or literally.

The particular practice they were about to indulge was one of her creations. It was a much cleaner form of torture.

The two men carried the basket up the steps to the top of the platform, where they set it down beside the prisoner and opened the lid. She could hear the hissing from where she stood. The defiant prisoner's eyes widened, but he remained where he was.

"Those are horned asps," she said. "Caught in the Slags and bred for one purpose: to inflict pain. I've seen men chew their own tongues off with just a single bite from one of these creatures." She nodded at the two men holding the basket, and they poured the snakes inside the barrel.

The snakes' poison would not kill, but one bite from a horned asp would make you wish you were dead.

"I'll not ask you again. Tell me who sent you." She didn't care if the first man talked or not, as long as one of them did. And after seeing the horrific experimentation that they had been performing on those they'd kidnapped, she almost didn't care if they talked at all. They deserved to suffer.

The prisoner on the platform tightened his fists, his eyes sharp as a razor. He bowed his back in defiance as he looked her in the eyes. "You'll never stop what's coming." And before she could order the guards to throw him in, he jumped in himself.

To say she was surprised would have been an understatement. She stood there with mouth gaping. Looking around the room, she wasn't the only one. She didn't know what to say, and clearly neither did anyone else, since the only noise in the room were the screams coming from inside the barrel.

High-pitched squeals and shrieks erupted from the barrel, setting the hairs on her arms on end. First, they came in long drawn-out waves, then in short bursts. Kira started to wonder if they would ever stop.

Eventually, they did, and the room went silent.

Normally, those watching would have been cheering, calling out wagers as to how long the man would last, but this time was different. No one said a word, all eyes on the barrel.

"Well, that was unexpected," she said.

"What do you think he meant by *we'll never stop what's coming?*" Yorik asked cautiously.

This was going horribly wrong. She was supposed to scare the prisoners into talking, not her own people. She needed to do something before she lost the entire room. Taking a step toward the barrel, she turned and looked at the other two prisoners. "Next!"

One after the other, they walked the prisoners up to the platform, questioned them unsuccessfully, and watched as they threw themselves inside.

"Clearly, they are more afraid of whoever they work for than us," Shilvin said, scraping the side of the barrel with his nails.

"I don't know if I should be impressed or terrified by that fact," Kira said as she started around the barrel, Kerson in her wake. "Slit their throats if they're still alive and get rid of the bodies." The poison from one asp wasn't enough to kill, but with repeated strikes, she doubted they'd survive.

The crowd parted as she headed for the door; the look on her face was enough to keep them quiet as she passed. She needed to do some thinking. Whatever was going on, it was bigger than some secret sect of wielders experimenting on people. The man's final words kept playing over and over in her mind.

You'll never stop what's coming.

Shutting the door to her chambers, she walked over to her bed, grabbed a pillow, and screamed into it. At least one good thing had come from this. It was clear the Warrens was going to need to get more involved, and after a display like this, the other heads were sure to agree that they needed to take a stronger stance with these kidnappings.

Chapter 26 | Amarysia

ARE WE SURE WE KNOW what we're doing?" Asa whispered to the other three, keeping his voice lowered so as not to be heard by their rather shifty-looking escorts. "I've heard stories of this place that'll grow hair on your back." He looked at Amarysia and cleared his throat. "I mean no offense, of course."

Amarysia chuckled. "None taken." She knew Asa to be one of the most forthright of Tolin's former captains, with a reputation for his gruff exterior, but as loyal as a setter hound. Asa was shorter than the other two men, with a red ducktail beard and leather patch over one eye. He looked like a man who'd seen one too many battles and lived to tell about it. "Besides," she added, "I think the last thing Barthol needs is more hair."

Asa laughed, and so did Tolin.

"You got that right," Barthol said. "I've got plenty enough to go around." Barthol looked more animal than man lately, with the heavy whiskers on his face he'd let grow to mask his appearance in public, since he was supposed to be dead.

"You've actually been here before?" Tolin asked, walking to Amarysia's right. He wasn't quite as tall as Barthol, but he was still a good head over Asa. Tolin had a strong face, very handsome, with a well-groomed beard that was showing his age. Streaks of grey ran through his dark hair, gathering around the temples and filtering toward the back, which gave him a very distinguished look.

She nodded. "Yes. Not exactly a place I'd care to revisit, if I'm honest. The last time I was there, I was nearly killed. A man standing behind me had a knife plunged into his chest. Not exactly fond memories."

"How'd you manage to get out?"

"Ayrion." She didn't need to say more.

Barthol, who'd remained mostly quiet up until this point, tugged on his lengthening whiskers. "I can see why you wouldn't want to return." He looked at the others. "So, is it wise for us to be going there now? We could have had this meeting at my place."

Asa hmphed. "And let the heads of the Warren clans see exactly where you live? Yes, that's a brilliant idea."

"Especially now that Tirana and I are sharing that same dwelling with you," Tolin added.

"I've been meaning to ask how that was going," Asa said with a sheepish grin as he spared a passing glance at Barthol. "Surprised you didn't kick this ornery ol' cuss out weeks ago. I've had to share a tent with him on more than one occasion." He pinched his nose. "Not a pleasant experience."

"Shut it," Tolin threatened, "or I'll tell them about the time you—"

"Okay, okay," Asa said, throwing up his hands in surrender. "You win."

"You don't even know what I was going to say."

"Don't need to. I'm sure whatever it is, it's best left unmentioned."

"Wonderful," Amarysia said. "Now I'm going to spend the rest of the night wondering what you were going to tell us."

The three men chuckled.

The old city was covered in darkness, no streetlights to guide the way on a moonless night. The only light came from the lanterns their guides carried to keep from wandering off the path and getting lost, which would have been easy to do since all the old buildings looked the same. The only sounds were the haunting echoes of their feet as they trudged along the broken cobbles between old brick and stone of what had once been the origins of Aramoor back during the time of King Torrin himself.

Now, this lonely part of the lower town saw nothing but vagrants, pickpockets, and cutmen. Only the brave, or the very stupid, wandered these streets. The last time Amarysia had been here, it hadn't been of her own volition. Their party was being led by the same tall, angular, dark-haired man that had participated in her and Ayrion's capture the first time. The same man Ayrion had left naked in Kira's bed. He had been a childhood acquaintance of Ayrion's; she believed his name was Po.

They came to a stop just outside what looked like a large stone latrine.

Amarysia knew it for what it was: one of the entrances to the Warren underground. This time it felt different, though. This time she was here by her own choice, not bound and gagged and dragged bodily into the depths below. Still, it didn't mean that their visit wasn't dangerous. She knew from personal experience that any time she had dealings with the Warrens, she was likely putting her life on the line. She only hoped that once inside, Tolin and the others wouldn't react in a way that would see them never being allowed to leave.

The door to the latrine opened, and Po stepped inside.

"You don't expect us to go climbing in there, do ya?" Asa said, his mouth gaping. "I ain't crawling around in no hundred-year-old dung."

"It's not what you think," Amarysia said over her shoulder as she waited for her turn to step in. She could hear Asa grumbling behind her as she walked through the rusty door and down the winding stairs toward the bottom landing. The moldy smell of moist dirt was only cut by the strong scent of pitch rising from the torches on the wall.

The steps leading down into the Warrens were smooth, the corners rounded from centuries of use. Soon enough, she circled the final bend and reached the bottom, stepping out of the tunnel and into the round antechamber where she found herself waiting in front of the enormous metal disc that was the door leading into the Warrens. Ayrion had been right—the pattern of crisscrossing lines engraved on the door did appear to be some sort of map, possibly of the tunnels themselves. Who knew how extensive they were and how far they ran under the city?

A pair of muscular sentries stood watch at the entrance, waiting for the rest of their party to make it out of the tunnel before opening. Barthol was the last, nearly bumping his head on the archway leading into the antechamber.

"Quite the place you have here," Asa remarked to no one in particular.

Po stepped forward and cleared his throat.

"*When hope is all but lost,*
And light has turned to dark.
There will a sign be given,
The rising of the marked."

The two guards grabbed the wheel at the center and began to spin it to the right. A loud grating sound filled the room as whatever mechanism that held the door in place slowly released its grip. The circular disc parted slightly, and the two men pulled, their muscles tightening as the door swung fully open.

Tolin, Asa, and Barthol moved up to flank her, their hands close enough to their weapons to be drawn at a moment's notice. She smiled. Even knowing that they were there by request of the clans' chief, she felt a whole lot safer having three battle-hardened veterans standing at her side.

They followed Po through the door and into the main hall, which was filled wall to wall with people. It was a proper Warrens welcome, one that left her weak in the knees as they walked through the onslaught of the city's dregs. The men's leering eyes had Amarysia scooting as close to Tolin as she could without tripping him. She had tried to dress more modestly, knowing where they were heading, but apparently it hadn't been enough.

The crowd parted just enough to leave a narrow walkway from the door to the front of the main platform, where the heads of the clans sat waiting on their thronelike seats. Kira sat on the top tier all by herself. Below her sat two others, and below them two more.

It didn't take the positioning of the seating to set the heads of the clans apart; their dress alone was enough to tell they held some form of notoriety.

Unlike the threadbare clothing worn by most of the men and women they'd passed on their way to the platform, these five seemed dressed to imitate royalty, their garments an interesting mix and match of attire thrown together by people who'd clearly never been trained in any real high society. Cravats that didn't match vests, belts that didn't match boots, hats that didn't match with any other stitch of clothing they wore. It almost seemed that the more ridiculous the items they put on, the higher class they felt they appeared.

If they were to have attended any real social gatherings, they'd have been thrown out by the butlery before making it through the front door.

Kira was the only one of the lot who looked like she had an ounce of common sense when it came to clothing. However, she wouldn't have made it past the front gate with what she was wearing. She reminded Amarysia of Ayrion. She wore the same long leather jacket with matching pants and boots. The only difference was the color. Unlike Ayrion's, which were raven black, hers were blood red, a sharp contrast to her thick raven hair, which hung halfway down her back. Kira certainly stood out from the rest, which Amarysia had no doubt was the clan chief's intention.

Why had Ayrion chosen to be with Amarysia when he had someone like Kira desiring his company? They seemed to have been a perfect match, not to mention they shared a past. Amarysia clutched a wad of her dress and tried pushing those thoughts aside. They were meaningless now, and the last thing she needed here was to start getting choked up.

"Well, if it isn't the mighty Tolin, come to pay us poor souls a visit," one of the men sitting on the platform said. There was something off about his fingers.

The tips looked more like claws than nails. "Oh, how the mighty have fallen."

Tolin looked puzzled at first. His expression said he recognized the speaker but wasn't sure where from.

"I see you no longer wear the king's crest," the man mocked. "What a pity."

Tolin's eyes brightened. "And I see they give deserters and cowards a place of notoriety down here."

The man on the platform sneered. "I was no deserter! I was relieved of duty. By you!"

Tolin showed no sign of emotion. "Yes, if memory serves me, you had a problem with killing."

"Hah!" The clan head gripped the hilt of his sword as he stared Tolin down. "That's what we were paid to do."

"Yes. But you tended to enjoy it a little too much."

The clan head glared for a moment, then his face softened into a smirk. "A man should take pride in his work."

"And when that man starts wearing his work around like a trophy, he ceases being a man and becomes a rabid animal."

The clan head seethed as he pointed to a group of men near the front. Next thing Amarysia knew, she was being shoved to the back, behind Tolin, Asa, and Barthol as several armed men rushed their position. Tolin's and Barthol's swords were already in hand, and Asa's axe was in motion.

Kira shouted for them to stop, but it was too late. By the time she regained control of those around the platform, all six of the cutmen were lying dead, and Tolin had rushed the stage. The man with the strange clawlike nails didn't even get a chance to draw his weapon before Tolin had the edge of his sword pressed to his neck. The man slunk back in his seat, not willing to do much more than growl.

"Enough!" Kira shouted, turning to the monster of a man on her left, who Amarysia recognized as the man Ayrion had defeated the last time she set foot in the Warrens. "Kerson! Kill the next person who makes a move on my guests."

Kerson moved down to the front of the stage, wielding an axe that was at least twice the size of Asa's. He was even bigger than Barthol, if that was possible.

Kira stood. "If I see another weapon drawn in this chamber, I'll stick that person in the barrel! You got that?"

Those closest to the platform quickly scooted back, giving the newcomers plenty of space. Whatever the barrel was, it was clearly something that the rest of the room wanted nothing to do with.

Kira looked at the clan head Tolin had pinned to his seat. "Shilvin! I have half a mind to let him finish the job. You picked a fight with the wrong man. Now apologize so we can get down to business."

The words were practically dragged from his mouth, but in the end Shilvin did manage a mediocre apology, which sounded more like he was sorry for having failed than for having tried in the first place. But it was enough for Tolin to release him and take his place alongside Amarysia and the others.

Tolin wiped the blood from his sword on one of the fallen's cloaks, then turned and looked at her. "You all right?"

"I'm fine," Amarysia said, still in shock at how fast the battle had taken place, and how quickly it had ended.

"These four have free rein of the Warrens," Kira said to those gathered. "They are under my protection."

Whispers trickled through the crowd, but nothing loud enough for Amarysia to understand.

Kira turned back to those huddled around the front and raised her arms. "Welcome to the Warrens, Commander Tolin, Overcaptain Asa, Captain Barthol." She looked at Amarysia and added, "And hussy." There was a friendly sort of smile on her face as she said it. She walked down the platform steps to stand in front of them. "You were gracious enough to open your home to me. What kind of host would I be if I refused to do the same?" She opened her arms out toward the main hall. "My home is yours."

"Our gratitude at the warm welcome," Tolin said.

Asa coughed.

Barthol stood there in silence, as he and Kerson seemed to be in the middle of a stare-off as the two looked each other over. They both stood head and shoulders over the rest. Kerson maintained his grip on his axe, and Barthol kept his on his sword. Overcaptain Asa and Commander Tolin might have been military trained, but Barthol had been trained by Ayrion. Amarysia had no doubt he could take care of himself, even against someone as big as Kerson.

Kira walked down the steps of the platform and wrapped her arms around Amarysia, whispering in her ear. "It's good to see you again." She stepped back to address those on stage. "Come, we have discussions to attend to." She turned to all those gathered. "You're dismissed."

The crowd slowly dissipated to their respective tunnels, most keeping an eye on the stage to see if there would be any more skirmishes. Several stayed behind to clean up the bodies lying near the bottom step.

"If you'll follow me," Kira said, starting for the tunnel behind the left side of the stage. The drapery hanging over this particular tunnel's entryway had been drawn to the side to allow passage. Each of the six tunnels leading off the meeting room held similar draperies, each with their own colors and crests.

This particular tapestry bore the image of a large black cat on a field of red. It was a ferocious-looking creature, claws up and ready for the kill. She'd seen a similar beast at the palace during one of Dakaran's feasts. It had been brought in by a traveling circus to entertain the guests, and she remembered the attendees being more frightened than entertained.

They passed by the tunnel Amarysia and Ayrion had taken the last time she'd been in the Warrens. Its colors were plum and bronze, and the crest on the front was of an enormous bird with wings spread and talons poised.

Kira and Kerson were the first into the tunnel, Kerson ducking under the tapestry and holding it high enough for the other four heads of the clans to follow suit. Amarysia walked just behind Tolin, with Asa and Barthol bringing up the rear. Po was the last through, keeping a close eye on Amarysia's party. He tended to glance away anytime he caught her looking. She wondered if he was still embarrassed about her last visit, when he had ended up naked in Kira's bed.

Guards stood outside most of the doors on this particular tunnel's corridor. Kira stopped in front of one on the right, and the guard quickly unlocked and opened it for them to pass. The room was made of stone, with a rather tall ceiling despite being underground, with a fire roaring in the hearth. Amarysia wondered how far up the flue went in order to release the smoke. Their walk down from the privy above had been fairly extensive.

"Please, take your seats," Kira said, motioning to a large circular table at the center of the room. Enough seating had been arranged for everyone to get their own, and still there was room left over. It was quite an impressive piece of furniture.

Amarysia took her seat, taking a moment to read the inscription carved in the wood: *Kaiwin*. She wondered if it was the name of one of the clan heads. It seemed feminine. She passed a quick glance across the table to the only female clan head in the room besides Kira.

The woman nodded in return but didn't smile. She was lithe of build and dressed in similarly ill-matched fashion as her male counterparts, including a rather bold choice of gold, violet, and white. Very few of the women in the Warrens wore dresses, and this Kaiwin was clearly no exception, but she did seem to favor more lace around the collars and cuffs than the men.

Amarysia joined the others in taking a small sip from the chalice in front of her seat. It was a deep-red wine that warmed her insides. She relaxed against the high back of her chair as she waited for Kira to begin formal introductions.

Kira went around the table from right to left, giving everyone's name, title, and rank—or in the case of Tolin, Asa, and Barthol, their former rank. Amarysia soon discovered that what she thought was a clan head's proper name was the name of the woman's clan. She was glad to finally put names to the faces staring back at her. Surprisingly, Kira had introduced Amarysia by her proper name, and even included her title as chief lady-in-waiting to the queen, as opposed to her usual term of endearment.

"I've asked our guests to join us this evening," Kira said, looking to her right, where Tolin, Amarysia, Asa, and Barthol sat, "to discuss the changes taking place within our fair city, including these recent kidnappings. I also wanted my clan heads to hear firsthand the information you presented to us during our last meeting. There's still some debate as to whether such a meeting even occurred."

There was some grumbling over near Shilvin's side of the table.

"Most didn't believe me when I told them that the Queen Mother herself had been in attendance. Not that I blame them. If Yorik over there," she said, pointing to the shortest of the clan heads—he had brown hair cut short enough to be almost shaven and shifty green eyes that spoke of someone you didn't want to turn your back on—"had told me he'd been in a secret meeting with the Queen Mother, I'd have slit his throat for lying." She noticed the look of horror on Amarysia's face and recanted. "Fine, I wouldn't have slit his throat, maybe just pulled a toenail or two." Kira smiled playfully. She seemed to enjoy getting a rise out of Amarysia.

Kira turned to Tolin. "Having you here, Commander, I believe, is proof enough for my fellow clansmen that such a meeting did indeed occur." She sat silently staring at the commander as though waiting for a confirmation.

Tolin leaned forward with a nod as he looked across the table at the other heads. "She is correct. We did meet to discuss some very troubling events, and yes, even though unexpected, Queen Ellise was in attendance, since the news was that of the events surrounding the death of her husband."

The clan heads seemed satisfied with Tolin's answer, all but Shilvin, who wasn't going to be satisfied with anything that had to do with his former commanding officer. He sat quietly with his head back against his seat while picking at the tips of his sharpened nails.

Kira turned and addressed her fellow clansmen. "What was not mentioned in our previous session was that there was treason on the battlefield with Cylmar. Treason from within the king's own family."

The other heads sat quietly as she filled them in on what had truly taken place. Even Shilvin stopped picking at his nails long enough to listen.

"Dakaran was the one responsible for the king's and the guardian's deaths." Kira tightened her grip on the stem of her goblet. Amarysia wasn't sure if anyone else picked up on it.

"Good riddance if you ask me," Shilvin said. "One king's as bad as another, and Ayrion was nothing more than the king's lapdog."

Kira launched her goblet straight at Shilvin's head. He barely ducked as the goblet smacked against the headboard, showering him with wine and staining the front of his green-and-gold doublet. He started to draw his sword but stopped.

"Just give me an excuse," she said. Two daggers had already appeared in her hands as if by magic.

The others sat and watched. Tolin had his sword halfway out of its scabbard, waiting to see what happened. One look around the table, and Shilvin sheathed his sword.

"What was that for?" he finally asked, slowly regaining his composure.

"That was for being an oaf! In case you didn't notice, Rhydan and Ayrion were the only ones willing to help the Warrens. Whether you liked the king or not, he was good for us. Dakaran's backside has warmed the throne two months, and look where the city is now. People afraid to leave their homes at night. Riots in the streets. Men roaming through Cheapside kidnapping anyone they see, white uniforms everywhere we look. This city has gone to the Pits. And if you're too stubborn or too stupid to realize we are all in this mess together, then you don't deserve a seat at this table."

Shilvin leaned forward, his eyes fierce. "No one has the right to get rid of a clan head, except that clan. Not even you," he added with an open note of contempt.

Kira took a deep breath and released. "Perhaps not. But if you don't have the common sense to see what's right in front of you, then it won't be long before your seat is challenged by another."

Shilvin didn't respond, just sat back in his seat and began picking at his nails again.

Amarysia's heart was pounding. How in the name of Aldor did Kira live like this? They'd been there barely an hour and already they'd killed a handful of men and almost had a standoff between clan heads. This was a terrible way to live life, always looking over one's shoulder, never knowing when someone was going to stab you in the back.

"Kira is correct," Tolin said. "We are all in this together."

"Aye," Asa interjected. "With those flaming sons of goat suckers, the Black Watch, taking up permanent residence, ain't none of us safe. The White Tower's taken over the entire city. If you ask me, it might be best if we were to get out while the gettin's good."

"That's coward's talk," Ren said, glaring across the table at Asa. "And you don't look like a coward."

Asa stiffened in his seat. "No, I look like a man with enough experience to know when to draw a weapon and when not to. Wars aren't necessarily won by the brave, but by those who know when to walk away."

Ren looked confused. "Explain."

"There comes a time when the smartest move is to not move at all, but to wait for the other side to move. That way they might just tip their hand."

Ren and Asa stared at each other from over the table, neither speaking. Amarysia couldn't exactly tell what either was thinking. They almost seemed to be measuring each other. It grew awkward enough that Tolin finally spoke up.

"What my illustrious friend is trying to point out is that we barely know who the players are, let alone what they intend to do. If this had just been Dakaran, I might have seen his reason for getting rid of me and Asa. We were loyal to his father, and he wouldn't want us around after his succession. But that wouldn't account for his sudden decision to disband not only the High Guard but most of the Elondrian Lancers as well, replacing them with none other than the Tower's guards. There's more at play here than we know."

"Perhaps that's what they meant by *we won't be able to stop what's coming,*" Tolferd said.

"What's he referring to?" Barthol asked. It was the first time he'd spoken since they'd entered the room. Amarysia had almost forgotten he was even there.

Kira proceeded to tell the four of their experience with the kidnappers they had captured the night before, who'd been spotted wandering through the city, looking for more victims. She finished with their last words just before killing themselves.

By the time she finished, Amarysia had to rub the hairs on her arms back down.

"You mentioned having a few senators you trusted enough to confide in," Kira said, looking to Tolin. "Is that still the case? Have you managed to reach out to them as of yet?"

Tolin shook his head. "I've spent the last couple weeks trying to relocate. As soon as I can make safe arrangements, I'll find a way to reach them. We must be careful, though. The wrong word in the wrong ear, and we could find ourselves being hunted by the crown."

"And what is it you expect to tell them?" Yorik asked, his bright-green eyes glued to Tolin. He looked to be calculating some dark and devious plot. Something about him gave Amarysia the chills, even more so than Shilvin and his pointed claws.

"The Senate is the only body, other than the Provincial Authority, that has the power to overturn the king's decisions. If they were to find out that he had committed treason, they could act."

"And how do you expect them to act?" Yorik asked. "It's always been my belief that those in power tend to want to stay that way, which always leads them to act in their own self-interest. Is it in their interest to depose Dakaran, or to use him?

Let's face it. He's a pathetic sort of human being, weak as water and bendable as a hook worm."

Asa burst out laughing. "He's got ol' Dakaran pegged, that's for flaming sure."

"Yes," Tolin said thoughtfully, "but put enough wind behind it and water can be one of the most destructive forces we know. Caution is warranted. But there are times when taking a risk is as well. It is true there are many on the Senate who I wouldn't trust with my privy pan, but there are those that I would trust with my life."

"It's not just your life that's at stake," Ren said, her eyes continually drifting over to Asa.

"Then it's a right good thing we have someone on the inside," Asa said with a stout clap on Amarysia's shoulder that had all eyes turning in her direction.

Her tongue was suddenly as dry as old book leather. She couldn't even find enough spit to swallow as she attempted a smile, but it was so forced she was sure everyone in the room could see right through it. "I . . . I will do my best," she finally managed to squeak out.

"No one expects more," Tolin said.

"Aye," Barthol agreed with an encouraging wink. "Ayrion trusted you. The queen trusts you. That's good enough for us."

"Yes," Asa agreed. "Getting close enough to that pig sucker to find out what they're up to could very well prove to be the most important role of us all."

"So, no pressure, then."

Kira studied her from across the table. Amarysia couldn't tell if she was judging whether Amarysia was up to the task, or if there was something else ticking away in that methodical brain of hers. With Kira, she never knew.

The chieftain finally turned to Tolin. "We are agreed, then, that the next step is to reach out to your contacts within the Senate and let them know of Dakaran's treachery?"

Tolin nodded. "Agreed."

The meeting continued a while longer, everyone discussing possible strategies on how to best deal with these kidnappers. Everyone had their own opinions as to what the kidnappers had meant by not being able to stop what was coming. The only thing everyone could agree on was that they couldn't agree on anything, so the meeting was adjourned with the knowledge that another would be set for some point in the future.

Amarysia felt almost faint as she rose from the table, Asa's words playing over in her mind: that she might very well have the most important role of all.

Chapter 27 | Ty

IT HAD TAKEN NEARLY two days to finally break free of the tall grass, and another five days across rugged terrain for them to reach the foothills of the mountains they had first seen after Breen dragged Ty out of the river. For all their walking, they still had no idea where the mirror had transported them.

The mountains that had at one time loomed in the distance now stood before them like a great wall, blocking their way. Ty had expected to find the lower plains filled with mountain pine, like he'd seen surrounding the foothills of the Angoran Mountains back home. Instead, he found nothing but sporadic patches of dry, yellow grass across large chunks of grey rock.

They had found what looked like a small road leading from the plains toward the peaks ahead and decided to see where it went. So far, it seemed to be traveling in the same direction the compass was leading.

"I'm starving," Ty said, feeling the all-to-familiar rumble in his gut. They'd eaten most of what was left of the rabbit Breen had killed two days prior.

"I'm more worried about water," Breen said. They hadn't come across a clean spring in over a day, and with as much walking as the brothers were doing, water tended to get used fairly quickly.

"Any guess as to what we'll find at the end of this trail?" Ty asked, long tired of the continuous crunch of rock underfoot or the constant thump of his sword against his leg.

"No idea," Breen said. "But from the ruts, we might find a small village. Looks as though this trail has seen a steady flow of wagons at some point, which generally means civilization." He shrugged. "Or it could just be an old mining outpost, and the workers have gone home for the winter."

"I hope it's a village," Ty said. "We're running low on supplies, and I wouldn't mind sleeping in a bed for once, or even a nice pile of straw." Sleeping in the outdoors back home wasn't too difficult, with easy access to fallen leaves, pine needles, or thick grass, but the only thing they seemed to be able to grow around here was rock and more rock. What was worse, Ty had lost his bedding along with his pack, which meant he had to share with his very large brother. He just hoped they were able to find some sort of shop where they could replenish some of what had been lost.

By late afternoon, they crossed over a small ridge and caught their first glimpse of what lay ahead: a wall of sheer stone. At the base was a haphazard collection of ramshackle dwellings that could barely be described as a settlement, let alone a village.

"Not too promising," Ty said. The road they were traveling led straight through the center of the buildings and directly into what appeared to be a large fissure in the side of the mountain. It was too far away to see how far in it went. "Looks like you were right. Some kind of mining community." He watched some of the people inside milling about. "Looks like they haven't left for the winter yet. What do you think they're mining?"

Breen hefted his pack a little higher on his shoulders. "Let's go find out."

They followed the trail toward the first cluster of buildings ahead, each step weighing heavily on Ty's nerves. What few patches of grass there had been poking up between the rock disappeared. There were no sounds of birds or even insects, not that they'd seen much of either on their way across, but there was a stillness about this place that left Ty on edge.

The townsfolk had apparently seen them coming and assembled a welcome party just outside the first of the dwellings. They were about the poorest-looking people Ty had ever seen. Their clothes were extremely threadbare, and their skin had dark spots that Ty had at first thought must have been from whatever they had been mining for, but on closer inspection he realized it wasn't dirt or dust, but strange patches of discolored skin. It was on their hands, arms, necks, and faces.

"I don't like this," Ty whispered to Breen, trying not to move his lips. "They look sick."

"Greetings!" an older woman near the front said and took a couple of steps toward them. She hunched as she walked, balancing her weight with a simple wooden cane that bore the same discolored blotches. Straight white hair draped her back and shoulders like a thin shawl, and her dark-brown eyes seemed to look right through him.

Ty almost took a step back, but he managed to hold his ground. Whatever was wrong with these people, he didn't want to get too close and wind up catching it. "My name is Tirana. Welcome to Karpaath." The old woman's smile looked a little too eager. Her words were in Aldoran, but they seemed strange, an accent Ty wasn't used to hearing. "The last stop before you enter. It has been many moons since a paladin has ventured here. And today we are blessed with two." She threw up her arms. "There will be celebrating tonight!"

Cheers rose behind her, cheers that had Ty wanting to turn and run. These people here were cracked in the head. For all he knew, their idea of celebrating was to cook him and Breen for dinner. "This is a bad idea, Breen."

"Don't see we have that much of a choice. That compass of yours sent us here, so this is where we need to be." He turned and looked at Ty. "Just don't get too close."

"Come," Tirana said, motioning for them to follow.

With little other option, they started after the miners.

From closer up, the place did appear to be a small village, a very rundown, unkempt village, where the buildings seemed to be as in need of repair as those dwelling in them. Ty poked his brother in the side and pointed toward the front of one of the first buildings they passed.

Breen nodded. "Yeah, I see it." The wooden planks were covered with the same dark blotches as the townsfolk.

People up and down the street stepped out of their homes to get a look at the newcomers. One look at Ty and Breen, and they all fell in line behind them, some clapping, some even going so far as to dance in the street as they formed a parade through town behind them.

"What is wrong with these people?" Ty asked. "You'd think the high king had just come to town by the way they're acting."

Breen didn't say anything, just kept his eyes on those closest, while keeping one hand close to his sword.

They finally came to a stop outside the largest building in town. It was resting up against the side of the mountain, using the rock to keep it in place. And just like all the other buildings, it, too, was covered in dark splotches.

"One thing's for sure," Ty whispered to his brother. "We won't be getting any supplies here." They had now walked from one side of the village to the other, and there wasn't a single shop in sight. *How do they live?* he wondered.

Tirana waved the two brothers forward, and they slowly made their way through the crowd, doing their best to not brush up against any of the villagers.

They walked to the front of the procession and stepped up on the porch. "Tonight," she said, "we feast! For tomorrow, we die!"

Ty grabbed for his sword, stumbling backward away from the crowd. Breen grabbed a set of throwing knives out from his coat and joined him. They backed all the way to the front of the building, stopping just shy of the front wall.

"We don't want any trouble," Breen said, holding up his knives.

Ty was ready to cut down the first one of these crazy villagers that stepped foot on the porch. Without even thinking, he reached for his magic, letting the familiar heat spread through his body and out to his limbs.

The villagers suddenly went still.

Ty glanced over his shoulder at the mountain. They weren't too far from the fissure.

"Let's make a run for it." He caught Breen looking as well.

"Wait!" Tirana shouted, raising her hands submissively. "You misunderstand. We are not here to hurt you. We are here to help you."

Breen pointed at the old woman with one of his knives. "Talk fast." The old woman took a step toward the porch, and Breen raised the knife. "Don't come any closer. I'm warning you. I won't miss."

She didn't seem all that worried, but she stopped nonetheless before setting her foot on the first step up. "You are a paladin," she said, as if Ty or Breen had any idea what she was talking about. "We are the caretakers." She looked at the brothers as though she made perfect sense, as though everyone should have automatically understood what she was raving about.

"Caretakers to what?" Breen asked.

"To what lies beyond." She turned and pointed a crooked finger over to the opening in the mountainside. "We have been here for centuries guiding young seekers like yourselves toward their destiny, waiting for the day when the rightful heir would arrive." She looked at Ty when she mentioned *rightful heir*.

He lowered his sword. Something in the old woman's eyes, and of those gathered, read of desperation.

"Do you know why we're here?" Ty asked.

"Of course. We've been waiting for centuries for the true seeker to come and break the curse."

"Curse?" Ty shared a concerned look with Breen. "What curse?" As if this quest wasn't already dangerous enough.

"The curse that holds us captive, the curse that made us like this," she said, holding up her arm to point out the dark blotches. "We tried to steal the talisman from the wizards when they first placed it here, and our punishment has been to never leave this place until the true seeker recovers it. We've been waiting a long,

long time for someone to set us free."

Ty looked around at the dingy, desperate faces staring back at him. "What do you mean by never leave?"

"A boundary has been set around our village. It starts at the fissure and stops a little way beyond the first home you passed on your way in."

"How have you kept your village this size all these years," Breen asked, "and not outgrown the boundary?"

"Look around," the old woman said. "Do you see any youth? Do you see any children?" Ty hadn't really noticed until now, but she was right—the youngest looked to be no older than Breen. "We have been rendered incapable of reproducing."

Ty shook his head. "Then how have you managed to replenish your numbers?"

"We haven't," she said, looking at him like she couldn't understand why he wasn't getting it. "Our numbers have never changed."

"That's impossible," Ty said. "That would mean . . ."

The old woman's eyes brightened. "Ah, and now you understand. Not only are we unable to leave this place, and unable to reproduce, but we are unable to die as well." She took a step forward, clearly not caring whether Ty or Breen attempted to strike her down or not. If she couldn't die, there was little that the two brothers could do to stop them. Suddenly, Ty felt very vulnerable. "Please," she pleaded, arms outstretched as if begging for coin. "Please help us." Her focus was solely on Ty. "We can sense your magic. We know you are the one."

"How do you know—"

"We are bonded to it. We are bonded not only to the magic that keeps us here but to the magic that lies deep within the mountain." She looked at Breen. "He has it as well. But his is merely the spark of a candle compared to what burns within you. We have not seen such power, not since the wizards, and even they do not compare. You are the one we've been waiting for. Help us die."

As bizarre as someone asking you to help them die might have sounded, their earlier comments made a little more sense now. Breen looked at Ty, and Ty shrugged. "*Tonight, we feast, for tomorrow we die*," he said. "Well, *they* die. Not us. I don't want to die. At least, not yet."

Breen sighed and slowly lowered his knives, placing them back within the folds of his jacket as he took a couple of steps back, allowing Tirana up on the porch. Ty, too, sheathed his weapon and stood to the side, waiting to see what would happen next.

"Come," Tirana said as she opened the front door. "Tonight we feast."

Cautiously, Ty and Breen followed their host into the building, which turned out to be a large dining hall with a cooking pit set up in the center and a rusty spit overtop that didn't look to have seen much use in the last few decades. There were rows of tables lined with benches to either side. The villagers slowly filed in and gathered around the tables, each taking what looked to be an assigned seat.

Ty watched as the last of the villagers made it inside and took their seats. What did these people eat if they weren't able to leave the village? It wasn't like they could hunt for food. Except for the passing scavenger that might have the misfortune of wandering through their cursed little community, they had no way of feeding themselves.

Ty moved over beside Breen, who was resting against one of the larger posts holding the structure in place, and whispered. "Do you see any food?"

Breen looked around, as if noticing for the first time that the villagers were arriving empty-handed, and pursed his lips.

"Keep your knives ready," Ty said with a gulp, "just in case we turn out to be the main course after all."

Breen didn't exactly reach for his knives, but he did keep a close eye on the proceedings.

"Our guests of honor sit here," Tirana said from one of the tables closest to the open pit. There were two empty seats at the end across from her.

Ty looked at Breen, not sure what to do.

"Better sitting at the table than on the spit, I guess," Breen said, and he started across the room for the empty chairs.

Ty groaned and chased after him. This was getting stranger by the moment. Breen laid his pack and bow down behind his seat and sat. Ty noted that he didn't remove the overcoat holding his knives. Ty, not having a pack of his own to carry, simply plopped down on the end, closest to Tirana.

He sat quietly, watching those across from him and wondering why everyone was sitting up to empty tables, staring down at nothing. He even went so far as to swipe his hand quickly across his section of the table just in case there was something that he wasn't seeing. He tried to hide the movement by pretending to stretch his arms.

The table was empty.

He looked at Tirana. "What are we—"

She raised her finger. "Wait."

Suddenly a blinding light filled the room. Ty closed his eyes, but it hardly helped. Whatever it was, it was warm and inviting, but as soon as it appeared, it faded away. Ty lowered his hands and took a moment for his eyes to readjust. As soon as they did, his mouth gaped wide.

The room, which had been bare cracked planks and wooden beams with empty tables and a dead cooking pit, was now bustling with life. The walls were made of plaster and lined with colorful draperies and large murals. An enormous chandelier hung from the ceiling, providing a brilliant glow across colorfully tiled floors. The table in front of him was suddenly filled with dishes of every variety he could imagine, and the flames dancing from the cooking fire to his right provided a comforting warmth he hadn't enjoyed since his time at Douina's.

Even the people had changed. Their spots were gone, their clothes no longer torn and ragged but clean and pressed. He looked down at himself to see if he'd changed as well, but it didn't appear so. He then looked at Breen, whose eyes were as wide as persimmons. "What just happened?"

Across the table, Tirana, who no longer looked like death warmed over but more like a loving grandmother, smiled. "I told you, tonight we feast."

Ty's stomach growled as he stared at the incredible spread in front of him. He grabbed what appeared to be a leg of mutton, or something that appeared to be mutton, from the closest tray, half expecting his hand to slip right through it. He thought this might be a vision, similar to the one he'd created at the East Inn during Performance Night, but it wasn't. It was real, the bone warm in his hands, the juices leaving his fingers moist.

He watched as Breen lifted a piece up to his mouth and took a bite.

His brother's eyes widened. "It's delicious."

Ty didn't wait to see if Breen dropped dead or suddenly grew spots on his own arm before he was stuffing the hunk of meat in his own mouth and biting down. The juices seeped from the corners of his mouth, warm and flavorful. There was a strange sweetness to it, like cherries. Very unique.

Breen immediately grabbed some long sausages and stuffed half of one into his mouth and bit down. The look of delight had Ty gleefully reaching for a sausage himself. There were puddings and pies of all shapes and sizes; fruits and vegetables of every known variety; wheels of cheese both strong and mild; roasted meat both familiar and not; loaves of bread, rolls, and pastries the likes of which would have made Peyla, Easthaven's central baker, green with envy. He doubted even Lord Barl could have managed such a banquet.

"How is this possible?" Ty tried asking amidst chewing. He'd just taken a slice of soft white bread, stuffed a cut of cold pork and cheese into it, and dipped it into some sort of mushroom gravy. His words were nearly unintelligible.

Tirana lowered her fork, which held a sizable piece of fresh trout. "We don't really know. Twice a day, our meals are provided to us. Of course, they are not all the likes of what you see here. These are only given on special occasions, days on which we receive new seekers like yourselves."

"How does . . . it . . . know we are here?"

Tirana stuffed the fish into her mouth. "No idea. How does the magic keeping us here know how to do anything? It was set up by wizards."

"Where are we, exactly?" Breen asked, working through a helping of roast venison garnished with black beans, carrots, and onion. "I don't recognize the mountain chain."

"These are the Mountains of Escalor."

Both Breen and Ty stopped chewing.

"Of what?" Ty asked. "I've never heard of any mountains by that name. What kingdom are we in?"

"What do you mean by kingdom? These lands belong to the Rupoor. Or at least they used to a thousand years ago. Don't know who they belong to now. It's been a while since we've had a new seeker come this way to tell us of what is going on in the outside world."

Breen looked as confused as Ty. Even a thousand years ago, the Five Kingdoms had still been in existence. "What part of Aldor are we in? North, South—"

"This isn't Aldor."

Ty dropped his fork, part of the sweet potato he'd been chewing falling back onto his plate. "What do you mean this isn't Aldor? Where else would we be?"

Several of the other villagers sitting close enough to listen lowered their utensils, apparently as curious as Ty and Breen.

"This is Nusala," Tirana said, looking more intrigued by the moment. "Where did you say you were from?"

"We're from Aldor," Ty said, trying to swallow the other half of his potato. "You know, the Five Kingdoms: Elondria, Sidara, Briston, Cylmar, and Keldor. We are from Easthaven, the capital of Sidara."

Tirana looked inquisitively around the table at those seated nearby, and they all shook their heads. "Nope. Never heard of it. You're the first seekers who've ever come from any place other than Nusala."

Ty was barely able to contain his excitement as he turned to Breen. "Could we have been sent into the Westlands? It's clearly too warm to be the Frozen North. Or perhaps we've reached some land no cartographer has ever mapped."

Breen ran a hand through his shoulder-length brown hair. "Must be. I've never heard of Nusala or the Mountains of Escalor." He looked across the table. "You said these lands belong to the Ra . . ."

"The Rupoor," she finished. "Yes."

"Who, or what, are they?"

"They are, or at least were, a warring faction of the Emerald Scepter, the tri-ruling body of Nusala."

Ty's head was swimming with questions, none of which really mattered at this point. They weren't there to uncover a new world and catalog its intricacies. They were there to uncover a piece of a long-lost key.

"These Rupoor don't sound very pleasant. Will we be running into any of them in there?" Ty asked, motioning over his shoulder in the general direction of the mountain.

Tirana smirked. "Not unless they are corpses."

Ty gulped, suddenly losing part of his appetite, not to mention his curiosity over this new world. All he could think about now was what awaited them inside that dark crevice.

They finished up the rest of the meal with polite conversation, mostly answering questions from Tirana and other villagers over what was going on in the world, even if it wasn't their own. The villagers of Karpaath found Ty and Breen's description of Aldor to be rather delightful and not all that dissimilar to their own land. One thing that seemed to be universal, though, was the struggle between those with magic and those without. Apparently, no matter where you went, humans tended to share the same disagreements.

After the meal was finished, the brothers were shown to a small hut across the way, where they would be able to get some rest before their big journey the next morning. The hut wasn't much more than two rooms. The smaller room off the main held a couple of cots, a rickety table set up between, and a single candle with half its wick already melted down the sides, sealing its base to the top of the table.

It wasn't much to look at, but at least it was dry. Ty laid their one blanket down on the floor, not wanting to take the chance of catching the same blight that was infecting the village. Tirana had never really explained where the disease had come from and if it was contagious.

"I won't be able to sleep a wink," he said, staring up at the rafter above him. "What about you?"

Breen answered with a deep snore. Ty turned over. His brother's eyes were closed.

Ty shook his head. "Must be nice." He turned back around and began counting the beams. Next thing he knew, someone was shaking him. He jostled awake and sat up, wiping the sleep from his eyes with a deep yawn. He noticed Breen standing there, staring down at him.

"Why are you waking me? I'd barely gotten to sleep."

"You slept the entire night. Take a look." He pointed to a shuttered window on the other side of the room, and sure enough, there were faint traces of grey light spilling in through the cracks. "Get your boots on." He looked down at Ty's feet. "Oh, never mind. I see you slept in them."

Ty yawned, again. "In this cursed village, wouldn't you?"

"Good point." Breen stuffed the blanket into his pack, and they gathered their weapons and started for the front door.

Ty and Breen stepped outside and found Tirana waiting just off the porch. In fact, the entire town was there, all standing there with eager eyes, waiting to see what they would do.

"Good morning," Tirana said, fiddling nervously with her cane. "Did you get plenty of rest?"

"We did," Breen said with a curt nod.

"That's good. We are here to see you off."

Ty took a moment to stretch before following Breen off the porch and out into the middle of the road, where they joined the other villagers in walking toward the sheer slab of rock and the open crevice between. The fissure looked like a giant arrowhead. It stretched only about as high as a single pine, narrowing as it rose, eventually coming to a point. The widest part of the opening was at the base, barely room enough for three people to stand shoulder to shoulder.

They stopped a few feet from the entrance. "This is as far as we can go," Tirana said, leaning heavily on her cane as she looked longingly inside the open rift. "We wanted to wish you luck and swift speed."

Ty stood beside his brother, staring as far into the darkness as his eyes would allow. "How many have gone through there?"

"Hundreds. Maybe thousands. There were more in the beginning, brave warriors tempting their fate to find what they believed was some mythical lost treasure."

"Do you know what it is?" Breen asked.

"We do."

Ty was puzzled. "Then why didn't you tell them?"

"We tried at first, but no one believed us, so we gave up and told them what they wanted to hear in hopes that one of them would be able to break the curse."

"How many have returned?"

Tirana lowered her head slightly. "None."

Ty looked at Breen. His brother didn't look any happier about the news than he did. "Do you know what's in there?" he asked, unsure whether he truly wanted to find out.

Tirana twisted her cane, letting the end dig into the loose rock under their feet. "We don't. After the wizards caught us attempting to steal the missing piece, they devised a way to protect it."

Ty's head lifted. "What way?"

"Unfortunately, we've never been inside to find out."

Lot of good these people are. Clearly, they weren't going to learn anything useful from this lot. "We need provisions," Ty said, noticing the twinge in his stomach, not so much from hunger but from the overindulgence the prior night. "Food. Water."

Tirana waved one of the men over. "We can provide water from our well, but as you've seen already, we have no food, apart from what is provided to us daily. There are no leftover provisions to store."

"What happens to it?" Ty asked.

"Nothing. It simply vanishes."

"And your clothes?" Breen asked. "Where do they come from?"

"Once every few years they just show up, like our feast meals. The wizards thought of everything, the perfect prison." She shook her fist in the air. "But we will be free of it soon enough!"

Ty and Breen handed over their waterskins to the man and waited as he rushed over to a covered well several buildings behind them and filled both. Ty wasn't too keen about drinking anything that came from this place, but they didn't have much of a choice. The man came back and handed over the waterskins.

Tirana must have noticed their hesitancy. "The well is spring fed. Cleanest water you'll ever drink, I assure you."

Ty thanked her and tied his waterskin to his belt. He spared a quick nod at Breen and started for the crack in the mountain. Breen was right behind him, his boots crunching across the loose rock as they made their way inside.

Ty turned at the familiar sound of steel on flint. Breen dropped the striker tied around his neck back under his shirt as he held up a torch.

Behind them, the opening was still in view, with all the townsfolk gathered around the entrance, some even waving. Ty wasn't sure if it was for encouragement or if they were trying to hurry them on. Knowing these people had been waiting for nearly a thousand years to die, Ty guessed it was probably the latter.

Breen moved up beside him, holding his flame off to the side to keep from blinding them as they walked.

"I could have just used my own fire," Ty said, holding out his hand and calling on his magic. Blue flames burst from his open palm and lit the other half of the narrow gap between the rock.

"Best to save your strength in case we need it later."

It was a valid point, so Ty released the magic, letting it simmer back to a snug warming in his lower gut. He didn't feel safe releasing it completely. Who knew when they might have need of it.

Above them, the fissure stretched upward into darkness, farther than any torchlight could pierce.

Cautiously they continued on, until the light from the opening behind them shrunk down to a mere sliver, then disappeared altogether. Their footsteps echoed around them, the flicker of the torch and the dance of shadows it cast across the walls adding to the growing sense of unease. Ty might not have been afraid of confined spaces, but this was beginning to weigh heavily on his nerves. The thought of endless amounts of rock above him that could come crashing down at any time had him nearly panting.

"Take a deep breath and hold it," Breen said.

Ty listened and sucked in a deep gulp.

"Now release, slowly."

Ty did, surprised that he did indeed feel a little calmer.

"Again."

After the third time, his hands weren't shaking quite as bad and his breathing had calmed.

"Why aren't you panicking?" Ty asked.

"I am."

Ty looked at his brother. "Could've fooled me."

"If I were to tell you how I really feel, it would probably chill you to the bone."

"Thanks. That helps a lot."

Breen smiled. "My pleasure."

They walked for what seemed like hours, the tunnel widening in spots and narrowing in others but keeping a fairly direct route. At least Ty guessed it was. Without any sun or stars to check for guidance, there was no real way of knowing.

Ty's feet and legs were beginning to tire by the time the tunnel shifted directions. "I think we're getting close."

Breen glanced over his shoulder at the compass in Ty's hand. "How do you know?"

"I feel it."

Breen pursed his lips. "I don't feel anything."

About that time, a sliver of light appeared ahead. "Look. See?" Ty said, excited at having finally made it to the other side, even more excited with the chance to get out of the cave. He needed to see the sky. He had no idea how long they'd been walking, but it felt as though they'd been in there for days.

Ty hurried, anxious to reach the exit. They were all but running by the time they broke free, but he skidded to a stop.

They were on a precipice hundreds of feet in the air.

Ty gasped as he stared out at the valley below, stretching off into the distance. It was surrounded on all sides by sheer walls of rock, seemingly untouched by time.

He tried to speak, but the words wouldn't come.

It wasn't the deadly drop that had Ty's attention, or even the perfectly secluded valley that had been hidden away from the world for who knew how long.

It was what the valley held. The villagers in Karpaath had spoken of the wizards setting up a way to protect the shorlock, but Ty could have never imagined something like this.

The entire floor of the valley was covered for miles in all directions by the most incredible-looking stone labyrinth he had ever seen, a maze they could not hope to navigate.

"What do we do now?" Breen asked as he stood there dumbfounded.

Ty shook his head. "I have no idea."

Chapter 28 | Ty

T HE VALLEY WAS AS QUIET as a grave. Not even the smallest bit of wind rustled their clothing. Like stepping inside a glass bubble where the elements couldn't reach you, it was the most disturbing silence Ty had ever heard. He could feel it all the way to his marrow. "Is it too late to go back?"

The place was too eerie to even get a chuckle from his brother. Instead, they both just stood staring at the most incredible feat of stonework either could have ever imagined existing.

Ty had seen mazes before. His sister had prided herself on designing a few that had taken Ty an entire day to work through, but nothing even remotely comparable to what he was witnessing now. The entire valley was filled with crisscrossing walls of stone that formed patterns he couldn't hope to understand, let alone navigate. It was such a disheartening sight that he'd almost forgotten about the man's leg he was standing on.

"Gross." He hopped back, trying to keep from tripping over the skull in the process. Breen joined him, having just spotted the remains himself.

"Well, this doesn't exactly bode well," he said, reaching for his knives. "What do you think could have killed these people from up here? Looks like they didn't even make it down to the maze." Breen started back for the cave and hit something. "What's this?"

Ty stopped his examination of the long staircase on the left, leading down the mountain, and walked over to get a closer look. His brother had his hands in the air in front of him, pushing on something.

"What are you—" Ty's face smashed into something invisible. "Ow!"

It was a wall. An invisible wall.

The two felt their way along the entire opening of the cavern to find there was no opening after all. The crevice had been sealed.

"Looks like the wizards found a way to keep people trapped in here," Breen said.

"Would have been nice knowing that before we stepped through in the first place." Ty looked down at all the bones and rusted armor and weapons lying scattered across the open ledge. "I wonder if that's what happened to these people. They couldn't find their way through the maze and tried to get back. Maybe they starved, or something ate them." His first thoughts were of giant spiders climbing down the rock above them. Ty grabbed for his sword and looked up. He didn't see anything moving above, but that didn't mean they weren't there watching from some shallow crevice along the cliff face.

Just about the time he'd given up on the idea of an arachnobe dropping on his head, a loud cry, like the wail of a woman in labor but with a sharper pitch, sounded from somewhere off in the maze and echoed across the surrounding peaks. Ty and Breen raced to the edge of the shelf and looked out to see if they could spot where the noise had come from and what had made it.

"Ever hear anything like that before?" Ty asked.

Breen shook his head.

A thick fog covered parts of the maze, leaving some sections open to study and others completely shrouded. The fog appeared to be on the move, slithering through the maze like a giant serpent.

"There!" Breen said, pointing to a spot that had just been uncovered. "Did you see that?"

"See what?" Ty scanned the area his brother was pointing to, but the fog had completely enveloped it. "What did you see?"

"I'm not sure. Whatever it was, it was big." The two continued to stare out across the labyrinth, too afraid to pull their eyes away. Breen was the first to finally step back from the edge as he removed his carry pack and started digging around inside.

"What are you looking for?" Ty asked, joining him in front of the invisible wall, once again running his hands across it, still hoping for an opening. He could feel a slight tingling sensation from whatever magic was holding it in place. The wall was smooth to the touch but not slick. It gripped the skin if he placed his hand flat against it. Standing back, he punched it, surprised by the fact it didn't hurt or even bruise his knuckles like it would have had he punched a normal wall.

"I want to see how much food we have left."

Ty looked down at the two cloth-wrapped bundles his brother pulled from the sack and unwrapped. "Not much, apparently. Good thing we stuffed our bellies last night. Fated last meal and all."

"If rationed, we might get two days out of this," Breen said despondently. "If I'd known we weren't going to find other rations, I would have done a little more hunting before walking into Karpaath. I hope we don't end up like these poor souls," he said, sparing a quick glance down at the remains while packing what little food they had back into his satchel.

Ty walked back over to the edge and stared out at the impossible task that lay before them. "Faith, wisdom, strength, compassion."

"What was that?" Breen asked, walking over to join him at the edge.

"The four tests I have to pass in order to recover the four missing pieces of the shorlock." He looked down at the maze. "I wonder which one this is?"

"Look!" Breen said, pointing right, to a section of the maze that jutted up against the side of one of the mountain peaks. "Am I going crazy or did those walls just move?"

Ty watched in horror as several walls within the maze suddenly shifted positions to form a whole new design. "That's impossible. How are we supposed to get through a maze that is constantly changing?"

The brothers stood there in silence, watching for any other movement. After several minutes had passed with no other shifts, Breen finally took a step back. "Well, one thing's for sure. We'll never find out if we don't get started."

Ty stepped back from the edge as well, wishing he'd never seen the shifting walls. At least prior to then they'd stood a chance, slim as it had been, but now, they stood no chance at all. With a heavy sigh, he turned and started for the steps on the left. He sheathed his sword, wanting both hands free for balance. There might not have been any wind whipping through the mountaintops, but there was also no protective railing. One wrong move, and he'd find himself just another set of bones to add to the maze's macabre collection.

Carefully, they climbed their way down the side of the mountain, the pace slow, as they were forced to stop periodically to move more skeletal remains out of the way to keep from tripping. Along with the bones were numerous swords and spears of all makes and sizes, shields, helms. Full metal armor on some, nothing but thick leather guards on others.

By the time they reached the bottom, both had assembled a small selection of protective gear from the trove littering the steps above. With Breen's help, Ty had managed to find some forearm, shin, and chest guards made of thick leather, as opposed to the metal ones his brother had originally tried to get him to wear. Ty didn't like the way the metal felt against his skin. It wasn't all that heavy, just awkward, not to mention nowhere near his size.

Breen tried them on as well, but in the end the brothers decided to leave the metal armor behind, opting instead for the tough leather, if for no other reason than because the metal armor made too much noise when they moved. Best not to draw attention to themselves if they could help it.

"Not exactly built for comfort, are they?" Ty said, trying to wiggle his leg around. The top rim of the shin guards pressed against the backs of his knees.

"Better that than losing a leg," Breen said as the two stared up at the outer wall of the maze. The grey stone blocks stood at least twenty feet in the air, too high to climb with no discernable hand- or footholds. The stone seemed ageless, as though the maze had been built within the last year.

Ty turned and tilted his head even further, earning a wave of dizziness for his troubles as he looked up at the winding set of stairs they'd just descended. He paused a moment to let the world stop spinning before turning his attention back to the open archway ahead of them. It was their way in. For all he knew, it was the only way in.

At the top of the arch, carved into the stone, was the word *FAITH*.

"What was that ditty Nyalis quoted?" Breen asked.

"*Faith in oneself is important,*
but faith without wisdom can be misplaced,
and wisdom without strength can lead to complacency,
and strength without compassion can lead to tyranny."

"Seems to me it would take a lot of faith to be willing to step foot in this place."

"I don't know how much of it is faith," Ty said, staring at the piles of remains around the opening and scattered throughout the passageway ahead. "More like madness." He reached into his pocket and pulled out the silver compass.

The needle pointed directly ahead.

"Do you think it will guide us all the way through?" Breen asked.

Ty shrugged. "Only one way to find out."

Breen shifted the pack on his back. "Are you ready?"

"If I said no, would it matter?"

Breen rolled his shoulders. "Guess not."

"Then no," Ty said emphatically and took his first step into the maze. He tried reaching out with his magic, but it didn't seem to be working. Normally he could sense living things with it, but it was as though there was nothing alive in this place. In fact, he couldn't even sense his brother beside him, so it was like walking around temporarily blinded.

Ty didn't think he could have been any more unnerved than he had been looking out across the labyrinth from the cliffs above, seeing how impossible the task was going to be, watching as the living fog moved through the maze like a creature seeking helpless prey, watching as the walls shifted and spun on their own. Having stepped foot inside, it was a thousand times worse.

Another eerie screech sounded off in the distance, and he drew his sword, his heart pounding. To either side of the maze were large openings, passageways leading off in a variety of directions. He had no idea where they led, but as long as the compass needle continued to point straight ahead, that was the direction he took.

He could hear his brother breathing heavily beside him, could see his head shifting back and forth out of the corner of his eye. He hated to think what it would have been like to attempt all this on his own.

The way ahead rested within the shadow of the mountain behind him, but even in shadow, there was still enough light to see. Enough that Breen had extinguished his torch and replaced it with his bow and a nocked arrow. Up ahead, the passage ended, leaving them with two choices: right or left. Or they could backtrack and take any of the other forks they had passed along the way.

Ty held up his compass, and his heart sank. The needle hadn't changed position. It was still aiming straight ahead. What good was the compass if it wasn't going to show them where to go?"

"Which way?" Breen asked, noting the needle's fixed position.

Ty took a moment to glance down both passageways. There were no discernable markings, no structural variations, no runes to help make his choice. He simply had to pick one. "I don't know. What do you think?"

"You're the one with the compass. You choose. Besides, this is supposed to be your test, anyway. And if it's the wrong choice, I can always blame it on you."

Ty shook his head, then released a deep, frustrated sigh. "I've got no idea which way to go."

"Guess that's why they call it *faith*," Breen said with a grin.

"Very funny." Unfortunately, Breen wasn't wrong. Ty stared at the two passageways. He couldn't tell just by looking whether either one would take him in the right direction. A flock of ravens overhead cawed as they circled their position, not even having the courtesy to wait until they were dead to come calling. After taking a few more minutes to second- and third-guess himself, he finally took the left channel. "This way."

To Breen's credit, he never questioned him, just followed. It wouldn't have done him any good if he had. Ty had no idea why he'd chosen the one on the left. Perhaps it was because it seemed to have fewer bones. The corridor went a short distance, curving to the right before forking in three different directions. Once again, Ty took the left path, which seemed to be taking them right back to the mountainside instead of toward their destination somewhere deep within the center of the basin.

Another crossing point, and this time he took the right branch, watching the needle turn. They were finally starting to get back on—

Ty was suddenly yanked backward by the nape of his shirt, almost losing his compass and sword.

"What do you think you're—" Ty gasped when he lowered the compass long enough to see where his foot had been.

He'd been so focused on where the needle was pointing that he hadn't noticed the floor of the maze was no longer there. In its place was a hole. Actually, it was more like a nothingness. It ran the complete width of the passage and stretched at least a good ten feet ahead. When he looked into it, he could see no bottom, like looking at a sheet of solid black glass, but without a reflection.

Ty rubbed his neck where he'd been momentarily hanged by his collar. "That was close."

"You can say that again," Breen said. "If something happens to you, then I'm the one who's going to starve to death in here and have the crows feeding on me before I breathe my last." His brother sounded upset but actually looked more scared than anything. "Watch where you're going."

Ty stuffed the compass back in his trousers. It was proving less than useful in helping them navigate which tunnel to take anyway. He stared out at the black opening, judging the distance.

"Don't even think about it," Breen said.

Ty spotted a couple of bones near the side of one of the walls. They looked like they belonged to someone's arm. He grabbed two and walked over near the edge and dropped the first in. As soon as it hit the surface, it disappeared. Ty spun around. "Did you see that?"

"See what?" Breen had been looking at the passageway behind them.

"Here. Watch." Ty waited until Breen had made it to the edge before dropping in the second bone. It, too, disappeared as soon as it struck the surface. "That's the strangest hole I've ever seen."

Breen grabbed hold of Ty's shoulder and pulled him back from the edge. "Best we don't get too near. Let's go. We've got to find another way around."

Ty automatically reached for his compass but thought better of it. Besides, he could still see the mountain behind them, so he knew basically which direction they needed to go. Backtracking, they reached the first new branch, and Ty took the one to the left, then the next right, then left, then another left, then straight. Ty had given up on keeping a mental log of which direction they were heading, and instead simply chose whichever path looked like it had the least number of human remains.

By the time they stopped for their first break, Ty could no longer see the peaks behind them, leaving him with nothing but his gut to guide them. They were truly lost.

Their lunch was eaten quickly, and not just because there wasn't much of it, but because both were too on edge to stomach it. Ty did manage to get some water down before they started back up again.

Every now and then, they reached a passageway that allowed them to spot the sun. It wasn't enough of a view to navigate by, but it was enough for them to see that the day was beginning to wane. Ty didn't much care for the idea of spending the night in the place, but unless they were able to find a way out in the next few hours, they weren't going to have much of a choice. At this point, Ty didn't think they'd find their way out if they spent the next year looking.

Several more times, they heard the wail from whatever creature was roaming farther in. It seemed to be getting louder. Ty wondered how anything living could survive in a place like this. There was no way it could have remained fed, unless of course there was another way out and the creature only returned when a new source of food presented itself. Ty tried not to think about it. He was nervous enough as it was.

A thunderous scraping sound on their right had both brothers spinning—Breen with his bow nocked and Ty with his sword up and ready—but as soon as it sounded, it was gone. Ty stared up at the wall, and as soon as he did, the entire thing slid in their direction, like a giant hand about to clamp shut and squash them between.

"Run!" Breen shouted, and they raced forward.

The end of the passage was just ahead, but it was closing fast. Ty could see the shadow of it moving up beside him. They were now forced to run single file just to fit between.

"Faster!" Breen shouted desperately from behind.

Ty could hear the clanging of pots and pans from Breen's travel sack as they tore down the now very narrow passageway.

They weren't going to make it. Ty could have reached out and touched both walls with his hands, which was when he noticed the bloodstains smeared along the bottom with pieces of bone wedged partway underneath. He willed his legs to go faster. Ty's legs weren't as long as his brother's, but he also wasn't carrying all their supplies on his back. Ty could see the opening just ahead, but it was too far to reach. The walls were now barely wide enough to fit through.

Suddenly, Ty was hit from behind, and he flew through the air, landing just past the end of the wall. He turned in time to see his brother pressed up against one side, his eyes closing.

"No!" Ty shouted, raising his hands and reaching for any magic he could grab hold of. But it was too late. He couldn't think of a single ability he had that could stop the wall. All he could do was watch as his brother was flattened between.

Unexpectedly, the wall stopped, spun outward in an arc, and formed the side of a whole new tunnel passage. Breen stood there, still in shock, as he looked down at himself then at Ty. "I thought I was done for."

"So did I."

Breen's face whitened. "Move!"

The wall beside them began to move, along with the wall in front. Quickly, they ran through the shifting passageways, darting left then right, doing everything they could to keep from getting run over or separated by the moving pieces of this enormous puzzle. They reached the end of a newly formed corridor, and the rumbling behind them stopped, leaving behind small quakes in the stones under their feet.

Both were panting hard by the time they found a seat up against one side of a new passageway.

"I hate this place," Ty said, his knuckles white from strangling the hilt of his sword. He released the weapon and let it clang on the stone beside him.

"I say we stop here for the night," Breen said, looking up at the sky.

Ty looked up, surprised to find the first hint of stars beginning to shimmer in the grey heavens above. Time seemed distorted down here beneath the endless barrage of stone. "Should we attempt a fire? Kind of cold at night."

Breen unhooked his pack and set it between his legs. "I don't know. A fire might keep some things at bay, but it might attract others."

"I say we risk it. If something is out there, I prefer to see it."

"And where exactly are you going to find enough wood in this place?"

Ty grabbed a piece of armor and pulled out the leg that was caught inside and held it up with a smile.

Breen shuddered. "Afraid that isn't going to burn too well."

"Can't hurt to try. Either that or we sit here in the dark." With Breen's help, Ty managed to accumulate a decent pile of bones, and Breen used the tattered remains of what had been a very old uniform as tinder to get them started, but unfortunately, Breen was right. The material burned up rather quickly but never ignited even a single bone.

"Darkness it is," Breen said, scooting up against the wall.

"Let me try something else," Ty said and raised his hand. Blue fire burst from the top, and he doused the bones in flame, the heat strong enough to force Breen to raise his hand in front of his face.

This time the flames stuck, the bones unable to stand up against his magic. He smiled and reclined against the wall himself, satisfied with a job well done. Overhead, the sky had long since lost its color and was in the process of transforming from a drab grey to a dark charcoal. A few of the brighter stars were already waking from their slumber as the maze around them darkened.

Supper wasn't much more than a single rabbit leg and a thin slice of white cheese—the cheaper, stronger kind that left a sour taste in Ty's mouth—which was then downed with a couple conservative swallows from their respective waterskins. Ty tried to imagine himself back in Karpaath, sitting around the empty tables as the strange light filled the room with every wondrous type of food. All he managed to do was make himself hungrier, so he eventually gave up.

He had thought the maze creepy during the day, but it seemed to come alive at night. Howls, guttural caws, shifting stone, and the occasional wail from the maze monster Ty hoped they never crossed paths with was enough to keep anyone up. Not to mention the warmth of their fire was provided by the burning of human remains.

"I sure hope this Aero'set place is really worth it," Breen grumbled from the other side of the fire.

"And to think this is only the first of four tests," Ty added.

"I'm trying not to. The more I think about it, the more depressed I become."

A sharp skittering noise had both brothers reaching for their weapons. Ty stared down the darkened passage on the right as far as the light from their fire would allow, but he couldn't see anything. "I almost forgot," he said excitedly. "*Ru'kasha Kor.*" The passageway suddenly brightened, and he could see the stone walls all the way to where they ended about a hundred feet farther in.

"What did you almost forget?" Breen asked.

Ty turned back around and quickly threw his hands up over his eyes. "Oh, that's bright." His night sight was clearly not made to be used around a strong light source. "*Ru'kasha Sve.*" The light faded, and so did his surroundings. "Wow, that hurt."

"What are you going on about over there?"

"I was using a simple spell that the book . . . Mangora taught me for seeing in the dark."

"I wouldn't trust anything that old witch told you. Next thing you know you'll be sprouting a tail or growing fangs." There was a long silence before his brother finally spoke again, curiosity getting the better of him. "Did it work?"

Ty smiled. "Yes. It's amazing. You want to try?"

Breen threw a couple of arms and a backbone onto the fire and watched the sparks leap into the air. "Do I look like I want to go growing a tail?" There was another awkward silence. "What does it feel like?"

Ty sighed. "Just try it. I promise it doesn't hurt. You just have to use a bit of your magic and repeat the phrase: *Ru'kasha Kor.*"

Breen leaned back against the side wall with his arms crossed, but Ty could see the building interest in his eyes. "Fine. But only so you'll stop pestering me about it. What was it you said?"

"*Ru'kasha Kor.* But you've got to pronounce it exactly as I say it, or it won't work. Don't be frustrated if you don't get it on your first try. It took me—"

"*Ru'kasha Kor.*" Breen's eyes widened, and then he looked at the fire and quickly raised his hands. "Wow!" He stood and started down the darkened passageway ahead. "I can see almost everything. This is incredible."

Ty smiled as he stood. He didn't know if he should be excited at being able to share a bit of magic with his brother, or depressed at the fact that his brother had picked it up the very first time he attempted it. He opted for the former. "*Ru'kasha Kor.*" His surroundings brightened, allowing him to see his brother off in the distance. He was presently peeking around the next bend. "I told you you'd like it."

Breen walked back toward the fire, lowering his eyes the closer he came. "How do you get it to stop?"

"*Ru'kasha Sve.*"

Breen repeated the phrase and sat back down. "That is an extremely useful piece of magic. I can't believe she showed it to you."

"I don't think she believed I was going to be around long enough to use it."

Breen nodded and retook his seat by the fire. "Best we turn in." Another round of howling echoed in the distance.

"Don't know how much sleep we'll actually be getting, though."

His brother pursed his lips. "We can rest our feet at the least. I'll take first watch if you want to get a couple hours."

Ty nodded, and Breen tossed him the blanket from his pack, and Ty scooted over closer to the fire. "Don't fall asleep."

His brother chuckled. "Don't think you'll need to worry about that." Ty hunkered down and closed his eyes. Before he knew it, he was asleep.

Chapter 29 | Ty

T Y WOKE TO A HAND on his shoulder. His eyes opened slowly. It was still dark, the stars filling the night sky.

"Your turn," Breen said as he hunkered down near the fire.

Ty yawned and sat up far enough to stretch and take a look around. "Anything exciting happen while I was asleep? Like someone stopping by to drop off the missing piece of the shorlock?"

Breen's eyes were closed, but he smiled anyway. "Nothing exciting." He opened his eyes momentarily. "I'll give you the same warning. Don't fall asleep."

Ty yawned. "I'll try not to."

"Do more than try," Breen said, then turned over. Within minutes, he was snoring, leaving Ty alone to his thoughts. Unfortunately, his thoughts had a tendency to get away from him, and he began to imagine all kinds of horrific things, like what would have happened if that wall hadn't stopped when it did, or if Breen hadn't stopped him before he stepped into that black nothingness, or the crows pecking away on his rotting corpse.

Ty was so caught up in his imagination that he almost didn't notice the clicking.

It was faint at first, but it grew quickly, completely pulling him from his waking nightmares and back to reality. He looked around, trying to figure out where it was coming from.

Grabbing his sword from his lap, he stood and glanced down the left passageway, which they had come through earlier. Whatever it was, it was getting louder, more discernible. It almost reminded him of . . .

"*Ru'kasha Kor.*" Ty gasped.

The floor and walls of the maze were covered with large bug-like creatures. There were so many it looked like the stones themselves were moving. With the night-sight magic working, he couldn't tell their color, but they were between the size of a small rat and a very large horned beetle. He couldn't really make out what they looked like as they all moved as one, their legs clicking on the stone as they came.

"Breen!"

Breen shot out of his bed, tripping over his blanket and nearly landing in the fire as he grabbed for his bow. "What? What's going on? Where is it?" He managed to nock an arrow and make it to Ty's side of the fire. "What's happening?"

Ty pointed back down the tunnel. "Look!"

Breen turned. "*Ru'kasha . . . Ru'kasha . . .* Flaming Pits! What is that stupid word?"

"*Kor!*" Ty shouted back over his shoulder as he ran to snatch one of the bones off the fire. Behind him, he heard his brother finish the incantation.

"What is that?" Breen raced back to the travel pack and quickly stuffed his blanket in, then flung it and his bow and quiver over his shoulders. Arrows were hardly going to do any good against what was heading their way. They barely finished gathering the rest of their meager belongings when the first of the large insect creatures came into the light.

They were ferocious looking with hardened shells that ran down their backs, ending at a tail with a curved stinger. Their two front legs ended in pincers, and when they opened their mouths and squealed, Ty could see fangs similar to that of a rat.

The creatures reached the pile of burning bones and slowed at first, almost as if they were enamored by the flames. It didn't take them long to get over their curiosity, and soon enough they were rushing past the fire in a wave of scurrying legs and hissing shrills.

Ty sent out several lances of fire, but each time, the creatures would divide around those that had been scorched and continue coming. There were just too many of them.

"Come on!" Breen shouted as he pulled Ty back. They fled down the passageway in the opposite direction, taking the first branch to the left, then back right, then right again as they continued running, the sound of their pursuers growing. They couldn't keep going like this for long. Sooner or later they were going to hit a dead end, or worse, one of those black nothingness patches.

Ty sucked in deep gulps of air as he willed his feet to keep going, too afraid to glance over his shoulder to see how close the bugs were. He didn't need to. He could hear their feet skittering across the stone just behind them. Ty spared a passing glance at his brother, wondering how he was doing, carrying all their supplies. Breen barely looked winded.

Ty had hardly turned back around when his foot snagged on a loose stone, and he went down hard, rolling until he hit one of the walls, his hands and knees cut and bleeding. He barely had time to turn over before the creatures were on top of him.

His hands went up on instinct, and blue flames erupted from both, lighting the tunnel up like a beacon fire. Shrilling screeches echoed off the walls as the closest wave of bugs was incinerated in the blue wake. Ty was afraid to unleash too much of his magic. The last time he had, it had rendered him unconscious. Ty released it, and the flames in his hands disappeared, but the corridor continued to burn, a blue wall holding back what remained of the creatures—at least for the moment.

"Run!" Breen said, yanking Ty to his feet.

They turned and ran, taking one fork after another, running for what seemed like hours, until their legs couldn't run anymore, and they collapsed against the side of a random passageway, gasping for breath.

"I don't hear them anymore," Ty said. He was still holding on to his night sight, and as far as he could tell, they weren't still being pursued. "Our bone fire must have attracted them."

"Possibly," Breen said as he pulled off the heavy satchel from his back and dropped it and his bow and quiver onto the floor beside them. "And if that bone fire wasn't enough, the torrent you just unleashed is sure to attract every creature from here to Aldor." He shook his head. "Sounds funny just saying that: *Here to Aldor.*"

Ty smiled and leaned back against the wall with a heavy sigh as he listened intently for any signs of the encroaching bugs.

Before long, Breen was back on his feet. "I say we keep going. I don't know about you, but I don't expect I'll be shutting my eyes anytime soon, and with this new night sight, I'd prefer not to waste time sitting here when we could be that much closer to what we came for."

Ty groaned, but eventually he stood with his brother's help. "Want me to carry the pack some?" he offered, pointing at the large satchel leaning against the wall beside Breen's black bow.

"No," Breen said as he grabbed the pack and flung it over his back. "I prefer you to have your hands free in case we run into any more of those critters. Besides," he said with a grin, "you can barely keep to your feet now. I'd hate to think of how bad you'd slow me down with this on your back."

Ty wasn't going to argue.

With nothing keeping them there but their own fatigue, the brothers started back through the maze. They found themselves needing to stop more often, taking small breaks to rest their feet and sip on water. Their waterskins were down to about half. At least Ty's was. He didn't know if Breen's was any better. He'd been rationing his as best he could, but if they didn't find this missing piece of the shorlock in the next day or two, they were going to run out.

They could survive without food for a while, but they couldn't survive long without water. And it was pretty clear they weren't going to find some magical well just waiting around the next bend. The thought had his curiosity piqued, though, and he spent the next several hours thinking about Karpaath and their magical feast, wondering how the magic worked, how it compared to his own magic. With his magic, he could make people see things that weren't there, and even make them forget they had seen anything, but what they had experienced in Karpaath wasn't just an illusion. Ty had been able to touch it, taste it, smell it.

It was all very intriguing.

Slowly, they trudged on with nothing but the occasional wail of the maze monster—as Ty had officially deemed it—to keep them company. Several more times they heard the familiar thunderous grating of the walls shifting. How were they ever going to find their way to the center of this place? With no directions, no obvious pointers, no chart to guide the way, it seemed a hopeless cause.

Was he missing something? Something about this idea of *faith* . . . but faith in what? The farther they went, the less faith he had. At this point, if they did somehow manage to find the center of this place, it wouldn't be because of faith. It would be because of sheer dumb luck.

Ty's feet were beginning to hurt, the endless walking was taking its toll. When the stars had begun to wink from existence and the first signs of greying formed overhead, the two brothers decided to take a little break for an early breakfast. Neither was very hungry, but Ty would take any opportunity to get off his feet. He even went so far as to remove his boots, although he kept them close at hand in case he needed to throw them back on at a moment's notice.

"Where do you think we are?" Ty asked, using the time to once more pull out his compass for a quick peek. The needle was pointing off to the left.

"Lost is where we are," Breen said as he, too, removed his boots and began to slowly rub the soles of his feet. He closed his eyes and released a soft whimper when he reached his toes.

Ty could relate. He wiggled his toes, trying to get some feeling back in them before stretching his legs out in front and leaning back against a section of the wall that was completely free from bones. "How much food do we have left?"

His brother didn't even bother looking. "Not enough." Breen finished massaging his feet and leaned back against the wall himself. "I'm just going to rest my eyes for a little bit."

Ty joined him.

A loud screech brought them both awake and scurrying for their weapons, half tripping over themselves as their socked feet stumbled over loose stones and old remains.

"What was that?" Breen looked up. The sun was midway to its zenith.

Ty looked around, but it seemed whatever had made the noise was nowhere to be seen.

"I must have fallen asleep," Breen said, turning to look at Ty. "Why didn't you wake me?"

"Because I fell asleep."

Breen hmphed. "Great outdoorsmen we turned out to be. Glad Father wasn't here to see this."

"I wish Father *was* here," Ty added.

Breen smiled as he quickly put his boots back on. "Yeah, I miss him too. And Adarra."

"Well, I wouldn't get too carried away," Ty said sarcastically, causing Breen to laugh. Ty reluctantly stuffed his feet into his boots and stamped down, then strapped his sword back on and patted his pants pocket to make sure the compass was still there, something he found himself doing more often than not.

As soon as Breen managed to get his pack and quiver back on his shoulders, he grabbed his bow, and they started off once more. Again, Ty had no idea where they were going. In fact, he did his best to not think about the choices at all and simply let his feet guide him. There were several times his feet had taken them to dead ends, and twice they happened across sections of nothingness like the one Ty had almost stumbled into the previous day, leaving Ty to believe that no matter what this test was called, *faith* had nothing to do with any of it.

After a quick lunch consisting of the rabbit's leg he hadn't eaten the previous day, another thinly sliced piece of stinky cheese, and a very small slurp of water, they were off again. The occasional wail of the maze monster was definitely getting closer, which meant that they were at least heading in the right direction.

Rounding another bend, this one strangely wet, as though it had rained recently, they were once again forced to stop when they came upon another section of missing floor. Ty paused long enough to toss in a piece of rock and watch it disappear just like the rest. "What do you think these things are?"

"I don't want to find out," Breen said, already heading back the way they'd come. A slight tremor under their feet stopped him, and he turned around. "You feel that?"

Ty nodded and followed his brother back around to the intersecting branch they'd just exited.

"Is it the walls?" Breen asked, placing his hand on the nearest.

Ty didn't think so. It didn't have the same grating sound of stone rubbing against stone. This was different, more like the way the East River sounded during the spring, when the ice from farther north would melt and overflow its banks. Whatever it was, it was getting closer.

The brothers moved out into the center of the adjoining corridor, which formed an upside-down T, so they could try seeing what was coming and, possibly, which direction they'd need to run to get away from it. Not that it mattered. They only had two options: the right corridor or the left. The center branch, where they'd just come from, was blocked by the patch of black nothingness.

The earlier rumble was now shaking the entire corridor. Loose pebbles bounced on the stone at their feet.

Breen looked at Ty and shouted just to be heard above the uproar. "I've got a very bad feeling about this!" He barely got the words out when the first sign of movement burst into the corridor on the right, fifty feet from where they were standing.

Ty gaped as a wall of water flooded into the passageway.

"Run!" both brothers shouted at the same time and darted into the left corridor, barely making it into the passageway when another wall of water poured into that branch as well. They skidded to a stop, looked at each other, then turned and ran for the only passageway left, knowing full well what lay around the corner ahead.

Thoughts of being drowned all over again had Ty running hard enough to overtake his brother. He could see the black opening just coming into view. Behind them, the water from both the left and right branches collided in the middle, then poured into the central corridor after them. The wall of water was now at least ten to fifteen feet high. They weren't going to make it. At least he wasn't. Breen was the only one who stood a chance of leaping across the hole, but even with his longer legs and muscular frame, Ty doubted he could make it over on his own, not with that pack weighing him down.

Breen glanced at Ty and nodded reassuringly. "We can make it!"

Ty nodded back, but he could see the truth in his brother's eyes. They were going to die.

Five steps from the hole, Ty reached for his magic and slid to a stop. The water was nearly on top of him. With only a moment to spare, he raised his hands and hit Breen with a short burst of air just as his brother leaped for the other side.

The water hit Ty like a battering ram, but not before he saw his brother fly free of the hole.

He could hear Breen shouting his name as the water lifted him off his feet and straight for the nothingness. He held his breath but kept his eyes open as he was pulled straight down past his brother and into the blackness.

Light reappeared. He wasn't dead. Fighting with everything he had, he paddled and kicked his way to the top, breaking free with a deep gulp of air. He couldn't believe he was still alive. Even more surprising, he was still in the maze. Where had he gone? The rush of the current flung Ty from one side of the corridor to the other. It took every ounce of strength to keep his head above the water. He was dragged from one passageway to the next. All the corridors looked the same, since all he could see of them was the top half.

Even with the boost from the water, the top of the wall was still too high to reach, and with each new branching corridor he crossed, the water would split and lower. At times, some of the branches would rejoin, just to split again farther down the line. Where had the water come from? Had it been here the whole time? Again, he was thrown against one of the walls, this time with enough undercurrent to drag him below the surface, all the way to the bottom.

Panic set in as images of himself stuck on the tree under the river came flooding in. He could feel the burning in his lungs as the water was inhaled, the desperation he'd felt, the hopelessness, knowing he was going to die there all alone.

A piece of metal chest guard struck him in the side, half of the skeleton that had been wearing it still attached. The man seemed to be waving at him as he floated by. Ty didn't have time to watch. He was running out of air. As hard as he could, he kicked off the bottom and swam for the top, using the side wall to crawl to the surface. Breaking free, he gasped for breath, choking and coughing and spitting water as he did.

Back on top, he watched as the water continued to split and reform, glancing behind him every now and then to see if Breen had been foolish enough to jump in after him. At this point, knowing that the black nothingness wouldn't kill him, he hoped he had. Unfortunately, there was no sign his brother was following, and even if he were, there was no telling if he would have been taken down the same path or veered off at some other corridor.

Ty was still on the front edge of the wave when he rounded the next bend and struck an oncoming wave racing from the other direction. The merging of the two intersecting streams struck a chord. Was he back where they had first seen the water? He swam as close to the front as he dared as the wave tore into a third interconnecting channel. Ty's heart leaped when he saw the black nothingness ahead, and his brother standing just behind it.

Breen was shouting something, but Ty couldn't make it out. He tried shouting back but got a mouthful of water for his trouble. How was he going to reach his brother? Breen was doing something with his hands, swinging them about, but Ty couldn't quite make out why.

He was almost on top of the hole when one of their blankets landed in front of him in the water, floating just on top. He latched onto it and the short bit of rope it was attached to.

The water hit the black hole and dragged him down with it, but he held onto the blanket and rope for dear life. The force of the water slammed him up against the far side of the hole while at the same time pulling him downward into the nothingness. He held his breath for as long as he could as his head went under.

Inch by inch, Breen managed to pull him up through the water to the back edge of the hole, his lower half still hanging through. He looked down to find his legs and waist were missing.

"Pull!" he shouted desperately.

Above him, Breen heaved on the other end of the rope, shouting for Ty to hold on. Ty clung to the blanket and the rope with everything he had, ignoring the burning in his hands. With one final pull, Ty was lifted high enough to get his knees up over the edge and roll free of the water onto the other side. He lay on his back beside the hole, panting, watching as the torrent continued to pour inside. Pretty soon, the last of the water dropped through the opening and disappeared, leaving nothing but an empty wet tunnel behind them.

Breen dragged Ty back from the hole and propped him up against the left wall. "What were you thinking? You could have killed yourself."

Ty coughed up a mouthful of water. "I was trying to save you."

Breen wrapped his huge arms around him. "I'm the oldest, that's my job." His voice was trembling. He finally released Ty and scooted back. "I thought I'd lost you for sure."

"I thought you'd jump in after me."

"I almost did, but then I remembered how wet the tunnel had been when we first came down it earlier, and it dawned on me what these things might be."

"Yeah, a flaming death trap!" Ty said, fighting through another bout of coughing.

Breen rubbed his hand through his wet hair. "It only made sense that if the water had been through there recently enough that the sun hadn't yet dried the stone, then there was a good chance it would be coming through there again."

Breen scooted over to the wall and plopped down beside Ty. "Where did it take you?"

Ty shook his head. "No idea. I was too busy trying to stay alive to stop and see the sights. I was up high enough to see that we are a long way from the mountains. I'd say we've got to be getting close to the center of this thing."

Breen nodded as he looked down the left passageway in the direction they needed to go. "Best we keep going, then. I don't know about you, but I don't relish the idea of spending another night in this place."

The very thought had Ty scrambling to his feet.

Chapter 30 | Ty

TY SPENT PART OF THE afternoon trying to wring the water from his clothes, while Breen attempted to hold him still long enough to wrap his wounds. There wasn't much that could be done about the bruised ribs, but Breen had managed to pack enough swaddling to bandage Ty's rope-burned hands.

Thankfully, the sun was out, and it warmed Ty's skin as he stood in the center of the passageway wearing nothing but an embarrassed smile while Breen drained the last few drops from their clothes. He hated putting them back on while they were wet, but he hated standing there naked even more. His brother was too preoccupied with his own blanket, not to mention the coil of rope and Ty's sword—which Ty had surprisingly managed not to lose during his excursion through the waterlogged corridors—to pay any attention to Ty's pasty backside.

"This is going to be miserable," Ty said, walking over to test his shirt, which was lying prostrate beside his pants and socks and boots on the narrowing section of stone that was still within the sun's reach. He was half tempted to request they light a fire and dry the clothes out that way, but after their last attempt with fire, he had no intention of running into another horde of rat-sized insects.

Ty waited just long enough for the sun to shift beyond their channel in the maze before gathering up his clothes and redressing. The clothes weren't exactly soggy, but they weren't dry either. They were just wet enough to be uncomfortable.

The worst was his socks and boots. His socks were wool and dried fairly quickly, but the inside of his boots left him squishing and squashing for some time to come. Eventually, he grew accustomed to the stiffness of his trousers and tunic and set his mind to more important issues, like the wail of the maze monster and how close they were getting.

How was anyone supposed to survive these tests? The worse question was what happened if he failed? Would the wizarding school be lost for all time? Perhaps in another thousand years another half faerie would come along. Although, he doubted Nyalis would still be around to guide them if they did. Not that the wizard's guidance had proven all that useful so far. If it had just been left up to what Nyalis had told him, Ty would have been toes up before having ever reached the first test.

They continued on through the rest of the afternoon, until the sky filled with color and the sun dropped below the surrounding peaks of the Mountains of Escalor.

"Let's go ahead and eat," Breen said, stopping at the corner of another long intersection, "while there's still enough light left to see." He looked up at the soft rose-colored swirls and sighed. "I'm dreading the thought of another night in this place."

"You and me both," Ty agreed, stopping to admire the tapestry of color above him. It was hard to picture such beauty in a place like this, but he found himself smiling. He used to enjoy walking through the wheat field not far from his house. There was a small hill that he'd climb and then sit to watch the sun set. His mother would join him there and she'd share old stories passed down from her childhood, stories of her grandparents and how they'd first settled in Easthaven. Tears filled his eyes.

"What's wrong?" Breen asked, unwrapping what remained of their meager food stores.

"I was thinking of Mother. She would have loved to see a sky like this."

Breen stopped what he was doing and looked up, and they both stared quietly for some time before Breen finally turned his attention back to the food.

The meal was eaten in silence, neither able to express how they were feeling. But as Ty had observed, that was the way of men. Women, on the other hand, spent way too much time talking about their feelings, which must be why the Creator had put the two together, to balance each other out. Although, Lyessa seemed to be more of the kind of girl to punch you in the arm and tell you to get over it than to sit around and listen to you prattle on about your emotions. Ty found that oddly appealing.

Breen packed what was left of their supper—not much more than a few slices of cheese since they'd eaten what little was left of the rather picked-over rabbit—and slung the heavy pack over his shoulders and grabbed his bow and quiver. Ty strapped on his sword and brought out the compass once more to get their bearings. The needle pointed left, so they took the left branch and started back on their journey.

They hadn't walked far before the ground began to shake once more, but this time it was accompanied by the familiar grating of stone rubbing against stone. They quickly moved to the middle, watching the walls on either side to see which way they might need to run. Amazingly, neither of the walls forming their channel shifted. They waited until the final bits of rumbling stopped, then waited a little longer still before starting forward.

The color in the sky was gone, and the lighter grey had already begun to shift, revealing the first of the heavenly gems above. A spattering of clouds filled the sky. Ty could just make out their shapes as they passed. "*Ru'kasha Kor.*" The way ahead brightened.

Breen joined him. "*Ru'kasha Kor.* That's better." He smiled. "I love this magic."

Ty couldn't help but smile. That is, until another loud wail split the silence, sending the brothers scurrying for the side of the tunnel. After the echoes passed, they stepped back out and looked around.

"That was close," Breen said, slowly lowering his black bow.

Ty stared at Breen's weapon a moment, recalling what Nyalis had said about the magical weapon. He still didn't know what he thought about his brother wielding something that had been created to kill faeries. "Do you think your bow was probably created here in Nusala?"

Breen held it up. "I hadn't thought about that. You could be right. Nyalis said it was wielded by an elite group of rangers from the Westlands. Do you think he was talking about here?"

Ty shrugged. "Could be."

Breen chuckled as he lowered the weapon to his side. "It's seen more of this world than I have."

"It's also seen a lot more death."

"True. Let's just hope it doesn't witness ours." Breen started forward, and Ty followed just behind.

The tunnels in this section of the maze looked exactly like the tunnels in every other section they'd been through, but with far fewer bones. Apparently, very few of those seeking the fabled treasure had made it this far. Ty wondered how many other deadly traps had been included in this place.

So far, they'd seen moving walls, a horde of insects, transporting black holes, flash-flooding tunnels, and had heard several different kinds of ferocious creatures, not to mention the maze monster. The wizards who had created this place must have been placing bets on who could create the most ridiculous way to die.

They'd been walking for some time in silence, nothing but the echo of their boots on the stone below, when the hair on Ty's arms suddenly stood on end and he grabbed his brother's sleeve and pulled him to a stop. "Do you feel that?"

"Feel what?"

Ty didn't exactly know how to explain it. "Like we're being watched."

Breen raised his nocked bow and looked both ways down the channel, even glancing up at the top of the walls. "I don't see anything."

Just as quick as it had appeared, the feeling passed. Ty took a deep breath and moved away from the wall and back out into the passageway to see if he could sense whatever it was again. He shook his head frustratedly. "Whatever it was, it's gone."

They stood a moment longer, searching the tunnel for any sign of something out there, but finally continued on. They moved from one dividing branch to another, never really knowing which direction they were going, only that they needed to keep moving. Several forks later, it was Breen's turn to come to a halt.

Ty spotted him out of the corner of his eye and stopped as well. "What is it?"

"I think I'm feeling something too."

Ty sighed. "Good, I thought it was just me, but I didn't want to say anything and look foolish again."

The brothers stared up and down the passageway, listening intently for whatever it was that had them so on edge, but just like before, there was nothing. The stars lit the sky above them, and the moon's rays were just seeping over the top of the right wall.

"What do you think it is?" Ty whispered.

Breen just shook his head. "Why don't you try doing that thing with your magic where you can sense things nearby?"

"I tried that before we ever stepped foot in this place, but whatever magic went into creating it is blocking me from being able to sense other living things that way."

"Too bad," Breen said as he raised his bow and started forward once more. "We could have really used that right about now."

Ty agreed, but there wasn't much he could do about it. He found himself walking a little closer to his brother, his own weapon out and raised as he periodically spun to see if they were being followed.

They came to the end of another tunnel and took the left branch, following it around until it took a sharp turn back to the right. Ty had just rounded the corner when he jerked to a stop. Breen moved up beside him and raised his bow. The passageway ahead was blocked with a thick rolling fog. Ty looked up, but the clouds that had been there earlier were gone, the sky completely clear.

"I wondered how long it'd be until we came across this," Ty said. He'd seen it from their perch above the maze after first exiting the cave. It was like a long snake, moving slowly through the maze, stretched out through all the surrounding passageways.

"That feeling of being watched is back," Breen said.

"Yeah, I think it's coming from that. I think it's alive."

Breen shivered. "That's a troubling thought." He glanced behind them. "Let's try another route and see if we can't get around this thing."

Ty followed his brother, and they slowly backed around the corner and quickly made their way into an open channel leading to the right, hoping to avoid the fog but ending up running right back into it. "Let me try something."

Ty pulled on his magic and drew the air to him. He raised his hands and threw a blast of wind into the fog. Nothing happened. The fog didn't even budge, as though Ty's magic had just passed straight through, or maybe been consumed by it.

"Was something supposed to happen?" Breen asked.

Ty lowered his arms. "I don't think we have a choice. I think the only way to get to where we want to go is straight through."

"It's your test. You choose."

Ty looked at the menacing haze ahead. There was something in there. He could feel it calling to him.

If he had a lick of common sense, he would have run in the opposite direction, and perhaps a couple of months ago he would have. A couple of months ago, he'd have never volunteered to go on this quest in the first place. He wanted to believe his being there meant he had grown. Steeling his nerves, he raised his sword and started toward the fog.

The fog didn't move, slowly swirling in place as if waiting for them to come to it. Ty's hands shook the closer they got. He could feel a presence within. It was growing stronger. It felt . . . angry.

"You sure about this?" Breen whispered beside him.

"No. But it's the only choice we have."

"Wait," Breen said, stopping about ten feet from the edge of the mist. He lowered his satchel and dug around inside, coming out with the coil of rope he'd used to save Ty with earlier. He handed one end to Ty. "Tie yourself off so we don't lose each other."

"Good idea," Ty said, taking the moist rope and looping it around his waist with a secure knot. Breen tied his as well, and after testing both, he slung the travel pack over his shoulders and placed the arrow he'd been carrying back in the quiver and hooked his bow over his shoulder.

Ty looked at him funny. "Why are you—"

"A bow isn't going to do me much good in there," he said, reaching into his jacket and pulling out two of his larger knives. He looked at Ty's short sword. "Don't hit me with that."

"I'll try not to."

With a single nod, they started for the fog. The feeling of something inside waiting on them grew to the point Ty could almost see it. Ty was the first through. He quickly discovered that not even the magic of night sight could pierce the mist. He couldn't even see his sword. He felt for the rope and released a sigh of relief when he found it was still there, hanging to his left.

"Breen, can you see anything?"

There was no answer.

"Breen?"

The rope suddenly went slack.

Ty panicked, raising his hand to feel for where his brother should have been. "Breen, say something!" Ty no longer cared who heard him. "Breen!" He gathered up the loose end of the rope and kept moving, one hand in front of him as he tried to find his brother.

He smacked up against the side of one of the walls and turned in the other direction, eventually finding the other side, but with no sign of his brother. He tried feeling his way back in the direction they'd come to see if his brother had gotten turned around, but by the time he reached the next intersection, he realized the fog was everywhere. He quickly untied his half of the rope and wrapped it over his shoulder, not quite sure what to do with it.

His heart was pumping loud enough for him to hear. He raised his hand and called on his magic. Blue flames erupted from his hand, but they did nothing to scatter the fog. He was tempted to ignite the corridor but was too afraid he might hit his brother in the process. He tried gathering the wind once again, but no matter how many puffs of air he sent out, whatever this stuff was, it wasn't moving.

"Breen!"

Nothing but silence.

Ty finally relinquished his magic and let the flames die. They weren't doing him any good anyway. He grabbed the rope and wrapped it around his waist to keep it from dragging behind him, kicking himself for not thinking to do that sooner.

Breen was probably looking for him farther in. He had to keep searching. He started to raise his sword but thought better of it. What if he accidentally impaled his brother with it, not knowing he was there? Reluctantly, he kept the tip aimed down as he pushed forward, not willing to let go of it altogether, feeling at least a modicum of safety with it in his hands.

Every so often, he called his brother's name, not quite as loudly as before, but enough that if his brother was within throwing distance, he might have heard him. He still couldn't imagine what would have possessed Breen to untie himself. Whatever the reason, Ty couldn't understand how he had disappeared so quickly. One moment, he was there, the next he wasn't.

Ty kept one hand on the stone wall as he put one foot in front of the other. He came to what he thought was another intersection and, feeling his way along the outer walls, he headed right. The fog thickened, so much so that he could no longer see his hands in front of his face, which brought him to a stop as he tried to wait and see if it would pass. When it didn't, he started forward once more, slower now that he had no visibility at all.

That earlier feeling of something living within the mist was growing. He could feel a sudden barrage of emotions floating around him: anger, fear, desperation, but mostly despair. It left his skin crawling.

Ty heard a voice behind him and spun. "Who's there? Breen?"

Another muffled voice spoke directly behind him, and he spun back around, this time swinging his blade, striking the wall beside him. "Show yourself!"

Breen was the least of his worries at this point, so he swept his sword up and moved it through the mist around him like a blind man with his guiding staff, making sure no one was there waiting to pounce on him. He kept his shoulder to the wall as he scooted down the passageway. The voices were growing in number. He couldn't make out what they were saying, muffled as though through a heavy blanket. They whispered to him out of the fog, coming at him from all sides. He swung his sword left, then right, but hit nothing.

He took off running, not caring where he went so long as it was away from the voices. But no matter where he ran, the voices followed, only growing in number and intensity. He found himself wandering through the tunnels, hopelessly lost, growing more desperate by the minute. He screamed into the darkness, and the darkness screamed back.

Ty stumbled into a corner in the passage wall and curled into a ball. The voices were all around him. He could hear them now: some shouting at him to turn around, others enticing him to keep going. A man shouted that he needed to get back to his wife and kids, another threatened that if Ty didn't take him to the treasure, he'd kill him. A young lad begged Ty to save him, to take him out of this wretched place.

Pretty soon faces began to appear. Frightening, terrifying faces warning him to turn back while he still could. Faces of men and women, disfigured with rot, some so horrifying to look on that Ty was forced to close his eyes. But even with his eyes closed, he could see them. Bodies formed with the faces, just as desiccated, arms outstretched to him, begging for relief, begging for him to save them. But how could he? He didn't know who they were.

"We are the lost," they chorused, nearly shaking the stones he leaned against. There were thousands of voices all speaking as one. "We are the cursed! We are those who came before. Leave! Or you will join us."

The very thought of who these voices belonged to had Ty back on his feet and running. How was this possible? Was he to believe that these were the souls of all those who'd died within the maze? That their spirits had been trapped like those poor wretches in Karpaath? At least Tirana and her people were still alive, still had use of their bodies. These voices had been brutally killed trying to lay claim to something that didn't even exist.

Ty ran until his legs gave out and he collapsed against one of the walls. The voices and faces followed him, surrounded him. It felt as though they were inside of him. Was this what it was like to lose your mind? He couldn't block them out. He reached for his magic and sent his flames searing into the abyss, volley after volley, but it did nothing to stop the shades.

"What do you want?" he screamed.

"To be free!" they screamed back as one all-powerful chorus that shook the very foundation of the maze. "Release us!"

"How?" Ty demanded, tears running down his cheeks, the emotions threatening to completely overwhelm him.

"Finish your task."

He dropped to his knees as all the pain and anguish from these lost souls poured out of him. "How can I? I have no idea where I am."

As soon as the words came out, the mist parted, and a man stepped out, dressed in full armor similar to those Ty had seen scattered along the maze corridors. He was somewhat transparent, seemingly created by the same mist that made up the surrounding fog. "We have been waiting a long time. Come."

Ty could sense the desperation in the man's words, so he didn't argue. He got to his feet and followed him, wondering in the back of his mind if this had something to do with faith, though he didn't really see how. Unless, of course, one counted the faith it took to chase after a spirit.

The fog formed a thick wall both in front and behind, blocking off any attempt by Ty to escape. The warrior made no sound as he walked, his armor not so much as squeaking. Ty had no idea where they were going, since he couldn't see anything beyond the small hole that had been created for him to walk in, but he had a feeling that wherever they were going, it was important. The farther they went, the more he began to question what he was doing.

What if this is part of the test? What if the fog spirits were put here to lead me in the wrong direction? For all Ty knew, it could be taking him right back to the beginning of the maze.

Ty was about to turn around when the soldier came to a stop and raised his arm. "We are here."

The fog parted ahead, pulling back far enough for Ty to see that he was standing just inside the entrance of another corridor, and what lay beyond was a wide circular opening surrounded by dozens of other similar passageways. He looked at the warrior. "What about my brother?"

The man didn't say a word. He just stood there, pointing toward the center of the opening even after the fog closed in and swallowed him.

Ty turned back to the opening.

He'd done it. He'd finally reached the center.

Chapter 31 | Ty

HE VOICES AND FACES from within the fog faded into the background, but the fog itself remained just behind him, as if to bear witness, an audience of thousands pushing him forward, their freedom hanging in the balance. Ty's sword trembled in his hand as he slowly made his way out into the open center of the maze, his eyes darting left and right, expecting to see the maze monster lumbering out at him at any moment.

The center of the maze was an enormous circle with dozens of passageways all meeting together. Ty wondered why he hadn't seen this place from the cliffs back at the cavern, but then he remembered that most of the central section of the maze had been covered by the strange fog.

"Ty!"

Ty spun, ready to swing, but nearly dropped his sword when he spotted Breen racing out from another corridor three down from his own. "Breen!" Ty ran to meet him, never so glad to see his brother as right then.

Breen snatched Ty off the ground, and they embraced, Breen squeezing him so hard, Ty thought he'd pass out. Breen finally released him, and Ty took a step back. "Why did you untie yourself from the rope?" He handed Breen the coil from his shoulder. "Why did you leave me back there?"

"I didn't leave you," Breen said, taking a moment to look at the rope before stuffing it in his pack. "You left me."

"No, I didn't. I searched for you everywhere. At least until the voices came."

"What voices?"

"The voices in the fog. Didn't you see all the dead people? They were everywhere."

"Dead people?" Breen stared at him like he'd lost his mind. Perhaps he had. "I didn't hear any voices, and I certainly didn't see any dead people. When I saw we'd been separated, I started looking for you, and eventually ended up here."

Ty pointed back toward the mist, which had now engulfed all the branching corridors visible to Ty from where they were standing. "The dead people in the mist are the spirits from all the dead bodies we've seen in the maze. They say they're trapped here until someone claims the key."

"Trapped like Tirana and her people?"

Ty nodded. "I think so. Except these people are a whole lot angrier than those back in Karpaath."

Breen glanced around at the fog-lined corridors and frowned. "Then I guess we better get on with it. I don't know about you, but I want to get out of this place." With a knife in both hands, Breen started out toward the middle of the circle.

Ty followed beside him, stepping over another set of remains, this one with a full suit of armor and a long spear still clutched in his hand. Ty felt sorry for the man, to have made it this far and found out there was no treasure after all. He probably just sat down and died right there.

At the center of the circle, they found a rectangular piece of stone that stood at least ten feet high. Why would there be a single block of stone sitting here? There was no writing on it, no markings, no indication whatsoever that it was in any way relevant. Ty walked over and laid his hands on the stone while Breen circled to the other side. It was cool to the touch, but not all that different from—

"Ty! You might want to come take a look at this."

Ty walked around to the other side and nearly yelped with delight. A long piece of glass had been melded into the stone with ancient runes carved into the frame around it.

"Do you see anything that looks like a key?" Ty asked, studying the runes at the top.

"Maybe it's down there."

"Where?" Ty turned. He hadn't noticed it before, too preoccupied with finding the traveling mirror, but there was a hole in the ground a few steps behind them. It wasn't like the black nothingness they'd come across before. This one had a set of stairs leading down and inside. The closer they got to the hole, the warmer it seemed to get.

They stopped at the edge and looked down. The heat billowing out of the hole was intense. Ty wiped the sweat from his forehead.

"How far do you think it goes?" Ty asked.

Breen had sweat dripping in his eyes. "Afraid we're going to have to find out."

Ty grimaced and started for the hole, but his brother stopped him.

"No. I'll go first."

Ty immediately took a step back.

Breen frowned. "You could have at least pretended to argue the point."

"Oh, sorry." He grabbed his brother's arm. "No, Breen, I insist on going first!" He smiled at his brother. "How was that?"

Breen rolled his eyes and started into the hole.

Ty didn't want to wait and started down after him. The first wave of heat hit him in the face, and he nearly lost his breath. It was so strong he found he could hardly keep the air in his lungs. This was certainly one of those times Ty wished he was more adept with his magic. He was sure Nyalis would have known a way to keep the heat from touching them.

Reaching the bottom, Ty nearly had to push his brother out of the way just to see into the small antechamber. "What's going on?" He stepped around Breen and gaped. The room was empty, comprised of the same slate-grey stone as the rest of the maze, all except the back wall, which seemed to be made of fire. "*Ru'kasha Sve.*" The blinding light from the flames dimmed, but they also regained their color.

Breen joined him in releasing the spell.

Ty could hardly suck in enough air to speak. He felt as though he were being slowly roasted alive. "There," he said, pointing at the flames, which seemed to be moving in unpredictable patterns, coming together in some places, spreading apart in others, but only momentarily. Behind the somewhat translucent wall, he could just make out a pedestal with something floating above it.

"How do we get it?" Breen asked, almost doubled over, his hands up to protect his face from the heat.

Ty delved as deep as he dared and drew whatever air he could find to him. He was having a difficult time gathering it because the heat was eating most of it up. What he could find was coming from the stairs. Gathering what he could, he turned and threw it at the flames. They didn't extinguish. They didn't even budge. Apparently, this wasn't your average fire.

Just above the wall was an inscription: *FAITH*. Ty knew what he had to do and took a step toward the flames.

Breen grabbed Ty's arm. "Are you sure?"

Ty looked at the flames and tried to focus his thoughts. *I can do this.* He didn't know if it was bravery or stupidity forcing him on, but one thing was for sure: He hadn't come this far for nothing. He took one step forward, then another. He had both his arms up to protect his face, as it felt like the skin was peeling from his bones. Pretty soon, he was standing directly in front of the wall, the flames so hot he almost lost consciousness.

Drawing every bit of courage he could muster, he reached out toward the wall. His mind screamed for him to stop, begging him to pull back, shouting how stupid he was.

But he couldn't stop. Too many people were depending on him.

His arm barely scraped the edge of the flames, and he screamed, and everything went black.

". . . die on me. Ty . . . Ty, wake up."

Ty opened his eyes, and the first thing he felt was a cold gust of night air washing over his face. It was wonderful, for a brief moment. Then the agonizing pain struck, and he screamed again.

Breen grabbed Ty's arm. "Stop moving or you'll make it worse!"

Ty attempted to lift it high enough to take a look. What he saw was hideous. The fingers on his right hand were twice their normal size, and covered in white blisters, pus oozing from some, blood from others. Breen was attempting to wrap them, but even the faintest kiss from the evening breeze was enough to send the world spinning.

Breen finally managed to hold him down long enough to get the rest on. He even lathered the fingers with a concoction Orlyn had given them to help aid in the healing process. Breen looked beside himself with worry as he rubbed his hands through his hair. "I don't know what to do. I should never have let you try that. This is all my fault."

"No," Ty croaked between bouts of tears and spurts of whimpering. "It's my fault. I figured because I'm this so-called chosen one that I could just walk right through it. Stupid! Like being part faerie would somehow keep me from getting burned alive." He laid his head back down on his brother's lap and sobbed.

By the time Ty finished crying and had managed to sit up on his own, he found his hand had gone from a shrilling agony down to an overwhelming throb. At least the sky had stopped spinning. Orlyn certainly knew his herbs.

Ty conjured his night sight, and the center of the maze came back into view, at least the part not enveloped by living fog.

"What do we do now?" Breen asked, staring at Ty's bandaged hand.

"I don't know."

Breen glanced over his shoulder at the hole. "I could try."

Ty shot up. "Are you crazy?" He winced and quickly cradled his hand. "I'm not about to let you—"

A bloodcurdling wail broke the night.

Ty nearly toppled over trying to get to his feet with one hand.

Breen helped him the rest of the way up, then grabbed his bow and quiver, nocking an arrow as fast as Ty had ever seen. Ty went to draw his weapon, but then saw the white wrapping and realized it was his sword hand that had been burned, so he went for his magic instead. Blue flames encapsulated his left hand as he joined his brother in scanning the surrounding passageways, looking for where the wail had originated.

The fog parted from one of the tunnels directly in front of them, and they got their first good look at the creature. It was even more frightening than it sounded, standing at least half the size of one of the maze walls, looming far over either of them. It had four legs but seemed to favor using only two as it reared back and opened its maw to produce its ear-piercing wail. The front of its jaws were similar to that of a viper, with two prominent fangs at the top, but unlike the viper, it also had a full set of daggerlike teeth just behind them. Dark spikes protruded from pale grey skin across its shoulders and down the back of each arm, stopping at the elbows. Its tail seemed to balance its weight as it beat against the side of the tunnel, shaking down loose bits of stone and debris. Fur grew in patches along the back of the creature's hide, while the front was covered in tough sinew and scales, giving the maze monster the appearance of having been bred from several different species. Ty wondered if the wizards had created it or if it had lived in these mountains all along.

The creature dropped to all fours and slowly started for them, moving as though it had all the time in the world, a hunter knowing it had cornered its prey. The brothers backed all the way to the center of the platform.

Ty could feel the heat coming from the hole directly behind them. "Whatever happens, we need to protect that mirror," he said, sparing a hasty glance over his shoulder at the exposed glass on the other side of the hole. "It's our only way out of here."

His hand still felt as though it were on fire, but he had to push the pain aside to focus on the more immediate threat. The maze monster slowly circled their position.

"What's it waiting for, an invitation?" Breen asked, sighting his arrow. "Come on, you ugly thing, show me your eyes." The creature's eyes were tiny in proportion to its size, two black orbs no larger than peaches, and each protected by a thick, bony protrusion just above the lid. The creature's hide looked as tough as a razorback's. Ty remembered what happened the last time he shot one with an arrow: nothing. The arrow did little to slow it.

The monster reared once more and released another wail, then attacked.

Breen was the first to respond, sending one of the black arrows straight into the creature's open maw. The arrow buried itself into the softer tissue in the back of its throat, but the monster kept coming. Breen didn't have time to nock another arrow, which meant it was up to Ty.

Ty focused all his energy on his fire and sent it straight into the monster's face. The creature stumbled to the side, just missing Breen as it went down and rolled past. The tail clipped his brother in the leg, and Breen collapsed. He rolled back to his feet with a limp, trying to nock another arrow.

The creature rolled to the side, then tore into one of the nearby passageways and disappeared into the fog.

Another wail split the night, but this time it sounded like it came from somewhere on their left. The brothers spun on their heels, searching each tunnel.

"Where is it?" Ty said, continuing to spin, his back to his brother.

"I don't know," Breen said frustratedly, his bow up, searching the surrounding tunnels but seeing nothing but fog.

Ty didn't know which was worse, facing the creature head on or spinning in circles not knowing where it was.

Without warning, the monster burst out of a tunnel on the right, and Ty released another volley of blue flame, but the creature ducked, and the fire went straight over its head, disappearing into the fog on the other side.

Breen took aim and released, but the monster lowered its head, and the arrow struck the hardened protrusion just above its right eye and bounced off. The monster dove at them, and Breen shoved Ty out of the way just before the creature's claws punched three holes in the stone where Ty had been standing.

Breen was hit in the chest by the monster's lower arm and went flying backward, skidding to a stop several feet away. His bow had been flung free of his hands, and the monster turned and stepped directly on it. Ty's heart dropped.

The monster, seeing Breen lying there, swung its tail around to squash him, but Ty, drawing in all the air he could muster, hit the creature before it could. The force sent the creature careening into one of the tunnel walls. The walls groaned and cracked, raining stone down on the creature.

Ty ran for Breen, who was just managing to push his way up to his hands and knees, and grabbed him with his one good arm and attempted to drag him back toward the center. Behind them, the monster pulled itself from the rubble and disappeared back into the fog.

Breen winced as he made it to his feet, blood seeping from a gash on the side of his head. He rushed over to his bow and picked it up. Ty was astonished. It was still in one piece. He had been worried the creature had snapped the limbs in two, but there didn't seem to be even a noticeable scratch. Even the string was still taut.

They limped back to the mirror at the center of the platform and retook their places just outside the hole, Ty with his injured hand and Breen with his wounded leg and now bruised chest and head. Ty scanned each of the surrounding passageways, expecting the maze monster to come charging out of the mist at any moment.

"We can't keep going like this," Breen said, wiping the blood that was now trickling down the side of his cheek. "Even if we manage to kill it, we can't leave without that piece of the key."

"I know." Ty bit his lower lip nearly hard enough to draw blood as he weighed their limited options.

His brother was right. Whether they liked it or not, that piece of rounded metal below was their only hope at surviving. It didn't matter if they killed the maze monster. It didn't matter if there had been no maze monster to begin with. They couldn't leave without what they came for.

The ground began to tremble, and they both turned as the monster broke through the fog from a different corridor. Breen barely got another shot off, the black arrow burying itself to the fletching in a vulnerable spot just under the creature's arm. It screeched and stumbled forward, knocking Ty off his feet, but not before he was able to hit it with another fist of air. The force flung the creature free of the mirror and back into another passageway, where it vanished into the mist.

Breen drew another arrow and waited as Ty crawled his way back to his feet, limping as he did, pain shooting through his leg. He looked down and found a long gash on the side, probably from one of the monster's spikes. His pants were already turning red around the gaping tear.

They couldn't wait any longer. Biting back the pain, he hobbled over to the hole, took one last deep breath of fresh air, and started down. He didn't know if Breen had seen him leave or not. He didn't have time to find out. The sooner he found a way to complete his task, the sooner they could get out of there. Slowly, he made his way down to the awaiting room. The heat was unbearable, his breath coming in heavy rasps by the time he reached the landing below and stood in front of the searing wall of flames.

"*Ru'kasha Sve.*" He stared at the blinding wall in front of him. Why was faith so important? What was faith anyway? "*Believing in something greater than yourself,*" he heard his mother say. "*Believing in what you cannot see.*" Memories of his childhood flooded back.

"*Like the Creator?*" he remembered asking.

His mother smiled. "*Yes, Ty, like the Creator. We can't see Him, but we can see his handiwork all around us.*"

"And what if I choose not to believe?"

She patted him on the head. *"That's what faith is all about. Believing in something even when those around you choose not to. Faith is when you close your eyes and look with your heart."*

Ty closed his eyes for a moment, but her words filled his mind. What did he believe in? A loud wail sounded from somewhere above, and Ty's eyes jerked back open, but he forced the fear aside and focused on his mother's words. *Believing in something when everything tells you not to?* He kept his hands raised to protect his face. He was all but gasping for air at this point, the flames sucking up all the air in the room.

"I believe that if the wizards went to all the work of setting this up, they intended for someone to pass it. I also believe that, whether it's by the Creator's design or not, if I don't get that key, we're going to die here anyway." Ty took one last raspy gulp of air. "I believe this is going to really hurt!" Ty closed his eyes, raised his good hand out in front of him, and ran straight at the flames.

Pain like he'd never felt before racked his body as he hit the wall. He opened his mouth to scream and sucked in fire. It burned him from the inside out.

His charred fingers wrapped around something cold, and the inferno vanished.

Ty opened his eyes, surprised he still had eyes to open.

The pain was gone.

He looked down, almost afraid to see the results, only to find there wasn't so much as a single smoldering mark, not even the lingering hint of smoke. In fact, the pain from his first burning seemed to have disappeared as well. He unwrapped the bandages on his hand and found the skin smooth to the touch, not a single blister.

Ty held up the piece of metal. It was cool to the touch.

It looked like the outer ring of a medallion. It even had a braided leather necklace attached on one end. There were three evenly spaced gold insets around the outside of the silver casing, each with a single black stone at its center, and the casing between the insets was decorated with runes.

"All that death, for this?"

Ty turned to run back up the stairs but quickly learned that the deep gash in his leg hadn't disappeared along with the burns. He yelped. As fast as he could, he started up the stairs, noticing for the first time how quiet it was above. Ignoring the pain in his leg, he ran the rest of the way up.

Breen stood at the edge of the hole, staring off toward one of the passageways on the left. Ty grabbed his brother's leg on the way out, and Breen jumped with a shout, nearly releasing his arrow. He spun around and raised his bow as if to clobber Ty over the head with it when he spotted what was in Ty's hands.

"You did it!" He released the draw on his bowstring and helped Ty the rest of the way out of the hole. "Wait. How did you do it?" He quickly looked Ty over. "Are you burned?"

Ty shook his head. "No. As soon as I touched the key, the flames disappeared." He held up his hand. "And so did the burns." He looked past his brother to the fog, which was now encircling the entire perimeter, blocking the tunnels from view. "Where's the maze monster?"

"I don't know," Breen said, turning to look. "One minute it was about to cut me down, the next, it simply walked away and disappeared back into the mist."

The fog, which had been content up until that point to remain at the edge of the channels, slid out across the opening to where they were standing. Breen moved to protect Ty with his bow, but Ty grabbed his arm and lowered it.

"I don't think they mean us harm." At least he hoped they didn't. He no longer sensed the earlier feelings of anguish and hatred and despair. Now, there was a sense of peace, a calm that had him breathing easier as the mist completely encapsulated them.

The voices filled his head. "We are free." With that, the mist lifted off the ground and rose into the sky, vanishing as it went.

"I heard them," Breen said uneasily. "I actually heard them." He tilted his head and joined Ty in watching the last remnants of the dead drift into oblivion. "What now?"

Ty looked at the mirror. "Now we get out of this place once and for all." He took a moment to gaze back across what he could see of the maze, noting the Mountains of Escalor in the distance. He wondered if this would be all of the Westlands they'd ever get the chance to see. Quite the terrible first impression. "I wonder what happened to Tirana and her village?"

Breen collected their travel bag from where he'd left it in front of the mirror. "I was wondering the same thing. I hope they were finally able to go free."

Ty smiled. "We could always go back and find out."

Breen hmphed. "I don't want to know that badly." He offered a quick salute toward the mountains. "Good luck to them," he said, then turned back to the mirror. "Let's get out of here before that monster changes its mind."

"Don't think we need to worry about that," Ty said as he pulled the compass from his pocket and stared up at the runes around the mirror's frame. "You're right, though, it's time to go."

He reached for his magic, letting the heat radiate through him as he reached out with his mind and let the magic of the compass stroke the mirror's frame. Two names came to life.

"*Nigul Kaldieris. Vahalera Miyami.*"

Ty and Breen's reflection in the glass spun and swirled, replaced by darkness. It looked like one of the empty holes that had sucked Ty through earlier.

"I wonder where we'll end up this time," Ty said, hesitant to step through considering what had happened the last time he had.

Breen looked at him and smiled. "Only one way to find out, I guess." He stepped through the glass.

Ty followed him and stumbled to a stop just on the other side. For just a brief moment, he could see back through the mirror into the maze before the image swirled and vanished, leaving them in complete darkness. He could feel it pressing in around him.

"Is it night here?" Breen asked softly, his words echoing around their heads.

"I don't think it's night that we're seeing," Ty said, raising his hand and conjuring a small ball of blue flame.

The breath caught in Ty's throat. They were standing on a lone spit of rock not much wider than the front room of their house. Massive spear-like protrusions dangled over their heads. Behind them was the mirror they'd just traveled through, embedded in rock, and on the other side was a second mirror. It, too, was embedded in rock.

They had been transported into some sort of underground cavern.

The rock they were currently standing on was completely surrounded by water, water dark enough to see their reflections. They had been sent to the middle of an underground lake, with no key in sight.

Ty shivered as he made a complete turn. There was nothing there but water . . . and whatever was in the water. All Ty could think about was the monster that had been living just below the surface back in Reed Marsh. For all of the horrors they had faced within the maze, somehow this felt worse.

Chapter 32 | Adarra

ADARRA WIPED SWEAT from her face. She didn't think it was possible to hurt any more than she did right now. Her back hurt. Her arms hurt. Her head hurt, especially after getting clobbered by Fraya, who seemed to be picking up on Darryk's training unnaturally fast. Adarra sat down on the bench under the old willow in the corner of the courtyard and winced. Even her backside hurt.

"Tell me again why we're doing this?" she asked Fraya, who joined her on the bench after clearing some snow off from the previous day's fall. Fraya placed her bo staff on the ground beside Adarra's.

"We do it so we can defend ourselves when the time comes," Fraya said, looking very proud of herself after having swept aside Adarra's attack so effortlessly, once again leaving Adarra lying face first in the snow and sand.

Getting a mouthful of sand wasn't even the worst of it. It was doing it in front of Aiden, who never ceased to find the time to be there to watch her humiliation. Even he, of all people, was picking up the training faster than she was.

"If I try defending myself any more than I am now," Adarra grumbled, "I'll be dead."

Fraya chuckled. The young healer's black hair was pulled back and tied with a brightly colored ribbon, this one a deep pumpkin. Breen had complimented Fraya on her ribbons some time back, and now she was never seen without one.

"I thought you were very . . . graceful," Aiden said, trotting over in his rich burgundy suit to hand her his handkerchief.

Aiden was beautiful, certainly more so than she was with her straight brown hair, shorter legs, and freckles. Why he doted on her, she'd never know, but there came a point when enough was enough. The last thing Adarra wanted was for this beautiful man to be standing there dabbing the sweat and finely ground rock from her brow. Besides, she stank, her hair was disheveled, and she was sure her left eye was swollen from Lyessa's demonstration of "wind over water."

The wind had missed the water altogether and somehow ended up in Adarra's eye.

Worse yet, she still had to find the time to go see Jonas. Overlord Barl insisted the huge Tallosian be kept in the lower dungeon until they determined what to do with him, and had requested Adarra find a way to communicate with him. Thanks to her magic, she was the only one who could attempt to learn his language in the time needed to get some answers.

"Here," Fraya said, reaching over to place her fingers around Adarra's eye. "Let me help."

Adarra felt a cold tingling on the side of her face that sent a trickle of bumps down both arms. The twinging ache vanished, and she immediately reached up to gently press around the socket. It no longer stung at her touch. She looked at Fraya. "Thanks."

"My pleasure. And don't worry, you'll get there. You remember how bad I was when we first started. Didn't know one side of the bo staff from the other, and now look at me," she said, pulling up her sleeve and holding out her arm. "I only get half the bruises I used to."

Adarra sighed. "You would think that being a memoriae would somehow help me with my training. I can remember every word or image I've ever seen since I was born, and yet I can't remember how to hold a stick in the right direction to keep from getting hit by another stick." She shook her head. "I'm hopeless."

"Quit gawking at the women, Aiden," Darryk called out from the center of the practice ring. The burly trainer had his staff in hand and was waiting. "It's your turn. And what in the flaming Pits are you wearing? How many times have I told you to buy some proper clothing? That shirt's going to get ripped three ways from Eighthday. You might as well go shirtless for all the good that will do."

Adarra's attention perked, completely suppressing the complaints she had thought to levy against Lyessa for her insisting they learn how to fight. All the suffering might be worth it to just see Aiden sweaty and bare chested.

"Come on," Lyessa said to the two girls as she left the practice ring and passed by their bench on her way to the house. "Let's get washed up."

Adarra's heart sank. "But, but I . . ." She looked back at the practice ring where Aiden was just collecting his bo staff. With a heavy sigh, she finally stood and traipsed after the other two, glancing back over her shoulder periodically to see if Aiden would indeed take his shirt off. Alas, the cold weather won out, and he didn't.

The one saving grace about the training was the soaking that came afterward, something Adarra never got to enjoy at home. Their brass tub was hardly large enough to dip in, let alone spread out the way she could in Lyessa's. As usual, Gina had the three basins filled with hot water and scented oils, and she stood in the doorway waiting to collect their dirty clothing.

"Strip," she ordered as they started into the washroom. Lyessa's nanny clicked her tongue and shook her head when she saw the bruises. "I'm just gonna have to have another word with that brute down there. He should know better than to be treating three fine ladies such as yourselves in this fashion."

Adarra harrumphed. "Lyessa's the one you need to have a stern talking-to. This was all her idea in the first place." She passed a smile over to the redheaded young lady.

"And you'll thank me for it later."

"Don't hold your breath," Fraya added, wincing as she pulled off her tunic.

Gina collected the clothes, still clicking her tongue and shaking her head the entire time. Adarra thought it nice to have someone like Gina there to see to your needs. She often wondered what it was like living in the overlord's house, being waited on hand and foot, eating the best foods, wearing the latest fashions, riding around in fancy carriages. Amidst all of that, she had been surprised at how normal Lyessa had turned out. Well, *normal*, in someone's definition of the word.

Lyessa wasn't like the other wealthy girls in town. In fact, quite the opposite. Sure, she could dress up like the rest and put on airs, but it seemed a mask to hide who she really was—a fighter, and future leader of Sidara. Adarra liked her and liked the idea of her and Ty. Her little brother needed someone strong to keep him in line.

"Any word on your brothers?" Lyessa asked as if reading Adarra's mind. The overlord's daughter sank slowly into the soapy bubbles and exhaled. Fraya, who was already in her tub, stuck her head up high enough to see over the rim.

Adarra pulled off the last of her clothing and lowered herself into the tub on Lyessa's right. After taking a moment to adjust to the hot water, she finally replied, "Nothing new at this point. Don't know if we'll ever hear anything."

The room was silent for a moment as they pondered how frightening that would be, the possibility of never hearing from either of them again.

"Stubborn oaf," Lyessa mumbled under her breath, loud enough for everyone to hear. "He should have let me go with him. I could have helped. Sometimes, I wonder if he's got any brains up there at all."

"Just sometimes?" Adarra asked.

They all chuckled.

"At least he has Breen with him," Fraya added. "Breen will keep him safe."

"If Breen managed to catch up to him," Adarra added. There was no guarantee her brother could have tracked the wizard through the forest. Reed Marsh was enormous. There was no telling where her brother might have entered from.

"I'm sure he did," Fraya said, trying to stay positive.

"Then there's at least one person with a clear head," Lyessa said. "Oh, my father wanted me to ask how you're coming along with the Northman. Any progress in communicating with him? Not that I can think of a good reason why you'd want to. Best to kill him and be done with it. He seems the kind of man who'd rather die than sit in a cage anyway."

"I've made some progress," Adarra said. "In fact, that was my next stop."

"I don't know how you do it, Adarra," Fraya said. "There's no way I could face someone like that, someone who'd tried to kill me. He seems a vicious sort of creature."

"Nothing but animals, if you ask me," Lyessa said.

Justly earned as Lyessa's animosity was, Adarra still felt a twinge of pity for the big Tallosian. "That's what I had thought at first. But—"

"But?" Lyessa stopped her scrubbing and lowered her brush. "What's there to *but* about? They wear pieces of skulls on their faces. They wear the scalps of their enemies on their backs. Probably eat their kills as well." She sneered. "Animals, all of them. Even if you learned their language and somehow miraculously managed to teach him ours, I don't see how it would help. What can you possibly hope to learn from a savage like that?"

"I must admit I felt the same way as you at first, but the more I talk with him, the more I find myself sympathetic. His people had come to our shores out of desperation to find food for their families. It was Mangora who used them."

"They didn't seem all that conflicted about it when they tried taking my head off."

"I'm with Lyessa on this one," Fraya said. "How can you defend them after they nearly killed your entire family?"

"I'm not defending anyone. What they did was wrong. I'm just saying people will do things out of desperation that perhaps they wouldn't normally. They came to find food. Who knows what that witch said to convince them to work for her? She might have put some kind of obedience spell on them for all we know."

"There's no such thing," Lyessa said, though she had no way of knowing herself since magic was a topic she knew very little about.

"Is there?" Fraya asked, not quite so convinced.

Adarra shrugged. "I don't know. But that's not the point. The point is, we don't really know the circumstances surrounding their decision."

"I don't care what the circumstances were," Lyessa said, pointing the bristle end of her brush at Adarra. "Every man and woman is responsible for making their own choices. They better be ready to deal with the consequences. I hope he gets the rope."

Adarra could see she wasn't going to win this argument with Lyessa, and in all honesty she probably didn't deserve to. Lyessa was right. There wasn't a moment's hesitation in any of the Tallosians' eyes when it came to killing, except perhaps Jonas. It wasn't until Adarra had gutted his partner that Jonas had attacked. "I'm doing this because your father insists that I try, and I gave him my word that I would."

Fraya tossed her bar of soap at Lyessa, and the splash hit her in the face. The two shared a look, and Lyessa turned to Adarra. "I'm sorry. You didn't deserve that. I know how hard this has to be, and I know you'll do your best. If there's anyone capable of getting him to speak, it's you. I'm just having a hard time separating my feelings. Many of those lancers they killed had families, families that Father and I had to console."

"I understand," Adarra said, and she did.

Lyessa picked her brush back up and lathered the bristles with her soap. "I've got to meet Father in town later. Perhaps I'll see you there."

"Perhaps," Adarra said with a smile as she finished soaping off her legs. She looked over at Fraya's tub and could barely see her head over the rim. "What are your plans, Fraya?"

Fraya sat up so she could see the others, soap bubbles clinging to her hair and face. She looked like she'd grown a beard. At least a partial one. Half of it seemed to be slipping back down into the water. "I've got to go home and start dinner. Father will be wanting something to eat after another long day with my brothers dressing livestock. I'm surprised he's let me come and train as much as he has." She smiled at Lyessa. "I'm sure it didn't hurt to have the daughter of the overlord asking on my behalf."

Adarra wondered if her own father was still in town. It was now just the two of them at home, which made the days feel rather lonely. She didn't realize how much she'd miss her brothers until they weren't around. She even missed the aggravating way they'd hide her books when she wasn't looking.

Realizing she was just sitting, staring at her own reflection in the water, she looked up to see if one of the other two were watching. They weren't, each too preoccupied with scrubbing off the dirt. With Gina's help, Adarra quickly finished her scrubbing and was rinsed off, dried, and dressed before the other two had even washed the soap from their hair.

The dress she wore was one Lyessa had given her just after their incident with Mangora. It was a deep emerald, with a full skirt and dramatic sleeves that hung to below her knees. The round neckline and upper sleeves were adorned with matching white lace. It might have paled in comparison to some of Lyessa's evening gowns, but it was the most fashionable outfit Adarra had ever worn.

After a brief goodbye, Adarra left the overlord's estate and rode into town, feeling rather rejuvenated after the hot soak.

The sun was high and warm on her skin, tempering the cold easterly wind snaking its way down River Street as she passed through the north gates and started into the city proper. Snow clung to the cobbles, especially where it piled along the side of the walkways. The piles tended to grow with each fresh fall, as the shopkeepers would sweep it away from the front of their shops, making sure customers had a clear path inside.

The East Inn was just ahead on the left, but the traffic leading out from the Sidaran Assembly Hall on the right was so heavy that she decided to take a detour and enter the inn from the back. With the recall of the assembly and the formal meeting of the Provincial Authority, the Assembly Hall was one of the busiest buildings in Easthaven, a steady stream of carriages coming and going at all hours of the day.

With an hour or more to kill, Adarra decided to see if her father was taking his lunch inside. She knew he had business in town, she just didn't know with whom or for how long. Leaving Thistle with the stablehand, she walked across the back courtyard and entered from the side. The corridor was filled with men in green-and-yellow uniforms, all with the Sidaran crest of a great oak tree on the front. Easthaven seemed filled with lancers of late, a direct response to the attack by the White Tower.

The men stared as she passed. At least some of them did. She was sure it had more to do with her wearing one of Lyessa's frilly dresses than anything to do with her own appearance. Then again, give a man enough to drink and he'd find a toadfish appealing.

She caught herself sauntering and put a quick end to it. This wasn't her. She didn't prance around in front of men like some snobbish highborn. Of course, she'd never walked around town in such fancy clothes before either.

Oh no, she mused. *I'm becoming one of them.* Give her a pretty dress and immediately she turned into one of those prissy genteel girls who cared about nothing more than being noticed. After today, she was determined never to wear another fancy dress again.

The common room was unusually packed, even for lunch. Half the tables were being used, most with only a couple of seats taken, but it still made the place seem lively. There was even some live entertainment as Ethen—the local carpenter known for his exquisite decorative woodwork—regaled the audience with a few rounds of "The Miller's Daughter." The bar on the right was lined with mostly lancers, as they tended to prefer it to the tables. Only a few had gathered for a meal.

She smiled when she spotted her father at one of the tables near the front of the stage. He wasn't eating alone. A couple members of the council were there as well, including Sheeva, who was sitting uncommonly close to her father. Adarra hadn't been able to figure the woman out. Out of all the members of the council she could have befriended, she seemed to have bonded with her father, which bothered her. Adarra's mother had just passed. Did this woman have no sense of common propriety?

Then again, the woman lived her life in the shadows. She'd probably never had a real friendship in her life. Adarra guessed she could try giving her the benefit of the doubt.

"Adarra, come join us," Mistress Reloria said, spotting her from across the room.

Her father turned in his seat and smiled. "Perfect timing. We were just about to order." He grabbed a chair from a nearby table and placed it beside his. "What will you have?"

She took her seat, careful to not wrinkle her dress. "I'll have whatever stew they're serving today."

"It's lamb on Thirday," Feoldor said with an eager fluff of his whiskers. "And no one makes a better lamb stew than Bue Aboloff." He licked his lips. "I can taste those little red potatoes and onions already."

"They better hurry before Feoldor starts eating the plates," Orlyn said from Feoldor's right. His tall rune-covered staff shifted against the back of his seat as he leaned forward to take another sip from his tankard. The two men acted more like brothers than they did close friends, constantly picking on each other. It would have been annoying had it not been so amusing.

"How did training go today?" her father asked. "I hope Darryk went a little easier on you."

Adarra hmphed. "That man doesn't know the meaning of the word *easy*. You'd think he was instructing hardened lancer recruits. And Lyessa's no help, ordering us around like a drill sergeant at her first garrison posting." Adarra stretched her back. "I won't sit easy for a week."

The others chuckled. All except Sheeva, who looked like she'd eaten a sour persimmon. "It's good for a woman to know how to fight," the assassin said. "Strong here," she added, patting her arm. "And strong here," she finished, tapping the side of her head with her finger. "You should pay attention and not complain."

If Adarra hadn't felt uncomfortable around the woman before, she certainly did now. Her father tried smiling it off, but it came out rather forced and crooked. No one spoke until the food had arrived, and even then, it was just polite snippets of conversation to make the meal less awkward. Sheeva didn't seem bothered by the silence at all. In fact, she appeared to prefer it as she finished off one bowl and promptly asked for another.

Adarra had lost her appetite and merely picked at her stew before finally excusing herself. She thanked her father for the meal and left them to it. Sheeva was really beginning to get on her nerves, and it was high time she talked to her father about it.

Frustrated by the whole situation, Adarra decided to get a leg up on her work and ride over to the garrison early. After collecting her horse from the stables, she rode south toward the center of town and took Wood Lane west, where it eventually ended outside the south gate of the Easthaven barracks. She'd never seen it as full as it was presently.

The meetings with the overlords had lasted nearly two weeks before they finally headed home. Even still, the garrison was bustling with activity. Overlord Barl had recalled the lancers, and their numbers were increasing by the day. She'd never seen the city in such a state. She could almost feel the apprehension in the air.

She left Thistle tied in front of the main building, which also housed the underground cells they used for some of the city's more dangerous criminals. The city patrollers had their own cells in town, but those were mostly for purse snatchers and tavern brawlers. This building was also where the heads of the Lancer Corps kept their offices, preferring to remain separate from the rest of the enlisted men. After grabbing her satchel of books out of her saddlebag, she started up the steps.

"Can I help you, young lady?" asked an older gentleman standing guard at the front door. With so many new arrivals, the watch out front was continually changing, leaving her once again to have to explain who she was and where she was going.

"I'm here to see the Tallosian," she said, already anticipating the man's reaction, as it was the same for each new guard she spoke with. First, he'd smile as if Adarra were simply playing a joke, then when he saw she wasn't laughing, his demeanor would change to one of concern.

"Now see here, young lady, you don't want to go visiting a man like that. He's dangerous. Very dangerous." He kept shaking his head as if his persistence would somehow convince her he was right. "What's a nice woman like you want with a savage like that? Nope. Wouldn't be proper, me letting you down there and all."

As noble as his intentions might have been, the aging lancer was starting to grate on her nerves. "Please inform Commander Tiernan that Mistress Adarra is here for her scheduled meeting with the Northman at Overlord Barl's request."

The old man's eyes widened. "Overlord Barl? Well, I uh . . ." He glanced at some of the other lancers passing by and cleared his throat. "No need to bother the commander, I'm sure." He opened the door and directed her to follow him inside.

She straightened her shoulders and walked across the main room with her head held high as they made their way to the set of stairs leading down to the underground cells.

"Ah, Mistress Adarra," the sergeant said, rising from his desk at the bottom of the stairs. "You're early today." The jailer was a portly man with rosy cheeks, not much taller than she was. He grabbed his quill, dipped it into a small jar on the right side of his desk, and started scribbling into a ledger on the table. "I'll add your name to the roster." He glanced up from his writing. "And might I say you are looking quite lovely today."

Adarra smiled, blushing a little as she did. "Why thank you, Sergeant Finnly."

"My pleasure, ma'am."

The older guard beside her didn't seem to quite know what to make of it all, and simply kept his mouth shut.

"You can go back to your duties," Sergeant Finnly said to her escort.

The guard saluted. "Yes, sir." He glanced at Adarra timidly and tipped his hat. "Milady."

She nodded, and he headed back up the stairs, his sword clanging against his hip the whole way up.

"Good man, Orlis," Finnly said with a sad shake of his head as he watched the old lancer disappear over the stairs. "Bit long in the tooth, though." The jailer grabbed a set of keys off a hook on the wall behind his desk and promptly unlocked the door, motioning for her to follow. Once inside, he relocked the door and grabbed the torch from its bracket on the wall and started through the dark corridors. She followed quietly. As many times as she'd been down there, she could have found Jonas's cell in the dark.

Reaching their destination, Finnly stopped to light a torch hanging on the wall to give her some light to work with. The big Northman was sitting at the back of his cell, his back against the wall as he faced the bars separating him from his newly arrived guests. One look at Adarra and he immediately stood and walked to the front. "Spotted warrior."

She nodded to him, doing her best not to appear too flustered. "Jonas."

"Well, I'll leave you to it," Finnly said, giving the Tallosian a stern look. "If he tries anything, you just holler, and I'll have half the garrison in here."

"I'll be fine," Adarra said, then lowered her satchel and began pulling out her books, one at a time, her usual routine.

"I'll post a guard at the end of the hall, Miss Adarra, in case you need anything."

Adarra smiled. "Thank you, Sergeant."

Finnly waited a moment longer, giving Jonas one last looking-over, then proceeded back down the hall and disappeared around the corner.

Adarra looked at Jonas, taking a deep breath to calm her nerves. She didn't want to, but every time she looked at the man, all she could see was her mother. Jonas hadn't been the one to kill her, but that didn't mean he didn't hold some of the responsibility. Yet she had a job to do, and no matter what, she was determined to finish it.

Chapter 33 | Adarra

ADARRA ASSEMBLED HER books in a half circle on the cold stone in front of Jonas's cell, then plopped herself down between them. Jonas followed her down, sitting cross-legged with his knees pressing against the bars, as was his usual routine. Most of his face paint had washed off after having been provided a bucket of water to bathe with, revealing him to be younger than she had originally thought. He couldn't have been too much older than Breen.

The burn scar running down the side of his face also reached up into his hair line, leaving a bald area where the hair would no longer grow. The paint had a done a fair job in covering the pale pink area. Unfortunately, he was still wearing his thick cloak of human hair, unwilling to use the blanket they had provided for him. She wondered if it was a cultural thing, or a statement of defiance.

She opened *Aelbert's Guide to Understanding Languages* and placed it alongside *Roland's History of the Isle of Tallos*, which was one of the only helpful references on the founding of the Tallosian people and their breakaway from the Five Kingdoms. She had also collected several books on nonverbal communication, which had proven useful in better understanding Jonas's unique form of speech. She had the books memorized, even without her special gift, but she still found it comforting to have them close at hand.

Most surprising to her was how quickly the enormous Northman had picked up the Aldoran tongue, which might have had something to do with Tallosian heritage being derived from Aldor. According to the histories, the Tallosians had left Aldor during the Second Age, around the time that magic had begun to flourish. They had believed magic was evil and wanted to separate themselves from it.

For all his savage outward appearance, Jonas had an unexpectedly astute mind. He seemed to enjoy learning, with the way his mouth would curl upward when she spoke, or the intense way he watched her while she tried explaining things. She waved her fingers in front of her like ripples on water, then placed her thumb to her mouth, which was to ask Jonas if he'd been given enough to drink. From where she sat, she couldn't see any indication that he'd received any food or water.

He nodded. "Yas."

She smiled. "Good." She didn't bother trying to translate. He seemed to understand. "Now where did we stop last time?" She scanned through the notes she'd scribed in the leaves of her journal from their last visit. Not that she needed to, being a memoriae, but she found it helped her make connections between the things she remembered.

"How long . . . keep me?"

She looked up. There was confusion on his face. Did he expect them to just set him free? She suddenly felt a twinge of anger. "You killed many people," she said, using his dialect and hand gestures. "You will remain until the overlord decides your fate."

Jonas grew even more agitated, and he stood and paced the floor of his cell. He finally turned and grabbed hold of the bars. "You release me."

Adarra shot to her feet. "Why would I release you? You killed my mother."

Jonas looked confused and released the bars. "Mother?"

She nodded curtly. "Yes. You killed my mother," she said, going back to her signing and the Tallosian dialect.

He shook his head. "I no kill."

"You tried to kill me!" she said, taking an angry step toward the bars.

Jonas took a step back. His back straightened, and he stepped forward once more. Adarra had forgotten how big he really was until she was standing there looking up at him. She also had forgotten how close she was to the bars. Jonas was close enough now to reach through and grab her, but she had too much pride to scoot back now. She wasn't going to let him think he had intimidated her.

"Honor," he said, hitting his chest twice with the inside of his fist.

"What honor?" she asked. "You have no honor. You attacked without provocation." She had a hard time coming up with a way to make him understand, settling on them attacking for no reason.

"You won. Good fight. Now release . . . or you no honor."

"*Me*, no honor?" She wanted to reach through the cell and choke him herself, but then she remembered reading once about the Upakans, another segment of people who had distanced themselves from other societies. They, too, were a warring sect, but they also lived by their own specific code of conduct, with one rule standing above the rest: they weren't allowed to kill their own. Adarra wondered if this was something similar.

Unlike the Upakans, the Tallosians didn't appear to have any problems with attacking rival tribes or clans, or whatever they called their factions. The problem was when dealing with limited numbers, if you allowed constant skirmishes, there would soon be few people left.

She stared up at Jonas, holding his gaze, and began to sign. "What happens to those who lose?"

He thought a moment, as if making sure he understood her question, before answering. "Those in shame . . . pay tribute."

"What kind of tribute?"

"Victor's choice."

She nodded, almost forgetting her earlier anger at the prospect of learning something new. She walked over and grabbed her journal and began jotting everything down. "After tribute, what then?"

"Collect dead. Go home."

Now his request made a little more sense. It was a conflict of cultural customs. If someone were to walk around killing people in Easthaven, they better expect to suffer a similar fate. However, in their culture . . . Actually, she didn't know what it was like in their culture. Perhaps the Tallosians hadn't perceived this as having been a random murder. Maybe they had thought of it as an actual battle. Would they have attacked her family if Overlord Barl's guards hadn't been there? Did they look at them as . . .

She stopped her scribbling and looked up. "Would you have killed my family if the lancers hadn't been there?" She had to repeat it three times before he got the basic idea.

"No honor in killing a weaker foe."

She wrote down his words, feeling a little more relieved.

"When you release me?" he asked once more.

She set down her pad. How was she going to explain to him that in their custom what the Tallosians had done would be considered an atrocity? "What you did was—"

"Others come."

She stopped her translating. "What others?"

"The Dogar come."

The Dogar? That name sparked a memory, and she searched for it in her head, finding it in one of the Tallosian histories. The Dogar was the official name for the Northmen's hierarchy, similar to the Provincial Authority in Aldor, which consisted of the five Tallosian houses.

"Why would they come here?" she asked.

"Food."

"Is it that bad?" His people hadn't set foot in Aldor in nearly five hundred years. At least, that's what she'd overheard her father and Overlord Barl discussing.

"Black death. Kill harvest."

"Black death? Is that a disease?" She added the sign for sickness by touching her forehead and stomach with the first two fingers of both hands simultaneously.

Jonas shook his head frustratedly and used another word, adding an additional sign with it that symbolized wings. Now she was confused. A disease didn't have wings. She tried finding something in her memory that could be related but was drawing a blank.

He grunted and ran to the back of his cell and grabbed something off the floor. He came back and stuck his closed fist through the bars as if wanting to give her something.

Adarra stepped forward to take a look, and he opened his hand, revealing a large beetle-like insect. At least, she thought it was a beetle—it was almost too squished to tell.

Her eyes widened. *Insects.* He was talking about some kind of infestation. She'd heard of things like this before, but mostly in warmer, dryer climates. She remembered reading about a swarm of cyala, better known to most as wheat killers, that plagued the Rymiran Plains for two years before finally dying off.

By the time the bugs had finished, they'd eaten everything in sight, leaving a swath of devoured plants that severely damaged the food supply to not just Elondria, but every other kingdom in Aldor. Because of this plague, the other kingdoms realized they couldn't rely on a single source for something as important as grain, and began cultivating their own crops for harvest.

She held up the dead insect. "This is black death? This is what killed your harvest?"

Jonas nodded with a relieved smile. "Yas."

She smiled as well, excited that they were coming to a better understanding.

"You must release me."

Adarra sighed. They had come full circle, and she still wasn't able to explain why she couldn't.

"If not. They come. Search."

She understood that part. He had already told her that his group was nothing more than a scouting party to see where they could acquire what they needed. If the Northmen were really in that bad a shape, she doubted they would wait long before sending out others to see what had happened.

"How many will come? How many of the Dogar?"

His face grew pensive. "All."

Adarra took a step back. *All?* All five houses? Just a single scouting party had nearly taken down the overlord's personal guard and her family. What would happen if all five houses showed up at Easthaven's back door?

She needed to warn the overlord. Gathering her books, she stuffed them back in her satchel, stopping only long enough to explain to Jonas that she would speak on his behalf to their leader. She promised to return and let him know what was decided.

He thanked her, once again using his nickname for her: Spotted Warrior.

She left the garrison and rode back to the East Inn, hoping to find her father still inside. According to Noreen Aboloff, her father had left some time ago but had been seen riding in the direction of the Sidaran Assembly Hall. Adarra thanked the innkeeper and left. The congestion in and out of the main road leading to the Hall was just as thick as it had been earlier, so she decided to take a more roundabout approach and come in from the back.

She had just made it into the plaza on the left side of the hall when someone called out her name. She pulled Thistle to a stop and turned. Lyessa waved as she rode over, looking to have had the same idea to get to the hall.

"I thought that was you," Lyessa said, reining in alongside. "What are you up to? Have you talked with your Tallosian yet?"

Adarra noted Lyessa's use of *your*. "That's actually why I'm here. Have you seen your father? I need to speak with him."

"I don't know where he is right at this moment, but I know where he'll be this evening. He's arranged for an informal dinner at the house with the newly formed Easthaven security council. Your father will be there. Why don't you come and tell him then?"

"Oh." Adarra fidgeted in her saddle. "I don't know. I wouldn't want to interrupt an official meeting."

"Nonsense. Does what you have to say have anything to do with the Tallosians?"

Adarra nodded, and Lyessa smiled.

"Then it most likely pertains to the security of Easthaven."

That's an understatement, she thought as the two left the plaza.

By the time they rode back, they only had an hour to freshen up before Overlord Barl's guests arrived. Adarra remained in the same dress she'd worn into town, refusing to change all over again, though she did allow Gina to brush it for dust and horsehair after her ride into town.

Lyessa, on the other hand, changed into what appeared to be a formal riding outfit. Adarra didn't think she'd ever get used to seeing the overlord's daughter wearing men's trousers. Her bright-red hair hung over her soft white blouse and leaf-green jacket.

When she caught Adarra staring, she smiled. "It's only Father and a couple of military types. No one worth enduring getting strapped into a gown for. You, on the other hand . . ." She walked over and pulled Adarra's straight brown hair back behind her shoulders. "I'm sure Aiden won't be able to keep his eyes off you."

Adarra smiled. Aiden seemed to be taking advantage of the overlord's hospitality for as long as he would permit. She wondered when he would be returning home. His wounds had long since healed with Fraya's help, and he had clearly regained his strength, as demonstrated by his daily lessons with Darryk. Still, as much as she hated dolling herself up for anybody, she did enjoy his attention. She'd never had anyone fawn over her before, and she woke every morning wondering if this was the day he'd finally see her for who she really was and leave.

She ran her hands down the soft velvet front of her dress, admiring the way the fabric lay. "At least it hides all the bruises."

There was a knock on the bedroom door, and Lyessa turned. "Enter."

Piel, the chamberlain, opened the door and stuck his head in. He was wearing another one of his colorful feathered hats, which made him look even taller and skinnier than he already was. He bowed politely. "Your father's guests have arrived, and dinner is served."

Lyessa looked at Adarra. "Time to go. Are you ready?"

Adarra nodded, and they followed Piel down to the first floor and around to one of the dining areas. It wasn't the banquet hall—this was a smaller, more informal gathering—but it was every bit as big as the front room of Adarra's house, including the kitchen and possibly a couple of the bedrooms. The table had been set as if for a banquet, which for Adarra meant the addition of several types of utensils, plates, and glasses, where only one of each would have been necessary.

The men at the table stood as the two entered, including her father and Overlord Barl. She recognized Ambassador Lanmiere, who was no longer sporting his cast from the injury he'd received during the former king's hunting excursion. Ever since the wielder council had revealed itself, several of Barl's inner circle had requested the use of their healer. Fraya had been more than happy to comply, receiving compensation enough to help her family during a slow year of crops.

Along with the ambassador, Adarra also spotted Commander Tiernan, who she had come to know during her visits to the barracks. There were also two other gentlemen she did not recognize, and of course Aiden, who was sitting two chairs down from the overlord. Apparently, he'd been saving a seat for Adarra, as he pulled the empty chair next to his out for her. Lyessa took the seat beside Adarra's, which was directly to the right of her father.

As soon as the women sat, the men did the same. Adarra's father smiled at her from across the table. She smiled back, feeling more than a little embarrassed at all the preferential treatment. Being close friends with the overlord's daughter had its perks, but for someone like Adarra, who'd rather be curled up in front of a cozy fire reading a good book, the extra attention was wasted.

The meal consisted of five courses, each building in flavor until the final, leaving Adarra wishing she'd followed Lyessa's example and opted for a loose-fitting blouse instead of the over constriction of her dress. By the time dessert arrived, she could barely breathe, passing on it altogether. It was a shame, really, considering how delicious it looked with its almond crust, stacked with layers of sweet cheese, chocolate torte, and topped with a fruit gelatin and vanilla glaze.

Adarra kept waiting for the right time to discuss her meeting with Jonas, but it seemed that Barl didn't wish to talk business during the meal, and instead asked each member about their families. In fact, each time the conversation seemed to be drifting toward the reason why they had assembled, Lyessa's father would change the subject.

By the time they had finished eating and had retired into one of the larger sitting rooms off the dining hall, where a warm blaze and trays of drinks had been prepared for them, the sun had slipped over the horizon and the sky was awash with color.

Most of the men, including Adarra's father, pulled out their pipes as they sat around in cushioned sofas to discuss the reason for their summoning. Adarra never could understand men's infatuation with the pipe, and why so many men had felt it their duty to take it up, like a rite of passage.

She had snuck a puff from her father's a few years back while he was away, just to see what it was like and why it brought him so much comfort. She'd never coughed or choked so much in her life; it felt like she'd swallowed live coals. She swore never to touch the stuff again, not that it would be considered proper in polite society for a woman to do such a thing anyway.

"How's the Lancer Corps progressing?" Barl asked, staring over his goblet at Commander Tiernan, who was sitting in a seat next to Adarra's father and the ambassador.

Tiernan was a tall man, not quite as tall as her father, but close. His light-brown hair had strips of grey and was tied back with a leather strap. He had thick brows and strong cheeks, even more accentuated by the jawline beard that ran from his chin to his ears, tapering to a point just below the earlobe.

The commander pulled his pipe from his mouth, releasing a couple of quick puffs into the air. "We are almost at full capacity, milord. There are a few smaller companies from the farthest regions, like Niska and Aldwick and Storyl, which have probably only just received word, but I'm sure they will respond swiftly." His brow furrowed. "I am worried, though, that we haven't heard from Woodvale or Belvin. Not like them to be so quiet."

Barl thought a moment as he twisted his goblet in his hand. "Send some riders and see what you can find out."

Tiernan nodded. "I'll send some in the morning, sir."

Adarra gathered up the nerve to speak, but as she opened her mouth, the overlord turned to one of the men Adarra didn't recognize. He was sitting in a cushioned high-back chair beside the short settee that she was sharing with Lyessa and Aiden. He wore the green-and-white uniform of one of the city patrollers and was quite decorated by the ribbons on his arm. "How is morale within the city, Captain Noklis?"

Noklis was the youngest man in the room besides Aiden, but at least a good fifteen years older than herself. He was of average height, with a thick mustache under a hooked nose that made his thin frame look even more gaunt. He also had a unique smile, where only one side of his face lifted.

"Morale seems to be weighing heavily on most," the patroller said, "but they are Easthaveners, sir, tough as tree bark. The people seem to be more at ease with the increase in lancers. It helps them feel that their city is well guarded—that is, as long as we can ensure the men stay in line," he added with a not-so-subtle look in Commander Tiernan's direction.

"I'll make sure my men behave as long as yours do the same," Tiernan said.

"I'm sure everyone will play nice," Barl added, giving them each a sharp look.

The two men went back to puffing on their pipes and glaring at one another from opposite sides of the hearth.

Adarra squeezed her hands tight in her lap. This was her opportunity. She opened her mouth once more.

"Has the wielder council noticed any suspicious . . . things, happening around Easthaven?" Ambassador Lanmiere asked Adarra's father, who was sitting next to him on the sofa. "You know. Anything . . . magical?"

The ambassador was older, his hair shifting from grey to white as it curled under at his shoulders. He had a thin face, made even longer by his beard, which came to a point at his chest. Adarra could tell the ambassador was unsure how to approach the subject, almost as though he were afraid to offend her father.

"Is that wizard still around?" Barl asked before her father had a chance to answer the ambassador, not at all worried about sharing such information with those gathered. Perhaps they had already been informed of the wizard's presence because of their positions as heads of security.

Adarra's father shifted his long pipe to the side of his mouth. "Nyalis had other places to be. He left sometime last week."

"Will he be back?" Barl asked.

"With him, there's no telling," her father said.

Barl didn't seem all that pleased at hearing of Nyalis's departure, but the old wizard had a tendency to show up when needed. Hopefully, they wouldn't need him anytime soon. Besides, it was Ty and Breen who needed him right now, and yet they were the only ones Nyalis had said he wouldn't be helping.

"Troops have been dispatched along our southern and western border, milord," the second man Adarra hadn't recognized said, before she could get a word in. He was seated next to the commander and wearing a lancer uniform as well, the patch on his sleeve signifying an overcaptain's ranking. "We've also sent lancers to Kariss and Braedon, to watch for any possible breaches along the Razor Spine Mountains."

Barl nodded slowly, his lips pursed.

"What about the river?" Lyessa asked. "Seems the ideal spot to smuggle in troops."

Her father smiled. "Yes, we sent riders to Riverton to keep an eye on any traffic flowing north out of Briston. With winter setting in, though, this would be a harsh time of year to attempt anything by water."

It sounded like they had things well in hand, Adarra mused. They were keeping a close eye on all the usual and some of the not-so-usual routes. However, there was one place their attention had not been utilized: Tallos.

"I'm afraid there might yet be another source of hostility that hasn't been considered," Adarra said, drawing the others' attention.

Commander Tiernan lowered his pipe. "And what sort of hostility do you reckon we've missed?"

"The Tallosians."

Her father shifted slightly in his seat, still chewing on the tip of his pipe. "Have you learned something?"

"I believe I have. I think we should release the prisoner."

The room grew quiet. Not that it wasn't quiet before, but now even the random inhales and exhales of their pipes were temporarily halted.

"Are you crazy?" Aiden suddenly blurted, then realizing what he'd done, quickly apologized. "That came out badly."

"It might not have come out as you intended," Noklis said, straightening the stiff collar of his patroller uniform, "but it was worded quite appropriately, I thought."

"Why would you make such a suggestion?" Barl asked, setting his goblet aside altogether.

"He tried to kill the overlord," Noklis said, as though she hadn't been made aware.

Adarra's father finally pulled the pipe from his mouth and leaned forward. "Let her speak."

Noklis, and even Tiernan, paused to look at her father, but did as he suggested. When you were the biggest man in the room, others tended to listen. Her father looked at her and nodded.

"I visited Jonas this afternoon," she said, then paused to think. "Let me start by prefacing that the Tallosian culture is much different than our own, their customs are peculiar."

"In what way?" Barl asked, beating Tiernan to the punch as Tiernan had just set aside his own drink to speak.

"While the Five Kingdoms have grown, the Northmen seemed to have digressed. As violent as they may seem, though, they do still have a form of honor, or a code that they live by. From what I was able to glean, it seems that the factions within the Tallosian culture are quite dysfunctional, each attacking the others for dominance. But," she said, pausing for emphasis, "after a conflict is over and one side is declared victorious, the losing faction is free to return to their homes, provided they meet some sort of payment." She looked around the room, stopping on the overlord. "The point is, Jonas has conceded that he lost and is demanding his release."

"Not flaming likely," Aiden said. "The man tried to cut me in half. He tried to do the same to you."

"I agree with the boy," Noklis said.

Aiden's cheeks reddened at the notion of being called a *boy*.

"Blood for blood," Noklis finished.

Adarra looked down at her lap. Her hands were shaking. "There's more. Jonas says that if we do not release him, others will come looking. His small company was merely a scouting party for the Dogar."

"And what, pray tell, are the Dogar?" Commander Tiernan asked, eyes intent.

Adarra explained that the Dogar was the ruling body of Tallos, consisting of the heads of the five houses, and that they had recently endured a blight, which had demolished their food supply. "They've never seen the likes of it before. This *black death*, as they call it, is what has driven them to such desperation as to seek help outside their island. The witch approached them and promised them supplies in exchange for their help in capturing Ty."

"Even still," Barl said testily, "that doesn't negate what they did. Their actions would be considered an act of war by any kingdom in Aldor."

"I understand," Adarra said, "but we do have to consider that their customs are different, which I know doesn't excuse what they did, but maybe it can put things into a broader perspective."

"Release the man or not," her father said, finally speaking up. "There are other things here we must consider, more important than us seeking justice on a single individual." He pulled the pipe from his mouth and pointed the tip at Adarra. "If what my daughter says is true, then this might prove an opportunity for us."

"How is that?" Noklis asked, looking at her father like he didn't belong. To them, her father was just the overlord's gamekeeper and didn't deserve a seat on this new council, though none of them would openly say it to his face. Despite what they thought, her father wasn't just the tallest man in the room, he was by far the strongest, and if Adarra were to wager, probably the most cunning. He was also the chosen spokesman for the wielder council, due to his familiarity with the overlord.

Her father leaned back against his cushion. "Seems fairly obvious. Putting aside what the man did or didn't do, if his people are in serious enough need to leave their island and step foot on these shores again, then we need to take heed. The last thing we need is to turn potential neighbors into enemies."

"Seems that's what they've already done," Lyessa said, "by attacking us in the first place."

"She's got a point," Barl said.

"She does," her father agreed. "No one is disputing the fact, but before we turn a skirmish into an all-out war, perhaps we consider other avenues of recourse. For example, what if we offered assistance? Perhaps this could lead to some kind of ongoing trade."

"What could they possibly offer for trade?" Noklis asked skeptically. "Scalp cloaks?"

Aiden chuckled.

Adarra shivered at the thought. From what she'd seen of the Tallosians, they weren't exactly brimming with goods worthy of trade.

Her father was growing frustrated as he bit down on his pipe.

"We won't know unless we find out," Adarra said. "Besides, you never know when a favor from a battle-hardened people such as the Tallosians might come in handy."

The overlord spun his goblet in his hand as he contemplated what was said.

"It's clear we need more information." He looked at Adarra. "How soon do you plan on visiting the prisoner again?"

"As early as you wish."

"Good, then perhaps we can set a day later this week to accompany you." He looked around the room. "I'm sure we all have questions."

Adarra cleared her throat. "I'm not sure how open he will be with an audience. Jonas seems to be more talkative when it's just me."

Aiden's brows lowered. There was a hint of jealousy in his eyes.

"If you have something specific you would like me to discuss with him, please let me know. I like to prepare my questions beforehand, so I can rehearse them in his language. It takes a while to translate."

"I see," Barl said. He sat there a moment in silence. "I guess the most important question to ask is: How long do we have?"

Adarra nodded, thankful the overlord was going to allow her to question Jonas alone. She knew how nervous she'd be if they were all standing over her shoulder, pressuring her to ask their questions. It would have made her job that much more difficult. Regardless, she had some studying to do in preparation for her next encounter with the huge Tallosian. She only hoped he remained receptive.

Chapter 34 | Ferrin

ERRIN AND THE OTHERS had left the protection of the Sidaran Forest a few days back and were now trudging across the open country just south of the Grasslands of Tekoa, heading for Praxil Lake. Wasn't much in the way of grass to be found, as everything was covered in snow. It would have been easier to circle around to the main road, running from Woodvale to Hedgemont—which eventually crossed into Keldor—but they couldn't take the chance of accidentally running into Sylas along the way.

Ferrin didn't like leaving the shelter of the trees, but so far, they hadn't seen any sign of the strange reptilian birds since leaving Elondria. He figured the forest had had something to do with that, but it still didn't stop him from glancing up into the boughs from time to time. Another reason for wishing to remain sheltered was the weather.

The steady fall of snow over the last several days had slowed their progress, making it difficult to keep to a straight path. Eventually, they had found a small ravine from a dried-up creek bed and built a shelter to wait it out. Apart from a couple of trappers they'd come across earlier in the week, there'd been no other sign of anyone living this far out.

"The nights are getting colder," Myron said, handing Ferrin a steaming cup of tea. "We would have never made it without those supplies."

Ferrin nodded as he took the cup, casting a brief glance behind him to the sacks of goods sitting inside their makeshift shelter, which they had dug into the rocky side of a creek bed. It might not have been the softest place to lay your head, but at least it was out of the snow and large enough for even the horses.

Nola, on the other hand, seemed to prefer her seclusion. Ferrin hadn't seen the enormous wolf in the last day or two. She kept herself away from the others and only appeared when she wanted to get her ears scratched by Suri.

Ferrin blew over the brim of his mug and slowly took a sip, letting the hot liquid warm his insides. It was almost too hot to even taste the flavor, but after the initial burn settled, there was a lingering hint of juniper, which seemed to be one of Myron's favorite seasonings. He not only steeped their tea with it, he laced their meat with it as well. It certainly had a robust flavor.

He stared out at the slate-grey sky as much as the falling snow would allow. "Yes, it is getting colder, and it's not looking to be letting up anytime soon. We might not have any other choice but to press on, snowfall or not. We can't wait here for the Tower's guards to catch up with us."

"That's for sure," Myron said, sipping noisily on his own tea and whimpering in delight as he did. "How far do you think to Storyl?"

"In weather like this, I'd say a good six days yet. Maybe more, depending on how difficult it is to find shelter."

"I don't see anyone, including the white riders, chancing weather like this. If they're smart, they'll be doing the same thing we are. Except they'll be finding some town to shelter in, enjoying a hot meal and a warm bed while we sit out here in the freezing cold." Myron's teeth began to chatter, and he quickly took another sip.

Rae and Suri sat quietly at the back of the shelter, wrapped tightly in their blankets as they stared out of the burrow, seemingly transfixed by the snow.

"How about a piping-hot cup of tea?" Myron suggested, motioning for the two to join them around the fire.

Rae hesitated, but as soon as Suri opened their blanket and hopped out, she stood and walked over, accepting a cup from Myron that she blew on for several minutes before allowing Suri to take a drink. "I say we keep going," Rae said, still staring out at the snow. "The sooner we get to Rhowynn, the sooner we can leave. I don't like Sidara. All it does is snow."

"It doesn't always snow," Myron said diplomatically. "Only during the winter. Normally, it is a beautiful, lush place to live. In my opinion one of the more beautiful kingdoms."

"I still don't like it here," she said, shivering.

Ferrin looked at Myron, who simply shrugged and took another long, slow sip from his cup. "It's decided, then," Ferrin said. "We leave at first light."

No one argued, but no one looked overjoyed either. Except for perhaps Suri, who was smiling intently at her latest mouthful of tea as she waved Tippi through the air, at one point even offering the large pinecone a sip.

The next morning found them up and eating breakfast, which was nothing more than some cheese and biscuits warmed over the fire, along with an apple and another piping-hot cup of tea. The snow outside hadn't let up, and the ground was covered several inches deep, making it not only more difficult on the horses but more dangerous as well. Before they left, Nola made another appearance, her white fur making her seem almost wraithlike as she trotted out of the blanket of falling snow and made her way over to Suri.

She had another large rodent in her mouth, which she dropped at the little girl's feet in exchange for a good rubbing around the back of her ears and forehead, finished by a kiss to the side of her furry cheek. Rae always tensed, nearly as skittish as the horses, each time the wolf engaged with her daughter.

"It's time to go," Ferrin said, mounting his horse while trying to hold it steady as the animal backed nervously away from Nola.

Nola moved far enough away for Myron to help Suri up in the saddle in front of her mother, then watched as the riders left the ravine and started back on the trail. Ferrin occasionally caught glimpses of the big wolf through the snow as they started out across the wintery frozen plains, though it was hard to tell what he was seeing through the sheets of white. He could have very well imagined it. He had to admit, he did feel a sense of protection having Nola around. At the very least, they were sure not to starve.

The days and nights passed in the same manner, a slow trudge forward by aid of their compass and a cold shivering night that left little in the way of sleep or warmth. It wasn't until they caught their first sight of Praxil Lake nearly a week later that the snows finally began to let up. Ferrin had no idea which part of the lake they'd reached, so he turned the party north, and they followed the shoreline around for another day until they came across a farmer and his wife on the road to Hedgemont.

"Half a day's ride at most, if you wish to reach Storyl," the farmer said, his wagon laden with goods. The back was covered with a canvas tarp to hold off the snow. "I'd wager you make it before dark if you have a care, and if the weather permits."

The farmer's wife, sitting on the front seat beside him, looked at Suri. "You poor dear. You look half frozen." Suri held up Tippi for the couple to see. The woman smiled, then turned to Myron. "Have you been traveling long?"

"Long enough. We'll be right glad to find a warm place to lay our heads tonight. Can you recommend a decent inn?"

"Aye," her husband said. "You'll be wanting the White Pheasant. The Tulicks are good people. They'll treat you right. They don't put up with any of that unsavory behavior some of the other inns permit." He looked at Suri, not quite sure whether to continue. "Not the kind of things you want little ones exposed to, if you catch my meaning."

"The White Pheasant," Myron repeated. "We'll keep an eye out." He tipped his hat. "Much obliged."

The farmer tipped his in return and went to slap his reins, but Ferrin stopped him with an additional question. "Seen much of the white riders lately? The Tower looks to be spreading further north from what we've seen in our travels." He was careful how he worded the question and just as careful how he presented it, not giving any indication as to whether he was for or against the White Tower's involvement.

The farmer had no such reserve. He spat off the side of his wagon. "The Black Watch can burn in Aran'gal for all I care. Thankfully, we haven't seen their kind in some time, but if I ever see another one of those white uniforms, it'll be too soon."

Ferrin smiled and breathed a faint sigh of relief. "I couldn't agree with you more. Drown them all, I say." He nodded at the couple. "We appreciate the help. May the Creator return the favor."

"If only," the farmer said, kissing his first two fingers and then touching them to his forehead before offering up a ritualistic prayer. He slapped the reins, and the wagon rolled off down the road.

Ferrin turned to Myron. "That was fast thinking about the inn."

"I don't deserve all the credit," Myron said with a cheeky grin, then rubbed his stomach. "This might have had something to do with it."

Ferrin couldn't help but chuckle.

Even Rae smiled, if briefly.

"Good to know they haven't seen white riders about," Myron said. "Must mean we're ahead of them."

"I hope that's the case," Ferrin said, then grabbed his reins. "Well, you heard the man. Storyl by sundown if we don't dawdle." He nudged his horse, and they started forward, following in the tracks left by the farmer's wagon.

Ferrin didn't like the idea of stopping at another town. Every time they'd stopped so far, trouble had found them. But he also knew that if they didn't stop and get at least one good night's rest, they probably weren't going to make it much farther. Besides, they needed supplies. Hopefully, this time, they managed to get their supplies before they were run out of town.

The road to Storyl was a pleasant one. The snow stopped late morning, bringing with it a parting of overcast skies, releasing the sun for the first time in a week. The rays glistened off the waves of the lake on their left, leaving a bright but beautiful sheen across the water, especially around the edges where the ice was already beginning to form. Unlike many of the smaller lakes, Praxil didn't ice all the way over. Its currents were too strong.

"Mommy, look." Suri was practically standing up in the saddle to get a better view of the water, holding her pinecone up to make sure Tippi could see. Rae was just as in awe as her daughter as she stared out over the vast horizon of shimmering waves. "It's pretty, Mommy."

"Yes, it is," Rae said, then helped Suri back into her seat and re-wrapped her blanket around her.

Ferrin kept the small caravan at a decent pace, wanting to make sure they did indeed reach Storyl before the sun went down. He caught himself looking back from time to time across the snow-covered plains on their right to see if he could spot Nola. He never did, but he could still feel her watching.

All along the road, houses began to crop up. One or two at first, mostly fishing huts with rickety docks leading out to the water, but then as the numbers grew, so did their size and quality. Pretty soon, they were riding through the outskirts of Storyl, one of the larger townships this side of Praxil Lake. The place seemed a bustle of activity, more so than Ferrin would have expected this late in the day. The sun hadn't yet dropped below the horizon, but it was within a copper's throw.

Like most of the townships within Sidara, Storyl had no surrounding wall. They did, however, have a number of watch towers placed sporadically around the outside border, and a few randomly scattered atop some of the larger buildings in town. Several had what looked to be pyres built into the tops, most likely signal fires for when the fog rolled in off the lake and the boats needed direction back.

Riding into Storyl was another reminder of how close to home Ferrin was getting. The strong smell of fish off the water, nets hanging from every wall, barrels of fish and piles of rope decorating the empty spaces between buildings. Stalls were assembled along the main avenue, where men and women cleaned the catch of the day, getting them ready to sell the next morning, now that the weather was cold enough to keep.

Unlike Rhowynn, however, Storyl was built almost solely on top of the water, with canals running between the streets, and boats tied along boardwalks that ran the length and breadth of the city. Rampways and bridges were used to get from one side of each channel to the other, some tall enough to let the larger boats ferry through, others close enough to see your reflection in the water. Ferrin was glad they weren't toting a wagon, since some of the bridges didn't look wide or sturdy enough to carry such a load.

The largest of the boats, those big enough to support a full sail, were docked around the western perimeter of the city, each with its own pier that stretched out like fingers on a great wooden hand to gather the day's catch.

The city was a congestion of tightly crammed buildings, not plaster or stone like one might find in most sizable townships, but of wood. Wood that had been treated to survive the water, but still weathered all the same. The buildings were pressed together so tightly you could walk from one side of the city to the other if you could maintain your balance. The roofs were pitched as sharp as an arrow, with patches of wooden shingles peeking out through the snow. Each of the second and third floors had their own balconies overlooking the street, but in weather such as this, most lay empty.

The familiar sound of wood twisting and turning under heavy weight let him know they were no longer on solid ground. He could almost feel the sway of the planks under him as the city moved with the water below. It was an unsettling feeling to those who weren't used to its ways, much like the feel of a boat at sea.

No one seemed to pay their caravan much mind as they made their way farther into Storyl. The denizens were dressed in heavy fur-lined cloaks, mittens, and hats. Knowing that winter had come to stay, no one seemingly cared all that much about appearance.

The farther they went, the stronger the smell of fish became. At one point, Suri made a peculiar face, and Rae went so far as to hold her nose. One look at the two of them and Ferrin couldn't help but laugh. He hadn't realized how much he'd missed the smell of the water. His smithy in Rhowynn was located in the eastern section of town, not too far from the docks, so it was a smell he was very familiar with.

"Fish," he said to Rae. "It's only fish you smell."

Only two words proceeded from her mouth. "Smelly Trout."

This time it was Myron who laughed. "The Smelly Trout doesn't have anything on this." He took in a deep whiff. "It's been many a year since I've been through a proper lake town. By the Almighty, I'm not ashamed to say I've missed it. It's a smell you don't forget."

"Took the words right out of my mouth," Ferrin said as they crossed over the first of what looked like several bridges ahead. They stopped and dismounted, walking over to the railing to get a good look down one of the wider channels running through Storyl.

The water below was calm but still maintained a steady pulse. Boardwalks ran the full length of the water, and Ferrin watched as the townsfolk used them to get from one street to the next. Skiffs and dories of all shapes and sizes lined the edges of the boardwalks down below, waiting patiently for their owners to set them free.

When a storm came in, they would lash the boats to the boardwalk to keep them from either floating off in the surge or beating a hole in the side of whatever building they happened to be next to. Ferrin remembered seeing waves coming in off Lake Baeron high enough to cover the boardwalks altogether. You didn't want to be caught below when one came in, as you were just as likely to drown in the middle of town as in the middle of the lake.

Myron stopped a man who was carrying a large coil of rope over one shoulder and a spear hook on the other. "Could you point us in the direction of the White Pheasant?"

"Aye," the fisherman said, motioning with his spear in the direction they were traveling. "You'll be wanting to take the second causeway to the left and straight on till you hit the water. You'll find what you're looking for there."

Myron thanked the man, and they continued on.

Most people were on foot, with very few horses to be seen, which made their party stand out, but not enough to draw attention in a way that had people stopping to gander. Storyl was along the western trade route for Sidara, so they were sure to have a constant flow of new faces.

Ferrin took the second street to the left, as the man had suggested, and they followed it until it ended at another road, which looked to wind its way round the entire outer perimeter of the city. On the other side of the street was a three-story building wide enough to be considered three buildings in one. A green sign hung out front, bearing the image of a white bird with a black breast and red face. Its long tail feathers were spread out behind it. And if the image wasn't enough, there were thick gold letters above it that read: *The White Pheasant*.

Myron looked at Ferrin. "Guess we found it."

A small stable stood on the right just between the inn and the next building over, which appeared to be a cooper. There was a large selection of barrels, buckets, troughs, and vats sitting around the front of the establishment.

"Let's unsaddle first," Ferrin said as he walked the horses over to the front of the stable. He was greeted by a young boy sitting beside a stone pit, warming his hands over a small blaze. He hopped up when he saw them coming.

"Stable for the night, gents?" he asked and tipped his cap to them. Sandy-blond hair hung halfway over his eyes, blending with his pale features.

"How could we say no to an offer like that?" Myron said, not even bothering to ask the price before turning the reins over to the young lad. The barn wasn't much warmer inside than out, but there was fresh hay in the stalls and oats in the trough. Just being out of the wind and snow was a far cry better than what they'd been traveling through.

As soon as the horses had been unsaddled, the boy held out his hand. "That'll be three coppers for the stalls and one more for the feed and rubdown."

Ferrin dug around in one of the saddlebags, looking as though he were searching for something to pay the boy with. He made sure to keep his back to the boy while he pulled out one of their purses from an inner coat pocket and collected what he needed before turning back around. "What's your name, son?"

"Pin, sir. Short for Pinfagan." His mouth curled into a sneer. "It's a silly name."

"Nonsense," Myron cut in. "It's a strong name. One to be proud of. Pinfagan was a great general. It's said he stood at the vanguard of an enormous force and faced down the Kuhl hordes when they overran Aramoor. He stood his ground and drove the cursed creatures out of the Five Kingdoms forever."

Pin's earlier sneer was replaced with a proud smile. He even straightened his back. "Wow! Did he really do all that?"

"Sure did. You have a proud heritage in that name, and don't ever forget it."

"No, sir."

"Here you go," Ferrin said and placed five coppers instead of four in Pin's hand. "The extra is for you."

Pin bowed. "Mighty generous, sir."

"And there'll be a couple more coppers in it for you if you can keep us apprised of any of the comings and goings around the city."

"Not much of that, sir," Pin said with a shiver, "what with the frosty weather. Not much good for traveling these days. The road's been quiet."

Ferrin nodded approvingly. "How's the inn? Room to spare?"

"Yes, sir. Best rooms this side of Praxil."

"More importantly," Myron added, "how's the food?"

Pin rubbed his stomach and licked his lips. "Won't find tastier, sir. Mother's the best cook in Storyl."

Myron smiled and rubbed the top of Pin's head. "Good lad. Just what I wanted to hear."

They gathered their belongings and followed Pin out of the stable and around to the front of the inn. As soon as Pin was far enough ahead not to hear, Ferrin leaned over to Myron. "I've never heard of a general named Pinfagan."

Myron shrugged. "Neither have I."

Ferrin smiled.

Just inside the front entrance was a lobby with a desk on the right to sign in visitors, and a row of chairs around the wall for guests to sit and wait. Beyond was a set of stairs leading up to a second-floor catwalk that overlooked the common room. The main room stretched from the lobby clear to the back of the inn, where a wall of tall glass windows overlooked the lake and lit the room with an early evening sun that was barely hanging above the horizon. The sky had already begun to change color, a refreshing change to the dull grey they'd been staring at for the last week. It was a breathtaking view.

Suri jerked out of her mother's hand as soon as she saw the water and ran across the common room to take a look.

"Suri, come back." Rae chased after her, nearly tripping on her cloak as she gathered it up with her hands and wove her way through the tables. In all the haste of leaving Woodvale, they hadn't had the opportunity to tailor her clothes to fit her shorter height. Ferrin found it amusing, though he didn't dare let her know.

He scanned the tables, noticing more than a couple of the guests wore matching red vests. Seemed an odd choice.

"What can I do for you, sirs?" a teenage girl sitting behind the desk asked on approach. Her blonde hair was tied up with blue ribbons that matched her eyes. "Will you be needing rooms or a meal, or both?"

"We'll be having both," Myron stated, passing the young girl a friendly smile. "Definitely both."

She looked at Pin, who was languishing in one of the seats by the door, and cleared her throat. "Don't let Papa catch you sitting there."

Pin's eyes widened, and he shot out of the seat, scanning the common room. With a quick bow and wave to Ferrin and Myron, he made his exit out the front.

Ferrin walked over to the desk, loosening the drawstring of his purse from inside his trouser pocket. He could tell by touch which coins were which without having to pull the purse out for everyone to see. They'd learned that mistake the hard way back in Elondria, and nearly paid for it with their lives.

"Supper is served until eighth bell if you want," the young girl said.

"We do," Myron was quick to point out.

"We require two rooms," Ferrin said, trying not to chuckle at his friend's eagerness. "As long as they have at least two beds in one of them." He glanced at Myron, who was nodding profusely.

"Street side or lake side?"

"Lake side, of course," Myron said before Ferrin got a chance to even open his mouth. "Who would dare visit your fine city and not want to enjoy all the beauties that came with it? Oh, do you have any open rooms on the third floor?"

"Let me look," the girl said, trying not to stare too intently at Myron. It took Ferrin a moment to realize what she was looking at. It dawned on him it was Myron's nose, and he almost laughed. Poor Nostrils couldn't go anywhere without drawing some attention. It wasn't that it was abhorrent to look at, just different from most. People were always curious about what was different.

It didn't take her long to leaf through the last couple of pages of the book before lifting her head with a smile. "You're in luck. We have five. It'll be two silvers and four for the rooms, lakeside view, which will also include meals for tonight and breakfast in the morning."

"That will be fine," Ferrin said, already having pulled three silvers from the purse. He placed the coins on the desk, and she went about getting him his change.

"What name do I record?" the girl asked, swiping the coins up with one hand while holding her quill over the ledger with the other.

Ferrin stood a moment, unsure what to say. Clearly, they couldn't use their real names in case anyone came looking, but having been put on the spot, his mind went completely blank.

"Treehorn," Myron said. "Merrill Treehorn."

"Very good, sir." The young girl scribbled the name down, then replaced the quill and scooted away from the desk. "If you'll follow me, I'll show you to your rooms."

By the time they'd finished gathering their bags, Rae had managed to pull Suri and Tippi away from the glass and met them at the staircase.

"We are on the third floor overlooking the lake," Myron said with a twinkle in his eyes.

Ferrin had to admit, he was looking forward to seeing the rooms himself. They continued up to the third-floor landing and started down a long hall to the left. They passed several rooms on both sides before coming to a stop a few doors down from the end.

"You'll have this room and the next," the girl said, pointing to the door just beyond the one they were standing in front of. She pulled out a set of keys and proceeded to unlock the girls' room, leaving both keys with them. "I hope you enjoy your rooms. If there's anything you need, my name is Sarren. Supper ends at eighth bell, so don't be late." She walked back down the hall, leaving them to explore their rooms.

Myron looked at Ferrin with a cheeky grin and held out his hand for the key. "Let's see what we've got."

Chapter 35 | Ferrin

HE ROOM WASN'T EXACTLY what Ferrin would have deemed grand, but it was certainly the best they'd stayed in so far. Sarren hadn't been mistaken on the view either—it was every bit as wonderous as in the common room below. A door led out to a shared balcony with what appeared to be three other rooms, including Rae and Suri's.

The room itself was spacious compared to others they'd rented. Two full-size beds with matching quilts lay longways to either side of the balcony door. The heads of each bed butted up against their own window, the shutters open enough to let in the last rays of light, adding a touch of warmth. Beside each bed was a nightstand with a single unlit candle. A tall cabinet in the corner just opposite the hearth stood empty except for a set of spare sheets and two knit throws. There was plenty of room to deposit most of their belongings, and the trunk at the end of the left bed looked large enough to fit the rest.

A vase of winter daisies rested on a table just to the right of the door, their bright yellow centers adding a touch of friendliness to the place, and on the wall above the table hung a plainly framed mural, which, by the quality of the brush strokes, had no doubt come from one of the innkeeper's children. It was a portrait of the lake with a view from what looked to be their very room. Not exactly accurate in perspective, but pleasing nonetheless. There was even a washbasin and stand on the left wall, along with a fresh set of towels and a mirror above for shaving, if the need arose.

A head bobbed by the window, and soon after there was a knock on their balcony door.

Myron opened it, and Suri stuck her head in. "We're right there," she said eagerly, pointing back to her and Rae's room.

Myron stuck his head out the door. "So you are. Better get back before your mother wonders where you've run off to."

Suri giggled and ran back across the balcony.

Myron shivered and shut the door, then walked over to the fireplace on the right side of the room and, with a striker he pulled from his pack, lit some of the tinder under the wood, tossing on a couple extra pieces from the pile beside. "That's better," he said, holding his hands out before turning to warm his backside.

Ferrin walked over and looked at himself in the mirror and frowned.

Myron laughed. "Just think, I've had to look at that face for the last couple of months."

Ferrin smiled but found it hard to see under the thick red growth over his mouth. "You're hardly one to talk."

Myron stayed where he was in front of the fire. "Don't need to look to know I could keep crows out of a corn patch. The question is, should we wash *now*, or after we eat?"

Ferrin rubbed his hand across the back of his neck, which was crusty with dried sweat, then pulled the top of his tunic out far enough to smell inside. He winced. "I prefer not to run off all the inn's guests. I vote we bathe first."

Myron thought a moment, then smiled. "Running off the guests would mean more food for us."

"Perhaps, but one whiff of us might run off the servers as well."

Myron's head lifted and he frowned. "Good point. Bathing it is." Myron went for Sarren to see about getting themselves and their clothes washed while Ferrin finished up organizing their supplies in the large trunk. While he was gone, Ferrin walked next door by way of the balcony and helped Rae and Suri get the fire started in their room, which was nearly identical to his and Myron's. The only difference was their fireplace was on the left wall instead of the right, and the painting hanging over their table, while still the same subject matter, had been brushed in different hues, as though having been painted at a different time of the day or possibly a different season of the year.

It didn't take Sarren long to have the inn's staff fill the washtubs. Apparently, the White Pheasant was large enough to have their own bathhouse. Each tub had its own privacy curtain, with a female attendant to see to Rae's and Suri's needs, and a male attendant to see to Ferrin's and Myron's. Their clothes were taken to be scrubbed and dried, leaving them with a fresh set the inn kept on hand for such occasions.

Ferrin had never experienced such service before. Then again, his only experience with inns had been the Smelly Trout in Iraseth and the Smok'n Pig in Woodvale. Neither came close to measuring up to the White Pheasant.

As much as he wanted to linger and enjoy the heated water and soap, his stomach urged him to hurry. Of course, it might have had something to do with Myron continually pestering him about how long he was taking, reminding Ferrin how hungry Myron was. Even with Myron's urging, Ferrin did take the time to trim his beard and comb the knots out of his red hair before drying off and dressing in the clothes the inn had laid out for him. He kept his boots, but there was a clean pair of stockings laid out for his use.

"Are we ready?" Ferrin asked as he pulled back the curtain to his tub and found the others waiting.

Myron harrumphed. "What a silly question."

Myron was dressed in identical clothing to Ferrin, same dark trousers and white top, same matching red vests, which now made sense. He'd wondered why so many of the guests in the common room had been wearing red vests. Rae and Suri each wore a grey dress, with matching white collars and a red rope tied around the waist. They looked like twins, with their dark, unevenly chopped hair and pale-green eyes. Suri's skin wasn't quite as caramel as her mother's, closer to the color of a day laborer after spending a week in the fields. There was also a bulge in her pocket, no doubt Tippi coming along for the ride.

Myron stuffed their key in his pocket and headed out of the bathhouse and down the main hall toward the common room. Ferrin looked at Rae and Suri and smiled. "You two look nice."

Rae held her skirt up so it didn't drag on the floor. "It's too long." It was hard to find clothing that fit Rae, as short as she was. Most dresses her size were made for young girls, so they tended not to fit in other places.

"We'll try to find a tailor in town tomorrow," he said as they left the room and headed down the hall after Myron.

The common room smelled divine. The windows at the back were divided down the center by a great hearth, the blaze inside warming the room with its vigor. More than half the tables were empty, leaving them plenty to choose from. Suri made the choice for them, her little legs rushing over to the empty table closest to the glass. The beautiful sunset had long since vanished, and the sky was now filled with stars.

"I guess this will do," Myron said, looking forlorn at not being able to get a table closer to the kitchen.

They'd barely gotten their seats when a young man appeared to take their orders. He was older than Pin but bore the same cheekbones. An older brother perhaps. Ferrin wondered how many children the Tulicks had running around the place. He envied them to be able to work side by side with their family every day, and in such a wonderous location.

He wondered how Myriah was doing, how she had survived his absence. He wondered if she had ever learned how he had been betrayed.

"He'll have an ale, same as me," Myron said, pulling Ferrin back from his musings.

Ferrin looked at the lad. "Yes, an ale will be fine. And whatever is making that wonderful smell," he said, taking a long whiff. "I'll have that, too."

The boy smiled. "That'd be Ma's specialty. Rack of lamb with a red wine sauce."

Ferrin's mouth watered. "Make that two helpings for me."

"Three for me," Myron stated, not wanting to be outdone.

The lad cleared his throat. "Uh . . . extra helpings will cost more, gents." He looked embarrassed to admit it.

"This should cover it," Ferrin said, plopping four coppers down on the table for the lad to take. "Just keep our plates and tankards filled."

The lad tipped his cap. "Right you are, sir." He looked at Rae. "And what for you, Missus?"

"Same. Do you have cider?"

"Mulled or plain?"

She looked at Ferrin.

"Mulled is heated with spices," he said.

She looked at the lad. "Heated."

The boy bowed and scurried off.

It didn't take any time at all to get their first plates filled and served, which was a good thing. Ferrin had been afraid if they'd been forced to wait for any real length of time, Myron was going to move his seat into the kitchen. As it was, the meal was exactly what they needed. It was the finest lamb he'd had since one of Harlin's dinner parties for the Rhowynn wielder council—finer, in fact, since during those instances, he had been too put off by the company to enjoy it. Whereas here, he couldn't ask for better companions to share a meal with than those seated around him. They'd come a long way together, been through times that would have tested the patience of a Wengoby priest, and yet, they'd stuck with him.

He looked out at the sea of stars through the tall glass windows beside their table, admiring how the twinkling lights shimmered, wondering if his sister was looking up at those same stars. If she was thinking of him.

"Copper for your thoughts," Myron said, leaning back in his chair after finishing off his third helping. He looked very pleased with himself as he slowly sipped the ale from his tankard before pulling out his pipe.

"Just thinking about my sister. Wondering where we will go after I get her out of Rhowynn. What we will do."

"I believe you said something about Easthaven," Myron said, dripping the wax off one of the candles before using it to light his pipe.

"Yes. I owe a great debt that needs paying." He lifted his tankard and took a swallow, the ale cool and soothing to his throat as it went down. "But afterward . . ." He shook his head. "Who knows."

"As far away from the Tower as we can get," Myron said adamantly, then grinned. "Maybe we could join the Upakans. I suspect that would be the last place in Aldor the Tower will likely go."

The two men chuckled.

"What are Upakans?" Rae asked, her unusually pale-green eyes sparkling by the light of the candelabra on their table.

Ferrin smiled. "Myron was only jesting. He doesn't actually plan to go live with the Upakans."

Rae looked confused. "Why not? If the Tower will not go there, then why wouldn't we?"

Ferrin looked at Myron, who smiled and pointed at him to explain. "Well, first of all, the Upakans live underground in tunnels beneath the ruins of the Lost City. They are mercenaries. Their society is built around killing for hire. Not a place you want to pack up a family and move to." He cleared his throat. "Not that we're a family or anything . . . just saying." He cleared his throat again. "Besides, they don't let outsiders in."

Rae studied the two men, then reclined in her seat without saying a word. She did, however, turn and join her daughter in looking at the stars.

Ferrin glanced at Myron, who had an impish grin on his face. "What?"

Myron simply shrugged and continued puffing on his pipe. "What's our course from here? Do we continue riding north till we reach Niska?"

"It would be faster if we could find a boat. Unfortunately, most boats this time of year are heading south down the Taloos River, but if we could find one heading north, we could take it all the way to Lake Baeron and around to dock at Rhowynn. The problem will be finding a boat big enough to take the horses."

"Have you given any thought to what you will do with your property?" Myron asked, leaning forward and resting his elbows on the table. "That is, if your house and smithy haven't already been repossessed. If you leave, what happens to them?

Don't have time to go selling them off. You'll barely have time to pack your sister's belongings, and if she's like most women I've known, that's no easy task, being asked to leave behind all your worldly belongings."

Ferrin hadn't truly thought that far ahead. His only concern up until that point had been just getting there. The rest would have to work itself out. Myriah wasn't going to like being told to leave everything behind, but when the choice was that or enjoy the accommodations at the White Tower, it wasn't all that difficult to decide. "If we make it out of Rhowynn alive and manage to find some out-of-the-way place to settle down in, perhaps I could return after the dust has cleared to gather our belongings and sell."

The young server gathered their plates and topped off their drinks, letting them know that the kitchen was now closed but that the bar would stay open until eleventh bell. Ferrin hoped to be fast asleep by then. He looked over at Rae and Suri, who were busy watching the growing number of customers straggling in from outside and heading over to the bar, or the tables closest to it.

"We'll need to get some supplies tomorrow before heading out," Ferrin said, shifting in his seat. His backside was growing sore. "I also told Rae that I'd look for a tailor to help better fit some of her clothing."

At the mention of her name, Rae turned her attention back to the conversation.

"We'll also need to get some warmer overcoats," Myron said, motioning with his head at several men sitting around a table not far from theirs, who were just taking off their thick coats and placing them on the backs of their chairs. "Something completely fur-lined, not just around the collars."

Ferrin took one last sip of his drink, his gut swollen from the number of tankards he'd emptied. "How about this: tomorrow, while I go into town and gather supplies and look for a tailor, you see if you can't scrounge us up a captain willing to take us north, one with a boat large enough to transport the horses."

Myron filled his cheeks with a long deep inhale and slowly sent a couple of smoke rings up above their table as Suri watched with wide-eyed wonder, giggling and pointing. "I'll find us a ride if I have to build one myself, but," he said with a deep yawn, "I think it's time to hit the sack. I could sleep till Winter's Eve."

Myron triggered a sympathetic yawn from Ferrin. "Yes, I think we've done enough damage here for one night." He rubbed his bulging waistline as he scooted his seat back from the table and stood. "Got to save room for breakfast tomorrow."

"Right you are," Myron said, standing as well.

Back at their rooms, Ferrin and Myron bid Rae and Suri good night and waited until they were in and the door locked before heading into their own room.

They were surprised to see their clothes, cleaned, dried, and pressed, lying on their beds for them when they walked in. "Wow, now that is service," Myron stated, walking over to feel his shirt. He looked at the fireplace and the blaze inside. "How do you think they dried them so quickly?"

Ferrin shook his head. "No idea, but glad they did. That'll give us something to wear tomorrow when we go into town."

Myron tossed a couple more logs on the fire, then sat down on the edge of his bed and pulled off his boots, grunting as he did. He sprawled out on top of the comforters and yawned once more, barely having time enough to crawl underneath before he was snoring.

Ferrin sat on the edge of his bed for some time, just staring at the former captain as he slept, watching and counting the rise and falls of his chest. For some reason, Ferrin wasn't tired. He should have been. Spending half of each night on watch while the others slept and the other half shaking from the cold, he was surprised he hadn't fallen out of his saddle. One of the logs on the fire dropped, sending sparks up the flue and pulling Ferrin's attention back to the room.

He stood and walked over to the window above his bed and peeked out through the shutters. The cracks were too small to see anything, so he pulled on his coat, unlocked the door, and stepped out on the balcony, closing it quickly behind him to keep in the warmer air. He pulled his coat tight around the neck as he walked out to the edge of the balcony and leaned against the rail, wiping the snow away before he did. It was a beautiful night to look up at the stars, let alone look down and see them reflected in the water below.

The moon was up and partially formed, sending down plenty of light to see by. It had been a long time since he'd felt this at ease. Even knowing who was chasing them, he found he could put it all aside for a brief moment to enjoy the beauty of the place. He could feel the ebb and flow of the city under him, hear the water gently beating against the docks and piers below. Even the wind had died down enough to be bearable. He heard the squeak of a door hinge and turned, figuring Myron had gotten up to look for him.

It was Rae. She had her coat tucked snuggly around her as she walked across the balcony to join him at the rail, her caramel skin making her face blend in with the night. Her pale-green eyes sparkled in the moonlight, giving them the momentary appearance of glowing. She stood close, their arms touching.

"Beautiful night." It was all he could think to say. She didn't respond. Although, he thought he might have seen her head bob slightly. "Why are you helping me with my sister?"

He wasn't sure why he'd said it. It had just slipped out, the silence more unnerving than expected. There was something about her that always put him on edge.

She didn't answer, nothing but the warm air misting up from her mouth to let him know she was still even breathing.

"You could go anywhere. I'm sure it would be safer for you. You could head east to Easthaven or southeast to Briston, maybe even catch a ship to the Blue Isles. Anywhere would be safer than with me."

Her arm wrapped around his as she scooted closer. She held him for a moment without talking, the two of them looking out over the star-filled lake. "I'm right where I need to be." Without saying more, she released his arm, turned, and walked back inside, leaving him standing there with his heart thumping in his ears.

Chapter 36 | Ferrin

ERRIN WOKE TO THE pitter-patter of little feet rushing across the balcony outside his room. Sunlight was already filtering through the shutters, and his covers were pulled clean to his nose. The room was surprisingly warm, and he turned over to find a healthy fire still crackling in the hearth. Myron must have added a few more logs during the night, he mused, but then he noticed Myron's bed was empty.

He flung back his covers and wished he hadn't, as the chill in the air rushed in. Like Myron, he, too, had slept in all but his boots, too tired to bother undressing.

"He's awake," he heard Suri shout from outside his balcony door. Ferrin sat on the edge of his bed and stretched with a deep yawn. He could have slept a couple more days and still not felt as though he'd caught up with all he'd missed.

The door opened, and Rae stuck her head in. Seeing that he was dressed, she walked in and inspected the room before sitting down beside him. She was dressed in her usual attire, the grey dress and red-twine belt from the previous night gone. "You slept a long time," she said. "I didn't want to wake you."

Ferrin yawned once more after having the sunlight hit his face. "Where's Myron?"

"He went down to breakfast. Said I was to tell you that he'd be more than happy to eat your share as well."

Ferrin shot from his bed. "Did he, now?" He started to take off his shirt to change back into his regular clothes, then remembered she was still sitting there. She didn't seem all that keen on leaving either. He cleared his throat. "Do you mind?"

"No."

"I, uh, I need to change so we can go down to breakfast."

"It's not the first time I've seen you without a shirt. I doubt it will be the last." She finally stood and walked out the door, but she dragged her feet just to spite him. Once the door was closed, he stripped and changed, leaving the inn's clothing lying on his bed for them to collect once they left. It didn't take him long to finish. When he did, he stuck his head out the door to tell them he was ready, but the balcony was empty. He grabbed the smallest of their coin pouches and placed it in his pocket, then he placed the others in his boots. Myron had one as well. It was a lot safer than carrying it all in one large pouch.

He walked down the hall and knocked on the girls' door. Suri opened it. Rae was sitting in a chair by the fire, and Tippi was resting comfortably on a pillow on the only bed that looked to have been slept in.

"I'm ready if you are," he said.

Rae collected her cloak while Suri collected Tippi, and they walked with him down to the common room, where they found Myron sitting at the same table they'd shared the previous night. Myron waved when he saw them coming, his mouth bursting with griddlecake.

Ferrin pulled Rae's seat out for her but didn't bother with Suri's, as she was too preoccupied with pressing her and Tippi's faces against the glass as the boats made ready to set sail. If it hadn't been so frigid, Ferrin would have enjoyed taking his breakfast out on the terrace behind the inn. It was set with tables and chairs, but all of them were covered for the season.

A young serving lady walked over when she saw them arrive. She didn't have the same likeness as the rest of the young people. Probably an extra hired hand. "Can I get you something for breakfast?"

"We'll have whatever it is he's stuffing into his face so eagerly," Ferrin said, pointing at Myron.

She smiled. "Three servings of griddlecakes and eggs and sausage coming right up. Would you care for some hot tea? We also have some fresh dairy."

"Sounds delicious. I'll take both."

"Yes, sir." She looked at Rae, and Rae nodded in turn. With a half-curtsy, the girl disappeared into the kitchen, and before Rae could pull Suri away from the window, she was back with a tray of drinks. "Tea and cream for each of you. Careful with the tea. It's hot."

"Thank you," Ferrin said, warming his hands around the mug. "Just the way we like it."

The girl curtsied once more. "I'll be back with your food shortly, sir." With that, she headed back into the kitchen.

Ferrin turned to Myron. "Why didn't you wake me?"

Myron looked baffled by the question. "So I could eat your helping of breakfast, of course. Why else?" He laughed and stuffed a whole sausage in his mouth and bit down. Ferrin's mouth immediately watered. "I wanted to let you sleep," Myron said, washing the pork down with a stout gulp of ale. "You were resting so peacefully I couldn't bear to wake you."

Rae smiled. She tried to hide it with her hand, and when that didn't work, she turned and looked at Suri, who had gone back to staring out at the boats as they moved farther away from the city.

"And how did you fare, Rae?" Ferrin asked. "Was your sleep restful?"

Rae turned. "My pillow was too soft. I thought I might drown."

Myron bellowed out a laugh, causing him to lose half a griddlecake and turn all the heads in the room. "Well, if that doesn't take the pudding. A woman who doesn't care for the finer things. Let me guess, the mattress was too comfortable, so you slept on the floor?" When she didn't smile, but instead looked down, embarrassed, he stopped laughing. "Oh dear, I was just kidding. You didn't actually . . ."

"I prefer something firm underneath me. I don't care to feel like I'm sinking."

Myron looked at Ferrin, but Ferrin didn't know how to respond any more than Myron. Thankfully, Myron had enough common sense not to leave everyone sitting there in an awkward silence. "Well, if we do ever get out of this mess, I'm sure that given a little time you'll find some of these so-called comforts more pleasing. But if it makes you feel more at home to sleep on the floor, then you go right ahead." He leaned back and raised his glass in salute. "I don't care if you sleep on the ceiling like a scalenbat. If it helps you sleep, you do whatever it takes."

Rae chuckled at the suggestion of sleeping on the ceiling. "What's a scalenbat?"

"It's a type of large cave bat. Nasty little buggers. They don't bite, but they have very sharp claws on their wings."

The serving lady returned with a large tray holding three platters of food. She barely got Ferrin's down on the table before he was digging into the sausage. The server also left a small tin pitcher of honey for the griddlecakes. After their meal the previous evening, Ferrin hadn't thought he'd ever be able to eat again, but he found himself stuffing his face with the same voraciousness as Myron.

"Good, aren't they?" Myron said with a grin.

Ferrin's mouth was too full to speak, but he did manage a brusque nod.

Ferrin held off with just a single extra helping, knowing he had a lot of walking to do that morning. He didn't want to make himself sick. Also, as nice as it was to sit and talk last night, they didn't have the luxury of time. If it hadn't been so cold, and they hadn't been on the verge of collapse from riding through the snow for the last week, he wouldn't have suggested spending the night in Storyl. As it was, they'd needed at least one night of good sleep. It might be the last they got until Rhowynn.

"Daylight's burning," Ferrin said, looking out at the sails shrinking in the distance over the lake. "We need to get these supplies and be on our way. The longer we stay, the greater the risk of those behind us catching up."

Myron took one last swallow from his tankard before wiping his mouth and pushing back from the table. "I guess I better get to looking for a captain willing to travel upriver, which means a merchant transport. Most of the boats are local fishers. We need someone running trade from here to Rhowynn."

Ferrin stood from the table, and Rae and Suri joined him, having already finished their one helping of the cakes. They returned to their rooms long enough to grab a couple of their packs for toting around their purchases.

"Make mine green, if you can find one," Myron said. "I've always wanted a green coat."

"I'll look, but I can't promise anything."

They left their rooms, locking the doors after them, and headed down to the front lobby, where Sarren was working the desk. Ferrin stopped to ask her where they might find a chandlery and a tailor who could make fast alterations.

"You'll find most of the shops on Canal Street," the young blonde girl said. "As far as a good tailor, I recommend Mistress Hanley. Best seamstress in Storyl. You can ask anyone. A far sight better than any of the tailors, that's for sure. Her shop is just off Canal. When you come to the smithy, you'll want to take the next street to the left. You can't miss it. The sign will read Hanley's, and there will be a large pair of scissors painted underneath."

"And where would be the best place to find passage to Rhowynn?" Myron asked.

The girl thought a moment. "Most of the ships large enough for passage will be on the southside docks." She pointed out the doors to the road in front of the inn. "Bailer Circle will take you from one side of Storyl to the other by way of the water. Walk it south and you'll eventually reach the southern docks."

They thanked the girl and left.

Pin was sitting on a stool just outside the front entrance, waiting on guests. He hopped up when he saw them. "Good day, gents, missus." He tipped his hat. "Be needing your horses?"

"Not this time," Ferrin said. "Have you been keeping your eyes open for any newcomers?"

"I have, but other than yourselves, there's been no other comings and goings. Don't get much during the winter months." He gave Ferrin a curious look. "Anyone in particular I need to be looking for?"

Ferrin shook his head. "No. No one in particular." He didn't think it wise to tell him to be watching for white riders, as that could draw unwanted suspicion. He dug around in his pocket and tossed the boy another copper. "Keep those eyes open."

Pin tipped his hat and bowed. "Yes, sir. Thank you, sir."

They walked down the stairs and stopped beside the road out front. Ferrin looked up to see if he could see the sun, but it was blocked by the buildings on the other side of the street. "Let's meet back here at noon," Ferrin said to Myron.

"I'll have found us passage by then, even if I have to buy a boat myself."

Ferrin nearly choked. He couldn't tell if Myron was joking or not. "Let's hope it doesn't come to that."

Myron smiled, then started down Bailer Circle, south toward the docks. Ferrin, Rae, and Suri kept straight ahead on Mooring Lane, which was the road they had come down the day before when looking for the White Pheasant.

The streets were beginning to fill with shoppers as shopkeepers opened for business. Most paid them no mind, except for one of the stall owners who attempted to sell them some fresh cut bait. Suri stopped long enough to join Tippi in admiring the minnows swimming in the man's bucket.

They made it back to Canal Street, which was quite a bit more active than it had been last evening when they had arrived. Shopkeepers called out their wares, most for fresh-caught fish and eel. What had been a strong smell yesterday was almost abrasive today as they made their way down the busy street. Once through the heart of the fish market, they reached a section of street that appeared to be nothing but sleeping establishments and taverns.

Some of the inns were every bit as large as the White Pheasant, but perhaps not as well kept: the fronts not swept, the curtains in the windows, the signs showing wear.

They stopped on one of the bridges, and Ferrin hung out over the rail to see underneath. It was almost like a whole other city just below them. There were stairs on either side of each bridge leading down. If they hadn't been in such a hurry, he'd have liked to go below to see what was down there.

They came across the chandlery first. The sign bore an arrangement of white candles on a green background. It also had a basket of assorted fruits and vegetables with lettering below that read: Storyl Chandlery. Not a very original name, but effective. They didn't spend a long time in the shop, finding most of what they had on the list, even some hooks and line in case the need arose.

They filled at least one pack with supplies, and Ferrin paid the chandler and his wife for the goods and bid them a good day. Back on the street, they kept their eyes out for a shop selling coats. They found one not three shops down from the chandlery.

The clothing was hardly what one would consider fashionable, but then Storyl was a simple lake town, where the people cared more for comfort than keeping up with the latest fashion. They did manage to find several very durable coats, each lined with enough fur to keep the wearer warm during the cold winter months.

The coats didn't exactly have a wide selection of colors, mostly variations of brown, but they did have a decent assortment of furs. For those with not a lot of coin to spend, there was beaver, muskrat, and even dog, but for Ferrin, who opted for the more expensive, the shopkeeper brought out a selection of fox, rabbit, and wolf. If they were going to have to travel in such conditions, they might as well make the journey as pleasant as possible.

Suri all but started crying when Ferrin had shown her the wolf pelt, so he quickly decided to go with the red-and-grey fox instead. As luck would have it, the shop owner even had a couple of dyed coats with the more expensive fur that he kept for special occasions. They were faded, but one of them had a definite green hue. Ferrin snatched it up right away, holding out his arm to the sleeve to judge whether or not it would fit Myron. It looked close enough.

He purchased the coats, and they each put theirs on, exchanging their old ones for partial payment. The shopkeeper was extremely happy to acquire items from outside of Storyl, and believed they'd fetch a good price. Ferrin bid the shopkeeper a good day and stepped outside onto the sidewalk.

"You like your new coat?" Ferrin asked Suri, who was playing with the wooden buttons on the front.

She smiled. "Tippi likes it too," she said, tucking her pinecone inside.

"How does yours fit?" he asked Rae.

She was busy feeling the fur around the cuff. "It's warm, thank you." Hers was the lightest colored of the bunch, a very soft tan. Ferrin's was a medium brown, much the color of a deer's hide.

"Guess that just leaves the seamstress," he said as he directed them back to the street, and they moved back into the ebb and flow of the traffic.

The farther they went down Canal Street, the less reputable the inns and taverns became, causing Rae to pull Suri closer to her as they passed. In some of the upper windows, scantily clad women with painted faces waved to those passing below, some calling out improper invitations. At one point, several women standing out front in their bed clothes whistled to them as they passed. Ferrin couldn't imagine how they hadn't caught their death of cold.

Rae took Ferrin's arm as they moved through the street.

Spotting the smithy ahead on the left, Ferrin pointed. "We're close." He heard it before he saw it, the smith's hammer striking the anvil in repetitive fashion, bringing back memories of home. They passed the smith, who was standing under a lean-to outside his workshop, smelting a long piece of metal, most likely forging a sword.

Not far down from his shop, they turned down the first street to the left. Ferrin could see the seamstress's sign out front, with its pair of golden scissors painted clearly on a field of blue. "Guess this is it. Let's hope she's not too busy."

A small bell on the door announced their arrival. The shop was half the size of those on the main road through town, but it was clean and set in an orderly fashion, with shelves of material tucked away on the side and racks of clothing forming two aisles leading to the back. On one side, there were women's dresses and undergarments, and on the other, men's pants, tunics, and accessories. Not exactly a large selection, but from the way the girl at the White Pheasant spoke, the shopkeeper did most of her business through mending and alterations.

"How can I help you?" a middle-aged woman with light-brown hair, rosy cheeks, and a cheery disposition asked as she stepped out from a back room and stood behind her counter. She was short and plump and wore a red pincushion on one wrist, which she kept in place with a bracelet. It was filled with pins and needles of all shapes and sizes.

"Mistress Hanley, I assume?" Ferrin asked as they walked to the back of the shop.

The woman smiled. "I am." She glanced at Rae and Suri and inspected each of their outfits in turn. "Ah, yes, I see the problem," she stated, looking at Rae.

Ferrin placed the pack with Rae's clothes on a table beside the woman's desk. "We have some items that need altering."

"Let's see what you've got there."

Ferrin pulled out the skirts for her to inspect.

"Yes, definitely too long for someone of our height," she said with a wink, as the seamstress wasn't much taller than Rae.

Mistress Hanley laid the skirts out longways on the table, then grabbed a roll of sewing tape out from one of the front pockets of her apron and walked around the counter. "Hold still, girl," she said. "I need to make sure I cut this to the right size, or you'll be walking around town with your ankles hanging out for all to see."

Rae stood in place and let the seamstress move up and down her leg with her sewing tape.

"That should do it," she said, rolling up the tape and tucking it back in her pocket. "I can have this done by the end of the week."

"I'm afraid we don't have that long. We are just passing through on our way to Rhowynn, and—"

"Well, how long do you have?" she asked, placing her hands on her hips.

Ferrin looked at Rae and cleared his throat. "Noon today."

Mistress Hanley leaned back and roared with laughter. "Go on. I've got work to do. I don't have time for your nonsense."

Ferrin slapped the table with two silver coins, and the woman stopped laughing. "If you can have these done by then, they're yours." It was nearly as much as they had paid for their two lakeside rooms and meals.

Mistress Hanley stared at the coins lying on the table. Ferrin could almost see her calculating whether she could get it done.

"I was told by those at the White Pheasant that if anyone could do it, it would be you." Ferrin didn't know how long it took to cut material and sew it, but he figured for a seamstress of her renown, it could be done.

"Flattery will get you nowhere," she said, then smiled. "But that doesn't mean I don't like to hear it." She grabbed the skirts off the table. "Fine. You've got yourself a deal." She looked at Rae. "Take it off, deary, I've got to have it too."

Rae passed Ferrin an uncertain glance, and the woman shook her head. "Ain't nothing your husband hasn't already seen."

Rae looked at Ferrin, then shrugged and started unbuttoning down the side.

"What if someone were to walk in?" Ferrin asked. Rae didn't look all that worried, but Ferrin quickly busied himself inspecting some skirts on one of the racks behind him.

"Here," Mistress Hanley said, guiding Rae back around the counter. "You can change in here if you're that worried about it. You'd think you two were newly bonded, the way your husband's acting." She chuckled as she opened the door to her workshop and ushered Rae inside while Suri waited with Ferrin.

"Do you have something for her to wear in the meantime?" Ferrin asked.

"I'm sure I can find something around here that might work." The door shut with Rae and Mistress Hanley inside, and a few minutes later Rae stepped out wearing a new skirt. It was nearly as long as the last. The color was a bluish grey, similar in style to what most of the other women in Storyl seemed to wear.

"It itches," Rae said, rubbing down the side of her leg.

"You won't have to wear it long," Ferrin said, then looked at Mistress Hanley, who was already pulling out a couple pairs of scissors. "We'll be back at noon with your payment."

She waved them on as she sat down at her workbench and laid out the first of Rae's skirts. Ferrin directed Rae and Suri back to the front door. "Let's drop our bags off at the inn and see if Myron has made any progress. We can come back later and see if she's been able to get the alterations completed." Ferrin hoped Myron was having as good luck with finding a boat willing to take them upriver.

Chapter 37 | Ferrin

ONCE BACK AT THE INN, they dropped their bags off in their rooms, but there was no sign of Myron.

"He must be having a difficult time finding a captain willing to take us north," Ferrin said to Rae as they stood on the balcony outside their rooms and watched the boats floating across the water. Some had sails, some did not, some carried long nets fastened to poles that stuck out from the sides of their boat.

Ferrin wondered what it must be like to spend days on the water trolling for fish, to come home every night to clean them and have them ready to sell, just to go out and do it all over again the following day. He guessed it wasn't much different from most jobs, where you found yourself performing the same repetitive tasks, grinding away just to put food in the mouths of your family. He wondered if he'd ever get the chance to find out what having a family was like.

Rae slid over beside him, her shoulder rubbing against his arm. "He will find one."

Ferrin looked at her and smiled. "I'm sure you're right."

"I'm thirsty," Suri suddenly pronounced, leaving the railing to carry Tippi back to her room.

Rae sighed, then looked at Ferrin.

Ferrin turned. "We'll all go down and see if they have any of that mulled cider available. How's that sound?"

Suri squealed, nearly dropping Tippi, and rushed inside, leaving the door open behind her. Rae gave him an approving smile, and even went so far as to lay her hand on his for a brief moment before following her daughter in.

"I'll meet you in the hallway," Ferrin said over his shoulder, taking one last look at the incredible view before heading inside himself. The sun was at its peak, warming his face against the cold gusts coming in off the water. Light sparkled across the tops of the waves, blinding him if he looked at it directly.

Leaving their gear, he locked the door and met Rae and Suri in the hall and walked downstairs. The common room was mostly empty, not quite time for the lunch crowd, and they found their usual table by the windows and waited for someone to serve them. The man behind the bar saw them sitting there and walked into the kitchen. A few moments later, one of the serving girls who'd delivered their breakfast appeared, rushing over when she spotted Ferrin looking. She offered a polite curtsy.

"Lunch isn't served until twelfth bell, I'm afraid."

"No need," Ferrin said, digging around in his pocket for his purse. "We aren't here to eat."

"I want cider," Suri proclaimed from the window, then looked at her pinecone. "Do you want cider, Tippi?" She looked at Ferrin. "Tippi wants cider."

Ferrin smiled as he turned to the server. "Do you have any of the mulled left?"

The girl nodded. "I can warm some, if you like."

Ferrin placed a couple of coppers on the table, and the girl swiped them into her hand and headed for the kitchen. After a while she was back with three steaming glasses, which she set in front of them.

"My thanks," Ferrin said, and the girl curtsied once more and walked back toward the kitchen. Instead of going inside, she sat on a stool beside the bar and chatted quietly with the young man behind it. At least until Mistress Tulick came out in her flour-covered apron, caught her, and ushered her into the kitchen, giving the young man behind the bar a harsh look as she did. Ferrin chuckled. He'd seen that look a time or two when he was younger, when a mother didn't much care for the attention her daughter was receiving.

"Will your sister like me?"

Ferrin completely forgot about the young barkeep and turned to look at Rae. "What?"

She looked down at her clothes. "Will she approve of me?"

"I don't understand. Approve of what?"

Rae touched her shorter cropped hair. "I'm not . . . I don't look like most girls."

"That's a good thing," he blurted out. "Of course my sister will like you. Why wouldn't she?" Other than when Ferrin had purchased Rae some new clothing in Iraseth, he'd never once seen her care about what others thought, especially about the way she looked. Although, her hair had been a point of contention for her ever since Sylas had taken a pair of shears to it.

"I don't know." She fiddled with her glass. "How do you look at me?"

Ferrin nearly choked on his drink and set the mug on the table.

"I saw the way you looked at those women at the inn," she said, turning Ferrin's cheeks a bright red. "Do people look at me like that?"

"I . . . I wasn't staring at those women," he said adamantly. Was she talking about the brothel? "I was . . ." He shook his head. "They were hanging out the windows whistling at us. I couldn't help but see them. But I wasn't staring."

"You didn't look at Mistress Hanley like that."

"I didn't look at Mistress Hanley at all. Well, I mean, of course I looked at her. I was talking to her. I had to look at her. What was the question?"

"Do people look at me differently?"

"No. Of course not. What do you mean?"

"You don't look at me like you did Mistress Hanley."

"How do I look at you?" he asked, almost afraid to hear her answer.

"You look at me more like you did those women at the inn."

Ferrin swallowed the lump building in his throat. Rae had never been in any common society before or had any notion as to what was proper and what wasn't. As far as he could tell, she'd never even had a true friend before, let alone any other type of relationship. Men, to her, were nothing more than something to fear or loathe, and who could blame her? He only wished he understood what it was she was trying to ask.

"Do you think I look different, like those women?"

His breath caught in his throat, and he glanced briefly over at Suri, who was using Tippi to chase a drop of melted ice down the windowpane. "No." Her face grew pensive, almost hurt. He quickly leaned forward and tried placing his hand on hers, but she pulled back. "I think you look different, but not like those women in the brothel. I think you look like no other woman I've ever met. In a good way," he added, when he saw the worried look in her eyes. "If people look at you, it's probably because they are intrigued, not because there is anything wrong with you."

"Some men look at me like the men in the Tower."

"Those men are pigs and don't deserve to look at any woman. There are men out there who lust after what they cannot have. They see a beautiful woman and believe they have the right to her, no matter the cost."

Rae pursed her lips as she pondered what he'd said, then finally looked up at him. "Do you think I'm beautiful?"

Ferrin blinked. That's what she took away out of that whole conversation? He was stuck between a rock and a hard place. If he said yes, she might start to think he was like those other men, but if he lied and said no when she was hoping he said yes, it might force her back in her shell. Why were women so difficult? "I, uh . . . I—"

"There you are!" someone called out behind them, nearly causing Ferrin to jump out of his seat.

Ferrin turned to find Myron sweeping across the room for their table and breathed a deep sigh of relief. Perfect timing. Ferrin pulled out a seat, and Myron gladly took it. He plopped down with a soft moan. Rae, however, didn't look quite so happy as Ferrin for Myron's abrupt return.

"I've walked from one side of this city to the other, and my feet are killing me." He pulled off his boots right at the table and began rubbing the balls of his feet. "That's much better."

"So?" Ferrin asked with bated breath. "Did you find us a ride out of here?"

"Sort of."

"What does that mean?"

"It means I found a captain willing to take us upriver, but his ship isn't large enough to carry the horses."

Ferrin winced. "There were no other ships heading to Rhowynn?"

Myron shook his head and grabbed Ferrin's mug and gulped down what was left of his cider. "Oh, that hit the spot." He looked at Ferrin. "There was one ship, but he wasn't setting sail for another three weeks."

"That's disappointing."

"One good thing, though," Myron said, "was that the captain was willing to take a trade on the horses as fare for our passage."

"Those horses are worth five times that."

"Yes, but we're desperate, and worse yet, he knows it. Word of a group of travelers looking to get passage to Rhowynn had already reached his ears before I made it as far as Canal Street. Gossip spreads as fast as a northern wind around these parts."

Ferrin went to take a swallow of his cider, forgetting Myron had just drained the rest of it. With a disappointed grunt, he lowered the empty mug back to the table.

"How did you three fare?" Myron asked, noticing Rae's new grey skirt.

"We managed to acquire all the supplies on our list, and even found a seamstress willing to alter Rae's clothing in quick order, but it's going to cost a pretty coin to do it. I told her we'd pick them up by noon."

"Then you don't have much time to spare." Myron pointed to the window. "Sun's reaching its peak."

Ferrin glanced out the window. Where had the morning gone? His stomach grumbled as he turned back to Myron. "While you pack our belongings and clean out our rooms, I'll retrieve the skirts from Mistress Hanley."

"I'm coming as well," Rae said, standing from her seat. She looked at Suri, who was busy trying to offer Tippi a sip of her cider. The little girl finally ended up placing her finger in the cider and dropping some of it on the top of Tippi's head. "You stay here with Master Myron," Rae said. "I'll be right back."

"But I want to go with you."

"I can collect the outfits on my own," Ferrin said. "You don't have to come."

"Yes, I do," Rae said insistently, pointing down at the borrowed skirt she was wearing.

"Oh, I forgot about needing to return that." He looked at Myron. "We'll be back as soon as possible, maybe even find time to grab a small lunch before we go."

Myron smiled. "I like the sound of that."

Ferrin left Myron and Suri sitting at the table and headed across the common room for the lobby, Rae rushing to keep up. After their awkward conversation earlier, he had been hoping for some time alone to think through what she had said. Apparently, she had no intention of giving it to him, or she might have actually just wanted to try the skirts on. Either way, there was nothing he could do about it now. The sooner they got there and back, the sooner they could depart.

Ferrin looked around the front porch for Pin, but he wasn't there. He wasn't in his other usual spot in front of the stables either. Not wanting to waste any more time, Ferrin started back up Mooring Lane toward Canal Street. Rae had to almost jog to keep up with his longer legs. She finally grabbed him by the arm.

"Slow down. I'm going to trip over this skirt." She had fabric clutched in each hand to hike up the bottom enough to walk in.

Ferrin slowed. "Sorry, I just want to get the stuff and get back as soon as possible."

"Is that why you didn't want me to come?"

That uncomfortable feeling was beginning to creep back in as a small warning bell rang in his head. "No. I just . . ." He thought a moment. "I just figured it would be faster if I went alone."

"I'm fast. I can keep up."

Ferrin chuckled inwardly. When Rae set her mind to something, there was little use arguing. The little healer was a force to be reckoned with.

"You're looking at me like that again," she said.

"What?" Ferrin hadn't realized that he'd been staring, and quickly focused on the street ahead. "Sorry. I, uh . . . Sorry."

They reached Canal Street and had to slow. It was even more congested now than it had been when they'd gone through earlier that morning. They were halfway down the street, just passing the shop where they'd purchased their coats, when someone called out behind them.

"Hey, mister."

Ferrin didn't stop. Whoever it was could have been referring to anyone. Then he heard it again, louder.

"Hey, mister. Mister, wait up!" Something in the voice had him turning.

Pin beamed when he saw Ferrin spot him, and he rushed through the crowd to catch him. The little boy was out of breath by the time he reached them. "I spotted some new arrivals like you asked."

"Oh?" Ferrin moved them to the side of the walkway to keep from getting trampled.

"There was six of them, not friendly looking at all. My friend Trick said he saw them ride in from the south gate."

"Six of who?" Ferrin asked. "What did they look like?"

"Didn't I say? I thought I did." Pin looked confused, then finally raised his head. "Black Watch."

Ferrin scanned the street behind them, searching for any sign of white in the crowd. He looked up the street in the direction they were heading and did the same, but nothing stood out. They could be anywhere. "We need to go back."

"No!" Rae said. "I need my clothes."

Ferrin grabbed a coin out of his purse, not caring what it was, and slapped it in Pin's hand. Pin's eyes widened when he saw the silver gleam. "Run back to the inn and tell my friend what you just heard. Tell him we'll meet him . . . Just tell him we'll meet him. He'll know what I mean. Now run!"

Pin disappeared into the throng.

"I don't like this," Ferrin said, turning to Rae. "They could be behind us. They could be in front of us. We don't know." He looked up to see if he could spot any black shapes flying over their heads. The sky seemed clear enough.

"We have to be quick," he said, raising the hood of his coat. Rae did the same. He grabbed her hand, and they took off down the sidewalk, weaving through the shoppers, keeping an eye out for any hint of white uniforms. They crossed several bridges with no sign of the Tower's guards. The brothels were just coming into view, the same women hanging out the windows of the upper floors, but Ferrin was too busy looking for white riders to notice.

They were all but jogging by the time they caught sight of the blacksmith ahead. The street began to empty, as the more frequented shops had ended at the last bridge. Ferrin released a faint sigh of relief when they finally reached the smithy on their way to the next street up.

"You there! Halt and identify yourselves."

Rae's hand clamped tight to his.

Maybe it's just the city patrollers. Ferrin turned, and he could feel the sweat break out across his forehead as four men in white uniforms stepped out of the blacksmith's shop and started their way

Chapter 38 | Ferrin

ALONG WITH THE FOUR members of the Black Watch was a fifth person, walking out front and wearing a simple grey robe. Their hood was also raised, and by their size and shape, it was clearly a man. Ferrin didn't see Sylas amongst them—or the body he'd been occupying—and the wielder he'd fought in Iraseth had been a woman. In fact, he didn't recognize any of this lot.

They came to a stop a few feet away.

"We're the Tinkersons, sir." It was the first name that popped into his mind. He had no idea where it had come from. He didn't know anyone named Tinkerson. "We're on our way to Mistress Hanley's, just around the corner. My wife," he said, putting his arm around Rae and pulling her up against him, "is getting some dresses hemmed." He took a step back, pulling her along with him. "We'll just be on our way, sorry to bother you."

"Remove your hoods," one of the guards demanded.

Ferrin released Rae, letting his arm drop slowly behind his back, where his dagger lay sheathed at his waist. "It's a bit chilly today, sir." Had they been demanding that everyone remove their hoods? Then it dawned on him why they had been coming from the blacksmiths. They were looking for him.

"Lower your hoods," the man said once more, his hand sliding toward his sword.

"We don't want any trouble." Ferrin reached up with his free hand and pulled back his hood.

The guards stared a moment, but none of them showed any recognition. The man in the grey robe looked at Rae, and she did the same. He took a step forward and pointed.

"That's her!"

Ferrin pulled his dagger and threw it straight at the man. It was a perfect shot. It flew from his fingers with precise accuracy, then struck nothing and deflected into the street. The man was a wielder. Ferrin grabbed Rae and ran, practically carrying her down the sidewalk as he raced for the next street up. If he could just—

Something hit him in the back, and he was thrown forward. Rae shrieked as she was flung with him. They landed on top of each other and rolled to a stop.

Ferrin tried making it back to his feet, but something held him down, an enormous weight pushing him into the wood. He yelled as the force of it pressed him flat. He felt, as well as heard, what sounded like the boards under him snapping, but the pain told him it wasn't the boards. It was his ribs. He wanted to scream, but all the wind had been crushed out of him.

Suddenly the pressure was gone, and he took a deep gulp of air, then cried out from the searing pain in his chest. He looked up through tear-soaked eyes to see the man in the grey robe standing over him, the other members of the Black Watch waiting just behind.

Rae was lying beside him. He tried reaching over to touch her arm, but the men in white were on top of him, yanking him to his feet. The stabbing shock from the movement was so excruciating he vomited his entire breakfast across the men in front of him.

"Ahh! Yuck!" One of the men punched Ferrin in the face, and Ferrin's head snapped to the left.

"Look what you did to my uniform."

Ferrin turned his head and watched as they pulled Rae to her feet. She didn't appear to be in the kind of pain he was, at least he didn't think she was. He was having a hard time seeing through the tears. Two of the guards held her arms as they stood her in front of the man in the grey robe.

Why grey? he wondered. The woman he'd faced in Iraseth wore black robes with a white insignia. This man had none of that. Then again, everything was blurry under the pain.

"The inquisitors have been lost without you, Rae," the man said. He had a nasal voice that made Ferrin want to stuff his fist in the man's mouth just to keep him from talking.

Ferrin's legs gave out from under him, and he nearly toppled the two men holding him as he landed on the wooden street.

"Fix him," the man in the grey robe said to Rae, and they dragged her over to where Ferrin was kneeling on his hands and knees, trying his best not to move, or even breathe, as every breath felt like being stabbed in the chest by a dull blade. She knelt to lay her hands on him.

"Wait!" the man said, and he walked over and pulled something silver out from beneath his cloak.

Ferrin took one look at the durma collar and tried to crawl away, but the pain overwhelmed him, and he landed on his face, screaming. He tried getting back to his knees, but something invisible grabbed him and flipped him over on his back. He jerked and twisted, biting down against the sharpness in his chest as the man in the grey robe walked over and clamped the round piece of smooth metal to his neck. He could hear it snap into place.

As soon as the collar was attached, he felt his magic recede. It was still there, but not where he could reach it, not even if he had Rae's crystal. The invisible barrier that had been holding him vanished. He tried flipping over when his body erupted with what felt like a jolt of lightning.

Every muscle in his body seized at the same time. He wanted to cry out, but his throat had seized as well. He couldn't breathe.

"Stop!" he heard Rae scream. "Stop! You're killing him!"

The pain eased, but the aftershock on his body didn't as he went into a state of convulsions. He'd felt this pain once before, back when he'd first been captured. He opened his eyes. Even through the tears he could see the metallic rod hanging from a chain around the man's neck. Ferrin had seen a similar key before. The rune on the end of the rod was glowing.

"We have quite the fighter here," the man said in that same whiny, irritating tone. "Although, I see nothing special about you. Why does the archchancellor want you so badly?"

Ferrin looked up at the man. Didn't he know who Ferrin was? "Where's Sylas?" he asked, his voice cracking under the pain.

"Sylas?" The man looked confused. "How should I know where the inquisitor is?"

Ferrin took another deep breath to slow his heart. "Isn't he with you?" Ferrin looked at the surrounding buildings as if expecting the inquisitor to come walking out at any moment. "Where's the other one? Lenara."

"Lenara isn't here," the man said, a spark of understanding lighting his eyes. "I'm Taggert, first apprentice to Bulradoer Rukar. The archchancellor sent out several teams to look for you. We just happened to be the first to catch you." He looked at his men and grinned. "And we'll be rewarded handsomely for this, and I will finally earn my black robes." He looked at Rae. "Now, heal him. I don't want to have to carry him all the way back to the White Tower."

Rae knelt beside Ferrin in the street and laid her hands on his chest. There were tears in her eyes, a desperation he hadn't seen since their time inside the Tower. He felt the familiar chill of her magic work its way inside. He didn't need to look to know what was happening. He cried out as the bones moved back into place and resealed. The pain, he knew, would be temporary, and he bit back against it. Soon enough, the burning was gone.

By the time she was finished, they had pulled Ferrin back to his feet, tied his hands, and were quickly marching the two of them back down Canal Street toward the south gate.

The people on the road were quick to move, heads lowered, eyes diverted to the other side of the street. No one wanted to be caught looking. Even the brothel ladies with the painted faces closed their windows when they saw them coming.

The man in the grey didn't seem to mind, or even notice. Two guards walked alongside Ferrin, leaving one to walk with Rae and one to take up the rear.

Ferrin had no idea how many of the Tower's guards were in Storyl, but after seeing the contingent following Sylas, he doubted it was just these four. They must have split up to search the city. If there was any hope for escape, it was going to have to be before they caught up with the rest of their group.

They crossed the first of three bridges leading back to Mooring Lane, its side rails low enough for Ferrin to see the water channel and the boardwalks below. He watched helplessly as the people went about their lives without a clue as to what was happening, or even caring. They passed by the shop with the fur coats, then started up another bridge, this one a little narrower than the last, forcing the pedestrians on their side to cross the road just to get out of the Black Watch's way.

He'd sworn he'd never allow them to collar him again. He'd rather kill himself than be dragged back to the Tower.

He'd tried to free himself from one during his first escape from the Black Watch in Syrel, back when they were first taking him to the Tower. A blacksmith had used a wedge on it, hammered it until the end of the wedge had bent under the strain. It hadn't left so much as a scratch on the collar. It hadn't been until a Black Watch captain named Hatch had shown up with the key that the durma had unlocked. The collars had no key holes. Ferrin had spent hours, days even, sliding his fingers along the smooth exterior before finally giving up and agreeing with the other wielders in the prison transport that it was a hopeless cause.

They passed the chandlery on their right and started up the final bridge before reaching Mooring Lane. He only hoped Myron and Suri wouldn't come looking once they heard from Pin. He hoped they got out of Storyl. No matter what happened, Ferrin wasn't going back. He didn't care what he had to do. He would never step foot inside the White Tower again.

Ferrin didn't have time to warn Rae. He threw his weight into the two guards walking beside him, throwing them off balance long enough for him to turn and kick the guard holding Rae. The wielder in front turned, reaching inside his robe for the key, but Ferrin grabbed him with his bound hands and pulled him over the side of the bridge.

The wielder didn't even have time to scream before they hit the water. It was like hitting solid ground. The water was so cold it ripped the breath right out of Ferrin's lungs and felt as though someone had peeled the flesh right off his face.

The wielder under him jerked and thrashed, his hands tangled in his robes as Ferrin fought to keep him from the key. They were sinking fast. If he didn't stop him now, they were both going to drown. With his hands still tied, Ferrin wrapped his arms around the man's neck and pulled with everything he had. A searing jolt of pain wracked his limbs from where the wielder had managed to get his hands on the key, but Ferrin held his grip and twisted the man's head as hard as he could. A moment later the pain subsided, and the man went limp.

Desperately, Ferrin kicked his feet, holding on to the dead wielder as he fought to break the surface. His head broke free and he gasped, sucking in as much water as air. The current had carried him down from the bridge, but not far enough that he couldn't see the four guards standing at the top watching to see what had happened to their leader. Ferrin couldn't see Rae anywhere. Where'd she gone? He spun in the water and happened to see her head bobbing up and down near the boardwalk on the other side, her arms flailing.

Relief flooded through him. He was afraid she hadn't jumped.

He swam as hard as he could, dragging the man's corpse with him. He was completely numb, his breath coming in short raspy gasps, each harder than the last. He could feel his life fading, his legs barely moving. The weight of his clothes, along with the dead wielder, pulled him downward, the icy fingers of Praxil Lake beckoning for him to just let go. But letting go was the last thing he was going to do. He'd come too far to give in now. He was nearing the edge of the boardwalk, just a little farther. As much as he willed them to keep going, his legs stopped moving, and he sank beneath the water. He wasn't going to make it.

Suddenly, he was being lifted back up to the surface. People on shore were fishing him out with pole hooks. As soon as he reached the edge of the walk, the people standing around fished them out. He could see Rae being laid on the planks a few feet down, coughing up water. She was still alive.

One man unbound his hands, and Ferrin turned toward the bridge. The Tower's guards were no longer there, but he was sure they would be coming. They needed to get out of there, but he was too weak to even stand, let alone even crawl down to where Rae was lying to see if she was all right.

Ferrin shook uncontrollably, his teeth chattering to the point of chipping. He was careful to keep his tongue out of the way for fear of biting it off. The people gathered around were examining the wielder's body, checking for life. Drawing on every ounce of strength he had, he turned over and yanked the man's hood back, stuffing his hand down his shirt, acting as though he, too, were checking on the man. His fingers wrapped around a chain, and he pulled it out.

With shivering hands, he wrapped the chain with the small silver rod around his neck. The chain held a couple of other items as well, but Ferrin didn't have time to look. All he cared about was the key.

He started to turn back over but felt a familiar icy chill spread through him. It was a different sort of cold than the frigid touch of the water. He looked down to find Rae lying at his feet, with her hand up his pants leg. He could feel his strength returning, but before she could finish, her eyes rolled up and her head hit the boardwalk. "Rae!"

With what little healing she'd been able to offer, he managed to get to his feet and lift her in his arms. "I need to get her to the physicker!" he shouted and took off down the boardwalk in the opposite direction of the bridge.

People behind him were shouting for him to stop, that the healer was the other way, but stopping was the last thing on his mind. He had no intention of finding a physicker, and every intention of getting to the south docks where he was hoping and praying that Myron and Suri were still waiting.

The cold wet of his fur-lined coat clung to him like death's fingers waiting to finish the job. If he had had the time, he would have stopped to take it off, but he didn't.

He half ran, half stumbled down the boardwalk, the boards bending and creaking under his feet. Those on the walk scooted to the side when they saw him coming, partly because he was carrying a woman in his arms, but more so from the desperate look on his face, a look that said no one better stand in his way. The sky above them disappeared altogether as the boardwalk moved up under the next bridge.

It didn't stop there. It made a sharp turn south, and Ferrin found himself in what appeared to be a whole other city directly under the one above. Perhaps this had been the original city back when it was first built. There were shops and residences and narrow streets leading from each boardwalk, an entire community most visitors would never see.

It took Ferrin a moment to get his bearings, but when he did, he started running once more. As small as she was, Rae was getting heavy in his arms. His weakened condition was hardly conducive to a full-on sprint across the city. Rae had managed to keep him alive; now it was his time to return the favor. He reached the end of one street and took the next, doing his best to maintain the right direction.

"Stop! Stop in the name of the White Tower!"

Ferrin glanced over his shoulder, nearly tripping over his feet. Behind him, several men in white uniforms came charging around a corner, several shops down. People scattered when they saw the armed guards rushing down the street. Ferrin could see light coming from a street to his right, so he took it, his breath leaving a faint trail of mist behind him.

The hard clops of boots striking wood and the clang of swords striking legs let him know they were gaining ground. He ran until he lost all feeling in his legs. He knew at any moment he was going to drop Rae and it would be over. Maybe it was better to try fighting the men off.

No. He knew he didn't have the strength.

He looked for a place to hide, somewhere to at least keep her hidden while he led the men away, but other than a few short barrels, there was nothing to protect her. He reached the end of the underpart of the city, and the sun hit his face as he rushed out onto another boardwalk, once again dodging and weaving his way through those traveling its course.

Ahead was a rampway leading back up to the top, and he took it, his arms and legs shaking as he went. He spared a swift glance back and saw the soldiers pushing their way through the people. He wasn't sure if they'd seen him take the ramp or not, so he did his best to blend in with those already on it. He stopped running and melted into the crowd, doing his best not to draw attention.

At the top of the ramp, he could see the lake in front of him just on the other side of the street. This had to be Bailer Circle, which ran the entire perimeter of Storyl. He wondered if he was north or south of the White Pheasant. He spotted sails rising above some of the buildings on his left. Quickly, he moved off the street and started down the sidewalk, keeping as close to the buildings as possible, hoping to hide himself from those following. He stopped at the corner of what looked like an apothecary and tried to catch his breath.

He set Rae down in the alley against the side of the building. She wasn't moving. Except for the slow rise and fall of her chest, there was no indication she was even alive. He knew how the healing weakened her, and she'd already healed him twice. On top of that, she'd nearly drowned. It was a miracle she was still breathing at all.

"Don't you die on me." He leaned over and kissed her forehead, and her eyes flickered open.

"Ferrin? My clothes . . ." She was too weak to talk.

Of all the things to be worried about. "We had to leave them, remember?" Her eyes started to flicker shut. "We can get more," he said. Her eyes closed, and they didn't open again. Behind him, the guards reached the top of the ramp and were searching up and down the street. Half went north, the others heading in his direction. He had to keep going.

With a deep gulp of air to steady himself and hopefully slow the spinning in his head, he hefted her back into his arms and started down the sidewalk, moving through the people at what felt like a snail's pace. His legs and arms were shaking so hard he wasn't sure he was moving at all. He'd lost all feeling in them some time back.

He could hear footsteps running up behind him. He willed his legs to go faster, but they wouldn't. There was nothing he could do.

"Master Ferrin, is that you?" Ferrin turned to find a familiar face running up behind him.

"Pin? How did you—"

"Master Myron told me to come find you. I heard the shouting and saw you take off down the walk. You're a fast man on foot. I almost lost you at the ramp."

"Where's Myron?" Ferrin asked, not having the time to listen to Pin's story about how he had found them.

"They're waiting for you at the boat. This way."

Ferrin almost felt like crying as the little boy directed him off the street, down a narrow alley in the direction of the water, and onto another boardwalk that encircled the backs of the shops on the road. He could see the waves between the boards under his feet as they struck against the massive pylons. Boats lined the outer rim of the walk, and up ahead were several piers running out to the larger anchored ships.

Ferrin stumbled after Pin down the first ramp leading to the lower boardwalk and docks below. Myron and Suri were waving from the bow of the third ship. It was larger than some of the others but had a sleek curve to the frame that hinted it would be swift on the water. It was also crafted from a dark wood that, paired with its single black sail, made it stand out.

One look at Ferrin and Rae, and Myron rushed down the dock to meet them. He gathered Rae in his arms. "What the flaming Pits happened to you two?"

"No time," Ferrin said as he watched Myron carry Rae down the pier and onto their ship. "Tell the captain to cast off, now!"

Ferrin fumbled over to a barrel and leaned against it for support, his legs finally giving out. He dug around inside his waterlogged pocket and pulled out three silver coins and handed them to Pin. "Take two of these to Mistress Hanley and apologize for us not being able to pick up the clothing. The third is for you, my appreciation for what you've done for us."

Pin gasped when he saw the coin.

"You need to go," Ferrin said. "Take a different way home. Stay as far away from the men in white uniforms as you can."

Pin hugged Ferrin, nearly knocking him over, then took off running down the boardwalk in the opposite direction.

Shouts arose behind him. "There they are! Don't let them get away!"

Ferrin barely had time to turn when four of the Tower's guards rushed down the ramp for him. They were only about twenty feet away. He tried running down the pier for the retracting gangplank, but his legs gave out, and he stumbled forward onto the dock. He hit the planks, barely making it to his knees as the ship began to move down the dock.

"No!" Myron shouted at the men on board. "We can't leave yet!" He yelled at Ferrin, "Get up, you fool! Run!"

Ferrin struggled to his feet, but by the time he made it up, the guards were already on top of him. One of the guard's fists connected with the side of his face and Ferrin went down again. He threw his hands up to block another strike, but the man suddenly disappeared. Shouts of anger and excitement were replaced with screams of fear.

Ferrin crawled to his knees. The boat was halfway down the pier. He grabbed a barrel and pulled himself up, turning to find himself standing face-to-face with a muzzle of blood-soaked fangs.

"Nola? How in holy shades did you get over here without being seen? Not that I'm not glad to see you, but . . ." He looked over his shoulder at the ship that was now pulling away from the dock. "I'm afraid we might be too late."

The wolf bowed under Ferrin's arm, and he realized she wanted him to climb on her back. He struggled to get his leg over and had barely grabbed hold of a fistful of her fur when the enormous wolf charged down the dock. Those standing in her path dove into the water as she approached, crying for mercy at the sight of her.

The world was darkening around him, shifting from unconsciousness to flashes of dock and boats and men leaping into the water. Ferrin fought with everything in him to hold on. He could see the end of the pier ahead. They weren't going to make it. Suddenly they were in the air, soaring over the water. Ferrin flew across the boat and slammed against the rail on the other side. All he could hear were shouts and curses before everything went black.

"Ferrin?" a voice called out, pulling him from the blackness. "He's waking."

Ferrin wasn't sure who had spoken; everything was still a blur. His eyes fluttered open. He was lying in a bed. Why was he in bed? Where was he? The memories flooded back, and he tried to sit up. Pain ripped through his right arm, and he cried out and dropped back onto the pillow.

"Don't move, you fool. Your arm's broken, probably a few other things as well." Myron sat on the edge of his bed, looking down with a smile. "Never seen anyone fly across a ship before. Thankfully the rail on the other side stopped you before you went into the drink. Although, by the state of your clothes, looks like you've already taken a dip."

"How is he?"

A tall man with a hard face and a beard that came to a point just below the chin stepped out from behind Myron to get a look at Ferrin. His skin looked like tanned leather, and he wore a long green leather coat that reached almost to his knees, with gold buttons and wide cuffs at the sleeves. In his left hand he carried a triangular brimmed hat with a full plume. Beside him was a woman with features alike enough to be related. Probably his daughter. She wore a long coat of similar cut, but instead of green, it was a deep burgundy, matching the thick waves of dark-red hair running down her back.

"He'll recover, Captain."

The captain took a step closer. "You're on board the *Wind Binder*. I'm Captain Treygan. This is my daughter Ismara."

The woman nodded stiffly, her hand resting on the hilt of her sword.

"I don't know what sort of trouble you've gotten yourselves mixed up in," Treygan said, "but by the way those Tower guards were chasing you, it doesn't look to be too good." He raised his hand, the sleeve sliding far enough to reveal a long scar running up his forearm. "No one said anything about harboring fugitives."

Ferrin didn't like where this was going.

"As it stands," Captain Treygan continued, "I don't have much love for the White Tower or its goons, so I'll keep you on board. But the price just went up. Doubly so for that ferocious creature you have sleeping on the bow of my ship. Won't let anyone get near her without acting like she's going to eat them. Only person she responds to is that little girly running around with her pinecone. A bit sun-touched that one, if you ask me."

Ferrin didn't bother explaining who the little girl or her pinecone were, but he did agree to the increased transportation costs.

"Good," the captain said. "I'll see that Kettle brings you in some dinner, and a plate for your little friend as soon as she wakes." With that, Treygan and his daughter walked out the cabin door.

Ferrin pushed himself up on his good elbow. "Rae? Where's Rae?"

Myron placed a hand on his chest. "She's fine. She's resting right over there." A small cot had been laid out on the other side of whatever room they were in. She was curled up under her blankets, nothing but her head sticking out from the top. "Thought we'd lost you there for sure. If it hadn't been for Nola, we would have." He chuckled. "Thought we were about to lose the crew when she jumped on board."

Ferrin felt for his neck.

"It's still there. We had no idea how to remove the crazy thing." Myron pinched his chin. "It's the first time I've actually seen one up close. Did you know there's no keyhole? Not even a latch."

Ferrin lifted his head and removed the silver chain he'd grabbed from the dead wielder back on the boardwalk. "Here," he said, handing the silver rod up for Myron to see. "Use this."

Myron took the rod and inspected it, noting the rune on the end. As soon as his hands touched it, it started to glow. "What's this?"

"It's the key."

"How does it work?"

"I'm not sure. I think you need to touch it to the collar."

"Well, that all seems a little vague. Where on the collar?" Myron lowered the rod slowly but quickly jerked back when the collar began to light up as well. "Is it supposed to do that? It's covered in runes."

"I don't know."

Myron took a deep breath and tried once more, this time holding the rod low enough to touch the metal. "I think it's working, a hole just appeared."

"Then use it."

Myron nodded. A moment later the collar snapped free, and the key stopped glowing.

Ferrin pulled the collar off his neck and threw it across the room, where it bounced against the back wall and landed beside a wooden chest.

"What do we do with this?" Myron asked, holding up the key.

Ferrin took the chain and placed it back around his neck. "Keep it safe."

"What about the collar?"

"I never want to see it again."

Myron walked across the cabin and picked up the piece of metal. "Something like this could come in handy. Best we keep it as well."

"Throw it into the lake for all I care," Ferrin said, "just so long as I never have to look at it again."

"I'm sure I can find somewhere to hide it." With that, Myron left, and Ferrin lay there quietly watching Rae as she slept. He was glad to be out of Storyl, but their journey was still a long cry from being over. Even still, there was an ache in his chest, more than just the bruises he'd sustained from his fall or his newly healed ribs. He was going home, something he'd been dreaming of for nearly a year. The thought of seeing his sister's face once more had him trembling. But her face wasn't the only one he wished to see. There was another, a face that burned bright at the forefront of his mind. *Harlin.* The man who'd betrayed him.

Ferrin closed his eyes and dreamed of how he was going to get his revenge.

Chapter 39 | Lenara

PLEASE, LENARA, YOU HAVE to listen. I can feel him. Right here." Joren pressed his hand to his head as he lay on his bedding with her kneeling beside him. "He's taking control. I'm waking less and less. Pretty soon I'll just be gone." He looked at her, tears forming in his eyes. "Lenara, I'm afraid. I don't want to die."

Lenara kissed him and placed both hands on his head. "There is one thing I can try." It was the one thing she didn't want to. "But it's very dangerous." The last person she'd seen magic like this performed on had been left so damaged in the head that they might as well have been dead.

"What is it?" he asked, his words sounding as though he were in pain.

"It's something I've seen used to communicate with those in death sleep. It's a way to look at what's inside the head."

"Try it. Please."

"I've never performed it before. I've only ever seen it done. It might leave your mind ruined."

"Look at me, Lenara. I'm already ruined. If something isn't done now, I'm afraid it will be too late. It might already be too late." He looked up at her and placed his hands on her wrists, holding her hands to the sides of his head. "I trust you."

She stared at him a moment, then took a deep breath to calm her nerves. Was she perhaps acting too hastily in suggesting this now? Joren was right, his ability to take back his own body was quickly disappearing. She didn't know how many times he had left. She smiled at him, not sure who she was trying to still more, him or her. She'd never cared for any man like this before, and now that she had experienced what it was like, she couldn't let him go. She wouldn't.

Joren had changed everything. He'd caused her to question her very existence, her duty to an idea that she'd held on to since she was a child. The belief that what she did, she did for the good of Aldor. The ends always justified the means, didn't they?

She hated feeling this way, torn between her choices and seeing things from his perspective. There were times she wished she'd never met the young guard. Things would have certainly been a lot easier. Every time the idea surfaced, though, she knew she was lying to herself. It was a clash of conscience, one being performed in front of her as though on a grand stage.

Two men sharing the same body, both as different as blood from water.

Watching the two, it wasn't hard to know which she preferred. Yet, for all of it, there was still this pull, an overwhelming desire to serve, something that had been instilled in her since her arrival at the Tower nearly twenty years ago. It was a bond not easily broken, but if there was ever a cause to sever that tie, it would be this.

The brief moments they shared were more rewarding than all the years she'd spent in service to the Tower.

"Don't move," she said, and slowly pushed her magic into him. She'd never done anything like this before, but time was running out, and desperation was driving her forward.

"What are you doing?" he asked. "I feel strange."

"Lie still," she said, her magic penetrating deeper into him. She could feel Joren's presence, and not just physically. It was more than that. She could feel his essence, what made him who he was. She could sense his fear, his frustration, his anger. But there was something else there as well, dark and foreboding, resting quietly around the edges, hiding in the shadows like a predator waiting to pounce.

And the shadows were growing.

"I don't know how much longer I can hold on," Joren said.

She could see the weariness in his eyes. It was a familiar sight, one she'd seen on the faces of those imprisoned within the Tower, those wielders who'd been brought in to keep the world safe. Sure, it was a strange paradox, wielders sent to hunt down wielders, but as the archchancellor always said: "Sometimes the only way to stop a fire is by using more of the same."

Yet things were never as simple as that. Look at what they had done to Joren, the lengths Valtor was willing to go just to capture one man. Where was the justification in that?

"You must hold on," she said, still cupping the sides of his head. "You can't give in now. You've got to keep fighting. Do it for me." She pressed even harder, trying to push back against the shadow of what she knew was Sylas. Maybe she could grab hold of the darkness and draw it out, or even burn it back in some way.

No. She didn't dare try that. She might end up killing Joren.

Her magic stroked the darker parts of Joren's mind, and the shadows pushed back, grabbing hold of her like an arm around the neck. She fought back, pushing pulse after pulse of her magic into the blackness in order to hold it at bay, but she had no idea what she was doing.

Joren began to convulse, his body flopping in his bed like a fish out of water. She tried breaking free, but the shadows clung to her. She was scared to simply release her magic in case the darkness somehow pulled her inside as well. She panicked. She could feel Sylas squeezing the life from Joren.

Joren screamed, and she immediately released her magic, panting and gasping for breath as she did. Joren's body went lax. Was he alive? She quickly felt his neck for a pulse and sighed when she found it, nearly collapsing beside him as she did. What had she done? That was stupid. She'd nearly killed them both.

A soft moan beside her had her up on her hands and knees, checking to see if she had done any permanent damage to Joren. He opened his eyes. She could see pain, but it was still him. "How are you?"

He winced, putting his hands to the sides of his head. "I've been better. What happened? Did it work?"

Her head lowered. "I'm afraid not. I almost lost you and had to stop. I just don't know enough about what I'm doing."

"Try again," he said desperately.

She shook her head. "If I were to try again you wouldn't survive."

He lay there for a moment in silence, looking up at the stars.

She looked beyond him toward the other side of the camp, where the rest of the Black Watch had settled in for the night. They knew better than to pay any attention to what was happening on their side. After the incident in the woods where they'd lost half a dozen men to wolves and bears, no one had stepped so much as a toenail out of place, most bending over backward to appear helpful.

She looked at Joren. There was anguish on his face, pain she wished she could take away. She leaned in and kissed him once again, tenderly. She could feel the weight he was carrying melt away. The kiss grew more passionate, hungry even. He snatched her by the neck and jerked her in close. Something was wrong. She elbowed him in the chest and stumbled backward to catch her breath. "What do you think you're doing?"

He sat up. "Giving you what you want."

She wiped her mouth, tasting blood. She could see the hardness in his eyes. Joren was no longer there. Sylas had returned. He'd never before been able to take back control once asleep. Was Joren really that weak, or had she just done something terrible?

Sylas scooted toward her. "Quit being such a tease. I can see the desire in your eyes even now." He reached for her leg and tried pulling her to him, and she conjured a pocket of air that sent him sprawling into the snow. He got back to his feet, fire in his eyes, and came for her again.

By this time, the guards were out of their beds and grabbing weapons, unsure what to do. A couple of the men went so far as to retreat into the surrounding trees.

Lenara pointed at Sylas. "Stay back! I'm warning you!"

Sylas didn't listen and started for her once more, a look on his face that had her cringing.

Lenara conjured another fist of air and knocked him to the ground once more. "Don't you ever lay your hands on me again! You so much as look at me in a way I don't like, and there won't be enough of you left to bury."

Sylas made it back to his knees, gasping for air after it had been knocked out of him. He looked up and smiled, blood on his teeth.

She could see it in his eyes: This wasn't over.

He raised one hand toward the woods, and a couple of wolves flew out of the thicket, one lunging straight for her throat. She spun and hit the first so hard it nearly snapped in half. The second, she called roots out of the ground that grabbed it and pulled it under, howling and screaming the entire way down, a trick she'd learned from a very resourceful wizard she fought years ago.

She grabbed Sylas by the neck with an invisible hand of hardened air and threw him up against the trunk of a nearby tree. His face flushed as she squeezed, his lips darkening.

"Remember your place, Sylas," she spat as she walked over to stand face-to-face with him. "You're an inquisitor, but I'm a bulradoer. Don't ever for one moment believe you could challenge me."

"I'm the chancellor's emissary," he hissed. "He'll hear about this."

Lenara leaned in until their noses were touching. "You think Valtor gives a flaming fig about you?" She laughed. "The only reason you're here is because of your time spent with this swordsmith. You cross me again and I'll peel your skin off and wear it for a blanket."

Sylas laughed, a disturbing I-hold-all-the-cards sort of laugh that had her skin crawling. "You don't think I know?" He grinned as he held her gaze. "Your threats have no weight. You'd as soon hurt this body as hurt yourself."

Lenara loosened her grip on his neck and took a step back, the bumps growing on her arms.

"You don't think I've been watching the two of you?" Sylas said. "Pretending like I didn't know." He laughed again. "I've been watching you since we left the White Tower."

She gaped, still holding his gaze. "Then why didn't you . . ."

"Why didn't I say anything?" He licked his lips. "Because I was enjoying it so much."

She punched him in the face before she could stop herself. His head spun to the side, blood running from a busted lip. She bit her own lip in anger at letting him goad her.

He turned, the disturbing grin still plastered on his face. "Did that feel good? I'm sure your precious Joren enjoyed it."

Lenara balled her fists.

"I can see it in your eyes. You want to kill me. But as long as I'm in here," he said, rubbing his hands down Joren's body, "you can't touch me. So if I were you, I'd sleep with one eye open."

He was right. She wanted to kill him like she'd never wanted to kill anyone before, except perhaps for the man who'd murdered her sister. She could almost taste the hatred, bittersweet. She released him, and he dropped to his knees in the snow.

Her hands trembled as she walked back to her side of the fire. She should have been worried by the fact that she was now going to be forced to watch her back, but instead, all she could think about was whether or not she'd hurt Joren in any permanent way. More importantly, she now realized that any moments shared between them would have to be shared with Sylas. The thought turned her stomach.

She crawled into her tent—one of two they had purchased in Hedgemont after the first of the snow had begun to fall—and lay on top of her blanket but didn't go to sleep. Her head was close enough to the entrance to watch the stars twinkling above. There was no doubt in her mind: at this point, if Sylas got the chance, he was going to kill her.

Travel for the next several days was quiet, a rare treat under most circumstances, since it meant not having to listen to Sylas boasting about his ingenuity in creating some new and wondrous way to get people to spill their guts, figuratively and literally. However, this silence had the hairs on the back of her neck standing. She could feel him looking at her, plotting.

The snows had finally passed, giving the corax a better chance to continue their search. The winged hunters had managed to pick up their trail in Woodvale, only to lose them again with the onslaught of a weeklong storm. The corax were part reptilian, which meant they couldn't control their body temperatures, so naturally they hated and feared the cold, but Sylas had been insistent they continue their search, pushing them beyond what they could handle. They lost nearly half the praad to the freezing weather. After that, they refused to fly in it, no matter what Sylas demanded.

The next several days dragged on—especially without the constant threat from the weather to keep her mind occupied—and the nights were spent in silent meditation as she tried to keep her mind awake. She knew if she slipped that Sylas would slit her throat in her sleep, or call in another attack, or send a snake into her bedroll. At this point, she almost wondered if it would be better for her to leave, perhaps track them from a distance. She needed sleep. Without it, she wasn't going to make it much farther.

She'd come to setting up her tent on the opposite side of the encampment from Sylas, with the Black Watch guards now forced to sleep in between, something they weren't too keen to do, since it put them directly in the middle of any confrontation. Regardless, they seemed to be sleeping with one eye open as well, or at the least keeping one of the night watch inside the camp.

She had even gone so far as to attempt to bribe one of the guards to stand watch by her tent so she could sleep, but if there was one thing the Tower's guards seemed to hate worse than Sylas, it was a bulradoer. Most bulradoer weren't known for their empathy. She heard stories where some had killed their entire regiments for failure to capture their intended targets. The white guards also despised the bulradoer because they felt they represented everything the White Tower stood against, but they feared them too much to ever risk angering one.

By the fifth day, she could hardly stay in her saddle. She nearly slid out of it at one point, grabbing the saddle horn in time to catch her fall. She glanced over her shoulder and found Sylas smiling. She gritted her teeth and turned back around.

Sylas pushed the men all the harder, leaving little time for sleep. They were making good time in their quest for Rhowynn, but at this rate, by the time they arrived, they'd be half dead themselves. She didn't know what was driving him more, his hatred for the young healer who'd taken his daughter and left him for dead on his own rack, his fixation on recapturing the weaponsmith, or his desire to push Lenara to the breaking point. Either way, she knew she wasn't going to be able to keep this up another night.

They made camp alongside the Taloos River, sheltering in a small gully to block against the strong northerly winds that had them all drawing close to the fires. Once again, she set up her tent on the opposite side of the camp, keeping the white guards between her and Sylas. Every time she passed a glance in his direction, she found him staring at her, smiling as though he knew something she didn't. She had to keep reminding herself it was just his way of getting to her.

It was working.

It took her quite a while to unpack the bedroll from her saddlebag and scrounge up enough floating deadwood to keep her own fire going for the night. Her legs were wobbling by the time she dropped onto her blankets. The world seemed to be spinning. She hadn't slept in days, except for the occasional dozing she'd done while in the saddle. A twig snapped behind her, and she immediately attempted to conjure a shield, her befuddled mind making it difficult to hold.

She turned to find nothing but tall grass and large rocks. Sylas had animals watching her. She could feel their eyes on her at all times. Her skin never ceased crawling.

She had to leave, gather her thoughts. She needed sleep. She could think better once her mind wasn't in such a fog. Leaving might be the best thing for Joren as well. If anything happened, she couldn't be sure she could control herself enough not to kill him.

The only thing that had kept her from simply trussing Sylas up like a chicken, killing off the rest of the Tower's guards, and leaving, was her duty to the Tower, knowing that if she did there would be no going back. The decision was proving harder than she thought. But she knew she had to make it.

She'd do it tonight. Wait till they were all asleep and sneak out.

She lay quietly, doing her best to keep some thought at the forefront of her mind in order to stay awake. Thinking of Joren helped best. She imagined what it would be like if Sylas were no longer there, if the two of them could simply run away, leave the White Tower and all its responsibilities behind. What would it be like to live a normal life, to take him away from all of this, to find some small corner of the world and settle down?

It was something she had never considered before. She didn't even know if she could. Her life had always been bound to the Tower. Could she simply just walk away? She knew she wanted to, and the thought of obtaining freedom such as that was intoxicating. The idea of controlling her own destiny fueled her excitement, of creating her own desires and dreams.

She thought she might enjoy being a wife, having children, Joren's children. She tried to imagine what they would look like. She smiled at the thought of waking up every morning to see his face, to feel him there beside her. He was so handsome, those warm, caring eyes. He turned in the bed and knelt over her, leaned down to kiss her softly on her forehead, her eyes, the tip of her nose, then her mouth. She wanted to drink him in.

Joren held the kiss to the point she was finding it hard to breathe. She tried pushing him away, but he didn't move. He was no longer kneeling over her, but sitting on her, squishing her into the bed. She heard a snap, and everything changed. Something was wrong. Her eyes ripped open to find Sylas sitting on top of her, his hands around her neck.

He released her and stood, several of the guards standing around to watch.

She tried conjuring a wall of air large enough to send them all across the camp and threw it at them. A couple ducked, the others looked around, then they all started laughing. What was happening? Her mind was foggy. Was she still asleep? She leaped from her tent and tried again, this time throwing her arms out to send a wave of energy to disperse them.

They laughed all the louder.

Pain like she'd never felt flooded through her body, and she dropped to the ground, convulsing. Sylas stood over her, holding a small silver rod that was glowing at the end. The breath caught in her throat as she reached up and felt around her neck. Her fingers wrapped around the metal collar, and she panicked, crawling back to her feet once the initial pain had subsided enough to move.

"How dare you collar me! I'm a bulra—"

She felt as though she'd been struck by lightning, every muscle in her body seizing at the same time. She screamed and dropped into a fetal position, vomiting all down her front. She wanted to die. She wanted to kill Sylas. She screamed until her voice gave out.

The pain finally stopped, and she turned over and retched some more, barely able to breathe.

"I told you to sleep with one eye open."

She opened her mouth, but any threat she made would be empty. How had she let him do this to her?

"I had no idea how well these worked," Sylas said, studying the metal rod. "I'm going to have to incorporate them into my questioning." He lifted the rod once more, and the pain seared her from the inside out. She rolled across the hard ground, not even feeling the rocks below her. She tried crawling backward through the snow to get away from the key, but then collapsed as a new wave struck, causing her to lose all dignity as she soaked her lower robes.

"I'm going to kill you!" she shouted, but the words never actually came out.

The pain suddenly ceased, and she fell backward, sprawling on the ground in front of Sylas and the entire contingent of Black Watch soldiers.

"You are no longer a bulradoer," he said, turning to look at the men. "Take her robes. She won't be needing them any longer."

"No!" Her robes were the symbol of who she was, what she had spent her life achieving. To take a bulradoer's robes was like taking a piece of their soul.

The guards hesitated.

"What are you waiting for?" Sylas said, growing angry. "Strip her!"

A couple of the guards started forward slowly.

"She can't hurt you," Sylas said. "In fact, whoever gets her clothes off first can have her for the night."

Over half the men rushed her at once.

She fought and kicked and even resorted to biting, but there was little she could do to stop them.

What they couldn't rip off, they cut off with knives, leaving her to curl in a ball to fend off unwanted hands.

"Take her to my tent," Sylas demanded.

"Wait," one of the men called out near the front of the pile, his hand pressed against her thigh. "You said we could have her."

Sylas flicked his wrist. "I lied. If I were to leave her with you, she'd probably be dead by morning." His face darkened. "Well, what are you waiting for? I said take her to my tent!"

The guards grumbled but finally grabbed her by her arms and legs and carried her across the camp, tossing her inside Sylas's tent. Lenara grabbed the blanket and covered herself, fighting back the tears as she did. For the first time since leaving the Tower, she almost didn't care if she killed Joren or not.

She wanted Sylas dead.

Chapter 40 | Ty

 U'KASHA KOR." Ty saw nothing but blackness. "Well, that didn't work."

Breen called out the same incantation. "Huh? You're right. I can't see a thing."

Ty raised his hand, and blue fire ignited from his palm, forcing him to squint.

"A little warning would have been nice," Breen said, lifting his hand to cover his eyes. "It looks like this night-sight magic doesn't work without at least a little light." He turned and looked out across the backside of the shelf of rock they had been stranded on. "Oh, wow."

Wow was right. The cavern had been unsettling enough without being able to see what it looked like. Now, it was a thousand times creepier, with sharp fang-like protrusions hanging from the ceiling, the walls of the cavern plastered with what looked like waterfalls that had turned to stone, as if whatever was growing above their heads had slowly slithered its way down the sides of the walls. The water was so still it looked like a sheet of glass, and the reflection cast from the rock above made it seem as though there was no water at all, just an enormous underground hole.

Unfortunately, Ty knew better, and the eerie dripping from the hundreds of hanging protrusions over their heads was plenty to remind him. He stepped over to the edge of the water and looked down. All he could see was his own reflection.

Breen was right, he almost wished they could see what they were facing and get on with it. Not knowing was proving far more frightening.

"Hey, look," Breen said, pointing to the cave wall on the right side of the island.

Ty turned and held up the blue flames. The wall was about thirty or forty feet from their shelf, with a large inscription carved into the stone about ten feet over the top of the water. It read: *WISDOM.*

Breen climbed over the boulders to where he had left his travel pack by the first mirror at the back of the island. He opened the pack and pulled out the torch he had created from a thigh bone he'd found in the maze and a strip of wax-soaked cloth he'd packed before leaving home. Ty had packed some as well, but his had been lost to the river. Breen lit the torch with his striker and the orange flame burst to life, allowing Ty to release his magic.

"There we go," Breen said, walking back to the middle of the island and finding a crevice in the rocks large enough to wedge the torch into. "No offense, but those blue flames of yours give me a headache."

Ty didn't disagree. It was a little disconcerting to see everything in blue, but without it, they would have probably walked right off the edge of the rock and into the water.

Breen walked down to the edge of the island and studied the inscription on the wall. "A lot of good that does us," he grumbled. "If we had any wisdom, we wouldn't be here in the first place." He stared at the letters a while longer. "Do you see anything that resembles a key, or even a clue as to where we can find it? For that matter, do you see any indication as to where in Aldor we even are? If we're in Aldor at all."

He sat down on one of the larger rocks behind them and ran his hand through his hair, tucking one side behind his ear. "I'm getting tired of all these riddles!" he shouted at no one in particular, his words echoing off the cold stone. "Just show us what we need to overcome and let us get on with it." He looked at Ty. "You're unusually quiet."

"I think I don't like it here."

"That makes two of us."

"The maze was bad enough, but this . . . this somehow feels worse." He stared out at the surrounding darkness and shivered. "I'm afraid of what might be out there."

"Now why did you have to go and say that?" Breen griped, looking out over the water. "Great. Now I'm going to be imagining all sorts of horrible things."

Ty smiled, then thought about it. There was no telling what all might be lurking out there under the water.

"What now?" Breen asked. "I don't see any tunnels leading out of here. Do you?"

Ty shook his head, then looked back at the word carved in stone across the water. "The last time we saw the name of a test written out like that was at the entrance to the maze, marking the beginning of the trial. Perhaps that does the same here."

They both stood at the edge of the water and stared out at the letters.

"Yeah," Breen said, "but I'm not seeing anything that looks like an entrance here. I don't see so much as a crevice in the stone."

"That's what I'm afraid of," Ty said, still staring at the large WISDOM engraved in the wall across from them. "I've got a bad feeling that what we're looking for isn't up here. It's down there."

Breen joined Ty in looking down at the water and grimaced. "Of course it is. It's wizard work. Why would we expect this to actually be easy?" he shouted.

Ty smiled. "I don't think they can hear you. They've been dead for centuries."

Breen picked up a rock and threw it across the water, striking dead center between the S and the D. "Stupid wizards and their meddling. Sometimes I think the world *would* be better off without all this magic. It's done nothing but cause us grief. Flaming faeries couldn't be satisfied with their own realm, had to come poking their noses into ours." He looked at Ty, and his brows rose. "Sorry, I don't mean you. Just frustrated."

"I know. Sometimes I wonder what it would be like to be normal as well."

Breen looked at the cavern wall and sighed. "Guess if the wizards had made it easy, then anyone could have gotten their hands on the key."

Ty nodded and turned to take another look at the rest of the cavern. From what he could see, Breen was right. There were no indications as to what they needed to do next. It wasn't like the maze, where there was a clear starting point. Here, there was nothing. Nothing but water. He heard Breen fiddling with something behind him and turned. "What are you doing?"

Breen was sitting on one of the rocks, struggling to pull off one of his boots. "We can't just sit here hoping this key falls in our laps." He paused halfway through pulling off his sock. "Although that would be really nice." He waited a moment as if half expecting one to, then grabbed his second boot and started to tug. Once his boots and socks were off, he removed his jacket, then his trousers and tunic, leaving him in nothing but his skivvies.

Thankfully, the cavern wasn't nearly as cold as it had been in the maze. In fact, the temperature was fairly mild. Breen walked over to the edge of the island and stuck his toe in the water. "It's not too bad, considering."

Ty walked over and dabbled his fingers in as well, having been too afraid to even touch the water until now. Breen was right. It was chilly, but not like what it should have been in the heart of winter. "You sure about this? It should probably be me going out there."

Breen raised his head. "Okay, if you want to."

Ty's eyes widened, and Breen laughed.

"Yeah, that's what I thought." Breen carried his torch over to the edge, and they both stood staring out at the water before Breen finally handed him the torch. "Get that fire of yours ready, would you?" he said, looking at Ty's hand. "Just in case."

Ty walked over and grabbed the torch, then conjured a ball of blue flame as he waited to see if Breen would actually go in. Part of him hoped he wouldn't, wanting him to stay safely on dry rock with him, while the other part wanted to get this test over with as soon as possible. "Are you sure about this?"

Breen looked out at the water. "No. But do you have any better ideas?"

Ty shook his head reluctantly. He wished he did. Something about that black water unnerved him to no end, and he didn't like the idea of his brother swimming out in it.

Breen strapped a knife to his right leg, tying the sheath's thick cords around his calf and securing the hilt with a strap. He looked at Ty and nodded, then slipped into the water. "It's actually warmer than I thought," he said as he treaded for a moment to get used to it.

Ty raised the torch out to give his brother more light. Breen finally pushed off from the rock with his feet and started out into the blackness, the echoes of his strokes filling the cavern.

Ty's hands were shaking as he watched his brother move farther and farther away from the safety of their island. His toes curled inside his boots, something they did whenever he saw spiders. He asked the Creator to keep Breen safe and held the torch and his flaming hand up as high as he could while continually scanning the surrounding water for any sudden disturbances.

Breen reached the side of the cavern and stopped. The carved letters were above his head, just out of reach. Ty watched as his brother felt along the stone from one side of the engraving to the other, but he didn't appear to find anything.

A faint splash had Ty spinning toward the water on the other side of the island. He couldn't see any ripples. He quickly turned back around to warn his brother. "Breen, I think I heard . . ."

His brother was gone.

Ty leaped up on the highest rock and thrust out the torch, his eyes frantically searching the water around the cavern wall. There was no sign of his brother, only the ripples moving outward from where he had been.

"Breen! Breen!" He tossed the torch on the ground and released his blue flames as he began yanking off his boots as fast as he could. Another splash had him snatching up the torch and racing to the island's edge in his socks.

Breen was back above the water and moving toward him. Ty heaved a deep sigh of relief as he watched his brother's steady strokes pull him closer to the island. He conjured his blue flames once again, keeping the torch held high until his brother reached the island. Quickly, he released his magic and helped his brother out of the water. As soon as Breen made it to his feet, Ty punched him in the arm.

"Hey, what was that for?"

"For scaring the Pits out of me! One minute you're there, then I turn around and you're gone. I thought something had grabbed you for sure, you stupid oaf. I was about to jump in after you."

Breen looked down and noticed Ty standing in his socks, then smiled. "Good to know you wouldn't have left me out there to die." He shook himself off, coating Ty with an onslaught of water droplets.

Ty wiped his face and looked down at his clothes. "Thanks for that."

"That's for turning around."

"Huh?"

"You said one minute I was there, then you turned around and I was gone. Why were you turned around?"

"I thought I heard something."

Breen's grin vanished. "Where?"

Ty turned and pointed toward the water behind them, and they both climbed over the rocks to take a look. After searching the other side without seeing anything, they headed back.

"Well, what did you find?" Ty asked anxiously.

Breen attempted to dry himself off with his blanket roll. "Good news is, I think I found the entrance to wherever it is you're supposed to go. Bad news is, it's underwater. This lake might not have been here when they first put this test in, or perhaps it rose unexpectedly over the years, kind of like that first mirror dumping us out at the bottom of a river."

"Or," Ty said grimly, "it's exactly where they wanted it."

Breen looked over at the WISDOM scrawled into the stone and shrugged. "Maybe. The question is, what now? Whether it's supposed to be there or not, there's no way we're going to be able to swim down to the tunnel and see where it goes. It took most of my breath just getting down to it and back up. I've got no idea where it leads or how far you'd have to swim to get to wherever it's taking you. All I know is, we'd drown for sure if we tried." Breen wrapped his blanket around him and sat down on one of the smaller boulders behind them.

Ty stood there, torch in hand, staring at the word. Wisdom. What were the wizards wanting from this test? The last trial had to deal with faith, which at least made sense once they had managed to find the center of the maze. Only faith could have seen him through the wall of fire at the end. Without it, they wouldn't have the first piece of the key. Ty felt for the cylindrical part of the shorlock hanging from his neck.

"I wonder how the wizards defined wisdom?" Breen suddenly asked, echoing Ty's own thoughts. "Each of these trials has supposedly been created to test a specific character trait. So if we want to figure out what this one is about or how we are going to pass it, then maybe we need to figure out what it is. When I say wisdom, what is the first thing you think of?"

"An old person."

Breen laughed. In fact, he laughed so hard he almost tipped backward off the rock.

"You know what I mean," Ty said, feeling a bit foolish. "Clye Durran always said his white hair was a sign of great wisdom." Ty took his cap off and made a point of rubbing his own head of white hair. "Guess that means I'm really wise."

Breen rolled his shoulders and grunted. "What that tells us is that white hair doesn't mean anything except you got white hair. 'Cause neither you nor Clye has a lick of common sense half the time."

"Then what do *you* think it means?"

Breen thought a moment, staring out across the open water. "I think wisdom can come from knowledge. Take Father for example. He knows a great deal about a great many things. He's always careful with what he says, thinks before he speaks. He's smart, you know, up here." Breen pointed to the side of his head. "I've heard more than one person refer to Father as having a great deal of wisdom."

Ty nodded. He'd heard the same, but was knowing things the same as being wise? "Yes, but look at Adarra. I don't know of anyone who knows more than she does, and I've watched her walk straight into a wall while reading one of her books." He shook his head. "And just look at the way she acts whenever Aiden's around, a complete buffoon. I don't think her knowledge has made her all that wise."

Breen chuckled. "I wish I had even a fraction of her knowledge right about now. I'm sure she could think of something clever to do."

Ty nodded. It would have been nice to have his sister along. Then again, it would have been nice to have had his whole family along, and Lyessa, and Fraya, and while he was at it, about a hundred Sidaran Lancers.

"So," Breen said, running his hands back through his wet hair, "the question is, how do we get into that tunnel without drowning?"

All Ty heard was the words *tunnel* and *drowning*, and it hit him. "Gilly!"

"What about him?"

"Don't you remember what he did with Saleena after Father shot her with the arrow?"

Breen's face lit up. "That's right. He carried her upriver from under the water." Breen stood. "Do you think you can do that?"

Ty looked out at the water, then shook his head. "No. Not really."

Breen flung his arms out to the side. "Then why did you just bring it up?"

"It was the first thing that popped into my head."

"Then try it. What can it hurt? Or do you want to just sit here and slowly starve to death?"

"I don't know anything about being a voda. I've never tried doing anything with water before. I wouldn't even know where to start."

"You found a way to use Feoldor's gift, didn't you? If you can manage to wield like a vanti, then I would think you could do the same as a voda. Water and air aren't that different."

Ty looked at him like he was crazy. Air and water were nothing alike.

"Besides," Breen said, "I've already seen you manipulate water."

"Huh?"

"Sure. At Gilly's underground cave you managed to lower the water in the well before you . . . Well, before you tried killing us all."

"Yeah, but that wasn't me. That was Mangora."

"She did it through you, which stands to reason that you should be able to as well, doesn't it?"

"I don't know that. I don't know anything." Ty was growing frustrated, and he wasn't sure why. He was the one who'd mentioned Gilly in the first place, which just went to show that having white hair had nothing to do with wisdom. "Fine, I'll see what I can do. But don't get mad if it doesn't work." He handed Breen the torch and walked over to the edge.

Breen followed.

"You might not want to get so close," Ty warned. "The last two times I experimented with magic, it didn't go so well. The first time I set Adarra on fire, and the second I nearly punched a hole through a Northman's chest."

Breen scooted back.

Ty took a deep breath and tried remembering what he'd done when he'd first connected with the wind. He reached out and attempted to feel the water, using his magic in the same way he would to sense the life around him. He let the magic slide its fingers across the glassy surface, attempting to get a sense of what the water felt like, but he couldn't quite find what he was looking for.

The water didn't exactly have a life of its own. Sure, it could move and sway, but only if it was acted upon by an outside force, like someone throwing a rock, or a fish swimming by, or the wind whipping across the surface. The water itself wasn't alive. Then again, neither was the wind when he'd attempted to harness its power.

"How's it going?" Breen asked impatiently.

Ty kept his eyes shut. "It would be going better if I wasn't getting interrupted." Breen didn't say more, and Ty turned his attention back to the water.

He wasn't sure what he was supposed to do, so he mimicked what he'd done with the wind and held out his hands and imagined himself pushing it. He peeked through his lids, but the surface was unchanged, not so much as a ripple.

Frustrated, he tried again, imagining himself hitting the top of the water with his hands. He peeked again. Still nothing. He released an exasperated breath. "This isn't working."

"Don't give up. It looked like something might have been happening the last time."

Ty perked. "Really?"

"No." Breen grinned. "But that doesn't mean you should stop trying."

Ty rolled his eyes, imagining what it would be like to toss his brother back in, which gave him an idea. He walked back over to the edge, and, instead of reaching for the water, he reached for the wind instead, gathering it to him. His hair and clothes whipped about as he drew a pocket of air around him and then struck the water with it. A wave ricocheted and completely soaked his clothes.

Breen fell backward off his perch laughing, until he noticed that the water had also soaked his clothes where they were piled on one of the nearby rocks. "Flaming Pits!" He rushed over, turning his boots upside down and gaping as water ran out.

Ty chuckled. "Serves you right."

He turned back around to try again, but this time he tried directing the wind into a single funnel down into the water. Instead of using it like a club to force an opening, he used it more like an airtight container that could be slid down into the water. The pocket of air slowly broke the surface, and Ty maintained his grip, forcing it deeper and deeper into the dark waters.

The farther down it went, the harder it was to control. Pretty soon his concentration slipped, and the air pocket shot to the surface and exploded upward, hitting one of the hanging spikes of limestone about twenty feet from where he was standing. The force snapped the large spike off, and it hit the water, sending a wave crashing toward their island. Both brothers grabbed their gear and clothes and torch and jumped up onto the higher boulders as the water crashed over the lower level.

"Well, that was just brilliant," Breen said, trying not to set his clothes on fire as he juggled the torch, his clothes, and his pack. Finally, he dropped the pack with his bow and quiver on the rocks along with his clothes and sat down.

The water receded quickly enough, but it left the lower rock covered in small pools where the water had collected. Ty took his socks off, which at this point were just as wet as the rest of him, and stuffed them in his boots for safekeeping. The cool air in the cavern was already causing him to shiver.

Breen climbed back down, looking for a safe place to lay his bow and quiver. "Whatever you're doing, it's not working." He stuffed them between two large boulders and placed his travel pack on top. "No need to swim down to the tunnel to drown when you're going to do it for us right here."

"If you think you can do better, then give it your best shot," Ty said angrily.

Breen sighed and looked up at the missing piece of rock Ty had split. "Why were you using Feoldor's gift and not Gilly's? We want to control the water, not the wind. Another accident like that in the wrong place, and you might bring the entire cavern down on our heads."

Ty gritted his teeth. "I was using the wind because I can't seem to do anything with the water. You're the one who told me to try something. *It can't hurt*, you said."

"Well, obviously I was wrong." Breen sat on the boulder behind him. "Sorry. I shouldn't have snapped like that. You're right. I did tell you not to give up." He balled his fists. "I hate feeling helpless. What good is having perfect aim in a situation like this?"

Ty snorted. "What good is having all my abilities when I don't know how to use them? I don't even know what abilities I have." He looked over at the wall and read the inscription out loud. "Wisdom." He shook his head. "This is pointless. We don't have enough wisdom to even start this test."

"Maybe that's the point," Breen said, suddenly sitting forward. "What if this *is* the test?"

Ty turned. "What do you mean?"

"I mean, what if we've already started the trial? What if that tunnel down there isn't the entrance but the destination?"

"You think the missing piece is just lying down there in the tunnel?"

Breen shrugged. "Could be. Obviously they wouldn't have placed it close enough for us to simply swim down and grab it. That would be too simple, especially after what we went through to get the first piece of the key."

"Obviously," Ty said.

"So maybe the test is to see if we can reach the key at all." He looked out across the empty lake and raised his arms. "Consider this our maze. We have to find some way to get through it in order to get the key."

Ty stood a moment, staring out over the water separating him from his goal. Perhaps Breen was right. Maybe this was the test. Reaching the key was just as difficult as acquiring it, which meant he had to find a way to search the tunnel without drowning. And there was only one way he knew to do it.

He closed his eyes and reached out once more.

Chapter 41 | Ty

TY TOUCHED THE WATER with his mind, letting the fingers of his magic break through the surface. It was cool to the touch, refreshing. He could almost feel it in his hands, so why wasn't he able to do something with it? He remembered how frustrated he'd been when first using his vanti gifts during their battle with the Tallosians. Nothing was more distracting to learning how to use something for the first time than a huge Tallosian swinging his bloody cleaver at your head.

What Ty had discovered, though, was that using his gift as a vanti wasn't the same as conjuring the blue flames of an incindi. With the flames, it was as though the fire was coming from out of him, and every time he had tried using the wind in the same way, it had ended in failure. So perhaps instead of trying to move it himself, he needed to allow the water to do the work for him. With this in mind, he reached out once more, but instead of sliding the fingers of his magic into the water and attempting to move it, he let himself connect to the water on a different level, as though allowing part of himself to become the water, to give the water its own life.

"Something's happening," Breen said, joining Ty at the edge of the rock.

Ty didn't open his eyes, holding his concentration. He could feel sweat breaking out on his forehead as he called the water to him, enticing it instead of forcing it. He pictured in his mind what he wanted it to do. A familiar burning sensation seared his arm, just below the elbow, letting him know he was pushing his magic in new directions, the markings on his arm growing. It was nowhere near as painful as it had been at previous times, but then again, he wasn't exactly using a great deal of magic either.

"Ty, you're doing it!"

Ty opened his eyes. The water at the edge of the rock had separated, leaving a short empty pathway down before it met the new edge of the water a few feet below. He smiled and released his hold. The walls collapsed, and the water struck the side of the rock, soaking the brothers' legs.

Breen leaned over and smacked his arm. "You did it!"

Ty yelped and grabbed the sensitive area where the new markings had just formed. "The only thing I did was prove how little I really know about this stuff."

"Maybe so, but it was a good first step. Try it again."

Ty groaned, but inwardly he was as excited by the prospect of learning some new piece of magic as he was of finding the next piece of the key and getting out of there. He spent the next couple hours trying to gain better control of it but found the progress very slow. By the time he'd managed to move enough water out of the way for two people to walk down about ten feet, he'd nearly passed out from exhaustion. It didn't help that he hadn't had a decent night's sleep in the last couple of weeks, or that the last full belly he'd received was from a magical feast that he wasn't quite sure he hadn't hallucinated.

Needless to say, he was tired and hungry, and neither of those was conducive to the use of magic.

"You need to rest," Breen said as Ty yawned deeply. "Won't do us much good to have you walk us halfway across the lake and then collapse from fatigue."

Ty yawned again and rubbed his eyes. "I wouldn't be averse to a couple hours of sleep."

"Go ahead. I'll keep watch."

"I also wouldn't say no to some food," he added with a cheeky grin.

Breen smiled. "I'll see what I can find."

For the length of time his brother spent digging around in their pack, Ty was expecting a feast. What he got was a soggy biscuit, a piece of hard meat, and half of a spotted apple. Still, it was better than nothing, and it was quickly consumed, core and all. Finding a comfortable spot on a pile of rock was quite difficult. Ty was worried that his wet clothes would have hindered sleeping altogether, but as soon as his head hit the wadded blanket, he was out.

He had no idea how long he'd slept, since there was no sun or moon or stars to judge the passage of time, but when he did finally open his eyes, he felt ready to take on the world. Even the gash on his leg from where he'd been struck by the maze monster was throbbing less. Orlyn's rub was doing its job splendidly.

"How long was I asleep?" Ty asked, twisting in his bedding to find Breen staring out at the water on the other side of the island. Breen had redressed himself while Ty was asleep, clearly hoping not to have to go swimming again.

Breen left his perch and crawled down off the higher rocks and took a seat. "I'm not really sure," he said with a grin. "I kind of fell asleep myself."

Ty stood and stretched. "You look like you needed it as much as I did." He looked out at the water. "At least we weren't eaten in our sleep. I'm starting to think there's nothing out there after all." Even saying it, he didn't believe it.

It all came down to whether he could control his magic long enough to get them down to the tunnel and to wherever it led.

"You feeling up to trying again?" Breen asked.

Ty yawned once more. "I think so."

Breen tossed him another apple. "I was saving this last one for a special occasion. You getting us out of here qualifies, I think."

"It's the last apple?"

Breen rolled his shoulders. "It's the last everything. We finished off what was left of the meat before you slept."

Ty looked down at the sad excuse for a piece of fruit, then back at his brother. "You want to split it?"

Breen shook his head. "You need it more than I do. It's your magic that has to get us out of here, which means you need all the strength you can muster."

Ty didn't argue, practically swallowing the shriveled fruit whole. Breen was right. If he didn't do it now, he wasn't going to have the strength to do it later.

Pushing his worries aside, he left his bedding and walked over to the edge of the island where he could see the inscription on the wall. He was surprised to find that his night sight was still working, even after a full night's sleep. The word seemed to taunt him, a reminder of how little wisdom he really had. He was sixteen, which meant he was a man now, but barely just, and not experienced enough to have garnered the kind of wisdom he needed to keep himself and his brother alive.

Breen clapped him on the shoulder. "Come on, little brother. You can do this."

Pushing everything else aside, Ty reached out with his mind and once again connected with the water. He could feel it moving just as before. This time he delved a little deeper, bringing up a little more of the magic he'd been careful not to overuse earlier. He could feel the water dividing, moving backward from the island and opening a pathway down. Breen gasped, and his concentration faltered, but only for a moment. He quickly recovered and pushed even further. He was beginning to sweat, the heat of his magic building inside him.

The deeper he went, the heavier the water became, growing more difficult to control. He finally snuck a quick peek just before everything collapsed. He had managed to part the waters at least twenty feet down, a corridor of dark liquid. It was quite wondrous to behold, but that wonder only lasted for a brief moment before everything buckled.

Breen tried to turn and run, seeing what was coming, but he didn't make it as the wave crashed against the rocks and sprayed over half the island. Ty, on the other hand, didn't move, letting the water hit him full force. He stumbled backward but maintained his footing, his clothes completely soaked once more. All he could do was laugh.

"What are you laughing at?" Breen asked, slinging water from his shirt and coat as he sloshed over to where Ty stood waiting at the lake's bank. "You not only soaked our clothes but our gear as well." He tossed their travel pack down at Ty's feet. There were water droplets beaded all across the outer surface.

"What else am I going to do? Cry? Shout? Right now, it could go either way." Ty sat down on one of the rocks behind him and let his soggy sleeves flop over his legs as he stared out at the enormous amount of water between them and the tunnel below. "I just can't do it. I'm not strong enough. If Gilly were here, he could probably do it while napping, but I'm not Gilly. I just don't know enough about what I'm doing to pull this off." He looked up at the inscription. "There! Are you happy? I have just enough *wisdom* to know when I'm beaten!"

Breen sat down beside him, his longer hair plastered to his face, making him look almost scary. "I doubt the wizards would have created something that was unbeatable. The point was that when the right person came along, they would make it through."

"Then perhaps I'm not the right person, because there's no way that I can move all that water."

They sat there in silence for a while as they watched the waves turn to ripples and eventually flatten back to a calm surface once again.

"What if you're not supposed to?"

Ty cocked his head. "What do you mean?"

"You said it earlier. Gilly didn't divide the East River—he found a way to walk around inside it. Instead of holding up two sides of a lake, what if you only held up enough for us to move around in. That way you aren't having to control the whole lake, but just the area around where we are walking? Is that possible?"

Ty stood and walked over to the edge and looked down at his reflection. "No idea." He closed his eyes and reached out with his magic.

"Wait," Breen said, breaking Ty's concentration and forcing him to release his hold. "We don't know how much strength you have left, so let's get our things ready. If it works, I say we go for it. No need to waste your energy just to test it out."

Ty nodded, and after wringing out his socks, he pulled them and his boots back on. Breen, who was already soaked from head to toe, folded their bedroll and stuffed it back inside his pack before collecting his bow and quiver, which had been shielded mostly by the larger boulders.

"You ready?" Breen asked, holding their torch. He had left it up near the first mirror where he'd kept watch, and it had managed to survive the soaking.

"As ready as I'll ever be, I guess." He closed his eyes and reached for the magic, letting it run through him and out into the water. This time, instead of trying to split the water in half to create a passageway, he imagined a bubble forming at the edge of the water and allowed it to grow, leaving an opening large enough for them to step into. He opened his eyes and found an open pocket reaching down into the lake.

One look at Breen and they stepped off the island and inside the opening. They climbed down the wet stones, and Ty closed the bubble behind them as they continued down. It was an extraordinary feeling, walking through the lake. It seemed the bottom was much like the top, covered in rock with protrusions that seemed to be growing up instead of down.

Ty felt a tickle in his throat that started to grow. Pretty soon it was burning, and he began to cough. Breen was coughing as well, almost uncontrollably. Ty's eyes were watering so bad he couldn't see. Panic set in, and they both realized what had happened at the same time.

They were running out of air.

Quickly, Breen shoved the end of their torch through the closest wall of water. "We've got to go back," he shouted somewhere on Ty's left. Ty couldn't see him, since their only light source had just been extinguished.

Ty could hear his brother trying to climb back up the rock behind them, and he turned to do the same, fighting to hold on to the magic long enough to get them back. What air they had burned his insides, and he was suddenly taken back to the flaming wall of fire inside the maze and what it had felt like when he stepped through. His concentration buckled, and the magic collapsed, along with the bubble. Next thing Ty knew, he was swimming for the top, or at least he thought it was the top. There was no light above the surface to guide the way, and he was weighed down by a thick coat. Panic set in, and he began to flounder.

A hand grabbed his arm, and suddenly he was being lifted. His head broke the surface and he gasped for air as Breen hauled him up onto the rocks at the edge of the island. Ty coughed up some of the water, drinking the rest as a way to stave off the burning from the smoke of the torch. He dry-heaved a couple of times, then raised his hand and conjured some fire. "Well," he said, continuing to cough, "that was one of the stupidest things we've ever done."

Breen was bent over a rock doing the same. "Reminds me of the time that bird's nest got stuck in the flue, and when Father tried lighting the first fire of fall, we had to clear the house for two days."

Ty chuckled. "I remember. My clothes smelled like smoke for months, even after washing them." He looked at the water. "Now what? We can't exactly go wandering around the inside of a lake without light."

Breen pointed at Ty's hand. "I guess we use yours. Your fire doesn't seem to burn anything when you're holding it. I've never seen it smoke."

Ty stared at the flames dancing across his fingers. "I hadn't actually thought about that before. It doesn't smoke, does it?"

"No, but it does get hot. I can feel it from here." Breen stared out across the water toward the cavern wall. "Maybe we can get down there and back before the heat becomes too unbearable." He sounded unsure. "If not . . ."

"If not . . . what?" Ty didn't like the way Breen was looking at him.

"You might have to go down there on your own."

Ty didn't care for that idea at all. "I'm sure we can go quickly enough. I could always make the bubble bigger or use less flame."

"But can you do both at once? We're talking about using two different magics at the same time. Takes concentration, which might be exactly why Nyalis said that you should probably go alone. The more people that come with you, the more magic you are forced to expel."

"I can do it." Ty wasn't about to go walking around down there by himself.

Breen stepped over to the edge of the rock and poured the water out of his quiver. There was no helping any of it now. The food was gone and everything else was waterlogged. Breen stuffed the wet torch back in the top of his pack and slung it and his bow and quiver over his shoulder, then looked at Ty. "Up to you now."

Ty held his flame-covered hand up to see where the rock ended and the water began. He found he didn't need quite so large a flame with their use of night sight, and released most of it, letting it taper off until all that was left was a single finger's worth. It almost looked like he was holding a candle, a pale, skinny candle.

He took a deep breath and once again closed his eyes. He'd never attempted to use more than one gift at the same time before. At least, not on his own. Under the witch's control, he'd been forced to perform all kinds of magic when fighting back the wielder council. If it hadn't been for his brother . . . He paused. "Did I ever thank you for helping save me from Mangora?"

"What?" Breen turned his head. "Where did that come from?"

"I was just thinking about the last time I found myself using magic like this. If you hadn't been there, who knows what I might have done."

"Nyalis did most of the work."

"Yeah, but it was your shot that destroyed the numori."

Breen's brow furrowed. "I thought you were going to quit blaming yourself for what happened. You've said you were sorry more times than I can count. You don't need to say it again."

"I know, but I never got to say thank you."

Breen stared at him a moment. "Well, you're welcome. Now open this water so we can get that key."

Ty smiled and turned back around. His magic seemed to come a little easier with each new attempt, growing more familiar. Slowly the bubble began to form and grow, and once again they found themselves back inside, completely surrounded by the lake. The blue light was dim, but enough to make out the rocky outcropping below their feet as they made their way downward into the lake's depths. It was deeper than Ty had anticipated.

He held his focus on the shape of the bubble, not wanting to decrease it any further than it was already. The bubble was large enough that the brothers could stand back-to-back at the center, raise their arms, and still have at least three feet before reaching the outer wall. "Let me know if the fire gets too warm."

"It's not. I think the cold water is helping to temper it."

Ty couldn't feel the fire himself. He never had been able to, which was a good thing. It wouldn't prove a very efficient gift to have if every time he conjured it he burned himself.

After a long climb down the rocky slope, they reached what Ty guessed was the bottom of the lake. It wasn't much different from any other part of the cavern, except it seemed to level off some, allowing them to walk, more than climb, their way forward.

Unfortunately, all the stone looked the same, which left him unsure as to which direction they needed to take to reach the tunnel his brother had found. "I'm going to extinguish the light for a little bit."

"Why?" Breen asked. "What's going on?"

"Nothing. I just don't really know where we are. I need to try feeling my way ahead and see if I can locate the entrance to the tunnel, and I don't want to take a chance at using three different types of magic at once and lose control of all of them."

"Yeah, let's not do that. Feel free to get rid of the fire. We can stand here while you do. Wait a minute," he said, and Ty held back.

"What?"

"If you can use your magic to feel for the tunnel, then why in the name of Aldor didn't you tell me that before I swam all the way out there?"

Ty frowned. "Sorry. I didn't even think about it. The only time I've used it before was to look for other signs of life. Like I did with the arachnobe when we tracked it to its lair. Honestly, I have no idea if this will work or not."

Breen frowned, but he finally motioned for Ty to go ahead.

Ty nodded. "Here goes." He released the flame, and the darkness enveloped them. Once he was sure the bubble wasn't going to collapse, he slowly sent out a web of magic, little feelers searching for what lay ahead. He wasn't sure how exactly to direct them to a specific location, so he did what he always did and sent them out in all directions. He would then keep his focus on those heading in the general direction of where he wanted to search.

His feelers reached the wall in front of them first, since it was the closest, and it didn't take long for them to work their way up the wall and find the hole. He smiled. It worked. And they hadn't traveled too far off their course, maybe a slight adjustment to the right and they should be fine. He went to release the web, and something pricked the hairs on the back of his neck. Quickly, he conjured his flames and spun to the left.

"Woah! Try warning me next time," Breen said as he covered his eyes. "What's with all the light?" He noticed Ty staring off to the left and turned. "What are you looking at? Are we that far off?"

"No." Perspiration broke out across Ty's forehead as he tried staring deeper into the murky waters. "We need to run."

"Run? Why? What's going on?"

"I think I just woke something. Something big."

Chapter 42 | Ty

TY RAN STRAIGHT FOR the inscribed wall with Breen hard on his heels, both casting frightened glances over their shoulders as they raced forward. Spear-like protrusions threatened to block their way, and they wove their way around them, climbing over large boulders and loose rock as they did.

"What did you see?" Breen asked, looking up at the water over their heads. "Do you have control of the bubble?"

Ty didn't bother answering, his focus solely on reaching the hole ahead. He could feel something approaching. Flashes of memory of the water monster he'd seen back at Reed Marsh flooded his thoughts, and he picked up his pace. Whatever this creature was, it was even bigger.

They scrambled up the rock on the far side, leading toward the tunnel ahead. Something flashed through the water, and they both turned.

"What was that?" Breen asked, drawing both his knives.

A giant tentacle struck the side of their bubble and tossed them to the right. Breen grabbed Ty by the collar of his coat and lifted him back to his feet. "Keep going!"

Ty fought to maintain his grip on the magic, but he could feel it slipping. Another one of the creature's slimy arms hit them, and this time came through. Ty held the water in place as Breen dove on top of the enormous slimy arm and plunged both daggers in, nearly cutting it in half. Warm black liquid shot from the wounds, covering the front of Breen's chest and the side of Ty's face. The long tentacle slithered back out, and they kept climbing.

"It's on top of us!" Breen shouted.

Ty looked up. Before he'd even realized it, he'd unleashed his flames. Breen covered his face, pulling back from the heat. The fire tore through the bubble and lit the water around them, revealing an enormous mass of dark flesh, tentacles, and teeth. Dozens of long, spongy arms crawled through the water, and at their center, a mouth lined with rows of deadly fangs. It was the same as the marsh monster that Douina had dangled him over, except at least twice its size.

Ty's fire didn't die in the water, but it did miss the intended target, burning two of the creature's arms off on the right. He sent out another lance of blue flame, and it struck just above the mouth. The creature shrilled and released a cloudy black substance that temporarily hid it from sight. Its cry created a wave strong enough to throw the bubble backward.

"Climb!" Ty shouted, ignoring the pain in his arms from the new growth of marks he'd just acquired from his overuse of magic. The bubble was beginning to shrink and had been cut by almost a quarter, leaving them even less room to maneuver. He was beginning to feel the strain of the magic, amazed at the fact that he'd been able to hold the bubble together for this long, desperation more than anything driving him to do it.

Breen was back on his feet and scrambling up the side, pulling Ty with him.

Ty could feel the tunnel just ahead. They were close. Very close. "We're almost there." If they could just make it inside, they'd be safe. The creature was far too big to fit through.

They fought their way up the rocks. Ty could feel the creature behind them as its hunger and rage spurred it into another attack.

Two more tentacles broke through. The first struck Breen in the back and flung him to the other side, where he landed hard against a rock. The second came straight for Ty. He dodged to the left and sent another lance of flame at the snakelike arm and sheared it in half, soaking himself in blood. The black liquid stank nearly as bad as arachnobe blood, and he quickly spat it from his mouth. The severed piece of tentacle writhed and bounced across the stone. Several of the small suckers on the inside of the arm latched onto his pants leg, forcing him to stomp on it to get them to release.

Breen was back on his feet, but with a notable limp as he cautiously started forward once more. "You all right?"

Ty nodded, but he could still feel his hold on the magic slipping, the bubble shrinking by the moment. "We've got to hurry."

The tunnel appeared just above them. Breen climbed up to it and reached down for Ty just as another set of tentacles ripped through. Breen was thrown straight through the wall of the bubble and into the water-filled tunnel behind them. Ty spun to help, but another arm pinned him against the side of the cavern wall. It pressed against his chest, and his breath whooshed out. He fought with everything he had left to hold the bubble in place. He could feel himself slipping. He was losing consciousness.

Water rained down on Ty's head as Breen broke through the bubble and landed on the arm holding Ty, cleaving it in two. Ty sucked in a lungful of air, and before he even managed to turn around, he felt himself being lifted back to his feet. His head rang like the school bell in Easthaven, announcing the start of a new day. Everything spun. Breen yanked him into the narrow passageway of the tunnel and dragged him backward as far as he could.

"Are you hurt?" Breen asked, standing in front of him protectively with his long knives up. The creature seemed to have lost them for a moment as the tentacles flipped and flopped across the cavern wall, searching for where they had gone. One of the smaller arms found the hole and thrust inside. "Move!" Breen shouted, half lifting Ty off his feet as he propelled them farther into the passageway. The tentacle missed them—barely—as they pressed against the side and quickly scooted back far enough to keep out of its way.

The arm felt around the tunnel's surface, then finally pulled back out and moved on.

"We've got to keep going."

"We need to hurry," Ty said, his head still pounding. "I don't know how much longer I can—"

The bubble collapsed and sent them flying up against the ceiling of the tunnel. His head struck the top. Shooting pain tore through his skull, leaving him completely disoriented. He tried opening a new bubble, but the air was already gone. He couldn't see anything. He had no idea how far back the tunnel went, or if there was any air to be found. The only other choice was to try swimming back out into the arms of the creature in hopes of reaching the surface.

Something grabbed his arm and yanked him around. There was a pinprick of light up ahead. As hard as he could, he tried to swim, his legs and arms flailing, weighed down by his thick clothing. The light was getting bigger. It looked like a passageway leading up.

He fought for consciousness. His chest was on fire, and he thought his head would explode. They weren't going to make it. He sucked in a mouthful of water, unable to stop himself, and his body began to convulse. He grabbed his brother and reached for whatever magic he still had and latched onto the water.

Without thinking about what he was doing, he pushed them forward, not with his feet or legs or arms, but with the water itself, like a great hand moving them through the tunnel. They reached the light. It was another passageway, and it went straight up.

All Ty could think about was Gilly's underwater cave and the way Mangora had forced the water to lower them down into it. If he could just do the reverse.

Suddenly they were moving upward, the light above growing in intensity, then everything went black.

Turning, he retched. Something behind him was striking his back. "Cough it up. That's it. Get it out."

Ty retched again, emptying his lungs until he caught his first breath. It was half filled with water, but it was precious. He coughed some more, the pain in his head decreasing slightly, while the fire in his chest remained.

He opened his eyes, blinking slowly against the light. "*Ru'kasha Sve,*" he said in a raspy, garbled whisper.

The brilliance dimmed, and he found himself in a small cavern not much larger than Overlord Barl's study, except the ceiling was at least thirty feet high. A hole in the rock over their heads filtered in enough light to see without having to use magic, which was a pleasant change. Evidently, they weren't too far from the surface. He wondered if there was anyone up there, and if so, if they had any idea of what was just below them.

"I was worried I'd lost you back there."

"How do you know you didn't?" Ty said as he took another shallow breath. He felt half dead. He rolled over to find his brother kneeling behind him, looking about as bad as Ty felt. His pack and bow with quiver lay a few feet away. Ty placed his hands on the sides of his head and pressed against his temples in hopes of lessening the pain, or at least slowing the spinning.

It didn't work.

"How did you do that back there? We were actually moving through the water."

Ty shook his head, then wished he hadn't. "I don't really know."

"It was like the water grabbed us and shot us straight up that hole," Breen said, pointing behind him to the circular opening in the rock at the back of the room. "It spewed us out like one of those mud spouts Clye Durran is always going on about. The ones he saw during his so-called expedition into the Valley of Bones."

Ty rolled his eyes. "Like he'd know. The farthest that man's ever traveled is his barstool at the East Inn."

Breen chuckled.

Ty wanted to but he was hurting too badly to try. He took another couple of deep breaths, and the spinning began to slow. He could handle the burning in his chest and even the pressure in his head, but the spinning was too much. With Breen's help, he made it up to wobbly legs, and they both walked over to the water-filled hole and looked inside. "I can't believe we made it out of there alive."

"You and me both." Breen picked up a rock and tossed it in. It disappeared not far past the surface. "And to think we have to go back down there to get out."

Ty nearly collapsed at the thought. They both turned, and for the first time, Ty was able to get a good look at the room, his eyes going straight to the three pedestals on the other side. All three stood in a row, directly under the beam of light coming from the hole in the ceiling, almost like it had been planned that way.

They hobbled over to get a closer look. Each pedestal had a small identical object floating over it, in the same way he had remembered seeing the first piece of the key floating behind the wall of fire. It also reminded him of the floating bowl of silver liquid he had seen during his time spent in Y'tarra with Nyalis.

Each pedestal was also an identical replica of the next, no discernable differences, from the black marble to the gold inlay designs that wrapped like vines down to the rectangular base at the bottom. All in all, they looked like three giant candelabras made for just a single candle.

Ty started to lean forward to get a closer look at the floating pieces when Breen grabbed his arm and pulled him back. "Careful," he said, pointing to an inscription in the floor just in front of the three pedestals that read:

A barrier to block the flesh of man.

Only one choice will thus be given.

Ty stared at the inscription, not bothering to get any closer than they already were. The last piece of the shorlock he'd tried to get had nearly burned him alive. "What do you think it means?"

"Seems clear enough," Breen said. "You only get one chance to choose."

Like the pedestals, each of the pieces floating above were identical. The second piece of the shorlock seemed to be made of the same aged silver and gold as the first. It, too, was round in shape and bore the names of each of the four character traits: Faith, Wisdom, Strength, and Compassion. Along with the inscriptions, there was a decoratively braided knot that encircled the piece just below the words. The braid had no discernable beginning or end.

"How do we know which is the right one?" Ty asked, more to himself than expecting an answer. "For that matter, what does wisdom have to do with any of this?"

"I guess you're supposed to use wisdom to figure out which one to choose."

"But how? They all look the same."

Breen took a step back and pursed his lips as he studied the three pieces. He finally shook his head. "I don't know. What did that proverb say that Nyalis told you? Faith in oneself . . . something, something." He looked over at Ty to finish it.

"Having faith in oneself is important. But faith without wisdom can be misplaced."

"Okay," Breen said, stopping him. "So, what does that mean? What does it mean that faith can be misplaced?"

"It means we can put our faith in the wrong thing."

"For example?"

Ty thought a moment. "Like the White Tower. Look at how many people trust it."

"Good. And why do you think that is?"

"Because they've been lied to."

"We've been lied to as well, so why don't we put *our* faith in the White Tower?"

"Because we know it's a lie."

"And how do we know that?"

"Because we've seen it for ourselves."

"Right again. So, the people of Aldor believe one thing because of what they've been told, and we believe another because of what we've seen."

Ty thought he understood where his brother was going with this. "What you're saying is that wisdom isn't just gaining knowledge. It's understanding how to use it."

Breen nodded. "You can have all the knowledge in the world and still be as stupid as Fraya's milk cow. Like you said, those in Aldor have been lied to, and so they put their faith in the White Tower. Faith is important, but without the wisdom to know where to place it, faith can lead to some pretty bad things." Breen looked at the three pedestals and the three circular pieces floating over them. "So, how do we use the knowledge we've been given here correctly? How do we use it to figure out which key is the right one, especially knowing we only get one chance?"

"Simple," Ty said. "We take them all?"

Breen laughed. "I don't think that's what the wizards had in mind."

"Me either." He looked up at the hole in the ceiling and the light pouring through. "What do you think will happen if I chose the wrong one?"

"Let's not find out."

Ty looked down at the inscription in the floor. "The second part is pretty clear. We only get one choice, but what do you think the first part means? A barrier to block the flesh of man."

Breen thumbed his chin. "I imagine it's saying we can't step through the light. Don't forget what happened when you tried to reach through the last barrier."

Ty cradled his hand. "Don't remind me."

They both stood in silence for what seemed the longest time, staring at each piece in turn, hoping to spot some indication as to which was the right one. Ty even got down on his hands and knees and followed the gold spiraled designs from the tops of each pedestal to the base, eager to find a difference in the three, but as far as he could tell, they were completely the same, down to the curved teardrops that wrapped around the bottom.

"This is crazy!" Ty said, throwing his hands up. "We could be here the rest of our lives and never figure out which of these is the one we want."

Breen made one more sweep around the three, keeping good and clear of the light, finally stopping alongside Ty and releasing an exasperated breath. "You might be right. I can't see any differences. They all look the same. Even the decorative braiding looks identical." He took a step forward, standing not more than a foot away from the light. "Can't say how *wise* it would be, but if we don't try something, then what's the point?"

Ty took a step forward as well. He stood directly in front of the middle pedestal. "Are you sure?"

"No," Breen said, keeping his eyes on the floating pieces of metal. "But how much sense does it make to sit here until we starve to death? Besides, the inscription reads that the barrier is there to block the flesh of *man*. You're not a man."

"Hey, watch it!"

"No, I mean you're not completely human. You're also half faerie."

Ty's head shot up. "You're right. I didn't even think about that. If this test was designed to keep out all but a faerie, this was the perfect way." He slowly raised his hand out toward the center dais, stopping just in front of the light, his fingertips nearly brushing the outer rim.

Somehow this felt wrong, but like his brother said, what other choice did they have? None that he could see. He could go ahead and make a guess, or they could sit there for days, weeks, maybe even years, and never figure out which was the right one. Maybe nothing would happen at all. Maybe this whole test was just to see if he would be stupid enough to sit there and do nothing.

Taking a deep breath, he inched his hand forward. As soon as his fingers broke the light, the room started to shake. He quickly yanked his hand back.

"Look out!" Breen shouted.

Before Ty could even turn around, Breen had grabbed him and yanked him backward to miss being hit by one of the hanging protrusions that fell from the cavern's ceiling. It shattered when it hit the floor, scattering pieces everywhere.

The quaking slowed, then stopped altogether, and Ty turned to Breen and gave him a sharp look.

"Hey, don't look at me. It was your hand."

"But you're the one who told me to do it."

"You're the one with the faerie blood. Besides, how was I to know the entire place was going to come down on our heads?" He looked back up at the ceiling and quickly took a couple steps to the right when he spotted another stalactite hanging just above him.

Too afraid to remain where they were, both brothers walked across the cavern to the pool of water and took a seat. Ty's stomach growled, another reminder of the predicament they found themselves in. "I need to rest," he said, pulling his drenched bedroll out of Breen's travel pack and wadding it up to lay his head on. "I can hardly keep my legs under me. Maybe with a little sleep, we can try again later."

Breen nodded. "I'll take first watch, not that it seems we have too much to watch for, except maybe getting clobbered in our sleep from falling debris."

Ty glanced up at the ceiling, feeling very unsure about the situation before deciding there wasn't much he could do about it, so he rolled over and closed his eyes. By the time he opened them again, he found Breen standing on the other side of the room in front of the keys once more, examining each in turn. Ty yawned.

"How long was I out?" He felt like he'd been asleep for days. The throbbing in his head was gone and the prickling in his chest from where he'd swallowed half the lake had settled as well. Even without having something to eat, he could tell he was strong enough to conjure again. How much, he didn't know.

Breen turned. "Quite a while."

"Why didn't you wake me?"

"You needed the sleep. If you don't have enough strength to get us out of here, it doesn't matter if we find the right key or not."

Ty looked up at the light shining down through the hole above and cocked his head to the side. Something felt off with it, but he couldn't quite put his finger on what.

"Yeah, puzzling, isn't it?" Breen said, following Ty's gaze. "I would have expected the sun to have gone down by now, but that light hasn't changed once, not so much as to shift positions."

Ty got to his feet and walked over to join his brother in front of the pedestals.

Breen was right. The light hadn't moved at all, as though the sun stood still in the sky with no intention of setting.

Breen chuckled as he stifled a yawn. "But what about these wizards isn't strange?"

"True enough." Ty left the pedestals and walked back over to the hole in the floor and studied the water. He reached out with his magic and connected to it. Now that he knew what it should feel like, it was a much easier process. He raised his hand, and a thin stream of water lifted from the center of the well. Like pinching the middle of a piece of lace spread on the floor and lifting it in the air, the rest of the water rose as well, forming a small thin spire standing about waist high.

"I watched Gilly do something like that with a cup of water," Breen said, giving up on his examination and walking over to see what Ty was up to.

"I remember." Ty concentrated, and the water slowly shifted, forming a crude hand with its palm facing the ceiling.

"Wow! Don't remember seeing Gilly do that. Try something else." Breen was really getting into the spirit of the magic. "Try making a fist, or make it wave at me."

Ty pictured the image of a fist in his mind and linked it with the water, and the fingers immediately balled. Breen grabbed the short sword from Ty's waist and swung at it. The blade cut right through, but the fist remained intact.

Ty turned to Breen and grinned.

Breen raised his hand in warning. "Don't you even think about—"

The fist shot from the well, and Breen dove to the right, but not before it had struck the side of his arm, sending him rolling backward and sloshing water across the cavern. Ty laughed as he released the arm, and the water dropped back into the well.

Breen crawled back to his feet and shot Ty an exasperated look as he flung the water from his coat.

Ty shrugged sheepishly, and they both walked back over to the pedestals to continue their examination. Both Ty and Breen made a complete circle around the perimeter, each in opposite directions, meeting back up at the front. Ty shook his head. "I just don't see what it is we are supposed to be—" He tripped over one of the pieces of the stalactite and nearly fell through the light.

Breen grabbed him just before he hit and pulled him back. "Watch where you're going."

"It was that stupid rock." Ty turned to kick the piece of broken shard and stopped. "Breen, look!"

"What?"

Ty pointed at the piece of rock he'd just tripped over, which was now hanging halfway through the light barrier. "No quakes," he said, looking up briefly. He looked back down at the rock, and to prove his point, he nudged it farther into the light with his boot.

Nothing happened.

"But that means . . ." Breen looked at Ty, and Ty could see they were both thinking the same thing as they turned and looked at the well on the other side of the room. "Will it reach this far?"

"Let's find out."

Chapter 43 | Ty

TY REACHED OUT WITH magic and latched onto the water from inside the well, almost as though he were holding it in his hands as he lifted the water out the same way he had earlier. Except this time, he needed it to stretch all the way across the room. He watched as the water rose above the stone and began to form, but instead of creating a hand, he shaped it into a long tentacle.

Breen moved to the side to allow the water room to make its way over to the three pedestals. Surprisingly, the arm managed to keep its shape, moving much the same way Ty had seen the lake monster's tentacles move. The pointed end of the tentacle stopped between the two brothers and waited as if for instructions.

Ty looked at Breen, and Breen nodded for him to continue. "But don't actually touch anything," Breen said nervously. "We still don't know which key is the right one."

Ty refocused his attention back on the tentacle, but instead of moving it forward by drawing more water from the well, he had the arm shrink down so that the end stretched outward to a smaller point, piercing the light barrier as it did. They looked up at the roof of the cave, but so far it seemed to remain intact. Ty looked at Breen, and they both smiled.

The light seemed to split as it entered the water, casting rays out below.

"That's one part of the test down," Breen said as Ty retracted the long tentacle and sent it back down into the hole on the other side of the room. "Now the other part. Figuring out which key is the one we want."

"Which leads us right back to where we started," Ty said as he joined his brother in front of the three keys. "Neither of us having a clue."

Breen scratched the back of his head, looking a little disheartened. "Right." He walked around the back of the pedestals to get another look from the other side.

Ty, on the other hand, studied the woven design on the front. He wondered if it had any significant meaning or if it was merely decoration. "I wonder how the two pieces fit together?"

Breen pursed his lips as he looked between the pedestals. "I hadn't even thought about it."

Ty reached into his shirt and pulled out the first piece of the medallion, where it hung from his neck by a cord. He held it up as close to the light as he dared, letting its ambience reflect off the silver casing to see if he could find any latches or indentations where the second piece might connect. "I don't see how the two—"

"Wait!" Breen said, holding up his hand. "Did you see that?"

Ty took a step back from the pedestals. Had he gotten too close? "See what?" He spared a nervous glance up at the ceiling in case of more falling rocks. "What is it?"

"Over here," Breen said, walking around to stand in front of the first pedestal. "I think it moved."

Ty walked over to the front of the pedestal, but nothing happened. The piece looked just the same as it always had.

Breen sighed and shook his head. "I could have sworn . . ."

"Maybe it's the key itself," Ty said as he grabbed the first piece hanging from his neck and held it up. The piece on the first pedestal pivoted clockwise. The movement was almost imperceptible, but it had happened.

"There! Did you see that?"

"I did!"

"Move it a little closer."

Ty slid the medallion as close to the light as he could without breaking the barrier. The piece hovering over the first pedestal began to spin, the words rotating to the point they were no longer recognizable, just a blur as they followed along the outer rim.

Breen chuckled. "And sometimes wisdom is nothing more than common sense." He shook his head. "We never even considered using the key."

What his brother said gave him an idea, and before Breen could stop him, he grabbed the back of the first piece and slipped it through the barrier and into the direct light. The three stones on the piece that Ty was holding flared to life.

"Breen, look!" About the time that Breen started to raise his head, the second piece flew off the pedestal.

Ty flinched, raising his hand to block the oncoming disc, and breached the barrier in the process. The second piece connected to the first piece at the center, spinning into place, and the three stones faded.

The cavern immediately began to shake, and Ty yanked his hand back out of the light. Maybe he should have used the water after all.

"Run!" Breen shouted, already racing across the room for his pack and weapons.

Enormous pieces of rock began dropping from the ceiling, landing all around them, shattering as they hit and sending shards across the ground, some high enough to catch the brothers' legs.

Breen snatched up his pack and weapons on the way to the water, and Ty grabbed his sword and the bedroll. Breen jumped into the well feet first, yelling at Ty to hurry. Ty skidded to a stop just as a huge chunk of rock dropped from the ceiling, heading straight for Breen.

Without thinking, he raised his hands and hit it with a fist of air the same way he had struck the Tallosian during their battle with Mangora. The enormous boulder shifted slightly and landed just beside the well, missing Breen by a hand or two.

"What are you waiting for?" Breen shouted.

Ty sent his magic into the water and stepped off, but instead of breaking through the surface, he brought a bubble of air with him from the cavern.

The two plunged downward through the tunnel until they hit the bottom and the adjoining corridor leading out to the lake. Ty reignited his flames to give them light enough to see, shrinking the bubble down in size and using the water to push them forward, much in the same way Gilly had done to propel their boat down the East River. Breen had a childlike smile on his face as they flew through the tunnel toward the lake ahead.

"Guess we could have handled that a bit differently," Breen said. "At least we got it."

Ty smiled but put all his focus into the magic. He could see why Gilly loved it. It was almost like flying. Ty quenched his flames to just a single finger, and both brothers conjured their night sight.

Just before they reached the exit, he slowed, coming to a stop just inside the opening. He looked at Breen. "What if it's waiting for us?"

Breen studied the blackness ahead. "The creature in the maze left as soon as you recovered the first piece. Perhaps this one has as well?"

"But we didn't exactly abide by all the rules on this one."

Breen shrugged. "It's not like we can go back."

Ty used the water to push them farther back into the tunnel. Concentrating on what he needed to do, he reached out and drew the water behind them, and they shot through the entrance and out into the deep.

As soon as they burst clear of the tunnel, a bubbling howl rose from somewhere just below, and several arms swung into view.

Ty refocused his hold on the water and pushed even harder, dodging and weaving through the mass of tentacles as he fought to get them to the surface. Each time one of the arms came close, he was forced to veer in the opposite direction and then pull them back to make sure they were still heading in the right direction. The creature was moving up behind them fast.

"Hold on!" Ty shouted, and they flew out of the water like a bolt from a crossbow. Ty used the water to soften their fall as they landed near the center of their island. By the time they were back on their feet, the first of the lake monster's arms broke through the water and swung straight for them.

"Get to the mirror!" Breen shouted, his daggers in his hands as he chased after Ty up the rocks toward the stone frame on their right. "Hurry!"

Ty scrambled up the rock toward the second mirror. Nearly there, he glanced over his shoulder, but Breen was no longer there. He turned and found his brother standing several boulders away, stabbing and slashing at the long slithering tentacles as they fought to crush him against the rock.

His brother was powerful, one of the biggest men in Easthaven, but nothing compared to what they were facing. He was a mere rodent to be toyed with.

Ty shoved his hand into his pocket and grabbed the compass. The runes on the mirror flashed to life. "*Urgala Nurishtu!*" he shouted, reading the name at the top before another name halfway up on the left burst to life. "*Fintora Coscosa!*"

The glass swirled, and the room filled with light. "I got it!" He turned to see how close Breen was, and the only thing he found was his brother's bow and quiver. Breen was gone!

Ty raised his hand and sent a ball of flame into the air, lighting the water around the island. That was when he saw him. Breen was suspended about twenty feet in the air with several tentacles wrapped around his legs and arms, holding him in place. His brother wiggled and shook, fighting to break free as the enormous slithering arms pulled him out over the water just above where the monster's mouth was rising up out of the darkness.

"No!" Ty jumped up on the higher rocks behind the mirror on the edge of the island and raised his hand, blue flames bursting into the air. He was about to throw his first volley when it hit him: if he hit the creature and caused it to drop his brother, Breen would land right inside the monster's mouth.

Ty released his flames and frantically looked around for something else to use. His brother's bow was there, but it was still the same. If he did anything to the monster, it would kill his brother.

Breen managed to free one arm and slice through one of the smaller tentacles. The arm flung sideways and hit the water near the island, soaking Ty, but it gave him an idea.

The water. He could use the water. Pushing his fear aside, he drove his magic down into the lake.

His brother was now hovering just over the creature's mouth, nothing but rings of teeth waiting below.

"Ty, do something!" The lake monster released Breen, and he plummeted straight for the gaping hole.

Ty raised his hands, and another tentacle broke the surface, this one made of water. It wrapped around his brother's waist and yanked him to the left, just before he was swallowed whole.

Ty drew the watery arm back to the island and deposited Breen on the rocks beside him. The creature shrilled at the loss of its prey and swam for the island.

"Quick! Grab your bow," Ty shouted. "I don't know how long the mirror will stay open."

The lake monster shrilled once more, and Ty turned just in time to duck before one of its tentacles took off his head. He could hear Breen rushing back up the rock behind him. Concentrating, he gathered the water near the island, and like he had with the fist inside the well, he hit the monster as hard as he could.

"Ty! Hurry. Let's go!"

Ty released the water and ran for the mirror, but not before one of the tentacles had latched onto his leg. He landed on his face and spun around, unleashing a bolt of blue flames that severed its arm. The creature was now pulling itself up onto the island. It had looked big underwater, but as it crawled toward them, Ty realized just how massive it was.

Breen snatched Ty off the ground, and they both dove through the glass. Ty sent another wave of fire behind him as he did. He could hear the creature's shrill from the other side just before the mirror began to spin. A single tentacle drove through the glass and latched onto the two of them with its suckers, only to be sheared in half as the mirror reformed and the underground lake disappeared.

They kicked the enormous snakelike arm to the side, where it continued to bounce around before eventually going still.

"Great," Breen said, picking himself off the sand-covered stone and looking around. "Another cave. Just our luck."

Ty stood as well. Thankfully, this cave didn't appear to have an underground lake. And unlike the blackness in the previous cavern, there was light visible with his night sight from a passageway on the left. They were standing in a chamber not much smaller than the one holding the three pedestals. Behind them, encased in the rock, was the mirror.

"One thing's for sure," Breen said as he started for the light, "I don't think we're going to need our coats."

His brother was right. Ty was already beginning to sweat. They removed their waterlogged garments, and Breen tied them to the top of his pack before heading into the tunnel.

"Look," Breen said, stopping to point at the top of the entrance.

It was another inscription: *STRENGTH.*

Breen shook the water from his head before tucking his hair behind his ears to keep it out of his eyes. "So far, we've seen faith and wisdom. I wonder what kind of test we'll need to go through for strength?"

"If the last two are any indication," Ty grumbled, "I don't want to find out." They stared at the word a moment longer, then Ty followed his brother into the narrow crevice in the rock as it wove through the mountainside.

The farther down the tunnel they got, the brighter the light became. Soon enough, they had released their night sight just to keep from being blinded. Reaching the end of the passage, they stepped out of the tunnel and found themselves staring out across a vast sea of nothingness, endless mounds of sand stretching across the entire horizon.

"This is certainly different," Breen said, his hand up in front of his eyes to block the sun.

"At least we won't have much difficulty drying our clothes," Ty said, wanting to sound optimistic.

Breen grunted as they both stared out across the barren wasteland in front of them. "Drying our clothes is going to be the least of our problems. Besides, I have a feeling we'll be begging for that water soon enough."

Chapter 44 | Ayrion

YRION STARED AT THE blade in his hand. The warm light from their campfire reflected off its dark sheen as he turned it over, then turned it again, admiring the durability of the steel, or whatever metal was used in its crafting. He had no memories of where the twin swords had come from, but it was clear they had been forged with magic.

"Those are quite the weapons," Bek said as he took a seat beside Ayrion on one of the downed logs they were using around the campfire. He picked up the second blade where it was resting against the wood between them and pulled it from its sheath. Bek tested its weight. "In the hand, they balance surprisingly well." He finally placed it back in its sheath and laid it against the log. "This was made by a skilled craftsman, indeed."

Behind them, Zynora and Nell were busy putting the children to bed, leaving Ayrion, Tameel, and Bek to enjoy the serenity of the fire. Their breath misted in front of them, mixing with the smoke from the newly applied wood. They'd been traveling north along Virn Run for almost a week, the first couple of nights without much sleep. Ayrion wanted to get as far away from Minotha and Endric Talmanes as possible. There was no telling what the young lordling would do once he saw what was left of his father's estate.

They'd barely made it ten miles from Lake Wenigapu when the first of the snow had begun to fall, and it hadn't let up since. Seven days and it was still tumbling out of the sky like a giant sifter shaking overhead with no end in sight. The thick powder had slowed their progress, which worried Tameel and Zynora, since they weren't sure whether the passes would still be clear enough to travel through. Tameel said they were treacherous enough during the summer months; he hated to think about traveling through them with thousands of pounds of snow just waiting to slide down the mountain and sweep them away.

Ayrion didn't like the sound of that, but there wasn't much they could do about it at this point except carry on. He wondered if there was some place they could shelter for the winter if the passes were indeed impassable. One thing was for sure: they wouldn't be going back to Minotha.

Ayrion stared at the black blade a moment longer, then slid it back in its sheath and propped it alongside its twin. "I wish I could remember how I came by them." He stood and walked over to a pile of wood they'd gathered before the sun went down and grabbed a couple of pieces and tossed them on the fire. Sparks billowed up out of the flames from where the smoldering cinders underneath had been disturbed. While up, he lifted the kettle from the fire and refilled his cup.

The aromatic tea was hot on the tip of his tongue, so he sipped it slowly as he sat back down. He enjoyed these times in the evening, when the women would gather in the wagons to rock around the kettle stove and enjoy each other's company, as the men did the same around the fire. He stared up at the thick canopy of fir overhead. It seemed to be holding back the snow almost as well as any shingled roof, not to mention sheltering them against the harsh northerly winds coming down off the Angoran Mountains.

"Tell us about Wellhollow," Bek said. "Never made it that far north myself. Always wanted to go, though. Heard it can be kind of a tough place." Bek was covered from head to toe in his usual hides and pelts. About the only part of him Ayrion could see was the man's eyes, peeking out just below his red fox cap.

Tameel took a long pull on his pipe, filling both cheeks, then sent a steady stream curling up around his head. "It's a quiet community, Wellhollow. Strong mountain folk. Don't care much for outsiders, but since me and the wife have been traveling these roads for decades, they've grown to tolerate us. Somewhat," he added with a dull grin. "They don't take kindly to people interfering in their business, but as long as we mind our own, I don't believe we'll have too much of a problem."

Ayrion hoped they didn't end up running into another situation like they had in Woodvale or Minotha . . . or Belvin for that matter. In fact, perhaps the safest thing would be to not visit any communities with more than half a dozen people in them.

"As long as we can get through the passes," Tameel said, "we should be safe until at least Manù or Toff when the sun warms enough to melt the snow."

"That late?" Bek asked, stuffing his pipe from a pouch Tameel had loaned him. He used a thin piece of tinder to light it. Tameel had offered Ayrion a pull from his pipe months back. Apparently, he wasn't supposed to have inhaled. After spending half the next hour or more coughing, he decided that smoking was something he didn't care to try again. Besides, if he wanted a mouthful of smoke, there was plenty to be had from the fire each time the wind changed.

Tameel pulled the pipe from his mouth and pointed north. "The snow in those mountains can reach as high as a roof, not including the drifts if a strong enough wind decides to blow. Snow like that can take months to melt."

Bek nodded, letting the smoke from his pipe seep from his mouth before amusing himself by producing several perfectly shaped rings. Tameel smiled and tipped his pipe to Bek before sending up a couple rings himself. Ayrion, on the other hand, found he didn't need a pipe, as he opened his mouth and released a mouthful of warm air into the frosty night.

Both Tameel and Bek laughed.

Yes, Ayrion enjoyed their evenings together. He found they didn't need to do much in the way of talking. It was enough to simply be in each other's company. Ayrion wished every day could be as pleasant as these last few. It was such a change of pace to find himself not being chased by angry townsfolk, or set upon by bandits, or battling ancient corporeal generals with armies of white-skinned crazies.

The next morning found them on the road again. In fact, they remained on that same road for the next couple of days, passing a scattering of houses along the way, houses that grew in number up until the road ended against the banks of Virn Run, where a ferry station had been set up alongside the river.

"Welcome to Wellhollow," Tameel said, pulling the old green-and-gold tinker wagon to a halt. Ayrion brought Shade up alongside Tameel and stared out across the river to where the city of Wellhollow rested on the other side. The river itself was quite a distance more than a stone's throw at this juncture, too wide for a bridge.

"Thought you were worried about passes," Ayrion said, staring at the buildings on the other side.

Tameel smiled and leaned back in his seat. "We haven't reached our destination quite yet."

Bek pulled his and Nell's red-and-gold wagon up alongside Ol' Lerra and looked at the ferry ahead. "Will that thing support the wagons?"

Tameel smiled. "Never had problems before, but we'll have to take them over one at a time."

The front window behind the driver's seat opened, and Zynora stuck her head out. "What's going on? Are we there?" She spotted the river. "Oh. I hate this part." She quickly closed the window back, and Tameel sighed.

"She doesn't do well over water."

Ayrion remembered them talking about that back when they had first rescued Taylis from the highwaymen. If he were honest, looking at the steady flow of the current, he could see why she would be a little on edge, especially when loading something as big and heavy as Ol' Lerra.

Tameel climbed down off the wagon, and Ayrion followed, dismounting Shade to let the horse graze on some of the winter grass poking through the snow. Ayrion had barely managed to help Zynora down from the back when something latched onto his leg.

He looked down to see Marissa's big brown eyes staring up at him fondly. She held out her arms to be picked up. Ayrion couldn't help but smile as he leaned over and lifted the little girl off the ground.

"Let's see if the ferryman is available," Tameel said as he and Zynora started for the front of the house. It was very reminiscent of Bek and Nell's cabin outside Belvin—single story, chinked log, with a stone chimney stack on the side. However, it didn't seem to possess the softer aspects of Nell's yellow curtains, or the flower garden in the front. Instead, the front porch was covered in tools, old lumber, and sawdust.

Tameel knocked on the door, and they waited.

"What's your business here?" a voice on the left called out, causing everyone to turn. A short, stocky man stepped out from around the left side of the house, carrying an axe. He was covered from head to toe in hides with a thick fur coat that hung halfway to his knees, and a beard that covered the majority of his face and hung to his chest.

Tameel stepped off the porch to meet him. "Greetings, Master Tofflin. Would you be running your ferry today? We have goods to trade in Wellhollow."

"Running a bit late, aren't ya?"

"We got a slow start, I'm afraid," Tameel said.

Tofflin walked around to the front of the porch as the others stepped down behind Tameel. He looked everyone over in turn, pausing a moment on Bek as if trying to decide if he was someone he should know. When he got to Ayrion, he took a step back. "What's his kind doin' here? I won't take no Upaka over, not if you's under contract."

"He's with us," Tameel said. "No contract, I assure you. He left those ways years ago."

Tofflin looked at Ayrion, then at the two blades sticking up above his head. "Don't look to have left his ways too far behind. Looks to be wantin' to cause some trouble."

"You have my oath as an Upakan," Ayrion said, having no idea if an Upakan's oath was worth anything. "I have no intention of causing trouble . . ." He paused a moment before adding. "Unless, of course, it comes looking for me."

Tofflin chuckled gruffly and spun his axe. "You'll find that trouble 'round these parts will be more than ya bargained for." He looked at the two wagons. "The river's neck up, but not enough to stop a crossing." He looked them over once again. "You's sure you wants to cross now? Poor time to be trad'n at Wellhollow."

"And why's that?" Tameel asked. When the ferryman didn't answer, Tameel shrugged. "We didn't come all this way to turn back now."

Tofflin tugged on his beard. "Don't say as I didn't warn ya." He started up the front porch steps. "Give me two shakes, and I'll be with ya shortly."

"What do you think that was all about?" Ayrion asked, staring after the ferryman.

Tameel shook his head. "No idea. I told you. They're set in their ways up here. Don't care much for strangers."

Ayrion followed the others around the side of the building and over to the ferry to get a better view of the water. It was moving at a quick pace, but it seemed calm on top. The ferry shifted with the current as it beat against the large wooden braces on the left side, which had been placed there to keep it from floating away.

The road continued all the way down to the water, with very little incline, making passage onto the ferry much easier for those with wagons and carts. Taylis walked down and stuck a finger in the water, then quickly pulled it back out. "Brrr! That's cold."

"Come," Tameel said, walking back to the wagons. "Let's get the teams into place."

Ayrion guided the front horses by hand down to the water while Tameel sat in the front seat. Bek brought his team around behind and waited for Tofflin to arrive and get the first wagon on board. It didn't take the short ferryman long to finish whatever business he had inside before he was stepping out the back. Another young man came out just behind him, probably his son. They walked over to the flat-bottomed boat, and Tofflin pulled Tameel to the side to haggle about the price.

Ayrion watched Tameel pull out his purse and drop some coins in Tofflin's hand. Tofflin promptly stuffed the coins in his trouser pocket, and he and his son climbed on board. With Ayrion's help, they managed to lay a ramp down at the front of the boat for the wagons, then stood to the side to let the first one on board.

From the front seat, Tameel gave the reins a soft flutter, and the horses started forward. "Careful now," he called out. "Easy does it." The horses carried Ol' Lerra across the rampway and onto the ferry, stopping just shy of the rope-lined rail on the other side. It was a tight fit, but after they managed to chock the wheels to keep them from rolling, Tameel climbed down to stand with the horses and keep a firm hand on their reins. In truth, Ayrion didn't think Tameel liked the idea of sitting on top of the wagon while crossing in case the wagon tipped.

Ayrion helped Tofflin and his son to drag the ramp aboard before Tofflin tied off the back with a rope to keep anyone from falling off. They loosed the mooring lines from the pilings on the left side, and the ferry slowly slid away from the bank. Bek and Taylis waved from shore as they stood beside the other wagon, waiting for the ferry's return. "We'll see you on the other side," he called out.

Marissa waved enthusiastically from the back of the ferry, with Nell standing beside her, her hands planted firmly on the little girl's shoulders in case she got too excited and decided to rush forward. Zynora kept herself as close to the center of the boat as possible. Ayrion, on the other hand, grabbed hold of the thick rope stretching from one side of the river to the other and helped Tofflin pull.

The ferryman didn't seem to be in much of a hurry as he and his son and Ayrion walked the rope down the side of the boat, released, then marched back to do it again. A flash of memory caught Ayrion about halfway back, and he nearly tripped on one of the boards as he found himself standing on another ferry, very similar to the one they were on now. This time, he was just a boy. He remembered the ferry snapping free from the rope and the ferryman flying into the water. The next thing, he was in the water himself, swimming toward the fallen man. There was something very familiar about him. A name on the back of his . . . *Hobb!*

"What you lookin' at?"

Ayrion turned, realizing he was just standing there staring out at the water, and nodded. "Sorry, I . . . I thought I saw something."

Tofflin looked out at the water as well, but when he didn't see anything, he grunted. "Don't you be quittin' on me now. We've got a furpiece left to go yet."

Ayrion grabbed the rope once more and started toward the back of the ferry. He had newfound energy, as the excitement of having recovered another small piece of memory drove him onward. He wondered who this Hobb character was, and what had led them to nearly drowning in the muddy waters of whatever river they had been trying to cross. He hoped the same circumstances didn't happen here.

They were nearing the far shore when something struck the ferry from underneath, and the boat lurched. Ayrion clutched the rope, suddenly imagining the ferry tipping. Behind him, Zynora released a quick shrill and latched onto one of Ol' Lerra's front wheels. Nell yanked Marissa away from the back rope, where they'd been watching Bek and Taylis, and Tameel stumbled to his knees, still clinging to the horses' reins.

"No worries! No worries!" Tofflin shouted, seeing their reactions. "Ain't nothin' but a downed tree wedged in the mire on the bottom. She'll right herself." Sure enough, the ferry straightened, and they continued on.

As soon as they reached the other side, Zynora was off the boat before Ayrion and Tofflin had managed to drop the ramp at the front. She barely missed the water, leaping from the planks into the ankle-deep snow covering the road. From the lack of tracks, it didn't look like anyone had traveled that way since the last snowfall.

Ayrion helped Tameel back up onto the front seat, and Tameel guided the horses off the ferry and up onto the waiting road. He pulled the wagon to a stop a few dozen feet away from the river and climbed down. "Everyone in one piece?"

Zynora mumbled something under her breath and disappeared inside the back of the wagon. Tameel simply shook his head with a cheeky grin and pulled out his pipe as he sat on the back ledge and waited for the ferry to return with the other wagon. Ayrion walked down to the water and helped Tofflin and his son with the ramp, then watched with Marissa and Nell as the ferry made its slow journey back across.

It took at least a full hour before the ferry made it back to the other side, picked up the red-and-gold wagon, and returned. Taylis waved from the front as they neared, shouting something about almost drowning. Ayrion hopped back on board as soon as the boat came to a stop and helped them lower the ramp for Bek, who was waiting quietly for the two to finish before snapping the reins and leading the second wagon off the boat. Shade trotted along after the wagon, having been forced to wait for the second ferry since most of the travelers had ridden on the first. He snorted at Ayrion on the way by, letting him know he didn't appreciate being left behind.

Ayrion ignored his horse's ire and helped them lift the front ramp and placed it back on board.

"Much obliged," Tofflin said hesitantly. Ayrion turned to rejoin the group, but Tofflin grabbed his arm and pulled him back around. "You's might have forsaken your ways, but I reckon I can see the fight in them eyes. You watch out for the little ones and the womenfolk, ya hear? Keep 'em safe."

Ayrion thought it a strange thing to say, but he nodded reassuringly.

Tofflin held his gaze a moment longer, then finally turned back around.

"Warned 'em, I did," he mumbled to himself as he climbed back aboard the ferry. "Can'ts do much more than that."

Ayrion watched as Tofflin and his son grabbed the thick rope and the ferry moved away from shore.

"What was that all about?" Bek asked just over Ayrion's shoulder as he watched the boat pull away from shore. The big trapper had a tendency to sneak up on people unexpectedly, his zabatas making his steps rather silent.

"Not really sure. He wanted to make sure I was going to watch out for the little ones and the womenfolk."

"Odd." They both stared after the ferry.

"You two going to stand there gawking at the river all day?" Zynora asked from the back of the wagon, clearly anxious to be underway.

Bek laid a hand on Ayrion's shoulder. "Keep your eyes open."

Ayrion nodded. "You do the same."

Swinging up onto Shade, Ayrion directed the big warhorse around to the front of Ol' Lerra and nodded to Tameel, who seemed to be waiting for everyone to get aboard.

"If this is Wellhollow," Ayrion said, "then what was all this talk of not reaching our destination?"

Tameel scratched the top of his head, where his purple headwrap covered most of his white hair. "Ah, that's an interesting topic, and a point of some contention. Wellhollow is really two towns. A lower and an upper."

Bek listened from the other wagon.

"Rumor has it," Tameel continued, loud enough for both to hear, "that many, many years ago there was an argument between two families, a debate as to the ownership of a specific piece of land, something they all held as sacred." He shrugged. "No idea what it was, but it caused such a rift that the town itself split in two. The family that lost the argument moved down off the mountain to the foothills and started their own city, which they decided to call Wellhollow as well."

"So this . . ." Bek said, pointing toward the town in front of them.

"Yes," Tameel answered. "This is the second Wellhollow, or *Lower* Wellhollow, which as it stands, ended up growing and thriving into the community you see here. The original town is up there," he said, pointing to the mountain peaks on their left. "They keep to themselves, coming down only when the need arises."

"That's quite the story," Ayrion said, wondering what piece of land could have caused the split of an entire town.

"As I said, it's nothing more than rumor." He smiled and snapped the reins, the frozen wheels creaking along under the wagons, leaving fresh tracks in the snow behind them.

Lower Wellhollow lay nestled within the crook of several adjoining mountains. It looked to be larger than Minotha, but not by much, crafted solely from local timber. The town, however, seemed on the poorer side, its buildings weathered and its people more so.

Gruff, dull eyes stared out over thick beards and heavy furs. One man wore an entire bear pelt across his back, the bear's arms wrapping around his neck like a collar. Like most of the communities they'd passed through, no one seemed pleased to see them, everyone stopping what they were doing just to watch them pass. Most people in polite societies would have at least waited until they had driven by before turning to stare at the newcomers, but not in Wellhollow. They wanted to let you know they'd seen you and were keeping an eye on you.

Most eyes passed over Bek, who fit right in with his badger pelts and beard; some even seemed to recognize Tameel with his colorful robe and white hair, but everyone made sure to let Ayrion know they didn't recognize him and didn't much care to. Those faces he could see tightened—lips curling, eyes narrowing—when they caught the first glimpse of his eyes.

The center of town was just ahead, where another road, as wide as the one they were on, cut northward toward the mountain. Ayrion wondered how difficult it was for Tameel and Zynora to sell up here, where the people seemed to give visitors the cold shoulder, both figuratively and literally. They started into the town square, and Tameel slowed as another wagon laden with some sort of vegetable Ayrion didn't recognize passed by.

"Get inside," Tameel said.

"What?" Ayrion turned to see who he was talking to.

Tameel was looking directly at him. "Hurry, don't ask questions."

Ayrion hopped off Shade and headed to the back of the wagon. What was going on? He tied Shade onto the back and climbed inside, shutting the door behind him.

Zynora looked up, in the middle of kneading some dough. "What can I get you?" she asked.

"Nothing. Tameel told me to get inside. I thought perhaps you needed my help."

Zynora dropped the dough and wiped her hands on the front of her apron, then walked over to the front window and opened it. "What's going on out there?"

"White riders," Tameel said nervously. "And they're coming this way."

Chapter 45 | Ayrion

HE TOWER'S GUARDS RODE two abreast as they headed straight for them.

"Change your outfit, and quick!" Tameel said back through the opening. "Looks like we'll be testing those mountain passes after all." He jerked the reins to the left, and the wagon veered around the outside of the square toward an adjoining street, which headed in the direction of the mountains.

Zynora shut the flap, and Ayrion quickly slid out of his jacket.

"And hide those," she said, pointing at his swords. "The last time we ran into the Black Watch, they recognized them."

Ayrion gritted his teeth. He didn't like leaving his weapons behind, but she had a point, so he pulled them off and stuffed them under one of the cots, opting instead for one of the older swords they'd been unable to sell in Minotha.

"Here," Zynora said, tossing Ayrion a fur coat. "Put that on."

It wasn't quite as long and heavy as Bek's, but it did its job well enough. Grabbing a knife on the way out, he tied it behind his waist and stepped out the back.

Quickly, he hopped up into the saddle and fell back in place, riding directly behind Ol' Lerra so he could keep an eye on Bek as well as the company of Tower guards about to ride through the center of town. If luck held, the Watch would simply pass by behind them. They reached the end of the square and were just starting down the next street when the white riders suddenly turned.

"You there, halt!"

"Keep going," Ayrion said to Bek. "Act as though you didn't hear them. Maybe they'll—"

"I said you there, on the wagons, halt in the name of the White Tower!"

Ayrion glanced behind him and could see the entire company was heading their way. "Stop the wagon," he said and turned his horse back to meet them.

Ayrion lifted his hood and rode over, stopping several feet from the first of the riders. "Our apologies," he said, keeping his eyes lowered enough to hopefully not attract attention. "We didn't know you were referring to us. Is there something we can help you with, Captain?" Ayrion noticed the same patch on the man's arm that he'd seen on the guard outside the Smok'n Pig. "Would you care to do some trading? We have some fine tobac available, and I'm sure we could find you a nice vintage of ale for these cold nights."

"We aren't looking to trade," the man at the front said sharply, the bottom of his white mantle rustling behind him in the strong mountain breeze. He wore a long fur-lined cloak over his cape. "What's your business here?"

"We are tinkers, sir, been trading along this route since the fall." By this time, Bek and Tameel had climbed down and were on their way over. "This is our last stop for the winter. You sure we couldn't interest you in some extra blankets or candles, or perhaps some scented soap?"

The captain looked at the two wagons. "We are looking for wielders. Who all do you have with you?"

"Good day to you," Tameel said, walking up alongside Shade, Bek just to his right. "My name is Tameel. What brings our illustrious protectors this far north? Could we interest you in—"

"No," the captain said adamantly. "Your man here has already given me the spiel. We aren't looking to trade. We're looking for wielders."

"Wielders?" Tameel shrugged. "Afraid we are fresh out of those, good sir."

Ayrion was half tempted to kick Tameel in the foot. He hoped the Watch didn't take Tameel's humor the wrong way.

"What's in the wagons?"

"Nothing but our wares, I assure you. My wife is in the green one up front, preparing dinner, and Bek's wife and their children are in the red, doing the same."

"Open them."

"As you wish." Tameel walked over to the red wagon, since it was first in line, and knocked on the back door. Nell opened it a crack. "May we take a look inside, my dear?" He glanced over his shoulder. "Afraid we don't have much of a choice."

Ayrion dismounted and followed the captain and three other guards over to the first wagon. He needed to get to Ol' Lerra and warn Zynora, especially with his swords lying under his cot, but if the captain saw him leave, he might grow suspicious. Nell stepped out of the back of the red wagon, bringing Taylis and Marissa along with her, and let a couple of the guards take a look inside. After a couple of minutes of poking around, they stepped back out and shook their heads. "No one else inside."

The captain nodded, and they moved on to Ol' Lerra.

Ayrion wrung his hands. What happened if they found his swords? What if they recognized them? Even if they didn't, they'd have to wonder how an old tinker couple had come across such exquisite craftsmanship, not what they'd expect to sell from the back of a wagon. He rested one hand on the hilt of the sword, not that it would have done all that much. They couldn't fight off an entire company of Black Watch, not with the women and children. And who knew if there were more.

Zynora was already waiting outside the door when the guards arrived. Her charms hung proudly from her headdress, jingling in the wind as she waited with crossed arms for the men to poke and prod through the guts of their wagon.

"Captain," one of the guards inside called out.

This was it, Ayrion thought, reaching for the knife at his back. There were only four of them. Perhaps he could kill the other three and use the captain as a hostage, at least long enough for them to get into the pass. The guard inside the wagon stuck his head back out.

"We found these." He stepped out with a small armful of swords and polearms.

The captain turned to Tameel. "What's this?"

"Part of our trade, sir. We purchased these in Belvin from a swordsmith for a very reasonable price after throwing in a cask of Black Briar. We have been selling them off a few at a time with every stop that we make. You'll be surprised how many people nowadays are looking for a sturdy weapon. Times are dark indeed with so many of these wielders on the loose. I'm just thanking the Creator for the White Tower and what it does to keep us safe. How about a pint of Keldoran brandy for you and your men, as a token of our appreciation for what—"

"Thank you, no," the captain said, turning back to his men. "Anything else inside?"

Ayrion held his breath.

The man shook his head. "No, sir." The two stepped out from the back of the wagon and joined the others.

The captain nodded. "Fine." He turned to Tameel. "Be on your way."

Ayrion released a sigh of relief as he climbed back up onto Shade. How had they not found his swords?

"What about these?" the man holding the weapons asked.

The captain pointed at the wagon. "Leave them."

"Thank you, Captain," Tameel said grovelingly. "May the Great Father's light shine upon you."

The captain left them standing there and walked back to his horse. Ayrion could hear him giving orders, and the entire line of white riders started down the street in the direction of the ferry. None of their group moved until the last of the guards had disappeared from view.

"That was a close one," Bek said, wiping his forehead.

"Too close," Zynora added, looking at Ayrion.

Ayrion knew exactly what she was referring to. "How did they not find them? I'd placed them under the cot."

"I know. When I saw them searching the other wagon, I grabbed them and a couple other items and hid them along with the rest of our more valuable cache under the floor."

Ayrion lifted his head. "Did I know we had a secret hideaway under the floor?"

Zynora smiled. "You do now."

"Right," Tameel said. "I think we've seen quite enough of Lower Wellhollow. What you say we head on up into the mountains and see if there are fewer uniforms up there? Can't say as when I've ever seen the Black Watch this far north."

"Agreed," Bek said and hustled Nell and the two kids back toward the red wagon.

Ayrion turned to find Shade standing behind him. "Hey, boy," he said, rubbing the bridge of Shade's nose. "I forgot all about you. Glad you didn't wander off." He swung into the saddle and nudged him with his boots, and they rode to the front of the line as they made their way through the back half of town.

The road narrowed as they left the last of the cottages behind and started up to the entrance of the first pass. Ayrion pulled back to ride alongside Tameel. "How far in is this Upper Wellhollow?"

"Far enough to take the rest of the afternoon to get there, depending on how the road holds up," Tameel said, looking up at the snow-covered peaks they were about to cross between. Tameel pulled the horses to a stop and climbed down, motioning for Ayrion to do the same.

Ayrion dismounted, dragging Shade along with him as they walked to the back of Ol' Lerra, where Tameel motioned for Bek to join them. "Gather the others," he said, keeping his voice lowered as he did. Within a few minutes, the entire group was gathered inside the green wagon and sipping on some hot tea. "Best we eat lunch now, because once we start into the pass, there won't be any stopping."

Zynora handed out fresh biscuits, the same ones she'd been working on while first riding into Lower Wellhollow. They stuffed them with some salted pork and cheese, followed by a couple dried apple slices. The tea had been sweetened with honey, not to be indulgent but enough to cut the stronger taste of the sage.

"From here on in, we make as little noise as possible," Tameel said. "The snow that covers these mountains has a tendency to slide. They call it an avalanche. It's said that when they first constructed Lower Wellhollow, they built it right between the convergence of two peaks, and during a particularly cold winter, one of those avalanches wiped out the town, taking nearly a third of the townsfolk with it. Zynora and I have seen one ourselves, and believe me, it's a fearful sight to behold."

Zynora nodded as she went about cleaning up the meal. "Loud noises can cause this to happen, so take care of the horses as we go and keep the children quiet."

Bek looked at Nell, and she placed her hands on the top of Taylis's and Marissa's heads. "You hear that?" she said, looking them both in the eyes. "You will need to keep as quiet as you can."

The two children nodded.

"I'll keep an eye on them," Nell said to Tameel.

"Good. Then let's be off. The sooner we get a move on, the sooner we get through."

Ayrion untied Shade from the back where he'd simply draped the reins around one of the hooks. He never really bothered with tying them off, since it seemed Shade never had a tendency to wander very far. Their bond kept them close. Ayrion opted to keep the fur coat Zynora had given him, thankful for the warmth. His black leather duster was comfortable and maneuverable, perfect for a fight, but it wasn't exactly warm, at least not the kind of warm he needed this far north.

Ayrion took the lead, staying only a few paces in front of Ol' Lerra, as the small caravan started into the pass. He didn't care much for riding in the middle, especially in narrow spaces, because the wagons blocked his view. The wind whipping through the winding mountain passageways was the only sound to be heard, apart from the thump of the horses' hooves into the packed snow and the creaking of the wheels as they moved the wagons onward.

The peaks above them were covered in snow, some sheer enough to have gathered no more than a light dusting with patches of dark rock showing beneath, and others that looked deep enough to cover a mountain pine. Ayrion pulled the hood of his coat over his head and raised the scarf up over his nose. The wind was sharp and cold, causing the run from his nose to freeze.

He glanced back over his shoulder to see how Tameel was faring, but the old man didn't seem too bothered. He kept the reins tight to his chest, blowing into his gloves occasionally and patting the thick wooly cap on top of his head. He seemed more preoccupied with the surrounding mountains than anything else. At one point, he startled to the point of jumping when Zynora stuck her head out and offered him a steaming cup of something to keep him warm.

Ayrion continually rubbed his gloved hands across Shade's coat, which was beginning to build a lather. He worried that if their climb grew any steeper, the horses wouldn't be able to continue pulling the wagons. As it happened, every time the way forward looked as though it was about to become impassable, it would flatten off, giving them time to allow the horses to rest before moving on. Twice they stopped at interconnecting passageways—trails which looked to lead to other parts of the mountain chain—long enough to rub the animals down and offer them some water and feed. In both instances, everyone went about their tasks without so much as a whisper, relying on hand gestures to communicate what was needed.

A couple of hours in, the pass began to narrow as the mountains shifted their direction, all but encapsulating them between the peaks. It was the steepest and closest of the inclines they'd traveled thus far, leaving only enough room for a single wagon to pass at a time, and even then, it was a tight fit. Ayrion left Shade tied to the back to walk with the horses up front. He kept his hands on the reins, guiding them forward as he kept his eyes on the sides of the wagon and how close they were to the rock walls.

Several thin falls of snow dropped from the sides of the cliff face, covering the top of the wagon as they rode underneath. Ayrion had to move to the other side of the trail to keep from getting hit. He couldn't imagine what it would be like if one of those huge slides dropped. It would fill the entire pass, drowning them all. The weight would probably be enough to crush the wagons on impact.

The thought of it had Ayrion pulling the horses all the faster, urging them to make it through. He didn't have a fear of tight spaces that he was aware of, but the surrounding rock and snow was certainly edging him in that direction. The narrow channel twisted back and forth, snaking itself through the mountainside, each step echoing off the rock and leaving Ayrion's hands shaking from more than just the freezing cold. He could almost hear his own heartbeat pounding in his ears as he stared up at the edge of what looked like a wall of snow above, just waiting to be released.

Behind them, Bek followed closely in Ol' Lerra's tracks. His fur-lined coat and hat had turned from brown to white after passing underneath one of the snow falls. Other than shaking his head, Bek didn't bother wiping it down, his hands preoccupied with keeping the horses moving in the right direction.

They were nearing what looked to be the end of the stone corridor when the trail suddenly steepened. Ayrion had Tameel wait as he went to let Bek know to keep the red wagon there while they tried getting Ol' Lerra up the hill. He let Bek know that he would then come back and do the same for the red wagon. Bek nodded with a wave, letting him know he understood, and Ayrion walked back around and grabbed the straps between the horses.

Slowly, they worked their way up the hill. Ayrion slipped more than once as he attempted to walk backward, not keeping a close eye on his foot placement. Each time, the wagon would slip farther back, forcing him to crawl back to his feet and pull all the harder. The horses were struggling, but the snow seemed to lock their hooves into place, giving them a surer grip. Before he knew it, they'd reached the top, and the old green-and-gold wagon rolled to a stop.

Ayrion had to raise his hand to shield his eyes from the late afternoon sun shining in from the opening on the left. He was standing at the back of a large plateau, surrounded on three sides by rock. He could see the tops of several peaks branching out around them, signaling they were nearing the uppermost pinnacle of this particular chain.

His eyes had barely had time to adjust when he found himself surrounded by a group of armed men, covered in fur and growling like a pack of wild animals. Several had spears, some bows, a few had axes. All were pointed at him. One thing to say for Upper Wellhollow: They certainly knew how to throw a proper welcome.

Chapter 46 | Ayrion

HAT HAD LOOKED LIKE nothing more than walls of rock and stone at first glance was an entire community, where the dwellings had been built right into the mountainside itself. Each crook and cranny and crevice had a door or window sticking from it. There were footpaths that had been carved into the rock, leading all along the cragged surface as they wound their way up the mountainside from one dwelling to the next. There were other dwellings even farther up, but Ayrion didn't have time to stand and gawk, not while surrounded by some of the most fearsome-looking people he'd ever met.

"We mean you no harm," Tameel said, arms raised to show he carried no weapons.

"What brings you to our sacred ground?" a man said as he walked across the plateau in their direction, flanked on both sides by a personal guard. He carried a double-sided broadaxe, letting it swing from his hand as he approached. Like many others, he wore what appeared to be a bear hide for his cloak, except his bear still had its head attached, which sat atop the man like a hat, giving him the impression of being half beast. Red hair draped his shoulders, blending in with a full beard that hung halfway down his chest. The hair on his face was thick enough to braid, which was exactly what he'd done, one on either side of his cheeks. His dark-brown eyes were sharp and cunning as they scanned the wagon.

"We have come to trade," Tameel said, climbing down from his seat and walking over to greet the man, who was every bit as wide in the chest as Bek, but about fifteen to twenty years his senior, which showed in the streaks of grey that mixed with the red. "May the Great Father bless you with long life and grandchildren to sit on your knees."

The big man and his entourage stopped a few paces away, and he pointed his axe in Tameel's direction. "I see the Great Father has kept that slick tongue of yours as sharp as ever." He handed his axe to one of the men beside him and walked over and grabbed Tameel in a huge embrace, nearly picking him up off the ground. When he finally lowered Tameel back to his feet, he turned to the wagon. "Where's that enchanting beauty of yours? Hiding herself away to keep from succumbing to my charms, I take it?"

"The day I succumb to your charms will be the day they throw dirt on my face," Zynora said, stepping out from around the back of the wagon.

The man laughed and gave his long beard a good tug. "You haven't aged a day."

Zynora walked over and stood beside Tameel. "And you, Ozlin Beartooth, look and smell as vile as ever."

The man laughed again, and so did those holding Ayrion at spearpoint.

Ozlin hugged Zynora as well, lingering long enough to force her to push him away. "So, who is this?" the bear-clad man asked, pointing at Ayrion.

"My apprentice, Jair," Tameel said, and Ozlin walked over to get a good look at Ayrion, stiffening when he caught his first glimpse of Ayrion's eyes.

"Apprentice, be hanged! That man has the look of death about him." He sniffed the air. "Smells of it too." Ozlin reached back and snatched his axe back from the man who'd been carrying it.

"He's Upakan," Zynora said.

"I know what he is. I have a great respect for his kind, as long as they keep their business far from me." He pointed his axe at Ayrion. "Speak. Have you come to make trouble? If so, you've come to the wrong place." Ozlin spat off to the side, forcing Zynora to take a step back so as not to get hit. She glared, but he didn't seem to notice.

"I am not under contract," Ayrion said, keeping his hands out for everyone to see, "if that is what you're asking. Tameel and Zynora saved my life, so now I travel with them."

Ozlin thought a moment, his lips pursed under his beard. "That sounds like a story worth hearing. But I warn you," he said, raising his axe threateningly. "If you so much as look at one of my people the wrong way, I'll mount your head above my mantel."

One look in the man's eyes and Ayrion could see he meant every word. Ayrion nodded, but Ozlin kept his gaze a moment longer before finally turning back to Tameel and Zynora.

"Come! You will stay with me as my personal guests."

"We have another wagon with us at the bottom of the ravine," Tameel said. "May we have your permission to bring it up?"

Ozlin motioned for the men standing around Ayrion to lower their weapons, which they did hesitantly, then they followed their leader over to the edge of the plateau for a better look. He sent five men down to help bring the red wagon up, and Ayrion went with them so Bek didn't get the wrong impression and think he was under attack.

Before Bek had time to even warn those inside, the men had the wagon up the slope and parked alongside the other. Bek hopped down and brought Nell, Taylis, and Marissa out from the back. Everyone seemed to welcome the group quite readily, but they continued to keep their distance when it came to Ayrion, no one coming within weapon's reach. Even with his new furry coat, he blended in about as well as Ozlin would have at high court. He was starting to wonder if he actually did smell of death.

"Come," Ozlin said as he started toward one of the larger dwellings on the other side of the plateau, which overlooked the bluff.

"What about the wagons?" Tameel asked, not wanting to leave his goods behind.

"And the horses?" Ayrion added, patting Shade's neck.

"They will be seen to, I assure you," Ozlin said. "But first, we eat!"

Tameel walked around to the back of the wagon and locked it, then looked at Ayrion. "Can't be too careful."

Ayrion smiled and followed Tameel across the plateau, taking that time to get his first real look at Upper Wellhollow. He was surprised to see how high up some of the dwellings went. Each home had people standing in the doorways and windows, as everyone wanted to get a glimpse at the new visitors. Then again, they might have just been excited at the prospect of having a tinker come. No telling how often these people got the chance to purchase things from outside their community.

Several of the upper residences had balconies built to communicate back and forth with those living nearby. It was like nothing Ayrion had ever seen before. Granted, he couldn't remember what he'd seen before. Ayrion stopped with the others alongside the waist-high wall at the front of the bluff on the left of the plateau and stared out over the enormous drop. The view was breathtaking. He could see for miles. In fact, if he looked hard enough, he could even see part of Virn Run as it snaked between sections of forest in the lower foothills.

"Come, come," Ozlin said impatiently as he summoned the group away from the incredible view and walked them over to the front of his home, which sat directly off the bluff.

Ayrion brought up the rear, and behind him was the same group of men that had been there to meet him when he first arrived, all of whom were keeping a close eye on him. He was beginning to wish he'd kept his blades after all. Whoever these people were, they seemed as tough and unyielding as the mountains themselves.

Ayrion was the last one inside, pausing long enough to kick the snow from his boots on the doorstop. Inside, he was greeted by a tall thin man in a dark suit with a thick mustache that curled on the ends. His hair had more grey than red in it, except for his eyebrows, which for some reason had remained untouched by time.

"Can I take your coat, sir?" the man said, not having noticed Ayrion's eyes as of yet. The man shut the door, leaving the armed guard to stand watch on the front stoop.

Ayrion removed his coat and handed it to him, though he wished he hadn't. The inside of Ozlin's home was nearly as cold as the outside, at least until they reached the second door on the right, where Ozlin beckoned everyone to enter. Ayrion was met with a welcoming wave of heat as he reached the doorway.

"Please take a seat," their host said. "Supper will be served shortly." He turned to the tall butler who'd greeted them at the door. "Kuwa here will see to your needs. He's been with my family since he was a boy. His family has served the seat of the magistrate for generations." He clapped Kuwa on the shoulder. "Make sure they get something to drink." With that, Ozlin excused himself and slipped out of the room and down the hall.

Kuwa walked over to the corner and tossed their overcoats haphazardly on a chair off to the side, then turned back around. "I'll see to your drinks. Please," he said, motioning to the wooden sofa and chairs around the stone hearth, "make yourselves comfortable." Before anyone had time to actually sit down, Kuwa had disappeared as well.

There wasn't quite enough seating, so Ayrion stood beside the fire, noting the broad rack of antlers hanging over the hearth. Whatever they had belonged to was unlike any deer he'd ever seen. Looked more like two trees with interconnected branches running all along the trunks.

"Pretty incredible to see an entire town built right into the mountainside," Bek said, gazing around at the slate-grey stone walls, ceiling, and floor. There were several small insets along the walls, much like those they passed in the hall, each filled with a single candle to light the room. However, most of the candles in that particular room were unlit, since they already had not only the light from the fire but also from a window to the left of the hearth that overlooked the same view they had seen from the wall outside. "I'd heard of such things," Bek continued, "but never thought I'd see it for myself. I can see the appeal."

Ayrion nodded. "Completely defensible. It wouldn't matter what size army you faced, that narrow corridor leading up here would be more than enough to hold off any and all attackers. And there is no possible way to scale the cliff face." He nodded. "Yes, very secure indeed."

"Actually," Bek said, "I was just referring to the solitude."

Tameel chuckled. "It's a nice place to visit, but not to stay. Too much rock. Just give me a cozy vale, a warm fire, and a sky full of stars, and I'll die a happy man."

Bek nodded. "You're probably right. I would miss the sounds of the forest, but this is nice as well."

Zynora smiled. "Ever the pacifist."

Before anyone else had a chance to state their opinion, Kuwa returned with a tray of wooden goblets and two large wooden pitchers filled to the brim and foaming over the sides. Before pouring the drinks, he first handed Taylis and Marissa two smaller tankards. "We have fresh cream for the younger ones."

Ayrion wondered where they had gotten fresh dairy. It wasn't like they'd passed a pasture of cows on the way up. They must still trade with Lower Wellhollow.

Taylis scrunched up his face. "This milk tastes funny."

"It's goat milk," Kuwa said. "Very good for you."

Marissa didn't seem all that bothered by it, nearly downing half her glass in one gulp. She lifted her head with a smile, revealing a white smear across her upper lip, which she tried to lick away before going in for her next swallow.

Ayrion accepted his tankard, resigned to merely sipping the rather strong ale as opposed to gulping it down as Tameel was doing. Not caring all that much for the taste, Ayrion placed the tankard on the stone mantel above the hearth and let it sit.

"I hope you have healthy appetites," Ozlin said, patting his midriff as he walked back into the room. "I've told the cook to prepare extra." He noticed all the seats had been filled, so he walked over to the chair holding their coats and tossed them on the floor, then dragged the chair over to the front of the hearth and sat down. "How long's it been?" he asked Tameel and Zynora, who were seated between him and the sofa that Bek and Nell were presently occupying. Taylis and Marissa were over in front of the window, staring out at the surrounding mountains.

Tameel leaned forward, shifting the fur hide over the back of his seat far enough to see that the chair had been crafted from pieces of antler. "At least two cycles."

"Three," Zynora clarified.

"Too many," Ozlin said, picking at his teeth with one of the claws from his bearskin coat. "Don't hear much from the outside world apart from your visits."

"Count that a blessing," Bek said, drawing Ozlin's attention.

"You don't seem much of a tinker to me. Where are you from?"

"Belvin. Well, what's left of it."

"Left of it?" Ozlin stared at Bek a moment, then looked at Tameel and Zynora, waiting on someone to explain. But before they got the chance, a woman about Ozlin's age, with thick wavy hair every bit as red as Ozlin's and with just as many grey streaks, stepped into the room. She wore a dress made of heavy wool and hides, along with fur slippers that reminded Ayrion of Bek's zabatas. "Dinner's served, my dear."

Ozlin hopped to his feet. "To be continued in the next room," he said as he ushered everyone out the door, down the hall, and into another room, where a table had been set and waiting. Ayrion took his seat somewhere in the middle, while Ozlin's wife took hers at the far end, opposite the magistrate.

"This is Hanani," Ozlin said, motioning to the other end of the table. "Mistress of this house."

Ayrion echoed the others' sentiments in relaying his pleasure at making her acquaintance.

She smiled as she scanned the table, stopping when she came to Ayrion. "You brought an Upaka into our house, husband? Have you lost your mind?" She reached for the knife beside her plate.

Ozlin chuckled nervously, looking more embarrassed than anything. "He has given me his word he will cause no trouble."

"And you trust the word of an assassin?"

Ozlin looked at his wife. "My dear, if he wanted us dead, I have no doubt we would already be so. Besides, the tinkers have vouched for him, which is good enough for me."

Hanani might have released her grip on the dinner knife, but her face said she would be keeping an eye on him while he was there. Ayrion wished he had a better way to disguise his heritage, or better yet, change everyone's perception about his people. Hanani studied his eyes a moment. "I've never met one of your people before. Is it true you are trained to fight from birth?"

Ayrion smiled at the thought of training an infant to fight as it lay there on its back, blowing bubbles from its mouth and sucking on its toes. "We are trained from a very early age." At least that was what Tameel and Zynora had told him.

Hanani nodded slowly. "Is it true the Upaka live completely underground?"

"It is." Again, another piece of information learned secondhand.

"Sounds both intriguing and exhilarating. It appears our peoples have at least one thing in common. Neither of us cares much to involve ourselves in the woes of common society."

"Yes," Ozlin butted in. "We were just discussing some of those troubles. But before we continue . . ." He raised his hands and clapped them together twice. "Bring in the food."

A man and a woman appeared in the doorway carrying trays of meat with stewed potatoes, vegetables, and several loaves of dark bread. They set the food down across the table for those gathered to serve themselves, then disappeared out the door.

"We don't stand on ceremony here," Ozlin said, leaning forward with his belt knife to stab a large cut of meat from off the platter nearest him. He flopped it on his plate and started for the next dish over. The others followed suit, dishing out their own helpings and passing it on to the next. By the time all of the dishes had made it around the table at least once, Ozlin was already eyeing the meat platter for his second helping.

Ayrion found the meat somewhat tough but flavorful. It was a little spicier than he was used to, but appetizing nonetheless, warming his insides as it went down. The potatoes were exceptionally good. They had been stewed in a butter sauce mixed with juices from the meat. He found he enjoyed dabbing at the juice with his bread, then folding some of his meat inside. It was by far one of the better meals they'd eaten in some time.

"Now, you were discussing Belvin, I believe," Ozlin said, his mouth full and his beard catching the overflow. "Something about what was left of it? Care to elaborate?"

Bek took a small swallow from his goblet. "Yes, well, that is quite a long story." For the rest of the meal and quite some time afterward, they discussed the recent events in Belvin and what had ultimately led to Bek and Nell leaving their home. It was a tale so incredible that both Ozlin and Hanani let the food on their plates grow cold as they sat and listened.

They started with the tragic events that had taken place at the rover camp, careful not to go into too much detail with Taylis and Marissa sitting there, then they moved on to explain the arrival of the vulraak and Argon. They told of the raising of their army and their stand in Belvin, finishing with the creatures' eventual death inside the mines.

"I have no doubt the White Tower had something to do with it," Tameel said. "Their hands seem to be in everything nowadays. With the old king now dead, the Tower grows even more powerful, spreading itself as it never has before. This new king is barely a shadow of his father. A spoiled whelp if you ask me, more interested in himself than those he professes to rule. There's hardly a place left in Aldor to travel that hasn't been influenced by the Tower. The Black Watch is everywhere."

"Yes," Ozlin interrupted. "Our spies tell us that the white riders have been seen below. No doubt brought here to take our lands from us. Few from the White Tower have stepped foot in Upper Wellhollow. Those that did took the quick way down." There was no need to guess what he meant by the *quick way*.

"They claimed to be looking for wielders," Ayrion said. "But I got the impression they were looking for something specific."

Ozlin passed his wife a troubled look. "You don't think . . .?"

She nodded. "They're here for the oracle."

"What oracle?" Zynora asked. "You've never mentioned anything about a seer living here."

"She is sacred to our people."

Hanani leaned forward, concern on her face. "We need to find out what she knows, Ozlin."

Ozlin wiped the loose crumbs from his beard. "She doesn't like to be disturbed."

"It seems it can't be helped. If they are here for her—"

"If they're here for her, she'll likely already know."

Hanani glared at him from across the table.

"Fine," he said, throwing his hands in the air and slinging bits of meat and potato from the cuffs of his sleeves along with them. "We'll pay her a visit tomorrow."

Hanani crossed her arms. "You'll pay her a visit tonight."

Ozlin's lips tightened, his face hard, but under his wife's unyielding gaze, he finally caved. "Fine, we'll go tonight." He shook his head. "I don't know why I put up with you."

She smiled. "As if you had a choice."

With that, he stuffed a potato in his mouth and began to chew.

Chapter 47 | Ayrion

B Y THE TIME THEY finished their dessert and collected their coats, the sun had already set, and the stars were beginning to dot the sky.

"I'll stay with the children," Hanani said. "No need for them to go."

"What?" Ozlin stopped just inside the front room doorway and turned. He looked ready to chew stone. "This was your idea! And you aren't even planning on going?"

"Why?" Hanani pooched her lips. "Are you frightened of the little old woman?"

Ozlin cleared his throat, his cheeks turning as red as his hair. "No. But she likes you better than she does me. You remember what happened the last time I went to see her."

Hanani chuckled. "Yes, that was a very disturbing vision, indeed."

Ozlin hmphed and walked out of the room. "Well, are you coming?" he said as he headed down the hall toward the front door, Kuwa chasing after him. "Let's get this over with."

Ayrion threw on his coat and followed the others out.

Nell opted to stay with the children and keep Hanani company. It was clear by the look she gave Bek that she had no desire to learn their future. After what had been done to her in Belvin, it was no wonder.

The sky was clear, and the stars looked close enough to pluck. The earlier wind had died down since the onset of evening, but the occasional moan could be heard moving through the upper peaks and down to circle the plateau. Torches lined the outer walls between dwellings, lighting the way as Ozlin led them toward the back-left corner, where they found a couple of guards standing in front of what looked like a hollow in the rock.

"We have come to see the oracle."

"She's already expecting you, Magistrate," the guard on the left said with a hint of a smile around the corners of his mouth.

Ozlin shuddered and shifted his bear hide up higher on his shoulders. "I hate it when she does that."

"Leave your weapons," the sentry said. "They are not permitted beyond this point."

Ayrion waited to see what the others would do, but as soon as Ozlin gave them the nod and unhooked his battle-axe, he removed his sword and belt knife, leaving them propped against the outside wall with the others.

Ozlin nodded for them to follow. "Guess we shouldn't keep Her *Highness* waiting," he said, then grabbed a torch from the rack just inside the opening and started into the mountain.

Tameel and Zynora were next in after Ozlin, then Bek, followed closely by Ayrion.

The tunnel ahead was wrapped in darkness, lit only by Ozlin's torch as it wound its way farther into the mountainside. Ayrion thought it a very dismal place to live.

"Where does this lead?" Tameel asked. "We've never been in here before."

Ozlin stopped. "This place is sacred. It was entrusted to my people many generations ago, and we were sworn to its protection."

"Protection from what?" Bek asked.

Ozlin tugged on his beard and eventually shrugged. "Don't rightly know."

"And what, pray tell, are you protecting?" Zynora chimed in, looking every bit as anxious to see what lay ahead as the rest.

Ozlin smiled like he had some great secret to tell. "You shall see. Come."

"I thought we were going to see an oracle."

"We are."

"Why is it so dark?"

"She prefers it that way."

Zynora didn't respond further. She did, however, give Tameel a curious look.

The scuff of their boots on the hard stone followed them as they wound their way deeper into the mountain's throat. Ayrion was beginning to wonder how far in they were going to have to go before they reached their destination, when Ozlin finally brought them to a halt not far from the opening of a small cavern. The only light inside was the spillover from Ozlin's torch, and a cooking fire on the far right that wasn't even big enough to light its corner of the room.

Ayrion moved out from behind Ozlin to get a better look, but Ozlin kept blinding Ayrion with his torch as he waved it about to get a better look himself. The constant flicker of the light in front of his face left Ayrion temporarily blinded, much the same way it would if he stared at the sun for any short period of time.

"What are you waiting for, Ozlin Beartooth?" an aged voice called out from somewhere on the right. "I can smell you from here."

Ozlin gritted his teeth and turned to whisper to the others. "I told you the old cave bat didn't like me."

"This is where the oracle lives?" Tameel asked, trying to peer into the large empty chamber. "I can't see a thing."

Bek took a step forward beside Ayrion to try peering into the darkness. "I'm getting a nervous feeling about this place. Wondering if maybe leaving our weapons wasn't the best idea after all."

Ayrion nodded, then wiggled his right boot to make sure he could still feel the knife inside.

"We have news," Ozlin all but shouted from the tunnel.

"Then by all means stop lingering in my doorway and step inside and present it. If you force me to carry these rickety bones over to you, I'll be sure to see something exceptionally awful in your next viewing."

"We're coming, we're coming," he grunted, waving the others along.

Once inside, the torchlight was all that Ayrion needed to get a good view of the place, barren as it was. It looked like any other small cavern he'd ever seen, nothing but solid rock, apart from the tunnel they'd just exited and a second opening directly across the way. It was too dark to see where it led. A smattering of simple furniture gave the stone chamber a slight homey feel. A table with two chairs sat on the right, and behind them was a bed with a small end table filled with books.

Several rugs lined the floor around the bed and table, creating a makeshift pathway around the cavern that ran from the bed to the table and from the table to the small pit on the right side of the room, where half-baked embers lay smoldering inside. There was also a line of rugs leading from one tunnel to the other.

Ayrion wondered how the old woman kept herself fed, but then he spotted a large basket on the other side of the table with some bread and cheese poking out from between a cloth.

On the far side of the bed sat a rocking chair with several piles of books stacked against the wall behind it. The oracle was sitting in the rocker, her legs covered with a long quilt, her white hair hanging out from underneath a fur hat all the way down to where her arms rested comfortably in her lap. She appeared to be looking in their direction. Her skin was well aged, her eyes gaunt to the point of seeing the sockets, but she wore a keen sort of grin as she waited for them to approach.

Ozlin stopped about five feet from the rocker and cleared his throat. "Should I tell you our news, or would I be wasting my breath?"

"If you are so inclined as to warm my den by expelling some of that hot air, then by all means, please do so."

Ozlin tightened his grip on the torch. Ayrion was surprised it hadn't been thrown at the rocker yet for all the goading the old woman seemed to be giving the magistrate. He wondered what sort of bad blood had passed between them to cause such animosity. Then again, he'd seen Tameel and Zynora do the same on many an occasion, except their petty bickering was more a sign of endearment than actual hostility.

"The Black Watch have been spotted in Lower Wellhollow."

"Yes," she said, "but they have been here before, so it's not so uncommon."

"True, but they seem to be here with purpose." He paused and looked at the others.

"Well, spit it out," she scolded. "You believe they are here for me?"

"The thought had crossed my mind." He waited for her to answer, but when she didn't, he added, "Have you seen anything?"

"I have seen a great many things. It's hard to know what is relevant to right now and what is still yet to come."

"Should we prepare for battle?"

The oracle rocked in her seat for a moment, the wooden legs creaking under her weight. "I have seen the arrival of the white riders, but I can't be certain why they've come. The images tend to blur together. What is for certain is that their arrival signals great change. Whether it's a beginning or an ending, I do not know. The future is uncertain to me. I see a great many paths that lead to a great many outcomes. Some for the better, others . . ." She didn't need to continue. "We are living in dangerous times, and I believe our little community will play a pivotal role in what's to come."

Ozlin grunted. "I don't much care for the sound of that. Rather ominous."

"More than you know."

The room grew quiet as everyone pondered the oracle's words. Even though no tangible details had been divulged, the overall sentiment left Ayrion feeling like he'd stepped in it again. Someone up there really had it out for him. Was there nowhere he could escape what appeared to be a very dismal fate?

Ozlin shrugged it off and turned. "I have brought some visitors. They have traveled a great distance to be here."

"I was wondering how long it would take you to introduce them." She motioned Ayrion and the others forward. "Come. Don't be shy. I won't bite—hard." She smiled, purposefully baring her teeth.

Ozlin held up the light as they made their way across the rugs and over to where the old woman sat. Her clothes were made of wool and very plain, not so much for looks as for warmth.

Tameel hesitated, but Zynora pulled on his arm, and he stumbled forward. "My name is Tameel," he said, his voice shaking notably, "and this is my wife, Zynora. We are of the—"

"Dar'Rhivanni," the oracle finished. "Yes, I can hear it in your voice." She smiled once again, this time not so menacingly. "My name is Angioma, keeper of the Hall of Record, guardian of the Doors of Light."

Tameel looked at Zynora, then for no apparent reason, waved his hand in front of the old woman's face. Ayrion shifted to get a better look.

"Yes," she said. "I am quite blind. A consequence of overuse of magic, I'm afraid. I pushed the boundaries of my gift in my youth, and it pushed back."

From where Ayrion had been standing behind the others, he hadn't noticed the film over Angioma's eyes, or the way they never seemed to look directly at who she was addressing, but now that he was closer, it became more evident. Suddenly, things around the stone chamber began to make sense: the layout of the rugs as a way for her to direct herself to where she needed to go, a path of sorts to navigate the cave; the lack of candles or lighting of any type. What was the point in wasting good wax when you couldn't enjoy the benefit? He did find himself wondering about the stacks of books along the back wall. Perhaps it was from, as she said, her youth.

"What are these Doors of Light you speak of?" Tameel asked before the oracle could give them their viewing, earning him a reproaching elbow from Zynora.

Angioma smiled and grabbed her cane, which was leaning against the left arm of the chair. Before she stood, she turned to Ozlin, or in the general direction of where he was standing. "Be a dear, Magistrate, and grab my amulet from the stand beside my bed, would you?"

Ozlin walked over and lifted a chain necklace with something attached at the bottom. He carried it over and placed it in her outstretched hand. She took a moment to feel around the emblem at the bottom. Finding the side she was looking for, she hung it around her neck. The amulet was gold plated and fashioned into the shape of an eye. At its center was a large crystal. Ayrion wondered if it had any significance to her gifts as an oracle, or whether it was merely symbolic of being a seer.

Angioma stood from her seat and tapped her way across the rugs with the bottom of her cane. Ayrion, along with the others, was quick to move out of her way as she passed.

Ozlin slid in behind her, holding out his torch as if she needed it to see where she was going. "Are you taking them to see it?" he asked.

"Yes."

Ozlin turned and smiled at the others. "You asked what it was we protect. You are about to see."

Angioma followed her rugs past her bed and nightstand before working her way around the table and chairs. She stumbled over the wicker basket that was lying behind the table, and Ozlin quickly caught her before she toppled all the way. She turned and hit it with her cane, smashing the top of one of the loaves sticking out. "Curse you to the Pits!" She pointed in the general direction of the basket and tapped Ozlin on the arm. "Be a dear, won't you?" She shook her head as Ozlin scooped up the basket and stuck it on the table. "No matter how many times I tell them, they never listen. Place your gifts on the table. Don't leave them on the floor." She hmphed as she started forward once more. "I swear, sometimes I think they are trying to get rid of me."

"If we were only so lucky," Ozlin grumbled.

Angioma ignored him and followed the rugs to the center of the room, and from there left toward the tunnel at the back. This new tunnel was roughly the same size as the one they had arrived through, and they followed it deeper into the mountain. Ayrion wondered how much farther they could go before they came out the other side.

The pace was slow, as it was set by Angioma, her legs growing shakier by the moment. She stumbled but caught her balance. Ayrion thought Ozlin was going to have to carry her, but she never stopped, and eventually they reached the end, which turned out to be another cavern, this one larger than the one she was living in. Ozlin held out his torch, and the light barely reached halfway across. The chamber seemed empty at first, apart from an enormous set of stone doors on the far-right side of the cave and two waist-high troughs of oil that ran down the outer walls from the tunnel to the doors.

"Wait here," Ozlin said as he walked over and stuck his torch inside the trough on the right wall. The fire ignited and ran down the right wall, stopping at the side of the stone doors. He then walked over and lit the second trough on the left side, and it did the same, stopping just left of the doors. By the time he returned, the entire cavern was aglow, letting Ayrion see firsthand that it wasn't nearly as bare as he had originally believed.

The walls held a vast array of artwork, entire scenes chiseled into the rock, with rows of indecipherable writing between each. The light from the troughs sent shadows dancing across the sculpted figures, tricking the eye into believing they were actually moving.

"This is the Hall of Record," Angioma said, swiping her arm in a circle, causing Ozlin to duck or get hit in the face. "The ancient text. This is our people's legacy."

"It's incredible," Bek said, staring wide-eyed up at the giant murals sculpted into the stone. "Never seen anything like them." He stared at the ancient text surrounding the murals. "What does it say?"

The others turned and looked at Angioma as she stopped for a moment and looked upward, as if studying the depictions herself. "No flaming idea."

Ayrion almost laughed. He was liking the old woman more and more. She certainly didn't have any qualms with speaking her mind. Regardless of whether the oracle understood what the inscriptions said or not, Bek was right: they were extraordinary.

"And that right there," Ozlin said, pointing to the far side of the chamber with his torch, "is Harok Laos. The Doors of Light."

They all stopped what they were previously looking at to gawk at the enormous stone archway.

"Where does it lead?" Zynora asked.

The oracle shrugged. "Wish I knew."

Ayrion turned from looking at the doors to study the walls. Some of the murals that caught his early attention were that of winged beasts with people riding atop them, while others had ships without sails that appeared to be floating through clouds. There were depictions of great battles, one in particular showing an enormous circle of robed individuals surrounding some sort of mist, a dark cloud that reminded Ayrion of Argon in a way. Ayrion couldn't read the inscriptions around the scene, but the next image in line showed that same mist being locked away underground in what Ayrion could only describe as the Pits of Aran'gal."

"The Defiler's final defeat," Zynora said, walking over to get a look at the sculpted artwork. "This seems to be a history of some sort."

"Yes," Angioma said, leaning against Ozlin's arm as they stood near the entrance. "That is what we have come to conclude. Please," she said, motioning them over to the side. "If you will, I will give you each a viewing." Ozlin helped her over to a jut of rock on the left of the tunnel opening, wide enough for her to sit on and rest her legs.

Bek was the closest, but he kept back, allowing Zynora and Tameel to go ahead of him.

Angioma held out her hands. "Come, place your hands in mine."

Tameel and Zynora stopped in front of the oracle, and each of them placed a single hand in hers. Ayrion stood to the side with Bek and watched. Her eyes opened, but instead of a filmy glaze, they had turned pure white, even more so than his own eyes, as though she had no irises at all. Her breathing grew raspy and her head shifted back and forth as though observing something the others could not see.

Finally, after what felt like a very long, uncomfortable moment, she released a heavy sigh, keeping a tight grip on their hands. "Your viewing is unlike any I have seen thus far. It's as though it is yet undetermined. So many images. So many possible conclusions that will affect more than just your lives."

She paused, and Tameel looked at Zynora. She carried the same perplexed look as Tameel.

"Most of those I see are simple viewings," Angioma continued, "their lives lived out as you would expect. Some continue until they are too old to stand, others taken much sooner than they would like. There's love, marriage, children, grandchildren, with joy and sadness along the way. However, your paths are very much intertwined. The fate of one will be shared by the other."

"I wouldn't have it any other way," Zynora said, bringing a soft smile to Tameel's cheeks as she reached out and took his other hand in hers.

"I also see great hardship and pain. Your journey is fraught with danger."

"Tell us something we don't already know," Tameel said jokingly.

"One wrong step along the way could lead to ruin. You walk a fine line. But your lives are not your own, they are entangled with another." They both turned and looked at Ayrion at the same time. "This union will be your greatest triumph and your greatest sorrow." Their faces darkened as they turned back around, and she released their hands.

"That's it?" Tameel asked. "Seems a bit depressing if you ask me."

Angioma chuckled. "Yes, that tends to be the case more often than not lately. I will leave you with these words of encouragement: as long as you remain together, you may yet make it through."

Tameel and Zynora stepped aside to let Bek have his turn, walking over to converse quietly with themselves on the other side of the tunnel. Bek looked a bit peaked, his face whiter than normal as he took a deep gulp and stepped forward, placing one of his huge hands in hers. Her fingers barely wrapped around half, but she maintained a steady grip nonetheless. Again, her eyes went pale and her breathing slowed as her gift took over and she was overcome by her visions. After a moment, she released a heavy exhale as though she'd been holding her breath through the entire vision. Perhaps she had.

"Yours is much the same as the last. Undetermined. You, too, share a great fate, dark as it may be. I see cloaks of white bathed in red, a pair of hatchets looking for their master. Your path is also inexplicably linked with the others. Pull the wrong thread and the weave might collapse. Your strength does you justice, but it can also be your undoing. Don't be afraid to listen to the counsel of others, no matter who they may be."

She released his hand, and he walked away scratching his head. Ayrion couldn't help but agree. Some of what the old woman said made sense, other parts, not in the least.

"Who's next?" Angioma asked, her hands outstretched, waiting for Ayrion.

"I'm not sure I want to know my fate," Ayrion said.

Angioma smiled. "Then you are a wise man, or perhaps a fool, depending on the reasons."

"Do you believe our fates are set? That there is no way to change them?"

Angioma lowered her hands into her lap. "I believe the Creator has a plan, but that doesn't mean I don't believe in free choice. I could wallop you upside the head with my cane and say that it was the Creator's plan so you have no cause to be upset with me. Or I could choose to believe that I have been given the right to make my own choices and be willing to live with the consequences of what might happen after I conk you a good one." She smiled. "But I have a feeling that isn't exactly what you're asking."

Ayrion shook his head, forgetting she couldn't see.

"Personally, I believe there is a plan for our lives; whether we seek it out or it's dropped on us remains to be seen. However, I also believe that we, out of our own pride or greed or cowardice, can stray from that plan to the point that the Creator is forced to take it from us and give it to another. To say that the Creator needs any of us to work His will is hubris indeed. Not every man or woman born into this world is meant for greatness. Most are happy to simply go about living their lives in peace. Those are the ones who tend to have the greatest flexibility in their choices.

"Nevertheless, there are those who play a much larger role, those whose decisions can ripple outward, sending a wave so large it can wash away entire kingdoms. Those are the ones whose choices tend to be less flexible, as the hand of the Creator guides them in the right direction, if they allow."

"So how do you know which is the correct path to take? You say that your visions are indeterminate, the outcomes constantly changing. How do we know we are making the right choices?"

"By sticking to a righteous path and trusting He'll not lead you astray."

"And if you don't know if you believe in the Creator?"

Angioma laughed, and it came out as more of a cackle, which led to a hoarse coughing. "Then I would say you haven't opened your eyes." She held out her hands once more. "Are you ready to see what I have to show you?"

Ayrion looked at the others, but they were little help, all too preoccupied by what they had been shown. In the end, he stepped forward and placed his hands in hers.

Her head snapped back so hard he thought she'd broken her neck. Ozlin leaped forward to grab her, afraid she would send herself off the rock, but she held him back, her strength greater than Ayrion realized. "You!" Her head lowered slowly, those same two pure white eyes looking straight at him, or perhaps straight through him.

Ayrion tried to jerk his hands away, but her grip was too strong, her fingernails digging into his palms, blood pooling at the centers. He was so startled he barely felt it. He could feel a connection between them, a link he hadn't expected. It was a tingling sensation that ran from his hands, through his arms, and into his chest. Had the same thing happened to the others when she read them?

"I know you, Ayrion, son of the night. Death walks in your shadow. You have haunted my dreams since I was a child. Our fates are intertwined, you and I, which means my end is near."

"What are you saying, Oracle?" Ozlin looked at Ayrion and started to reach for his axe, but then he remembered it wasn't there. He raised his torch to clobber Ayrion over the head, but Bek managed to grab the man by the arms and pull him back.

"He will not harm her, I assure you," Bek said.

Angioma ignored the others and continued, still caught within her trance. "I see an underground city in need of saving, something dark and ancient lurking just beneath. I see a black horse riding at the front of an enumerable host, its rider carrying a set of twin blades. I see those long passed, returning. I see a queen with a broken heart. The name Guardian Protector is rightly given, one it seems is forever branded into the fiber of your soul."

Ayrion's head was reeling from the onslaught of information, but there was only one question he needed an answer to. "My memories. Will I find them? Will they return?"

She released his hands and slumped forward.

Ozlin, who had finally jerked out of Bek's grip, rushed to the old woman's side.

"It is unclear," she said, still panting from the experience. She turned to Ozlin. "I must rest." She reached up and grabbed the magistrate's arm. "Take me back."

Ozlin put his arm around the old woman and gently helped her back through the tunnel, leaving the others to stand quietly where they were, contemplating what had just taken place.

"What do you think she meant by hatchets looking for their master?" Bek asked.

Tameel shook his head slowly. "I wonder what she meant by our union being our greatest triumph and our greatest sorrow."

Zynora placed her hand on her husband's arm. "Best not think about it. It will give your head a good hurting."

Ayrion barely heard their discussions. All he could think about was her reaction when she had touched him. She had told him that he would be her end. What had she meant? Was she saying that he would be responsible for her death?" A prickling sensation rose in the back of his mind, telling him that the answer to that question would find him sooner rather than later.

Chapter 48 | Valtor

ALTOR HURRIED THROUGH the never-ending number of corridors in the upper tower, his wolf-head staff clicking away on the stone tiles beneath his feet. He was running late for a scheduled meeting with Dakaran back in Aramoor, and he still, as of yet, had to prepare for the weekly banquet with the Elondrian Senate that evening. It was a gluttonous waste of time and gold that could certainly have been put to better use, like filling the Tower's coffers. Unfortunately, at this point, they still needed the Senate's sway, as they were the ruling body of lawmakers for the kingdom. It would require their participation to see that the correct types of laws were being introduced, laws that would benefit the Tower's plans.

Thankfully, as with most people in power, they tended to want to stay that way, which meant setting their own ambitions over that of the people they were supposed to represent. Valtor was always amazed at how easily an aristocrat could be persuaded to his point of view. A favor here, a favor there, and he would have them voting in step with whatever he desired.

Unfortunately, there were still a few idealists within the ruling class who could not be persuaded to use such tactics, forcing Valtor to find alternative methods. If bribery wouldn't work, there was always blackmail, and if there wasn't enough to use for blackmail, then an unmarked missive threatening the lives of their family typically did the job.

Thankfully, those still holding out for the people were few and far between. It seemed with the death of the late king that the true colors of the ruling class were now being flown, their own lust for power and wealth guiding their decisions his way.

Up ahead, voices could be heard just around the next bend. It sounded like laughter. He wondered why anyone would be this far away from the common areas. There wasn't anything in the upper levels that would have required anyone's presence, which was why he had chosen this spot for his second mirror. Valtor rounded the corner to find several grey-robed trainees surrounding someone they had backed against the wall. Valtor couldn't see who it was, as the others were blocking his view.

"Go on, toad face," a young man said, shoving the person hard against the wall. "Croak for us." The group laughed.

Valtor stood back, watching the scene unfold, curious as to who these new recruits were hazing. Whoever it was, if they couldn't learn to stand up for themselves now, then they were useless to him.

"What's wrong, a faerie got your tongue?" the same man said mockingly.

"Look," a young woman said, pointing to their victim, "you've made the freak cry." She started laughing, as did the others, and suddenly three of the six flew backward across the hall and slammed into the wall on the other side, giving Valtor his first glimpse of who they were hazing. *Rowen?*

The recruits scrambled to their feet, joining the other three, who had already thrown Rowen up against the wall with magic of their own.

The first young man wiped blood from his mouth after he punched Rowen in the gut. "Not so tough now, are you?"

Rowen dropped to his knees. Rowen was no stranger to magic and could have defended himself in a fairer fight, but when facing six-to-one odds, Valtor's young apprentice was hardly up for that kind of challenge.

Tears streaked Rowen's deformed cheeks as the young man looked between his attackers' legs and saw Valtor standing at the corner.

"Master, help."

"He can't hear you," another boy said and kicked Rowen in the side while he was down.

Valtor's knuckles whitened around his staff, and he conjured a wall of hardened air and hit the entire group of trainees with it from the front, flinging them backward against the wall on the other side of the corridor. Before they could even turn to see who had attacked them, Valtor unleashed a bolt of flame so strong he actually watched the flesh melt from their bones. Their screams lasted only a moment, and by the time the echoes had faded, the only thing left were several piles of smoldering flesh and melted cloth, along with the rather unpleasant smell of overcooked meat.

By the time he made it halfway down the hallway, his crippled apprentice had pulled himself back to his feet. Rowen looked as though he were going to hug him at first, but thankfully he didn't, and instead walked over to admire what remained of the trainees' corpses.

"It's time I taught you how to defend yourself," Valtor said. His apprentice had spent countless hours watching Valtor in his study, gleaning off the ideas of how magic worked, but so far, he'd never put it into practice, and Valtor couldn't be around to protect him every moment of every day. "For now, best you stay away from the new inductees. The bulradoer know not to bother you, but these new recruits are too stupid to care."

Rowen nodded eagerly, a hungry gleam in his eye at the thought of being trained himself.

"We'll set up a schedule sometime next week."

"Where are you going?" Rowen asked. "Can I come?"

Valtor shook his head. "I'm meeting with Dakaran. Remember to stay away from the grey robes, and if you ever see any of them wandering about where they shouldn't be, let me know."

"Yes, Master." He bowed and limped off down the corridor in the opposite direction.

Valtor stared after him for a moment, a sense of sadness overtaking him as he contemplated his apprentice's disease. So far, he'd been unable to find anything that resembled a cure. If the growth continued to spread, he wasn't sure how much longer Rowen had.

Gathering his robes, he swiftly made his way down the hallway, taking another empty stairwell up three levels and making his way to the hidden room with the traveling mirror. He shut the door to the room, locking it behind him, then walked over to stand in front of the ancient frame. "*Nothleen Filaurel. Galaerion Sugethru.*"

The mirror shifted, sparking to life as his reflection disappeared, replaced by an image of his chambers in the royal palace in Aramoor. There didn't appear to be anyone in the room, so he stepped through. He turned and watched the image on the other side disappear, replaced once more with his reflection.

He studied the man looking at him for a moment. He almost didn't recognize the older face staring back: his gaunt features, pale leathery skin, dark circles surrounding sunken eyes. His black hair looked almost out of place, white being more fitting for a face that aged. He flung the dusty canvas lying on the floor back over the mirror and started for the door.

He really needed to hurry.

Leaving his chambers without so much as stopping to catch his breath, Valtor made his way down from the top of his lonely tower near the back of the palace and passed through dozens of winding corridors until finally reaching the grand veranda leading down to the main hall. Like the Tower, he wished he had some mirrors set up throughout the widely spread labyrinth to avoid walking such great distances. By the time he got to his next destination, his feet and legs were already cramping.

"Where've you been?" Dakaran shouted from across the foyer, waving a goblet in one hand as he sat on a cushioned settee near the front entrance. The goblet was no doubt nearly empty by now.

Valtor waited to answer until he reached the lower landing and had made it halfway across the checkered marble tiles. "I beg Your Majesty's forgiveness. I was unavoidably detained with affairs of state."

"What affairs? I'm the *head* of state, those affairs should have been made known to me first."

Valtor bowed, more to give show for those standing around than for any real gesture of deference. He kept one hand on his staff and the other on his mitre to keep it from tipping off his head as he straightened. "The affairs I was referring to were in reference to the banquet for this evening. Last-minute preparations."

"I see." Dakaran looked less than satisfied with Valtor's excuse as he stood. "And is everything in order?"

"Of course," Valtor said with a reassuring grin. "Nothing to worry about."

Dakaran straightened his crown, his stylish blue cape hanging clear to his feet. It was trimmed at the bottom and top with the exotic fur of a white snow leopard, making Valtor's velvet archchancellor robes pale in comparison. "I hate these constant processions," Dakaran griped. "Can't we stay in today? I have a lot to prepare before the feast tonight. Do you know how difficult it can be to find the right outfit?"

"Your people need to see you, Your Majesty. They need to think that their king is alive and well and working on their behalf."

"Who cares what they think? I'm the king. Why should I be expected to parade myself around like the prize bull at a village auction?"

"Appearances, Your Majesty. It's all about appearances." He motioned toward the doors. "Shall we?"

Dakaran released an exasperated swell of air, then marched over to the entrance, which was opened by three guards before he arrived, allowing him to walk through without slowing. The king's golden carriage sat waiting at the bottom of the steps with an entire regiment of mounted Black Watch guards in procession. The long line of horsemen stretched in a circle around the entire inner courtyard fountain and partway under the tunnel overhang leading to the outer bailey.

Valtor waited for Dakaran to climb into the open carriage and situate his cape before climbing in himself, where he spent some time adjusting his own clothing so that it wouldn't wrinkle under him. He placed his wolf-head staff against the seat beside him. "It's a beautiful day for a drive, don't you think, Your Majesty?"

Dakaran raised his glass in mock salute. "Let's get on with it."

Valtor nodded at the driver, and the convoy started forward. They rode under the tunnel opening leading to the bailey, then through the main gates and across the bridge that spanned the merging of the Shemoa River and the Bay of Torrin. Valtor stared out at the sparkling waters in the bay as they passed, the wind beating hard enough for him to snatch at his mitre before it flew off. It was a cumbersome article of clothing to have to wear outside, but he did appreciate the way it stood erect on his head, signifying his status as the respected head of the White Tower.

Ahead, people stood on both sides of King's Way West, watching as a couple of trumpeters near the front of the parade announced the king's arrival. The people clapped as the carriage drove by, prompted by the armed men in white uniforms who stood behind them.

Dakaran waved occasionally, doing his best to maintain a polite smile, which was more than what the majority of Aramoor's citizens seemed capable of as they scowled and sneered and glared at the king and Valtor as they passed. Thankfully, Dakaran was too enamored with his drink to notice. The only attendees who appeared sincere in their efforts were the Cylmarans, whose numbers were increasing by the day after they had opened the borders between the two kingdoms in an effort to expand Elondrian territory. As soon as the patrols along the border had been recalled, the gates of Aramoor had been flooded.

The Cylmarans were fairly easy to spot. Besides their plain, threadbare clothing, they had an olive complexion, not as dark as those of the Blue Isles, but certainly enough to stand out from the rather pasty nature of those living within Aramoor.

Periodically, Valtor spotted a blue-caped member of the Aramoor patroller's office within the crowd, looking no more enthused about the king's arrival than the rest of the people. Valtor was going to have to replace them like he had the High Guard and the Elondrian Lancers. With the might of the lancers now beholden to him and not the crown, he no longer had to worry about the throne and its former threat to keep the Tower in line.

They reached the eastern gate and stopped. "While we are here, Your Majesty," Valtor said, "I thought we could do an inspection of the wall. It always seemed to lift your spirits in the past." In truth, Valtor rather enjoyed his visits to the wall as well. Rarely did he get the chance to view the city from such a height, to look down across the vast network of buildings and streets that he would one day control. That time was in the not-too-distant future.

Dakaran leaned back and stared up at the enormous white stones as they rose into the sky overhead. They were too close to the wall to even see the top. "I guess it wouldn't hurt to take a quick look." And before Valtor could get to his feet, Dakaran was out of the carriage and heading straight for one of the lifts.

Valtor followed him over, though not quite so eagerly, climbing up the stairs to the waiting platform, where a couple of loaders held the front gate open for them to enter. They bowed deeply as they did, never once looking higher than the men's chests.

"Your Majesty. Your Grace."

Valtor nodded to the men, acknowledging their regard, even though they never looked high enough to notice. Once aboard, they were accompanied by several of their armed patrol. The Tower's guards nearly started a brawl right there on the steps of the lift as they fought to see who the first ones on would be. They would have all packed aboard if the head haulers hadn't stopped them, allowing for only five to enter, as the platform could only hold so much weight. Those that didn't make it grumbled as they walked back down the steps to watch from the ground.

"Here, Your Grace," one of the haulers at the back said, holding out a rope to Valtor. "I will need to tie this on for your safety, if you will permit."

Valtor nodded, but since the man wouldn't look him in the eyes, he had to resort to a verbal affirmation. "Proceed."

"Nonsense," Dakaran stated near the front, drawing Valtor's attention away from the rope being tied around his waist. "If you don't need a support, then neither do I."

"But, Your Majesty, it is required of all passengers," the lead hauler stated rather uneasily. "It is for your safety."

"If you're not wearing one, then I don't see why I should either."

The man looked at the other haulers a moment and nodded. "Fine. Then we will secure ourselves as well."

Dakaran wasn't pleased, but he did finally allow them to tie one of the ropes around his waist. Although he insisted it be under his cape, as he didn't want to blemish the fur.

Valtor left the king to his grumbling and took a seat on a small stack of crates in the middle of the platform, having no desire to stand near the edge as they were lifted. Magic was a wonderful thing, but magic couldn't help him if he were to tumble over the side, not from the height they were about to travel to. Looking up, all he could see were the wooden braces that hung out over the top of the wall to hold the ropes and pulley. They were hardly a speck in the sky from where he was sitting, making his stomach queasy, as he knew what they were about to do.

Dakaran, on the other hand, seemed to enjoy tempting fate when it came to getting a better view. He stood near the front, moving back only far enough to allow the haulers room to shut the gate, and then he was back at the edge once more.

"Take care, Your Majesty," Valtor said. "One wrong move and you will go down in history as having the shortest reign of any Aldoran king. Not something you would wish to be remembered for."

Dakaran took a single step back from the rail, but no more. At least he didn't bring his cup with him, Valtor mused. Valtor had noticed that even though Dakaran's goblets seemed a staple of his outfits, the king didn't seem to drain them quite as fast as he used to. In fact, it seemed to take more and more of Valtor's magic to sway the young ruler in the direction Valtor wanted him to go.

Dakaran's drunkenness had always been both a blessing and a curse. However, Valtor was finding he almost preferred the tipsy Dakaran to the more clearheaded one. This newer Dakaran tended to have more opinions. He wasn't sure what had brought on the change, but he had a feeling it had something to do with the Queen Mother's first lady-in-waiting. He didn't like the influence Amarysia held over the king, and he would have to find a way to deal with it.

The huge ropes overhead, hanging down from the pulley mechanism that connected with all four sides of the platform, suddenly went taut, and the platform jerked, causing Valtor to grab hold of one of the ropes beside him that secured a stack of crates on his left. "Going up!" one of the haulers shouted, and the platform was lifted off its base and started its ascent.

Valtor clutched his staff in one hand and rope in the other. He hated this part. If it wasn't such a hard climb, he would have preferred to reach the top through the circular stairwell at the guard station. It wound its way up to the top by means of hundreds of steps, reminding him, in a way, of the White Tower and its central stairwell. Needless to say, the stairs were rarely used, most opting for the lifts if they were available.

The first time Valtor had ever visited the wall, he'd taken one look at the rising platform and promptly decided to take the stairs. However, the stairwell was so tight that he found himself feeling more than a little anxious, to the point of needing to be helped the rest of the way up. It was an embarrassment he didn't plan to repeat, so from then on, nerves or not, he took the lifts.

The wind was cold and sharp as it beat across Valtor's face, forcing him to conjure a small barrier of hardened air directly in front of his head just to keep his teeth from chattering. Thankfully, that type of conjuring was such that wouldn't be spotted by anyone other than another wielder.

Dakaran seemed unaffected by the harsh breeze as he stood as close to the edge as he dared and looked down. He chatted with several of the haulers, who appeared nervous at their king's insistence of enjoying the closer view. As entertaining as it would have been to watch the young king plummet over the side, the crown would most likely be passed to the Queen Mother, and that was something Valtor could not take the chance of happening. So, unbeknownst to Dakaran or anyone else on the lift, Valtor conjured a barrier just off the front-right corner where the king was standing, just in case he happened to slip.

The buildings across the street dropped from view as the lift continued to rise. Valtor spared another glimpse up toward the top and quickly changed his mind, as everything began to spin, the lift having not even reached the halfway mark. Taking a deep breath, he contented himself with reading the labels on the barrels beside him and imagining what madness the city had encountered to have forced the wizards to create such a protective barrier as this.

Most of the containers around him seemed to be either food provisions for those on watch or stockpiles of weaponry, which were kept in the many storage spaces built along the wall's fortifications. They were supplies that would most likely never see use, as it had been centuries since Aramoor's last invasion. Those guarding the wall, however, took their jobs very seriously. The city watchers were one of the last vestiges of military personnel that had not yet been replaced by the Tower's guards. They tended to think of themselves as a separate unit from the Elondrian Lancers, and even had a separate chain of command, one that Valtor needed the king to get rid of.

About halfway up, Valtor spared a quick glance out at the city, having already memorized nearly every container label within eyesight. They were already well above most of the buildings, except for perhaps the four large towers just north of the merchant district, near the Elondrian Senate Hall. The size of the city was breathtaking. Several of the upper rooms in the palace towers held grand views of the city as well, but none compared to the wall.

The higher up they went, the stronger the wind became, rocking the platform slightly as it swayed in the breeze, causing Valtor's stomach to turn as his hands tightened on the ropes. His body tensed with each new rock. Near the top, a particularly strong gust hit the side and shifted the platform enough to slide the boxes Valtor was sitting on forward several inches.

Valtor yelped, his shields collapsing as he dug his heels desperately into the platform to keep from sliding farther. In front of him, Dakaran lost his balance and stumbled forward. He hollered as he hit the railing, but before he went over, a couple of the haulers grabbed him and yanked him backward onto the floor.

The king's guard, those not clinging to the rope for dear life, jumped into action and pulled the king out from under the haulers and dragged him back toward the middle of the platform, planting him firmly on a box not too far from Valtor. Valtor was still too shaken to say anything as he held his chest and panted.

"That was quite the excitement," Dakaran stated, his face pale, but with a sliver of delight in his eyes. He reached behind him and felt for the rope. "Good thing we had them tie us off, aye?"

Valtor managed a stiff nod, still trying to catch his breath from where his stomach had leapt into his throat. He didn't look up again, keeping his eyes on the planks beneath his feet until they came to a complete stop. Valtor released a heavy sigh of relief as the lead hauler behind them opened the back gate. "Watch your step as you exit," the man said, lending a hand to those getting off.

Dakaran was the first one to take that offer, just as soon as they managed to untie his harness. There was a slight gap between where the platform ended and the wall began, easy enough to trip on if you weren't careful, so Valtor grabbed the lead hauler's arm when it was offered and stepped off, using his staff for balance.

His legs were shaking as they headed down a short walkway from the loading platform to the wall itself. The men and women on both sides—both guards and those managing the winches—moved when they saw who was coming. They bowed as the two passed, not quite so deeply for Valtor as for Dakaran, but enough that he didn't take offense. Then again, his attention had been too diverted by the ride up to care. After that experience, Valtor was actually contemplating taking the stairs.

One of the watchers, who bore a captain's insignia on the sleeve of his uniform, rushed over, looking more than a little confused. "Your Majesty. We weren't told of your coming, or we would have organized a more formal reception."

The man was at least twenty years Dakaran's senior and stood half a head taller, with streaks of grey in his chestnut hair and beard. He had a strong chin, sharp green narrow-set eyes, and a wide forehead that made his receding hair look even more pronounced. His uniform, as with the uniforms worn by most of those on the wall, was neatly pressed, unlike that of the Black Watch, who seemed to be less worried about appearances and more worried about what they would spend their pay on at week's end.

Dakaran waved the captain off. "If it makes you feel any better, I wasn't told of it either."

Valtor didn't miss the sharp edge to Dakaran's statement, or the passing glance over his right shoulder in Valtor's direction.

"I'm not here on any official inspection, Captain," Dakaran continued, "so please, go about your business as though we were never here."

The captain bowed, but he was hardly going to leave the king unattended, so he and a small group of watchers followed closely behind. They kept far enough back from the Black Watch guards to not appear obtrusive, but close enough to be there if the king had a request. Valtor wished the Tower's guards were half as attentive, but when your ranks were filled with men whose sole reason for being there was either gold or the chance at staining their blades red, it was hard to expect too much.

Valtor followed Dakaran over to one of the guard stations on the right that overlooked Aramoor. There was a small platform that led up to the top of the turret, where the watchers could stand for the best vantage point between the crenelation. Valtor walked up the steps and stood beside the king, looking out over the royal city. It was no wonder that Aramoor and its wall were considered one of the great marvels of the world.

The city was enormous. Valtor could see all the way across to the bay and the white spires rising from the top of the palace on the other side of the Shemoa River. The palace looked even bigger from this distance now that he could take it all in at once. To the left, he could see all the way to the old city and beyond, to the deep-blue waters of the Rhunarin Ocean, which filled most of the horizon.

He turned his attention back to the city proper, taking a few moments to name off the different individual districts, from the northern lumbermill to the old city, which the Warrens had confiscated for themselves.

As obtrusive as the Warrens were, they served their purpose. Where else would the nobility find disreputables to hire to do their dirty work, the kind of jobs they didn't want their good names sullied with? Hypocrites, the lot of them. But even the aristocracy had their usefulness at times, seeing as how they controlled most of the wealth and power in Elondria. Valtor squeezed his staff. The political ruling elite believed that because of their station in life, they had been given a type of divine right to rule over the likes of all others, and most of them acted accordingly, their own laws and regulations not applying to themselves.

These fools, who had never worked an honest day in their life but had grown wealthy either because of family birthright or off the backs of others, had no idea what true power was. For all their conniving and scheming, they couldn't see past the ends of their noses, too worried about maintaining their station to see what was really going on below the surface. This was something that could be exploited.

Valtor, on the other hand, had worked for everything he had, and one of these days, after he had milked the overindulgent Elondrian lords and ladies for all they were worth, he would be sure they received their just rewards.

"What is that?"

Valtor turned, noticing for the first time that Dakaran was no longer standing beside him. In fact, Valtor was quite alone on his turret, apart from two watchers that stood at the bottom of the steps. They each nodded as he passed, unlike the full bending of the waist they had been giving Dakaran. Somehow that little gesture was enough to make him grit his teeth. It was petty, he knew, but it showed their lack of respect for his office over that of the king. Just another item on the list of things he would eventually set right.

Dakaran stood atop another turret behind him, overlooking the opposite side of the wall. In the distance were the rolling foothills of the Sandrethin Mountains, and on the left, the meandering waters of the Tansian River as it flowed down out of the mountains, straight through the city, before finally merging with the Bay of Torrin.

"What is Your Majesty looking at?" Valtor asked as he moved alongside Dakaran and leaned out over the wall to get a better look at what had the king so enthralled.

"Explain that," Dakaran asked, pointing down to a vast array of makeshift shelters and canvas bivouacs that spread outward from the eastern gates, all along the road for nearly half a mile. Dakaran had barely stepped foot outside the palace since returning from the Battle of Belbridge, let alone left the city itself, so he had no idea what was taking place outside his small sphere of influence, which consisted mostly of his mother, the ladies-in-waiting, Valtor, and his cupbearer.

"Those are Cylmarans, Your Majesty."

"Cylmarans?" Dakaran continued to stare down at the growing community of hovels that clung to the eastern wall like a swollen tick. "What are they doing here?"

"Ever since we opened our western border, they've been flocking to Aramoor by the droves."

Dakaran studied the ramshackle dwellings below. "That's a lot of people."

"There are even more inside the walls."

"But why Aramoor?"

"Because they see you as their de facto leader and expect you to provide for them."

"Can't they provide for themselves? I'm not wasting Aramoor's resources on another kingdom's outcasts."

Valtor was confused. "That's why you proposed the new citizenry tax to be levied on all those living and working within Elondria, as a way to help provide for the newcomers."

A spark of recognition finally ignited in the king's eyes. "Yes, well, I didn't realize there would be so many."

"Look at this as an opportunity, Your Majesty."

"Opportunity for what? To impoverish the kingdom?"

"To expand the Elondrian territories. Think about the fealty these people will bestow upon you if you were to show them even the smallest amount of kindness. They're poor; it's not like they need much. But in return, their numbers are growing, and loyalty like that can't be measured in currency. Their support could prove valuable in the near future." Valtor almost cringed at his own words and how similar they made him appear to the aristocracy.

"And how are we supposed to help them? Our coffers aren't exactly overflowing."

Valtor smiled, as it was the perfect segue to a topic he'd been meaning to discuss with Dakaran for the last couple of weeks, and the sole purpose of bringing him to the wall in the first place. "I believe we should look into increasing the citizenry tax and using part of that funding to build stable housing for those outside the walls. Something more than the canvas tents and wooden shanties they are using now." Besides, Valtor could use the rest as a buffer for the White Tower to shore up their funding now that the expansion had really begun to take off.

The White Tower might be filled with magic, but until it learned how to create gold from rock, it still operated on currency, of which theirs was sorely lacking what with the heavy increase in new recruits. The Black Watch was a necessary part of the Tower's future protection, but that protection didn't come cheap. They relied almost completely on funds from the crown to stay afloat, and those funds were quickly running dry. Valtor needed more, and the only way that could happen would be through taxation. It wasn't like the Tower had a way to generate funds themselves without consorting to thievery or their own form of taxation, which would only ensure the people of Aldor would rise up against them.

No. For now, it was best to remain as much in the shadows as possible, slowly working their way into a position of power so entrenched that there would be no way of it being usurped. And when the time was right, there would be no one left to stop what he had planned. But until that day arrived, Valtor would need to continue to play the humble advisor.

He looked down at the tumbledown dwellings and shook his head. "If we don't do something, I doubt half of them will survive the winter."

"Seems like that's their problem."

Valtor filtered more of his magic into Dakaran, attempting to shift his attitude more toward the empathetic. "Which could turn out to be your solution. I've learned the hard way to never let a bad situation go unused. Besides," he said, stepping back away from the edge, "I'm sure we can find a way to put them to good use. Imagine the labor force that could be spun from such a horde."

"And what possible labor could these wretches provide? Most Cylmarans are uneducated and unskilled. They hardly seem of quality merchant stock."

"Menial labor, Your Majesty. Street sweepers. Dung haulers. They can be placed in charge of the city's refuse." Valtor had some other ideas in mind as well, but nothing that he could mention—a horde of fresh bodies to be exploited for his experimentation, for one. Unwanted people that no one would miss.

"And I suppose you want me to convince the Senate this evening during our festivities?"

Valtor rolled his shoulders with a faint hint of a smile. "I'm sure a word here or there from their king would go a long way toward making it happen."

Dakaran grunted, not looking quite as convinced as Valtor would have liked. At least he didn't continue to argue the point as he stepped away from the edge and started down the steps and back toward the lift. Valtor tightened his grip on his staff when he thought about stepping back on that swinging platform.

"Did Your Majesty care to tour any of the guard stations or weapons caches?" the watcher captain asked as Dakaran and Valtor passed.

Dakaran shook his head. "No. I believe we've seen enough. Everything seems to be in order. Thank you, Captain."

The watcher bowed once more. "It was my pleasure, Your Majesty."

Valtor followed Dakaran down the walkway to the lift, but before stepping on, he demanded they go ahead and tie the rope around his waist. It wasn't much, but at least it made him feel a little more secure. He then retook his seat in the middle, this time sitting directly on the platform, as all the crates and barrels had been offloaded already.

"All aboard?" the same lead hauler called out behind him, and Valtor clutched his wolf-head staff, which was now lying across his lap. The sound of the back gate being shut echoed off the wall just before the platform shuddered and began to lower. Valtor closed his eyes and focused on the banquet ahead, and how the senators would react to another increase in taxes.

Chapter 49 | Dakaran

AKARAN TOSSED HIS CLOAK on the bed and walked over to the hearth and sank into the plush cushioned seat in front of the fire. Beside him was a short table empty of all but his goblet and a newly poured pitcher of Bristonian red. He preferred the white, as it had a sweeter taste, but the red tended to leave him a little more lucid. He filled the goblet halfway but left it untouched as he pondered which outfit to wear for the evening's events.

He wondered what colors Amarysia would be wearing for the banquet so he could dress accordingly, but since he wasn't exactly privy to that information, he decided to stick with the blue that he'd already chosen for that day, since it was the color of her eyes, and she tended to wear it more often than not.

He relaxed farther into the chair, finally taking a sip of the wine as he let the warmth of the flames melt away the tension in his back from where he'd wrenched it in his near fall off the lift. The wine was bittersweet, enticing him to take another, but he denied his fancies and placed the goblet back on the table. He wanted Amarysia to see him strong tonight, and not the way he got after overindulging, which was something he had done quite a lot of when Ayrion had been around. But with the street rat finally out of the picture, he felt like he had a fresh start on life, a chance to do things differently.

He stared into the fire and imagined Amarysia staring back with those bright blue eyes, the kind of eyes he could get lost in and never wish to be found. She'd been distant of late, even more distant since Ayrion's passing, never around when he went looking, almost as though purposefully sequestering herself away. He admitted his earlier attempts at wooing her had gone afoul, partly because she hadn't gotten over her obsession with Ayrion, but also because his approach had been all wrong. He knew that now. She wasn't like the other women he'd fancied. She didn't seem to find his dominance all that pleasing or desirable. She didn't even care for the title, something he certainly wasn't used to.

He needed to try a different approach.

A knock on the door jolted him out of his daydreaming. "Enter," he shouted from across the room, and Witler, the master of the robes, stuck his head inside.

"Are you ready for your fitting tonight, Your Majesty?"

Dakaran yawned. "What time is it?"

"Close to sixth bell, I believe." Witler was an older man, with well-groomed grey hair that hung straight to the shoulders and then curled inward toward the neck. His back might be bent with age and his failing eyes forcing him to continually adjust the spectacles on the tip of his nose, but Dakaran wouldn't have traded him for anyone. The man had been dressing him since he was a child and knew precisely which direction Dakaran's taste tended to lean.

"That late?" Dakaran waved the man in as he stood and walked over to the three-piece mirror that stood beside his dressing room. Behind him, several attendants were ushered in through the front door along with Witler and made a line straight for the fitting room, where they lit several lanterns and began digging through the king's rather vast wardrobe. "I want blue," Dakaran said as he studied himself in the mirror.

"I will see to everything, Your Majesty," Witler declared as he clapped his hands at his attendants, encouraging them to hurry, nodding his head in agreement or shaking it in disagreement as each one carried out a separate item of clothing to be inspected. Soon enough, the attendants were removing Dakaran's clothes and preparing him for his evening engagement.

His regimental grooming took longer than he expected, since he spent a good deal of time arguing with Witler as to the appropriate color of doublet that would offset his cape without proving too flamboyant or distracting. They eventually settled on a decorative white with gold trim and buttons. By the time he'd made it out the door to where a procession of Royal Guard stood waiting, it was nearly seventh bell.

The white-uniformed members of the Black Watch escorted Dakaran from his chambers down to the main hall, which had been three days in the preparation for his guests. In fact, it seemed that was all the palace staff ever prepared for. These co-weekly banquets had at first proven rather fun, much more entertaining than the ones his father had hosted, which had been few and far between, but now they were growing tedious, as it seemed that each one had a hidden agenda. Valtor had encouraged him to pamper the senators as best he could. He would need their support if he had any hope of seeing the changes he wished to take place.

The Royal Guard marched to the beat of its own drums, one barely in step with the other. There were times he wished he hadn't disbanded the High Guard so hastily. For all of Ayrion's faults, Dakaran could say this for him: Ayrion had known how to whip his men into shape. They had been the most elite fighting force in Elondria, probably in all of Aldor, but as dedicated as they had been to their job, their dedication had been to Ayrion, first and foremost, and that was something Dakaran couldn't allow.

The Black Watch, though rowdy, unscrupulous, and loyal only to the point that they received their gold, were also Dakaran's safest choice. And yet sadly, right now, he'd never felt more unsafe in his life.

Servants in the halls stopped and bowed as the procession made its way through the numerous corridors and stairwells, finally reaching the main hall, where several couples stood waiting outside a set of gold inlay doors for the announcer to present them. Dakaran waited until the last had been heralded before approaching. Inside, he could see the tables were filled, each elaborately decorated with floral wreaths, table runners, and candelabras, interspersed between crystal chalices and gold cutlery. A quartet of trumpeters standing to either side of the doors sounded a fanfare, and those seated around the tables stood and turned, applauding the king as he entered the great chamber and proceeded around to the head table.

Valtor was already there, standing in front of his seat just left of Dakaran's, with that ugly staff of his leaning against the back. His mother and Amarysia were there as well. He spotted Amarysia's gown, and his countenance fell. It was *green*. Walking up the steps, he stifled his disappointment with a pleasant smile in her direction as he passed. Blue or not, she still looked radiant. He even stopped long enough to offer his mother a kiss on the cheek.

She flinched.

What was that about? He took his place and lifted his hands, signaling the orchestra to halt their playing. "Please, be seated." With help from two of the ushers, he sat, and the music commenced. The guests waited until the king was fully down before sitting themselves, a light rumble of conversation once more filling the room as they sipped on their drinks and casually peppered each other with the latest gossip while waiting for the first course to arrive.

As wearisome as these meetings had become, Dakaran preferred holding his assemblies in the palace as opposed to the cold, stuffy chambers of the Elondrian

Senate Hall. He found the senators to be much more agreeable to his point of view with a leg of lamb in one hand and a glass of wine in the other, especially when that point of view had something to do with the collection of gold. The Senate had been less than enthused with his last proclamation of additional aid to the White Tower through taxation, or of his suggestion of a citizenry tax. It wasn't until Valtor had assuaged the senators' fears by announcing that they themselves would be given waiver from such taxes that they had finally agreed.

At least, most had.

There were still a few who were adamantly opposed to such a tax. Thankfully, their numbers were seemingly few, at least those bold enough to be outspoken about it. Looking around the room, he noticed several of those same senators were not in attendance. In fact, over the last couple of meetings, he'd noticed more and more of their seats remaining empty. Had they taken ill, or were they showing their opposition by not attending his banquets? He would have to remember to speak to Valtor about this when he got the chance.

"How was your outing this afternoon?" his mother asked, not sounding quite her jovial self. Dakaran attributed it to her having another one of her spells. Ever since news of his father's death, his mother had been inconsolable. He had thought she was finally pulling out of it when, for no apparent reason, she suddenly had a reversal. So much so that he was finding it hard for her to even look at him. If he didn't know better, he would have thought she knew something about his father's death.

But that was impossible.

"I saw the carriage leave from one of the library windows," she added.

His mother tended to frequent the library more than just about any other room in the palace, even more so since his father's passing. There were times he thought she must be sleeping there, since she had been spotted entering and exiting the stacks at all hours of the night. He wondered what had her so engrossed.

"We rode to the eastern gate today and took one of the lifts up to the top."

Valtor coughed at the mention of the lift and promptly dabbed his mouth, as he had been in the process of taking a sip from his goblet at the time.

"It has been a while since I've been up there," his mother said. "Not since . . ." Her face tightened, and Amarysia laid her hand on his mother's and smiled. His mother nodded and gently patted Amarysia's in return. "I'm fine." She looked at Dakaran. "Perhaps you can let me know the next time you visit the wall, so I may accompany you."

He gave her a puzzled look, but then smiled. "That would be nice."

Dakaran leaned forward to catch Amarysia's eye. "That is a lovely gown. Have you worn it before? I don't believe I recognize the make." It was a deep forest green, but unlike most gowns that hung from the neck down, this one wrapped around her body like swaddling on a child. There were bands at the elbows where the sleeves widened outward toward the hands, and the material was covered in an array of delicately stitched designs. It certainly hugged her body in all the right places, making it all the more difficult to keep his eyes from lingering.

"Thank you, Your Majesty," she said with a notable lack of fawning looks and batting lashes he would have normally expected from a woman he had just complimented. In fact, she didn't appear overly pleased with his praise at all. She simply looked composed. He wished he could read her better, but her eyes were stoic and didn't give away anything of how she felt. "I don't wear it all that often," she added, "but when the Queen Mother suggested green for this evening, I pulled it out."

"Ah, well, you should wear it more often. It certainly does you justice." He smiled, not knowing what else to say, and the ensuing awkward silence was thankfully ended by the arrival of the first course—a very thin chowder with bits of fish, crab, and shrimp. Very tasty indeed. He spent several minutes savoring the bisque while trying to think of another topic to raise. "Did you know there are Cylmarans building a ramshackle borough outside the eastern gates? I saw it from the wall. Quite the eyesore."

"Yes," his mother said, looking uneasy as her earlier smile for Amarysia slipped from her lips. "There seems to be more of them arriving every day, and they don't appear to be leaving."

"Valtor believes they can be used to our benefit if we'd be willing to help them."

Valtor coughed again.

"Yes, I'm sure he would," his mother said, not bothering to even look in his advisor's direction. Valtor quietly worked on his chowder, but Dakaran could tell his advisor was listening in. He was always listening in. "Using people because they are in need is hardly the way an honorable king should behave." There was a sharp edge to his mother's words that seemed to be meant for more than just Valtor. "Your father . . ." She stopped, no doubt seeing Dakaran's hand tightening on the arm of his chair.

He was sick and tired of hearing about what *his father* would or wouldn't have done. He didn't care. He was the king now, not his father. Why couldn't she see that? Why couldn't she just—

"What is it you wish to do for them?" Amarysia asked, assuaging the situation.

Dakaran took a deep breath as he felt a soothing wave of stillness wash over him, leaving him feeling much more in control, even to the point of wondering why he had gotten so incensed in the first place. "We are considering building them a more stable place to live."

"And how do you plan on doing that?" his mother asked, still clinging to her soup spoon.

Dakaran thought it an odd question. "By just . . . doing it."

"Do you plan on building homes for every poor visitor who shows up at Aramoor's gates? If so, then we are about to have a whole lot of visitors. And what about the poor who already live here? Are you going to build homes for them as well? If not, you're going to end up with a lot of very angry citizens."

"I, uh . . ." He hadn't exactly thought that far ahead.

"Are you going to start feeding them and clothing them? It won't do much good to have a shelter over their heads if they starve to death or freeze without proper clothing."

Dakaran's lips pursed. His mother was right. They would need more than a place to sleep. How much would that cost?

"And are these people going to work, or simply expect to live off our people's generosity?"

There was a notable clang on Dakaran's left as Valtor's spoon struck the side of his bowl. Why wasn't Valtor saying anything? This was his stupid idea in the first place.

"I'm sure they can find work in the city," Dakaran said, though it sounded more like a question than a statement.

"If so, then whose jobs will they be taking?"

"What do you mean?"

"If Aramoor is flooded with people and there are only so many jobs to go around, then those already living here would likely lose work for themselves, would they not?"

"I guess. I hadn't really thought about it."

"There are plenty of ways these people can be of use, Your Majesty," Valtor cut in, finally, his smile as sharp as a dagger as he leaned forward to address the Queen Mother. "Our streets are in dire need of repair, especially those in the southern districts and the Maze. We could put them to work on street crews. There are plenty of jobs that have been going by the wayside, as our own people don't have the desire to do them, jobs like street sweepers, dung haulers, and canal cleaners."

"True," his mother said, "but what is to entice them to work if you are already guaranteeing them shelter and food and clothing? In fact, when word spreads that Aramoor is offering free board to any who wish it, what's to stop every vagabond from the Wengoby Desert to the Ozrin Sea showing up on our doorstep with their hands out?"

She looked at Dakaran. "There's a reason why Aramoor disbanded such practices decades ago, although they do tend to creep back in from generation to generation. I've read through the histories and have seen the chaos that ensues with such . . . *generosity*, as you put it. I was young, but I remember when your great-great-grandfather attempted such an act, believing it would curry favor with the citizens of Elondria. Apart from nearly bankrupting the kingdom, we ended up filling Aramoor with the wrong sort of people. And when the city gets to the point that it can no longer sustain that generosity and your gold runs out, which it inevitably will, those same people grow violent as desperation takes over."

Dakaran didn't know much about his great-great-grandfather's rule or the earlier times within the city—perhaps this was the reason. "What happened?"

"What happened was that your great-great-grandfather died of consumption and passed his failed rule on to his son, your great-grandfather, who became known as the King of Blood."

"King of Blood?" He knew his great-grandfather had been a hard ruler, but he'd never heard that title before.

"By the time he took reign, the city of Aramoor had nearly collapsed in on itself, entire sections razed to the ground as mobs demanded what they believed were their just dues. The citizens of Aramoor feared for their lives, keeping indoors, no one leaving for fear of being mugged in the streets. Work came to a complete halt across the city as the looters took over. They burned down the city patroller offices, their first act before moving on to the shops. Half the merchant district was pillaged and burned, which is why they are now located on the Island instead of the western quarter where they had been."

"And how did Great-grandfather deal with the problem?"

His mother sighed, momentarily glancing down at her half-empty bowl of chowder. "He did what few kings have ever been forced to do. He unleashed the Elondrian Lancers, turning the streets of Aramoor into a battlefield. It took nearly a month to quash the rebellion and round up its perpetrators. Those that hadn't been killed fled to the Warrens. It was a very dark time in our city's history."

"If you can believe such revisionism," Valtor added with a hint of contempt. "In my experience, I've found that history tends to favor the victor." Dakaran's advisor wiped his mouth with his napkin and pushed his seat back before the ushers behind them had a chance to step forward and move it themselves. "I believe I will retire for the evening. I have a full day tomorrow and need the rest."

"But what about our discussion with the senators?" Dakaran asked. "Concerning a raise in taxes?"

Valtor passed a hesitant glance toward the Queen Mother. "It can wait."

Dakaran could almost see the little veins on the side of his advisor's head throbbing as he bowed.

"By your leave, Your Majesty?"

Dakaran nodded with a simple wave of his hand, and his advisor turned, but then stopped and looked back. "Just remember, Your Majesty: It's never wrong to help those in need." With that, Valtor left the table and exited the great hall by way of one of the side entrances.

His mother frowned. "Yes, that has been the motto behind every form of tyranny since the beginning of time. Because, honestly, who doesn't want to be seen helping people? The fact is, though, you're not helping anyone by making them dependent on you. That's called control. If you want to do something good, help them rebuild their own land."

Dakaran stirred his soup. This banquet had gone completely afoul. Was he still expected to hold a formal Senate meeting or not? He certainly had no desire to do so with his advisor having up and left, and after listening to his mother's retelling of the histories, he was definitely rethinking his earlier idea of providing shelter and goods to those outside the walls. The last thing he wanted was to bankrupt the kingdom. Perhaps a brief moratorium on the issue was in order, which would give him a little more time to consider the issue further.

His advisor had made some valid points, not the least being that if they didn't do something for the Cylmarans now, most of them wouldn't survive the winter, whether they decided to let them stay or not. And how would that make him look? Yet his mother made some very disturbing points as well, from what seemed to be Aramoor's history. But the fact was, Cylmar was no more. Their overlord had been executed, their armies vanquished, their entire kingdom left in turmoil. Even if he decided to provide temporary shelter and food, how was he to stop these people from flocking to the city in the first place? There was no way they could house an entire kingdom.

His head was beginning to ache, and without thinking, he had already grabbed his goblet and downed half the glass. The pain eased, but only slightly. As much as he had craved the idea of sitting on the throne, it was times like this when he wished the responsibility on someone else. He didn't like being the one who got blamed when things went wrong, which for him seemed almost a certainty.

At least without the extra burden of having to press the senators for more funding, he could enjoy the evening's festivities unhindered. It would be the first time in a long while that he'd been able to do so. With a wave of his hand, an army of servers rushed into the room and gathered up the bowls of chowder from the tables to make room for the next course.

Dakaran leaned back and listened to the orchestra, sparing several passing glances in Amarysia's direction as the dancers and acrobats and jugglers entertained the guests. He had a lot to consider, but it could wait. Right now, he just wanted to enjoy himself as he lifted his goblet and drained it to the last.

Chapter 50 | Ty

TY LOOKED AT THE COMPASS and then back up at the blinding sea of sand in front of them. "It says we should be going in that direction," he said, pointing just off to the right before placing the compass back in his pocket. His tongue stuck to the roof of his mouth as he fought back the urge to ask for another swallow from their nearly empty waterskin.

They had been traveling the dunes for a couple of days, after resting up inside the small mountain chamber where the traveling mirror from the underground lake had been placed. They had also spent a good deal of that time trying to scrub the lake monster's blood from their skin, using the only thing available to them—sand. It hadn't worked. The dark liquid had permanently set in, and without water or soap, they were forced to resign themselves to the fact that it wouldn't be coming off anytime soon.

The days were sweltering hot and the nights uncomfortably cold. It had only taken them half the first day to realize that traveling while the sun was up was a very bad idea, and so they waited for the sun to drop before starting back out again.

Neither was absolutely sure where they were, but it was a good guess that they were somewhere inside the Wengoby Desert. Unless, of course, there was another desert somewhere inside the Westlands that they didn't know about. The only other uncharted territory shown on any map he'd seen was that of the Frozen North, beyond the Gates of Bel'Taag, dividing the Angoran Mountains from the

Northern Heights. Ty had always wanted to visit those gates. They were said to be one of the great wonders of the world, along with the great wall of Aramoor.

From what Ty could remember of the world map he'd studied in school, the Wengoby Desert was on the outer western boundary of Aldor, separated from the mainland by the Khezrian Wall, a long mountain chain that ran from the Rhunarin Ocean up along the western border of Cylmar and Keldor before cutting farther into the Westlands.

"Ever wonder how big the Westlands really are?" Ty asked as he trudged along behind his brother, doing his best to walk the ridge of the dune to keep from sliding down either side. His sword bumped uncomfortably against his leg as he went. "The sand could go on for hundreds of miles. Who knows, maybe it goes on forever." It certainly felt that way after having spent the better part of three days crossing it without seeing so much as a blade of grass or a speck of brush. They had now traveled far enough that they could no longer see the mountains behind them. They were completely surrounded by sand.

The night sky was bright with stars, and the pale moonlight gave the dunes an almost wintery look, as though they were walking across great mounds of snow. Ty blew on his hands. He still couldn't believe that a place this hot during the day could be so cold at night. It didn't make sense.

Breen didn't say anything as he focused on the placement of his feet, leading them in the general direction of where Ty had just pointed. Breen had taken a knife to his bedroll on the first day, giving them each an equal half, which they tied over their heads to shelter against the beating sun and to shade their eyes as best they could from the occasional gusts of sand.

It was a strange feeling, stepping through a mirror and landing in a place so vastly different from where they had just been—an open sky instead of rock, sand instead of water, heat instead of cold, at least during the day.

As bad as the heat and thirst were, he preferred being able to see where they were going to the underground cavern they'd just escaped from. He didn't think anything could be as frightening as swimming out into those black waters, not knowing what was lurking underneath. He shivered just thinking about the creature that had almost eaten them.

"We can't keep going like this," Ty said. "This was a stupid idea."

"It was your idea," Breen grumbled, not bothering to turn or even slow down.

"Then you need to quit listening to me."

"The compass pointed us in this direction, so this is the direction we go."

"Yeah, but I didn't know how far it was going to take us. It's been three days, Breen. This is crazy. We're going to die of thirst before we get to wherever we're supposed to be going." Ty grabbed the back of his brother's pack. "Stop. I need a break." His legs and back ached, and his chest felt as tight as Veldon's waistcoat as he tried catching his breath.

Breen turned around, his red, sun-kissed skin plastered with sand as it clung to his sweat, especially around the hairline, lips, and neck. He looked diseased. Ty looked down at his own hands, which was the only skin showing on his arms, and found they were just as red and just as covered. At least around the areas not already marked by lake monster goo. He tried rubbing the sand off, but only managed to smear it further.

"I guess it couldn't hurt to take a small break," Breen said, glancing around at the empty dunes. "Here, help me get this off." He lowered his right shoulder, and Ty pulled down one of the straps, letting the travel pack slip from his brother's back and onto the hot sand.

Ty unhooked Breen's bow and quiver from around his own neck and dropped them on top of the travel pack just before his legs buckled and he landed in the sand beside them. He was too tired to try unstrapping his sword. His brother didn't fare much better, as he made it only halfway down before his legs gave out and he landed on the opposite side of the pack. Ty wiped his forehead with his sleeve, smearing sand from one side to the next, the grit grating on his skin. He wanted to rub his eyes, but he remembered what had happened the first time he had tried.

They'd barely made it a couple of dunes out from the rock crevice housing the next mirror when Ty thought he'd gotten some sand in his eye. He immediately tried rubbing it with his shirtsleeve, not realizing the sweaty piece of material was coated in the stuff. They wasted precious water flushing his eyes, water that they now needed to keep going.

"How long do you figure till sunrise?" Ty asked, too tired to even look up to find the moon.

Breen raised his hand over his eyes and searched the sky. "I reckon we still have a few hours left. The moon seems to rise and set fairly quickly out here." He looked behind them and out across the dunes they'd already traveled. There was nothing there but a line of footprints to mark their passing, footprints that would soon be swallowed up by the ever-shifting sand. Breen untied the waterskin from the side of their pack and jostled it. "We don't have much left. If we don't find water soon, nothing is going to make a difference."

"I don't think I can go much farther tonight," Ty said. "I'm just too exhausted."

Breen pointed to the bottom of the dune they were sitting on. "Then let's set up camp down there, between the dunes. There's not enough room up here to lie down on without sliding down the sides."

With Breen's help, Ty managed to make it back to his feet and helped his brother carry their gear down the side of the dune to the bottom, where they used their split bedroll and a couple of Breen's arrows to set up a temporary shelter from the coming sun. Ty lay beside his brother, trying not to think about how hot it was about to get and how difficult it was to sleep while lying in his own sweat. He was thankful for the sweat, however, as it meant he still had at least a little water left in him. It was when the sweating stopped that they really needed to worry.

"Breen, how long do you . . ." His brother was snoring before Ty could even finish, so he lay there on his back and stared up at the woolen blanket flapping over his head, imagining himself anywhere but there, but with the sun beating down overhead and the scorching sand underneath, it seemed almost an impossible task.

Closing his eyes, he listened to the sound of the wind as it whipped over the sides of the surrounding dunes. Unlike the light whistling it made when rustling through the leaves or the high-pitched hiss when blowing across an open field of grass, this was a deep, lonely sort of sound, a rumbling of lost souls bemoaning their fate. Very eerie and yet at the same time, somehow soothing. Before long, the weariness took over and Ty slipped into unconsciousness.

He woke to Breen shaking his arm. "What is it? Are we there?" Ty's mouth was so dry he could hardly speak, his lips blistered and cracking. It took a moment for his head to clear enough to realize where he was.

"It's time to go," Breen said, passing the waterskin to Ty as he started breaking down their flimsy shelter. "We've slept all day."

Ty felt around the bottom end of the waterskin, barely able to tell whether there was anything in it. "Have you gotten some yet?"

"Sure, just before you." The crackly sound of his brother's voice said the opposite, but Ty didn't argue. Gently, he tilted the waterskin back, keeping his tongue pressed against the opening so he didn't accidentally pour too much. As soon as he felt the warm water caress his tongue, he released for a single gulp and quickly stoppered the top. It was barely enough to even swallow, but it felt like bathing in a cool mountain spring on a hot summer day. He could almost feel his strength returning, at least until he tried to stand and ended up back on his buttocks as his feet sank into the sand and he lost his balance.

Breen pulled him back up, and Ty took a moment to get his bearings as a momentary wave of lightheadedness washed over him. "I'm fine," he said while his brother looked him over. "Just a little dizzy when first getting up." As soon as his head cleared, he turned and helped his brother undo the last of the bedding, which they tied back over their heads once more. They didn't need them so much for the sun as for the sand, as the wind would periodically whip it up around them in small cyclones.

After stuffing the last of the gear in the pack, Breen turned to Ty. "Which way?"

Ty pulled out the compass. "There," he said, pointing straight ahead. He stuffed the small instrument back into his pocket and watched his brother heft their pack. "You want me to take the pack for a while?"

"No, I got it." Ty helped him swing it over his back as he hooked his arms through the straps, and then looked at Ty. "Ready?"

"Just about." Ty strapped his sword back to his waist and hooked Breen's bow and quiver over his shoulder. From there, they started up the side of the now bluish-colored dune, the sand still warm from the day's heat as it gave way under them. It was a slow trudge up the side, but they finally reached the top and started across the ridgeline.

Ty had to admit, the trek was easier without the might of the sun beating down on their heads. The air, though cold, was easier to breathe. Ty had never seen so many stars. The entire sky was lit with them. He could see where the poets had gotten the phrase *a sea of stars* from. He wondered if it was the same with sailors out on the open water.

His mind began to drift as he thought about water. His first thoughts were of the East River and the fun he and his brother would have each summer spending their days traveling its ever-winding course. He also thought about Crystal Lake and his time spent fishing with his father, as well as the incredible boat ride he'd taken with Gilly from Meerwood all the way home. His mind then drifted to the bog waters of Reed Marsh and eventually landed on the underground lake and the monster living underneath, which was enough to startle him back to reality.

As beautiful as the stars were, they were telling his body that he should be sleeping, not slogging across a Creator-forsaken desert. He yawned, catching an unexpected mouthful of sand as another small twister, no taller than himself, swirled up behind him without him seeing. It disappeared as quickly as it had arrived, melting back into the dune under their feet and leaving him with a mouthful of sand. He spat as much of the grit out as he could and suffered the rest, since he didn't have enough saliva to even swallow.

They continued on for what felt like hours, the moon barely moving as it lit the sky. It was large enough for Ty to actually see some of the dark splotches across its surface, something he'd never seen before, at least not in such detail. He wondered what they were.

"Incredible, isn't it?" Breen said, stopping to rest his legs as he stared up at the bright milky object over their heads.

Ty smiled with a nod. "Never seen anything like it." His voice was hoarse and crackly from the lack of water. "I want to sit down, but I'm afraid if I do, I won't make it back up."

"I know the feeling. Are we still heading in the right direction? It's been a while since we looked."

Ty stuck his hand in his pocket and came out with the compass. "A little more left."

Breen nodded, and they pushed on. Ty could see his brother was having a difficult time. His pace had decreased considerably, and he seemed to be floundering whenever they hit a spot of deeper sand at the edge of the dunes. A couple of times he went down to one knee, but eventually righted himself. Ty had offered several times to carry the pack, but his brother refused, always using the same excuse that Ty needed to conserve his energy in case his magic was needed.

At this point, Ty didn't think he could light a candle, let alone wield anything useful enough to fight with, but he kept it to himself, not wanting to worry his brother any more than he already was. The nights seemed to be getting colder, their jackets barely enough to keep the chill off.

Breen stumbled once again, and Ty tried to catch him, but instead of holding his footing, Ty ended up on his back with the full weight of Breen on top of him. Breen rolled off, and neither brother spoke, both panting as they lay there, staring up at the endless stars.

"I can't keep going," Ty said. "I don't have enough strength to even turn over."

Breen grunted but didn't move, his breathing heavy as if having chased Acorn across half the front paddock. It was Acorn's favorite place to graze. The sand shifted under Ty, forming a natural cushion, and within minutes, sleep had overtaken him.

He woke exhausted, but not quite as exhausted as he had been a few hours ago. He pulled his bedroll off his face, where he had left it to keep the sand out of his eyes, and turned to find the sun creeping up over the horizon behind them, like a great cat about to pounce. It was a new day, and Ty didn't see how they would survive it.

He turned over to find his brother still lying in the same place he'd left him, on top of their pack. It didn't look like he'd even shifted positions. In fact, it didn't look like he was moving at all. Without thinking, Ty swung his arm over and hit his brother in the chest. "Breen!"

Breen shot up with a shout. "What is it?"

Ty released a heavy sigh of relief. "I thought . . . I thought you . . . never mind." He turned. "The sun is almost up. We fell asleep." He looked at the waterskin on the side of the pack. "Is there any water left? I think now might be a good time to try a little, at least enough to wet our tongues."

"I'll look." Breen's lips were blistered and chapped. Ty knew his were as well

without having to touch them. His tongue felt twice its normal size. His brother
untied the waterskin and once again felt around the bottom, then looked at Ty,
worry in his eyes.

"What's wrong?"

"Not much more than a swallow left." He looked at the dried skin for a
moment, then passed it to Ty. "Here. You drink it."

Ty shoved it away. "No. You drink it. You're the one carrying the heaviest
load. You need it more than I do. All I'm carrying is your bow and arrows."

"You're the one who has to make it out of here, not me. You're the only one
who can assemble the key and bring back the wizard fortress. I'm not even
supposed to be here, remember?" He shoved the waterskin into Ty's hands, and
Ty pushed it right back at him.

"No! You drink it. You don't think I've noticed you not taking your share?
You've been holding back. Now take it!"

"No! You—" Breen's head lifted, and his eyes went wide. "What is that?"

Ty turned, his breath catching in his throat as the horizon behind them
suddenly darkened, the sun disappearing completely from view. He stood slowly,
still holding on to the waterskin as he joined his brother in silent wonder at the
vanishing horizon. A gust of hot air struck Ty hard enough to make him stumble
backward into his brother. "It's a sandstorm."

Ty had only ever heard of such a thing. He never thought he'd actually see
one firsthand. Now that he was standing face-to-face with it, he wished he hadn't.

"Run!" Breen shouted as he lifted their pack and grabbed Ty by the arm,
yanking him up with such force that Ty lost his grip on the waterskin and it flew
down the side of the dune.

"Our water!" Ty started to turn, but Breen jerked him away.

"Leave it! It won't save us now!"

Ty held on to Breen's bow and quiver as he struggled to keep up with his
brother's longer legs. With everything they had, they plowed through the sand with
as much speed as they could muster, given their feet sank up to the ankles with
each step. Ty glanced behind him. The storm was coming fast, the wind picking
up to the point that Ty was forced to keep his hands in front of his face just to see.
Pretty soon, he wasn't going to be able to see at all.

"Breen, stop!" He grabbed his brother's pack, and Breen turned. "We can't
outrun it," he shouted just to be heard over the wind. "We need shelter."

Breen spun in a circle, but neither of them could see much more than ten feet
in front of them. "Down there. We dig in at the bottom."

Ty didn't even have time to agree before the two of them were sliding down
the side of the dune. The wall of darkness was nearly on them, maybe three dunes

back. They reached the bottom and raced for the back edge, the sand cutting his face as the wind rose to an unbearable level. Quickly, Ty helped yank the pack off his brother's back, and they dug out a hole and climbed in, throwing their blankets over their heads just as the wall of sand flew over the dune and down on top of them.

The howl of the storm was deafening. Ty could feel himself being covered as he fought to hold his blanket in place to protect his head. He just had to keep breathing. As long as he could breathe, he was okay. Breathing was everything.

The storm continued, and the weight of the sand on top of him was growing, making it harder and harder to breathe. Panic set in, but he forced himself not to give in to it. All he wanted to do was run, but he knew if he did that it would be over. Instead, he focused on his breathing, concentrating on taking small, measured breaths as he listened to the storm.

After a while, the shrilling of the wind finally began to lessen, eventually returning to a dull moan before vanishing all together.

As soon as he thought it was safe to move, he tried getting up, but the sand over him was so heavy he couldn't move. He couldn't so much as budge. Desperation set in all over again, and he started to scream. About that time, something scraped his ribs. Whatever it was, it was moving, then it slid across his back. He stopped squirming just as a hand latched onto his arm, and he was slowly lifted up out of the mound he'd been buried under.

Sunlight hit his face, and he never thought he'd be so excited to welcome its embrace. He gasped for air as he dropped to his knees beside the indention in the sand where he'd been.

"Thought I'd lost you there for a moment," Breen said, looking about as frightened as Ty as he dropped into the sand and exhaled.

"The pack!" Ty turned and started digging as fast as he could, scooping out handfuls of sand as he tried searching for their gear.

"It's fine. I've already got it." Breen's voice was barely above a hoarse whisper.

Ty stopped digging when he noticed part of the leather satchel sticking out from behind his brother. Giving over to the exhaustion, Ty collapsed back into the sand, then shot back up. "Wait! Your bow." He felt around his neck, but neither the bow nor quiver was there.

This time it was Breen who was on his feet. "Where did you last see them? Were they with you in the sand?" Before Ty could respond, Breen was digging down into the indention Ty had just emerged from.

"I had them with me. They couldn't have gotten far." Ty moved to the other side of where his brother was frantically digging and started shoveling handfuls of sand as well. That bow and quiver were nearly as precious to Breen as Ty's compass was to him.

Breen was growing more frenzied by the moment. The more he dug, the more the sand kept sliding down off the dune to fill it in.

In a last-ditch effort, Ty shoved his hand down as far in as it would go before the sand filled in the hole. "Wait! I think I feel it."

Breen turned and started digging down beside where Ty's arm was. "I got it!" Breen exclaimed, lifting out not only the black rune-marked bow but its quiver and arrows as well. He clutched them to his chest and dropped back on the sand, and Ty joined him as they stared upward at the blue sky.

The sun had risen behind them high enough to feel its heat, but not high enough yet to reach them as they lay against the front side of the dune, enjoying what little shade it afforded them. It wouldn't be long before there would be no hiding from it.

"Should we stay here and rest," Ty asked, "or try pushing on?"

They hadn't eaten in at least four days. In fact, the last real meal they'd tasted was during their stay with Tirana and the cursed village of Karpaath, just outside the Maze. Ty's stomach felt as though it was twisting in knots. It was one thing to go without eating for over half a week, but it was quite another to go without eating while swimming through underground tunnels, fighting off water monsters, and trekking across an open desert on foot. He tried licking his lips, but his tongue felt like sandstone and just opened up the blisters all over again.

When his brother didn't respond, Ty turned his head, the only part of him he had strength enough left to move. The look of sheer surrender on Breen's face as he lay there in the sand answered any question Ty had about pressing on. "Never mind. It was a stupid question." He turned back over and closed his eyes, pulling his blanket up over his face as he let the soothing sounds of the hot desert wind lull him back to sleep.

By the time he woke and pulled back the blanket, he felt worse than before he'd slept. His hands were burning, and he held them up just to make sure he wasn't somehow conjuring a flame. His hands were a deep red. He'd forgotten to cover them before falling asleep. "Great. That's all I need."

He was too exhausted to move. It didn't matter if he slept the rest of the day; he knew he didn't have enough strength left to even stand up. He turned his head to see how Breen was faring and realized his brother hadn't covered his face, which was now deep red and blistering. "Breen." His brother didn't respond. "Breen!"

Breen didn't so much as twitch. Ty couldn't tell if his chest was rising or not under his shirt. Desperately, he rolled himself over and shook his brother's arm. Breen still didn't respond.

"Breen! Wake up." Ty stuck his ear over his brother's mouth. He could hear a slight wheezing, but it was shallow and slow in coming. He looked around, but his eyes were beginning to blur as heat sickness took over.

He could barely see his own hands as the dunes began to spin around him. He managed to find Breen's bedroll and drag it up over his brother's head before collapsing beside him, his own shallow breaths growing harder to hold on to. He couldn't believe after everything they'd been through—finding their way through an impossible maze, walking through walls of fire, nearly drowning in an underwater passage, battling two ferocious monsters—they were now going to succumb to a pile of sand.

An image of the inscription in the stone flashed across his mind. STRENGTH. The one thing he was sadly lacking. So much for his magic. Little good it did him under the circumstances. It wasn't like he could conjure water, or block the sun, or invoke a feast. He almost felt ashamed at having been beaten by something as simple as the elements.

The steady moaning of the wind over the dunes pulled at his senses, tempting him with sleep, begging him to give in. He knew if he did sleep, he'd probably never awaken. But no matter how hard he tried to fight it, the pull of the desert's call was stronger. It was as though it called out to him, the voices growing louder, more distinct. He couldn't quite tell what they were saying, but . . .

Wait, there was something about those voices, something . . .

The blanket covering his face suddenly disappeared, and he fought to open his eyes, barely managing a simple squint. Everything was a blur, but it seemed as though the dunes were moving, or at least something was moving. He felt hands touching his face.

Who's there? he tried to ask, but nothing came out. Then an indistinct voice called out in a soothing sort of way as Ty felt himself being lifted.

"*Nuntaka kameedu. Nuntaka kameedu.*"

With that, Ty slipped into unconsciousness.

Chapter 51 | Ty

Y FELT SOMETHING COOL press against his forehead, and he attempted to open his eyes. They burned, and all he could see were fuzzy shapes. "Who's there?" His voice was weak, but it was at least there. "Breen?"

"Shhh," a soft voice whispered beside him. "*Benyami akoodu.* Go back to sleep." He couldn't tell who it was, other than it sounded like a woman's voice. He felt something press against his forehead once more, and the cool sensation of water poured down the sides of his face. "Sleep, young traveler. Sleep."

Ty let his eyes drift shut once more, and the darkness took him.

He woke to the sound of voices off to his right. He couldn't understand what they were saying. "Hello?" He opened his eyes, and this time they didn't hurt quite so badly as before, though they were still just as blurry. Several shapes moved over to surround him, but no matter how hard he tried, he couldn't quite tell who or what they were.

"Stubborn, this one," the same familiar woman's voice said. Other voices responded to hers, but not in any language Ty understood. "Open." He felt someone press their finger against his chin as they worked open his mouth. Next thing he knew, something that tasted like fungalwart was being poured down his throat.

He coughed and choked, spitting some of it back out. Again, the hand was there, pressing down on his jaw and pouring more of the vile stuff in his mouth, but this time the hand clamped his mouth shut, and he choked it down. As bad as it tasted, it did alleviate some of the burning in his throat. Pretty soon, he started to feel woozy, everything going blurry once more, then nothing but darkness.

There were no dreams in the darkness, no way to pass the time. In fact, no time passed at all that Ty could remember, and when he opened his eyes, he found himself completely alone. He wiped the sleep and dried tears from his eyes and turned his head, letting his eyes focus enough to see where he was. It appeared to be some sort of large tent, the front flapping in the breeze.

"Breen." He tried sitting up to get a better look and immediately heaved over the side of the bed as the nausea set in and everything spun out of control.

"*Tekima lura banitoo,*" someone said to his left, and they rushed over to hold him down and wipe his mouth. It was the same woman's voice he'd heard during his delirium. "Stay down," she said. "You are too weak to move."

She wasn't as old as he had pictured her voice to be, perhaps even his age. She had darker skin, somewhat similar to the boatmen that would journey up from southern Briston and the Blue Isles. Her hair was woven tight above her head with several strands of red cord. A single braid fell down over her shoulder, tied off with more of the same. There were white dots painted on her forehead which ran just above her brows around to the sides of her face, with several more on her cheeks up under her eyes.

She wore a gold band around her head and several more around her neck and upper arms, only noticeable because she wore a sleeveless top.

"Where's Breen?" he asked, his voice strengthening but still very weak and hoarse. "Where's my brother?"

"He rests," she said and placed a cool compress on his forehead. "Very bad shape." She stood there for a moment examining his face. Her hazel eyes were strong, but at the same time somehow comforting. She was beautiful in a unique way, unlike any other woman he'd known before. "Why do you walk our sands?" she asked, looking down at him, puzzled.

Walk our sands? His head lifted as he suddenly thought about why he was even there, and he reached for his chest but found nothing but covers. "Where is it? Where's my key?"

"Your what?"

"Where's the medallion that was hanging around my neck. Tell me you have it!"

"It is here," she said, grabbing the cord holding the two pieces of the shorlock and handing it to him.

He snatched it from her and quickly tucked it over his neck, letting it rest on his chest.

She didn't say anything for a while, just sat there staring at his awkward behavior. "Tell me. Why do you walk our sands?"

"It's a long story."

She nodded. "Good. Stories should be long. That way nothing is missing."

"I'm afraid you'll be disappointed with this story. There's not much I can tell other than to say that me and my brother are on a quest."

"Brothers? But you do not share the same look. Only the very old or very blessed have hair as you." She ran her fingers over his head. "You are very beautiful for a light skin."

"Thank you, I think."

"And what are these markings?" She ran her fingers gently down his shoulders and arms, where the growing designs of his magic had stretched just beyond his elbows.

"Another long story."

"One I would like to hear." She straightened her shoulders. "I am Princess Narendi of the Imbatoo. Who are you?"

"Princess?" He was suddenly aware of the informal way he'd been addressing her. "I . . . I am Ty of . . . of Easthaven, I guess. Are we still in Aldor?"

"You are on the boundary of the great sand sea. Home of the Imbatoo."

"Is this the Wengoby Desert?"

"Yes."

"But you live here?"

She nodded.

"Why?"

Her brows furrowed. "Because it belongs to the Imbatoo."

"It's a desert."

"It is my home." The fire in her eyes said not to push the subject further. "Where is your home?"

Ty almost laughed, trying to think how to explain. "My home is a long ways away, on the opposite side of Aldor. Do you know where the kingdom of Sidara is?"

She crossed her arms and clicked her tongue.

"Fine," he said. "My home is on the eastern side of that, on the edge of the Sidaran Forest. It's beautiful. You'd love it. Lush green trees that change colors in the fall, winding rivers, meadowlands for the cattle and sheep." The more he talked, the more he realized how much he missed it.

She shook her head. "I have never seen such things. Here, we have our beautiful dunes."

"But they're all the same, just big piles of sand."

"You know nothing of what you speak. They are alive, changing with the wind, always moving, like the Imbatoo."

Ty smiled and nodded, wanting to look agreeable. All he knew was that he never wanted to see another sand dune in his life. "Can I see my brother?"

"When he wakes. For now, you must rest and heal."

"What about our belongings?" It was the first Ty had thought about them. He reached for his pants leg and the compass and realized he was no longer wearing his trousers. In fact, he wasn't wearing anything under his blanket. Quickly, he tucked the sides up under his legs. "Where are my clothes?"

"They are no good. Better you wear that of the Imbatoo, keep you cool on the dunes."

"My compass. Where is my compass?"

"It was broken. We—"

Ty leaped from the bed, his blanket barely covering his front where he held it to his waist. "Where is it? Where's my compass? You don't understand, I have to have it."

Narendi stood with a smile on her face, giggling as she held her hand to her mouth.

"What? What's so funny? Don't you understand how important that compass is? I can't lose it."

She giggled even more.

"What?" Ty twisted his head around and realized his backside was bare. He quickly yanked the blanket sideways and wrapped it around himself like a dry cloth, almost too embarrassed to even look in her direction. "Why didn't you say something?"

"I have never seen a bottom so white before."

If it wasn't for his sunburnt skin, there was no doubt she would have seen every inch of his blushing embarrassment. Humiliation or not, he needed to find that compass. "Please tell me you still have it."

Narendi walked across the rug-strewn floor of the tent, over to the corner, where Ty could see a clump of something that he couldn't quite make out in the shadows. A few moments later, she returned with a small silver object in her palm. "Is this what you seek?"

Ty went to grab for it but nearly lost his blanket all over again.

She held it up to the light coming in from the open doorway. "See?" She pointed out, turning in a full circle. "It is broken."

"No. It's just . . ." How could he explain a compass that didn't point north? "It is very sentimental to me. It was . . . It was a gift from my grandfather." *Close enough*, Ty thought.

She held it out, and he took it about the time that several large men marched into the tent, all wearing loose flowing robes of different shades of blue. Ty gulped, realizing he was standing there half naked with their princess, and quickly stumbled back to the bed he'd been lying on. The men gathered around Narendi, each carrying a curved blade at their side.

Ty reached for his magic in case he had to defend himself, barely able to grasp it in his weakened state. "I . . . I wasn't trying to harm her," he said, his voice shaking, and this time not from dryness by the sun. "I . . . I was just getting my compass. You see?" He held up the silver instrument, but it didn't seem to make any difference.

The men looked positively frightening, even more so with their dark skin and sharp eyes, all staring directly at him. He hadn't thought about it until now, but he hoped this wasn't one of those tribes he'd read about that ate people.

All of the armed men suddenly turned toward the entrance. Standing in the doorway was a man whose size would have given his father and brother a run for their money. He wasn't quite as tall as his father and brother, but he was every bit as wide in the shoulders and arms, maybe even more so.

Like Narendi, he wore a sleeveless vest with long baggy red pants and a yellow sash. A golden bracelet was clasped around both his upper arms like Narendi, and a gold band circled his head. He, too, had several rows of white dots on his forehead and face, reminding Ty in a way of the Tallosian hunters, though these seemed more symbolic and decorative than for effect.

The man stepped into the tent, and the others bowed, even Narendi, as he made his way over to stand beside the young woman. Ty didn't move. He sat there wrapped in his blanket roll, wondering if he should simply take off running or try to talk his way out of whatever mess he'd gotten himself into.

"*Ana m toogu* Diawandy Unsala," the very large dark-skinned man said, his hand on his chest.

Ty looked at him, then at Narendi.

"He said his name is Diawandy Unsala. He is king of the Imbatoo . . . and my father."

Ty gulped again, his mouth as dry as it ever had been out on the dunes. He stood and grabbed his blanket so it didn't fall off and humiliate him further, then bowed. "I am Ty of Easthaven. And I want to thank you for helping me and my brother." He looked at Narendi to translate, which she did, and her father nodded in return before inquiring about why the two of them were out there wandering the dunes in such a state.

Ty noted the way the king kept looking at Ty's hair but attempted to ignore it as he went on to explain the same as he had with Narendi. After Narendi translated Ty's words, Diawandy sighed and shook his head, then spoke.

"You seek the treasure of the priests," Narendi translated.

"What priests?"

"The Wengoby priests. Their temple lies to the west. It is a very dangerous journey. There are few who attempt it." She clicked her tongue and shook her head.

"What?"

"There is no treasure," she said. "We try telling those who come, but they never listen. And soon enough, they are swallowed by the desert. Never see them again."

Diawandy spoke again, pointing at Ty's shoulders, and Narendi answered. "My father was inquiring about your markings, and if they symbolize your tribe."

Ty had no way to answer, so he nodded, figuring it was as easy an explanation as he could give. "Something like that."

Narendi and her father spoke some more. "My father says that you will be our guests until you are well enough to travel, and it will be up to you when you choose to go. But he says you should forget this treasure and turn back."

"I wish I could," Ty stated solemnly. "But there is more at stake here than just our lives. Far more. I don't seek treasure. I seek salvation."

Narendi hesitated a moment, then translated. Her father grew pensive as he stared at Ty, almost as though he were measuring Ty's words, or perhaps his chance at success, which by what they had told him seemed little to none. Her father finally spoke, then walked out before Narendi had a chance to translate. The other men, apparently the king's guard, left with him, leaving the two of them alone once more.

"What did he say?" Ty was curious by the way her father had looked at him.

"He said that when you are rested, *and dressed*," she added with a smirk, "he has something he wishes to show you."

Ty stood from the side of the bed. "I can get dressed now." As soon as he reached his feet, the room began to spin once more, and he sank back down onto the bed. "On second thought, a short nap might be in order after all."

Narendi walked over to the side of the bed. "Lie down." She grabbed his blanket and untied it, leaving him grasping at the edges to keep himself covered. She laughed and turned the blanket right side up and spread the bottom part over his feet, leaving him to adjust the top. She also lifted his head and fluffed the feather pillow underneath. Once finished, she looked down at him and smirked.

"What?" Ty lifted his head to see what she found so funny, afraid that something hadn't been covered. However, lifting his head brought on another wave of nausea, and he quickly lowered it back to the pillow.

"Have you thought about why your clothes are missing, or why you are no longer covered in sand?"

Ty hadn't considered it until right then, and his cheeks reddened.

"Someone had to bathe you."

Ty's mouth gaped. "Are you saying that you . . ."

She giggled and started for the front of the tent. "I will return to check on you." She grinned and walked out, closing the flaps of the tent behind her.

If Ty hadn't been embarrassed before, he certainly was now. The thought of Narendi giving him a bath while he was unconscious had him reaching for one of the pillows and throwing it over his face. But as soon as it touched his skin, he yelped and pulled it off, another reminder of why *light skins* shouldn't be wandering about the desert.

Ty closed his eyes, but sleep was slow in coming as his mind filled with images of him and his brother baking in the desert sun, and all those who had supposedly come before in search of the famed treasure. Ty wondered who these Wengoby priests were that Diawandy spoke of. Ty couldn't imagine someone setting up a temple out in the middle of a desert. He also considered what Narendi and her father had said about the journey to the temple being a dangerous one. How could it be any more dangerous than what they'd already been through? If it wasn't for the Imbatoo coming along when they did, Ty and Breen would be nothing more than rotting corpses under a pile of sand right about now.

His dreams were plagued with terrifying images of sandstorms and dry bones and a very attractive dark-skinned princess trying to take off his clothes in order to wipe him down with a wet cloth. It was all very disturbing, and Ty woke in a sweat to find Narendi sitting on the edge of his bed, wiping his forehead with a wet cloth, no doubt the reason for his strange dreams.

"Your sleep was restless. You spoke much."

"I did?" Ty was suddenly worried about what he might have said, what he might have given away about himself or his mission. "What . . . what did I say?"

She smiled. "I believe you are very beautiful too."

Ty wanted to sink into his pillow. What would Lyessa think if she ever found out that he was having dreams of another girl? He cringed. "I have to inform you that I am already pledged to another," he said, hoping that would quash any further attempt at Narendi's flirting. Of course, he and Lyessa had made no such pledge, but if it kept him out of any further embarrassment, then it was worth it. He didn't want the princess to get the wrong impression. She was intriguing, but his heart belonged to another.

"I am pledged as well."

"Oh. That's good." Ty breathed a sigh of relief.

"My father has three wives. I am of the first."

Ty gaped. *Three wives?* Why would anyone want three wives? He couldn't imagine the infighting that would cause and was glad that Aldorans only had one. His mind did briefly stray into other aspects of having three wives, but the sudden thought of three Lyessas bossing him around was enough to frighten him out of it.

He needed to change the subject, and quickly. "How is it you know my language so well?" He wondered why he hadn't asked her that before.

"We have found others over many years who search for the treasure. Some are persuaded to turn back, some even decide to remain with us," she added with a hint of encouragement. "One such man was Iridanus. In exchange for allowing him entrance into the tribe, he taught me my letters and to speak as the light skins do. We find it easier to dissuade travelers when we can openly communicate."

"You speak it very well."

She smiled, then grabbed a small bottle off the table next to his bed and uncorked the top before helping him into a sitting position and pouring a small portion into his mouth. "Drink. It will help you heal."

Ty nearly choked at the bitter flavor but managed to swallow it all with a straight face. She laid his head back on the pillow. Her skin smelled sweet. He didn't recognize the scent but found it pleasing as he lay there breathing it in.

"How do you feel?"

"Better. Not quite as dizzy. How's my brother?"

"Do not worry. His sleep is deep for him to heal."

Ty nodded. Once again, he found himself lying there staring up into her warm hazel eyes as she stared back with an overt sense of longing that made him extremely uncomfortable. She stroked his hair, something she seemed rather curious about.

"Do many of your people have such hair?"

Ty shook his head. "Only those with great age."

She leaned over, and Ty thought she was going to kiss him, but instead she examined the white strands further, even plucking one and holding it up to the light. "It is not painted?"

"Painted? Why would I paint my hair?"

She stared at him a moment as she sat on the edge of the bed. "You will stay with us, and I will be your first."

Ty gulped. "My first what?"

"Your first wife. We will be bonded, so you can't leave."

Ty sat up, his blanket dropping to his waist. At this point, he hardly cared. "I cannot be your husband. I have a quest I must fulfill. I cannot stay. Besides, I told you, I have already given my heart to another."

"You can give it to me too. Do you not think me beautiful?"

"No. I mean, yes. I mean . . . It doesn't matter what I think. I have to leave, or a lot of people are going to die." He reached out and took her hand. "I think you are very pretty, and if the situation were different . . ." He shook his head. "But it's not."

She pulled her hand away and stood. "You will change your mind. A princess does not pledge herself at will. It is a great honor for me to choose you."

"You don't even know me. I could be a very bad person."

"But you are not."

"How do you know? We've only just met."

"I've looked into your eyes, and I know." And before Ty could try to think of anything to say to counter her ridiculous comment, she left.

Ty hoped Breen's healing was swift, because they were going to need to get out of there as soon as possible before Ty found himself unintentionally married.

Chapter 52 | Ty

TY SLEPT THROUGH THE rest of the day, still unable to get out of bed without everything spinning. He couldn't believe how sick he'd been, how close to death. He did manage to wake the next morning to find things had calmed. Rather, he didn't feel like retching whenever he sat up. In fact, he managed to find the strength to have a walk about the tent, mostly to look for something to wear, but also to check their gear to see if anything was missing.

Surprisingly, other than the waterskin they'd lost during the storm, everything seemed to be there. Most importantly, Breen's Sol Ghati bow and arrows were still there.

"That is a very fine weapon," a voice said behind him, causing Ty to jump. He set the bow down and turned.

Narendi stood in the entranceway. She was wearing another one of her sleeveless tops, this one purple with a long, flowing skirt about the color of the dunes outside. She still bore the gold bands around her arms and neck and head, but instead of her hair being pulled up with red bands and a single braid, it hung loose around her shoulders in dozens of tiny wound locks, making her appear even more alluring, which Ty reckoned was exactly what she had intended.

He did his best not to act like he had noticed. "It's my brother's. He and my father are the archers in the family."

She nodded. "That is the news I came to tell you. Your brother is awake and requests to see you. Took three men to hold him down." She chuckled. "You should hurry before he tears the tent apart."

Ty started for the front flaps without even noticing he was still wearing nothing but his blanket. "My clothes?"

"They are being cleaned. We have other clothes."

"How soon will I get them back?" Ty wanted to be ready to leave as soon as possible, especially with the Imbatoo princess wanting him to stay.

"Your clothes are no good here."

"But I'm not always going to be here." Ty hmphed, almost throwing his hands in the air in frustration, but he remembered they were holding up his blanket.

"Here," she said, walking over to a pile of blue material lying on one of the rugs in front of his bed. Ty had thought them to be extra sheets. "Wear these."

He carried the folded material over to the bed and laid them on top, picking up what he believed were the bottoms. It was hard to tell. The material was just as wide as the other piece. He turned it over and held it up to Narendi. "How do they go on? Are these the bottoms or the top?"

Narendi sighed and clicked her tongue as she walked over to where Ty was flipping the item of clothing in a circle to figure out which part went where. "That goes underneath," she said, and without warning, yanked off his blanket.

Ty screeched and lowered the material in his hand down to cover himself. "What do you think you're doing?"

"I already bathed you. Quit acting so foolish." She grabbed the item of clothing from his hands and turned it right side up. "You stick your legs in there."

He did this as fast as he could.

"Good," she said, tying a thin strip of material around his waist to hold the bottoms up before reaching for the much longer piece. "This goes over." She helped him find the sleeves, and before long the outfit was complete. The top hung down to just above the knees, almost like wearing a dress, or at least what he imagined a dress would feel like.

Lastly, Narendi wrapped a long blue scarf loosely around his neck and up over his head, then took a step back and looked him over with a smile. "Very pleasing. It matches your eyes."

Ty was still too busy trying to catch his breath from the horror of having her rip off his blanket to acknowledge the compliment. He tried his best to look composed but failed miserably. The clothing was very loose, and his sleeves hung nearly to the end of his fingers.

"Here," she said, pulling off one of her golden arm bracelets and handing it to him. "Wear this." She placed it on his right arm, but it only went as high as his forearm. He was able to use it to keep the baggy sleeve in place.

"Thank you." He walked around the tent to see how the clothes fit. It was surprisingly comfortable, the loose material breathing in a way that left him feeling much cooler than he had with his own clothes. Maybe there was something to these baggy robes after all.

"Come. We will go to your brother before the Mzwati are called."

"Who's the Mzwati?"

"The dune runners."

Dune runners? That didn't sound good. Ty chased after her as far as the front of the tent but stopped just outside, as the sunlight blinded him. The scarf she had placed over his head helped, but it didn't stop him from keeping his hands over his eyes until they had adjusted. Once the brightness wore off, he found himself in the middle of a much larger community than he had first thought.

They appeared to be on the edge of a large pool of water with trees and green brush growing around the outer bank. The village itself encircled the lagoon, with two enormous dunes flanking either side like the walls of a city. At the back, running between the two mounds, was a plateau of rock, which then left the front of the canyon open to the desert.

It was a small oasis inside a barren wasteland.

"What is it?" Narendi asked, walking back to where Ty stood staring out across the water and strange plants that looked more like tall parasols than trees.

"It's beautiful. Not something I would have expected to find in the middle of a desert."

"Yes, we called it to us when we first settled here. Now come. Your brother is waiting." She left before Ty had a chance to ask her what she meant. He paused a moment longer to look at the water, then ran to catch up.

Taking his hand, she led him through the maze of tents as they made their way around the lagoon to the other side. Those they passed smiled and waved, whispering amongst themselves as they caught sight of Ty. Or was it the fact that their princess was holding his hand?

Ty tried not to let it bother him as he focused on where they were going. "Why is my brother's tent so far away?"

"He is with our healer. His sickness was much worse than yours."

Ty wondered how long his brother had gone without taking his share of the water. *Foolish clod. Trying to kill himself to save me.* Ty didn't need to guess which tent was his brother's. He could hear Breen shouting from three tents away, drawing a sizable crowd around the front.

"Where's my brother?" Breen hollered from inside. "I demand to see him! What have you done with him? Let go of me or I'll knock the front of your face out the back!"

Ty rushed into the tent along with Narendi. "Breen! I'm here."

Breen was at the back of the tent with five men trying to hold him down.

Narendi said something to the men, and they released him. Quickly, he snatched up his blanket and wrapped it around his midriff before racing over to give Ty a huge embrace.

"Are you hurt?" Breen asked, looking Ty over.

"I should be asking you the same thing," Ty said. Breen's forehead was slick with sweat, and his face was covered in deep-red splotches. His skin was peeled and blistered, although the blisters did seem to be drying up, and he had some sort of white cream plastered on top. His hands looked as bad as Ty's. Thankfully, Ty's blanket had protected his own face from most of it.

"I'm fine," Breen said, looking anything but. "They wouldn't tell me where you were. Wouldn't tell me anything at all. I don't think they speak our language." He stared at the men who were now taking up a protective stance between the brothers and Narendi. "We're going to have a hard time communicating if we can't—"

"Breen, let me introduce you to Narendi Unsala, princess of the Imbatoo."

Breen turned and looked at Narendi, then back at Ty. "How do you know who she is?"

"I told him," Narendi said with a quirky grin.

Ty smiled. "She can speak Aldoran."

"Then why wouldn't they listen to me when I told them I wanted to see you?"

"Because there aren't many of her people who can."

Ty turned to Narendi. "Princess, this is my brother, Breen of Easthaven."

Breen looked at Narendi and bowed, trying to maintain his grip on his blanket. "It's a pleasure to meet you, Princess." His brother looked unsteady on his feet, especially after leaning over. Ty recognized the dizziness, though his brother was doing his best not to show it.

Narendi smiled. "It is a pleasure to meet Ty's brother." She walked over and bumped Ty playfully with her shoulder. "I will leave you to talk, but I will return later with food." She looked at Ty. "You may wish to show him how to put on his clothes." She giggled and left the tent, motioning for the men inside to follow her out, which they did in haste.

"What was all that about?" Breen asked as he stumbled back to the edge of his bed and sat down. "Do you know where we are?" He put his thumbs to the sides of his head and rubbed. "How long have I been out?"

"You were pretty sick, or at least that's what they tell me," Ty said, clearing his throat. "Apparently, someone wasn't drinking his water when he said."

"I don't know what you're talking about," Breen said.

Ty walked over with the intent of punching his brother in the shoulder, but instead just sat beside him on the bed. "Were you purposefully trying to kill yourself?"

Breen didn't answer.

"We were rescued by Narendi's people. They call themselves the Imbatoo. They live here in the desert. Can you believe that? You ought to see the large pool they have outside. Can't imagine where water like that came from in the middle of this wasteland."

"And what do they want?"

"What do you mean? They want to help."

"No one wants to help without expecting something in return."

Ty shrugged. "I don't know. I've been talking with Narendi for the last day and a half, and it doesn't seem like they want anything. From what she says, there have been many others, like at the maze, who have tried crossing the desert to find some ancient treasure that belongs to the Wengoby priests, whoever they are. Narendi's people tell the venturers to go back, but most don't listen. Her father, King Diawandy Unsala, said we are welcome to stay as their guests until we are fit to travel, which I hope is soon." Ty glanced back at the doorway to make sure no one was standing outside listening in. "I think Narendi likes me."

Breen chuckled. "Isn't that a good thing?"

"Not when she's talking about choosing me as her husband."

Breen's chuckles turned to laughter.

"It's not funny. I think she really means it. We need to get out of here before they have me performing a bonding ceremony."

"I'm sure she was just giving you a hard time."

"You think so?"

"What father is going to want to give his daughter away to you?"

Breen made a fair point, but Ty wasn't completely convinced. "How are you feeling? The sooner we can be on our way, the sooner we can get the next part of the key."

Breen pulled his feet up on the bed and rolled over until his head was resting on the pillow. "To be honest, the room is still spinning a bit. It might be a while before I'm strong enough to do anything."

"So much for us passing this test," Ty said grimly. "I didn't even have enough strength to get us to the key. If it wasn't for Narendi's people, we'd both be dead and buried back in those dunes."

"But we're not." Breen closed his eyes and took a deep breath, releasing slowly. "I'm sure when the time comes, we'll have enough to keep going."

Ty watched the steady rise and fall of his brother's chest as Breen slowly drifted off.

Not feeling all that tired himself, and growing bored of counting his brother's snores, Ty decided to take a walk outside and explore the encampment. Those he passed smiled. The youngest children pointed or waved, while their mothers hung wet clothing across lines that ran from the side of one tent to another. Everyone seemed friendly and inviting. He was hard-pressed to find even a single scowl, which was more than he could say for those in Easthaven.

Sure, there were plenty of very happy people in Easthaven, but most wouldn't go out of their way to stop and smile, or wave, or even acknowledge you were there. Most were too busy worrying about their own lives and their own needs to pay much attention to those around them. It was a strange comparison. Here, the Imbatoo, who seemingly had little in the way of modern comforts—or what Ty would have considered comforts—seemed more content with their situation than those on the other side of the Khezrian Wall.

Breen's earlier response to the Imbatoo's kindness validated it. His brother's initial reaction had been to ask what the Imbatoo wanted in return, but the more Ty wandered through the encampment, the more he came to realize they really didn't want anything in return. They simply helped because they believed it the right thing to do.

Ty sat on a small patch of grass at the edge of the pool and stared out over the water as the sun's rays shimmered across the top. He watched as women carried their pitchers down to fill while children splashed in the water on the embankment. How would a community such as this survive within the Five Kingdoms? They would no doubt be taken advantage of because of their giving nature. The only thing keeping their society safe from outside influence was their location. No one other than the craziest of treasure seekers would be caught wandering around in a place this deadly.

Ty was about to leave when he noticed a herd of animals being ridden down to the water to drink. "Are those . . ." He watched as the long-legged creatures stopped beside the pool, their riders climbing down out of the saddles to lead them closer. Those had to be sherakin. He'd only ever seen drawings of the desert animals from books. They were much taller than horses, their legs alone reaching nearly halfway up a horse's neck. They had thick sandy skin, the same color as the dunes, with long necks and a narrow back. Their movement was awkward, much slower than a horse, but their longer legs probably helped stabilize them as they traveled through the dunes.

Ty watched until the last one had filled its belly and left before he stood and followed them around the pool toward the back of the village. He could hear someone shouting in the Imbatoo tongue, followed closely by ferocious grunts and what sounded like the clapping of wood. Ty gently wiped his brow as sweat continued to form, his skin burning from the already inflicted damage. Passing through the last of the tents, Ty found himself looking out across an open area of sand between the village and the rock formation at the back.

The sherakin were being herded to the left, toward one of the large dunes, where they had several sections roped off for the animals to graze. There was another, much smaller pool at the back, covered halfway around with layers of green brush for the animals to feed on.

Out in the open, between the last of the tents and the rocks behind, marched a parade of men and women dressed in robes similar in color to the sand, with curved swords at their waists and long spears in their hands. They stood in formation as someone in front shouted out orders and the rest moved and struck with their spears in perfect harmony. Ty walked down the line, keeping well back as he watched the group run through their routines, the spears all moving as one as they grunted and roared with each new simulated strike. There was a crowd gathering farther down, but Ty kept his distance, not wanting to interfere, especially since he spotted Narendi and her father amongst those in attendance.

Instead, he remained where he was as he watched the warriors pivot and lunge and strike and block, all in perfect synchronization. They were quite impressive. Not wanting to be spotted by Narendi, he turned to leave, but fell backward with a yelp as the sand suddenly shifted under his feet and a row of armed combatants leapt out from under him.

The warriors roared and thrust their spears in the air, scaring Ty so badly that without thinking, he reached for his magic and hit the closest with a wall of air that sent half the line flying backward. Before Ty could apologize, the entire formation of warriors he'd been watching rushed to the aid of their fellow warriors, their spears up to throw.

Were they attacking? Without thinking, Ty hardened the air in front of him to shield against the spears. To the right, he could hear Narendi shouting, but whatever she was saying, it didn't stop or even slow the charge. He leapt to his feet, his legs still wobbly. He didn't have much strength, but he couldn't let them see it. He raised his hands, and blue fire ignited from both, so bright even he had to squint against it as he faced the oncoming Imbatoo warriors.

The entire contingent came to a sudden stop, all but a few dropping to their knees at the same time and chanting the same phrase over and over again. "Mazota Wanjenga, Mazota Wanjenga."

Even Narendi stopped. Although not kneeling like the others, she seemed almost frozen in place. Ty could see the astonishment in her eyes, as it was in everyone else's, but he could also see the fear. She shouted something back over her shoulder to her father, who then shouted at the warriors, waving them back.

Slowly, the entire armed contingent stood and began to retreat, their spears no longer up, but down in respect.

Ty lowered his hands, and the fire receded, but he kept the invisible shield up just in case. As soon as the blue flames winked out, Narendi made her way over, her steps slow and cautious. She looked at him as though she were seeing him for the first time, the playful flirting no longer there.

"Are you Mazota Wanjenga?"

Ty shook his head. "I don't know what that means."

"Are you the fire spirit we watch for?"

"Fire spirit? I don't know anything about a fire spirit. Look. I'm sorry for hurting your warriors. I thought I was being attacked."

"They are fine. They are the Mzwati."

"The dune runners you told me of earlier?"

She nodded, but before she could say anything further, King Diawandy and a small gathering of other colorfully clad officials walked over, most keeping their distance, but Narendi's father walked over to stand beside her. He looked at Ty's arms, then rattled off something in their tongue, only two words of which Ty recognized: *Mazota Wanjenga*.

Narendi looked at Ty, then back at her father as they conversed back and forth for a while before both turned and looked at him. "I told my father you do not know about Mazota Wanjenga."

"Well, I don't."

"He says we are to take you to see the Zwaneri a Wakale."

"What's that?"

"It is the ancient temple ruins of the Wengoby priests. It is a dangerous place that many seek but few find, and those that do, do not return."

"That has to be what I'm looking for." Ty's heart was racing. They were one step closer to getting the next piece of the key. "Why does he want to take me there?"

"If you are the fire spirit, then you must go there. It has been written."

"Written? I don't understand."

She turned to her father, and they talked once more while Ty waited for her to finish and translate. "Once you rest, we will take you to see the scrolls."

"What are they?"

"Ancient foretellings. You will see. But for now, you must rest and regain your strength."

Ty looked out at the Mzwati, who were still standing in formation, waiting for orders. "I think I've caused enough damage here. I believe I'll return to my tent." His legs were already feeling wobbly. He hadn't had much strength in the first place. There was no telling how much longer he could have bluffed his way out of that fight. If Narendi hadn't stopped it when she did, his flames would have collapsed in on themselves, and he would have been left defenseless. He had gotten lucky and he knew it.

Narendi translated Ty's words to her father, who then half nodded, half bowed to Ty before walking over to rejoin the small gathering of officials to the side. They whispered amongst themselves, passing furtive glances in Ty's direction as he pretended not to notice. Diawandy looked as on edge as the rest, which for a man his size seemed strange and gave Ty a nervous rumbling in his gut. Who did they think he was supposed to be?

Ty smiled at Narendi, hoping to alleviate the tension. He almost would have rather had her flirting with him again than the uneasy way she was looking at him now. "I don't know how much sleep I'll be getting, though," he said with a chuckle, "as hot as it is." He dabbed at the sweat that was now openly dripping from his face, wincing at his sensitive skin.

"Come," she said. "I will apply more of Isha's cream."

"Isha?"

"Isha is our healer."

News traveled fast through the encampment, as those they passed stood anxiously at the entrances to their tents and stared, faces filled with a mixture of wonder and dread. The children clung to their mother's skirts as they watched him pass, no longer pointing and waving, but in a sense hiding.

"Why are they looking at me like that?"

"We have been waiting for the Mazota Wanjenga to come for many generations. And if you are him . . ." She shook her head and clicked her tongue. ". . . then the world is about to change."

They made it back to Ty's tent without being harassed, but Narendi did close the front flaps and light the oil lanterns to give him some privacy from all those standing outside, all wanting to get a glimpse of the Mazota Wanjenga, the great fire spirit. Ty lay back on the bed and let Narendi spread the gooey balm across his face and the tops of his hands. It was tacky and smelled of milk and mint, but it was cool, and he could immediately feel the heat seeping up from his skin.

"Feel better?"

"Much," he said, releasing a pleasant sigh as he relaxed further into the pillow. He lay there a moment with his eyes closed, enjoying the momentary lack of pain. In fact, he was so relaxed he almost dozed off when he felt something slide along his left hand.

"Show me."

Ty opened his eyes. "What?"

"Show me."

"Show you what?" With the intense way she was looking at him, Ty started to sweat all over again.

She lifted his hand. "Show me your fire."

He sighed. "I'm not so sure that's a good idea." The last time he'd seen someone this interested in his magic was with his sister, when they spent the day recording all his known abilities so she could keep it in her memory. Of course, that demonstration had gone terribly, ending with her dress catching fire.

She leaned over and stroked his cheek. "Show me." Her skin still bore a hint of that sweet scent he didn't recognize but would have loved to have gotten more of. It was dangerously alluring.

Shaking off a sudden bout of improper thoughts, he sat up and scooted to the edge of the bed. If it would keep her from touching his cheek in such a manner, he'd do just about anything. "Stand over there." He pointed to one of the posts several feet away, and she walked backward to it.

"Are you ready?"

She nodded enthusiastically.

He took one quick look toward the lowered flaps to make sure no one was there and drew on his magic, conjuring a blue tongue of flame in the palm of his hand. By the time he looked up, Narendi had left her spot against the post, crossed the tent, and was ogling the novelty with her nose no more than a few inches away.

"Careful," Ty said, pulling his hand back just a little to keep from lighting her hair on fire.

"It's beautiful," she said, completely mesmerized by the way it danced in his hand. She moved over to sit down beside him on the bed. "Does it hurt?" She held her hand out over it and quickly retracted. "Ow! It's hot." She looked at Ty. "Do you not feel it?"

Ty shook his head. "It doesn't affect the one conjuring it."

She watched it a moment longer, then looked at him. "You *are* the Mazota Wanjenga."

He wanted to tell her that there were other wielders out there who could conjure fire as well, even better than himself, but he wasn't sure if that was a good idea or not. As long as they thought he was this Mazota Wanjenga, then hopefully they would lead him to the temple ruins they were talking about.

The front flap of his tent flew open, and both he and Narendi jumped.

"What's this I'm hearing about you being some kind of whopping jinga?" Breen all but shouted as he pushed his way inside. He looked at the two of them sitting on the bed. "What's going on here?"

The fire withered in Ty's hand. "Mazota Wanjenga."

"What?" Breen crossed his arms.

"They are calling me Mazota Wanjenga. It means fire spirit."

"I don't care what it means. The whole village is in an uproar. What have you gone and done this time?" He shook his head and threw his hands in the air. "I swear, I can't leave you alone for a minute."

Chapter 53 | Ty

INSTEAD OF GOING ALL THE WAY back to his brother's tent, which Ty doubted Breen would even be capable of by the way his legs were shaking, Ty helped Breen over to his own bed, and he and Narendi laid him down, followed by Narendi pouring some of her terrible-tasting tonic down Breen's throat. Breen's face curdled, but he managed to swallow the lot without spitting before relaxing onto one of the pillows.

As his brother lay there shivering, Ty proceeded to tell him of everything that had happened since leaving his tent earlier, including his unintentional foray with the Mzwati. By the time he got around to discussing the Mazota Wanjenga or that Narendi's father wanted to take them to Zwaneri a Wakale, Breen was good and snoring. Ty finished his story anyway, knowing he'd have to retell it once his brother woke.

"You should rest as well," Narendi said, pulling a couple of the pillows from the bed and laying them on the rugs on the floor. Ty couldn't argue the point, especially since he hadn't stopped yawning since they'd made it back to the tent. "If the floor is hard, you can sleep in my tent." She smirked.

Ty cleared his throat. "No. This is perfect." He plopped down on the stiff rugs and pretended it was the most comfortable thing he'd ever slept on, ignoring the disappointment on her face.

She knelt beside him, and he closed his eyes, hoping she would take the hint.

"Would you like me to rub more of Isha's cream—"

"No," he said more forcefully than intended, and he opened his eyes and smiled. "I have plenty still, thank you." He forced out a fake yawn, since this was the one time he actually needed it and it wouldn't come. "I think I'll just rest a while this afternoon. We can talk more later."

She grunted, not looking very happy with the brush-off. She leaned over and kissed his forehead and spat to the side. "Yuck! That is very bad tasting." Clearly, she had forgotten about the cream. She wiped her tongue and stood, and Ty closed his eyes, waiting to see if she would leave. After a few minutes, he heard the tent flap rustle, and he peeked through his lids. The tent was empty. Turning over on his side so he could breathe a little better, he closed his eyes and relaxed, letting the ache in his legs and back and arms fall to the wayside as he drifted off to sleep.

He woke to the sound of Breen moving around the tent, his blanket wrapped around his waist. "There you are," his brother said from somewhere off in the corner, and Ty opened his eyes. Breen was holding his bow and arrows protectively to his chest. For a moment, Ty thought he was going to kiss them.

"Everything is there, except our clothes," Ty said, moving up to a sitting position. He stretched his arms with another yawn. He felt much better. Stronger even. Now he just needed to get something in his stomach, which of course growled at the very thought of food.

"Where are they?" Breen asked, still digging through their pack.

"Being cleaned, evidently."

"Cleaned? That would be nice. I wasn't going to mention it, but you were beginning to ripen."

"Speak for yourself." Ty walked over to a familiar pile of blue material lying beside the doorway and picked it up. "Narendi said our clothes were no good for the desert." He laid the pieces of material on the bed. "This is what they have for us to wear. To be honest," he said, waving his arms in the air, "they're actually quite comfortable."

Before Breen had made it over to the bed to inspect his new outfit, the tent flaps opened and Narendi strolled in. She had the worst timing. She looked at Breen. "How are you feeling?"

"I'm fine," Breen said, trying to hold his blanket up. "Apart from needing to get dressed."

She walked over and joined them beside the bed. "I can help if you want." She looked at Ty and winked.

"No," Ty said, stumbling for his words. "I, uh . . . I can show him how they work." He quickly ushered her out the door. "Thanks for stopping by."

She smiled. "I will wait here until you are ready."

Ty nodded and shuffled back through the flap and over to the bed where Breen was already trying to figure out what piece went where. Soon enough, Ty had it sorted, and Breen was able to finally get rid of the blanket roll. They had barely gotten the waist belt cinched when Narendi poked her head in. "Are you clothed?"

"Yes," Breen said, and she stepped the rest of the way in.

"King Diawandy would like to invite you to share his table this evening."

Ty looked at Breen, who was waving his arms about as he tried out the new clothing. "Are you feeling up to it?"

Breen lowered his arms and looked at Narendi. "We would be honored to share your father's table."

Narendi smiled and then adjusted the golden bracelet she'd given Ty up a little higher on his arm. "I'm glad you still wear it." She took his hand and turned it over. "You can show your fire to my mother."

Ty pulled his hand away with a grunt, not finding the thought of being the evening's entertainment all that agreeable. He looked at Breen, who simply shrugged. It wasn't like Ty could protest. They were dependent on these people to survive, which meant if he had to resort to being the king's family's amusement, then that's what he would do. Besides, it sounded as though the Imbatoo had knowledge about him that he desperately wanted to get his hands on. A fair trade in exchange for dazzling his hosts with a bit of fire magic. He was the fire spirit after all.

As soon as Ty agreed, Narendi took his hand and pulled him through the flaps to find a sizable crowd still gathered around the front. Narendi didn't seem at all ashamed to be seen holding Ty's hand, as awkward as it made him feel. In fact, she seemed almost proud of the fact, as though she wanted the other women to know that he was being claimed by her and they would have to look elsewhere.

The sun had already begun its descent over the western horizon, having dropped behind the plateau in back of the village and setting what few clouds still remained in the sky bursting with colors. Those closest to the rock formation had a deep gold hue that spread outward to red then purple and finally a dark blue. Absolutely breathtaking. Along with the sun's exit, the heat of the day was just beginning to break, the temperature cooling faster than how it normally would anywhere else.

"Follow me," Narendi said, guiding them through the onlookers and into the sea of tents as they made their way around the right side of the pool toward the back. She stopped in front of a very large tent that was at least three times the size of the others, set up so that it faced the edge of the water. This particular tent had been placed on top of the thicker grass growing around the water's edge.

King Diawandy stood just outside the front opening, the flaps having been tied back to welcome them. Surrounding the king were three women and a throng of children, ranging from those still giving suck to a couple that looked at least Breen's age, maybe older. Did these all belong to Diawandy? Ty felt sorry for the man. Then again, the king didn't look too unhappy with the situation as he stepped forward and raised his arms out to them.

"*Kwango mia a dwiyumba.*"

Narendi released Ty's hand and turned to look at them. "My father says: 'Welcome to my home.'"

Her father spoke again, this time pointing to the three women on his right, starting with the first and working his way to the last.

Narendi translated: "The king wishes you to know his wives. First, my mother, Nyota," she said proudly as she pointed to the finely dressed woman in purple and gold, standing directly to Diawandy's right.

Narendi's mother bowed in response to her name being called, but after looking at Ty's arm, her face seemed to harden.

"Next, Waseme." The second and tallest of the three women, who was dressed in red and gold, bowed as well when she heard her name. "And Maskima." A hefty lady on the end, wearing blue and gold, bowed as well.

King Diawandy wore an extremely proud look as Narendi went through the introductions. Ty and Breen both bowed to each in turn. "We are very honored to be here, and to meet your wonderful, and very large, family," Breen said.

Ty then quickly added, "And we pray the Creator's blessings on this home." Ty had heard his father say something similar when dealing with some of the more prominent members of Easthaven society. It sounded like as good a place as any to use it.

Narendi smiled as she translated. Ty watched their faces, feeling a little nervous at his addition. Not everyone believed in the Creator. He hoped he hadn't offended them.

Diawandy smiled broadly and spread his arms once more as he addressed them in the Imbatoo tongue.

"My father thanks you for your blessing and invites you in to dine." As soon as she finished, her father turned and walked inside, while his three wives and all their children moved to the side, making room for their guests to enter next.

"Come," Narendi said as she led Ty and Breen through the opening and inside the main room. Narendi's mother kept a keen eye on Ty as he passed. Ty wondered if Narendi had spoken of him to her, or worse, spoken of her desire to be his first wife.

Ty did his best to smile as he passed, keeping at least a step or two back from Narendi so as not to give the wrong impression, not that the wrong impression hadn't already been given when Narendi had shown up with his hand in hers.

The inside of the tent was lavish, with several large gatherings of pillows for sitting. Ty noticed they didn't seem to have a formal table, but instead there were a number of cordoned-off sections where food had been placed on the floor in between where the pillows had been arranged. The largest of the sitting areas was at the back, where the king stood, waiting for them to arrive. He motioned for them to take their places around the spread.

Ty removed the covering over his head and let it hang around his neck, drawing more than a few gasps and hushed whispers as the king's wives and children all stared at his unusual white hair.

The room smelled of incense and coriander, with a hint of pepper, a combination Ty was unaccustomed to. It wasn't bad, just different, nearly causing him to sneeze at one point. He was glad they had left the front flaps open to circulate the air.

Ty waited for the king to take his spot at the center, then followed Narendi's example and took his seat directly opposite him, while Narendi's mother and the other two wives took their seats on either side of Diawandy. The children all had their own sitting areas on the other side of the tent, causing Ty to wonder if they had been divided by family. He wondered how much contention having three wives with separate children caused. Ty, himself, was part of a divided family. Neither of his parents were his by blood, but he still looked to them as his own.

Diawandy pointed at the empty wooden bowls in front of each of their places. "*Tuwa.*"

Narendi looked at Ty and Breen. "Please eat."

Ty watched the others and followed their example as they began dishing out the food with their hands and plopping what they wanted into their bowls before using those same fingers to dish it into their mouths. Ty looked at Breen, who shrugged and pinched off a piece of stewed meat and dropped it in on top of some rice and beans. It was an interesting experience eating an entire meal with your hands, but a fun one. He used the dark bread to dish up the looser parts of the rice and beans and sop up the leftover juices. All in all, it was a very favorable meal, spicier than he would have liked, but savory nonetheless.

Along with eating with their hands, it seemed the custom was to burp as often and as loudly as you pleased, the louder the burp, the more that person showed their enjoyment of the food. By the time the meal was complete, Ty and Breen were burping with the best of them, laughing as they did at the peculiarity of it all. The king seemed to find their laughter a positive affirmation of his role as host and laughed as well, not really understanding why it was they were laughing in the first place.

The meal ended in joyful merriment, the laughter even spreading to the other seating areas where the king's children had been eating, most of whom were keeping an eye on Ty, still admiring his hair.

The king clapped his hands, and several men and women rushed in and cleared the food, offering bowls of water for them to wash their hands in before they reclined against the surrounding circle of thick pillows. All of the king's wives stared at Ty and Breen, but Nyota seemed to stare the hardest. She was a very elegant, proud-looking woman, even more so with the greying hair and strong features.

"I saw sherakin drinking down by the water," Ty said, eager to open a conversation and end the silence. "I've never seen one in person before. Are there many around here?"

Narendi translated for the others, and her father replied, which she then translated back. "The *pulah*, as they are called in our tongue, are many. They are as much Imbatoo as we are. Their strength carries our burden. Their hides provide our shelters." She pointed up at the tent overhead. "And their meat gives us food."

Ty cringed at the thought of what they had just eaten.

"The pulah are sacred to the Imbatoo. Without them, we would not be."

Ty understood. "It's like our horses and cattle back home. Although, we don't eat our horses. Just the cows." He felt foolish for having mentioned it, since he doubted they had any idea what he was referring to. "You don't need to translate," he told her. "Just tell him we understand."

"How did your people come by such a great body of water in the middle of the desert?" Breen asked.

Ty's head shot up. "Yes. You mentioned something about drawing it to you?"

Narendi translated their questions, and the two brothers waited for her father to finish answering. Whatever he said, it was definitely a very lengthy answer, followed by several back-and-forth discussions between him and Narendi.

When he finally stopped, Narendi turned with a smile. "I will do my best to interpret. My family are water diviners. Not all, but some. It has been given to us for generations. My grandmother had the gift. I have it, as does Safiri." She pointed to one of the girls in the third section of seating on the left.

The girl, who was at least four or five years Narendi's junior, looked confused, not knowing if she was needed for something. She stood and started toward them, but Narendi waved her off and said something that had the girl walking back to her seat.

"What is a water diviner?" Breen asked.

"We can feel the water, so we know where to dig our wells."

"You are voda, then?" Ty asked. He looked at Breen. "They must be water wielders like Gilly."

"What is voda?"

Ty scratched the back of his head. How could he explain? "A voda is a wielder, who can—"

"Wielder?"

Ty exhaled slowly. This was going to be difficult. How much did these people know of Aldoran history? Did they know anything of magic and where it came from? He might be opening a box here that wouldn't get shut. "A wielder is someone who is born with magic."

She shook her head, looking confused, which was exactly what Ty was afraid of. Still, he went on as best he could, with the occasional help from Breen, to explain what magic was, where it had come from, and how it existed in the world today, also going into some detail about the White Tower and their mission to bring about a war between the jun'ri and ven'ae. It was a very long conversation that had to be stopped every so often to give Narendi a chance to explain what was being said to her father and the others. Surprisingly, the words *jun'ri* and *ven'ae* were old enough that they had been seen in some of the Imbatoo's ancient texts, but it didn't appear that what the words represented had been passed down with them.

The talks lasted throughout the rest of the evening and well into the night as Ty and Breen explained some of the political structures in Aldor, and how they stood in relation to what was taking place. Narendi and her family were quite taken aback to hear of so many types of magic. Narendi said that when their people first moved into the valley, it was her great-grandmother who had called the waters to her. She had been the only one in the family to be able to do such a thing. Those others born with the ability to be a water diviner could only sense the water, not actually call it.

"Did your great-grandmother have a transferal crystal?" Breen asked. "Makes sense that if she was able to call the water, then she had to have had one of the faerie rocks."

Narendi asked her father, but he looked as mystified by the proclamation as she was. "I can call water if I have a crystal?" Her eyes lit up. "I have many crystals." She jumped up from her seat and was about to rush out of the tent when Ty stopped her.

"No. It's not just any crystal. It is a transferal crystal. A piece of the faerie homeland. They are the only ones that will work. But to answer your question, yes, I think if you had a transferal crystal, then you would be able to call the water as well. The fact that you can sense it says to me that you're a wielder."

"Like you?" she asked almost nervously as she retook her seat beside him.

"Uh, not exactly." Ty wasn't sure how much he should reveal about who or what he was. The hesitant look on Breen's face said he felt the same.

"Because you are a fire spirit?"

"I don't know what I am," Ty admitted. "Perhaps we will see more when we take a look at the scrolls you mentioned."

"Yes." She turned to her father, and they spoke. "My father says he will take you to them tomorrow."

"Are they in the Wengoby priests' temple you mentioned? Zwaneri a Wakale? Did I say that right?"

"Yes, and no. The scrolls are not there. They are safe within the rock."

"You mean the plateau behind the village?"

She nodded and turned to her father, and they conversed for a moment. Then the king stood, along with his wives. "My father wishes to sleep. He will take you to the chamber of records tomorrow."

Ty and Breen both stood as well, and Ty helped Narendi up, which drew a raised brow from her mother, especially the way her daughter's hand lingered on Ty's arm.

"Please thank your father and his . . ." Ty shook his head. "Just, thank everyone for their hospitality."

Narendi did as he asked, and the two brothers left the tent. Most of the younger children had already retired for the evening, but some of the older ones were sitting outside near the water, watching as they left.

Narendi had started after them, but her mother called her back, the tone in her voice and harsh look on her face said she didn't want her daughter spending so much time with them, Ty in particular. He glanced over his shoulder. Narendi didn't look very happy with the situation but did manage a small wave before Ty and Breen disappeared into the surrounding tents.

"Well, that was interesting to say the least," Breen said. "I've never had to explain what magic was to someone before." He shook his head in disbelief. "They had never even heard of the Fae. You would have thought that at the very least whoever had taught them their numbers and letters would have mentioned it, even in passing."

Ty shrugged. "Narendi said she was young when she had learned our language, and the man who had taught them died not long after. Perhaps she just doesn't remember."

"Perhaps."

As late into the night as they had sat there discussing the histories of Aldor, they had only managed to scratch the surface of what her people didn't know— not that Ty and Breen were well versed in Aldoran histories, not like Adarra—but that might have been a good thing. The Imbatoo lived a more simple, peaceful life, not encumbered by the worries of magic or those who craved it. Maybe it was better not knowing. Creator knew there had been plenty of times Ty wished he didn't.

Breen walked Ty to his tent first, then decided to go back to his for the evening, since the bed wasn't big enough for the two of them, especially with as much tossing and turning as Breen tended to do. It took him a while, but Ty did manage to finally get his new outfit off, which he didn't even take the time to fold properly, tossing the clothes and the bracelet on a rug before plopping down on the bed. He quickly crawled under the blankets, as the temperature had dropped considerably.

He lay there for some time imagining what these scrolls might have to say about him, or if they were about him at all. He was anxious to find out, and the sooner he went to sleep, the sooner the morning would come. He closed his eyes, but instead of the blissful darkness of slumber, his mind continued to play through the evening's conversations with Narendi's family and the fact that they literally had no knowledge of magic, or of the White Tower, or even of the Fae.

He wondered if their dunes would spare them from the rising conflict that now looked almost inevitable. Would their isolation be enough to keep them safe?

Chapter 54 | Ty

TY WOKE TO SUNLIGHT spilling between his tent flaps, thin lines of dust revealing the angled rays of light as they reached for the floor. Yesterday had been the first full day he'd spent out of bed. By the time he'd crawled in last night, he'd certainly felt the effects of it, but this morning he was feeling his chipper self again. He didn't reckon it would take too much longer before he was back to where he had been prior to leaving on this quest in the first place.

It almost seemed a lifetime ago.

Ty sat up and stretched, taking a moment to realize how much he missed his underdrawers. Quickly, he reached for his new pants and yanked them on, worried that at any moment Narendi was going to burst through the front and surprise him.

He was in the process of tying his belt when a rustle at the front announced Narendi's arrival.

"I was worried you would sleep all day," she said, walking over to give him a hand. She grabbed the top robe from off the bed and handed it to him, then slowly ran her fingers down the front of his chest as though completely fascinated by the color of his skin. Unlike the rest of his family, he had never seemed to be able to darken during the summer months. His skin tended to burn and peel. She took his hand and raised it, examining the blisters and flaked skin on the outside. "I'll put some more cream on before we go."

Releasing his hand, she helped him with his top, shaking it loose so it fell over his pants and down above his knees. Ty hadn't noticed until she had bent down to help him that her hair had been styled differently than the previous two times. The first had been up, with a single braid hanging over the shoulder. The second had been down, woven into dozens of tight locks. This time, the locks and braids were gone, and her hair had been brushed, leaving thick waves to hang over her shoulders and back. A single partial strand hung over one eye, which she continually flicked out of the way. Was she doing this for him?

Her dress was a pale green, and like the tops she had worn previously, it was sleeveless, her left arm bearing the same gold bracelet she'd been wearing since they'd met. He had seen many of the other women wearing similar ones. Her clothing and hair might have changed, but the dots on her face seemed to remain the same. He wondered if they had to be applied anew every morning. Seemed a lot of work to go through.

"Your hair looks . . . very nice." If she had been going to all the trouble to do it for him, the least he could do was acknowledge it.

She smiled shyly and ran her hands through the lower half. "I am glad you noticed."

"Hard not to," he added, then wished he hadn't by the flash of excitement in her eyes. He turned back to his bed and straightened the blanket and pillows, anything to give him an excuse not to stare. He tried picturing Lyessa walking into the tent and seeing them there, hoping that would refocus his thoughts in the right direction as he turned back around. She was still smiling. "When do we go to see the scrolls?"

"Later," she said, and walked him over to his bed and sat him down.

He hopped back up immediately, warning bells ringing. "How about breakfast?"

She pushed him back down on the bed. "Stay."

She turned to the table beside his bed and removed the wax paper from one of the clay jars and stuck two fingers inside, coming out with more of Isha's cream. She then gently rubbed the balm across the tops of his hands, taking the time to look at his face to see if he needed more there as well. Thankfully, she didn't seem to think he did. It was his hands that had suffered the worst of the damage, but even they were healing, the skin more of a light pink than the deeper red it had been. Whatever was in the cream seemed to work very well. He might need to try getting the recipe for Orlyn to add to his apothecary.

"Come," she said. "I'll see to your brother."

Ty wrapped the long scarf around his neck and up over his head, taking care not to smear any of the cream on it, then walked over and grabbed his compass from their pack and placed it in his pocket before following her out. He didn't want to take any chances of losing it. They walked along the waterfront, around to the other side of the large pool where Breen's tent had been placed. The villagers stopped and stared, no friendly smiles and waves as the day before, only long faces filled with curiosity and disquiet.

If he could have gone back and done things differently during his brush with the Mzwati, he would have taken better care not to spook so easily, or resort to magic. Although, he was admittedly impressed by the way he had instinctively used his magic to defend what he thought was an attack. It was good to know that he wouldn't simply freeze if the time came to really defend himself, and that air shield had proven quite the lifesaver.

He was still running over yesterday's skirmish when they reached their destination and Narendi tapped on the tent's flap. "Are you dressed?"

"Hey," Ty said. "Why don't you ever ask me that?"

Breen called out from inside. "Yes. Come in."

Narendi smiled, and before Ty could stop her, she leaned in and kissed him on the cheek. "Because I am pledged to you."

"You're not pledged to me." He shook his head adamantly. "No. There will be no pledging. I told you, I'm already pledged to someone else."

The front flap opened, and Breen stuck his head out. "Did you hear me?" He took one look at the two of them and pulled it back in. "Never mind."

"You can have more than one pledge," she said, arms crossed as she glared at him.

"I don't want more than one. It's not . . . it's not proper."

"You have already accepted my pledge."

Ty shook his head. "No, I haven't."

She pointed at his arm. "Then why do you wear my band?"

"What band?" He looked at the gold bracelet on his arm. "This? I thought you gave it to me to hold up my sleeve." She clicked her tongue at him, and he pulled the bracelet off and held it out for her to take.

She looked at him, stunned. "What is this? You cannot give that back to me. It would bring shame to me and my family. They have already seen you wear it. To reject it is to reject my family, reject the king."

Breen cleared his throat and stuck his head out once more. "Uh, Ty, can I have a word with you for just a moment?" He grabbed Ty by the arm and pulled him into the tent. "We'll be right back," he said to Narendi and shut the flap, leaving her standing in the doorway nearly in tears. "What do you think you're doing?" Breen scolded, keeping his voice lowered. "Are you trying to get us killed?"

"I didn't know the bracelet had anything to do with pledging," Ty said, holding the band up in front of Breen. "I just thought it was part of the outfit. You don't expect me to go marrying her, do you?"

Breen hmphed. "Of course not. But it wouldn't hurt to play along at least until we get our strength back and figure out where we go from here. It sounds like this desert temple you keep mentioning might be where we need to go, and if we can get them to lead us there, then all the better. But that's not going to happen if you shame the king's daughter by publicly rejecting her." He rolled his shoulders. "Besides, she is pretty."

"What does that have to do with anything? What happens if she tries demanding that we marry? She might hand me a pair of shoes to put on, and next thing you know, that means we're bonded."

Breen sighed. "I doubt wearing a pair of sandals is tantamount to a union, but we'll deal with it if the time comes. For now, just be nice, and try not to give her the wrong impression."

"A bit too late for that, don't you think?" He waved the bracelet around once more.

Breen tried to smile, but it came out half bent as he walked over and opened the front flap and tied it off, allowing Narendi to enter. "I'm very sorry for my brother's lack of manners, Princess. I believe you caught him off guard. It was a lot to take in. He really had no idea of the symbolism behind wearing your bracelet. We don't have such customs where we are from." He paused a moment. "Actually, I guess we do. But it has to do with rings for your—"

Ty elbowed his brother.

"Anyway," Breen finished. "It wasn't intentional, and he is sorry." He looked at Ty intently. "You are sorry, right?"

Ty nodded and slowly slid Narendi's bracelet back on his arm.

"Do you have something to say to her?" Breen prodded.

Ty cleared his throat, wishing he had one of the Mzwati spears in hand to club his brother over the head with. "I would be honored to wear your bracelet, Narendi. And to accept your pledge."

She stared at him a moment, the tightness around her eyes and mouth softening. "Good to see you show some wisdom. Only a foolish man brings shame to his family and his bond mate."

Ty wanted to roll his eyes, but he held back the urge. He had to keep reminding himself that they needed these people. Breen was right. Whatever it took to help them get the key was what they needed to do. At worst, even if she demanded some kind of union, it wouldn't be considered legitimate back home under such circumstances, and when they did manage to get the next piece of the key, he and Breen could jump through the mirror and never worry about seeing any of them again.

Narendi strolled past Ty in a huff, not so much as looking in his direction as she took Breen's arm and led him over to the bed. She sat him down and applied more of Isha's paste to his hands and the burnt areas on his face, which were growing fewer. Ty had even noticed a discernable difference in his brother's skin from the previous night.

"That cream seems to work well," Ty said, hoping a conversation would lighten the mood. "What's in it? I know of an apothecary who would love to get his hands on the recipe."

"What's an apo . . . apoth . . ."

"An *apothecary* is someone who uses herbs for medicinal purposes, like your cream."

As if having heard her name being called, an older woman with curly grey hair that stuck out around a colorful blue, gold, and white striped headwrap stepped into the tent. Her skin was tight and leathery except where it wrinkled around the eyes and cheeks and mouth, and she walked with a noticeable stoop. Ty had seen her once before, during the worst of his delirium, but he hadn't put it together that she was Isha. She spoke to Narendi in Imbatoo, and Narendi said something back as she held out the bowl to the older woman and stepped aside, letting Isha get a closer look at Breen.

Isha took her time, having to get very close to Breen's face to be able to see the damage. She nodded, and with shaky hands applied a little more of the white paste to a couple of the most damaged spots and handed the jar back to Narendi, saying something in the Imbatoo tongue.

"Isha says that the healing looks good."

"Ask her what she uses to make her balm," Ty said.

Narendi spoke back and forth with the old healer for a bit, Isha continually shaking her head as she did, before Narendi finally turned back around. "Isha says that her cream is a secret, passed on for generations through her family, and she will not break that trust."

Ty sighed. He knew how much Orlyn would have loved to have gotten his hands on such a salve.

"However," Narendi said with just the hint of a grin, "if you were to give Isha a look at your Mazota Wanjenga powers, she might be persuaded." She looked at Isha and winked.

Isha smiled, the wrinkles around her mouth and eyes lifting at the same time.

Ty sighed, once again feeling rather used, but decided it was a small price to pay for the outcome. He nodded at Narendi, who in turn smiled at Isha. Isha took a step closer and grabbed Narendi's arm for support as she waited on the fire spirit to impress.

Ty drew on his magic, taking a moment to make sure he wasn't standing too close, or underneath anything that might accidentally catch on fire. He turned to Breen. "Do you mind?" He motioned toward the open flap on the tent, and Breen walked over and untied it, letting it fall back into place. As soon as he was assured that no one outside was watching what happened, he raised his hands and called his magic to light.

Both hands ignited in blue flame.

Isha gasped and stumbled backward, though she maintained her grip on Narendi's arm. Clearly it was more than what she had been expecting. Ty didn't fuel the fire as strongly as he had when facing the Mzwati, but it was definitely more of a show than what he had demonstrated privately with Narendi. Isha didn't bother getting any closer to it than she was. She did whisper the name Mazota Wanjenga.

Ty released the flames, and Isha motioned to be taken to the bed, where she sat down and then had Narendi transcribe the ingredients she used in her healing salve. Narendi copied down her words and their amounts onto a single piece of rolled skin in Imbatoo, then added the translated words beside it with Ty's help. It appeared that sherakin milk was one of the main components, along with several herbs Ty recognized like mandrake and tulfer weed, which are used to lower swelling and take away pain, and one herb that he didn't recognize.

"What is this here?" he asked, pointing to the one word she was unable to translate. "Wamini."

Narendi took a look at the page. "Wamini is a plant that grows in the shade of the rock behind our village. The meat is dug out and boiled along with the other ingredients." She looked at Isha and they spoke for a minute. "Isha says that the wamini is what helps the skin to grow."

Ty wondered if they might be able to grab a couple of those plants before leaving. He would need to remind himself to look when they went over to the plateau later to search through the scrolls. Ty thanked Isha for entrusting him with the recipe, and she nodded with an approving smile. She seemed pleased enough with the tradeoff.

Narendi walked Isha over to the front and opened the flap for her to leave. The old healer passed one last look over her shoulder at Ty before slowly hobbling off and disappearing around the corner.

"I will have food brought before we see the scrolls," Narendi said and disappeared out the door herself.

"You're becoming quite popular around here," Breen said darkly. "I hope they don't demand you stay. We need to be careful not to tell them why we need to see the temple ruins. If they get the notion that we intend to leave, they might not take us."

Ty sat down on the edge of the bed. "With Narendi already pledging herself to me, it's a good bet you're right." Ty sighed. "To be honest, I almost wonder if me staying here might be the best thing for everyone. With me out of the way, it might keep Easthaven safe."

Breen scrunched his face. "And if you believe that, then you're as conked in the head as Narendi suggested. The White Tower won't care if you're in Easthaven or not. Anyone that stands in their way is going to be fair game to them, and Easthaven has well proven itself a threat to the Tower's goals, which is why we need to get our hands on this key."

Breen would have said more, but Narendi walked back in with two men following close behind, carrying trays of food and drink. Ty wondered if they had been waiting just outside for the speed at which they had arrived.

She directed the men to place the trays on the floor near one of the support posts. They filled each of the three wooden mugs with what appeared to be a thick cream. The two men bowed and exited the tent, scurrying back to wherever they had come from.

Narendi pointed toward the pillows. "Please, sit."

Ty and Breen walked over and took their seats, waiting for Narendi to take hers first—she was royalty after all. The trays held at least two types of cheeses, a couple loaves of dark bread already sliced, cuts of thinly sliced meat that were still warm to the touch, and several pieces of fruit that Ty hadn't seen before, each with a grey, prickly outside and a soft red center. The cream in the mugs was stronger than what Ty was used to, but it had been sweetened with honey, giving it a rich flavor.

The meal was delicious, and by the time he finished everything on his plate, he felt ready to take on anything, even the dunes. As fast as Breen's face was healing, Ty reckoned they only needed a couple more days to recover before they were ready to press on.

"When do we visit the scrolls?" Ty asked anxiously.

Narendi wiped the cream from her upper lip and belched. No matter how hard Ty tried not to let it bother him, he still found a woman openly belching rather unsettling. She smiled afterward, knowing it irritated him. Ty tried to manage a burp himself, but all he got was a backwash of the milk he'd swallowed earlier. He quickly grabbed his cup and took another swallow to rinse it down.

"We will depart after morning muster."

"What's that?" Breen asked.

Narendi pushed her plate away and stood. "You shall see. Come."

They left Breen's tent, and she led them toward the back of the village, where Ty had had the confrontation with the Mzwati. In fact, from the sounds of shouting ahead and the clanging of sticks, that was exactly where she was taking them. They passed through the last of the tents to find the Mzwati back in formation, running through their forms. They were precise in their movements, deadly in their strikes. Ty wondered why they needed to maintain such a prestigious fighting force. Who else was out here that they needed to defend against?

"Do not be frightened or kill anyone," Narendi warned with a smirk as once again a line of warriors suddenly came jumping up out of the sand a few feet ahead.

"Whoa!" Breen startled and pointed at the group. "That was impressive. I would have never known they were there."

"Yeah," Ty said. "I walked right over them yesterday."

"How do they stay under for so long?"

"We use our bakas," she said, pointing to the Mzwati headdresses, which were similar to the long scarves Ty and Breen wore that wrapped around their necks and up over their heads. "We also carry tikoo reeds for breathing." She produced an olive-colored reed out from her robe, no thicker than Ty's little finger.

"What do you mean *we* carry tubes? Are you saying you are one of the Mzwati?"

She smiled proudly. "Yes. All the king's children train once they reach age."

Ty found himself looking at her in a whole new light. Probably similar in manner to the way she had looked at him after he had set his hands ablaze. After holding the short pipe up to his mouth and testing out how accessible it was to breathe through, he handed it to Breen to test as well.

The reed reminded him in a way of his flute pipes. It was the one thing he wished he had packed with him, but at the same time he was grateful he hadn't, since it would have no doubt been lost to the river along with his pack when he had traveled through the first mirror.

"Very useful," Breen said, wiping the end of the reed off with his robe and handing it back to Narendi.

"Do you have more?" Ty asked, an idea suddenly popping into his head.

"More?"

"Tikoo reeds."

"Yes. Would you like me to get you one?"

Ty nodded. "I'll come with you."

They left Breen to watch the morning muster and walked back through the village toward the pool. Narendi found several batches of reeds growing on the far side, and Ty rolled up his pants and waded out to take a look. He found quite a few larger ones he thought might work, some large enough to make more than one pipe. Narendi handed him a knife, and he cut several before handing it back.

"What do you do with these?" she asked.

"It's a surprise." He stuffed the reeds into his pocket, and they walked back to the practice field to join Breen. "Did we miss anything?"

"No. They've been running through the same routines since you left, only they switched from spears to swords."

Ty watched as the silver blades caught the sunlight in a mesmerizing show of flourish and form as they simulated strikes, lunges, and parries. Ty was going to have to spend more time with Darryk, Lyessa's trainer, when he got back. After seeing the precision of technique achieved by the Imbatoo as they moved in all directions without a single falter, Ty knew he had a long way to go.

Lyessa had been firm with him on not relying so heavily on magic, reminding him that she had been forced to save his life on multiple occasions during their battle with the Tallosians. Of course, he knew nothing of his magic at that time, unlike now, where he seemed capable of manipulating air and water more freely, along with his flames. Still, he knew she was right. Magic tended to weaken him. Learning and understanding conventional weapons would go a long way to keeping him safe.

Ty watched the rows of fighters work their way through the last of their routines. One fighter in particular caught his eye, or maybe it was better to say Ty caught his. Every time Ty looked his way, he found the man looking back, and not in a friendly way. It was the man leading the drills. Every time he would shout an order, the entire company would shift positions.

Voices rose behind them, and Ty, Breen, and Narendi turned to see who was coming. King Diawandy and several other older men and women, dressed in matching white robes with long golden sashes that hung from their shoulders across to their waists, walked out from the tents and over to where the three were standing at the side of the practice field.

Diawandy waved in their direction and said something official sounding in the Imbatoo tongue. Ty and Breen both bowed with a smile, not knowing what else to do, since Narendi didn't interpret what had been said.

"Who are they?" Ty asked.

"Those are the Wazeri, keepers of the scrolls, chosen at an early age to learn. Those who pass are educated in the written word so that they, too, can one day become recorders of Imbatoo history."

"Aren't all Imbatoo taught their numbers and letters?" Breen asked.

Narendi shook her head. "Very few. Other than for recording, learning our letters and numbers isn't all that important out here."

The royal entourage joined them at the edge of the field and watched as the Mzwati continued their training. Ty noticed the way the men and women in white robes—the Wazeri as Narendi had called them—kept turning to look at him when they thought he wasn't looking. He didn't care for all the attention.

Narendi must have noticed it as well, as she took a step closer to Ty and reached over to hold his hand. Ty's first instinct was to pull away, but his brother's warning came to mind and he simply let it happen. It wasn't like he didn't enjoy her attention, especially knowing it came from a princess, but his conscience wouldn't let him fully enjoy it, since it continually pricked him with images of Lyessa in tears after finding out her affections had been replaced. Worse was having it happen right after Ty had demanded she stay behind.

Ty shuddered to think what might have happened if she had come along. First, they would have never made it this far. Even if they had made it through the maze together, there was no way he would have had the strength to keep both her and Breen alive inside the underground cavern. And if by some miracle they had made it through, Lyessa would have surely challenged Narendi to battle by now, and who knew how that would have ended up. Ty had never seen Narendi fight, but he had seen Lyessa, and he knew how good she was.

Ty shook his head, trying to clear his thoughts. Why was he thinking about Narendi and Lyessa fighting?

"Are you well?" Narendi asked, putting her hand to his forehead. "You are sweating more."

"I'm fine. Just another hot—"

A single shout rose from the Mzwati drill instructor, and Ty turned, but the man wasn't looking at the ranks—he was looking at him. He shouted something else and without warning, he lifted his spear and charged . . . straight for Ty.

Chapter 55 | Ty

OR ALL OF TY'S blustering about how he had instinctively used his magic to defend himself the previous day, he just stood there in complete shock. Was the man really attacking, or was he showing off for the king, who happened to be standing not five feet from Ty?

The instructor was halfway across the field when he threw his spear. Ty hardened the air in front of him as fast as he could, but by the time the shield was in place, Narendi had already jumped in front of him, using her own body as a shield. Before Ty could grab her and pull her out of the way, Breen released one of his knives, hitting the spear hard enough to send it off course, and it flew just over their heads.

Diawandy shouted at the man, but he didn't stop, didn't even slow down. He drew his curved sword and continued running.

In a panic, Ty forced Narendi out of the way and gathered the air to him. He focused it into a single strike, but not before his brother had leaped in between him and the oncoming lunatic. "Will you people get out of my way!"

The instructor raised his sword as he came within striking distance, and Breen kicked up a foot full of sand straight into the man's face. He swung anyway, and Breen barely deflected the blow with one of his longer knives. Before the Mzwati could turn for another swing, Breen's elbow connected with the man's chest, and he was stopped midair. His sword flew from his fingers as he landed in the sand at

Breen's feet, the wind completely knocked from his lungs. Sometimes Ty forgot how strong his brother was.

The king and Narendi rushed over, both yelling at the same time. Breen, thankfully, had enough good sense not to finish the man off, but instead stepped back to let the others deal with him. It took a while for the Mzwati instructor to catch his breath long enough to be able to speak. A hit like that, it was a wonder he could speak at all.

After several rounds of back and forth with the king, with Narendi jumping in as angry as Ty had ever seen her, they finally helped the man to his wobbly feet. Narendi left her father and the instructor and walked over to speak with them.

"What was that all about?" Ty asked. "Who's that man?"

"He is Bolo. He was my first pledged."

"First pledged?" Ty looked at the man, seeing nothing but rage in the eyes staring back at him. The man looked too old for Narendi, at least in his thirtieth year.

"I rescinded that pledge some time ago, but he believes we will still be bonded. When he saw you with my pledge . . ." She didn't finish. There was no need. It was written all over the other man's face. He wanted Ty dead. She took a step closer. "I do not wish to be his first. I wish to be yours."

"So, what do we do now?" Breen asked, receiving just as many scowling looks as Ty.

She turned to Ty. "Bolo has challenged you to combat for the right of my pledge, but my father has denied him that because it is my right to give my pledge to whom I wish. Also, Bolo is a good warrior, and my father does not wish to see him killed."

Ty saw this as an opportunity and removed the bracelet from his arm. "Then perhaps for the sake of keeping the peace we should wait on our pledges." Her eyes hardened, but before she could say anything, he continued. "I don't need to wear this bracelet to know you want to be with me, and me not wearing it doesn't mean I care for you any less. So if it will keep Bolo from sneaking into my tent tonight and slitting my throat, I would prefer we keep our pledging less . . . visible."

Even Breen appeared to agree with a curt nod.

Narendi, on the other hand, didn't even stop to consider. She grabbed the bracelet and shoved it back on Ty's arm. "I will deal with Bolo. You are my pledged. I am not ashamed of it, and neither should you be." With that, she walked over to have more harsh words with Bolo and her father, and by the time she was done, Bolo was limping off the practice field with the king's arm around his shoulders.

Ty shook his head. That wasn't exactly what he had meant by hiding their pledge. He looked at Breen and shrugged. "I tried."

Breen tucked his hair back behind his ears, his scarf having fallen down during his fight with Bolo. "I've never seen anyone with such terrible luck. The sooner we get out of here, the better."

Seeing their instructor being carted off the field, the rest of the Mzwati left as well, staying clear of the small group surrounding Ty.

"Father will be back shortly," Narendi said, joining Ty and Breen at the edge of the open sand. The congregant of Wazeri remained huddled as they nattered away amongst themselves in hushed conversation, occasionally coming up for air long enough to look at Ty, then back down for more.

"Had you been pledged to him for long?" Ty asked. "He seems kind of old."

"Bolo is a good man. My pledge to him had been when I was young. It was my father's decision. He wanted my joining to be with a man who could one day help me rule."

"How wonderful for you," Ty said, not sparing the sarcasm. He would have hated to think of his father picking his bride one day. His father would have probably made his decision based on how tasty her cantermelon pie was. No. His father would have cared more for how well she knew the forest. Either way, he was glad his family wasn't the one making the choice for him.

"You sound jealous," Narendi said with a smile creeping around the corners of her mouth.

Ty's head shot up. "I do not."

Breen nodded. "You kind of do."

Thankfully, Narendi's father interrupted them before Ty had to explain why he'd been so defensive about who Narendi was pledged to. Diawandy spoke to Narendi, and she then translated.

"My father wishes to thank you for not taking your kill," she said to Breen. "You were within your right to have judged Bolo for the attack. It was cowardly. He says you would make a fine Mzwati warrior. He has never seen a knife thrown like that before. Very impressive."

"Tell your father that I am honored he believes me worthy of the Mzwati, and that I am glad we were able to end the conflict peaceably." He leaned toward Narendi. "It is over, isn't it? We don't need to worry that Bolo will try again, do we?"

Narendi shook her head. "He will not try again. To do so would bring shame to his family, and the king would be forced to exile him." She relayed what Breen had said to her father, and the king smiled. Diawandy pointed toward the stone plateau on the other side of the practice field and then spoke with the Wazeri, who were still huddled at the side. They immediately left their cluster and started slowly across the sand toward the rock.

"My father says we are to see the scrolls now." Narendi walked alongside her father, leaving Ty and Breen to bring up the rear.

Ty pointed to the roped-off areas with the sherakin over on the left, near the dune. "I watched them drinking yesterday," he said to Breen. "The Imbatoo ride them, with saddles and everything."

"Maybe we'll get to ride one on our way to this temple they want us to see."

Ty's heart raced. He hadn't thought of that. Now he had even more to look forward to. The sand was hot beneath their sandals, some of it creeping between the bottom of Ty's feet and the hardened leather as they trekked across the open field. The sun was directly overhead by the time they reached the plateau, not leaving much in the way of shade.

Like the Khezrian Wall they had left nearly a week past, this slab of rock had a hollowed-out opening leading inside. However, unlike the last one they'd climbed out of, this one had a door with engraved columns and an archway that had been decoratively cast into the stone. Around the entrance between the door and the pillars were engraved inscriptions, most likely written in Imbatoo since Ty didn't recognize any of it. Hanging directly to the left of the door was a large gong.

The first of the Wazeri stepped up to the door and picked up a wooden rod with a fur-wrapped end and struck the gong. A very low-sounding rumble echoed off the rocks. Ty could feel the vibrations in his chest. He wondered what the purpose of the gong was, as they all stood there staring at the door, no one bothering to go inside.

By the time Ty had decided to walk over and ask Narendi what was going on, the sound of grating metal and a snapped latch stopped him. The heavy wooden door parted, revealing two more white-robed individuals with golden sashes inside, one holding a lit torch.

Without a word, those in front started through the doorway, each stopping long enough to kiss their fingers and touch part of the inscription around the doorway.

"Why are they doing that?" Ty whispered to Narendi, who had stepped back to walk alongside the two brothers.

"They are asking for blessing from the forefathers."

Neither the king nor Narendi participated in the finger-kissing ritual, so Ty and Breen refrained as well, though Ty did stop to take a closer look at the inscriptions. They weren't runes, nor were they written in any tongue he could read. He followed the others in, Breen right behind, as they passed one of the white robes waiting just inside the door. As soon as Breen was in, the man shut it behind them, then lowered a large brace. Whatever was in these scrolls, the Imbatoo clearly didn't want anyone getting a look at them.

The stone passage was lit with tallow candles that had been placed in small alcoves carved into the side walls every few feet, filling the narrow corridor with a strong, unpleasant smell. The tallow was most likely created from sherakin fat. However, unlike other caverns Ty had found himself wandering through, this one didn't smell of mildew. The tunnel looked to have been dug out by hand instead of being a natural occurrence, leaving Ty to wonder how long something like that would have taken.

Ahead, the tunnel ended outside another door, with a single passageway leading off to the right. Like the one they were in, it retained the evenly spaced candle insets, revealing one or two other doors farther down, all shut. One of the Wazeri opened the door in front of them and waited for the rest to enter before shutting it. The room on the other side was quite cavernous, nowhere near as massive as the underground lake, but much larger than any of the others they'd been through so far.

This chamber had clearly not been dug out by hand, as the ceiling rose several dozen feet overhead. Life-size statues lined the outer perimeter of the chamber, mostly men as far as Ty could tell, but there were some women interspersed throughout as well. Each one had its own unique look, whether it be the headdress or clothing, or the size and shape of the individual person. Most of the statues carried weapons and shields similar to that of the Mzwati; a couple held armloads of books. One of the women held an infant in each arm.

On the left side of the room, sitting in front of a statue of a shorter man wearing a spiked helmet and carrying some sort of ceremonial staff, was a small gathering of young children. A tall lanky man wearing the same white robes and gold sash as the others was teaching them, but he stopped when they entered and walked over to greet them, pausing when he caught a glimpse of Ty and Breen. His tightly curled white hair receded toward the top of his head, and he had a thick white beard that seemed almost odd against his dark features.

He spoke with the king a moment, then turned to Narendi, and they had a few words. He then turned to the brothers. "I am told you speak in the light-skin tongue," he said, his words pronounced just as well as Narendi's, if not better. When Breen nodded, he continued. "Greetings. I am Mshindu." He made a sweeping gesture with his hand to the surrounding statues. "These are the ancestral heads of the Imbatoo."

"You speak our language very well," Breen complimented.

"I thank you," he said with a slight bow. "It is not an easy language to learn. You speak very fast."

Ty and Breen smiled. Ty had never thought about it before, comparing the

Aldoran tongue to other languages. There weren't many living within Aldor that didn't speak at least some close dialect of Aldoran. Other than the Tallosians and some of the islanders off the southern coast, the Imbatoo were the first Ty had come across. Was Aldoran that much more complicated?

"I can't imagine learning more than one language," Breen said. "I've a difficult-enough time with the one."

Mshindu smiled and directed the small group over to the side to observe the students in training. "These are the novice Wazeri. They learn their letters and numbers so that they can one day record the histories and teach them to the people."

"What histories are you referring to?" Breen asked.

Ty was wondering the same thing, since it seemed no one here knew anything of Aldoran history, from the coming of the Fae and magic to the Wizard Wars and the Great Purge.

"We record events."

"What sort of events?" Ty asked curiously, wondering if it had anything to do with him.

"Events of note."

"The histories are very detailed," Narendi said. "Your arrival will be recorded. Even Bolo's actions earlier will be recorded."

Ty whistled and the echo filled the room, drawing all eyes to him. "Sorry. That just seems like a lot of recording."

Mshindu smiled. "It is. Come." He took them toward the back of the cavern, which was covered in shelving, each shelf filled to overflowing with large tomes. For a people that only taught a select few how to read and write, Ty was surprised by the amount of written words they had collected over the years. "These are the histories," Mshindu said with pride.

"How far back do they go?" Breen asked.

"To before our time here. Before even the Great Freeze."

Ty had no idea what the Great Freeze was. He couldn't remember reading or being taught in school anything about a Great Freeze. "Are these the scrolls?" Ty asked, anxious to find something in them about the Mazota Wanjenga.

Mshindu shook his head. "No. The scrolls are sacred. Only the heads of the Wazeri are allowed to see the scrolls."

Ty stared at the man. If they weren't allowed to see the scrolls, then what had they come all this way for?

"My father wishes to see the recordings of the Mazota Wanjenga," Narendi said.

Mshindu looked confused. "Why would he wish to see the foretellings?"

"He believes the Mazota Wanjenga has come."

Mshindu didn't move. He seemed almost frozen in place, much like the statues he guarded, his face showing no emotion. He looked at her in the same way Ty had his father when his father had first revealed to him that Saleena was still alive after Ty had watched his father shoot her. "What do you speak of?"

"The Mazota Wanjenga is here," she repeated, then grabbed Ty's head scarf and pulled it off.

Mshindu's eyes bulged, fear and what looked like hatred filling his face at the same time. He shouted something in Imbatoo, startling Ty so badly that he barely noticed the Wazeri teacher reaching into his robes and pulling out a knife. Mshindu lunged at Ty, but there was no time to prepare, no time to even reach for his magic. All Ty could do was raise his hands in stunned silence and hope they were enough to stop the blade before it entered his chest.

Narendi struck Mshindu so fast Ty barely saw it happen. A single flash of reflected steel from a blade she had somehow produced out of thin air, and the Wazeri instructor went down, his own knife clanging on the stone below as he clutched his arm, his white robes quickly staining red. By this time, the king was shouting, Narendi was shouting, Mshindu was shouting, and the other members of the Wazeri were swiftly gathering up the children and rushing them out of the room.

Ty was yanked nearly off his feet as Breen pulled him away from the Wazeri instructor. He noticed Breen, too, had one of his knives in hand. They stood watching from several feet away as the king and Narendi argued back and forth with Mshindu as Narendi went about bandaging the man's arm with his belt.

"What do you think that was all about?" Ty whispered.

Breen shook his head. "I don't know, but I'm getting awfully tired of being attacked around here."

"Imagine how I feel."

After a few more rounds of heated discussions, Mshindu was helped to his feet, and the three of them stood looking at Ty and Breen like they'd done something wrong.

"What is it?" Ty asked. "Why are you looking at us like that?" Ty turned to make sure no one was sneaking up behind them. He kept his magic on the tips of his fingers, holding an invisible shield between them and the three Imbatoo. "Will someone please tell me why it is that every time we turn around, we are being attacked? It was safer out on the dunes."

Narendi walked over, and Ty moved the shield closer. She stopped a few feet away. "Mshindu believes you are an evil omen." She glanced back over her shoulder to where the Wazeri instructor stood cradling his arm next to her father. "There is division amongst the Wazeri as to the interpretation of the scrolls over the coming of the Mazota Wanjenga. Some say the Mazota Wanjenga will be the Imbatoo's deliverer. He will rise up to protect us against great evil and will lead us to safety."

"Am I missing something?" Breen said, his knife still in hand. "That sounds like a good thing to me."

"Yes, but there are others, like Mshindu, who believe different. They say the Mazota Wanjenga *is* the great evil, and his arrival will mark the destruction of the Imbatoo, and he will force us from our home."

"Okay, granted, that doesn't sound quite so pleasant as the first, but you still have yet to prove that Ty is this Mazota Wanjenga person in the first place."

"Like we've already explained," Ty said, keeping his shield in place as he took a step forward. "There are other fire wielders out there. Magic is growing in Aldor, you yourself are a wielder of it and you didn't even know it." Ty noticed Mshindu's face harden at the mention of Narendi being a wielder. The Wazeri instructor caught Ty looking at him and quickly averted his eyes. "You knew this already, didn't you?"

Mshindu ground his teeth and stared down at the floor.

Narendi turned. "What is it he speaks of?"

"I know nothing of what he speaks," the man hissed.

The king spoke to Narendi, clearly not liking the looks on everyone's face as they all stared at Mshindu. She must have filled him in on what was happening, because the next thing Ty knew, Diawandy had grabbed Mshindu by the front of his robes and was reaching for his sword.

"Speak!" Narendi demanded. "What do you know of magic?"

Mshindu spoke in Imbatoo, and Narendi translated. "The oldest of our histories talk of a time when strange people came to our world. They had great power. Could do incredible things." Mshindu went on to explain a very basic version of the faerie arrival and even the battle in which they were sent away, but it seemed a very watered-down version, as though from a distant spectator and not from those who had lived it firsthand.

Diawandy's eyes grew hotter with each new unveiling of truth that had been kept hidden from him for years.

Ty had a thought. "How did you explain to your people what past water diviners were able to do? Narendi told us that her ancestors at one time were able to not only sense the water but call it to them. She told us that they were the ones to bring the water outside that has kept your people alive. How did you explain that away? And for that matter, what ever happened to their transferal crystals? If what you say is true and your histories are made up of meticulously kept events, then it would stand to reason that those would be recorded as well." Ty looked at all the books behind where Mshindu and the king stood. "Which of these volumes speaks of those events?"

Narendi raised her blade. "Answer!"

Mshindu clenched his fist. "None of these speak of those events."

"Why not?" Ty asked.

The king shouted, and Narendi spun in the direction of the door and raised her sword. Ty and Breen spun as well, Ty's shield suddenly blocking several arrows that had been fired at him from a group of armed Wazeri who were rushing into the chamber. The arrows ricocheted off in different directions. Breen's bow slid off his shoulder, and in a single motion, it was nocked and the string pulled to his cheek.

"I'm really beginning to hate this place."

Chapter 56 | Ty

O!" TY SHOUTED AT BREEN. "Don't shoot. The shield." He didn't want the arrow to accidentally ricochet off the hardened air and come back to hit one of them.

Breen released his draw but kept the arrow nocked.

"Protect the king," Narendi shouted, rushing in front of her father as she raised her scarf up over her head and wound it around her face, blocking everything but her eyes. She now looked like one of the Mzwati.

Several more arrows were released, even a couple of spears, as over half a dozen Wazeri raced across the chamber at them, all shouting, all holding that same look of fear and hatred Ty had seen in Mshindu's eyes. Ty tried extending his shield to protect Narendi and her father, but he wasn't fast enough, and a couple of arrows flew past.

Diawandy grabbed Mshindu and used him as a shield, two arrows burying themselves deep in the Wazeri's chest. A look of stunned horror crossed the man's face before he dropped to the ground.

Most of the white-robed attackers were now halfway across the room and coming fast. Two remained by the door with their bows, another two stood separate at the back. They looked more scared than anything. Ty pulled back his shield and nodded to Breen, who released his arrow, killing one of the two archers before they managed to reload.

Ty delved a little deeper within his magic and, still holding his shield, he unleashed his fire on the first three. The cavern filled with their screams. Those behind took one look at the three piles of melted flesh and cloth and bone and immediately fell to the ground, calling out something in Imbatoo that Ty took to be: "Don't kill us."

The one remaining Wazeri near the door tossed her bow and joined the others on the ground, as did the two who had been standing at the back. Ty's hands were shaking by the time he finally released his hold on his fire. He had just snuffed the life out of three people in the blink of an eye. The smell of their charred remains turned his stomach. He held a tight grip on his shield, having no intention of getting caught off guard again, as he and Breen cautiously made their way over to where Narendi and her father were standing beside Mshindu, who strangely enough was still alive despite two shafts sticking out of his chest.

"How many of the Wazeri are left?" Ty asked Narendi as he kept his eye on the door. "Do you think more will come?"

Narendi did a quick head count. "I believe that is all."

"Why did they attack us? I thought only part of them believed that the Mazota Wanjenga was evil?"

"I do not know," Narendi said as she knelt beside Mshindu and lifted his head, blood running down his mouth, staining his white beard. Diawandy and Breen kept a close watch on those lying on the floor, Breen with his bow up and arrow nocked, and Diawandy with his curved blade in hand.

Ty knelt beside Mshindu and looked the dying man in the eyes. "I'm not here to hurt your people. I didn't even know the Imbatoo existed until a few days ago. Once I find what I'm looking for, I will leave."

Narendi gave him a stern look at the mention of him leaving but didn't say anything.

Mshindu coughed again, more blood running down the sides of his chin. "The scrolls have foretold it. They do not lie."

"Then they've been misread or something. I am not the great evil." Ty wanted to say that that honor went to the White Tower and Aerodyne.

Mshindu grabbed Ty's sleeve and pulled him close. "I pray you are correct." He gasped twice, and his eyes went blank. Ty had never stared into the eyes of someone as their life passed before. It left him shaken. He unhooked the man's fingers from his robe and stood as Narendi closed the Wazeri instructor's eyes and laid his head back down on the ground, covering his face with part of his robe.

Narendi stood and spoke with her father, and he in turn walked over to where the other members of the Wazeri were still belly-down on the floor and began talking with them. Talking might have been a polite way to put it. Demanding would have been more appropriate. "My father demands answers. He demands to know where these histories are that speak of such things as magic and why they have been kept hidden from the people."

"This," Breen said offhandedly, still keeping his eyes on the open door on the other side of the room, "is why learning your letters can be very important. When you are forced to put your trust in others to tell you what is true and what is not, with no way to examine it for yourselves, then they hold all the power."

"We have always listened to the Wazeri," Narendi said, almost defensively. "Knowing our letters doesn't help us put food on our tables. It has never helped us put shelter over our heads. It is also very difficult to teach without proper materials. We have barely enough parchment to instruct the new Wazeri, let alone all Imbatoo."

"I hadn't considered that," Breen said. "Even still, if the Wazeri have been keeping the truth about magic hidden from you, then what other things have they kept hidden? Recording history as they want you to see it."

Narendi's jaw tightened as she looked at the white robes. "Something we will soon discover."

On the other side of the chamber, Diawandy gathered up the remaining members and marched them across the room, where they were directed to sit in single file in front of the stone shelves at the back, the same shelves holding the Imbatoo histories. He walked up and down the row, pointing the tip of his blade at each member as he passed, speaking to them in Imbatoo as Narendi translated his words quietly to Ty and Breen.

"He is demanding to be shown the hidden histories, and those who do not will be sent to the feeding grounds."

"And don't forget the scrolls," Ty added. "If they are what hold the foretelling we were nearly killed over, then we will want to see them as well."

Narendi passed that along to her father.

"Wait," Ty said. "What do you mean by feeding grounds?"

"It is where we go to prove we are of age."

"Huh?"

Before she could answer, Diawandy spoke with Narendi, and she passed his response to them. "The Wazeri say the scrolls and histories are kept in a separate chamber, but Father says we cannot see them until we decide what needs done with these. He desires me to bring the Mzwati to keep watch of the prisoners while we search the scrolls. Will you be fine here?"

Ty realized what she really meant was: would her *father* be safe if she left. He looked over at the Wazeri as they knelt in front of the books. "We will keep an eye on them."

Narendi nodded and raced across the room and out the door, disappearing down the hall on the other side.

Ty turned to find most of the Wazeri staring in his direction. However, one look from him and they hurriedly averted their eyes, all but the two on the end, one of whom was the woman the king had been speaking with. It was the same two who had remained at the back of the chamber, unwilling to join the fight. They seemed more curious than fearful.

Not wanting to stand there staring, Ty turned to Breen. "I thought being this Mazota Wanjenga was going to be a good thing. Now I've got a princess wanting to marry me, former pledges wanting to kill me, and a sect of desert historians claiming I'm the end of their world."

"Yes, being you is such a burden."

Ty snarled. He studied the cowering Wazeri on his left, then glanced at Breen's black Sol Ghati bow. "You can probably put that away, don't you think?"

"Not until I can be sure no one else is going to suddenly jump out and try to kill us, which around here means I'll probably be sleeping with it tonight."

Ty chuckled. "Next thing you know the statues are going to come alive and try killing us."

Breen frowned and turned to look at the closest of the life-size stone men and women. "Great. You just had to go and open your mouth."

Ty's smile vanished as he, too, turned to look at the menacing-looking figures. He shivered. They did seem to be staring at them. He walked over to get a better look at the closest and examined the man's sword, which was held point up in his right hand. It was the strangest-looking weapon he'd ever seen. In fact, it looked more like a bludgeon than a sword. The blade itself seemed more akin to an upside-down flower vase, with the widest part of the blade being closer to the tip than near the hilt like every other sword he'd ever seen.

From there, Ty moved on to the next statue, studying them one by one, at least those statues closest to the back. He didn't want to get too far away from Diawandy in case the Wazeri did somehow manage to overcome their fears enough to try overpowering the king. Not that he thought they could. Diawandy's arms were as thick as Ty's legs, and the look on his face said he almost hoped they would try. By the time Ty had made it halfway around, noises from outside the room drew his attention, and he started back across the chamber toward his brother and the captives.

A line of Mzwati warriors rushed into the room, their scarves covering their heads and the bottom half of their faces, similar to how Narendi had covered hers when the battle had started. Their swords were drawn, their spears tied around their backs the way Breen carried his quiver.

Ty raised his shield when he caught sight of Bolo, who was at the front of the line, limping slightly as he came, though trying not to show it. He managed a passing glare at Ty before stopping in front of the king with a bow.

Narendi was directly behind Bolo, but she broke off from the group before they reached her father and walked over to talk with the two of them. "The Mzwati will keep the Wazeri in line." She turned back around when she heard her father speak. "My father says we will go to see the scrolls now."

Ty's heart started to race. Finally. He and Breen followed Narendi to the left where they were joined by the king, Bolo, and one of the Wazeri. It was the woman on the end who had been staring at Ty earlier. She was shorter than the rest, and old enough to have lines of grey intermingled throughout her tightly wound curls. She had a wide face with very pronounced cheeks and a notable gap in her teeth.

Bolo walked in front of the king, keeping a safe distance between Diawandy and the Wazeri lady as she led them past the statues and toward a tunnel whose entrance had been blocked from view by one of the stone memorials. The tunnel wound its way through the plateau, passing doors and candle insets and other passageways as it went. Clearly, the Wazeri complex was more extensive than Ty had at first thought.

They stopped outside a set of double doors, and the woman produced a key. She unlocked the doors and stepped aside for the king to enter. Bolo opened the doors and walked inside first, no doubt wanting to make sure it was safe for the king. A moment later he walked back out and nodded, and the rest of the party entered the room. It was a small chamber, not much bigger than Ty's tent. Like the hallways outside, it appeared to have been chiseled out by hand, but instead of candles and torches giving light to the room and its valued contents, there were evenly spaced lanterns hanging over several long stone tables, which were covered in stacks of aged parchment.

The far-left wall was covered in a honeycomb of diamond-shaped inserts, each hole housing a single furled scroll. This had to be what they had come for. "Where are the scrolls that speak about the Mazota Wanjenga?" he asked.

Narendi translated Ty's request, and the Wazeri woman walked to the back of the room to where a stone chest with no lid sat open on the floor. She knelt and lifted out a large tome that took up both of her arms and toted it to the closest table, where she laid it out on the stone.

"What is the difference between the books out in the main chamber and the scrolls hidden away back here?"

Narendi passed his question along to the Wazeri woman. There was a brief back and forth before Narendi answered. "Atiena says that the books in the hall are filled with Imbatoo histories. The scrolls here are the foretellings."

"You mean prophecies?"

She looked at him curiously. "I'm not familiar with that word."

"Things that haven't happened yet. Future events, instead of past events."

Narendi nodded. "Yes."

"Where are these events being recorded from?" Breen asked.

"They were recorded long ago by Juma. He was a great man among the Imbatoo." She pointed to the honeycomb of collected scrolls at the back. "These are all his foretellings."

Ty glanced over at the wall. "He certainly had a lot of them. Any of them come true?"

Narendi smiled. "Many."

"Where did you get such a large collection of parchment?" Breen asked, an odd question, Ty thought, until he considered it further. Apart from the strange parasol-looking trees and scrub brush growing around the lagoon outside, Ty had seen nothing in the way of pulp materials to explain such a sizable stockpile of writing goods, and he doubted they had killed enough of the sherakin to produce skins for the considerable amount of vellum it would have taken to fill all the books out in the larger chamber.

"We make trade with those from the other side," Narendi said.

"From the other side of the Khezrian Wall?" Ty asked. "There's a way across?"

"There are passes if you know where to look. Twice a year, those from the other side cross through the Biyana Pass to trade. They always bring new parchment."

Breen looked as though he wanted to ask more about the pass, or the trading, but Atiena finished flipping through the pages and turned, saying something that had the others walking over to join her at the stone table. Ty moved to get a better look as well, not that it would have mattered, since everything was written in Imbatoo.

Atiena pointed to a specific portion of text that she read aloud.

"What is she saying?" Ty whispered to Narendi, anxiously shifting from one foot to the other.

She raised her finger for him to wait. He tried studying the others' faces in hopes of getting at least a brief idea of what was being read, whether good or bad, but all he could come away with was that everyone seemed to be thoroughly engrossed. After Atiena's finger had made it down and across two full columns, Narendi finally stopped her and turned to Ty and Breen. "The writings are unclear. Atiena says that they speak of a man who will come and bring great change."

Breen poked Ty in the shoulder. "I guess that leaves you out."

"What? Why?"

"She said a *man*."

Ty kicked him in the shin and turned back to Narendi. "I don't understand. How does any of that equate to the Mazota Wanjenga being evil?"

"It also talks of great famine and disease, and to the Imbatoo being exiled from their home."

"Okay, well, that doesn't sound quite so good, I guess, but are you saying that the fire spirit is going to make these things happen?"

"I'll ask." She turned to Atiena, and they spoke, then the Wazeri looked back down at the book and started reading once more.

Ty waited patiently until they came to another stopping point. How could he, if he was this fire spirit, be responsible for bringing about famine and disease? It was starting to sound more and more like this Mazota Wanjenga person wasn't him after all. At the end of the page, the woman stopped her reading, and they all turned to look at Ty.

"What? What did she say?"

Narendi paused a moment as if to figure out how best to translate what she'd just heard. The longer she waited, the more nervous Ty became. Ty was about to ask once more when she finally spoke. "The book says that there will be great destruction, a storm so vast it will swallow the sky, and there will be no shelter for the Imbatoo to hide."

Ty stood there a moment to let what she had told him sink in. It was clear to him that he wasn't the Mazota Wanjenga. How could he create a storm so vast it would swallow the sky? Not to mention the obvious question: Why would he want to? "I'm not sure I understand what part of that could be interpreted differently," he said. "It sounds like this fire spirit is not a very nice person."

Narendi turned and conversed with Atiena before answering. "Atiena believes that the writings can also be read to mean that the Mazota Wanjenga doesn't come to drive us from our lands, but to lead us away from our lands to safety. She believes he isn't a destroyer, but a savior."

Ty pursed his lips. "I think I like that interpretation best. But still, whether the Mazota Wanjenga is good or bad, whether he comes to drive Imbatoo away or lead them away, I still don't see how you think that I am this person. Like I said, there are other people out there who can wield fire. Some much better than me. And I certainly can't create a storm like that."

Narendi spoke once more with Atiena, and Atiena then turned back to the book and flipped the page, and everyone stood in silence as they stared at the other side. Ty and Breen both scooted over to get a better look. Ty's mouth gaped when he saw what they were looking at. There was no writing, only a single image.

A man stood at the top of a dune. He was dressed not in the typical desert garb, but in what would have been more fittingly worn by those on the other side of the Khezrian Wall, with trousers and a tunic and a long, flowing cape or coat that whipped out behind him in the desert breeze. In each hand he held a ball of fire, and behind him rose a great darkness, which Ty interpreted to be the storm the book was referring to that would destroy the Imbatoo.

However, it wasn't the man, or his clothing, or even the storm behind him that had Ty's attention. It was the fire in his hands. Whoever had created the drawing had gone to great lengths to make sure it captured a true essence of what this Mazota Wanjenga looked like. The man's face was too far in the distance to be clearly seen, but the one thing that was clearly visible was his white head of hair, and the fact that the flames in his hands were painted blue.

"Kind of hard to argue with something like that," Breen said, gawking at the drawing along with the rest. "Have your people been suffering any famine and disease lately?" he asked Narendi as he studied the image, unable to take his eyes off it.

She shook her head.

"There, you see? That proves that whatever this is saying isn't true."

"Besides," Ty said, "the last storm I went through, it wasn't me that saved anyone. It was you. If you hadn't found me and Breen, we'd both be dead."

She nodded slowly and relayed what Ty had said to the others, who looked about as unsure as Narendi did.

"I say that the best way to make sure this doesn't happen," Ty said, still staring at the image, which was clearly him, "is for us to leave. The sooner, the better."

Narendi balled her fists at the mention of Ty leaving but translated nonetheless. Her father seemed to agree with Ty as he offered a curt nod, and even Bolo looked hopeful, more for the fact of seeing Ty gone and away from Narendi than for anything in the book. The only person who didn't look happy by the idea was Narendi. Ty could almost see the wheels of her mind working to figure out a way to keep him there.

Ty looked at the king. "If we can take one more day to rest and gather enough provisions to continue our journey, then we will be out of your hair once and for all." He wasn't sure his colloquialism of being out of their hair had been clearly translated, but they seemed to get the meaning well enough.

Diawandy was the first to speak, and Narendi translated, looking none too happy with what she was being forced to say. "My father says he will see to the provisions you require, and even though he would be honored to have you stay, he would not wish to stand in the way of the Mazota Wanjenga's journey. He would ask that you accept his help in escorting you to Zwaneri a Wakale."

"The temple ruins?" Ty asked.

Narendi nodded, her father waiting just behind to see what Ty's answer would be.

"We would be more than honored to accept an escort across the dunes," Ty said, delighted with the prospect of finally being gone from the place, almost as much for getting out of a union with Narendi as for hopefully finding another missing piece of the key. They had spent way too much time on this particular portion of the test as it was.

Chapter 57 | Ty

HE NEXT DAY WAS spent gathering supplies, packing their carry bags, and resting when they could. Narendi had surprised Ty with a satchel of his own. It wasn't as big as the one he'd lost, but it was sizable enough to carry his bedding, a spare set of robes, his boots, a jar of Isha's cream—along with some of the harder-to-find ingredients required to make it, including stems from the wamini plant—and some extra food supplies. He even had enough room left over for his newly made pipe flute, something he had stayed up late through the night making.

Each reed was cut to the correct size to match a specific note, then sealed and dried over a fire. Afterward he stacked them in ascending order, with the longest on the left, producing the lowest notes. He then took two pieces of reed that had been split lengthwise and glued them on either side of the pipes, using an animal skin glue to hold them together. Afterward, he bound them with cordage, making sure the pieces were good and sturdy.

The instrument was crude and sounded nowhere near as clean as the pipe flute his father had made for him, but the notes were true and the familiarity of running his lips across the rough openings gave him a small piece of home to carry with him. Since he only had so much room in his bag to carry the instrument, he was forced to compromise by making this set of pipes on a higher scale, using shorter pieces. It wasn't exactly what he was used to, and he certainly preferred the lower, more haunting register with the longer pipes, but he found the melody it produced soothing all the same.

By the time he'd crawled into bed, he could hardly keep his eyes open, and he was just as exhausted when he woke to someone running their fingers through his hair. He opened his eyes to find Narendi sitting on the edge of his bed. Her hair was back to the dozens of tightly wound locks, but instead of wearing them loose, they were all pulled back into a single long braid, which had been tied back with red cord. He wondered how long it had taken her to do it. He had to imagine it had taken a good bit of time. Perhaps she had others doing it for her.

"Today is the day," she said.

Ty was afraid to ask what she meant by that as he threw back his blanket and rolled over, still wearing his pants, having been too tired after building his flute to try undoing the belt to take them off. "I suppose it is." He smiled inwardly as he automatically reached for the pieces of the key hanging from his neck. They were finally about to get back to their quest, leaving the Imbatoo village behind once and for all. No more having to be woken to a girl running her hands through his hair, no more of that girl's pledges trying to kill him, no more historians seeking his demise because of what they had read in a book.

In some ways this third test had already been just as deadly as the other two, even more so if he added in their near-death experience at the hands of the desert. One way or another, Ty was ready, almost looking forward to what awaited them next. Apart from a small bout of tired eyes, he felt raring to go. He glanced past her to the tent flap, which was hanging far enough back to see that it was still dark outside.

Hopping from his bed, he started to pull on the top half of his blue robe, but Narendi stopped him. "I have these for you to wear," she said as she grabbed a neatly folded set of Mzwati robes. He hadn't even noticed them lying there.

With Narendi's help, whether he wanted it or not, he dressed himself in the new set. The material was light and breathable, just like the other, the only difference being the color. And the fact that the outer robe on these was split up the center from the bottom to the waist, giving his legs a much wider range of motion.

After folding his older robes, he placed them, along with the remainder of his provisions, inside his new carry bag. This particular bag only had one long strap, unlike his brother's, which had two shorter ones to make it easier to carry across the back. However, once it was hooked over his head to the opposite shoulder, he found it balanced rather well. He shifted it to hang over his right side to free up his sword. Last, he slung his scarf around his neck and up over his head. The less of his white hair he showed, the less he hoped the others in the village would be prone to stop and stare.

By the time he finished, Breen was standing in the doorway. "How'd you sleep?" he asked with a deep yawn while scratching his stomach.

"About as well as you, apparently."

Breen smiled. "Thought as much. Have you eaten yet?"

"No," Narendi answered for him. "My father wishes you to eat with him. It is tradition to greet the sun before we cross the dunes."

"You mean before *you* cross the dunes?" Ty corrected. "You said *we*."

"Yes," she said as she marched out of the tent. "I go with you."

Ty looked at Breen and gulped.

Breen just shook his head. "Why do I get the feeling this is going to go very badly?"

The two brothers rushed to catch up with Narendi, who seemingly wasn't planning on slowing for them as she marched through the maze of tents. They caught up with her about the time she reached her father's tent.

Diawandy was sitting on one of a dozen flat rocks arranged between his abode and the edge of the water. At the center of the circle was a small cooking fire with a large piece of meat searing overtop. It smelled wonderful, forcing Ty to swallow back his hunger.

Diawandy stood when he saw them. He raised his arms and offered a formal greeting, which Narendi didn't bother translating. Both Ty and Breen bowed and offered their appreciation for his invitation. The king didn't wait for an interpretation either and simply nodded and motioned for them to join him.

Several other people were there waiting as well, one of whom was Bolo, as he stood off to the side with a group of Mzwati, occasionally pausing to glare in Ty's direction. Ty was determined not to let it bother him as Narendi directed him and Breen to a couple of stones to the left of the king. She sat between Ty and her father, while Bolo and the other six Mzwati took their seats on the opposite side.

Last to their gathering was Atiena. The Wazeri was wearing her ceremonial white robes and gold sash, along with a very giddy grin that never seemed to let up. She looked about how Ty felt: delighted to finally be leaving.

Ty leaned over to Narendi and covertly pointed to Atiena when she wasn't looking. "Why is she here?"

Narendi looked at Ty as though wondering why he'd asked such an obvious question. "To record events."

"Oh." He guessed that made sense. What better way to capture a historical moment than to live it firsthand? Atiena had a small satchel leaning against the side of the stone she was sitting on, from which Ty could see the parchment sticking out. She had clearly come prepared, and if these temple ruins did in fact hold the next piece of the key, Ty could see where she might end up using every single one of those sheets and more.

With Mshindu having been killed during his failed attempt to kill Ty, Ty wondered who would end up taking his place as head of the Wazeri. Atiena would be the most logical choice, as she had been the most outspoken toward believing the Mazota Wanjenga was a savior and not a destroyer. More importantly, she had been one of only two who hadn't joined in the attack and had been the most willing to allow them to see the hidden scrolls.

Ty started to ask Narendi about it when the king raised his arms and spoke. After he was done, Narendi looked at Ty and Breen. "My father has asked Ayo to bless our journey."

"Who's Ayo?" Ty asked.

Again, she looked at him like he'd grown a third eye. "Ayo is the great provider, the bringer of sun, wind, and water. He is the one who gave the Imbatoo this land."

Ty nodded, wondering if Ayo was just another name for the Creator, or if it was the name of one of the faeries who had come through the rift. From what he'd been told, many of his kind had set themselves up to be like the Creator, expecting to be worshiped because of their magic. He wondered if that was maybe what had happened here, and the Imbatoo people had continued to pass on the tradition down through the centuries.

Feeling too hungry to discuss theology, he instead focused on the sizable helping of meat which one of the preparers had just dropped on his plate. Along with the meat was a bowl of porridge mixed with small green berries that had a sweet taste at first, but quickly turned tart if not swallowed fast enough. He washed it down with a very mild wine the Imbatoo consumed with most of their meals. Narendi had said it was made from the sap of the strange parasol-looking trees growing around the waterfront.

Ty refrained from drinking too much of the wine, and instead opted mostly for his cup of cream. The wine was mild, but if consumed in quantity would leave him lightheaded. The last thing he wanted to be right before embarking on a journey of this magnitude was unsteady.

The meal was finished in quick order as those gathered ate in silence. When they were ready to leave, the sun had yet to rise in the sky. Ty and Breen had been two of the first to lower their plates, even after asking for another helping, not knowing when the next time they might get another good meal would be. They had packed their gear with provisions, but that was still no guarantee.

Overhead, the stars were beginning to fade, and the sky was shifting from black to grey when the king finally stood. As soon as everyone had gathered their weapons and belongings, they were joined by four more men, all of whom were carrying several large tote bags over their shoulders. They wore similar garb to the Mzwati but carried no weapons. Ty recognized one of them as the man who had served Ty his food earlier. Ty wondered why they didn't just take a couple of sherakin, which seemed a better way to convey their supplies than to force these men to bear it themselves. Plus, he had really been looking forward to riding one.

The party, now fourteen men and two women, made their way across the practice field, passing the holding pens on the left, and headed straight for the plateau ahead. However, instead of making their way to the door leading inside the Wazeri compound, they veered right, where a set of stairs had been carved into the stone, leading up to the top. It now became clear why they weren't taking the sherakin, as the long-legged animals would have never been able to scale the rock.

The steps were steep but well kept, and by the time they reached the top, the sun was just beginning to peek over the horizon behind them, setting the sky on fire with red, orange, and gold. Ty could feel the warmth on his back as they stood on the opposite side of the plateau from where they had climbed and gazed out over the vast sea of dunes they were about to cross. The sight was both exhilarating and exhausting.

Eagerly, Ty reached into his pocket and pulled out his compass, doing his best to keep it hidden as he glanced down to see where the needle was pointing. It seemed to be pointing straight ahead. He looked over at Breen, who had spotted him getting the instrument out, and nodded, indicating they were still heading in the right direction.

Beside him, Narendi fidgeted with her spear, adjusting the strap so it sat higher on her back and then checking the curved sword at her waist. She, along with everyone else, besides Atiena, wore the sand-colored robes of the Mzwati, no doubt to keep them hidden during their travels. The question was: *hidden from what?* Ty still had yet to determine why the Imbatoo needed the Mzwati in the first place. Who were they planning on fighting?

Diawandy spoke a few short words, then waved them toward the stairs leading down the backside of the plateau. Without having to be told, Bolo took the lead, directing half of the Mzwati to the front of the line and the other half to the back as they made their way carefully down the dark side of the rock to the awaiting dunes below. By the time they reached the bottom, Ty had wrapped his scarf—or *baka*, as Narendi had called it—up over his head to block the sand-filled wind from getting in his eyes. The others were quick to do the same.

In single file, they left the great rock behind, taking their first steps toward whatever adventure lay ahead. Ty glanced back over his shoulder as the sun's first rays reached over the peak behind them and struck him in the face. He wondered if he'd ever see the village again, and whether he cared one way or the other. Sure, his life had been threatened on more than one occasion during his stay, but the Imbatoo people as a whole had been gracious hosts, nursing him and Breen back to health, providing food and shelter while their bodies healed, even going so far as to allow them access to their most revered relics, the foretelling scrolls.

Ty felt a small sense of sadness as he turned back around. There was something to be said for living so far from all society, a peaceful sense of safety he hadn't felt in quite some time. Still, it was just a dream. People were relying on him, people he loved. As tempting as it would have been to have chucked it all aside and stayed with the Imbatoo, it was just a passing fancy. He knew his own conscience wouldn't allow it, and so with a surprisingly heavy heart, he set his face westward, keeping to the footprints of the person in front of him. He didn't look back again.

As the sun rose in the sky, drops of sweat began to form, causing the sand to stick to his face. His headdress blocked the brunt of it, but, like wading out into the East River and expecting to stop its flow with your hands, it could only do so much. The desert wind was like the river in other ways. Its strength came and went at random intervals. During the moderate times, they would keep walking, pulling their bakas a little tighter around the sides of their face to block the sand. When the worst arrived, they stopped altogether and lowered themselves to the ground, pulling their bakas completely over their heads as they waited it out. Those times of stronger gusts typically only lasted a few minutes, and then they were off once again, keeping to the dune's ridges as their sandals sank foot deep into the sand, deep enough to slow their pace, deep enough to prove an annoyance.

They stopped every so often, sometimes to test the wind, sometimes to get their bearings, and sometimes to simply rest their feet. Atiena, whose place in line was directly behind the king and just in front of Narendi, was having a difficult time keeping up. Her older legs were wobbly, and she seemed to be spending most of her time moving her satchel from one side of her body to the other. On several occasions Narendi had been forced to call a halt as the woman had tumbled to her knees, having either tripped over her own sandals or simply had her legs go out. Ty admired the woman's tenacity. She never seemed to complain, always insisting there was no reason to stop on her account, and that they should keep going.

Bolo, who thankfully remained at the front of the line and kept well away from Ty, carried a small compass, which he used, along with the angle of the sun, to determine their destination. Each time they stopped, Ty checked his own compass as well, which surprisingly showed them almost exactly on course. They did seem to be drifting a little south, but not bad enough for him to believe that this ancient temple they were heading for wasn't exactly where they were intending to go.

The few rests they took were short-lived, and the swallow of water they each received was even more so, but nonetheless, each time, Ty was glad to get back underway. If they were walking, then Bolo wasn't standing there glaring at him and Narendi.

The rest of the day went about the same, although their breaks grew more frequent and lasted longer as their strength began to wane. At one point, Ty thought they were going to have to carry Atiena, after a particularly nasty tumble into the sand that had her rolling halfway down one of the dunes before finally stopping. But in the end, after several of the Mzwati had helped her back to the top, she pushed them off and declared she could keep going. And to her credit, that was exactly what she did, though Ty did notice Narendi moving up closer behind the Wazeri to keep her from going over the side again.

By the time the sun had made its long trek across the sky and slowly sunk below the horizon in front of them, they reached an opening in the dunes. It was a flat area lined with what looked like small batches of white rock on the far side that stretched a good distance to the north and south, as far as the eye could see. Ahead, the dunes themselves seemed to taper off into the distance as well, no longer the deep crevices and peaks, but more ripples across water. In a way, it reminded him of one of the sandy beaches on the east side of Crystal Lake, where he and Breen and his father would go to fish a couple times a year.

"We make camp here," Narendi said softly, after Bolo had stopped to address the group in a notably hushed voice as well. Ty glanced around to see why everyone was talking so quietly, but as far as he could tell, there was no reason. He looked at Breen with a cocked brow and received a shrug in return.

With the sun down, the temperature was dropping quickly. Ty was already finding himself blowing into his hands to keep them from stiffening. He didn't bother unhooking his carry bag until the others had begun to lay their gear aside, forming a wide circle around what looked to have been a pre-dug pit. He couldn't tell how long it had been since the pit's last use. The ashes one would have expected to find inside were no longer there, but with the relentless wind blowing across the open dunes around them, it was no wonder.

Attempting not to appear too obvious, Ty walked slowly around the pit, waiting to see where Bolo would lay his roll before finding a spot on the direct opposite side to lay his own, as far away from the man's angry glare as possible. As soon as he and Breen had found their place, digging away some of the hardened bits of sand underneath to lay their bedding on, Narendi and Atiena strolled over and dropped their satchels down beside them. Narendi stuck her spear in the sand at the head of her bedding. The other Mzwati did the same.

Once their bedrolls had been placed, the four men who had been carrying the brunt of the supplies began to prepare the fire for the evening meal. Everyone seemed to be too tired to hold any conversation longer than a few words, and most of those were Diawandy giving direction to Bolo, and Bolo, in turn, doing the same to the other members of the Mzwati.

Several of the Imbatoo warriors took their spears and made their way over to the other side of the flat area, the side closest to where the scattering of white rocks marked the edge of the dunes ahead. Clearly, they were setting up a perimeter watch, not that Ty could figure out why.

Ty had just finished unrolling his blankets and was reaching for his flute when the ground beneath him rumbled. Everyone hopped to their feet. The Mzwati that hadn't gone out on patrol grabbed their spears. Everyone was looking westward beyond the white rocks. Even those preparing the meal stopped what they were doing and turned.

Ty and Breen stood with the others, gazing out toward the dunes and the last rays of sunlight fading over the horizon. "What's going on?" Ty whispered to Narendi, but she didn't answer, at least not right away, not until the tremors subsided.

Ty clung to his flute, too preoccupied with not knowing what was happening to even think of putting it down and grabbing something a little more useful, like his sword. Beside him, Breen was holding his bow with an already nocked arrow as he scanned the horizon.

"Do you see anything?" Ty whispered.

Breen shook his head but kept a firm grip on the string.

Once the last of the tremors had passed, the group slowly returned to whatever tasks they were previously doing as though nothing had happened, as though they hadn't all just been standing there, weapons in hand, looking like they were about to do battle.

Ty pulled Narendi aside so he and Breen could get some answers. "What's going on? Why was everyone staring at those white rocks as if expecting a horde of desert marauders to come riding in?" Ty looked at the rocks and the dunes beyond. "There aren't desert marauders out there, are there?"

"Marauders would never be so foolish as to come here. This is Mhina Duwapa . . . the feeding grounds. And those," she said, pointing to the piles of white rock at the edge of the dunes, "are not rocks. Those are bones."

"Bones?" Ty felt an icy chill wash over him, strong enough to overpower even the campfire.

"I know I'm going to regret asking this," Breen said, his bow still clutched firmly in his hand, "but feeding grounds to what?"

"To the orms."

Orms? Ty's stomach sank. Breen was right. Ty regretted him asking.

Chapter 58 | Ty

SLEEP THAT NIGHT had been slow to arrive and quick to leave, as Ty had spent most of it shivering under his blanket, weapon in hand, waiting for the next tremor, which would have them all back on their feet and staring out at the moonlit dunes ahead. Ty did manage to doze once or twice between tremors, each time imagining some giant wormlike creature burrowing up out of the sand and sucking him down. Each time, he woke with a start to find Narendi lying in her bedding beside him, staring. Her persistent watch over his well-being was almost as uncomfortable as the thought of what they were about to walk through once the sun came up, which it did all too quickly.

Ty had only ever heard of orms. No one he knew had ever laid eyes on one. There had been descriptions and drawings of the creatures, which almost seemed more myth than real. Who had ever heard of a sand worm large enough to swallow a man? Ty fished with worms. He couldn't imagine one so big it could eat him. He didn't want to imagine it. In fact, he did everything he could to avoid it, but the harder he tried, the more difficult it became, until he was consumed with nothing but giant people-sucking worms rising up out of the sand to feast on their flesh.

He had planned on playing his new instrument for the others that night, but after learning about the orms and observing the hushed silence around the camp, he thought better of it. With his luck, he'd start playing and find the orms enjoyed

- 529 -

a good ditty as well as the next and show up just to listen. Not that orms could hear, since from what he remembered studying about them in school, they sensed vibrations. Needless to say, it had been a very sleepless night.

Morning came to find Ty standing with the others at the edge of the dunes. While the others stared out at the open sand as the first of the sun's rays rose behind them, Ty stared at one of the piles of bones on his right. He couldn't believe he'd mistaken them for rocks. It was pretty clear, now, what they were. All shapes and sizes, some human, some not. Ty wondered how the bones came to be here, and in such well-preserved piles. Orms didn't have hands, and even if they did, he doubted they would have gone to the trouble to stack their leftovers.

"After they eat the flesh," Narendi said, noticing what Ty had been looking at, "they come here to purge the remains."

Ty didn't say anything at first, doing his best not to let his imagination run rampant. Besides, there wasn't much to say after hearing such a horrifying explanation. His stomach turned at the thought of what would happen to anyone who was sucked into one of these creatures. "Is there no way to go around?"

Narendi shook her head. "The Mhina Duwapa is very big. Stretches for days." She pointed both north and south. "We would not have water to make it."

"Are you saying we're going to have to travel for days out there before reaching the temple?"

She shook her head once more. "The temple is one day's journey through," she said, pointing directly ahead. "We should reach it before the sun sets, if we make fast speed."

Ty looked at Atiena, who was preoccupied with whatever Bolo was saying, and wondered how they were ever going to make good speed with her along. The poor woman had barely made it this far and had slept no better than the rest of them. Ty didn't want to end up stuck out here because she couldn't keep up. "Perhaps Atiena should remain here until we get back. I wouldn't want—"

"No," Narendi said adamantly. "A Wazeri must always record."

Ty would have argued that it would be safer for all of them if she didn't, but the resolution in her voice was enough for him to realize he wasn't going to win the argument. So, he turned his attention to the front where Bolo was giving out what sounded like some type of instructions. Ty waited for Narendi to interpret.

"Bolo says we are to walk divided. Space between. Less movement. Less sound."

Ty nodded and fell in line behind the others as they waited at the edge of the dunes and watched as the person in front of them started in. With each new person, Ty's hands shook a little more, counting down the time till he was next. By the time it had come to him, his heart was racing. Narendi, who had been in front of him in line, was about fifteen to twenty feet into the low-rising dunes ahead. Ty felt his brother's hand on his shoulder and turned. Breen nodded encouragingly, and Ty took a deep, dry breath and started in.

He could almost feel the sand shift under his feet, a sense of something moving underneath him. Whether it was just his imagination or not, Ty had no idea. All he could do was take the next step. Once again there was something deadly below him that he couldn't see. Only this time, he didn't exactly have all his magic to fall back on. He had been able to control the water to an extent, but this wasn't water.

Ty glanced over his shoulder in time to see Breen entering the dunes, with the carriers and several of the Mzwati waiting just behind for their turn. Turning back around, Ty willed with all his might for the group ahead to pick up the pace. The faster they went, the sooner they'd get through. At this point, he didn't give a toss about the ancient ruins, the temple, the priests, or even the flaming key. He just wanted to get out of the feeding grounds.

Feeding grounds? He hadn't thought about it before, since he hadn't known about the orms, but that seemed a terrible name for this place. Why would the Imbatoo name it in such a fashion? Were they feeding the orms, and if so, what? Ty felt a tremor and froze. The sand shifted unnaturally under his feet. It wasn't a big tremor, but it was enough to know he hadn't just imagined it. The others stopped as well, at least those he could see. Bolo was too far in the lead, with too much space between, for Ty to keep track of, as were those of the Mzwati bringing up the rear.

Ty reached out with his magic to see if he could find whatever had made the tremor, so as to keep as far from it as possible. He struck something solid off to the right about forty feet out and about ten feet down, and one of the dunes split open and the orm came shooting out. Ty grabbed his mouth to keep from yelping. The orm was even bigger than he had expected, rising a good fifteen feet up out of the sand.

From the side, it looked like what the books had said, nothing more than an enormous worm; however, unlike every other worm he'd ever tried scaring his sister with when he was younger, the front of this one had a wide, gaping maw lined with circular rows of tiny spiked teeth, perfect for ripping the flesh off anything unlucky enough to find itself inside.

Ty released the magical net he had thrown and drew his fire, flames crackling in both hands.

"Don't move," Breen shouted behind him.

Ty had no intention of moving.

Another tremor struck, this one even stronger, and another, even larger orm came ripping out of the dune on the left, this one close enough to spray sand across

Ty's face. Again, he didn't move. He wasn't sure if it was because he didn't want to alert them to his presence or because his appendages had been seized by fear.

The two monstrous creatures turned and dove back into the sand, the smaller sliding in the way it had come, the larger bending over and tunneling a new hole, which was soon covered over as the dune sank in behind it. Ty wheezed, not realizing he'd been holding his breath. No one moved for some time, waiting for the tremors to cease. After what felt like a good ten minutes of standing there waiting for one of those creatures to come up under them, the others in front finally started moving once again.

Behind him, Breen had his bow up and arrow nocked as he swung back and forth, keeping a close watch on both sides in case they came back. The Mzwati behind Breen all had their long spears in hand, which finally made sense. What better weapon to have than something that allows you to attack from a distance? The thought of going up against one of those things with nothing more than a sword or dagger was laughable.

Ty extinguished his fire but kept his magic up and ready, though he had no intention of using his feelers again. He wasn't sure if his magic had been what set the orms off, or if it had just been pure happenstance, but one thing was for sure: he wasn't about to take another chance.

Off in the distance, several more orms appeared, some so big they almost didn't look real, but they were all far enough away that Ty never even felt their tremors. The rest of the party must not have been too worried, as they continued on.

For once, Ty had no qualms with not stopping for lunch, though Bolo did stop infrequently for water, and to give Atiena a chance to catch her breath. Ty was surprised the older Wazeri woman had been able to keep up so far. Of course, a single glimpse of one of those monsters and you'd be astonished at what you can force your body to do.

They continued on through the morning, the heat growing more intense as they reached the afternoon. And with the heat came a notable rise in orm activity. The sand beneath their feet seemed to be in a constant state of flux, the tremors never really ceasing. Ty had hoped they'd been through the worst of it back near where they had spent the night and found all the bones, but it seemed he'd been wrong. Along with the increased rumbling was an increase in orm sightings as they broke through the surface only to slide back in and have the sand cover any trace of their appearance.

Ty was thankful he wasn't carrying a sword or spear or bow like most of the others. Had he been, his white-knuckled hands would have no doubt been clamped so tightly to the weapons that he'd never be able to pry his fingers free again. The tremors grew not only in number but in size. There were times he could actually see the sand near the surface shift as one of the creatures tunneled by.

At one point, Breen stumbled to his knees, rolling over on his back with his bowstring pulled to his cheek as one of the orms passed so close it nearly broke the surface. Ty waited for his brother to make it back to his feet before continuing. It seemed they were no longer stopping for the tremors, as the tremors themselves had ceased to stop.

Ty shifted his pack on his shoulder as he sank one foot after another into the steps of the ones before. All the while, he kept his eyes glued to the surrounding dunes, anticipating the tremors as they came, judging by the way they felt as to how close or how big the orm underneath was. He found that the size of the tremor didn't always correlate with the size of the orm. Sometimes, the largest of the tremors was due to the speed at which the orm burrowed through the sand and not its size.

Another tremor struck, and this one was large enough to have him stopping in place, frantically searching the sand around him. It was close. He raised his hands, blue fire ignited in both as he held his breath. Beside him, the orm came plowing through the dune. The sand under his feet shot up and threw him back as the creature's jaws spread to eat him. He tumbled backward, sand in his face. He barely got a single shot of his fire off as he rolled partway down the other side of the small dune.

He dug his hands in the sand to stop his tumbling and flipped himself over in time to see Narendi charging the creature, spear up and face covered. She struck the orm in the side, burying her spear quarter deep. Breen fired one of his non-Sol Ghati arrows into the giant orm's side. The monster squirmed and released a barrage of popping noises as it turned on Narendi. She pulled her spear free just as the creature opened its mouth and bent down to suck her up.

Frantically, Ty unleashed his fire. It slammed into the creature's side and threw it backward against the sand, long enough for Narendi to get out of its way. There was a gaping hole in the orm's underbelly, still smoldering as the enormous creature jerked and wiggled and eventually managed to slide back into the ground. Ty reached the top of the dune just as the sand was covering what was left of the orm's passing.

Both Breen and Narendi were there to help him the rest of the way up. "Are you hurt?" Breen asked, giving Ty a good looking-over.

"Nothing that Isha's cream can't fix," he said with a forced smile.

Narendi stuck her spear in the sand and began to wipe off the orm's blood, which reminded Ty in a way of the white gooey substance on the outside of most dirt worms they used while fishing. "That was close," she said, standing once again, spear in hand and at the ready. "Too close."

Someone screamed, and they all spun to see Atiena down on her back as an enormous orm burst through the sand in front of her with one of the Mzwati hanging out of the top of its jaws. It was one of the warriors who'd been assigned to help her make it through. The warrior cried out as he pulled out his knife and hacked away at the top of the creature's mouth. A moment later, he was sucked inside, and the ghastly shrills that followed had Ty nearly emptying his stomach as he ran to help the old woman. He sent another wave of fire crashing into the beast as Bolo, Diawandy, and two other Mzwati attacked from the other side.

One of Breen's arrows buried itself into the side of the monstrous creature, and it dropped on top of those spearing it from the back. One of the Mzwati barely managed to push the king out of the way before the creature landed on top of him, burying the warrior under it as it burrowed quickly out of view. All that could be seen of the Mzwati who'd risked his life was the top half of his head and one leg. It was evident by the blood pouring from his eyes that the man was beyond help.

Chucking caution to the wind since caution didn't seem to be working any longer, the group raced ahead, those behind hurrying to catch up as they fought to get free of the growing number of orms. Two of the Mzwati who had been at the rear ran to the front to help Bolo protect the king while those carrying the bags struggled to keep their footing as they raced to catch up. The distance between the members shortened as they charged ahead, no one wanting to be too far away from the others. Narendi had one arm around Atiena, since the older woman was now having a difficult time keeping to her feet.

Three more orms rose out of the dunes, two on the left, one on the right. Ty sent his flames into each, and the Mzwati attacked with their spears. Screams in back had Ty spinning as another orm surfaced, but instead of simply rising up out of the sand, this one leaped from the side like a great sea serpent flying out of the water.

The orm struck from the left, grabbing two of the carriers at once and diving straight back into a dune on the other side. Ty hit it with his flames, slicing the back tail nearly off, but it was too late. The two men didn't even have time to scream before they were dragged under. One of the men was still holding his bags as he was sucked from view.

Orms were rising from everywhere now. It was all Ty could do to keep up, blue flames barreling into each, cutting the smaller in half, burning gaping holes in the larger. But it just wasn't enough.

Ty was thrown backward as Breen grabbed him from behind just as one of the orms dove overtop. Breen unleashed another arrow, and it was buried to the fletching in what could have been the creature's eye. It released a loud set of clicking noises and slithered back into the sand.

Ty dropped his bag. He needed his hands free. He turned to find Atiena rolling down one side of the dune, while Narendi, her father, and Bolo danced between three orms as they stabbed and retreated, stabbed and retreated. "Hold on!" Ty shouted at the Wazeri and charged down the dune after her.

Atiena's rolling saved her life, as one of the giant creatures tore through the sand directly where she'd been. Ty hit the orm with his flame and cut it in half. The top half tumbled straight for Atiena, threatening to squash her just like the last Mzwati had been. Without thinking, he released the fire and called on the wind, snatching her out of the way just as the creature landed. He rushed over and helped the elderly woman to her feet, then carried her up the dune to where the others were battling for their lives.

They weren't going to make it. There were too many of them, more arriving by the moment.

"Why do they attack like this?" Narendi shouted. "They never attack like this!"

Ty shuddered. Was this his fault? Could they somehow sense magic? Or had his magic sent vibrations into the sand that drew their attention? There was only one way to find out. He turned to Breen. "Get the others out of here!" He shoved his brother with a pocket of wind toward Atiena, then ran straight down the dune in the opposite direction, firing fistfuls of hardened air into the ground as he went. Craters in the sand erupted with each strike, like an invisible giant punching holes in the sand with his fists.

If this didn't draw them away, nothing would.

Behind him, Ty could hear his brother shouting for him to stop, but Ty didn't have time to turn as he continued pounding the ground with fists of air while running as fast as his sandals would allow. A giant orm rose up out of the sand on his left where he'd sent the last fist, then another on his right.

It was working.

He sent three more pockets of hardened air deep into the sand about twenty feet ahead of him, showering everything in debris. Two orms tore through the exact spot, hitting each other as they fought for what they thought was their next meal.

Ty didn't stop running. He sent wave upon wave deep into the ground, exploding sand with each new strike as the orms tore through the surface. He didn't know how far he'd gone. By the time he had glanced over his shoulder, he could no longer see his friends behind him. But he didn't let it stop him as he pounded the sand as hard and as often as he could draw the wind to him. He sent each new strike a little farther ahead, until finally he was barely able to see where his magic was hitting, only judging strikes by where the orms were surfacing off in the distance. Pretty soon the tremors slowed, then stopped altogether.

Barely able to keep going, Ty dropped to his knees, panting as he struggled to catch his breath. He knelt on his hands and knees and watched the great orms shrink into the distance, then disappear from view. Why hadn't he thought to do that sooner? Those men might not have died if he had. Their screams came back to haunt him.

He pushed himself back to his feet and lowered his baka further on his forehead to cover his eyes, as the sun was now slipping down toward the horizon and shining directly in his face. Had they been fighting for that long? He looked behind him. Nothing but sand in all directions. His footsteps were only visible as far as the next dune before the harsh northerly wind swept them away.

A sudden panic rose, and he quickly felt for the key. His hand latched onto the medallion and he breathed a huge sigh of relief. Then he remembered the compass and quickly reached for his pocket. His fingers brushed against the small round object inside, and he smiled. He hadn't lost it. Ty pulled out the silver instrument that didn't point north and followed its bearing with his eyes. Again, nothing but sand as far as he could see.

By the time his legs had stopped shaking enough to continue on, he realized he was no longer carrying the satchel Narendi had given him. He hoped his brother had seen it and thought to grab it before leaving. Worse yet, his waterskin had been tied to his pack.

He screamed his frustration into the wind, wondering, perversely, how bad it would feel if he hit himself with a pocket of wind. Maybe just a small one, small enough to knock some sense into his thick skull.

How far was he going to get without water? Not very far if he didn't keep going. Picking up speed, Ty forced himself onward, following the compass's guidance. The only solace he could take was that Narendi had said the temple was supposed to be but a single day's journey, and the sun was quickly heading in that direction. Maybe there was hope yet. Ty stopped again and turned back around, a single thought gnawing at the back of his mind. If he knew his brother, which he did. He knew Breen wouldn't just leave him out in the dunes to die on his own. As soon as the orms were gone, he would have tried looking for him.

He scanned the dunes on his right, back in the direction he had run from, but saw nothing but sand in the distance. This was bad. There was no way his brother would know where he was. Breen didn't have the compass. Ty's head lifted. But he knew Ty had it, which meant he knew Ty would be heading in the same direction, hopefully. Either way, Ty couldn't just wait out there on the dunes, hoping someone would show up. He had to keep going.

Determined not to let this beat him, and with the occasional tremor reminding him that the orms hadn't vanished altogether, Ty pressed on. Twice he was forced to stop as the wind whipping over the dunes rose to the level of not allowing him to see, and each time he dug a hole and used his baka to cover his head as he waited it out.

His legs were tiring, and his stomach let him know with each new step how angry it was with Ty for not thinking to grab his satchel before running off into the middle of the desert like some flaming stupid hero. Heroes were supposed to die in battle, not die of thirst on some forsaken sand dune.

By the time he stopped to rest his legs, the sky above him was lit with a beautiful fusion of purples and blues as the sun dropped below the horizon ahead, taking with it the worst of the heat, but leaving behind a chill that Ty knew would only get worse. He pulled back his baka and let the warm desert breeze blow across his face. All he wanted to do at that point was lie back and let the sounds of the desert lull him to sleep, but as much as he needed the rest, especially after having expended so much of his energy on his magic, something inside of him told him to keep going. Probably the same *something* that had told him to go running off like a crazy man into the dunes in the first place. He needed to quit listening to that *something*.

Reluctantly, he crawled back to his feet and started walking. His tongue was already beginning to swell, and what little saliva he had managed to hold on to after the battle had dried up hours ago. His skin burned and his muscles ached, but that paled in comparison to the thirst, the inability to even swallow as each breath cut like a thousand tiny blades down his throat.

The colors in the sky faded, shifted to the monochromatic, leaving shadows to float across the horizon in front of him, silhouettes of objects Ty was certain to be nothing more than his imagination. Every so often he would see broken towers and crumbling walls ahead as his mind played tricks on him, making him believe he was getting close, but then stripping it all away as soon as he reached the next dune.

Only the brightest of the stars were visible overhead, as night had not yet come to claim the land, though it did seem to be lurking just around the corner. His fingers were starting to numb from the cold, forcing him to continuously blow on them. Now he had to contend with the possibility of freezing to death on top of everything else.

Behind him, there was no sign of the rising moon, and everything was awash in pale grey. In front of him, Ty could once again make out the tops of spires rising in the distance. They looked like tall misshapen monsters rising out of the deep to block his way forward.

The closer he got, the more defined their shapes became. Not only could he see small towers and crumbling walls, but windows and pillars and doors. It all seemed a fanciful dream, one Ty was sure to wake up from at any moment. It wasn't until he had reached the end of the dunes and was walking across a flat open area of hardened sand and rock that he realized it wasn't a mirage at all. It wasn't the night playing tricks on him.

He had reached his destination. He had found Zwaneri a Wakale.

Chapter 59 | Ty

"TY!" SHADOWS CHARGED OUT of the night from what looked like an entrance through the main wall surrounding the ancient temple ruins. It was too dark to see who it was, but Ty didn't need to. He knew the voice and stumbled toward it. He tripped over his own feet and plummeted straight for the ground, but two enormous arms were underneath him before he hit, pulling him up and squeezing him tight. "You had us worried. I can't believe you did that." There was a slight pause. "Actually, yes, I can."

Ty wanted to tell his brother how overjoyed he was to find him there, and alive, but nothing but grunts and garbled words came out of his parched throat.

Narendi was there as well, running her hands through his hair and saying something about how brave he had been. Something about saving their lives. Something about being very, very stupid. Ty couldn't argue there.

"Water," was all he could manage to say as Breen helped him through the gate, which was nothing more than a large hole in a decrepit wall with no actual gate in sight. Beyond the wall was a long stone porch with half-formed pillars covering the front of the main complex. Even in the dark, Ty could see the temple's massive size, much bigger than it had appeared from a distance. The outside looked barely a shell of itself, with piles of chipped stone crumbling around the outer walls, windows without glass or framing, doors that looked barely able to keep to their hinges.

It was a strange place to hide a key; then again, no stranger, he guessed, than the other two places they'd been. He only hoped that the key hadn't been lost to time. This place didn't look like it had seen visitors in centuries. He wondered what Diawandy and Narendi had been referring to when they talked about priests living here. It was clear that no one lived here.

One of the double doors at the front stood ajar, and Ty was helped inside. He gasped as they passed through the overhead archway, pulling Breen to a stop.

"Fascinating, isn't it?" Breen said, practically holding Ty in his arms, as Ty's legs felt like buckling.

Fascinating didn't even come close to describing it. The inside looked nothing like the out. He had expected to find parts of the roof missing with fallen beams, overturned stone, and dust-coated floors. Instead, the inside looked as though it had been built sometime within the last couple of weeks, with the main hall as welcoming as the East Inn—if the East Inn looked as luxurious as the Sidaran Assembly Hall or Overlord Barl's estate.

Clean-swept marble floors of deep blue and gold and white covered the entranceway from the doors to a grand staircase at the back, leading up to a spiral balcony with corridors that led off in a multitude of directions. The room was modestly decorated—compared to the elaborate blue-and-gold fluted pillars along the sides, interspersed by tall stained-glass windows that stretched nearly the entire height of the walls—with colorful tapestries, gold sconces, and ornamental vases carrying arrangements of flowers that could never have grown in such a climate as this, and yet there they were.

As incredible as it was, nothing compared to the enormous tree that sat at the center of the rotunda, its branches reaching up and out over the pool of water it rested within. The tree was green and full of life, even in a place as dry as this. Surrounding the pool were several short white marble stands that had a single strip of soft cushioned leather covering the top rail, along with a thick leather cushion near the floor that Ty could only guess was a place to stop and kneel on, which made sense if the priests came here to pray.

The wonder of it all had Ty nearly forgetting his thirst. Looking around, he half expected to find Tirana and the rest of the Karpaathians standing there waiting on him for another one of their magic feasts. Instead, he found Diawandy, Bolo, Atiena, and the two remaining carriers, along with the three remaining Mzwati, sitting around a large stone table on the left in front of an even larger hearth. The blaze inside was warm and inviting, melting away the chill from outside.

Clearly, some powerful magics were at work. But which was the lie? The outside ruins or the inside splendor?

Breen directed Ty over to one of the empty chairs at the table, which Narendi had already pulled out for him. Diawandy and the others stood when they saw him coming, greeting him in their native tongue. Bolo was the last to speak, and Narendi graciously offered an interpretation. "Bolo says that he would be honored to stand beside you in battle if ever you need it. Your bravery saved lives. It will not be forgotten."

Ty wasn't quite sure how to respond, considering the man had tried to kill him, but he did manage to pass a firm nod and a smile to the Mzwati warrior, though the smile might have been directed more toward the pitchers of drink sitting on the table in front of his seat. Narendi poured him a glass, which shook as he lifted it to his mouth and slowly emptied it of the warm spicy liquid inside. It burned at first, but once the back of his throat was good and coated, he downed one more, forcing Breen to cut him off before he made himself sick.

Ty set the goblet on the table and sat back in the seat, noticing for the first time that it had a cushioned back. He watched the flames from the candelabras on the table dance to some unheard melody, their flickers all in perfect harmony as they swished and swayed to an unfelt breeze. Ty closed his eyes and let the pain slowly release from his body. He didn't want to move. Someone touched his hand, and he opened them to find Narendi rubbing white paste across the top of the reddest skin before moving on to his forehead and cheeks.

Isha's cream felt wonderful, almost as wonderful as the gentle way Narendi spread it on. He found himself once again closing his eyes and enjoying the sensation. He was too tired to worry about what the others might think of her attention, especially Bolo. In fact, he was too tired to open his eyes at all.

Suddenly, he felt himself being lifted, and he peeked through his lids long enough to see the table and those sitting around it moving away from him as Breen carried him over to the side.

"Where are we going?" he asked, at least he thought he asked. He didn't remember ever hearing an answer as his eyes closed once more.

Next thing he knew, he was waking to find himself lying on a long sofa against the side wall, staring over at the table in front of the hearth. How long had he been out? The windows at the front showed no light coming in, which meant he hadn't slept through the night.

He was feeling stronger as he sat up and stretched. Breen stood from the table when he saw Ty was awake and walked over. "How are you feeling? You looked pretty out of it."

"How long was I asleep?" His throat still burned as his eyes drifted back to the now empty-looking pitchers on the table.

"Not long. You ready for some food? The priests were kind enough to offer us lodging for the night."

"Priests?" Ty glanced around the room but saw no one but his own traveling companions.

"They've already come and gone."

Ty could smell something pleasant wafting from the direction of the table, pleasant enough to have him standing all on his own and looking to find the first empty seat available. Two of the three Mzwati stood watch by the doors at the front. The third was nowhere to be seen, most likely patrolling the grounds outside, or perhaps searching one of the many passageways leading off the main hall.

As soon as Ty sat, Narendi went about filling him a plate. She put a little bit of everything the priests had offered, which wasn't much more than meat, bread, fruit, and nuts, but it was the best meat, bread, fruit, and nuts he'd eaten in some time. At least, that was the way it felt to him.

He went to stick a slice of something that resembled an apple into his mouth, then paused. "How sure are we of these priests?" This was part of the next test after all. "Is it safe to eat?"

"We have come here for many generations," Narendi said. "They are very generous."

Good enough. Ty stuffed the fruit in his mouth and chewed. It was softer than an apple, more the consistency of a ripe pear, but not as moist. "Why would anyone want to come here? We barely survived."

"We send our young ones here on pilgrimage. They come to prove they are no longer children."

Ty paused in chewing his first bite of the meat, which he found had a pleasantly mild flavor, not strongly spiced like the Imbatoo tended to cook theirs. "You send your children out here? Are you crazy? Why in Aldor would you do that?"

"It's their Pkana Undari. The rite of passage to become an adult, at least those that wish to train as Mzwati."

"How do you have any Mzwati if you send them all through there?"

Breen nodded. "That does seem a good way to kill off your younger generation."

Narendi looked frustrated as she shook her head. "It is not like that. Rarely do those on Pkana Undari ever see an orm. Those that do count themselves lucky if they get the chance. It is a rare thing to see an orm attack. I have never witnessed such a thing as what we saw today."

Ty lowered his fork. "That might have been my fault. I think they might have been attracted to my magic."

Narendi looked confused as she interpreted what was being said to the others who were sitting around the table. "But you were using no fire when they came?"

"No, but I was using another type of magic."

"Another type? I do not understand."

Ty sighed. He was tired of having to constantly explain everything. "I'm not like other wielders. I don't have just one gift." He refrained from explaining that he wasn't fully human. That would have been too much for them to take, but he did go about explaining some of his other gifts, at least those he knew about. The others seemed particularly interested in his flute magic after hearing the story about what had happened during Performance Night at the East Inn.

The best way to explain it would be to show them.

Breen carried over Ty's pack, which he had thankfully salvaged after the orm attack, and placed it on the table, where Ty quickly dug out his newly built pipe flute.

"When did you make that?" Breen asked.

Ty smiled. "The night before last."

"When you were supposed to be catching up on some rest?" Breen asked, giving Ty a harsh look.

"I couldn't sleep."

Ty tested the flute, making sure it hadn't been damaged during the battle. From what he could tell, it was still in good shape. None of the tubes were broken or loose. He ran his lips over it, releasing a soft continuous breath of directed air across each of the openings, sending their melody echoing throughout the open chamber. It sounded so much better inside the temple conclave than it ever did inside his tent. The single string of ascending notes carried on even after he had finished blowing, their tune reverberating off the walls and floor and ceiling as if by magic.

Everyone stopped what they had been doing to watch and listen.

It had been a while since he'd played anything. He was a bit rusty, but as soon the air escaped his lips and the first notes swelled from the pipes, it all seemed to come rushing right back to him, and he gave himself over to it. He could feel the warmth of his magic filling every note. He started slowly at first, letting the hauntingly airy melody sweep over them like the warm desert breeze as it moved across the dunes, the steady rhythm soothing and warm, like a soft blanket caressing the skin on a cold winter night.

He watched as the room folded in on itself. The walls and floor and table and hearth all being stripped away, and suddenly they were floating across the dunes. They were the wind, rising up and down as it pulled them along, floating slowly across the seemingly endless mounds of sand. The wind was warm, but not hot, comforting, like a long bath after a hard day's work. Ty could feel the tension slip from shoulders as he let the music carry him and the others wherever it desired.

The music shifted once again, and they were no longer floating over the dunes, but along a winding stream that grew in size as it cut its way through the heart of a lush green forestland, one that Ty was very familiar with. Beside him, Breen shifted in his seat at the sight of the Sidaran Forest and the East River. The others stared in blank wonder as their eyes darted from one tree to the next, staring longingly at all the water flowing underneath them.

He took them to his favorite spot within the birchwood grove. He took them to some of his favorite locations along the river that he and his brother had spent years exploring. He took them down past Easthaven, under the East Bridge and past Veldon's dockworks. He took them upriver past Gilly's sanctuary and all the way to Crystal Lake. He even let them see inside Meerwood Forest and all the places he had been that meant something to him. He ended his music on the shores of the river, taking them up the narrow footpath through the woods and eventually over a small wooden bridge that led around to the side of a cottage that looked like it had been built right out of the forest.

He was finally home.

Tears streaked down his cheeks, and Breen's as well, as he finally released his hold on the last note, and the vision vanished and the temple returned. He laid the pipe on the table in front of him and was surprised to find Narendi's arm around his. He hadn't noticed her taking it during the performance, but she was scooted up tight against him, staring like all the others at the wooden instrument on the table as if it possessed all the magic itself.

Narendi was the first to speak, though still staring at the flute. "I do not know how to express my feelings. I've never seen beauty such as this."

Ty smiled. "I wanted you to see my home."

Narendi let the others know what it was they had seen, most looking as though they were still in shock.

Several of those on the other side of the table stood, staring at something on the other side of the room. Ty turned in his seat to find a group of green-and-gold-robed clerics all gathered behind the tree, each with a long staff in hand, and all with their hoods up. There were even more watching from the balcony, all carrying staffs, all with raised hoods. Ty got the uncomfortable feeling that the other boot was about to drop.

Four clerics broke from the rest and made their way across the room, skirting the great tree at the center, and over to where Ty and the others were gathered at the table. The man at the front of the group stopped a few steps from Ty's seat and bowed. "We are the Wengoby priests," he said in unexpected clear Aldoran, "Keepers of the Temple of Divine Order and protectors of the Treasure of Tmoksuween. We have been awaiting your arrival."

Ty stood from his seat, as did the others. "Yes. Sorry about that, I was running a bit late. I got a little lost in the dunes and wasn't here with the others when you first greeted them."

The priest pulled back his hood to reveal an older man with a thin face, thick dark brows resting over even darker eyes, and a bald head with some sort of decorative runes tattooed across the top. "We have been waiting much longer than that," he said with a smile. "If you are the one, then your coming has been foretold for nearly a thousand years. And by the glamour you just performed, I would say you might be the one we have anticipated." He took a step forward and pulled back the collar of Ty's robe, revealing his left shoulder. One look at the markings, and the priest released the material. "Yes, I believe you are."

Ty looked at Narendi. "Do you need to interpret?"

"Interpret what? He speaks Imbatoo."

"No. He's speaking Aldoran."

"A simple language spell," the priest said with a smile. "Those that listen can understand in whatever tongue they speak."

"That's a handy gift," Breen noted.

Ty nodded before turning back to the priest. "Whether I'm the one or not, I'm here for—"

"Yes, we know," the priest interrupted before Ty could finish. "But first you must rest tonight. Gather your strength. You still have quite the journey ahead of you. Come." He motioned for the group to follow as he and the other three started toward the back, where they found a passageway behind the stairwell, leading further into the temple complex.

The long corridor was lit with bronze sconces that released some sort of scented flame that had Ty wanting to yawn. They passed several doors and adjoining hallways, stopping only once at a large circular intersection with three branching tunnels.

"We have rooms for each of you," the priest said, pointing down the corridor on the left. "I hope you find them to your liking."

The bald man remained in the antechamber and watched as several of the other priests directed the travelers to their rooms. None of the priests spoke or removed their hoods. They simply pointed to a specific member of Ty's group, then to a random door. Ty's was third from the end. A woman in green robes pointed to the left, and Ty opened the door and stepped inside.

It wasn't at all what he expected. The room was small, two single beds on the left, a dresser on the right, walls of plaster and wood, with a wooden plank floor and a single shuttered window on the far side of the room. Even without the shutters, there was no way that Ty could see out, since the room wasn't on a direct outside wall. Then again, nothing was certain in this place. Putting aside the sheer strangeness of finding a window in an interior room, it was the room itself that had Ty almost jumping with excitement.

The bedstand between the beds was exactly the same, even down to the off-sized leg on the right that made the table lamp wobble whenever bumped. He had always meant to get around to fixing it. The comforter was the same, so were the sheets and pillows. He walked over and practically leaped onto the far bed. He recognized the tug on the ropes in the center, the familiar squeak whenever he would turn over on his left side. He couldn't believe it.

It was his own bedroom.

How were these priests doing this? Were all the bedrooms like this, or was it just his? He laid his head on his lumpy feather pillow and found he didn't really care. With a full stomach and the comfort of his own bed, Ty was out as soon as he shut his eyes, too tired to have stopped himself had he wanted to, which he didn't.

Chapter 60 | Ty

TY WOKE TO EARLY MORNING rays seeping in through the shuttered window, feeling more rested than he had since leaving home to begin this insane quest. He'd lost count of how long it had been. The days seemed to blend together. The lamp beside his bed was still lit, the wick inside never seeming to burn down.

Rolling over, he sat on the edge of his bed and started to slip back into his sandals but thought better of it. Instead, he opened his bag and pulled out his pants and tunic and coat. He then pulled on his boots and slipped the sand-covered robes back inside his satchel before strapping on his short sword and belt knife. If they were to make it through the next test, it was highly unlikely they'd end up inside another desert.

Placing his carry bag on the bed, he walked over to the window and pushed open the shutters. His breath caught in his throat as he found himself staring out over the winding stream behind their house. He could see the old oak tree on the other side, even the wooden marker indicating where his mother lay at rest. Tears rolled down his cheeks. He didn't know if it was from the sight of his mother's grave or just being able to see his home once again. Either way, he didn't care. It gave him the strength to press on.

Behind him, the door opened, and he heard a slight rustle. He turned to find Breen standing in the doorway, back in his original clothing as well, and carrying his pack and weapons. "I wondered what your room would have been. I should have known."

"What was yours like?" Ty asked.

"I slept out under the stars on a bed of soft pine needles, with nothing but the crackling of a good blaze to lull me to sleep."

"Figures." Ty walked over to his bed and snatched up his satchel.

"How do you think they're doing this?"

Ty shook his head.

"I wonder if it's anything like your . . . what did they call it last night? Glamour magic?"

"I don't know, but it's way more powerful than what I was doing. I wonder what the others' rooms were like." Stepping into the hall, Ty took one last look around his room before shutting the door.

"How was your sleep?" a voice behind them asked.

Ty and Breen turned to find Narendi in her Mzwati robes, walking down the hall in their direction, staring curiously at Ty's door. She looked like she wanted to open it and see where the temple had taken him, but she refrained; instead, taking the time to look at their change of outfits and frown. "Those are no good for the desert."

"We don't plan on being in the desert for much longer," Ty said.

Narendi shifted her pack and spear higher on her shoulder. "The others are waiting. The priests have prepared a morning meal."

"You've been here before, haven't you?" Ty asked. "When you underwent your Pkana Undari?"

"Yes."

"Why didn't you tell us about this place?"

She smirked. "Why? Where did your room take you?"

"It took me to my bedroom back home. It was incredible. Every detail exactly the same, right down to the smell of my pillow."

She smiled. "I know. It is of the Divine."

"It is of magic, is what it is."

"Magic like yours?"

Ty shrugged. "I guess."

She looked at his arm, and her face grew pensive. "Where is my pledge?"

Ty groaned inwardly. He had hoped she wouldn't notice that he was no longer wearing the bracelet, especially since he had changed clothes, but apparently, he wasn't going to get away with it. He took a moment to dig around in his satchel before producing the gold piece of jewelry and tucking it up snug on his arm.

They both stood there for a moment staring at it until Breen finally interrupted. "I believe the lady said something about food," he stated as he started down the hall back toward the rotunda.

Ty and Narendi rushed to catch up. "Where did your room take you?" he asked.

She blushed. "It took me to, uh . . . It took me to a tent."

Ty noted she said *a* tent and not *her* tent. "So, it took you home?"

She hesitated once more. "Uh, yes. Back to the village." Again, she kept her answer vague. She didn't say more, and with the embarrassed look on her face, Ty didn't press. He had a feeling he would regret it if he did.

They followed the scented sconces back to the main hall, where they found the rest of the group sitting at a sizable spread of breads and cheeses, porridge and honey, a variety of fruit, some cut meat, and pitchers of cream and spiced ale to wash it down. Ty felt that after finishing off more than one plateful from the previous night, he'd be too bloated to eat more, but one look at the food and he started filling his plate once again.

By the time they had finished, having spent the majority of the meal discussing the variety of sleeping arrangements they had each undergone, the priests returned. The balcony was once again filled as the rest of the green-robed clerics stood around the great tree, each with their hoods up, each carrying the same wooden staff, clearly a symbol of their order. The bald man who had spoken with them the previous night greeted them once again, his hood the only one lowered.

"It is time," was all he said. It was all he had to say.

Ty looked at Breen, and his brother nodded. "I'm ready."

The priest raised his staff over his head and turned to those gathered around the room. "The seeker has come in search of the shorlock!" His voice rang throughout the empty hall. "The time has come, brothers and sisters. The time our forefathers bade us to be vigilant for." He looked at Ty. "What is it that you seek? Fame? Fortune? Power? They can all be yours if you choose the correct door."

Ty thought a moment. Was this part of the test? What door was he referring to? He didn't care about fame, fortune, and power, but if this was part of the test, he wanted to make sure his answer was a good one. This led him to consider whether either of those three could be used for good. After careful deliberation, and believing he had reasoned out a sensible answer, he responded.

"I seek *fame* only in that it will draw those who need my help. I seek *fortune* only in that it will aid in our fight against those that wish to destroy us. I seek *power* only in that it will allow me to stand against the coming darkness." He studied the cleric's face, trying to read whether his answer had been the right one or not, but saw no sign one way or the other. He spared a passing glance at Breen, who seemed rather proud of Ty's well-versed response by the staunch smile on his face and the encouraging nod.

The priest conferred quietly with a couple of the other clerics standing nearby, which had Ty second-guessing his answer. The priest finally turned back around. "To be honest, that wasn't exactly what I had expected." He studied Ty's face a moment as if looking for something hidden within, but then finally continued. "We shall put it to the test."

He waved his staff in the direction of the great tree, and the air began to shimmer as two stone arches appeared out of nowhere in front of the garden pool. It was similar in the way things appeared and disappeared whenever he played his flute. Each archway had a single door, both of which appeared to be the exact same, both of which were closed.

The priest walked over between the two and directed Ty to approach, which he did, as did the others of their company. "If what you seek is fame, fortune, and power, you will find that behind this door here," he said, pointing with his staff to the arch on the left. The door to that particular portico opened, and Ty, along with everyone else, stood there in dumbfounded wonder. "The treasure of Tmoksuween."

The room inside was a vast chamber filled with piles of gold, with golden statues, jeweled chalices, rings, necklaces, crowns, and weaponry, gems without measure. It was a treasure beyond any imagining.

"But," the priest said, turning to the archway on the right, "if it is something else you seek . . ." He raised his staff, and the second door opened to reveal a small empty stone room with nothing but a single raised dais with a small metal object floating overtop.

Ty didn't hesitate. He walked over to the second archway and stepped through, lifting the medallion from around his neck as he did. As soon as he held it up, the third piece shot from the dais and connected at the center. The piece reminded him of a compass needle. However, instead of a single needle, this one had three, each like the head of a spear with strange ridges that worked their way from the base down to the tip. They spun freely on the medallion, leaving only one piece left, an open socket at the center for something round to fit into. He had a feeling it was probably some sort of jewel or crystal, no doubt what gave it its power.

He hung the key back around his neck and tucked it under his tunic before turning and stepping out of the doorway and back into the main hall, where the others watched in silence. He turned to the priest, a little confused. "Was that it?"

The cleric looked confused as well. "What more did you expect?"

"Well, to be honest, after everything we went through for the other two pieces, I was expecting flaming darts, or boiling water, or a giant rat trying to eat me. I don't know. Something more. This was a test of strength, wasn't it?"

The priest chuckled. "Son, if you've made it this far, then your strength has already been tested. No. This was a test of the strength of your character. Only someone truly desiring of this key would have walked through that door. Anyone else would have surely chosen the other."

Ty turned to look at those gathered around, but most of them were still too busy staring at the famed treasure of Tmoksuween to pay much attention.

"You see my point," the priest said with a smile, then waved his staff, and both doors shut and the two archways vanished altogether, drawing everyone's attention back to the priest. "Sometimes the most difficult tests are the ones that challenge us in ways we do not expect. A test of character can be far more difficult to overcome than flaming arrows, or boiling water, or even rats."

Ty guessed that could be true, though it did have him wondering what this last test would be. He'd suffered through three of the four so far: Faith, Wisdom, and Strength. Now for the final test: Compassion. He hoped it was as easy a choice as this one had been. Although, getting to the test had proven much more difficult and time-consuming than the other two combined, giving him a slight pause as he thought about where they might end up next.

"What will happen to you now that your guardianship of the key is complete?" Ty asked, looking around the great room at all the green-robed individuals standing about, even those encircling the balcony. Where had they all come from? Surely they weren't all there just to protect the key. What did they do in the meantime?

"We have more than just the key we keep watch over."

As interested as he was in finding out what other secrets lay hidden within the magical walls of this temple, Ty had other more pressing concerns, like claiming the final piece of the key. "Is our mirror close by?"

The priest smiled. "Of course." He turned and headed for the right side of the room where one of several large tapestries hung, its tassels scraping the top of the marble tile underneath. One of the clerics took hold of a gold-colored cord beside the tapestry and pulled, lifting the tapestry as he did.

The mirror rested just behind, its frame built directly into the temple's wall. Ty and the others of his party walked over to take a look. He reached into his pocket and grabbed the compass, two of the runic names around the frame suddenly beginning to glow as they became legible enough to read. Before he called them out, he looked at those gathered behind him, stopping on Narendi. "Tell your father I wish to thank him for his generosity. If it were not for your people's help, the desert would have taken us long ago."

She interpreted, and her father stepped forward and offered both Ty and Breen his arm, speaking to them as he did. "My father says that it has been his honor and privilege to serve the Mazota Wanjenga. And he wishes you and your brother safe journeys, long life, and . . ." Narendi blushed. "Many children."

Ty offered the king a smile before releasing his arm, then turned to the Wazeri, who was busy documenting everything that was happening. "Tell Atiena to make sure she records these events accurately." He grinned. "Make sure she mentions something about my heroicness with the orms."

Narendi groaned but relayed Ty's message to Atiena anyway. The Wazeri woman bowed in turn and then went right back to scribbling on her papers, no doubt recording how Ty had demanded they make him look good in the histories.

Ty finally turned to Narendi. Now for the difficult part: letting her down easily. "You're an incredible woman, Narendi, and you will make a great leader of your people one day." He paused to see how she was taking it so far, and surprisingly, she seemed to be taking it pretty well. No weeping, no begging him to stay, no demanding they bond. Perhaps she now realized the importance of his mission. Of course, when he had an entire sect of secluded magical priests all calling him the destined one, and her own people's scrolls declaring much the same, how could she argue with that? "I am very honored to have gotten to know you and your people."

She smiled, still no tears or demands for marriage, which Ty took as a good sign. He quickly turned back to the mirror and called out the two names before she changed her mind. She would be better off with one of her own people. Bolo seemed a good man. Ty was sure he would do everything he could to make her happy . . . or die trying. "*Siwazuri Batwana. Radanja Dubravska.*"

The mirror sparked to life, the reflections of those gathered disappearing as a new image took its place. It was the image of a small circular room that reminded Ty of the first mirror he had traveled through in Reed Marsh, the one inside the great tree called Abinayu. There was a similarity to the walls, much like the hollowed-out inside of a tree. Several covered lanterns hung around the circular chamber, and at the center of the floor was a painted triangle with strange markings covering all three sides. There didn't appear to be anyone in the room, but wherever this mirror was, it was clearly being used by someone, so they needed to hurry.

He turned to all those gathered. "If the Creator wills it, we will meet again."

"Sooner than you may think," the bald priest said as Ty stepped through the glass and out the other side, leaving Ty wondering what he could have possibly meant.

Ty quickly moved out of the way in time for Breen to step through as well. He turned to wave goodbye to Narendi and the others before the glass shifted and saw her with her head buried in her father's chest. Ty had broken her heart. He only hoped she would forgive him. The glass started to shift, and Ty opened his mouth to wish her farewell, but before he got the chance, Narendi released her father and dove through.

She hit Ty with the full weight of her body, and they both went down. "What have you done?" He pushed her off and scrambled to his feet. "Have you lost your mind? I don't know if I can get you back."

He looked at the mirror—the temple now gone, leaving only their reflections—and grabbed the compass. None of the names lit up. He tried as hard as he could to remember what the two names had been, but no matter how hard he tried, they were gone. He attempted several variations of what he thought they'd been—even Breen gave a guess or two—but the mirror remained silent and unmoving.

Ty stood there with his mouth open. "I can't believe you did this."

Beside him, Breen was still too much in shock to know what to say, both of them staring at the Imbatoo princess as she glared defiantly right back at them.

"I am now yours," she said. "Where you walk, I walk. Where you go, I follow. I belong to you, and you to me."

"No!" Ty shook his head adamantly. "No, you don't belong to me."

"I have already performed the Ritual of Anaka," she stated firmly, pulling off her baka and revealing a head every bit as bald as the Wengoby priest. "It's done."

Ty gaped. "Where's your hair?"

She ran her hand over her smooth scalp. "My father performed the ritual last night, giving me his blessing."

"I don't understand. What does that have to do with you cutting off your hair?"

"It is the way Imbatoo women show that they have chosen their mate."

"Wonderful, but I didn't make a choice, other than to wear this bracelet." He quickly took it off.

"It is not for you to choose," she said. "It is the woman's right to choose who she will give her life to, and I have chosen you. I will be your first."

Ty shook his head till he thought his brains might fall out. "That is not how *we* do it. I told you, I have already pledged myself to someone else, and I have no intention of being married to more than one woman." He felt like pulling his hair out. He turned to Breen. "Say something. Tell her."

Breen just stood there, looking as perplexed as ever. "Tell her what?"

"Explain to her why I'm not her husband."

Breen turned to Narendi, who was practically shooting spears out of her eyes. "In our culture, being bonded is not the choice of just one partner. It is a consensual choice between both the man and the woman."

She hmphed. "With my people, the woman makes the decision, and her father discusses the arrangement with the man, who in turn has to show that he is capable of providing for her and their children."

"There, you see?" Ty butted in. "Your father never discussed anything with me. I can't provide for you. I can't even provide for myself. I'm only sixteen. I haven't even chosen an apprenticeship yet." At the rate things were going, he never would. He had thought at one time to apprentice with Orlyn. The idea of working with all the plants within his apothecary had always been a fascination of his.

"I am an Imbatoo princess," she stated. "No man denies me. I have performed the Anaka. I am now yours. Where you go, I go. Where you walk, I—"

"Yeah, I heard you the first time. Where you walk, I walk, where you go, we'll all go, apparently." He groaned. He wasn't getting anywhere with this, and it was clear as glass they weren't going to be able to return to the temple. He didn't see any other choice. He was stuck with her for now, whether he wanted it or not.

"We can't stay here," Breen said. "We need to keep going. Whether or not you two are legitimately bonded remains to be seen. For right now, though, we need to figure out where we are and how to get to the final piece of the key. So, if you two can put aside this awkward situation for the moment, we have more important things to worry about."

Ty took a deep breath and grabbed his satchel from off the floor where it had fallen and hooked it over his shoulder. This was the worst test of all. He'd rather face a horde of maze monsters, or cave creatures, or even orms, than Narendi claiming him as her bonded husband. Most guys would have probably killed to be in his shoes, a beautiful princess wanting to give herself to him, but then again, he wasn't most guys, and his heart already belonged to another, never more so than right now.

Doing his best to take Breen's advice and put this terrible situation aside, he started for the set of stairs at the back. The circular well was much longer than Ty had anticipated as the stairs wound their way ever upward. They must have been deep within the roots for such a long climb. Ty noted the chill in the air, a good sign that they were back in Aldor once again.

They reached the top of the very narrow staircase and found a single door, short enough that Breen was forced to duck as he went through first, demanding Ty and Narendi wait for him to make sure it was safe. After a brief look around, he motioned for them to follow, and Ty stepped out. A freezing gust of wind struck him in the face and set his teeth to chattering.

Narendi gasped and grabbed Ty's arm when she realized they were standing far above the ground on a very wobbly wood-and-rope walkway. The rickety balcony wrapped around the trunk of the enormous tree they'd just climbed out of. Several rope bridges led off in different directions, connecting their tree to other giant trees nearby. Even with all his years in the Sidaran Forest, Ty had never seen trees this size before.

Far below, the massive root systems spread out between the trees, most of which were completely surrounded by water. There was no dry ground in sight.

Boats floated in and around the roots, leading to docks and stairs and doorways, where people could be seen scurrying about with no more care than shoppers passing in the streets of Easthaven on their way to the next merchant. It was a good thing Ty wasn't afraid of heights. If so, this might have proven one of the worst tests yet. Then again, they had yet to cross one of those rickety-looking bridges.

Chapter 61 | Adarra

ADARRA STOPPED OUTSIDE the door to the Harbor House. Her breath misted in front of her face, slowly rising up to join the thick cloud of chimney smoke hovering over the rooftops of Easthaven. The lonely alley in back of the house was as quiet as a frozen creek and covered in ankle-deep snow. She looked at Lyessa, who had joined her on the back stoop. "I need to warn you. You will be one of only a few non-wielders to step foot in here. There might be some heated debate as to whether you will be permitted entry."

Lyessa held her head high. "I'm not worried." She was certainly her father's daughter, and not just because her long fur-lined coat cost more than Adarra's entire wardrobe. A sword hung low on her waist, giving her a confident edge that contrasted her rich clothing.

Adarra, on the other hand, wore her typical dark-red wool cloak over her light-grey wool dress. No frilly lace or fur lining, no decorative stitching down the front or around the sleeves, just a layer of solid, dependable material thick enough to keep her warm. She rapped on the door and waited. There was a notable scraping of wood from the other side just before the hinges squeaked and the door opened wide enough to spew warm light across her cheek. "It's me, Master Eliab."

The door opened the rest of the way to reveal the old gatekeeper with a lantern in one hand and his double-bolt crossbow resting in the other. He took one look at Lyessa and pursed his lips. "I don't know . . ."

"It will be fine, Master Eliab," Adarra said, motioning for Lyessa to follow her in. They stepped into the kitchen, and Eliab stuck his head out the door. It was soon followed by a satisfied grunt before he stepped back inside and placed the lantern down on the table. He promptly shut the door and slid the bracer back into place.

"If you'll follow me," he said with his all-too-familiar lisp, giving a slight bow toward Lyessa. "My lady. Everyone ith already here and waiting. Not in the betht of moodth, it would theem. I can hear them all the way up here."

Adarra just smiled, and they kept walking, taking the stairs in the adjoining room down to the cellar. They passed guest chambers on the left and right, where they kept the wayward wielder looking for a dry place to remain hidden. From there, they wound through layers of barrels and stacks of crates before coming to a stop just outside a thick wooden door on the far side, light seeping around its edges. Adarra could hear raised voices on the other side. Feoldor's being the most prominent.

"What did I tell you," Eliab said with a disgusted shake of his head as he knocked on the door. He glanced at Lyessa, who appeared unshaken by the situation, and smiled awkwardly.

"If that's you, Eliab, open the door." Adarra recognized Veldon's voice, the head of the Easthaven wielder council.

Eliab stuck his head in. "Pardon, but Adarra has arrived with company. Lady Lyessa."

The room on the other side exploded with conversation, a range of opinions being fired across the table at one another like arrows from her father's bow. Adarra waited patiently with a polite smile as the group inside continued to argue, feeling more embarrassed by the moment. "Sorry. I told you it could get quite heated. They mean well."

Veldon's voice finally broke through the cacophony, forcing the others to quiet down. "Show her in."

Eliab opened the door and stood to the side as Adarra and Lyessa stepped into the council chambers, which wasn't much more than a long room with a long table at the center. Eliab had been right; every seat but one was filled, which meant the entire council had shown up for the evening's meeting.

The men stood from their seats, Feoldor grumbling under his breath as he did, which wasn't anything new. It was when he wasn't grumbling that they truly needed to worry.

"Welcome, Lady Lyessa, to the Easthaven wielder council meeting," Veldon said from the head of the table on their right.

"It is an honor to be invited," Lyessa said, causing a few furtive glances to be passed around the table, most of which were leveled at Adarra.

"I believe you know most of those gathered," Veldon said, then pointed toward the far side of the table, where Adarra's seat lay empty between her father and Fraya. "Kellen, would you be so good as to get our guest another chair?"

There were two extra seats at the back of the room against the wall, seats that had belonged to Adarra's brothers but now rested empty, collecting dust. It was a constant reminder that she might not ever see them again. Her father grabbed the closest and set it between Adarra's seat and Fraya's, who was now sitting at the far end of the table. Fraya waved at the two girls as they made their way across the room and sat down.

"I apologize for the delay," Adarra said as the men retook their seats.

Veldon leaned forward as he looked across the table at Lyessa, his barrel chest and thickening waistline pressed against the table as he did. "There are few non-wielders who know this place exists. We hope that you will take that into consideration. The lives of those we protect depend on it."

"I assure you," Lyessa said, "your anonymity is safe with me."

"And yet," Feoldor grumbled from his seat directly across from Adarra, "we keep letting them in. And this time the overlord's daughter, no less." He glanced at Lyessa. "No offense, of course."

"None taken." Lyessa sat with her hands in her lap, seemingly unaffected, though Adarra did note Lyessa stroking her sword's pommel.

"I believe she has earned that right," Adarra's father said, his enormous arms crossed in front of his chest. "It's not as though our presence remains any great secret."

"It does still to most," Feoldor rebutted.

"True, but none of them have raised their sword in our defense or been willing to shed their blood to protect our own. The overlord and his daughter are allies of the ven'ae, and for my part will always be welcome within these walls."

There were a few head bobs from some, others still bore a look of hesitation, which under the circumstances wasn't that unexpected. When you'd spent your whole life hiding, change wasn't something that came naturally.

Orlyn pulled a small pot of soil from one of the many hidden pockets within his voluminous robes and stuck his finger inside. Adarra smiled and passed a quick glance at Lyessa, as did many of the others. She'd seen Orlyn perform this magic on several occasions, and it never grew tiresome. He lifted his finger out of the soil, and a green shoot burst from the pot, leaves forming from the newly sprouted stem, rising upward until a bud appeared at the top and slowly spread its petals to reveal a wash of purple and gold surrounding a pure white center. The tall apothecary slid the plant across the table to Lyessa. "For you, my dear. May it bring a moment of warmth on a cold day."

Lyessa smiled and leaned over to sniff the bloom. "It smells divine," she said. "Thank you."

Orlyn leaned back in his seat with a satisfied grin. It was difficult to hold a frown when witnessing something so glorious. The only other person seemingly excited by the magic was Sheeva, who wasn't sitting in her regular place on Veldon's left, but instead had taken Gilly's seat on the right. Adarra wondered if that was so she could be closer to her father. She still didn't know what to make of the white-haired assassin.

Lyessa released Orlyn's plant and scooted back in her seat. "I bring news."

Adarra's father stiffened. "There's been word from Ty and Breen?"

The room quieted.

Lyessa appeared a bit startled by the eager faces. "No. I haven't heard anything since he left. Have you?"

Adarra's father sighed. "Afraid not."

"No news is still good news," Reloria said, popping a small piece of candy in her mouth as she adjusted her gawdy red-and-green-striped hat.

Adarra wondered where that turn of phrase had first originated. No news didn't mean good news at all. It simply meant *no news*. Her brothers could be dead or dying in some obscure region of Aldor, and they might never hear from them again. That certainly wouldn't constitute good news.

"The news I bring is rather troubling, I'm afraid," Lyessa continued. "I just left a meeting with my father and Commander Tiernan. Word has reached Easthaven of some very troubling events that have recently taken place in the city of Belvin. Apparently, they had an outbreak." She paused a moment. "Honestly, I have no idea how to explain it. The best we can gather from the envoy was that dark magic was involved, turning people into monsters."

Monsters? Why hadn't Lyessa mentioned this on their ride over?

"What exactly do you mean by monsters?" Veldon asked.

"I mean the citizens went crazy. They started killing and eating each other and anyone else they came in contact with. From all accounts, they turned into some sort of white hairless creatures that had a taste for human flesh. They were being controlled by a creature called Argon. It sounds as though this plague started in Belvin and spread outward to other surrounding villages."

"Are you saying it's heading our direction?" Adarra's father asked.

"No. There was an uprising. With the help of a traveling group of warriors, several of the townships fought back and apparently defeated the creatures."

"So, we are sure the threat is ended?" Orlyn asked. "Plagues tend to spread rather quickly."

"The envoy says the threat is over. They were sent to ask for aid."

Feoldor tugged at his whiskers. "If the people went mad, then who exactly is rebuilding the city?"

"It seems that when Argon was killed, whatever magics he was using to control the people vanished, and they slowly have begun to revert back to their normal selves."

Feoldor looked around the room and blew out his lips. "Sounds a little far-fetched to me. Most likely a ploy to garner more gold at Easthaven's expense. I got to hand it to them, though, that's quite the tale. People turning into flesh-eating monsters, dark magic, a group of warriors there to save them in the nick of time. Sounds more like one of those fancy new adventure books stocking the shelves at BookBees."

Adarra smiled at the mention of her favorite book shop.

"Regardless of the believability," Lyessa said, "it's our duty to give aid where needed. My father plans to send an envoy of our own back to Belvin to see for ourselves the extent of the damage."

Adarra's father leaned forward. "Was there any mention where this Argon creature came from or how he was able to spread such a disease?"

Lyessa shook her head.

"Dark magic such as this doesn't simply appear for no reason," Adarra's father pointed out.

"A valid observation," Veldon said, fiddling with the flint and steel hanging from a chain around his neck. He looked at Lyessa. "Please keep us informed if you hear anything further."

Lyessa nodded in return.

"Have the overlords decided on their response to Dakaran's takeover of Cylmar?" Veldon asked, changing the subject.

Lyessa shook her head. "No news at this point other than what was discussed during the recent summit."

"A near catastrophe if I ever saw one," Reloria said, popping another small sweet into her mouth, this one looking like hard taffy.

"Yes," Orlyn agreed. "If the Tower had managed to wipe out the entire Provincial Authority in one fell swoop . . . I shudder to think."

"On the bright side," Adarra's father said, "it did give us a singular purpose to unite behind."

"I only pray it's not too late," Veldon said, receiving several grunts of agreement. The head of the council looked at Adarra. "Where are we with our giant Tallosian? The last we heard was something about a possible conflict looming."

All eyes shifted to Adarra, and she nervously tightened her grip on the pad of paper in her lap. Gathering her thoughts, she tried to remember what she had already told them, so as not to repeat herself. "Jonas made it clear that if we want to avoid a conflict with Tallos, we need to let him go. To be honest, he feels it might already be too late. The Tallosians can't afford to wait. The Dogar are sure to send out another convoy, and this time it won't be a simple raiding party, it will be a full-on incursion. We need to reach them before they do, and hopefully work out a peaceful solution."

"Aye," Orlyn said. "But will the Northmen share that same sentiment?"

"Jonas believes they will. They are in dire need of food, and an open hand might not be so easily turned away when what is inside is something they desperately need."

Adarra's father looked at Lyessa. "Has your father mentioned anything further about sending a delegation to meet with the Tallosians?"

"Commander Tiernan and Captain Noklis both share reservations for sending anyone. They believe it's a fool's errand, and nothing more than a ruse by Jonas to be set free."

"Sounds feasible to me," Feoldor said as he fluffed his whiskers. "Can't trust a Northman any further than you can toss him."

"My father isn't quite so convinced," Lyessa said, turning to Adarra. "And right now, the last thing we need is another battle looming over our heads. I believe he'll be willing to send a delegation on the off chance the prisoner speaks the truth."

"The question is," Feoldor said, leaning forward to rest his arms on the table, "who will they volunteer to go on such a suicidal mission?"

Adarra gulped as several of those at the table turned to look at her.

Chapter 62 | Ferrin

FERRIN OPENED THE CABIN DOOR and stepped out onto the deck. They'd spent the last two days traveling up the Taloos River toward Lake Baeron. The *Wind Binder* was quite the ship. Not as large as the ocean schooners, but what it lacked in size, it made up for in its sleek design and speed. Captain Treygan didn't seem all that intent on demonstrating it, though, as he chugged along at what felt like a snail's pace up the river.

Ferrin had even tempted the stubborn man with gold enough to outfit his ship and crew for the next year if he'd go faster, but Treygan wasn't a man to be pushed. He was a cautious man. His daughter, Ismara, wasn't one to be pushed either. She seemed the one in charge of the day-to-day tasks, while Treygan kept to his books and charts and made any final decisions that she felt she needed his opinion on.

The crew seemed more a family than a group of sailors earning their pay. Ferrin could tell by the way they worked together—they seemed to be able to communicate as much with a single look or nod than a bos'n shouting out his orders from the top deck. It was clear that these men had spent years in each other's company. Ferrin also didn't take their cordiality to mean they were a weak-willed lot. It was obvious by the way they handled themselves that these men had seen more than their fair share of action.

The first mate, Bones, seemed the most standoffish. He was a tall dark-skinned man with a painted face and wore a set of nasty-looking kamas that Ferrin was sure had ripped apart more than one man's gut.

"We should make port by tomorrow evening," Bray said when he saw Ferrin coming. The short, girthy man stood at the back of the ship, one hand on the rudder, the other holding a compass while keeping his eye on the next bend in the river. The others called him Needle. Ferrin had thought it was because of his obsession with his compass, but Kettle, the ship's rather overbearing and talkative cook, had joked that it had more to do with the quality of Bray's stitchwork than anything. The crew went to him whenever they needed to darn their socks and underclothing, since his needlework always seemed to hold up much better than their own.

"Thank you," Ferrin said, then walked back down the stairs, passing Whitey on his way up. The enormous man with his wide-brimmed hat nodded at Ferrin but kept his eyes on the two steaming mugs he was holding in his hands. Whitey tended to spend a good deal of his time helping Needle navigate, as his height gave him a clear advantage to see what lay ahead.

Ferrin reached the bottom of the stairs and crossed the main deck and over to the next set leading up to the bow, where he could generally find the captain staring out over the slow-moving water. It was also Nola's favorite spot, and he found her curled in a ball on the port side fast asleep, her enormous chest rising and falling. They had done their best, with Suri's help, to wash the blood out of her fur after she had killed those four guards on the docks at Storyl, but apart from dipping her fully in the river, there was only so much they could do.

"A fine night," Treygan said on Ferrin's approach, not even bothering to turn. The man had eyes in the back of his head. Treygan was a tough man with sun-dried skin and grey hair that showed his age. Despite that age, Ferrin wouldn't have wanted to test his steel against the man. The captain wore a long green trench coat that hung below the knees with a triangular captain's hat that tilted ever so slightly to the side.

"If by 'fine' you mean cold as a bulradoer's glare, then yeah, it's fine."

Treygan laughed as he continued to study the silhouettes of the passing trees on the far-right bank.

Ferrin joined him at the rail. "Needle says we should make port by evening tomorrow."

Treygan nodded. "Sounds about right. Anxious to get home, are we? How long has it been?"

Ferrin rested his elbows on the railing. "Not sure, really. Time seems to pass differently inside a windowless cell." After his battle with the White Tower's guards back in Storyl, Treygan had demanded an explanation as to what he had just gotten himself into, which Ferrin and Myron had done their best to give, even going so far as to let them know about his, Rae's, and Suri's wielding capabilities.

It seemed Treygan and his crew had no more love for the Tower than they did, but in a world where turning in your neighbors was rewarded with gold, one could never be too sure.

"Where's home for you?" Ferrin asked.

Treygan patted the top of the rail with his right hand. "You're standing on it. The *Wind Binder* has been my home for over thirty years. Spent most of that time running trade along the Shemoa River from the Slags to the Bay of Torrin. I've seen more of Aldor than most would ever hope to. Mind you, being a riverman isn't for everyone. It's got to be in your blood." He looked at Ferrin. "You seem to have a bit of the wanderer's spirit about you as well."

Ferrin grunted. "Not by choice. I've seen more of Aldor than I care to. Now, I want to find a nice quiet place to settle down and keep as far away from the Tower's eyes as possible."

Treygan pulled a bone-handled knife from his waist and began cleaning his nails. "From the sound of it, that might prove more difficult than you hope. Once the Tower has your scent, they're like a pack of bloodhounds, not easily turned away."

"True. They seem willing to go so far as to raise the dead to track you down. Not to mention those pesky corax."

"Aye. I've ordered the men to keep a sharp eye for any sign of them."

"We lost them in the storms between Woodvale and Storyl, but I'm sure they haven't given up."

"The sooner we get to Rhowynn and you collect your sister, the sooner we can be gone. I can take you anywhere along the Taloos you wish to go, or if you prefer to go further south, then we can ferry you down the Shemoa into Elondria."

Ferrin stood at the rail a moment, watching the mist lift in the air. "I appreciate the offer, but to be honest, I'm not quite sure where we'll end up. I do know that before I go anywhere, I have a promise to keep to an old friend, which requires me to reach Easthaven."

Treygan gave a slight tug on his grey beard. "Afraid that's one place we can't take you, unless you know of a way to sail a ship across land."

Ferrin smiled. "That's a bit out of my wielding capabilities."

"I've known a wielder or two in my time," Treygan said. "Can't say as they could make that happen either, though I've seen them do some pretty incredible things. One in particular. A boy. Actually, one of the Upaka."

"Upaka? Don't hear that name mentioned much lately."

"No. At least not in a good way. Of course, when was it ever?"

"I didn't know the Upaka were sending out children to do their dirty work."

"They aren't," Treygan said, "at least not in this case. The boy had been exiled from the Lost City and was looking for passage to Aramoor. It's been over twenty years, but I've never forgotten him, even went so far as to offer him a place on the crew. For a while I thought he would, but he had his sights set on the capital city. We've crossed paths a time or two since then, but it's been years now."

The two stood there for a while until the silence grew to an uncomfortable level, so Ferrin finally excused himself to go check on Rae. He stopped by the mess hall to pick up a bowl of soup from Kettle and walked back to the cabin to find that Myron had taken Suri up to see Nola.

Rae smiled as he dragged a stool over beside her bed and helped her to a sitting position. She was still very weak from having expended so much of her magic to save Ferrin during their battle with the Black Watch, not to mention the sickness she felt from the constant sway of the ship. She had managed to leave her cot long enough to take a few short strolls around the deck, as long as she kept close to the railing for balance. It was just too bad that those with gifts for healing were unable to heal themselves.

Ever since their time in Storyl and the intimate conversations they had shared on the balcony, Ferrin had done everything he could to find those few precious moments when they could be alone.

"How are you feeling this evening?" Ferrin asked, dipping out a spoon of the creamy broth and feeding it to her.

She took it and swallowed. "Stronger." She always seemed to perk up whenever Ferrin was there to feed her.

"Strong enough to eat on your own, then?" he teased.

She glared at him and opened her mouth, waiting for him to continue.

"Just checking."

She reached for the bowl. "If I'm too much of a burden . . ."

He pulled it away. "No. I like this side of you." He scooped out another spoonful.

She swallowed. "What side?"

"The side that lets your guard down long enough to allow someone to help you."

She bristled but allowed him to continue, staring up at him as he did. There was more passion in the way she looked at him than he'd experienced with any of the other young ladies he'd ever courted, not that there had been many. In fact, he could have counted his courtship attempts on two fingers.

Rae finished the rest of the soup, and Ferrin placed the bowl and spoon aside. He sat there a moment sharing her gaze, neither speaking. He was about to stand and leave when Rae's hand tightened on his arm, and she slowly pulled him down to her.

Is this wise? He feared causing problems for them down the road if things didn't work out. He decided he didn't care. He leaned in, and she closed her eyes.

The cabin door flew open, and Ferrin jerked away.

"Nola says she hopes you feel good soon," Suri exclaimed as she rushed across the room and hopped up on her mother's bed.

Ferrin scooted back, noting both the embarrassment and frustration on Rae's face as she looked his way.

"Sorry about that," Myron said, shutting the door behind him. He cleared his throat while trying to hide his smile. "Didn't mean to interrupt."

"You didn't," Ferrin shot back as he stood. "I'll see to the dishes." He grabbed Rae's bowl and spoon, along with a couple of tankards sitting on the table behind him, and walked out the door. He stopped long enough to glance back over his shoulder. Rae was staring after him.

He shut the door and took a deep breath, letting the evening winter air cool his blood. He couldn't believe that had just happened. Part of him said he needed to be careful, to take things slowly. He didn't want his affection to hurt her further after what she had endured in the Tower, but the other part was willing to risk anything to be close to her.

Leaving the cabin behind, and still feeling a bit lightheaded, he dropped off the empty dishes in the mess hall and made his way back to the forward deck once again. The captain was no longer there, only Nola, who sat in her usual place, her glowing yellow eyes following him from the stairs to the front rail. "Don't look at me like that. I couldn't help it."

He walked over and rubbed the top of the wolf's head, something she had only recently allowed him to do. He guessed their ride down the docks had somehow brought them a little closer together.

"I'm sorry about the untimely arrival back there," Myron said, joining Ferrin at the rail. Nola stretched her legs and stood as well, her head reaching as high as Ferrin's. "If I had known you two were wanting some time alone, I would have kept Suri away longer." He smiled. "I'm just glad to see you two happy. Can't think of two people who deserve it more."

"Happy?" Ferrin chuckled as he leaned against the side of the ship and watched the reflection of the moon glistening across the top of the water as it floated by. "I'd almost forgotten what that felt like." He smiled. "She's not like anyone I've ever known."

Myron leaned against the rail beside him. "She's not like what anyone has ever known, which is why you need to take extra care."

Ferrin turned, puzzled by the sudden shift in Myron's earlier enthusiasm.

"In a way she's almost like Suri," Myron said, "completely innocent of this world, but yet broken in ways we might not understand. The only men she's ever known are the ones she was forced to patch up, and the ones who saw her as nothing more than something to be used however they chose. From what you've told me of this Sylas character, there's no telling what sort of damage has been done to the way she views what we would call a relationship."

"I was there, remember? I was one of those men she had to patch up. Trust me, I know. I'm not trying to push anything." He turned and stared at the silhouette of the passing shoreline. *Am I pushing?* He couldn't help but wonder. Perhaps it would be better to keep his distance. "Are you saying that you don't think that what she feels for me is real?"

Myron hesitated a moment, then shook his head. "No. It's obvious she cares for you. But she has never known, or seen, a single example of an honest healthy relationship, other than what she has for Suri. At this point, it's not so much that she *desires* you as that she *needs* you. She needs that security and will probably do anything to keep it."

"The last thing I want to do is hurt her."

"Look, all I'm saying is: be careful. As they say aboard ship, slow and steady as you go."

"Aye, Captain," Ferrin said, then thought how ridiculous the comment had sounded, especially since that was precisely what Myron was, a Black Watch captain. Ferrin looked up at the blanket of stars overhead. "It's going to be another cold one, I reckon." His hands were already shivering.

"Best we turn in for the night," Myron said with a yawn. "I'm sure we'll have a long day tomorrow."

Ferrin nodded, and the two men walked back down to the cabin and crawled into their beds. Myron slept in the bed on the opposite side of the room from Rae and Suri, while Ferrin made do with the hammock in the corner. It was actually more comfortable than he had thought at first sight, its constant sway with the ship usually lulling him to sleep like a babe being rocked in its mother's arms. But tonight, even the gentle motion of the hammock didn't help as he lay awake contemplating what Myron had said, and the idea that Rae *needed* him. Ferrin didn't like the idea of her only needing him. Was that all it was for her? He cared about her in ways he'd never cared for anyone before. There was something so unique about Rae and the way she looked at everything with such wonder. It was intoxicating. What he enjoyed most of all was the way she made him feel . . . well, *needed*.

He groaned as he rolled over and faced the wall. Myron was right. She did need him, and now he worried that that need was the driving force behind his own attraction for her. Every man wanted to feel needed by the woman he cared for, and Rae had a way of bringing that out in him. He shook his head. *No!* The way he felt for her was not simply because of how she made him feel. It was a hundred different things. The way she sniffed at her food before eating, the excitement she showed when seeing something new, the way she looked at him when she thought he wasn't looking, the way she would finger the material on her dress, and a thousand other little intricacies. No, his feelings for her were more than his desire to be needed, but he would be careful. The last thing he would ever want to do was hurt her.

He closed his eyes and tried drifting to sleep, but each time he did, their *almost* kiss would replay in his mind and set his heart to racing.

Suri was up at the crack of dawn and bouncing around the room, making as much noise as she could in order to wake the rest of them up.

After one or two attempts of trying to get the little girl to crawl back in bed, Rae finally sat up.

Ferrin slipped from his hammock in time to help her to her feet. "How are you feeling?" he asked, keeping his arm out for her to balance with, which she clung to like her life depended on it.

"Better," she said, quietly glancing over at Myron's bed, where he had his blankets up over his head.

"Did you sleep well enough?" he asked.

"Better than you. I can usually hear when you sleep," she said with a smirk. "But every time I turned over, your corner was quiet."

"Yes, well, I had a lot to think about."

"Finding your sister?"

"That and other things."

Her smile said she knew what he was referring to. "I thought about things as well."

Suri ran over between them and grabbed one hand apiece. "Let's go see Nola, Mommy."

"Shhh," Rae said. "Master Myron is trying to sleep."

"And failing miserably," a voice called out from under the blankets.

"We are going to head top deck," Ferrin said. "Feel free to take advantage of the quiet."

"Don't mind if I do." The covers shifted as Myron rolled over on his side.

Ferrin helped Rae pull on her coat and then proceeded to do the same for Suri, kneeling long enough to get each of their boots on before tugging on his own and grabbing his coat on the way out. Rae kept one arm around his to steady herself as Suri took off up the stairs on the side of the ship. Ferrin let Rae set the pace as they slowly sauntered over to the starboard rail and gazed out at the rising sun off in the east across the snow-covered plains.

The sun was high enough that he could feel its rays on his face, but not high enough to reach the rest of him, so he carefully helped Rae up the stairs to the upper deck where they could bask in the sun's warmth. Suri was busy playing with Nola, who remained curled on the port side as the little girl crawled on top of her. Captain Treygan wasn't in his usual spot, but his daughter, Ismara, stood there stoically gazing out across the riverway. Her eyes were closed as they approached, no doubt enjoying the warmth of the sun as well.

Ismara wore a long coat like her father's, but while his was green, hers was a deep crimson with the same gold buttons and trim. She, too, wore a triangular captain's hat with a feather plume sticking from the right side. She had one foot up on the lowest rail, revealing a boot that ran all the way to her knee. "This is my favorite time of day," she said, her eyes still closed, demonstrating that she had inherited her father's keen sense of her surroundings.

"It is very quiet," Ferrin said as he walked Rae over to the rail. Rae stared at Ismara's long red hair as it waved behind her in the chilly breeze. She then reached up and felt her own dark hair, which had been chopped short by Sylas. Ferrin could almost see the longing in Rae's eyes. Truth was, Ferrin liked her short hair. It was different, unique, much the way everything about her was.

"Father says it's been some time since you were last this way. Are you looking forward to seeing the city once again?"

"I'd be lying if I said I wasn't. It's been my home for quite some time. A lot of memories."

"And there she is," Ismara said, gesturing straight ahead. "Lake Baeron."

Up ahead, the river basin widened as they reached the inlet leading into the lake itself. It was similar in size to Praxil Lake. You couldn't see the other side, waters stretching across the whole horizon. Ferrin took a deep breath, breathing in the smell of the water, not that it really smelled any different from what they'd been traveling up for the last couple of days, but to him somehow it did. At least his mind told him it did, which was all that really mattered.

"I hear you have a sister we are here to collect."

"A twin sister. Myriah."

"A twin? Don't know as I've ever seen twins before. She look much like you?"

"A bit, sadly for her."

"I doubt that. A ruggedly handsome man like yourself. I'm sure she has all the fellas gawking."

Rae's grip tightened on Ferrin's arm.

"There's only one man I want to make sure she holds no small acquaintance with."

"This lord you've been referring to occasionally, half a dozen times a day since coming aboard?" Ismara chuckled. "What's his name? Horrin?"

"Harlin. Lord Harlin. He's the coward who sold me to the White Tower."

Ismara shook her head. "Can't say as I blame you much. Only one fitting end to a traitor like that. Keelhauling."

Ferrin found the image of Harlin being dragged under the boat from one side to the other until he drowned more than entertaining. It was downright rousing, though he would have preferred a more hands-on approach himself. Not that he hadn't spent many a waking moment contemplating what he would do to the man if he ever made it back. In fact, he'd spent many a glorious hour in his Tower cell imagining all the horrible little things he would do if he ever made it back to Rhowynn. And after spending months at the hands of a true sadist like Cheeks, Ferrin had acquired more than enough training in the art to prove useful.

"Can't say as I wouldn't mind being there to see the man's face when you show up," she said as she started for the stairs down to the main deck. "Morning rations will be served shortly." She left them and disappeared down the stairs.

"I don't want you to see this Harlin," Rae said as she released his arm and walked over to the port side of the ship. She looked out at the disappearing shoreline as the *Wind Binder* sailed out of the southern mouth of the Taloos River and into the larger lake.

Ferrin followed her over. "Why would you say that?"

"Because it can lead to bad things."

"Yes, bad things for him."

"No. Bad things for you. I can see it in your eyes. You wish to do this man great harm. You don't wish for a quick death. You wish for an inquisitor death. One that lasts a very long time."

"Is that so bad? Look what he did to me. Does that not deserve justice? How many times would I have died if not for your intervention? Day after day, week after week, months of endless torture, all because of Harlin's treachery. Don't I deserve even a little satisfaction?"

"Of course, yes. But will that make you happy?"

Ferrin thought a moment. "Yes."

She looked him in the eyes. He hated when she looked at him like that.

"Fine," he said. "I guess not. But I could learn to live with it."

"I don't want you to be an inquisitor."

She wasn't exactly the most eloquent of speakers, but she certainly made her point. The very notion that she thought he could become like an inquisitor turned his stomach. "I can't promise I won't kill him, though."

She stared a while longer, then nodded silently and turned back to the water.

Chapter 63 | Ferrin

HE REST OF THE DAY came and went at a speed Ferrin wasn't quite prepared for. It seemed he'd barely finished his uneasy conversation with Rae when Captain Treygan was announcing their soon arrival at the docks of Rhowynn.

The sun was just beginning to set behind the distant Northern Heights, washing the city in its warm amber glow. Off to the north, storm clouds bordered the horizon and seemed to be drawing closer with each passing moment. He hoped it wasn't a foreshadowing of what might lie ahead. There was snow in the air. Ferrin could almost taste it. He stood at the bow of the ship and watched the colors in the sky fade to grey as the lights on shore brightened in the distance.

The city stretched out before him along the western horizon, shapes growing in the distance as the larger buildings toward the center came into view.

Rhowynn.

He was finally home. He never thought he'd see it again. Sure, he'd kept himself alive with the belief that he would one day make it back, but in his heart, he never believed it possible. And yet, here he was, freezing wind blowing through his hair, the slow fall of snow across the open water, and the fires of Rhowynn in the distance welcoming his arrival. It had been a long, difficult journey, but it was finally coming to an end.

The plan was simple. Get to his smithy, collect Myriah, and make a quick stop at Harlin's estate on the way out. Sure, the spoiled aristocrat's home was in the opposite direction of the docks, but that was hardly going to deter Ferrin. It was a good plan, and they couldn't have timed it better than to arrive under the cover of darkness at the close of day.

The crew lowered the *Wind Binder*'s sails as they reached the first of the long wooden piers. The docks stretched out from the boardwalk far enough to allow even the deepest of hulls to keep from scraping the bottom, something the *Wind Binder* would never need worry about, as its hull was built shallow for speed.

Needle, with Whitey's help, guided the *Wind Binder* into its berth with the skill of a seasoned navigator. Treygan stood at the bow, watching dockworkers scramble from the warehouse down to meet the ship.

Ferrin left the top deck and headed down to the cabin to finish packing. He carried little with him, speed and stealth being more useful for this trip than brute force. He had a couple of weapons and a little gold in case he needed to bribe his way past the harbor officials.

Standing just inside the cabin with Myron, Rae, and Suri, he waited for the captain to give them the all-clear to go ashore. They didn't want to get caught out in the open in case they were greeted by a contingent of Black Watch guards.

Nowadays they could never be too careful.

Nola, with Suri's help, had been sent belowdecks to the cargo hold, to keep from being seen. Nothing like an unnaturally giant wolf to have the dockworkers calling for a patroller enforcement.

"I want to come," Rae demanded for the dozenth time.

Ferrin knew why she wanted to be there—to make sure he didn't go too far when it came to Harlin—but there was no way, given her condition, she could go. "No. We've already discussed this. You're too weak to keep up. Best you stay here with Suri where it's safe."

"Then why does *she* get to go?"

By "she," of course, Rae meant Ismara. Ever since Ismara's "ruggedly handsome" comment concerning Ferrin, Rae had tried her best not to let Ferrin out of her sight.

"I don't have a say as to what the crew of this ship does or doesn't do," he said, "let alone the captain's daughter. If she demands to come, then my hands are tied."

"Then you can't tell me what to do either." Rae's eyes were fierce.

"Ferrin's right," Myron said. "It will do us no good to have you collapsing halfway down the dock. Besides, Suri needs you here with her in case something happens. The faster we can move across town, the faster we'll be back."

Rae crossed her arms in a huff and sat down on the edge of her bed, burning a hole in the back of Ferrin's head with her glare. He was thankful her gift wasn't that of an incindi. Ferrin walked over and sat down beside her, and she looked the other way.

"It's not that I don't want you to come," Ferrin said, reaching for the chain around his neck, holding Rae's crystal, reassuring himself that it was still there. "I do. But if something were to happen and you tried to use your gift so soon after the last time, you could kill yourself."

Rae turned. "I'm getting stronger by the day."

"Yes, you are, and as much as you want to go, you know you don't have the strength to be running all over Rhowynn." Ferrin looked over at the door to see if the others were listening in, then lowered his voice. "If anything were to happen to you because of me . . ." He stared into her warm hazel eyes and felt his heart start to pound. The longer he looked, the closer he leaned toward her—but Myron's warning stuck with him, and he stopped and pulled back.

Rae looked confused.

Ferrin stood and went about rechecking his list of items to bring. There was a knock on the door before it opened, and Kettle, who was still wearing his long apron, stuck his head inside.

"Captain says it's time to go ashore."

Myron nodded and then gave Suri a big hug before slipping out onto the deck. Suri chased after him, shutting the door behind her. Ferrin looked at Rae. "I'll be back as soon as I can." She didn't say anything, just sat there staring, and since he didn't exactly know what to say himself, he headed for the door.

He barely got his hands on the knob when Rae shot from her bed. She grabbed his coat and spun him around. He didn't even get a chance to open his mouth before she yanked him down by his tunic and kissed him. Ferrin didn't hesitate. He wrapped his arms around her and lifted her into the air as he kissed her back, all thoughts of Myron's warning flying out the ship's window as they clung to each other with such force it felt like they would merge into one.

Needing to catch his breath, Ferrin finally lowered her back to the floor and released. He couldn't believe that had just happened. He couldn't believe how badly he had wanted it to happen. The entire room was spinning as he backed awkwardly to the door. "I . . . I have to go."

"Promise you'll come back," Rae said, her words unsteady as she fought to catch her breath. "Promise me."

"I promise." Ferrin had to get out of there. It was all he could do to keep from racing back across the room and lifting her off the ground once more. As quick as he could, he turned the knob behind him and opened the door, the cold wind helping to alleviate the heat. He took a deep breath, and the world slowly came back into focus. With one last, long look at Rae, he slipped through the door and across the deck to where Myron, Ismara, and one of the younger crew—whose name Ferrin hadn't yet learned—waited for him to disembark.

Ferrin didn't turn around. He could almost feel Rae's eyes on the back of his head as he nodded to the captain and followed the others down the gangplank and onto the snow-covered pier below. He lifted his hood when he saw a couple of dockworkers waiting, not wanting to be recognized. His smithy had been one of the closest to the docks, so he was one of several that had been on a more permanent commission with the shipping companies to keep up with their supplies. He had never worn a beard before, so hopefully that would be enough of a disguise, as long as he kept his cowl up to hide his notably red hair.

Torches lit their way as the dockworkers escorted the small group up the pier and to the awaiting boardwalk, where several loading crews were busy carting freight from two other ships onto wagons, waiting to tote the freight to their respective purchasers in town. After stopping by the main office to sign in and pay their docking fee, the small group left the piers and started into town.

Smoke from a thousand chimneys rose into the air, mixing with the falling snow to produce a thick haze across the city. Golden windows lit the streets around them as the good citizens of Rhowynn kept to the warmth of their fires. The cobbles were snow-covered, grey stone showing through the most trafficked areas, especially along the sidewalks and at the edges of the streets where the wagon wheels had packed the powder far enough down.

Ferrin kept them off the main thoroughfares, choosing the back alleys and side streets in hopes they'd reach their destination without being stopped. Not that anyone would have needed to stop them, as they were doing nothing more suspicious than walking down the street, but after everything he'd been through to get this far, he wasn't taking any chances. A few people nodded as they passed, most in a hurry to get out of the weather.

The narrow alleys between the three- and four-story buildings did a fair job of blocking the snow from their heads, and with help from a lantern Ismara had procured before leaving the ship, they kept from stumbling over the boxes and crates and barrels that lined the passageways.

Ferrin was almost surprised by how little things had changed while he'd been gone. He held his breath as they passed by the tanner's, who tended to store his bleaching bins outside to keep the unpleasant smell from completely permeating his home. His wife had threatened on more than one occasion to run off with a traveling troupe of troubadours if he didn't keep them outside. Ferrin glanced in one of the windows as they passed just to see if she had finally made good on her threats. Not surprisingly, she was still there, pounding on a ball of dough in the kitchen with her roller.

Ferrin stopped at the edge of a small intersection to study the larger street before taking it to the right. The lamplighters had clearly already reached this part of town, as the flickering streetlamps guided their way up the road. Ferrin nearly broke into a run when he spotted their three-story wood-and-plaster home ahead. He did, in fact, start crying at the sight of the stone building attached on the right. He wiped his eyes with the sleeve of his coat, mentioning offhandedly something about getting snow in them.

He slowed. There were no lights in the windows. Myriah should have been home by now. Perhaps she was watching Lord and Lady Resdin's children, something she tended to do on occasion for extra money. Ferrin waved them forward as he worked his way around the back of the house and tested the door leading into the kitchen. It was locked. He reached for his magic with the aid of Rae's crystal, and the metal on the inside of the lock snapped. He opened the door and ushered everyone inside.

The house was cold, too cold for someone to have been there in the last day or two. Why was there no fire in the hearth? He ran his hand across the kitchen table and came away with a fingerful of dust.

"Doesn't look like anyone has lived here in a while," Myron said, noticing the worried look on Ferrin's face.

The house was in order. Nothing appeared out of place or broken. It just seemed as though whoever was living there had just packed up and left. All Ferrin could remember was the battle he'd fought with the Black Watch guards the last time he'd set foot in the place. Thankfully, his sister had been called away that evening to watch the Resdin children. Even still, the place had clearly been cleaned since then. So where was his sister? Ferrin left the others down in the main room and ran up the stairs to check the bedchambers.

Neither looked to have been touched. All of Myriah's clothes were still folded and resting inside their drawers. Ferrin's clothes, as well, had been neatly packed away in his own room, untouched, but like the furniture downstairs, everything held a notable layer of dust.

Had the Black Watch come and taken her as well? Was she at the White Tower even now? Ferrin doubted Sylas would have gone to all the trouble to uncover information about his sister and threatened to use her against him if he had already had her under his thumb.

Still, that didn't mean they couldn't have picked her up at some later point. She could be in the back of some Black Watch wagon now, on her way with a load of wielders to the Tower.

Ferrin pushed the thought aside. It was too terrible to even imagine. He couldn't let himself be discouraged by what-ifs. If she was still in the city, he would find her. Not bothering to search the rest of the rooms other than to simply stick his head in long enough to make sure there were no dead bodies lying around, he left the bedchambers and walked back down the stairs.

"Anything up there?" Myron asked.

Ferrin shook his head, then looked around the main room. "Where's Ismara?"

Myron nodded in the direction of the hall on the right, leading back to his smithy. "She and the young one went to check out there."

Ferrin headed after them, passing the kitchen and dining room on the way. The door to his shop was open, a single lantern lighting the workspace inside. Everything seemed to be just as he had left it. Even the length of steel he had been using to fashion a short sword for the nobleman's son was still lying on the anvil where he'd left it the night of the wielder council banquet, the night he'd been betrayed.

"Cluttered," was all that Ismara said as she finished making her rounds and started back to where Ferrin stood waiting at the door.

"It's actually smaller than what I had pictured," Myron said, "from all the times you've talked about it."

Ferrin walked across the room, letting his hands drift across the tools and stacks of various metals, until he reached the back, where the stone hearth stood waiting, coals still stacked inside, eager to be set aflame once more. There was water still in the trough beside the bellows, but it had a thin layer of ice on top, something Ferrin had never seen happen inside his smithy before. It was always warm and inviting, as he rarely ever let the coals die out. They always took too long to heat back up.

An outpouring of emotions swelled deep inside as he made a slow circle around his belongings. He choked back the tears as he met the others at the door, and they walked back inside the house.

"What do we do now?" Myron asked as Ismara held up the lantern to better see everyone's face.

"We keep looking."

"Where?"

"The wielder council." If anyone knew what had happened to Myriah, it would be them.

"And can they be trusted?" Myron asked. "If I recall, wasn't it one of the council that sold you out to the Black Watch?"

Ferrin balled his fists. "And he will be dealt with." He thought a moment. "The others can be trusted, I think." There were some he wasn't quite so sure of, like Garreth. The last time he'd come face-to-face with the carpenter, they had nearly come to blows if not for Ella and her ability to sway emotions. "Elson. We can trust Elson." Ferrin smiled. "At least when it comes to anything but a game of batmyth. The man cheats like a bankrupt politician. He'll be able to tell us what's happened here."

"And where can we find this Elson?" Ismara asked.

Ferrin smiled. "At this time of evening, there's only one place I can think to look: the Four Horns."

Chapter 64 | Ferrin

THEY LEFT FERRIN'S HOME and made their way further into the heart of Rhowynn to a watering hole so disreputable that even Elson's form of gamesmanship would have been considered fair play. The four waited inside the shadows of an alleyway across the street and watched as the seedier side of Rhowynn made their way inside, occasionally bumping into those who were trying to stumble out.

"Not exactly what I was expecting," Myron said as they watched a drunken brawl break out in the street.

Ismara smiled. "Now that's my kind of tavern. You show me an alehouse that doesn't have a good tussle on a given night, and I'll show you an alehouse that sells watered-down rum that ain't worth a bent copper." She handed her lantern over to the young man, who Ferrin still hadn't learned the name of, and strolled out of the alleyway like she owned the place. She walked right up to the four men, clunked the first in the back of the head with the butt end of her cutlass, kicked the second in the gut, causing him to turn and retch on the third, who she punched in the face, sending a few teeth flying as he flew backward into a pile of snow. The fourth man took one look at her, then at the other three on the ground, and fled down the street, promptly colliding with several barrels, where he flipped over and landed on his back and didn't bother getting back up.

Ferrin crossed the street to join her in front of the tavern, where she waited patiently for the others, still holding her cutlass. "We're trying *not* to be noticed," he said frustratedly. "Maybe it's best if I go in alone. The last thing we want is to draw attention. None of you knows what Elson looks like anyway, so you'll be of little help inside. If he's here, I'll find him."

Ismara sheathed her sword. "If you think I'm going to just stand out here in the snow freezing my nips off while you go inside for a warm pint, then you don't know me at all." She didn't give him a chance to argue as she pushed by and headed for the front door.

"Fine," he said, rushing to catch up. "Then find a table out of the way and stay there. And do me a favor." He opened the door for her. "Don't go jumping into another brawl."

Ismara smiled as she sauntered past. "Can't make any promises."

Myron looked at Ferrin and shrugged. "I'll keep an eye on her."

Little good that will do, Ferrin thought. They'd learned quickly enough that if Ismara set her mind to something, there wasn't much anyone could do to stop her.

The entryway was filled to the brim with those either waiting for a table to open or those waiting for their heads to clear before traipsing off into the freezing cold streets outside. Standing at the back of the common room, it was fairly obvious that finding a table was going to prove more difficult than they had hoped. Not only was every table filled but so was the bar and most of the chairs that had been placed around the outer wall. For a snowy night like tonight, Ferrin guessed it wasn't that uncommon to see crowds such as this, especially at the end of the week.

The room was filled with smoke, almost to the point of being impossible to see through, reminding him in a way of some of the snowstorms they'd been forced to endure. This, of course, wasn't quite that bad, but even for the Four Horns, it was heavy.

The evening's entertainment consisted of a minstrel, an off-pitch baritone—who seemed a few sheets to the wind as he attempted a round of "King Torrin's Daughters"—and two jugglers. The jugglers struggled to keep their colored balls in the air, as they were also busy dodging flying pieces of fruit and vegetables from the more sloshed patrons in the front row. They did somehow manage to keep the balls spinning as best they could, never being able to make it beyond four at a time. The minstrel wasn't faring much better, his fingers continuing to slip on the strings as he, too, kept a close eye on those nearest the stage in case a random tankard came wandering in his direction.

What proved the most entertaining, though, was the stage manager who sat at the side with a long wooden rod that he would occasionally use to whack the rowdiest patrons over the head with when they attempted to hassle the paid performers. The last man to receive the manager's attention was knocked so hard he fell out of his seat, bowling into one of the servers, who in turn landed on top of him with a full tray of drinks. The man still hadn't gotten back up.

Ferrin turned. "Why don't you . . ." Ismara was no longer there. He looked around the room and spotted her halfway across the back. She walked over to a table with three gentlemen and a lady and pressed the tip of her knife against the back of one man while leaning over to whisper in his ear. The man hopped up, grabbed the woman, and rushed for the door, the other two quickly following. She turned and waved Myron and the young crewman over with a bright smile.

Myron looked at Ferrin, and Ferrin simply shook his head. He was already regretting having let her come. She was proving more trouble than she was worth. He hoped that bringing her didn't ruin his chance at finding his sister. He certainly hadn't clawed his way across Aldor just to have Ismara throw away his one chance at finding her by her *hit first, ask questions later* attitude.

Ferrin stood in the entryway, keeping his hood up so no one would recognize him as he watched the three take their seats, Ismara already waving over a server to take their orders. Ferrin only hoped Myron had the good sense to keep her from overindulging. Not able to watch any longer without getting his hackles up, he finally turned to scan the tavern for his friend, starting with Elson's favorite spot.

The Four Horns had several private alcoves built into the wall along the right side of the room, each with its own booth and a curtain to pull if the conversation was of a nature that needed to be kept from prying eyes and ears. Of course, with the type of ruckus one found at the Four Horns, they were lucky if the person sitting across from them could hear a word they were saying at all.

Two of the three alcoves had left their curtains open, those inside enjoying the evening's entertainment. Ferrin studied the one alcove that had its curtain closed. The thick green material hung low enough from the brass rings that Ferrin couldn't tell if there were more than one set of boots underneath. Unable to see anything from where he was, he slowly worked his way across the room, taking long enough to scan the faces at each table as he did. So far, he hadn't noticed anyone resembling Elson. In fact, he hadn't noticed anyone he knew at all, not that he expected to.

The Four Horns was one of the last establishments Ferrin cared to frequent, having only done so a couple of times to share a game of batmyth with his friend. It was the only tavern Elson would drag himself out of his house for, something about the other establishments being too clean. Elson always claimed he didn't trust a tavern whose floors were tidier than his own. He wanted a place that looked "good and lived in," a sad quality that the Four Horns held in droves.

Ferrin passed the bar on his right and, reaching the corner, started down the side wall toward the farthest alcove. Just beyond the alcove were the doors leading into the kitchen and a steady stream of servers rushing in and out. Ferrin moved to get out of their way and accidentally stepped on the foot of a man sitting just inside the second alcove. The man howled, then looked up at Ferrin's larger build and mumbled something under his breath about *watching where he was going* before turning his attention back to the performers.

Ferrin finally made it to the last alcove and put his ear to the curtain, but with the deafening roar of the crowd, there could have been a quartet of trumpeters inside and Ferrin wouldn't have known. Finally, growing too impatient to just keep standing there, he yanked the curtain back.

Two men jumped, scattering a pair of dice and knocking over a pile of cards across the board in the center of the table. "Can't you see this is a private room?" the man on the left shouted, quickly gathering up his tipped hand.

Ferrin breathed a deep sigh of relief. *Elson.*

Elson's hair had grown longer and was more unkempt than usual, hanging below his shoulders, and his eyes were red and swollen from lack of sleep and too much drink.

The short, rotund man on the right, whom Ferrin had never laid eyes on before, barely managed a squeak as his beady eyes stared up at Ferrin's dark silhouette in the doorway. He had a mustache that curled from his nose to the tops of his cheeks, but one look at the shadowy figure standing over their table and both sides began to droop.

Elson reached for his sword. "I said be off with you before I run you through."

The single candle at the side of the table cast deep shadows across both sides of the booth, accentuating the anger on Elson's face while at the same time bolstering the fear on the other man's.

Ferrin took a step farther into the alcove and pulled back his hood.

Elson's mouth gaped. He sat in dumb silence for a moment before suddenly yanking a long dagger from underneath his cloak and waving it in the other man's face. "Get out, or I'll cut you!"

The man's eyes nearly popped out of his head as he grabbed a small pile of coins in front of him and swiftly bolted past Ferrin and scurried through the tables toward the back of the tavern.

Ferrin pulled the curtain shut and sat in the now-vacant seat across from Elson.

Elson grabbed the candle and held it up to get a better look. "Is it really you, or am I dreaming?"

Ferrin smiled. "It's really me, old friend."

Elson lowered the candle back to the table. "Where've you been, you flaming whoreson? You had us all in ruin, thinking you'd been taken by the Tower. Harlin said the Black Watch had rounded you up in the middle of the night." Elson grabbed the tankard in front of him and drained it to the last drop, finishing with a loud belch. "Clearly he didn't know what he was talking about."

"Oh, he knew exactly what he was talking about, since he was the one who sold me to them!"

"What?" Elson looked confused. "What do you mean he sold you? Are you telling me you really were taken by the White Tower?" He looked at Ferrin a moment, then shook his head. "Of course not. How could you be here if you were?" He paused a moment, then his eyes widened. "Unless they turned you."

"Turned me?"

Elson looked at the curtain as if expecting Black Watch soldiers to come pouring in at any moment. "You're one of them, aren't you? You've come to hunt us down!"

"I've come to do no such thing, you drunk fool. I escaped."

"No one has ever escaped the Tower."

"Then I'm the first."

"How?"

"With help."

Elson collapsed back against his seat. "So, it's true?" He ran his hand through his hair. "I mean . . . what was it like? What did they do to you?"

"It's a place of nightmares. I can't imagine the Pits of Aran'gal being much worse."

Elson leaned forward, scooting half out of his seat to pat Ferrin on both his shoulders. "You still have all your limbs?"

"Yes. But only because of the healers. The inquisitors tortured us for information. They would torture us to the brink of death and then use a healer to revive us long enough to do it all over again. For months."

Elson stared in silence, then took a swallow of his ale. "What kind of . . . things did they do?"

"You don't want to know."

Elson gulped. "How did you escape? In fact, when did you escape? You've been gone for nearly a year."

"It's a long story. But my cellmate was a seer, and he was the one who helped me get out, along with the healer I mentioned, her daughter, and a Black Watch captain."

"One of the Black Watch helped you escape? And you didn't think that strange? What if he did that just to get you to lead them right back to us?" Elson glanced once more nervously at the curtain in front of their booth.

"He didn't. In fact, he killed several of his own men just to make it out, and we've been on the run ever since."

"And you brought them here? Have you lost your mind?"

"I had to. They threatened to take Myriah in order to force me to create weapons for them. I'm only here long enough to collect her and be gone, but when I went by the house it looked like no one's been there for months. What's going on? Do you know where she is?"

Elson looked at the table, his face shifting to something that resembled guilt or embarrassment. "What did you mean when you said Harlin sold you out?"

"Do you remember our last wielder council banquet?"

"The one where you and Garreth nearly did battle in the middle of the dining hall? Of course. How could I forget?"

"After I got home that night, Myriah was called out on another errand for Lord and Lady Reskin. As soon as she left, the Black Watch showed up. I fought them as long as I could, even managed to kill a couple, but there were too many of them, and they collared me."

"Do the collars really take your magic?"

Ferrin didn't have time to go into all of it. "Yes, and that's when I saw Harlin. He was outside collecting payment from the Black Watch. He told me that he'd be sure to take good care of Myriah while I was gone."

Elson began fiddling with his dagger.

"What is it?"

"I don't know how to tell you this, or even if I should, but . . ." Elson took a deep breath and finally looked up. "Myriah is now living with Harlin."

"Living? What do you mean by living?"

"They were married three months ago."

Ferrin's hands began shaking. In fact, his whole body was shaking. He grabbed hold of the edge of the table, and for a moment thought about flipping it. The man who had sold him to the Tower was now bedding his sister. He couldn't breathe.

He stumbled out of his seat and out of the alcove, scattering servers and patrons alike as he struggled to reach the door. Myron must have seen him, for by the time Ferrin had reached the front doors, the others were there to meet him. He stumbled out of the tavern and screamed at the top of his lungs.

"What's going on?" Myron asked, laying a hand on Ferrin's shoulder. "What happened? She's not dead, is she? The Tower hasn't taken her, have they?"

Ferrin staggered over to one of the benches on the porch and plopped down, his head buried in his hands. He was so angry, he couldn't even make out the conversation taking place beside him. All he wanted was to get his hands on Harlin.

". . . going on?"

"What's going on," Elson said, his words a bit slurred from drink, "is that the man just received the worst news a man could. He just found out that the man who apparently betrayed him to the Tower has now taken his sister as well."

Myron looked at Elson. "You mean . . ."

Elson nodded. "They were wedded three months ago."

Myron sat down on the bench beside Ferrin and laid his hand on his leg. "What do you want to do?"

Ferrin looked up, staring out at the snow-covered street ahead. "I want to kill him."

Myron looked at the others, then back at Ferrin. "Okay. How?"

"Slowly."

"No. I mean how do we get there? How do we break in without alerting the patrollers? What do we do with your sister if she . . . Let's be honest, you're talking about walking in and killing her husband. Not sure how open to the idea she'll be, if you know what I mean."

"She will when she hears what he did."

Myron looked at Ismara, but she didn't seem much help as she offered no more than a non-judgmental shrug. "I like the killing-him idea."

"We are talking about someone she has been sharing her bed with. I don't see this going well for you if you just walk in there and stick a sword through him while she's lying there."

As much as Ferrin hated to admit it, Myron was right. If he were to walk in there and kill the man just like that, he might alienate his sister altogether. He had to do this right. "We'll take both of them back to the ship. That will give me time to explain to her what happened, and if worse comes to worst, I'm sure we can drop him overboard at some point, far enough out that he can't reach shore."

Myron looked at the others. "I guess that's something. So, where does this son of a faerie live?"

Ferrin stood. "Follow me."

The snow was now coming down in droves, thick enough to make visibility difficult, thick enough to hide the streetlamps altogether as they made their way north through town, not bothering with taking back alleys, as no one could see them anyhow. Ferrin guided them toward the wealthier side of Rhowynn, where buildings slowly began to spread farther and farther apart as they grew more elaborate.

By the time they reached the street Ferrin was looking for, the estates were set back off the road with their own private yards and brick walls. Ferrin counted down the numbers on the gates out front of each until finding the one he was looking for.

"This is it," he said, and climbed over the short brick boundary fronting the small courtyard that led up to the front of the large home.

As cold as it was, it was no surprise they didn't find a watchman on patrol as they all—Elson included—gathered under the overhang at the front of the home. Ferrin took off his glove and laid his hand on the door handle, pushing his magic until the locking mechanism gave way. By now it was well past midnight, the owners having gone to bed some time ago. The thought of his sister crawling into bed alongside Harlin had him nearly biting a hole in his tongue as he clamped down with his teeth.

The door slid open silently, and the freezing band of kidnappers shuffled inside.

Myron blew out the lantern they'd been carrying and placed it on the carpet runner next to the door.

There was a scraping sound from the hallway closet on the right. Ferrin ignored it—probably rats trying to escape the cold. There was only one thing on his mind, and it wasn't exterminating vermin. Well, in a way, he guessed that was exactly what it was.

The front entranceway and main hall leading toward the back were lit by sconces, providing only enough light to keep from tripping over any of the finer furnishings as the group made their way quietly up the hall entrance, keeping to the side as much as possible. Every so often Ferrin would stop and listen, but there didn't appear to be any sign of movement other than the expected groan of the building itself and the occasional branch beating against the odd window shutter.

The staff, having no doubt retired to the servants' quarters hours ago, were nowhere to be seen. They passed the main sitting room on the right, embers still burning in the hearth. The table at the back, where he and Elson would play round after round of batmyth while the other members of the council gossiped, sat all alone and empty.

Ahead, on the left, was the dining room where the wielder council would take their meals and discuss any upcoming events of note. This time of year, they would have been taking requests for arrangements concerning their annual Winter's Eve celebrations. Following that, their New Year traditional sleepover, where very little sleeping would actually take place, as most would stay up until the wee hours of the morning getting so sloshed that carriages and drivers would be hired to cart the attendees home.

There were a lot of memories tied to this house, and now those memories were threatening to drown him alive. He wanted to burn the place to the ground, and Harlin with it. Quietly, they started up the single staircase on the right, adjacent to the dining hall. Ferrin was first, Elson right behind, his legs a bit wobbly, no doubt due to the excessive amount of drink he'd partaken of before Ferrin arrived.

Behind him was Myron, then Ismara and the young crewman.

They reached the top of the stairs and stopped. "Which way?" Myron whispered.

Ferrin shook his head. He'd never been up to the second floor before. He had no idea where the master bedchamber would be. He started to turn when Elson walked past and started down a corridor on the left.

"This way," he said right before Ferrin clamped his mouth shut with his hand.

"Shh." Ferrin wondered if he ought to gag the drunk just to be safe.

"Oh, sorry." He pointed to the far end of the hall, where it stopped outside a set of beautifully carved doors.

Ferrin nodded, and they crept down the hall, keeping to the long stretch of carpet at the center, which padded their steps and quieted their approach. They reached the doors, and everyone looked at Ferrin as if to say the rest was up to him. Ferrin drew his belt knife and slowly turned the handle. It was locked as well, so he pushed his magic inside and shifted the latch, just enough to finish the turn and open the door. It squeaked, so Ferrin stopped.

He listened for a moment, but as far as he could tell, no one had woken. Carefully, he walked over to the hinges and touched each, the metal smoothing as he did. This time when he pushed on the door, it slid open without so much as a peep.

Ferrin stepped inside, the others right behind, closing the door behind them. The windows on the side were shuttered, not that it would have mattered. As heavy a snowfall as they were having, there would be no light coming through to see with anyway. There were no candles, and even after waiting for his eyes to adjust, Ferrin couldn't see much more than faint silhouettes of objects scattered around the room.

On the far side of the room toward the right, Ferrin could just make out what he thought was the bed, and he carefully made his way across the tiles and over to the thick rug the bed was standing on. His hands were shaking, afraid of what he would find, afraid of how this would affect his sister. Myriah or not, Harlin was going to get what was coming to him. Ferrin scooted his way slowly up the side of the bed, still trying his best to make out which side Harlin was on and which side—

"Now!"

Flashes of light from his left momentarily blinded him, and he stumbled back from the bed. He drew his sword as men in white uniforms raced in from a door on the left side of the room. He barely got the blade up in time to stop a cudgel to the side of his head. He took the guard's hand off at the forearm and finished him with thrust through the chest, sparing a quick glance over his shoulder at the bed. There was nothing there but bunched-up covers overtop thick pillows.

How did they know we were here?

Ferrin fought his way backward toward the exit, where his friends were waiting. The youngest crewman ripped opened the door behind them for a quick escape, only to find several men with short spears waiting on the other side. The young riverman screamed as one of the white guards rammed his spear straight through him. He tried pulling the thick shaft free, his fingers sliding on his own blood, before finally collapsing.

Ismara yelled and dove at the first three men coming through the doorway. The spearman didn't even have time to yank his weapon free before she had removed his head with her cutlass and stuck her long knife in the neck of the next. Pulling the blade free, she plunged it into the eye of the third guard.

Ferrin turned and threw back two guards that were on top of Elson, who had stumbled over his own feet as he rushed to the right side of the room to get away from the armed men. Ferrin grabbed his friend by his coat and jerked him to his feet, shoving him back into the corner and out of the way before rushing to Myron's side, as the former captain was holding back the armed guards trying to force their way in from the side room.

Myron was using one of Ferrin's two magic-wrought swords that he'd built in Iraseth as he cut back the men trying to surround them. A sudden gust of wind, and Myron flew past Ferrin, rolling to a stop on the right side of the room near where Elson was cowering in the corner.

A streak of blue light flashed from the corner of Ferrin's eyes, and he dove to the side, just avoiding getting his head removed from his shoulders as a bulradoer suddenly appeared amidst the Black Watch.

This was impossible. How were they here?

Ferrin rolled back to his feet and met the next pass with his own sword. The man in the black robe looked stunned by the fact that his fiery weapon hadn't cut Ferrin's sword in two, and him along with it. He looked even more stunned when Ferrin deflected his flaming sword on the next parry, then cut off his head. The body barely had time to fall before three more white guards rushed him.

He couldn't hold them back. The first struck his blade, and Ferrin's magic spread from his own sword into the Tower guard's, and his weapon bent like a wilted flower. Before the man had time to realize what had happened, Ferrin plunged his own sword through his chest. The second two didn't carry swords, but each held a heavy cudgel, rendering Ferrin's abilities useless.

Behind him, Myron and Ismara fought side by side, doing their best to hold back those coming through the hallway door, but there were just too many of them. It didn't seem to discourage his friends, though. Ferrin could hear their steel clashing as he fought to do the same with those pouring in from the side door.

Suddenly, the guards pulled back.

"Lay down your weapon," someone behind him said.

Ferrin spun, panting hard as he tried to catch his breath. His heart sank when he saw both Ismara and Myron on their knees with blades to their throats. Ferrin didn't have a choice. There was nothing he could do. He dropped his weapon on the floor in front of him and raised his hands.

The guards took all three and moved them to the center of the room, Elson included. After being thoroughly searched for weapons and crystals, they were put in irons and dragged to their feet and lined against the wall behind them, just to the right of the hall door.

"Did you think you could escape me?" a familiar voice called out from the side room.

Sylas stepped through the doorway and into the light.

It couldn't be. "How did you get here before us?"

Sylas smiled. "After you left Woodvale and crossed the grasslands on foot, we took a ship from Hedgemont across Praxil Lake and up to Rhowynn."

A second bulradoer stepped out as well, though she didn't seem to have the same fire in her eyes as she had when Ferrin had fought her in Iraseth. In fact, her face, apart from the nasty-looking scar running down her left cheek, looked bruised and . . . Ferrin's eyes caught a flash of silver under her robe. Had she been collared? Which brought another question: Where had the bulradoer Ferrin had just decapitated come from? There had only been one with Sylas in Iraseth. Had he picked up more along the way? If so, how many?

Sylas stared at the prisoners. "Where is my precious Rae? And what have you done with my daughter?"

"I'm surprised you even noticed," Ferrin said, "what with ordering your guards to attack the way they did."

Sylas walked over to stand in front of Ferrin. He was at least half a head shorter and nowhere near as thick in the shoulders. "I'll not ask you again. Where is my little Suri?"

"Dead," Ferrin said, feeling awkward even saying it.

Sylas's expression never changed. He didn't even blink an eye. Any other father would have fallen to their knees weeping. Sylas studied Ferrin's eyes a moment, then smiled. "You are lying."

"She's dead to you. You'll never see either of the two of them again, I've seen to it." Lying or not, Ferrin rather enjoyed the sudden flash of anger that passed across Sylas's normally unresponsive face.

Sylas flipped his wrist. "It will make torturing the information out of you all the more enjoyable." With that, the inquisitor sauntered down the line of prisoners, inspecting each, taking a few extra moments with Ismara as he pulled back her coat to admire what was underneath. "Yes, she will make a fine new addition."

"You touch me, and I'll feed you your own fingers."

Sylas chuckled and moved on, eventually reaching the end and turning back around to walk them again. He stopped in front of Ferrin. He might have been wearing another man's body, but those same dead eyes were still there, that same despicable smile that no doubt meant he was imagining all the horrors he had waiting for Ferrin when they got back.

"What have you done with my sister?"

"Oh, she's safe. You didn't think I'd return without her, did you? No, the two of you are clearly a package deal. I will enjoy spending weeks, months, *years* getting to know every bit of her. I can only hope she holds out that long, that way I can spend as much time as possible."

Ferrin leaped at the man, his arms nearly pulled out of their sockets by those holding his shackles.

"Now, now, my dear smith, we'll have none of that. There will be plenty of time to play later." Sylas turned to one of the guards at the back, who was carrying a large case, and ordered him forward. "Collar them all. I don't want to take any chances. Except him, of course," he said, pointing to Myron. "No need to waste a collar on that one. He has about as much magic as you do. The infamous Black Watch captain who betrayed his own." Sylas grinned. "Better yet, kill him on the way out."

"No!" Ferrin fought to break free of his captors. It took four men to pull him to the ground, but in the end, all he could do was stand there and watch as one of the guards pulled out his sword and thrust it straight through Myron's chest.

Myron never even flinched. The guard yanked the blade free, and Myron dropped to his knees, spitting blood as he did. He managed to turn his head. "Save her." He took once last garbled inhale and tipped over on his face and went still.

Ferrin stared at his friend's body in shock. He then looked the inquisitor in the eyes. "I'm going to kill you, Sylas. I'm going to kill you in ways you haven't even thought about. I'm going to—"

Pain tore through Ferrin like he'd been struck by lightning, and he tried to scream, but nothing came out as his entire body went limp and he collapsed to the floor, right beside Elson, who was writhing across the tile, same as him. Ismara didn't seem to be affected. She stood there with a confused look on her face as she watched them eventually curl into a ball and retch.

Sylas released the glowing silver rod in his hand and looked at the guard holding the chest of durma collars. "You can remove her collar. Save it for someone else."

"Where's my sister?" Ferrin asked as he fought back against the aftershock still coursing through his body, tears clouding his vision.

Sylas looked down at him and smiled. "Don't worry. You'll be reunited very soon."

Chapter 65 | Lenara

LENARA WATCHED HELPLESSLY as the swordsmith and his friends lay on the floor, curled in their own spittle and waste. She knew the pain of the durma all too well, having been wearing one for the last two weeks. Apparently, Sylas had linked a second key to the other collars separate from hers. Had he not, she would have been on the ground in her own retch, same as them.

In truth, it would have made no difference had she worn a collar or not. Sylas knew as long as he was in Joren's body, there was nothing she would do to him, but it did give Sylas no end of pleasure to use it on her whenever she attempted to fight against his advances.

Perhaps there was some way she could use the swordsmith to her advantage, though right now the man looked broken. She remembered the fire in his eyes in Iraseth when she had stood against him. Now, seeing him on the floor, tears streaming down his cheeks, she felt only pity for him, something she would have never thought to feel before meeting Joren. She pushed the feeling aside. She had more important things to worry about.

It was lucky for Sylas that the Tower had a regiment of Black Watch in the area to make up for the losses he'd caused during their expedition over the last few months. If not for the additional recruits, this swordsmith and his friends might just have been determined enough to have won this fight, and Sylas might have been forced to free Lenara of her collar just to keep himself alive.

"What do we do with them now?" one of the guards asked, staring down at the newly collared prisoners.

Sylas stood by the door. "We stay here another night. I'm not about to go traipsing out in this storm and take a chance of losing any of them." He glanced around the room. "Put them in the back and keep a guard on the door. I need my sleep, and I don't want to be interrupted by them trying to escape."

"What about her?" the guard asked, looking at Lenara.

Sylas smiled. "Put her with the others." He walked over to Lenara and stroked her cheek with Joren's finger. "I'm sorry, my dear. I know how much you want to be with me tonight, but I'm just too tired to give you my undivided attention."

Lenara didn't say a word, didn't even change her expression, which at the time was as flat and uncaring as possible. She couldn't tell if Sylas was trying to be sarcastic, or if he actually believed that Lenara had come to enjoy his affection. He was conceited enough to believe she did. And right now, it was probably the only thing keeping him from killing her. His enjoyment of others' pain was going to be his undoing. She only hoped that end was at her hands, and only after she managed to excise him from her beloved Joren.

It had been over a week since the last time Joren had surfaced, and that resurfacing had only lasted an hour. Joren had attempted to remove her collar, but Sylas, as despicable and untrusting as he was, had given the collar's key to the Black Watch guards to keep at night, since he never knew when Joren might make an appearance. By the time they realized they couldn't get the collar off, Sylas had returned. That single hour together had been wonderful, though, during which time she had begged him to hold on, promising she would find a way to free him.

"What about the bodies?" another guard asked, looking down at the former Black Watch captain and the younger sailor.

Sylas looked at the two and wrinkled his nose. "Well, I certainly don't want them stinking up my bedchamber, now do I? Take them downstairs and toss them out back. We'll be long gone before anyone finds them."

Several of the guards grabbed the two dead men, along with those Ferrin and his group had killed, and hauled them away while another grabbed Lenara by the arm and marched her into the room where they had spent the last several nights waiting for the smith to arrive. Sylas had originally thought to lie in wait at the smith's home, but after learning that the smith's sister was now living with Lord Harlin, Sylas determined he would much rather wait there than at the smith's humble abode.

The dressing chamber was nothing more than a large room, stocked with racks and shelves of clothes, which opened on the other side into the washroom. The guard placed her down against the front of a shelf laden with a wide variety of boots and shoes to go with every possible occasion. Lord Harlin had been quite the fop, his excessive wardrobe more than proving it.

A lantern was hung to give the guards enough light to stave off any attempts to escape. Once everyone had been placed inside and their manacles checked, the guards stepped out of the room and shut the door. They left the washroom unattended, as there was nowhere to escape from inside. The dressing room door leading into the bedchamber was the only way in or out.

The swordsmith sat on the other side of the room, tears still filling his eyes, either from the residual pain of the collar or the death of his companion. He and the other wielder looked rather the worse for wear as they struggled to remain in a sitting position. The shorter one finally succumbed to his injuries and collapsed unconscious on the floor. Then again, it could have been the drink. She could smell it on him from where she was sitting. Either way, he was the lucky one.

The closest of the other prisoners to Lenara was the female sailor, her outfit giving her away as a person of some notoriety aboard her ship, perhaps even the captain by the way she fought. As soon as they placed the woman down, she took one look at Lenara and quickly scooted over beside the swordsmith.

"Where's my sister?" the swordsmith mumbled through clenched teeth as he glared across the room at Lenara. If he'd had an ounce of strength left, Lenara had no doubt he would have leapt on top of her and tried beating the answers out of her. "What have you done to her?"

"I've done nothing with her, or has it escaped your notice that I'm in here with you?" She couldn't help but let some of her own anger bleed through as she all but hissed at him. She pulled back her hood and grabbed the silver collar around her neck. "I'm unable to do anything."

The smith laughed. It was a very cold, unfriendly laugh. "So, he doesn't trust you any more than the rest of us? Aren't you a bulradoer? How do you let someone like him collar you? Where're those fiery whips you tried cutting me down with in Iraseth?"

Lenara bit her tongue to keep from lashing out. Each question was a slap in the face, a reminder of what she had become, what she was allowing herself to be put through, and all for something she had spent most her life spurning. Love was weakness. "I cannot touch him."

"And why not? He's nothing more than a sadist with a set of tools. You have real power. I've seen it."

Lenara ground her teeth. "If I hurt him, then I hurt Joren."

"Joren? Who in the flaming Pits is Joren?"

"The man whose body Sylas has taken."

The swordsmith looked almost stunned. "Are you telling me that he's still alive?"

Lenara nodded. "He returns at night when Sylas enters a deep enough sleep." She stared at the shackles on her wrists. "At least, he used to. It's growing harder now for him to make it out. He's slipping away." She stopped talking, afraid if she did, she would break down and start sobbing herself, not that she had much in the way of pride left at that point, not after what Sylas had been doing to her for the last two weeks.

The swordsmith and the sailor sat in silence, sympathy on their faces that had Lenara's stomach turning.

"And I thought I had it bad," the smith said. "I can't imagine what it would be like to actually be joined to someone like Sylas." He looked at Lenara. "Is he . . . Is he aware? Does he see what's happening?"

Lenara nodded, this time much slower.

"How did Sylas end up in his body in the first place?"

Lenara explained what had taken place inside the Chamber of Purging. The swordsmith surprised her by stating that he had actually been there once before to meet with the archchancellor. That was news to Lenara. She described as best she could the process that Joren had undergone in order to bring the inquisitor back, including the graphic nature of what the Tree of Souls had done to him, and how, apparently, something had gone wrong and Joren had remained.

By the time she finished, the female sailor looked like she was on the verge of retching. "And you took part in that?" she asked. "You would have to be a special kind of sick to do that to someone. I thought the White Tower was there to rid Aldor of magic, not collect it."

"Sometimes you have to fight fire with fire." She regretted saying the words as soon as they left her mouth, leaving her with a bad taste. She had quoted them directly from Valtor and every other archchancellor to have held that seat of power. "Sorry. I don't know why I said that. The Tower might have started out with a mission of purging magic from Aldor, but it has long since strayed from that goal."

"Then why were you there?" the female sailor asked, looking at Lenara like one would a woman with an abusive husband, who remains unwilling to leave him.

Lenara took a moment to think about it, realizing her answer wasn't much better than that of the abused wife. "Because I had nowhere else to go."

The female sailor shook her head. "My name's Ismara. And I take it you already know Ferrin."

"And that's Elson," Ferrin added, pointing to the still-unconscious man lying to his left.

Lenara hadn't remembered the swordsmith's name. Sylas always referred to him as *the smith*. "I'm Lenara."

Ferrin scooted back against the wall, attempting to straighten himself after being slumped over from residual pain. "You never answered my question. Where's my sister?"

"She is safe, for now. They have her with the rest of the Tower's guards just outside the city."

"When will they take us to her? Tomorrow?"

"I'm not sure. Sylas is using Harlin to flush out the rest of your wielder council. He has been assured his own safety if he's willing to give up the rest. Apparently, there's no honor among wielders."

Ferrin sneered. "Not when it comes to that coward."

His shackles snapped tight on his wrists. The man's eyes were practically glowing. He looked crazed enough to break down the door and try attacking Sylas in his bed. "Harlin's the one who sold me to the Black Watch in the first place. And I'll be hanged if I let him do it again!"

"You'll be worse than hanged if you try anything right now. Don't give Sylas an excuse, or he'll have you wallowing in your own dung just for the pleasure of it."

"He'll do that anyway," Ferrin said, then looked at Ismara. "How long till your father sends out a search party?"

Ismara thought a moment. "Not till morning, but that's not going to do us much good. Where are they going to look? They have no idea where we are, and in a city this size, the chances of them accidentally stumbling across us is not even worth thinking about, especially if she's right and they are taking us out of the city." She turned to Lenara. "Which route will this Sylas use in taking us back to the Tower?"

"He'll follow the water south down the Taloos into Elondria, and from there east along the Razor Spine Mountains. Why?"

"Because even if they can't find us in Rhowynn, they can always track us along the river. If we wait for the right opportunity, we might still find a way to escape."

"Who's they?" Lenara asked.

"My crew."

So, she was a captain as Lenara had suspected. "I hope they are prepared for a fight. Sylas has a full regiment of Tower guards, not to mention a few extra bulradoer that had been assigned to them."

"I was wondering why there were more of you here," Ferrin said. "Do all of your kind carry those fire weapons?"

"They're called ter'aks. And yes, those who've risen high enough in the ranks to wear the mantle of a bulradoer have them. Not that it seemed to help poor Eljin all that much, considering the way you lopped off his head. He'd barely just received his robes. Clearly the standards at the Tower are slipping." She studied Ferrin a moment. "As I've mentioned before, your swords are quite unique. The fact that they can stand up to a wizard's weapon is beyond impressive."

"Lot of good they did us. We've been captured, and my friend is dead."

"Still, dispatching a bulradoer so easily is no small feat." She looked at Ismara. "Let's hope your crew are as good at tracking as you say, because even if we had your weapons, which we don't, they aren't going to do us much good with these collars around our necks just waiting to be set off at any time. We will need someone there to divert attention away from us as we try to find a way to steal the keys back."

Ferrin smiled, a strange look for a man imprisoned by the Tower for a second time, and reached down into his pants, all the way into his underpants. A moment later, he removed a chain with a small metal rod, a rod that looked awfully similar to . . . Lenara gaped.

"I think that opportunity might be closer than you think," Ferrin said.

Lenara stared at the cylindrical object resting between the smith's fingers. "Is that . . . is that a durma key?"

Chapter 66 | Ty

HE BRIDGE BETWEEN TREES began to swing, and Ty stopped, Narendi all but climbing on his back as Breen kept a step or two behind. They held on to the rope railing on either side as they waited for the movement to stop, or at least slow to the point they could feel safe enough to continue.

It had taken quite some time to coax Narendi out onto the first bridge. Ty had to promise to carry her if she couldn't make it on her own. In the end, he threatened to leave her behind, and she immediately wrapped her Mzwati baka around her face and began marching out over the long drop below. Marching might have been a generous word. She moved in a cautious glide as she slid one foot after the other out across the rickety trestle. As long as she didn't look down, she seemed to be okay.

Safely reaching the other side, they continued on to the next bridge. So far, they hadn't seen much of this new and rather unique community, only enough to believe that they were somewhere deep inside the upper Riverlands, a place where everyone lived within the trees themselves. The trees in this part of Aldor were all but worshiped, said to have been brought over during the time of the faeries by the giants, if one believed in such tales, which of course Ty most certainly did, or wanted to.

Anyone who saw them would have had a hard time arguing differently. Only a giant could have planted a grove of such magnitude. No other logical explanation could possibly justify their size. A single tree could hold three separate homes and a full merchant shop. Most cities spread out horizontally as their numbers increased. However, here in the Riverlands, that expansion went upward instead.

It was an incredible place, and even though it took some getting used to, Ty was delighted the mirror had brought them there. Now, they simply needed to find a place to rent for the night before the snow got any thicker. The bridges were dangerous enough to travel across in good conditions—add in a blanket of snow and ice, and their next step could be their last.

"How much farther do we travel?" Narendi asked, giving Ty a good excuse to stop before crossing the next bridge.

He turned to find Narendi pressed as close to the trunk of the tree as she could get. "The lady we asked earlier said to take a left at the last tree, cross two bridges, and we'd find the inn on the right."

"Actually," Breen cut in, "she said we'd find it two levels down."

"See?" Ty said with a forced grin. "Nothing to it." He placed his hand on her shoulder, and she flinched. "Time to start moving again."

"So soon?"

Ty wanted to chuckle, but he didn't. Instead, he started across the next swinging overhang, sliding his feet rather than picking them up, just to make sure they stayed as close to the wooden planks as possible, assuring they would be less likely to slip off. They reached the end of the bridge and began to circle the tree, stopping momentarily to glance in the lit window of what appeared to be a cobbler's shop.

There were rows of shoes and boots lined in a simple display on the other side of the glass. They didn't exactly have the kind of variety one would find in Easthaven, but for being located in the middle of a tree, Ty thought it quite impressive. He was half tempted to stop in just to get a better look, but one look at the fear in Narendi's eyes and he decided to continue on.

They crossed one more bridge, regrettably passing a couple of locals coming from the other direction. Ty was forced to stop and wrap one arm around Narendi and the other around the right-side railing. The two shoppers passed by without so much as even bothering to hold the rail, even picking up their pace when they caught a glimpse of Narendi's Mzwati robes and long spear.

Ty didn't think he could ever get used to the instability of the bridges in that way, not even if he spent the next ten years living there, which of course he hoped didn't happen. It would be like living aboard a sea vessel, spending every day walking the deck, feeling the constant sway and tilt of the ship as it rocked back and forth in the current. His stomach started to turn, and he quickly released the image.

Once the shoppers had made it off the bridge and the sway of the ropes had lessened, Ty released Narendi, and they hurried for the other side. Like all the other trees they'd seen so far, this one also held a winding staircase that wrapped up and down the tree like ribbon on a pole, and with little prodding on Narendi's behalf, they headed down in search of their destination.

Sure enough, after passing between several jutting balconies on the way down, they reached a landing with a sign that read: *The Beetle Bark Inn*. Ty stomped the snow off his boots as best he could and opened the door. Narendi, shivering from head to foot, didn't bother and simply hurried inside, ducking low enough to keep her spear from catching the top of the doorjamb.

Ty looked down at her snow-covered sandals and frowned. With all the excitement of discovering this new and incredible world, he hadn't even thought about the fact that she was still dressed for the desert. She had to be nearly frozen. "We've got to get you some new clothes before you catch your death."

Narendi's teeth were chattering. "I will be fine."

"No. You'll be stiff as a poker. Maybe tomorrow we can find a clothing shop and get you something more appropriate to wear."

"We need to get her in front of a fire," Breen said, looking as ashamed as Ty for not having noticed her predicament sooner. "Look at your feet. They're covered in snow."

Ty walked over to a small desk on the right, where an older woman with white hair and a long apron sat napping and cleared his throat. When that didn't work, he coughed loudly, and she jerked awake. "Wasn't asleep. Just resting my eyes." She adjusted her spectacles. "Welcome to Beetle Bark. How can I help you? My name is Nishka." She gave the three of them a good looking-over, gawking at Narendi and her spear before turning her attention back to Ty. "Well, sonny, what will it be?"

"We need a couple of rooms for the night."

The innkeeper looked down at the large leather-bound book on her desk and scanned the pages. "Afraid we only have one left. You should have booked early. With the Live Market in town this week and next, you'll be hard-pressed to find a knothole to climb into. Just so happens, though, that we had a cancellation earlier today."

Ty didn't hesitate. "We'll take it."

"Very good," she said, picking up the quill and dipping it in the ink. "Can I get your names?"

"I'm Ty. That's my brother Breen, and this here is Narendi."

She jotted down their names in the ledger and placed the quill back in the jar, then grabbed a key off the wall behind her. "Number fifteen is ready as soon as you pay."

"You haven't told us how much the room is," Ty pointed out as he reached into his boot, where he kept the small pouch of coins his father had given him. It wasn't much, but since they had made it this far without the need to spend any of it, it would hopefully be enough to manage a room and meals for a night. There might even be enough left for a change of clothes for Narendi—if the room was small, the food but leftover scraps, and the clothes secondhand.

"I guess I didn't," she said with a slight chuckle that turned into a bout of wheezing. "Let's see, for the one room, and I take it you'll want food and drink, not to mention candles." She counted on her fingers. "That'll be one silver and six."

Ty's eyes widened. "One silver and six for one room for one night?"

"I told you, the Live Market's in town this week and next. Prices rise with demand."

Ty dug around inside his pouch for the silver and coppers and handed them reluctantly to the woman.

"Just follow the stairs up till you reach the third landing, take the hall halfway down, and you'll find your room on the left."

Ty thanked her, not exactly knowing why, considering the prices she was gouging out of them, and took the stairs up to the third landing, Narendi and Breen close on his heels. They followed the hall down to the second door on the left, which had a bronze plate over the top that was engraved with the number 15. "Guess this is it," Ty said as he unlocked the door and opened it.

The room was small but cozy, with a single bed on the right, along with a desk and chair and a small cabinet to hang their clothes. To the left of the door was a mirror and washstand with a folded towel and a bar of soap just beside. A fireplace with a stack of chopped wood beside took up the left corner of the room. Between the unlit hearth on the left and the bed on the right was a door that led out to a covered balcony, and while Breen went about lighting the candles, Ty dropped his gear on the floor beside the balcony door and walked outside.

"Shut it behind you," Breen said as he used one of the candles to start the tinder in the fireplace.

Ty shut the door and cautiously made his way across the balcony to the railing on the other side and looked over. Even in the failing light of the sun, he could see that the boardwalks below were busy with people. The sun seemed to set faster in the forest, the trees blocking the natural light with their wide-reaching branches. Even with the leaves having dropped months prior, the size and density of the arms was enough to keep everything in shadow.

It was an incredible view. He wished his father were there to see it. He knew how much his father loved the outdoors. This would have been the perfect retreat for him. Who knew, maybe one day he'd get the chance to bring him back here.

The door behind him opened, and Narendi stuck her head out. "Are you coming back in?" She wasn't about to walk across the balcony to where Ty was.

"I'm coming." He took one last look out across the waterways below before heading inside.

Breen finished stoking the fire in the brick hearth and went about unpacking his gear while Narendi pulled off her sandals and held her feet up to the flames. Ty couldn't believe she hadn't complained about the cold, not even once. Her toes must have been frozen stiff. "Here, let me take a look." He sat down beside her and examined her feet for frostbite.

They were stiff around the joints, but still moveable. "Can you feel my fingers?" he asked as he slowly ran them over each toe. The ends were showing signs of whitening, which had him concerned, but they seemed to move on their own.

She nodded. "I feel your touch."

He lifted each foot in his hands and blew on them, doing his best to work the blood back in as he gently massaged from the lower calf down. Growing aware of the enchanted look on her face, he released her feet and joined his brother in unpacking their bags. "First thing tomorrow, we find her some proper socks and boots."

Breen nodded. "Along with a few other things."

Ty looked at their one bed. Though a decent size, it was certainly not big enough to fit the three of them. "I think I'll go down and ask the lady for some extra blankets."

"Maybe they would have a spare cot or two," Breen suggested.

Ty left his half-emptied pack on the bed and started for the door.

"Oh, and ask them when supper is served," Breen said, drawing Narendi's attention as well.

"Fine. I'll see about a washroom, too. A hot bath would certainly help Narendi's feet." He left the room and headed back down the winding stairs to the front desk. Nishka was all but slumped over the top, resting her eyes once again. Only this time, she rested them with some very loud snoring. He had to practically shake her arm to get her to wake.

"Yes, yes. What is it?" she asked, rubbing her eyes and looking around as if trying to figure out where she was.

Ty gave her a moment to gather herself before asking about the extra cots and blankets.

"No cots, I'm afraid. But I'm sure I can scrounge up some blankets for you. I'll have Myrtle bring them up."

"Also, do you have a washroom with a tub that we can use?"

The old woman smiled. "How thoughtful of you, dear."

He gave her a confused look.

She explained. "Those traveling in for the Live Market aren't exactly the kind of people who care to wash that often. If you had any idea as to the smell some of these folks leave behind." She pinched her nose just below her spectacles. "Plum near have to burn the sheets on some of the beds. Ain't much better than the animals they're selling."

"What is this Live Market you keep mentioning?"

She raised her brow. "You're clearly not from around here. Once a year, hunters, trappers, and poachers gather to hold a live auction for the buying and selling of exotic animals, animals not legally found for sale anywhere else."

"So it's a black market, then?"

"One of the worst, if you ask me," she said, keeping her voice lowered as she looked up at the surrounding stairs to make sure no one was there to overhear. "You'd be surprised by the number of wealthy merchants and nobles who send representatives down to purchase from here. Something about having what few others do tends to keep them coming, and thereby keeps the poachers in business. You'd be best to keep as far away from the Market as possible, if you know what's good for ya. Mark my words, no good can come of it."

"Sound advice," Ty said, taking a moment to look around the small foyer. "So, where can we find this washroom?"

She looked at him as if not sure why he was suddenly asking about a washroom, then perked up. "Oh, right." She pointed to the large room just beyond the stairs. "That's the common room where you can take your meals. And if you follow that hallway there," she said, pointing to a small archway behind Ty on the left, "that will take you back to the washroom. I'll make sure Myrtle heats the water for you. Would you care to wash before you eat?" She looked at him over her spectacles as though letting him know the correct answer would be *yes*.

Ty smiled. "That would be fine, thank you." He left the desk and started up the stairs. Halfway to the first landing he leaned out over the railing and called back down to Nishka, who was already leaning back against the wall and folding her arms. "Don't forget the extra blankets and pillows."

The old woman jerked back up in her seat, glancing around the room before finally looking up. She waved. "Yes, extra blankets. I'll be sure Myrtle knows."

Ty smiled and waved, then headed back up the stairs for their room.

"What did she say?" Breen asked when Ty stepped inside. The room was already beginning to warm from just the short time it took him to go downstairs.

"She said that they didn't have any more cots, but that she would make sure to tell Myrtle to bring us up some extra blankets, and that she'd also tell Myrtle to warm the water if we wished to bathe before we eat. Which we do," he added with a smile.

"Who's Myrtle?"

Ty shrugged. "Nishka just said she'd let her know. Then again, when I went down, she was sleeping so hard she was practically drooling on the ledger, so there's no telling if she'll tell this Myrtle anything or not."

A knock on the door had Breen and Ty turning. Narendi, who was now standing in front of the fire, suddenly unwrapped her Mzwati robe from the front to warm herself. Ty nearly swallowed his tongue when he saw. Thankfully the robe was high enough at the back to keep them from seeing anything they shouldn't have.

Breen noticed it as well and shook his head.

Ty walked over and opened the door. A middle-aged woman with a brown dress and white apron stood in the hall. The white bonnet holding up her hair bobbed to the side as she attempted to peer around the stack of blankets in her arms. "I was told room fifteen wanted extra blankets."

"Yes. Thank you." Ty took the pile from her and handed it off to Breen, who in turn set the blankets on the bed.

"And I'll have the water heated for you shortly."

Ty thanked her again, and she hurried back down the hall. Ty hoped the poor woman wasn't the only member of the staff. It wasn't like she could depend on Nishka to be of much help. Ty doubted the older woman had climbed those stairs in years.

"I've never seen a place so cold," Narendi said, wrapping her robe back around her body.

Ty laughed. "You haven't seen cold until you visit the Angorans during a midwinter blizzard." Ty looked at Breen, who was back to unpacking their belongings. "We'll give her a few more minutes, then go down."

Ty spent the time unloading the rest of his pack. Unfortunately, none of them had a good change of clothes. The only other outfit they had with them was their Mzwati robes, which Ty had no intention of putting on. Last thing he wanted to do was stand out.

He wished he had a large enough purse to purchase them each a new outfit, but with the steep prices being charged for their room and board, he doubted he'd have enough to even afford a cheap pair of socks and boots for Narendi.

He sat on the edge of his bed for a while and played his flute, not bothering with his magic this time, simply playing it for the enjoyment of the music. He kept the tune soft and melodic, a calming ditty he'd heard during one of the Performance Nights a few years back. By the time he finished, Narendi was all but pulling him off the bed to take her down to the washroom. It was the most excitement he'd seen from her since they'd first stepped out of the mirror and realized where they were.

Ty wondered what the river people were doing with the traveling mirror, whether they even knew what it was.

Leaving his flute on the bed, Ty followed the others out, locking the door before heading down the stairs. They passed the front desk on the way by, taking care not to wake Nishka, who was once again propped up against the back wall with her arms folded and her chin resting against her chest. They took a moment to peek in the common room. It was on the smaller side, but given the fact it was in a tree, it was rather impressive to begin with.

Ty led them down a hallway on the left just off the lobby that ended at a door with another brass plate overtop that read: *WASHROOM*. He knocked, unsure if they were expected to just walk in. It would have been more than embarrassing to open the door and catch some unsuspecting guest just getting out. When no answer came, Ty slid the door open a crack. Steam billowed out from the around the edge as Ty called inside. "Is anybody in here?"

"It's ready for you," a voice said behind them, causing everyone to jump. Myrtle, who was carrying a bucket of steaming water, scooted past and pushed the door open with her hip as she headed into the washroom. There were two tubs with a privacy curtain around each.

"There's soap on the stool," Myrtle said after dumping her bucket in the tub on the right. She set the large pail to the side. "I'll leave you to it, then. There's a lock on the door if you need it, and you'll find drycloths over on the shelf," she said, pointing to a small cabinet in the corner. "Shout if you need anything. I'll be around." With that, she scurried out the door and on to her next set of tasks.

By the time Ty and Breen had decided which tub they would use, Narendi had unrobed, not bothering to pull her curtain, and slowly stepped into the one on the right, her back to them as she sank into the water. Ty and Breen were so shocked by her lack of modesty that they barely managed to get their heads turned before she was already in.

She released an enthusiastic moan. "I like this hot-water bathing."

Ty looked at Breen, and they both gulped and quickly pulled their own curtain.

"What are you doing?" she asked.

"We're bathing," Ty said, having just managed to get his shirt off. He poked his head out around the curtain. Narendi still hadn't bothered shutting hers. She was busy testing out the soap on her newly shaved head. Ty had to admit there was something rather sensual about it. He'd never seen a woman with no hair before, other than Mistress Baudry, but she was very old and rather sickly.

"Yes, but why do you hide?"

"Because we don't want you to see us."

"I bathed you. I have seen you already."

Ty groaned. "Don't remind me." Ty looked at Breen, who was just beginning to take off his bottoms. "You go ahead. I'll wait till you're done."

"You sure?"

Ty nodded and stepped outside the curtain and grabbed a couple of the drycloths. He set two by their tub and tossed one over near Narendi's, which was difficult to do with his eyes down. He took a seat on a stool near the door and stared at the side wall as he quietly waited his turn.

"Come scrub my back," Narendi said behind him.

Ty's eyes widened. "I'll do no such thing."

"It is your duty as my bonded mate."

Ty glanced over his shoulder. "I'm not your mate, and we certainly haven't bonded."

She held out the soap. "I can't reach. Please."

Ty hmphed, but finally got up from the stool and walked over, keeping his eyes on the floor as best he could until he managed to get behind her. He grabbed the soap, and she leaned forward and hugged her knees as he lathered it in his hands and started running it down her back as fast as he could.

"Ow. That hurts. Go slow."

He hmphed again, but he ran the bar over her skin in slow, soft circles.

"That is better."

Once finished, he dropped the bar into the water and walked back over to the stool, keeping his eyes averted as best he could while at the same time trying to justify looking. Maybe they were really married.

No! He shook his head. *What am I doing?* He conjured an image of Lyessa, and the ensuing shame quickly dampened his earlier longings.

"I'm finished," Breen said, and just in the nick of time. Ty shot up from his stool, not even bothering to look in Narendi's direction, and shuffled behind their privacy curtain. Breen was already half dressed, with one of the drycloths on his head, attempting to dry his hair. He grabbed his shirt and stepped outside the curtain. "It's all yours."

Ty quickly undressed and hopped in. The water wasn't quite steaming as it had been and held a layer of white sheen from the soap, but it was still very warm.

Ty lathered himself up with the bar, including his hair, and then sank completely under to wash it off, staying under longer than he probably should have as he let the water warm his face.

He came up to find Narendi standing over him with her own bar of soap in hand. Thankfully, she was clothed, and thankfully, the soap bubbles in his tub dampened his embarrassment, but it didn't stop him from hugging his legs all the same.

"Sorry," Breen said from outside the curtain with a notable chuckle. "I tried to stop her."

"You didn't try hard enough!"

"Scoot forward," she said and knelt down in back of the tub. Not seeing as he had much of a choice, he obeyed, and she slowly began rubbing her soap over his back. He tried not to look too uncomfortable, since she seemed to get some kind of perverse pleasure in watching him squirm. Perhaps if he acted like her presence didn't bother him so much, she wouldn't go to such lengths to make him feel awkward. Then again, how else was he to feel while sitting naked in his bath with a beautiful princess scrubbing his back?

"Would you like me to wash more?"

"No," Ty said with as calm a voice as possible. "I've already washed the rest. Thank you."

She stood there staring down at him, clearly not taking the hint.

"You can leave now."

Narendi rolled her eyes but did eventually step outside the curtain. As soon as she did, Ty hopped out and jerked on his pants, barely taking the time to dry off beforehand. Once dressed, they left the washroom and headed for the common room, finding a table near the doors at the back that led out to another covered balcony, where the guests would no doubt enjoy their meals during the warmer months.

As it was, they soon discovered the reason for the open table. There was a cold draft blowing in from the crack between the doors behind them, leaving their table quite chilled. But after having spent the last half hour inside a room full of steam, the cooler air felt refreshing. They ordered their meals, which had already been covered in the cost of the rooms, and even requested a second helping of the stew once they learned it was free. The stewed meat, whatever it was, had a pleasant taste, mostly due to the seasoned gravy overtop.

After finishing her first helping, Narendi wiped her mouth and released the loudest belch Ty had ever heard. Ty started to laugh but quickly cupped his hand over his mouth when he realized that all the guests were looking their way. Ty quickly tried explaining to her that belching after a meal wasn't held in the same regard in most societies as it was with the Imbatoo. Most people found it to be very rude or even offensive during a meal.

Both Ty and Breen finished their second helping quickly, embarrassed to sit there while everyone continued to stare. They headed back upstairs to catch as much sleep as they could before they decided what to do on the morrow.

Ty and Breen cleared off the bed for Narendi, who was too preoccupied with warming her backside in front of the fire to help. Once she finished, they rolled out their bedding in front of the hearth and lay down. Ty's blankets were closest to the wall and the farthest from Narendi. He could hear the ropes squeaking on the other side of the room as she crawled under her comforter. Breen blew out the last candle before lying down himself.

Their room, like every other room in the inn, smelled strongly of sweet wood, no doubt from the sap these particular trees produced. It was a very pleasant, relaxing smell that had Ty breathing in quite deeply as he finally closed his eyes and tried drifting off. Unfortunately, the harder he tried, the more awake he became as he lay there thinking about everything they needed to do, trying to imagine what this last test would be like.

Compassion.

With *faith*, he had to walk through a wall of fire. With *wisdom*, he had to figure out which was the correct key without the use of his hands, not to mention how to get to the keys in the first place. With *strength*, he had to make a choice between ultimate riches and the next piece of the shorlock. What could the wizards possibly have in store for *compassion*?

Ty slowly started to nod off as he relived each of the tests he and Breen had been forced to endure. He had just reached the attack of the orms when he felt something move beside him. At first, he thought it was the dream, perhaps an orm sliding up out of his blanket to eat him, but then cold feet wrapped around his, and he startled awake.

It took him a moment to figure out what was happening as he let his eyes adjust to the fire, but then something squirmed beside him, and he grabbed it, his hands finding nothing but skin.

He quickly jerked away when he realized it was Narendi. She had crawled into his covers while he was half asleep. Mortified, he looked over at Breen to make sure his brother wasn't watching, then breathed a huge sigh of relief when he saw his brother's back was to him. He turned back around.

"What are you doing?" he whispered as he reached out with his hand and once again caught only bare skin. "Are you—" He quickly yanked his hand back. "What do you think you're doing?"

"My duty as your first."

He wiggled out the backside of the blanket and let it wrap around her as she pressed against him. "How many times do I need to say this?" he said, finding it difficult to keep his voice lowered. "We are not married. You are not my first. I don't care how many times you cut your hair off, there will be no bonding."

She leaned over and kissed him softly on the mouth, and he pulled away, though he found it hard to do so.

"Do I not please you?"

Ty ran his hand down his face. "In more ways than I care to admit, but this isn't right. I am pledged to another. I love Lyessa, and I will not betray her trust." Ty glanced back over his shoulder at his brother, who was either in a very deep sleep or doing his best to pretend he was. For Ty's sake, he hoped it was the former. He didn't think he could handle it if Breen knew he was lying there with a naked woman in his bedding. He almost couldn't believe it himself, as though it were all some sort of strange dream brought on by a lack of sleep and an overextended imagination. It would be just like him to dream something as ridiculous as having a naked princess climbing into his bed. Unfortunately for him, though, he was wide awake.

Narendi stared at him angrily for a while longer, as if expecting him to suddenly change his mind, but when he didn't budge, she threw back the blanket and stood. "I will wait," she said, as Ty turned his head and looked at the wall. "But you will choose me."

He waited a moment longer, but when he didn't hear anything, he finally turned his head in time to catch her silhouette prancing back across the room and crawling back into her own bed. She was going to be the death of him. He pulled his covers back over himself, this time tucking them firmly underneath his body, just to make sure no one else decided to crawl in while he wasn't looking.

Turning over, he closed his eyes and tried thinking of anything but her lying there beside him, or the sight of her walking across the room, or lying in her bath. That proved to be more difficult than he anticipated. Breen released a slight wheeze and rolled over, giving Ty the perfect distraction to clear his mind.

He'd barely fallen asleep when someone called out, "Help us!"

Chapter 67 | Ty

TY BOLTED STRAIGHT UP in his bedding. "What?"

He waited a moment, but other than the crackling and popping coming from the hearth behind him, he heard nothing else. Had he dreamed it? He lay back down and closed his eyes. Narendi had really set him on edge. He took a deep breath and sank back down into his pillow, closing his eyes as he slowly drifted back off to sleep.

"Help us!"

Ty jerked awake. "Who said that?"

"Said what?" Breen mumbled, half asleep himself.

"Didn't you hear it?"

Breen rolled over and looked at him. "Hear what?" Even Narendi sat up to see what was going on, her blanket tucked under her arms.

"Someone asking for help." Ty got up and walked over to the door and unlocked it, sticking his head out in the hall. He waited a moment but eventually closed it and flipped the lock. He looked at the two of them and shrugged. "I'm telling you, I heard someone asking for help."

Breen and Narendi both sat there with heads cocked and ears perked, listening. Finally, Breen shook his head. "I don't hear anything. You must have dreamed it."

"I didn't dream it." Ty walked over to the balcony door and peeked through the curtain, but other than the random window light still aglow in a couple of the closest trees, Ty couldn't see anything that would have led to what he had heard, or thought he heard. Maybe Breen was right. Maybe he had dreamed it. He was tired enough. Leaving the door, he walked over to his bed and lay back down. Narendi had already done the same, leaving only Breen sitting there with a curious look on his face. Ty sighed. "Maybe it was just a dream. A very real one, if it was."

He crawled back under his blankets and closed his eyes as he listened intently to every creak and groan rising from the old tree, but there were no other calls for help. Giving in to exhaustion, he turned over and dozed back off.

It felt as though he'd barely reached unconsciousness when he heard footsteps creaking across the floor. He pulled his covers down off his face to find daylight sweeping through the balcony door's window, filling the room with a new day. Narendi and Breen were both up and dressed, and Breen was restoking the fire.

When he saw Ty looking his way, he stopped. "Did you ever hear whatever it was you thought you heard last night again?"

Ty shook his head and yawned, taking a moment to stretch before climbing out of his blankets. He walked across the room in his undergarments, something he would have normally been horrified to do in front of someone like Narendi, but since there was little either hadn't seen of the other, it didn't exactly make that much of a difference. He laid his clothes out in front of the fire before putting them on.

Breen chuckled. "Wish I had thought to do that."

Ty smiled.

"Guess we need to get some breakfast," Ty said as he pulled on his boots. "Then find Narendi some new shoes."

She didn't seem all that excited by the prospect, but given the choice of that or walking around in the snow in her sandals, she opted for the shoes. Ty still held out hope that perhaps he might have enough coinage to get her a new outfit. The boots and socks would help, but she really didn't need to be wandering about in the freezing cold with nothing more than a thin piece of material wrapped around her body. She needed a good coat and a pair of sturdy trousers, especially with all the climbing they were going to be doing as they moved up and down the trees.

Narendi started for the door, but Breen stopped her. "Um, you probably aren't going to need to take that with you," he said, pointing to the long spear she had slung over her back.

Narendi relinquished her spear reluctantly but was wholly unwilling to part with her curved blade, and since both Ty and Breen had theirs strapped on, they could hardly fault her.

Ty stuffed his coin pouch in his boot, then double-checked his pocket for his compass before heading out the door. The shorlock he didn't need to check, as he never took it off. It hung loosely around his neck, tucked safely away under his tunic and jacket. With a turn of the wrist, he locked their door and stuffed the key inside his trousers and joined the others as they walked down to breakfast.

They each had a plate of eggs, some peppered sausage, and a couple of cakes with honey, which they ate fairly quickly, this time having found an open table on the opposite side of the room from the leaky door. Narendi wore her baka, though she didn't bother with hiding her face while she ate. She did draw several looks from some of the other patrons, but only at first glance. No one bothered to continue staring, especially not if she caught them doing so.

All but licking their plates clean, the three finished their meals, this time catching Narendi before she decided to show her normal Imbatoo appreciation with a deep gut-wrenching belch. Passing through the lobby on their way out, Ty noticed the front desk was empty. He wondered where Nishka had gotten off to. Probably hadn't woken yet.

They stepped outside, and the first freezing gust had them all scrambling up the stairway as fast as they dared, leading to the cobbler's shop they had seen two levels up. A sign out front read: *KOVIAN'S*. The front window was dark, but that didn't stop Ty from trying the door anyway. It swung open, with a bell announcing their arrival as all three piled inside as fast as they could.

It wasn't much warmer in the shop, but just being out of the harsh wind seemed to help.

"Not quite open yet, gents," a voice called out from the back. "I'll be with you shortly."

Ty heard what sounded like logs being tossed in a fireplace and a metal poker stirring up the coals underneath as it scraped the stone. Soon enough, a middle-aged gentleman with chestnut hair and a full beard stepped out from around a work area that appeared to be covered in strips of leather, tack nails, hammers, and buckets of sticky paste. The man was clearly very busy either creating or repairing several pairs of boots.

He wiped his hands on the front of his apron, and with a cheerful smile, walked across the room. It was a smile that said he was happy to see the first customers of the day. "Welcome to my shop. My name is Kovian. What can I do for you?"

He took a moment to look them over, his dark-brown eyes pausing like everyone else on Narendi with her unique Mzwati robes and headdress. But, unlike all the rest, he also took the time to look at everyone's feet. He didn't give Ty or Breen's boots much more than a passing glance, but his eyes widened notably when he saw Narendi's bare toes peeking out at him through the tips of her sandals.

"Yes, I see the predicament. Don't worry. I may have just the thing." Without giving them a chance to even offer a quick greeting, the man flitted off toward the back, stopping first to shuffle through some stock on the right, then promptly moving on to another shelf further down. He mumbled to himself with pursed lips as he held up one boot after another before eventually placing each pair back on their respective shelves and moving on to the next.

"I hope he's not searching through his most-expensive pile," Ty whispered to Breen.

"I believe I've got it." The man made his way back to the front and held out a pair of brown jackboots with a wide cuff at the end that rose nearly to the bottom of her knees, flaring outward at the top. Ty couldn't help but admire them. They were stunning, which meant they had to be way out of his price range.

Ty cleared his throat. "Those are lovely, but . . . uh, do you have anything a little less, well, less?"

The shopkeeper looked down his nose at Ty, then over at Narendi. "I guess I have something in the back if your husband doesn't care how you look, or if you would rather walk around town collecting blisters."

Ty wanted to wring the man's neck for the way he was making him look in front of Narendi, but he couldn't afford to anger him, since he was probably the only cobbler in town.

"I have never worn purchased feet coverings," Narendi said, drawing the shopkeeper's undivided attention.

"You have never worn a pair of merchant shoes?" He looked down at her feet then over at Ty and shook his head as if Ty was some sort of womanizing oppressor. He glared at him the way others looked at a man who beat his wife.

Ty stiffened his back. "She's not from around here. And I'm not . . ." He didn't finish the statement. "Our gold needs to be put toward more profitable means than shoes, so if you have a nice used pair in the back, that would be wonderful."

"No," Narendi said, crossing her arms. "I want to try those."

The shopkeeper's smile widened as he placed the pair of boots in her hands. He then turned and shot Ty a victorious smirk, as if knowing that once a woman had made up her mind, there was little the man could do to dissuade her. The cobbler rounded up a stool for her to sit on and even a clean pair of socks to use before trying out the feel of the new boots.

The man knelt and helped her with her sandals, taking care to keep clear of the curved blade at her side, then carefully pulled on her socks before placing each of her feet into their respective boot. He then helped her up and led her around the shop, all the while watching her face for an affirmative response.

Narendi made it around the shop and back to the stool before finally offering the shopkeeper a very pleased grin. "I like them."

The cobbler clapped his hands together. "Excellent, madam. Would you like them wrapped or would you prefer to wear them out?"

"She would prefer to know the price," Ty exclaimed, still in shock at the shameless way the cobbler was trying to offload his product.

The cobbler clicked his tongue. "What is price with something that was clearly made for beauty such as hers? Just look at her, sir. Is she not radiant in those boots?"

"And she'll be just as radiant in a nice sturdy pair of used ones, depending on the price."

"I see you're a man of strict means." He looked at Narendi, then at the boots, then back at Ty. "I suppose I could be willing to part with them for say, two silver and three."

Ty nearly choked. "We'll take a look at those in the back."

"No!" Narendi suddenly exclaimed. "I want these."

Ty pulled her to the side. "We can't afford those. They cost nearly double our room and food. I'm sure he has a fine pair in—"

"How much can I get for this?" Narendi pulled a pouch out from her trousers and emptied its contents into Ty's hands. Ty's eyes bulged, and Breen quickly moved between Ty and the merchant to keep the cobbler from seeing the stack of gold coins Narendi had just dropped on Ty.

"Where did you . . ." Ty didn't finish, but what he did do was gulp and quickly stick the gold back inside her pouch as he turned back to the cobbler, who was all but standing on his tiptoes, trying to see what was happening. "We'll take the boots."

"Very good." The shopkeeper smiled and rushed back to the counter for them to pay.

Ty didn't want to use the last two silvers he had in his purse, so he nervously placed one of Narendi's gold pieces down on the counter. That way they would receive several silvers and coppers in return to use for other spending and to keep them from flashing their newly found wealth around for others to see. The cobbler's eyes lighted on the coin, and his countenance dropped. He looked like he wanted to kick himself for not having charged more. He passed seven silvers and seven coppers back across the counter, and Ty dropped them in the pouch, waiting till the shopkeeper turned before stuffing both his pouch and Narendi's into his boots.

"Where could we find a clothing shop in town?" he asked. "Also, depending on what is available, we might be back to look at a couple more pairs of boots." Of course, Ty had no intention of coming back. His and Breen's boots were perfectly suitable, but if the owner were to think he stood a good chance of repeat business, he might be more willing to help them.

The cobbler's eyes lit at the possibility of them coming back. "I recommend Lenka's. Best quality in town . . . for those willing to pay," he added with a sharp arch of his brow.

"And where can we find this Lenka?"

The shopkeeper walked them over to the front window beside the door and pointed out. "You'll find her shop at the bottom of the third tree," he said, pointing downward. "Her shop is right on the water. Can't miss it."

Ty thanked the man, and they left and started back down the tree, stopping back in at the Beetle Bark to drop off Narendi's sandals to keep from having to tote them around while they went to find her a new outfit.

"Where did you get all that gold from?" Ty asked as he tossed her old shoes on the bed.

Narendi gave him one of her *why would you ask me such a foolish question* looks. "My father is king of the Imbatoo. Why would I not have gold?"

Breen tossed another piece of wood on the fire. "The upside is that you no longer have to worry about whether or not we'll have enough coin to get Narendi some clothes."

Narendi smiled. "I like purchasing things."

Ty frowned at Breen. "We've created a monster." He looked at Narendi. "Just remember, you might have more gold than I'll probably ever own at one time, but you need to be careful not to show it around. You don't want to simply purchase something just for the sake of purchasing. Also, you'll want to negotiate the price. Most merchants plan to charge more than the goods are worth, especially if they don't know you and believe you can afford it."

"Where's my pouch?" she asked, holding out her hand.

"You don't want me to carry it?"

She didn't say anything, just kept her hand out, so Ty dug around in his second boot and pulled out her pouch of gold and handed it over. She then followed his example and tucked it into one of her own boots, at least far enough down so the bulge wasn't too noticeable. "I want to go purchase," she said, then headed out the door.

Ty looked at Breen, and all Breen could do was shrug. "Don't look at me. She's your wife."

Ty threw his arms in the air. "She's not my wife."

After locking the door behind them, Ty headed with the others back down the stairs and out into the early morning sun, which had now risen high enough to pierce through the thick branches above. He stopped long enough to grab his compass and get their bearings. He was curious as to where it would direct them next. It seemed to be pointing northward, deeper into the heart of the Riverlands.

They took the stairs down to the bottom, where they reached a wide boardwalk that was built over and around the enormous root systems that encircled each of the trees. There were walkways down to the water from the upper boardwalk that led to short docks with tied-off boats for easier traveling up and down the causeway, and for whatever type of fishing took place in this part of the world.

There were also bridges that spanned the water channels, reaching from one tree to the next. These bridges, unlike their much higher counterparts, were not made from rope and didn't sway in the breeze, which they were all thankful for as they stopped halfway over the first bridge to look down at the black water below. These bridges almost seemed like extensions of the trees themselves. Instead of board planks, the tops were covered in a soft padding of green moss.

Narendi stood at the railing's edge for quite some time, watching as the boats floated in and around and under the endless system of roots. "What are those?"

Ty and Breen turned to see several flat barges floating up the waterway, passing just underneath the bridge they were currently standing on. All three of them walked to the other side to watch the boats float back out. Each barge carried a number of cages stacked at the center, some tied down with ropes, some covered with tarps. Those they could see had animals inside, animals Ty had not seen before.

He looked around cautiously at those standing nearby, to make sure no one was watching, then reached out with his magic to touch the animals. He was hesitant at first, the memory of what had happened in the Wengoby when he had reached out with his magic had nearly gotten them all eaten by orms, and the time before that when he had woken the lake monster. He shivered at the thought but kept going regardless.

He could sense the creatures' fear. They had been snatched from their homes and brought to this place to be sold, a place so far removed from the rest of Aldor that moral obligation was nowhere to be found, allowing these trappers and poachers the ability to get away with whatever they wanted. Ty wondered who was in charge of keeping the market running in the first place.

He started to send his magic down into the larger cages, but Breen grabbed his arm.

"Let's go. We need to get Narendi those warmer clothes before she starts to freeze."

Ty pulled himself away from the railing, and the three stepped off the interconnecting walkway and onto the next boardwalk. From there they found a woman willing to direct them where they needed to go. Keeping strictly to the lower walkways and bridges, they made their way through what the river people considered "town," stopping occasionally to look inside some of the shop windows, or resting on one of the many benches scattered through the lower quarter.

With the help of at least two more passersby, the small group managed to reach their destination without getting lost. The shop was indeed on the first floor of the tree and appeared to be even larger than Kovian's shoe shop. A sign out front read *LENKA'S* while portraying a newly painted dress on the right side and a pair of trousers and a tunic on the left. Breen opened the door, and a wave of warm air struck them in the face, inviting them to come on in.

They each knocked the snow from their boots before entering, even Narendi, who found no small amount of enjoyment in doing so, giving her the opportunity to show off her newly acquired footwear.

"How can I help you?" a young woman about Breen's age asked as she walked over to greet them in the doorway. She was tall and thin, with straight black hair that hung to her middle back, accentuating her long neck. Her skin was nearly as fair as Ty's, and like Ty, she had blue eyes, but not quite as bright.

"Are you Mistress Lenka?" Ty asked.

"That would be my mother. She's in the back mending a couple of blouses. I'm Dunya. Is there anything I can help you with?" She glanced at Narendi, eyeing her Mzwati robes.

Narendi hiked up one of her loose-fitting pants legs and held out her foot. "They are store purchased. You like?"

"I do, indeed." Dunya made a show of examining Narendi's boots.

Ty slapped his forehead. At least she wasn't fishing out her pouch of gold and showing it off as well. "We have traveled a long way and are in need of something . . ." Ty looked at Narendi. "Well, something more appropriate for the weather."

Now that she knew what they were looking for, Dunya turned to Narendi. "Yes, I can see your predicament. But don't worry, you've come to the right place."

"Kovian pointed us in your direction," Ty added. "He said Lenka's was the place to find what we needed."

"He is correct. We have the largest selection of both men's and women's fittings. Is there anything specific you had in mind?" She seemed to be addressing Ty, but why was she looking at Narendi as she did?

"That is very colorful," Narendi said, pointing to a rack over on the left.

"That is also a gown," Ty added. "Not something you need to be wearing outside."

Dunya looked at Narendi, then turned to Ty. "I think I know what you have in mind. This way," she said, and motioned them into the second half of the shop.

Ty and Narendi followed her through while Breen stayed in the front, perusing some of the side shelves that had tunics that looked large enough to fit even his broad shoulders.

"I take it you're here for the Live Market. Am I correct?"

Ty nodded, not knowing what else to do. If he said no, she might ask what they were there for, which would require him to come up with some unknown reason for visiting. Best to keep it simple, even though the thought of being associated with black marketeers made him feel uncomfortable.

"Then I would suggest something more like this." She grabbed several items from off a nearby shelf, as well as a couple more from one of the racks, before walking over and laying them all longways across the top of a counter at the back. Ty couldn't have done better if he'd spent the better part of the day searching. There was a set of dark-brown canvas trousers with a leaf-green tunic, and a brown suede vest that hung just below the waist. To finish it off, Dunya had chosen a dark-green wool cloak with a thick fur collar to wear over it.

Dunya directed Narendi to the left corner, where there was a privacy wall set up for customers to try on the outfits. By the time they had managed to get Narendi's robes off and into the new set of clothes, Breen had made it into the back to see the outcome.

"What did she find?" Breen asked.

Ty smiled. "Wait till you see."

"Are you waiting?" Narendi asked, peeking around the wall to make sure Ty was watching.

"Yes," both Ty and Breen answered in unison.

Narendi stepped out from behind the wall, and Ty almost didn't recognize her. With the hood of the cloak up to hide most of her face, she looked like a ranger, or at least what Ty would have imagined a ranger to look like had he ever met one. Both mysterious and dangerous.

"Wow," was about all he could manage to say.

"You like?" Narendi pulled the hood back, revealing her bald head, which somehow lent even more to the mystique of it all.

"I like," he said.

She smiled. "Then I like." She tried moving around in it, even going so far as to jump in the air a couple of times and kick out with one leg. "It is heavy." She wasn't used to something quite so constricting, having spent her life wearing nothing heavier than a bedsheet everywhere she went. "I will purchase." She started to reach for her pouch, but Ty quickly interrupted by making it seem like he wanted to get a closer look.

"Here," he said, taking her hand. "Spin around. Let me see the back." She spun once, and Ty turned to Dunya, who was standing to the side, wearing a proud smile at her choice in outfits. "Do you have these in any other colors?" he asked, pointing to her tunic and cape.

She nodded and started over to the side. "We have a blue one, and also a crimson."

As soon as she was out of eyesight, Ty reached into Narendi's boot and pulled out the pouch.

"Hey, what are you doing?"

"Shhh. I'm trying to keep you from showing her that you have a bag of gold. You can't do that, remember?"

She hmphed, but didn't argue, more preoccupied with her new outfit as she walked over to a mirror on the wall to admire herself.

"She'll learn," Breen said, clapping a hand on Ty's shoulder.

"Hopefully not the hard way, when she shows it to the wrong person, and we all get jumped in the night."

Dunya walked back over with the additional colored tunics and capes and held them up for Narendi to see, and before Ty could politely tell her that they would stick with the green one, Narendi had already gathered them up in her arms and rushed them over to the counter. "I want to purchase."

Ty gulped and turned his back so he could grab one of the gold pieces out of the pouch without the shopkeeper noticing. He then walked over and handed her the coin before she started suggesting any other ensembles for Narendi's eager eyes to enjoy. Along with the gold piece, he found he needed an additional two silvers to cover the order.

"Let's get out of here before she decides to purchase something else," Ty mumbled to Breen as he handed him one of several wrapped packages.

"Gloves," Breen said. "We'll need some warm gloves."

Ty groaned.

"And some warmer hats," Breen added. "Especially for Narendi with that shaved head."

Ty took a deep breath and turned back to Dunya, who was more than happy to find them three pairs of gloves and two woolen hats for Breen and Narendi. Ty was still wearing the stocking cap Orlyn had given him.

Dunya didn't bother with wrapping the gloves or the hats, as they all decided to wear them out of the store. She walked them to the door and waved goodbye and encouraged them to visit again, which was about the last thing Narendi needed to hear, as she almost turned around and walked back inside. Ty grabbed her arm and directed her down the boardwalk.

"That was quite the experience," Breen said. "I don't believe I've spent that much while shopping since Father purchased our bows."

"Yeah," Ty agreed. "I'm about all shopped out, and all I got was a pair of gloves."

They headed straight back to the inn, not bothering to stop on the benches to watch the boats. Narendi was eager to get her new store-bought clothes back to their room so she could try the rest of them on. Ty was looking forward to getting back for some lunch.

As reluctant as Ty was to do any more shopping, they still needed to purchase a few extra supplies, like food. But that could certainly wait until later that afternoon.

Chapter 68 | Ty

REALIZING THEY MIGHT need their room for more than a single night, since all they'd managed to do so far was purchase new clothing, Ty used the rest of his silvers to secure it for the next two. He wanted to make sure that no one else came along and purchased it out from under them, seeing as how it might have been the last room left in the Riverlands during the Live Market. He breathed a little easier about spending the coins, having discovered Narendi's secret stash, but he didn't like feeling so reliant on the Imbatoo princess. It was just another thing they would be forced to share between them, which he was afraid would only bolster her belief in their unity.

"We still need to find some hardtack and fresh water," Breen said as they sat around one of the tables in the Beetle Bark common room, having just devoured a rather tasty helping of pork and potatoes with a mushroom gravy that left them feeling strangely lightheaded, as though having consumed a glass of ale that hadn't been quite so watered down.

"I'd like to get a look at this Live Market," Ty added with a not-so-subtle belch that had Narendi glaring at him. "Sorry, I couldn't help it. It just came out." He wiped his mouth with the cloth napkin beside his plate.

"I don't think visiting the Live Market would be such a good idea," Breen said, putting a hand on his head. "You know, I don't feel so good. Don't think this food sat right."

Narendi didn't seem too bothered as she played with the tasseled drawstrings around the neck of her cloak. "I feel good." She pinched her cheeks. "I cannot feel my face."

One of the servers rushed by, and Ty stopped her. "Excuse me. Could you tell us what was in this?" he asked, pointing at his plate. "Something didn't sit right."

The girl smiled. "Those are sauteed tellareen mushrooms." She looked at their plates and giggled. "Most people don't eat the mushrooms; they push them to the side." She shook her head. "And they certainly don't eat three helpings' worth. I hope you weren't planning on doing anything this afternoon. You might want to try sleeping it off."

She left, and Ty looked at Breen. "Wished they'd told us we weren't supposed to eat them," he said, his words slurring. "I think I need to lie down."

The three stumbled from their seats and, with Myrtle's help—who just happened to be passing by and spotted them on the wrong floor, attempting to unlock someone else's door—they finally managed to make it to their room, where they each dropped into their respective beds and didn't move for the rest of the afternoon.

"Please help us."

Ty sat straight up, then wished he hadn't, as the room was spinning in circles. He grabbed his head to stabilize himself and took in a couple of deep breaths. Pretty soon, the room slowed and then stopped altogether, and Ty turned to find the fire had gone out and the room had begun to chill. Beside him, Breen was snoring soundly, and Narendi was cooing softly in her bed, not having bothered to get under her covers.

Ty walked over and tucked her in, pulling her blanket up to her chin. He watched her for a moment before finally walking over to place a couple more pieces of wood on the fire and stir the coals underneath. Soon enough, a small blaze was roaring, and he walked over to the balcony door and stepped outside. The freezing wind helped to clear his head.

The sun, which he couldn't see for the trees, hung low in the sky by the direction of the shadows. They had slept the afternoon away. The door opened behind him and Narendi stepped out, her blanket wrapped around her like a Mzwati robe. She stayed on the far side of the balcony, not wanting to get anywhere near the railing. "How do you feel?"

Ty glanced over his shoulder and smiled. "Better. You?"

She nodded, her face still a bit pale. "I do not think I like those mushrooms."

Ty chuckled. "Me either." He looked down at the water, watching more boats heading upstream. "I heard it again."

"Heard what?" Breen asked with a wide yawn as he stepped outside and immediately shivered.

"I heard the voice again, asking for help."

Breen rubbed the top of his head. "If you're still hearing it, then it's proving less likely to be just a dream. Though," he said, running his hand back through his hair, "I've known you to have some strange ones."

"It's not a dream." Ty gripped the edge of the railing. "I don't know what it is."

Breen walked over to join him and glanced over the side. "That's a long way down." He turned back around. "I say we clear our heads and go take a stroll around town. We need to find a chandlery and stock up on supplies before dark."

Ty nodded. "Sounds like a good idea."

"I want to wear my new purchased clothes," Narendi exclaimed.

Ty turned toward the door. "You already are." He pointed at her green tunic and cloak.

"I want to try another one."

Breen chuckled. "We'll wait out here while you change."

Narendi shrugged as though it didn't matter to her one way or the other and walked back inside. Before long, the door opened again, and she stepped out with a bright smile as she took a moment to spin on the deck so they could admire her new change of clothes. Instead of the green tunic and green cloak, she now wore the red tunic and red cloak, and if Ty had thought the green had looked rather fetching, the red was even more so, especially against her darker skin.

The look on Ty's face must have been the reaction Narendi had hoped for, as she smiled all the more and stepped back inside. Ty and Breen followed her in, their hands shivering from having stayed out too long. They tossed a couple more logs on the fire to keep the room warm before gathering their things and heading back into town.

Finding a chandler didn't prove all that difficult. The Riverlands people seemed more than happy to point them in the right direction, one man even going so far as to walk with them halfway, stopping only when they came within eyesight of the shop. Ty thanked him, and they headed over a short bridge to a large platform that had been built between a grouping of several trees. It almost felt like a makeshift town square, with several shops all located around the small plaza.

They walked inside the chandlery but found its shelves a little on the barren side. The shopkeeper said it was due to the Live Market and the large number of traders that had shown up this year. Apparently, most of the food supplies around town had been bought out. Ty found it odd that they wouldn't have stocked up with extra inventory for such an occasion.

They did manage to find a few packs of hard biscuits, some salted pork, and at least one wheel of cheese. It was one of the more tasteless whites, but at this point they were just happy to find anything at all.

"Hopefully this will last us till we get to wherever it is we're going," Breen said as he stuffed the meager provisions into a sack the chandler had provided them. They also grabbed a couple extra candles while they were there. One could never have too many candles.

By the time they left the shop, the early evening sun was gone and the way ahead was lit by torchlight. On their way back, they stopped at the bridge overlooking the main canal through town. It was the same bridge where they had spotted the flatboats heading north through the woods. Ty pulled out his compass. The needle seemed to follow the river's course. "I have a feeling we'll be needing a boat."

Breen glanced down at the compass, then up at the riverbed. "It would appear so."

"What does it show?" Narendi asked, scooting over to get a closer look at the instrument.

"Somewhere out there," Ty said, pointing off down the channel.

Breen stared out at the thickening trees ahead. "I wonder how far in we'll have to go to find the last piece. Hopefully, not too far. I don't relish the idea of getting stuck in there, not while on the water." He looked at Ty. "I also don't like the fact that your compass seems to be taking us in the same direction as the poachers. Last thing we need is to get mixed up with this Live Market."

Ty placed the compass back inside his trouser pocket and started down the other side of the bridge toward their inn. "I guess we'll find out tomorrow. For now, best we enjoy a hot meal and a warm bed. Might be the last we see for some time."

"Now that's a depressing thought," Breen said.

Sleep was slow in coming, almost a distant memory, as Ty lay awake listening to the crackling of the wood behind him, along with the occasional snore from his brother and the creak of the ropes under Narendi's mattress. It also didn't help that Ty kept waiting for another cry for help from whoever was attempting to reach him. By the time the first grey shards of light shot through the balcony window, illuminating motes of dust across the room, Ty was more than eager to get out of bed and get the day underway.

As soon as everyone was up and dressed, Ty and Narendi began packing their gear and supplies while Breen headed down to the docks to see about chartering a boat. He took their coin pouch with him, since none of them had a clue as to how much it would cost to purchase passage upriver.

"How far will we need to go?" Narendi asked, taking great care in folding her new clothes and tucking them away inside the garment bag she'd received from Lenka's shop.

Ty stuffed his Imbatoo robes back in his sack. "When we first arrived in the Wengoby, we traveled for days before your people found us, then we traveled another two days from your village to the temple ruins. The second mirror, however, sent us to a cavern where the missing piece of the key turned out to be fairly close, but getting to it proved nearly impossible." He shrugged. "I guess what I'm trying to say is . . . I have no idea."

"Why make it so hard?"

Ty chuckled. "I guess to keep the wrong people from getting it. If it was easy, then maybe anyone could have gotten the key by now." Ty had just finished packing his haversack, leaving his flute for last, when the door opened, and Breen walked in. Ty turned. "How'd it go?"

"Well, purchasing a ferry upriver proved more difficult than I would have thought. None of the locals seem willing to charter us. I think it has more to do with where we are wanting to go than who they're carrying. As soon as I mentioned heading north up the main channel, which I found out is part of the Bul Isra River, every one of them shook their heads and told me to move along."

"How are we going to get to the key if we don't have a boat?" Ty asked. "Don't think we're going to be swimming our way there."

"I didn't say I didn't get us a boat."

"What do you mean? You just said no one will ferry us upriver."

"Yes, no one will, but that didn't mean they wouldn't sell us a boat outright."

"You bought a boat?" Ty bit his lower lip. "How much did that cost us?"

Breen smiled. "Not as much as you might think. I found a fisherman with two boats who's looking to leave the Riverlands. Something about having family in Carran and wanting to try his luck on dry land. Apparently, there's a lake on Virn Run that borders the city, and he plans on spending his days fishing there." Breen shook his head. "The man was quite the talker once he got started. He quieted fairly quickly, though, when I handed him full payment. The boat is waiting for us on the south side of the next tree over." He looked at their packs. "How's it going in here?"

"Just about ready," Ty said, tying off the top of his bag.

"I'm done," Narendi said, holding her small bag in her left hand. She was wearing the same red outfit she'd worn the previous night. After supper, she had changed into her blue tunic and cape to see what they looked like but decided that she liked the red best.

Ty agreed.

"I guess that leaves me." Breen's satchel was the largest, which meant he had the most to carry. Thankfully, he had packed the majority of it the night before, including the supplies they had purchased from the chandlery. Ty and Narendi waited on the bed as Breen finished up, not allowing them to help, as he was particular that it was packed a certain way. Ty's brother had always been like that. He would much rather do something himself than ask someone else to help and it not get done the way he wanted. *Self-sufficient* was what their mother had always called him. Ty, on the other hand, was more than happy to let others help, especially when it came to his chores. In fact, he all but demanded it.

"Are we ready?" Ty asked as he put on his cap and pulled it down far enough to cover the tops of his ears. He was both anxious and nervous to get underway.

Breen had just finished packing, and they all did a quick walk-through inspection of the room to make sure they'd left nothing behind. Ty walked out on the balcony to get one more look out across the Riverlands. He didn't expect they would be coming back, even though they were paid up for one more night.

He was going to miss the place, but it was time to move on.

They left the Beetle Bark Inn, stopping only long enough to thank Myrtle for her service, and to wake Nishka to wish her well. The elderly bookkeeper looked a little confused, as she knew they had rented their room through the next night. Ty didn't come right out and say he didn't think they would be returning, in case they didn't find what they were looking for. Instead, he simply said they'd be gone for the day and offered a friendly smile and wave on his way out.

They headed down the stairs, Narendi keeping as close to the tree and as far away from the rail as possible. She didn't look as flustered as she had been previously, but it was clear that she still wasn't very keen walking around those heights. It was strange, as she hadn't shown any sign of fear when traveling to the top of the plateau behind their village, but that might have had something to do with the fact that there were no rickety wooden planks and swinging rope bridges.

Once they reached the bottom, Breen directed them left, over a bridge spanning a narrow branching channel off the main waterway. They reached the other side and Breen took them around the back of the tree and down to a set of docks where several boats lay tied.

"Which one is ours?" Ty asked, eager to be underway.

"This one," Breen said, heading for the one on the end.

Ty sighed. "I was afraid you were going to say that." The boat Breen had purchased was an old dinghy whose wood had weathered with age. There were only two seats, which meant someone would be sitting on the floorboards at the front. It did have two oars. "Is it safe?"

"I took it once around the tree before purchasing," Breen said as he climbed down into the boat and dropped his satchel and weapons between the back and middle seat. "It doesn't look like much, but it should get us upriver. So, unless you plan on swimming, I suggest you toss me your bags and get in."

Narendi tossed Breen her bag and let him help her into the boat. Her legs were shaky at first as she tried to catch her balance. "I've never been in a boat." As soon as the boat rocked, she lowered herself to all fours and crawled to the front and sat down with her back against the seat, leaving just enough room for Ty.

Ty dropped his pack in the middle alongside Breen's and took his place on the front seat. Breen sat down on the back and untied the mooring before lifting one of the oars and pushing off the dock. Ty grabbed the second oar and dropped it in on the left side, opposite his brother. He was used to paddling in time with Breen, as they had spent their childhood growing up along the East River. "Which way?"

"Back to the main channel," Breen said, and slowly started them moving forward, Ty matched his brother's strokes to keep them in a straight line, speeding up as they reached the first turn back in the direction they'd just come from. They passed the tree with the Beetle Bark Inn and the cobbler's shop and headed left under the next bridge toward the middle of town and the channel leading north.

The bridges and boardwalks filled with people as the sun rose higher in the sky, the warm rays letting them know that, at least for the time being, they didn't need to worry about snow, though they did pass several patches of ice up under the tree's roots. The waterways were beginning to fill as well, boats coming and going, some ferrying passengers, some cargo, others with nets and poles and tackle.

The Riverlands were alive with activity.

They reached the main channel and started north, sticking as close to the sides as possible to keep out of the way of the larger flatboats that were making their way toward whatever lay ahead. By the time the bridges had begun to fade into the distance, Ty gave up searching for leaks in the boat. To his relief, the boat did actually seem to hold its own.

The trees thickened the farther from town they got, fewer and fewer being used for habitation. There were still some with doors and windows and stairs, but usually only two or three stories high, mostly residences. There were few in the way of bridges between the outer trees—most looked to use their boats for travel.

Occasionally, Ty would catch the rustling of curtains in the windows or someone walking out on a front balcony to peer at those passing by.

"How are we looking?" Breen asked, pulling in his oar to slow their advance.

Ty pulled in his own oar so he could take off his glove and dig around in his pocket. He pulled out the compass and held it up high enough so that his brother could see as well. Their course was steady, the needle pointing nearly directly ahead, perhaps just a little west, but enough to show that the waterway they were on was taking them in the right direction, at least for now.

"What does it say?" Narendi asked, twisting in her place at the front of the boat to get a better look.

"It says we are still heading in the right direction," Ty answered as he pulled his glove back on and dropped his oar back in the water.

Narendi grunted and turned back around. She sat with her back up against the front of Ty's seat, directly between his legs. It was the only comfortable way Ty could keep his balance as he propelled his paddle through the water. Most of the boats that had followed them out of town had either veered off to take other branches or had surpassed their small dinghy and scooted far enough ahead that they were no longer seen around the winding bends.

They stopped at one point to eat lunch, more to rest their arms than for the food, tying off against a root small enough to get their rope around. Narendi seemed hungry enough, having not eaten as much as the two of them the night before, but Ty was just happy to have the oar out of his hands. They were beginning to cramp. He'd forgotten how much work it was paddling against the flow of a river. After a quick meal of hardtack, salted pork, and cheese, they washed it down with some water from their waterskins and started back up once more.

Not far ahead, the trees began to thicken, nearly blocking the sun altogether as the channel narrowed slightly. It had been a while since they'd seen a boat, and the trees in this part of the forest were completely void of any habitation. It seemed no one wanted to live this far out, or at least not in this section of the Riverlands. The icy wind that had plagued their journey so far had all but disappeared, being cut off by the thicket of branches overhead.

Their boat almost seemed to glide through the dark water effortlessly, as the current had slowed through the winding passageways ahead. The calls of the birds had died out, leaving behind an unnerving silence. Other than the occasional splash, which had Ty's mind conjuring up creatures from the deep, there were no other sounds of life. There was, however, the constant croak of the frogs. No matter how cut off they became from the rest of civilization, there was always one thing they could count on: where there was water and trees, there were frogs.

Ty pulled in his oar and once more checked on the compass. "Stop."

Breen halted his oar halfway through his last stroke, keeping it in the water to hold their place. "What is it?"

Narendi turned. "Why do we stop?"

Ty held up the compass to make sure he was actually seeing it correctly. "The needle has changed. It's pointing back that way." He shifted in his seat and pointed back behind them on the left side of the river. "We've gone too far."

Breen looked at the compass, then shifted his position with the oar and turned the boat around.

"Sorry," Ty said. "I should have been keeping a closer watch, I guess." He laid the compass on the seat between his legs and lifted his oar. With long strokes, they made their way back around and over to the opposite side of the channel and followed it back the way they'd come. Ty kept a close eye on the needle as they all looked for a connecting branch that would take them where they needed to go.

They didn't have to go far before Narendi shouted excitedly and pointed to a narrow split in the water at the next bend up. They pulled alongside the opening and Ty took another look at the compass. The needle was back at the top once more, guiding them forward. "I guess this is it."

"I wonder if this leads to the Live Market?" Breen said. "I haven't seen any other boats coming this way for some time."

"I hope not," Ty said, though a knot tightening in the pit of his stomach said otherwise.

He lifted his oar, and they started into the trees. He couldn't tell if the sun had gone down or if the clouds had covered it, but the farther in they got, the darker it became. There was a light haze hanging over the water, snaking its way through the surrounding trees. Dozens of other passageways came and went, but they kept to the one they were in, following the compass through what seemed to be a maze of interconnecting shoots. If not for the instrument's help, they would have been good and lost a long time back.

The fog thickened, leaving an eerie silence that had Ty slowing the stroke of his oar. Even Narendi had grabbed her spear and held it out over the front of the boat as she nervously scanned the trees ahead. The haze was too thick to see much more than just above the roots, leaving Ty to imagine all sorts of horrible things crawling around above them, waiting to drop down on top of them when they least expected it.

A splash sounded on the right, and they all spun in their seats. Ty drew his sword, then raised his hand and called on his flames. Blue fire ignited from his palm, lighting the boat and surrounding water, but not enough to punch through the fog itself. At times, the channel was wide enough for a couple of flatboats to pass through, while others left their boat scraping the sides of passing roots.

"There's no way that any trader came through here," Ty said, ducking his head to keep from hitting it on another low-hanging branch. All the trees within sight were covered in a thick green moss. Strings of it hung down in places like drapes over a window, forcing Narendi to use her spear to push them aside so Ty and Breen could direct them through.

"Yeah," Breen answered back softly as he used his oar to push off the surrounding trees to keep them moving forward. "I'm starting to wonder if *we're* going to make it through. If this stuff grows any thicker, we're going to be stuck."

"If the roots grow any thicker," Ty added, "we could probably walk the rest of the way."

"What is that?" Narendi asked, and Ty and Breen stopped to see what she was looking at.

"What?" Ty didn't see anything but fog as he lifted the blue flames a little higher.

"No. Listen."

Sure enough, there was something breaking through the silence ahead, growing louder the farther they went. It was a hodgepodge of noises, like all the animals in the forest calling out at the same time. There were growls and barks and whistles and caws and shrieks and howls, noises no one would expect to find in the middle of a river swamp.

"Look," Narendi said.

Up ahead, the fog thinned, and the trees suddenly opened. They were on the edge of a large circular clearing, but instead of a lush meadow, it was a dark hollow, as if some great being had reached down and scooped out a portion of the swamp, leaving nothing but a water-filled hole.

At the center of the black lagoon was a mammoth tree, unlike any Ty had seen so far.

If the Riverlands were a family, this tree would have been its patriarch, the great-grandfather of them all. It was as wide as five of the largest trees combined, but unlike the others, the top of this tree opened into an enormous hand with its palm facing upward. From what they could see back at the edge of the swamp, there were six trees around the edge of the palm that reached up like gnarled leafless fingers, looking to snatch passing birds out of the sky.

"There," Breen whispered, "at the top." The flicker of torchlight could be seen around the outer edge of the palm, revealing movement, people walking around, too small to make out anything but their basic shapes. Lanterns hung from dozens of boats that had been tied off along a rickety-looking boardwalk that encircled the base of the tree, their cargo being transported to several great lifts that carried the freight from the docks to the top of the palm.

Along with the lifts was a winding set of stairs that wrapped back and forth around the front half of the tree from the roots to the top, passing through several covered huts that jutted out from the tree like large misshapen knots.

Ty took a moment to take it all in, then quickly released his magic and let the blue flames vanish. "I guess we just found the Live Market."

Chapter 69 | Ty

TY AND BREEN SLOWLY and quietly paddled the old dinghy around the backside of the tree. They had apparently taken an indirect route through the forest to reach the Live Market. Ty could just make out the main channel on the other side that everyone else had used as one or two more flatboats floated in.

"It's a wonder we found this place at all," he said as he stopped to take a look at the compass. Sure enough, no matter how far they paddled around the clearing, the needle continued to point in the same direction.

The grandfather tree.

"Do you think the missing piece is somewhere in the tree?" Breen asked as he, too, paused the rowing to stare at the compass's heading. "What if one of the traders up there has it?"

"Then we purchase it," Ty said. "It's a market after all."

"What does it look like?" Narendi asked. "This piece."

Ty lifted the medallion out from under his tunic where it hung around his neck. He pointed at the empty socket at the center. "My guess is that it is some kind of gem. Probably a crystal of some sort. A big one, by the size of this hole."

"Even if we find it," Breen said, staring up at the top of the tree, "I don't understand how we're supposed to demonstrate compassion in order to get it. If one of the traders has it, are we supposed to compassionately offer to take it off his hands? Somehow, I doubt the final piece will be as easy to come by as the previous."

Ty lifted his oar. "Only one way to find out."

They found an open section where no lifts had been placed or boats tied, and swiftly pulled their boat alongside a small stretch of dock jutting out from the boardwalk.

"What do you think we should do with our packs?" Ty asked, staring down at his lopsided bundle in the front of the boat. "We'll definitely stand out if we walk up there looking like we'd just spent the last week hiking along the Angorans."

Breen lifted his hat high enough to tuck his hair back behind his ears, then lowered it. "We take what we need and stuff the rest up under the seats as best we can. Just make sure not to leave anything you wouldn't want to get left behind."

Other than the extra food, Ty didn't have much in the way of valuables inside his pack. Most of it was filled with his bedding and a spare set of Imbatoo robes, which he was glad to leave behind for now. The only thing that gave him pause was his new flute. He'd spent a lot of time constructing it, but in the end, he left it behind as well.

Breen carried his bow and quiver over his jacket, along with his sword and a brace of knives. He looked ready for war. Narendi had her spear and curved sword, as well as her entire knapsack of clothing.

"I think you missed the point about taking only what we need." Ty chuckled.

"I need this," she said, the sharpness of her tone letting him know that he would be wise not to dispute the claim, which got him to thinking.

"What if the mirror is up there?"

Breen leaned back as far as he dared, trying to see the top. "I hadn't considered that."

"If it is up there," Ty said, "then we'll need our packs with us, unless we plan on making a whole other trip back down the tree to collect them. And for all we know, we might need to make a hasty retreat. That means we won't have the chance to grab our things beforehand, and there's no telling where we'll end up. I don't want to jump through another mirror without our food and bedding."

Breen sighed. "Then I guess we take them with us."

The trio looked like lost travelers as they made their way around the boardwalk to the front of the tree where the staircase began. They passed a couple of lifts. The first sat dormant. The second held a new flatboat that had just made dock, its men busily offloading cages from the boat to the lift.

The men of the vessel either nodded, bowed, or tipped their hats in Narendi's direction when she walked past. Apparently, they got the impression that she was there to purchase, and by the way they ignored Ty and Breen, Ty got the impression they thought them her hired servants or protectors.

"If anyone asks," Breen said, "Narendi is a buyer and we are here as her personal guard."

Narendi stopped on the fourth step and turned. "I like being the one to purchase."

Ty rolled his eyes. "Just don't let it go to your head. We aren't actually here to purchase anything, unless of course we find we need to purchase the missing piece of the key."

"Let's hope it doesn't come to that," Breen said. "Even with the gold, if this center gem is as big as we think, we still might not have enough."

"I do not want to use my gold," Narendi stated rather emphatically as she continued up the stairs, clinging to her sack of purchased clothes.

Ty looked at Breen, and he wore a similarly uncomfortable expression. If they did find the gem and Narendi refused to use her gold to buy it, what were they going to do? Would Ty be willing to take it from her? He hoped it didn't come to that, but how could he expect her to give up all that she had for him, especially after his poignant refusal of her vows? She would be stuck on the opposite side of Aldor, away from her home and family, and with nothing to support herself.

Ty squeezed the railing as they went up. This was turning out to be far more difficult than he had at first considered. He had never even really thought about what it must be like for her. He had been too upset at her for having jumped through the mirror and placing him in this position in the first place to stop and consider anything else.

They reached the first of the huts built onto the side of the tree and stopped to rest their feet, each taking a moment to get a sip from their waterskins as well.

"*Help us.*"

Ty nearly spit his water.

Breen and Narendi both turned.

"I just heard them again. This time they were—"

"*I know you are there. I can feel you. Please, help us.*"

Ty's eyes widened.

"What is it?" Breen asked.

"The voice said that it knows I'm here." Ty looked at his arm, forgetting his sleeve was there. "I just got chill bumps."

"Who do you think is doing this? Do you think there is someone else up there with . . ." He glanced at the stairs on both sides of the hut, making sure no one was coming. ". . . magic?"

"I don't know."

"Have you tried asking?" Narendi said offhandedly.

"Once, but I never got a reply." He shrugged. "I'll try again." He looked up toward the top of the tree and tried speaking with his thoughts. *"Are you there? I heard you. Can you hear me?"*

The voice suddenly reappeared. *"We are here. Please help us."*

Ty looked at Breen and Narendi and nodded excitedly, holding up a finger to Breen as he could see his brother was about to ask what was being said. *"Who are you?"*

The voice suddenly cried out in pain and went silent.

"Are you still there?" Ty asked. *"What happened?"*

He waited, but there was no further answer. He finally shook his head. "They've stopped talking." He started to try again, but there were footsteps and muffled voices on the stairs behind them, coming up from below.

Several men, the same that had been loading their cargo onto one of the lifts, stepped off the stairs and into the hut. When they saw the three of them standing there, the men decided not to stop but to continue on, each offering a polite nod in Narendi's direction, each, once again, ignoring Ty and Breen. As soon as they had left the hut and were well on their way up the stairs and out of sight, Ty turned to the others.

"I found a way to communicate with whoever it is, but before they could tell me who they were, they went silent. I haven't heard anything since."

"This all seems a bit strange if you ask me," Breen said, "and coincidental. We show up the very week that this Live Market just happens to be holding its auctions. What's the likelihood of that happening? Slim to this side of never if you ask me. And then voices start calling out to you in the middle of the night, somehow knowing that you're here." He shook his head. "For all we know we're walking into some kind of trap."

"How could this be a trap?" Ty asked. "How could anyone have known we were coming? It's not like they've been sitting here for a thousand years, waiting for us to arrive."

"Why not? Tirana and her village of cursed souls had been sitting outside the Maze for nearly as long."

Breen had him there. "True, but even they didn't know we were coming until we showed up in their village. I've been hearing this voice since the first day we arrived in the Riverlands."

Breen rolled his shoulders, straightening his bow as he did. "I don't know what to tell you. It just feels . . . off."

"I can't argue there. I've felt off ever since Nyalis told me to go on this stupid quest in the first place." Ty reached up to pat the bulge under his tunic. "I certainly hope all of this is worth it."

Breen nodded. "Me too."

"It better be," Narendi stated, looking somewhat cross with both of them.

"The bigger question is," Breen said, "who are they and what kind of help do they need?"

"One thing at a time," Ty said, finding that the more he thought about it, the more his head ached. "First, we see if we can find the missing key, then we look for whoever it is that keeps reaching out to me." With that, he started for the next set of stairs.

About halfway up, they stopped to rest just inside the largest of the five covered huts. There were a couple other people standing inside as well, a tall man in blue-and-white robes, with four attendants all dressed in common everyday garb. The man in blue stood near the edge, looking out over the swamp as his servants kept to his shadow, weighted down with several tote bags and chests, items he probably didn't want to risk sending up on the lift unattended. He had a long face, made even longer by the narrow patch of growth that started from just below his lower lip and hung halfway to his chest.

Seeing Narendi, he walked over. "I don't believe I've had the pleasure." He offered a slight bow of his head, clearly not wanting to presume to be too formal to someone he didn't know, someone who he might even consider below his station. "My name is Taturov. I travel from Delyum."

Narendi looked at Ty, wondering what to do, but Ty kept his head lowered, so she turned back around. "I am Narendi, princess of the Imbatoo."

Ty clenched his fists, and Breen actually groaned. They hadn't thought to tell her it might not be wisest to admit to something like that. There are those who would kidnap a member of a royal family just to sell them back for ransom.

Taturov raised a brow and then bowed once more, this time with a little more bending of the waist. "It is my honor, Princess. And where is it that you hail from?"

Narendi stared at the man in silence, then turned to Ty.

Ty kept his head lowered. "He asks where it is you have traveled from . . . my princess," he said, adding the last as an afterthought.

"I am of the Imbatoo," she said once more as though the man from Delyum should have known where her people were located.

Ty cleared his throat. "We hail from the Wengoby Desert, sir."

"Ah." The man looked a little taken aback. "Then you have traveled a great distance. I've been coming to these markets for years, and I can say I have never met one of your people here before. It is a pleasure. Are you here for something in particular?"

Ty held his breath. The man seemed to be fishing for something, perhaps wondering what Narendi was interested in buying so that he could learn whether he had competition or not in the purchasing. The question was, was Narendi smart enough not to just come right out and say they were looking for a crystal or a missing part of a key, or anything that might give away their true intentions? They should have thought about developing a better story before leaving the boat. How could she be expected to—

"I am here to purchase a white jaguar."

Ty released an audible sigh, and so did the man in blue, his shoulders relaxing. Apparently, Taturov had his eyes set on something else. "A white jaguar, you say." He thumbed his smooth but prominent chin. "A rare find indeed. Well, I wish you the best of luck, Your Highness." He smiled and offered another bow. "May fortune favor your journey." He turned without waiting for a response and started up the stairs, his four servants scurrying to keep up as they carried his belongings.

"That was close," Breen said.

"That was smart thinking," Ty added with a smile to Narendi. "I was worried you were going to tell them what we were actually looking for."

Narendi scrunched her face. "Why would you think me to do that?"

Ty spared a passing glance at Breen, then blew out his lips. "I was just worried, that's all. And from now on, it might be best if you don't mention that you are a princess."

Narendi clicked her tongue at him and started for the stairs. Before she got there, she turned and handed Ty her bag of clothes. "Here. Carry these." She then marched up the stairs, head held high.

Breen looked at Ty and snickered, then started up after her. Ty looked down at her bag and shook his head. What else could he do? He wanted her to act the part. And now she was.

The trek up to the top was proving quite long. They stopped at least twice more just to rest their feet, even passing Taturov on the way, who had found a bench and plopped himself down to rub his feet. And by *rub his feet*, the man had his servants remove his boots before lacquering his heels and toes with some kind of rub. Ty wondered if it was anything like Isha's cream.

By the time the three reached the top and stepped off the stairwell, they were all nearly out of breath, and Ty's legs were definitely twinging. He walked across the landing, onto the tree's open palm, and nearly doubled over. Something was wrong. He felt like something had reached down and ripped a piece of him out. The breath caught in his throat as he realized what it was.

His magic was gone.

Chapter 70 | Ty

ELCOME TO THE LIVE MARKET," a man standing just off to the right of the stairs said. He wore a green leather coat and vest, and even his pants were dark green. He was a big man, not quite as big as Breen, but certainly taller and wider in the chest than most of those wandering about the top. The hair on his face was every bit as black as that on his head, but the latter showed a faint hint of greying around the temples and hung down just past the shoulder from under his wide-brim green hat.

He looked at Ty a moment and smiled wryly. "Clearly this is your first time to the Market." He waved his arms outward. "This is Tulgava Rashuvi, translated as, a *meeting of equals*. At one time it was used as a wizards' summit, one of several hidden locations across Aldor where wizards could meet on equal footing. It is a sanctuary from any form of magic." He pointed down at the floor of the great tree's palm. The entire thing was covered in giant runic symbols, carved deep into the wood. "You'll be surprised how many envoys will attempt to bring along a wielder or two only to find them useless." He smiled jeeringly in Ty's direction as if to say, *Caught ya!*

Breen leaned in and whispered, "I felt it too."

Narendi pretended not to notice as the man in green turned to her, doing his best to peer beneath her cowl. "Are you here to sell or to buy?"

"We are here to buy," Breen said, offering his arm to Ty, who was still having a difficult time with the sudden loss of his magic, though, strangely enough, he found he could still sense the animals.

"Very good," the man said, not even so much as glancing in Breen's direction to acknowledge who had just spoken. "And can I have your name and place of origin, please?"

Before either Ty or Breen could answer for her, Narendi spoke. "I am Narendi, princess of the Imbatoo, the great peoples of the Desert Sea."

Ty bit his tongue, half from the discomfort he was now feeling at having lost a part of himself, but also at Narendi's defiance. She wasn't going to listen to a thing he said. If she did get herself captured and taken hostage, it would serve her right.

The man in green was clearly impressed by her introduction, bowing deeply at the waist. "We are honored to have you with us, Princess Narendi," he said with a notable gleam in his eye, whether because he saw a potential new source of ransom or simply because he believed her title must have come with a sizable purse to spend at the Market, Ty didn't know. Perhaps both. Those standing within earshot turned as well. They must not get a lot of princesses visiting the Live Market.

"My name is Dalibor, and I will be your host for the remainder of your time here with us. Feel free to peruse our vast collection of rarities. If at any time you have a question, don't hesitate to ask. I am here to serve. Please," he said, motioning with an outstretched arm, "enjoy your stay."

Narendi nodded politely and walked past, heading to the right, where the first of the great tree's huge fingers rose into the air. There were tables with crates and cages lined across the entire outer ring of the open palm, sections marked off for each of the traders to display their wares.

By the time they reached the first booth, Ty was just finding his feet once again.

"Are you going to be all right?" Breen asked. "There was a slight tingling sensation for me. I can't imagine what it must be like for you."

Ty stopped and took a couple of deep breaths, letting the tension melt from his shoulders. "I can't explain how unnatural this feels. It's like I don't recognize my own body. It almost feels the same as when Mangora had control of me."

Breen shivered. "Can you still walk? Do we need to leave?"

"No," Ty said adamantly. "We have to find that missing piece."

Narendi tapped Ty on the shoulder. "I think I found your mirror."

Ty nearly yanked his brother's arm off as he twisted around. Sure enough, built just inside the first finger was a long pane of reflective glass. Ty wasn't close enough to read the runic letters around the base, but he was close enough to know they were there. "At least we know how we're getting out of here," he said with a forced smile.

Breen nodded. "Now for the key."

They walked over to the first vendor, who had several small cages set up on tables around his booth, which also happened to be just to the right of the mirror. There were other buyers perusing the tables as well, taking their time to inspect each cage and the unique selection of animals inside.

With Breen's assistance, Ty worked his way around to the left of the booth, hoping to get closer to the mirror and inspect the runes. They were forced to stop periodically as Narendi, who was walking in front of them, kept stopping to look in the cages as well. Not wanting to appear out of place or draw attention to himself by telling the princess to get a move on, Ty spent the time endeavoring to get used to the new sensations he was feeling. The sooner he could come to grips with how it felt, the better his chance of claiming that final piece of the key would be.

The initial pain was beginning to lessen, and feeling was just now coming back into his extremities. There was an overall tingling sensation throughout his body, similar to having slept on an arm too long and cutting off the blood. The more he moved about, the more normal he began to feel. Well, as normal as one could feel having the equivalent of his soul snatched out of him.

Most of the cages around the first booth were filled with all manner of fowl. They were absolutely resplendent. The birds came in all shapes and sizes, color combinations like Ty had never seen.

One specific bird caught his attention. It was about the size of a bluebird, with teal and crimson coloring sprinkled with a dash of gold around the neck, but what stood out the most was the remarkably long tail that hung all the way from its perch down to the floor of the cage, where it draped across the metal bars further still. It had to have been quite the nuisance to fly with, making it easy pickings for predators. Maybe that was the reason for it being in the Market. A bird near extinction.

Ty reached the end of the booth and stared at the mirror just behind. He stuck his hand in his pocket and squeezed the compass, waiting for the two names to appear. Like all the rest, the mirror's name showed at the top, its runes glowing, but no other name presented itself. "That's funny."

"What is?" Breen asked, keeping an eye on the large gathering of sellers and buyers scattered across the top of the enormous tree.

"I can't seem to find the second name needed to direct the mirror where to go next. Without that name, the mirror's useless."

Breen looked at him, clearly not liking what he was hearing. "Are you saying this mirror is broken?"

"Maybe, or maybe this isn't the right mirror."

Breen helped Ty over to the side and away from prying ears as Narendi continued her rounds, flicking the cages with her fingers and chirping at the birds as she went. Breen stood just to the left of the mirror between the first and second booth. "Are you sure this isn't the right mirror? Try again."

"I can try, but it's not going to do much good." Ty reached back in his pocket once more and grabbed the compass, this time lifting it out of his pocket in case that made some sort of difference. Again, the runic letters at the top of the wooden frame lit for him to see, but all other runes remained unaffected. He placed the compass back in his pocket and shook his head. "Nothing."

Breen blew out his lips.

Ty turned to tell Narendi that they needed to keep going, but she was clear on the other side of the booth, staring at a cluster of tiny yellow birds with bright-red beaks and a very bizarre purple comb that ran from the top of their heads to the bottom of their necks.

"I'll go get her," Ty said.

"You need help?"

Ty waved him off. "I'm feeling better." He left Breen between booths and walked over to where Narendi had begun open negotiations on the birds. "My princess, might I speak with you a moment," he said, and pulled her to the side, whether she wanted to go or not. "What do you think you're doing?"

"What does it appear? I am purchasing these creatures."

"No, you're not. We aren't here for you to spend our gold on birds. We're here to buy the missing piece of the shorlock and then leave."

"It is my gold," she hissed, jerking her arm free, "and I will purchase what I wish."

"Fine," he said. There was little he could do to stop her. If she caused a ruckus, it was Ty and Breen who were going to be tossed out, and here, *tossed out* could very well mean being tossed over the side.

Ty left her and followed his brother over to the next booth, where an old couple sat smoking pipes in a couple of rockers while keeping a close eye on those passing by. Once or twice, they had to warn buyers not to stick their fingers in the cages, that they might lose a digit or two in the process. Ty stopped at the first cage. It lay on the floor underneath a long table holding several wooden crates with their lids conveniently left open for customers to view inside.

Inside the cage was one of the longest lizards Ty had ever seen. This particular lizard had deep-orange scales with grey designs that ran from the tip of its nose to the tip of its very long tail. He used the tail to hang from a branch and grab a piece of sliced fruit from a pile at the bottom of the cage. Holding the slice gently between two of its five clawed fingers, it lifted itself back up to the branch and fed the fruit into its mouth much like any human.

Ty stood and bumped into Narendi, or more importantly, he bumped into the cage of little yellow birds she was carrying in her free hand. "What are—" He took a deep breath and tried counting to five before quickly moving on to the next booth.

"Best not to say anything," Breen said as he rushed to catch up. "The more you push her, the more she'll push back. Next thing you know, she'll be buying a bucket of jumping turtles to go with it."

They made their way slowly around the next two booths before reaching the second of the great tree's fingers. Ty nearly choked when he saw another mirror resting just inside the wooden appendage. He grabbed Breen's arm about the same time Breen grabbed his.

Ty immediately reached into his pocket and grabbed the compass, watching the runes at the top of the frame begin to brighten, but once again, no other names presented themselves. He released the compass and shook his head.

Breen pointed at the third finger further down. "You don't think?"

Ty turned and counted the number of fingers rising from the great palm. "Six trees," he mumbled to himself. "Could be six mirrors."

"It would make sense," Breen said. "If this was some great meeting place of wizards, they would no doubt be coming from different locations. How better to facilitate that than with several mirrors?" Breen smiled. "What are we waiting for?"

"Wait," Ty said as he looked around at all the other buyers calmly moving from one booth to the next. "Let's just keep going. We'll eventually make our way around to each. Best not to attract attention."

"What are you looking at?" Narendi asked, walking over to stand beside Ty.

Ty wanted to ignore her, but he did that at all their peril. "We found two more mirrors," he said, pointing toward the second and third gnarled fingers. "We're wondering if there might be more, and if so, which one is the one we need to escape through. We'll take a look at each as we make our way around. Best we not appear to be too interested in them, though, or someone might grow suspicious." Ty noticed Dalibor looking in their direction. "Don't turn around, but it seems our host has an interest in Narendi."

Narendi frowned. "I have already given my vow. He wastes his time."

Ty sighed, and they moved on to the next booth. A large cage near the far side of the tree's palm began to shake. Several armed men in leather armor rushed over and began jabbing through the cage with long poles. "Quiet down!" they shouted.

"*Help us!*"

Ty grabbed both Breen's and Narendi's arms at the same time and pulled them to a stop. "The voices are back. And I think that cage down there is where they are being kept."

"Then we go see?" Narendi said, taking a step in that direction before Ty pulled her back.

"No. We need to wait. Remember, we need to blend in. If we go rushing over there right now, we will definitely cause a scene."

"Ty's correct," Breen said. "Best to let whatever is happening calm down first."

Ty reached out with his mind, surprised he could still communicate, what with the rest of his magic having been taken. Perhaps this wasn't magic. "*I'm coming. What's your name?*"

The cages on the end stopped shaking. "*My name is not important. Please help us. Please help my child.*" Ty stopped Breen and Narendi once again, pulling them into the next booth, acting as though he were inspecting a couple of the cages at the back. "I don't know their names, but I think it's a mother and her child. There might be more, but those are the only two I've heard."

A deep growl rose from the cage next to them, and they all jumped back. Breen lifted the tarp overtop to find one of the most beautiful snow leopards Ty had ever seen. It growled again, and Ty could sense its anger. He sent a sense of comfort back through his connection with the great cat, and the leopard nuzzled up against the side of the cage and even went so far as to let Ty reach in and stroke the top of its head.

"Son," a voice behind them said softly. "Don't make any sudden movements. You need to pull your hand back out of that cage before it becomes a chew toy."

Ty removed his hand, not all that worried about bothering the cat or having his hand chewed off, but he didn't want to frighten anyone either. He turned to find a rugged-looking gentleman with a grey beard that hung to his navel, and a head of hair that would have rivaled any sheepdog. His green eyes were bulging as he stared at Ty. "I've never seen anything like that. You are either the luckiest lad I've ever met, or the dumbest."

"She's a beautiful animal," Ty said. "Where did you find her?"

The old man moved his pipe to the side of his mouth. "I'm surprised you knew it was a female. Most your age would barely know the front from the back." He released a garbled laugh. "I caged her along the northeastern Angorans."

"Don't know of many who hunt that close to the Gates of Bel'Taag," Breen said.

The old man smiled proudly, enough teeth missing to make chewing anything tougher than a boiled potato downright difficult. "Don't rightly know of many myself, just another reason why they sell so well here." He walked over and lowered the tarp back across the cat's cage. "Yes, they are beautiful animals, indeed." He stared at Ty a moment, then walked back around to answer some questions from a couple of gentlemen at the front.

Ty stared at the leopard's cage.

"Don't get any bright ideas," Breen said. "Remember what we're here for."

"I know, I know. I just hate to see something so beautiful locked away like this."

"It's not like you can take it with us," Breen said.

Ty left the leopard and started for the next set of booths. He stopped at the monkey cages, having never seen one in person before, and they gave him a momentary distraction. They were quite interesting to watch, some with long colorful snouts, some with bulbous paddle-shaped noses, some with short tails, others with tails longer than their bodies. Some looked as big and furry as a bear, others stood upright and appeared almost human. Ty couldn't believe how many types of monkeys there were. Where had these sellers found so many?

He didn't spot anyone watching the booth to ask, so they finally moved on, passing the third mirror. Ty reached into his pocket and grabbed the compass, watching as the runes at the top brightened. He started to release the compass when a second set of runes on the left side suddenly began to glow.

Shuta Ningiwa. Solnari Cushlora.

Ty grabbed Breen. "It's the one! I see the second name. We found it." He read the names three times each, careful not to speak them aloud, doing his best to commit them to memory in case they needed to make a hasty escape.

Narendi walked over from where she'd been playing with one of the smaller monkeys. "This is the one?"

Ty nodded. "Now if we can just find the missing piece of the shorlock."

"Find something you like?" a familiar voice behind them asked.

They all turned to find Dalibor in his green hat standing just behind them, staring at the mirror as well.

How much had he overheard? Ty cleared his throat nervously. "Princess Narendi was curious as to the strange pieces of glass inside the wood." Ty kept his head lowered as all good servants should and tried to sound as genuine as possible.

Dalibor straightened with a smile. "Ah, yes, well, they were used as a way to protect the wizards while they were in attendance during their forums. Since they no longer had their magic to rely on, they needed a way to make sure they could keep watch on the other wizards while they were here, a way to assure that no one was able to sneak up behind them."

Ty smiled. Clearly, Dalibor didn't have a clue as to what the mirrors were really for. It seemed a logical interpretation in its own way, and since Dalibor seemed to be trying his best to impress Narendi, there was definitely no reason to correct him, not that Ty would have, knowing what the mirrors were truly capable of.

"That is very interesting," Breen said as he shifted his pack higher on his shoulders. "Princess Narendi would be most interested in whether you carry other types of goods. Say, something one might wear around their neck?"

"And what a lovely neck it is," Dalibor said. "I believe we have what you seek over here." He directed them away from the right side of the palm and over to the left, where the final finger of the tree's hand rose high over their heads, its branches reaching upward, as if searching for the sun but never finding it. "Is this more of what you had in mind, Your Highness?"

The booth in front of the sixth mirror had several armed guards standing around it. And it was no wonder. Each of its four tables was filled with an impressive array of gems, some with colors Ty had never seen on any stone before.

"They are beautiful," Narendi said, her eyes sparkling in the light of the nearby torches as she gawked at the jeweler's wares.

Ty ran his eyes up and down the tables as he scanned the incredible display of stones. There were too many to look at. One of the guards growled when Ty got too close. How was he ever going to find the right piece with them staring over his shoulder?

He needed a distraction.

Chapter 71 | Ty

HE CAGE ON THE FAR back corner of the tree began to shake once more, all the animals surrounding them responding in kind. The monkeys screeched and whooped, the large cats roared, the birds squawked and chirped. Whoever was in those cages was affecting all the other animals. Wielders of some kind, no doubt.

"*I know you are close,*" the voice in his head spoke out. "*Please, you must free us. Save my child.*" The cages continued to shake, and men with long poles swatted at those inside. Ty couldn't make out who it was because the owners were doing a good job of keeping it covered, not to mention all those who had gathered around the front to watch the spectacle.

"What's happening over there?" Ty asked, but Dalibor ignored him, so Ty rephrased. "Is Princess Narendi safe?"

Dalibor looked at Narendi. "There's no need to worry," he said, laying one hand on the middle of her back. "Come, you can see for yourself."

They left the table and its jewels behind and started for the other side of the great tree.

"Did you see anything that looked like it might fit?" Breen asked, moving alongside Ty as they kept a step or two behind Narendi and Dalibor.

Ty shook his head. "I didn't have time. There were too many gems."

"To be honest," Breen said, "I was afraid if you got too close, the missing piece would do like the others and fly to you. Wouldn't that have been perfect. We would have finally found the last piece just in time to take a nosedive off the side of this tree once they got their hands on us."

"Who would have ever thought we would end up somewhere where magic couldn't be used? Without it, I'm about as useless as a sword without a blade." He tapped the hilt of his sword. "Remind me, if we ever make it back to Easthaven alive, to have Lyessa show me how to use this thing. The couple of lessons I had with Darryk was barely enough to keep me from dropping the crazy thing every time he struck it."

"Who knows," Breen said. "Without my magic, I might not be any better a shot than you."

Ty frowned. He hadn't thought about that. Ty had always been able to depend on Breen's marksmanship. "Let's just make sure it doesn't come to that."

Dalibor pushed his way through the crowd, which had already begun to disperse now that the excitement seemed to be over. "These are our most valued commodities," he said, stopping in front of the largest of the cages.

Ty stared up at the covered container. "What's so . . ." Breen nudged him, and Ty ground his teeth. "I mean, the *princess* would like to know what is so special about them."

"They are one of a kind," Dalibor said. "We have not seen their like in the Market for generations."

Ty's curiosity was piqued even more. Who in the world did they have under the canvas that would have everyone acting in such a fashion? Had they captured the king and his mother? Ty almost laughed. Wouldn't that have been something, Dakaran sitting in a cage waiting to be purchased. The only thing Ty knew was that whoever was under there was truly frightened, and more than that, they possessed magic, magic similar to his, at least when it came to communicating. It was strange. Ty had never known he could link with someone in such a way.

"Do you wish to get a look?" Dalibor asked, loudly enough for those around to hear.

"Yes!" Narendi half shouted before Ty could even open his mouth.

Dalibor walked over to the tall cage and grabbed hold of the canvas. He turned to all those that had gathered, which was just about everyone. Even the sellers had abandoned their stations to come take a look. The old man who had been in charge of the leopards stepped up beside Ty and winked at him. "Been waiting to catch a glimpse of these two for the last couple of days."

Dalibor waited until everyone had gathered around and all eyes were on him. "They are one of the last of their kind, a prize more valuable than all else."

Ty's eyes widened with anticipation. Who in the flaming Pits did he have in there?

"Help us, faerie!"

Ty nearly choked. *Faerie? How do they—*

"Dig deep in those pockets, my friends," Dalibor said, shouting to be heard above the din of all the animals. "I give you . . ." He ripped the canvas off in one swift pull, and Ty's breath caught in his throat. They weren't wielders. They weren't even human.

". . . Draakar!" Dalibor's eyes were positively beaming with excitement as the crowd gasped all at once. Many of those near the front jumped back as the two enormous reptilian creatures screeched.

Ty couldn't believe his eyes. They were unlike anything he'd ever seen or imagined before. He looked at Breen, but his brother was fixated on the two creatures. Narendi, as well, was frozen in place, her mouth open wide enough to stick a small apple in.

Many had talked about the draakar, but never from firsthand knowledge. One look and he knew the legends were true. They were beautiful and deadly all at the same time. From the side, they reminded Ty in a way of the razorback he'd seen in the marsh, but not as big. The larger of the two stood about as high as a small horse, but with thick powerful legs that ended in clawed feet.

Both creatures were covered from head to toe in red interlocking scales, though the smaller one's scales didn't seem to be as developed. They were thinner, with several patches of skin not yet covered. The younger draakar wasn't much bigger than a large wolf or coyote.

The mother's tail was spiked and stretched out behind her, curling against the back of the cage. Those same spikes ran partway up the back, stopping about midway, then starting once more near the base of the neck, up over the head, and halfway down the center of her nostrils. On either side of the mother's head was a pair of curved horns, each coming to a point about three feet behind her. Between the two horns were several smaller ones, running across the top of her head, giving the impression of wearing an enormous bone crown.

The smaller creature's horns were much less defined and quite a bit shorter, barely peeking out from the back of its head at all.

Their most captivating feature, however, were their wings, though they appeared stunted. Even Ty could have seen they were too small to ever lift either into the air. Maybe they were used as a defensive mechanism for scaring off predators, though Ty couldn't imagine what predators would be desperate enough to attack them.

The mother leaped forward and grabbed the front bars with her claws, her bright, golden eyes shifting through the crowd until they reached Ty's and stopped. *"I feel your power, faerie. Free us!"*

Ty's hands began to shake. He had been hoping that whoever had been communicating with him was a normal human being. It was just his luck that it was one of the more dangerous creatures in Aldor.

The draakar stuck out her neck and bellowed. Ty, along with everyone else, jumped back.

Breen grabbed his ears. "I've never heard anything so loud."

A few ran for the stairs on the far side. Ty was half tempted to join them, but somehow he managed to stay his ground, perhaps more out of fear than anything. Beside him, Narendi had unstrapped her spear and was holding it firmly in place.

"Help us!"

Ty took a deep breath and started for the cage, but not before Dalibor and half a dozen men charged in with spears. The mother draakar grabbed her child and shoved it back out of the way, taking the brunt of their attack. Most of the spears deflected off the thick scales at her chest, but a couple of the metal tips pierced the softer flesh near the base of her wings, and the draakar roared.

Breen grabbed Ty's arm and pulled him back, away from the men, who were swinging their spears wildly enough to possibly hit them. "What are you doing?" Breen asked, keeping his voice low enough to not be heard.

"I'm talking to her."

Breen gawked. "That's whose been communicating with you?"

Ty nodded and refocused his mind. *"If I set you free, how is that going to help? We are in the middle of the wetlands, and there's nowhere for you to go. You can't fly . . . can you? I would take you through the mirror with me, but you won't fit."*

"Save my child."

"If I release your cage, can you create a diversion?"

"Promise to save my child and you'll have your diversion."

"What's going on?" Breen asked.

Ty looked at Breen. "I'm going to free them."

"You're going to *what*?"

"That is a very bad plan," Narendi said, the three of them huddling close to talk. "They will kill us." Ty wasn't exactly sure if she was referring to the draakar or to the very angry men with spears.

"No. They won't. She's given me her word that if I free them and promise to take her child with us, she will provide the distraction we need to get the missing piece of the key and open the mirror."

"You want to take them with us?" Breen asked. "Have you lost your mind? Look at that thing. It'll kill us all."

"I don't think it will. It wants to get out of here as badly as we do. I can't just leave her child behind to die. Besides, I don't see how we have much choice. The stones are still guarded, and we have no way of getting to them. What better way to cause a distraction than to release a couple of draakar on everyone?" It was almost poetic justice, the hunters becoming the hunted.

"I hope you know what you're doing." Breen turned and looked at the cage. "How do you plan to release them? Walk up and politely ask Dalibor and those fine spearmen to kindly hand over the keys?"

"Hadn't thought that far," Ty said, then turned and slowly scanned the row of booths behind them, looking for something that could help. His eyes caught the leopard's cage.

Breen turned, along with Narendi, to see what he was looking at. "I'm not going to like this am I?"

Ty smiled. "Probably not."

They ran back through the crowd, not looking too suspicious, as there were plenty of others who were doing the same. They reached the large cats' booth, and thankfully the old keeper was nowhere to be seen. Probably still back at the draakar's cage, watching all the excitement. Ty pulled back the canvas covering and pushed a sense of urgency into the beautiful animal. *"Move back."*

The cat responded by circling to the back of its cage, where it waited patiently for Ty to open the door.

Surprisingly, there were no locks, because who would be stupid enough to try opening the cages? Ty chuckled as he pulled up on the lever and slid the handle back, and the door swung open. Breen held his bow at the ready, and Narendi kept her spear lowered. Both stayed just behind Ty.

"Go!" Ty said, pushing the thought into the leopard's mind. *"You're free."* The leopard stepped out of its cage and looked up at Ty for just a moment, then sauntered off in the direction of the crowd. Ty quickly turned and did the same to the others, releasing every last one of the big cats.

Before he'd gotten the last cage open, screams erupted on the back side of the palm. People spotting the big cats scattered, stampeding over each other as they fought to escape.

"Come on!" Ty said as he directed Breen and Narendi back toward the draakars' pen. Ty was knocked backward into his brother by those rushing to get out of the way of one of the panthers. The panther saw Ty and moved around him, still giving chase.

The spearmen were no longer guarding the draakar and were in the process of protecting Dalibor. He shouted with sword in hand as the men lunged and thrust at the hungry animals. The big cats had cornered them at the side. One of the spearmen managed to find its target, and the cat went down, but not before another one leaped on the man, sinking its teeth into his neck.

"This is a good enough distraction," Narendi said, her spear at the ready. "No need to free the draakar."

"I already gave my word," Ty said. He spared a quick glance across the palm to find the guards keeping watch over the stones fighting for their lives against two more cats. Perhaps Narendi was right. Maybe he wouldn't need to worry about releasing the draakar after all.

He shook his head. No. He'd given them his word. They reached the back of the cage holding the magnificent creatures and found the smaller one crouched in the corner. It stared at Ty as Ty made his way around. Ty could sense the creature through the same bond, but he hadn't yet heard the child speak.

Stepping over debris from upturned tables and broken crates, they made their way to the front of the cage. He grabbed the handle and pulled. "It's locked! I need a key!"

Before he could turn to tell the draakar that he couldn't open it yet, Narendi flew past and in the direction of the spearmen. "I'll get it!"

"*What are you waiting for, faerie?*"

Ty was getting tired of being called a faerie. "*Quit calling me that. I'm only half Fae.*"

"*Yes, I can smell the stench of your human blood. Now release us.*"

"*We're working on it. I have no magic here, so we need to get the key.*"

Breen pulled him down beside a stack of crates. "Don't let them see you."

Ty looked up at the cage. "*What's your name?*"

"*You cannot pronounce it in your tongue.*"

"*Then what do I call you?*"

"*The closest translation is Wuntara'solniici'ruvaraak.*"

Ty attempted to sound it out. "*Woon-tar-uh-sol-nee-see-roo-var-uck. How about I just call you . . . Tara?*"

The draakar growled. "*You humans and your short, pathetic little names.*" The draakar didn't sound very pleased by the reduction to hers, but she didn't come right out and say he couldn't use it.

"*And what is your child's name?*" Ty turned and looked at the young draakar cowering behind its mother. It seemed to be peeking out from behind to get a better look at Ty. "*What is your name, young one?*" Of course, Ty had no idea how young the draakar was. For all he knew, it was older than him.

The smaller creature stepped out from behind its mother. "*Laansilvic'kraeatori'dulfeyn,*" it said, its voice sounding feminine. The child was a girl.

Ty once again sounded it out. *"Lon-sil-vik-kray-uh-tor-ee-dul-fayn."* Tara was right. Their names were hard to pronounce. *"How about Sil or Vik? Silvik?"*

The young draakar shook her head.

"What about Tori? That sounds nice, doesn't it? Tara and Tori."

The draakar shook her head again, this time sticking out a long, forked tongue. *"Kraea,"* she said.

"Kraea?"

The draakar barked.

Ty smiled. *"Kraea it is."*

"What are they saying?" Breen asked, keeping an eye on the spearmen and the cats. "Are you still communicating with them?"

"You can use your normal tongue," Tara said. *"We are able to hear and understand. I just cannot speak it back. My mouth will not fashion your words."*

Ty turned to Breen. "Yes, we are talking. She can hear you."

Breen looked up at the creature. "She can hear me?"

"Her name is Tara. Actually, it's this really long name, but I shortened it to Tara. And her daughter's name is—"

"No one steals from the Live Market!" someone shouted from behind them.

Ty and Breen turned to find two of Dalibor's guards standing there with swords in hand, one of the blades covered in blood. Ty reached for his magic, forgetting momentarily that he didn't have it. When he realized, he jumped to his feet and grabbed his sword, drawing it about the time the two guards attacked.

He barely got it over his head before the blood-soaked blade connected. He stumbled back against the draakars' cage, trying to keep from getting hit. Beside him, his brother parried the second guard's sword with his bow, pulling the string back as he did and unleashing the arrow into the man's chest.

Ty swung left and right, blocking the man's advances as fast as he could, completely unable to get a swing in of his own. The guard stumbled on one of the crates and went down, swinging for Ty's legs as he did. Ty jumped to the side to keep from getting his leg cut off but ended up giving the man time to get back to his feet. The guard raised his sword and was hit in the side with a spear. He coughed blood and went down.

Ty turned to see Narendi running their way. "I have got it!" she shouted, dragging Dalibor by his neck, her sword pressed against the front. "Unlock the cage!"

Dalibor's eyes widened when he saw which cage she was referring to. "Are you mad? I'm not releasing those creatures."

Narendi pressed the edge of her blade higher on his neck, and Dalibor stiffened. He fumbled in his pocket for a moment and brought out a ring with three keys. Ty grabbed the keys and tried the first. It didn't work. He stuffed the second into the lock, and it snapped free.

"Hurry!" Tara said frantically. *"Those men are coming."*

Ty could hear shouts behind him, and he quickly lifted up the pin and flung back the bar. The door swung free, and Ty and the others quickly moved to the side of the cage to keep out of the draakar's way.

"Stay here!" Tara said to Kraea, then turned and released a roar that had even the cats running for the back of the tree.

The spearmen, those who hadn't been taken down by the cats, rushed the draakar before it had gotten halfway out of its cage.

"Leave him!" Ty shouted at Narendi. "We have to go!"

She threw Dalibor down against the side of the cage and pulled her spear free from the dead guard. She nodded at Ty, and they raced across the tree for the gems. There was no time to spare.

The jeweler was lying in a pool of blood beside two upturned tables, his throat looking like it had been chewed on. The stones were scattered across the floor, some near the edge of the tree. Ty prayed the one they needed hadn't gone over. Two of the guards were still there, but instead of protecting the goods, they were on their hands and knees, pocketing as many as they could.

They barely had a chance to turn when Breen and Narendi leaped on top of them. Breen knocked the first unconscious with a single punch to the side of his head. The second guard wasn't as lucky, as he was pinned to the floor with Narendi's spear. Ty fumbled across the ground, searching for anything that might resemble what he was looking for.

As Tara had promised, she was giving them the distraction they needed. She roared and swatted at the spearmen, using her claws and tail to keep them from getting too close with their spears. There were at least a dozen men surrounding her, and she fought to keep them back. She had little room to give, the edge of the enormous tree just behind her.

Ty yanked the key from around his neck and held it over the floor. "Do you see anything?" he shouted to Breen and Narendi. He looked up to find Narendi on the ground, stuffing her pouch and pockets with as many gems as she could get her hands on. "Hey! We need to find the key."

Breen was searching the far table, but so far, he didn't appear to have found anything useful. "It will have a round base," Ty said, looking once more at the empty socket at the center of the medallion. The floor was filled with hundreds of gems of all shapes and sizes and colors.

Behind him, Ty could hear Dalibor shouting out orders as the men continued to press their advantage of numbers against the draakar. Every so often, someone would cry out, no doubt having gotten too close to Tara's claws or tail.

"Hurry!" Tara pleaded. *"I cannot hold them back."*

Ty held the medallion out as he swept across the two tables that were still standing. "I don't see anything. None of the stones are moving." He looked over at Breen in a panic. "What if what we are looking for isn't a stone after all? What if we are looking for—"

"Wait! Look!" Breen pointed to the dead jeweler. "Look at his leg." His trouser pocket was glowing.

Ty ran and slid down beside the dead man, trying to keep clear of the blood, and thrust his fist into the pocket and pulled out a handful of large gems, the largest of which was pulsing a bright red. It was the biggest gem Ty had ever seen. He didn't remember it being displayed earlier. The jeweler must have been keeping it hidden until the time of the auction. Ty dropped the other stones and held up the one that was glowing. "This has to be it!"

"No!" Tara screamed and released an ear-piercing roar.

Ty nearly dropped the gem as he spun to see what was happening.

Tara was at the edge of the tree with nowhere to go, but instead of focusing on the spears in front of her, she was looking at the cage. Ty turned. Dalibor was inside the cage with two other men, and they had Kraea pinned to the back. She was crying out for her mother.

"Drag it out!" Dalibor shouted.

Breen was already pulling Ty toward the third mirror. "We've got the key. Let's go."

"Do not forget your promise, faerie!"

Ty pulled away from Breen. "No. I gave her my word I would take her daughter with us."

"You can't reach her," Breen said. "We have to go."

Ty started toward Dalibor and the spearmen.

"Stop this!" Dalibor shouted at Tara. "Or I'll kill your offspring!"

Tara lowered herself back to all fours as the spearmen held their line.

"Wait!" Ty shouted. "Don't kill her!"

"You!" Dalibor was practically foaming at the mouth. "You're the one responsible for . . ." Dalibor froze, his mouth widening. "What is that?" Dalibor had all but forgotten the draakar. His eyes were fixed on the enormous glowing stone in Ty's hand.

"It's nothing." Ty had forgotten he was still holding it.

"The flaming Pits it's nothing!" he said, drool practically running down the corners of his mouth. "That's the largest jewel I've ever seen. Worth a dozen of these creatures." He looked at Narendi. "Where did you get it?" He no doubt expected it to have come from her people.

"That's none of your concern," Ty said. "Now free the creature."

Dalibor laughed. "Or what? You forget, your magic is worthless here."

Ty ground his teeth. Ty could have wiped the floor with them if he had had his magic. But he didn't. He looked at Tara. The bottom of her left wing was ripped open, dark blood pouring from her side. Three of the spearmen were down, but there were still nine surrounding her.

"Don't leave without my child." Tara's words sounded more like a plea than a declaration. She knew she wasn't getting out of there. She had nowhere to go, which meant Ty was her only hope.

Ty stared at Dalibor, whose men were holding the tips of their blades to Kraea's lower neck, underneath one of her less-scaled regions. "I'm waiting, boy! It's clear you want the creature, so how about we make a trade? I'll give you the runt in exchange for that rock you hold in your hand."

Ty's breath caught in his throat. What was he going to do? He'd promised Tara, but the only reason he was there was for that final piece of the key. The lives of his family and friends, and so many more, depended on him getting it. His fist tightened so hard around the stone that he thought he might break his fingers.

"Look around," Dalibor said, growing more confident of his position with each passing moment. "You've got nowhere to run. Hand over the stone, and maybe I'll consider letting you leave."

Keeping his eyes on Dalibor, Ty eased his way back toward the third mirror.

"What are you doing, faerie?"

Ty stuck his free hand in his pocket and grabbed the compass. Two sets of runes lit around the mirror's frame.

"Well?" Dalibor said.

"What are we doing, Ty?" Breen asked. "You're not considering this, are you? We can't leave without that piece of the key."

"I know, but . . ."

"But what?"

"But what kind of person would I be if I broke my word and left them here to die so we could escape?"

Breen tightened the grip on his bow. "Quit acting so grown up, would you? It doesn't feel right." He sighed. "I can't tell you what to do. This is your quest. So, it's your decision. But I'm telling you now. I'm not coming back here a second time if we leave without that piece."

"Noted," Ty said, spotting a couple of Dalibor's men trying to work their way around the other side of the tree in order to block them from reaching the stairs. Ty turned and looked at Dalibor, his fist still clenched tightly around the stone.

"Honor your word, faerie."

"Well, what's it to be?" Dalibor demanded.

Ty bit his lip. Why was this so difficult?

"Fine," he said, almost not believing the words had come from his own mouth. "The stone for the draakar." Ty heard Breen grumble something behind him, but true to his word, he didn't try stopping him.

Dalibor's smile said no matter what he promised, none of them were going to be leaving there alive. "You have a deal. The runt for the stone. Now slide it over and I'll let the little one go free."

"And you expect me to take just your word on that?"

Dalibor flung his arms in the air. "Fine. We'll meet halfway."

Ty glanced at the mirror once more. The runic names were still glowing around the frame. *Shuta Ningiwa. Solnari Cushlora.* He repeated them over and over again in his mind, recommitting them to memory, before finally turning around and starting forward. Breen and Narendi flanked him as they went.

Dalibor and two other men marched Kraea in their direction.

"Mother." Kraea sounded frantic.

"Don't worry, little one. You will be fine."

Ty stopped about halfway, as did Dalibor.

"The stone," Dalibor said, holding his hand out at the ready.

Ty took a step forward. "Release the draakar."

"Why is this creature so important to you?"

"You wouldn't understand." Blazes, Ty didn't understand, not really. He was literally giving up everything to save a single life. Anyone with a lick of sense would have told him that was insane. What was one life against untold numbers? Ultimately, it came down to what he was willing to live with, and apparently leaving this mother and her child to die was something he couldn't.

Dalibor glanced over his shoulder at the two men holding Kraea and nodded for them to release her. Ty could see in Dalibor's eyes that none of this really mattered. Dalibor wasn't about to let Ty, or any of them, leave with the draakar. He just wanted to get his hands on that stone, probably before Ty threatened to toss it over the side.

Ty's hand was shaking as he raised it to get one last look at his failed mission. The stone was roundish in shape but with dozens of tiny edges. It pulsed a deep red, the inside almost seemingly moving. With a deep breath, he tossed the stone to Dalibor. Dalibor caught the gem and held it up against the surrounding torchlight. "It's exquisite."

"Go!" Tara shouted at Kraea, and Kraea leaped forward, nearly knocking

Breen off his feet with her tail. As fast as they could, without looking like they were intentionally fleeing, Ty, Breen, Narendi and Kraea backed their way toward the edge of the tree and the third mirror. *"Stay close,"* Ty told Kraea, *"and when I say to run, you run."*

"Mother," Kraea growled.

Dalibor lowered the stone, his face darkening. "I changed my mind," he said. "I want my draakar back."

"You already gave your word," Ty said, working his way past some of the fallen crates surrounding the third booth. Several snakes that had been inside the crates slithered away when they saw them coming.

"What can I say? You had a bit of an advantage, but now I have the stone, and you have nowhere to run." He gestured at the men over by the stairs, and they started toward Ty and the others.

Ty looked at Tara. *"Can you give me one more distraction?"*

Her lips parted, revealing her large fangs, and she snarled. Ty took that as a yes.

He turned and looked at the mirror. *"Shuta Ningiwa. Solnari Cushlora."*

The mirror burst to life, the image swirling as it revealed moonlit rocks covered in snow. Ty turned back around and smiled at Dalibor, whose mouth hung agape.

"Now!" Ty shouted, and Tara roared, spinning in a complete circle as she used her spiked tail to throw back the spearmen momentarily, most of them having been looking at the mirror.

She looked at Kraea. *"Run, my darling!"* With a loud roar, she burst through the men and leaped on top of Dalibor, sinking her teeth into his arm. With one final glance in Kraea's direction, Tara turned and leaped off the side of the great tree, dragging a screaming Dalibor and the gem with her.

"Mother!" Kraea started forward, but Ty jumped in her way.

"Run, Kraea!" Ty said, pushing her back toward the mirror. "Your mother said run!"

"Come on!" Breen shouted, Narendi having already jumped through. Ty and Kraea raced for the glass, the Market guards giving chase. Breen jumped through.

The guards were nearly on top of them. Ty gave everything he had, desperation willing him to run even faster. Kraea flew through the glass, and Ty dove through on top of her, just as several of the guards released their spears. Ty landed on his face in a pile of snow, and the spears flew over his head, ricocheting off the stone in front of him.

He'd barely turned over when he felt his body suddenly spark to life, a wave of heat tearing through him like a furnace, stealing his breath as it did. He smiled.

He could feel it.

His magic had returned.

He raised his hands and called on his flames. They ignited in both palms, bathing the surrounding stone in blue light. He turned to unleash a stream of fire back through the mirror and burn those guards to ash, but before he could send even so much as a spark through, he was struck on the back of his head.

He staggered forward and grabbed at the injured area. He looked down at his hand. There was blood. What happened? The world began to spin. He turned, and just before the darkness took him, a familiar face moved into view.

Mangora smiled. "It's good to see you again, my little faeling."

Chapter 72 | Ferrin

ERRIN WAS GROWING RESTLESS. They had spent the last three days sitting in Harlin's closet while Sylas was busy rounding up what remained of the Rhowynn wielder council. To make matters worse, he was left with nothing to do but relive Myron's passing, over and over again. Each time Ferrin didn't think he had tears enough left to cry, he'd find himself wiping his eyes once again.

His nerves were on edge. It didn't help that Elson had been caught in the throes of coming down off a pretty powerful bender, which had left him vomiting more than once, leaving them all to enjoy the aftermath. He had, of course, apologized profusely, but that did little to curb the smell.

It would have been easy to simply use the durma key in his boot, release Lenara, and between the two of them, kill every last one of the Tower's guards— that was, if the bulradoer she'd spoken of weren't nearby to stop them. Even if he could find one of his swords, it wasn't a match for a battle wielder. Sure, he could stop one of their flaming weapons, but if they decided to hit him with a ball of fire, there was little he could do but burn.

And to be honest, releasing their collars wasn't going to be all that beneficial unless they somehow found a bag of transferal crystals lying around, which was highly unlikely. Ferrin knew from experience that Sylas didn't wear a crystal himself. His innate ability had also been passed on to his daughter, Suri.

Worse, Lenara wasn't going to let Ferrin torture Sylas for the information, not while he was inhabiting Joren's body, especially as fragile as she claimed this Joren's hold to be. So that meant that even if they did manage to kill everyone else, they would have to rely on Sylas telling them where he had his sister hidden, and since he knew Lenara wouldn't allow anything to befall him, there was little Ferrin could do to force him to tell.

In the end, Ferrin's only option was to hold off on his escape until Sylas took him to where she was being kept.

It was the third night they'd been there, and the only time they'd been given permission to leave was to make a trip to the latrine in the next room. After his first involuntary spew, Elson had spent most of his time in the washroom, wallowing on the tile and threatening to never touch another bottle of wine again. Of course, when the guards brought in their supper, which included a flagon of watered ale, Elson was the first to grab his cup, which thankfully did calm some of his shakes, but not much.

Lenara kept mostly to herself, huddled in the corner. Ferrin felt sorry for the bulradoer and what had happened to her, which was strange, considering who she was. He remembered the first time he'd seen her. It was the day he first laid eyes on the White Tower. His prison transport had just crossed over the main bridge separating the Tower complex from the Pass of Arnon.

He had barely made it off the wagon when one of their group decided to make a run for it. Ferrin wasn't sure where the frightened man thought he was going to run, but wherever it was, he didn't get far, as one of the black-robed people waiting for them sent a stream of pale-green lightning to grab the man. He was lifted into the air and then exploded all over the cages. It was the most horrific thing Ferrin had ever witnessed.

Lenara had been that bulradoer.

Who would have thought that the short woman with the strange raspberry eyes could be so deadly? Ferrin remembered being more afraid of the utter look of indifference on her face after eviscerating the man than by the way she had accomplished it.

"What time do you think it is?" Elson asked, finally lifting himself up to a sitting position, his face pale even under the lanterns' amber light.

"It's time to get some sleep," Lenara said, irritation in her voice. She'd been quite vocal in her annoyance with Elson's lack of inhibitions when it came to his drinking, especially after leaving them all nearly retching after his initial spew. The smell had slowly faded over the last couple of days, the cold winter air helping considerably, but it did little to change the overall attitude of those stuck inside. In fact, everyone's nerves seemed to be on edge, the slightest thing setting them off.

Ferrin joined the others and scooted back down to the floor and closed his eyes, wishing for the sweet relief of sleep to wash away the cramped muscles in his back. As tired as he was, it came more swiftly than expected.

The door shot open, and Ferrin jerked awake, sunlight trailing in behind the white-robed guard, spilling around his arms and legs as he stood in the doorway. "Time to eat." The guard motioned toward the door, and two men stepped inside, carrying two trays of drinks, some freshly baked biscuits, and even some ham and eggs to go with them.

"What's the occasion?" Ferrin asked as he attempted to scoop the eggs into his spoon with cuffed hands.

"Sylas wishes you to join him today as he finishes with the last of your wielder council."

Ferrin suddenly lost his appetite and dropped the spoon back onto his plate. "You can tell him that I'd as soon lick the retch off these floors than spend an extra moment in his company."

"We aren't giving you a choice." The guards walked into the room and yanked him to his feet before he got a chance to touch his food and marched him out the door.

Elson called after him. "If you see Harlin, poke him in the eye for me!"

I'll poke him in the eye, Ferrin mused. *With a long dagger.* He smiled at the pleasant thought as the men took him through the master bedchamber. He was surprised to find a set of ropes tied to each of the four bedposts. He wondered if that had anything to do with Joren. Ferrin could have seen Sylas ordering himself strapped to the bed for safekeeping.

He wondered if the guards knew what was happening. They had to have suspected something. At least one of them would have known. There's no way Sylas could have tied himself to the bed.

Leaving the room, they headed down to the dining room. From the back, Ferrin thought it was Harlin at the table, and his heart skipped a beat, nearly risking everything to lunge at the man, but then the man turned, and Ferrin realized it wasn't Harlin at all, but Sylas wearing Harlin's clothes. It was strange to see Cheeks in such fine apparel, considering that dressing up for an inquisitor would have meant nothing more than having the blood washed from his whites.

The guards stood Ferrin behind a seat on the opposite side of the table, and one of them walked over and unhooked a chain from around his neck and handed it to Sylas. The durma key swung from the end.

Sylas hung the chain around his neck, then downed the rest of whatever was in his goblet before leaning back in his seat with a satisfied grin. "Who would have ever thought that one day you and I would be sharing a lord's table together?

Remarkable how things turn out, isn't it?" He raised his arms high enough to stare at his new hands, flipping them over in admiration. "Quite remarkable what magic can do." He glanced across the table. "We aren't so different, you and I. Cut from the same cloth. Aberrations that the world wishes to make disappear. The only difference is that you wish to run and hide, while I tend to embrace my differences and use them to my advantage."

"The difference," Ferrin said, "is that you're a flaming lunatic who gets his enjoyment through the suffering of others."

Sylas chuckled, then stood from the table. "Come, I have something for you. A gift."

One of the guards standing behind Ferrin stepped forward and hit him on the arm, signaling him to move. Reluctantly, he did, and followed Sylas out of the dining room, where they walked side by side down the hall toward the front door.

They stopped in the entranceway, and Sylas waved Ferrin over to one of the closets on the right. "I think you'll enjoy this." As soon as Ferrin was standing directly in front of the door, Sylas opened it.

Chapter 73 | Ferrin

ERRIN'S HEART SKIPPED A BEAT as he looked down at the man lying in the closet.

Harlin crawled to his knees, squinting against the sudden onset of light, but as soon as his eyes adjusted, he looked up, and the blood drained from his face. He jerked against his bonds, whatever he was saying completely muffled by the gag as he clawed his way back behind the coats. Oddly enough, it wasn't Sylas he was trying to escape from. It was Ferrin.

Sylas laughed and turned to Ferrin. "What, no witty remark? No long-awaited quip that you've been saving up all these months while wasting away in your cell? Come, come, my dear smith. The very least you could do is give him a good kick in the face. It will make you feel much better."

Ferrin looked down at the slobbering lord, and for the briefest of moments, he felt a twinge of pity . . . but it soon passed, and he kicked Harlin as hard as he could in the side of his face, sending his head ricocheting off the back wall.

Sylas was right, though Ferrin hated to admit it. That did feel good. "What do you plan to do with him?"

Sylas looked down at the sniveling weasel and thumbed his chin. "I haven't yet decided. Depends on how cooperative he will be."

Harlin started mumbling once again, bobbing his head up and down, practically doing obeisance on the floor as he tried to reassure Sylas that he would do whatever it took to save his own skin, even if it meant selling out his family, which by all accounts, the wielder council was.

Just looking at the way he was groveling before the inquisitor had Ferrin wanting to kick him again, but Sylas was already signaling the guards behind them, who had now grown in number. Ferrin moved aside and watched as the men lifted the coward to his feet and marched him out the door. He glared at Ferrin as he passed, blood running from his nose and the imprint of Ferrin's boot on the side of his cheek.

"If all goes well today," Sylas said, choosing a gaudy black-and-lavender fur-lined coat from the closet and sliding it on, "you might just be reunited with your sister by tomorrow morning. Now wouldn't that be nice?" He watched Ferrin a moment, then grabbed a silver-handled cane resting in the corner and walked out the front doors and down the steps to the carriage house, where one of Harlin's finest carriages was waiting on their arrival.

The wind was cold across the city, coming down off the Northern Heights, but the sky was clear, and the sun's rays warmed Ferrin's face as he followed the others down the sidewalk. He reached the covered carriage about the time they were tossing Harlin inside. Ferrin couldn't help but chuckle, but he did his best not to let Sylas see it. The man, for some unknown reason was trying to bond with him. In his own twisted and depraved mind, Sylas seemed to view Ferrin as something akin to a friend.

Of course, the inquisitor knew nothing of true friendship. An image of Myron's face appeared, and Ferrin's earlier enjoyment at Harlin's expense temporarily vanished, replaced with a momentary wave of grief.

With the guards' help, Ferrin climbed up into the carriage. It was one of the largest he'd ever been in. Most sat four comfortably, but this one had room to spare. He took the seat opposite Sylas, which happened to be the same seat Harlin was cowering on in the corner. Sylas smiled, admiring the plush interior, then looked at Ferrin.

"I could get used to this."

Sylas struck the top of the roof with the silver-handled cane, and the carriage jolted down the brick drive toward the front gates.

Ferrin glanced out the window, surprised to find no uniformed guards riding alongside. He turned and looked out the back. There were none there as well. The only others with them were the two men on the driver's seat. Ferrin's heart started to race. He was completely alone with the very two people he wanted to kill. It couldn't have been more perfect, except he knew he couldn't kill Sylas, not until he found out where his sister was being held.

But that didn't mean he couldn't torture the information out of him. Lenara wasn't there to stop him.

Ferrin leaped from his seat. If he could land one solid punch, he might be able to knock Sylas unconscious before he could use the key on him. He swung with all his might, and his fist slammed against an invisible wall, and he stumbled to the side. Suddenly, he was thrown backward against his seat with something pressing into him so hard he began to lose his breath.

Sylas laughed. "Did you think I came unprepared? You know me better than that, smith." Sylas pointed to the front window. One of the drivers was looking inside, his hand raised. "The Tower's bulradoer are quite handy to have around, don't you think?"

Ferrin hadn't given the dark-robed man more than a passing glance when first climbing aboard, assuming him to be just another footman. He'd been too focused on Harlin to pay more attention.

Sylas's smile faded. "You try something like that again, though, and . . ." He pulled his hand out of his pocket to reveal the durma key.

The pressure lifted from Ferrin's chest, and the man in the front seat turned back around.

Sylas grinned once more. "I've found that it is much easier to capture wielders when they don't see you coming. Riding up the drive of a house with a contingent of Black Watch tends to send the wrong message. This way, they invite you inside, and sometimes there is even a nice cup of tea."

Ferrin had suffered unholy amounts of abuse at the hands of the inquisitor, but this was a different type of torture. It sounded like Sylas planned on forcing him to be a spectator, helpless to do anything while Sylas rounded up his friends. "Where are we going?"

Sylas looked at Harlin. "I believe her name is Ella. Has the ability to control emotions, so I hear."

Ferrin gritted his teeth. The last time he'd seen Ella was at the wielder council dinner party, the night of his betrayal.

They drove through the center of town, stopping just beyond the garment district at a couple of bunched-up buildings used to house some of Rhowynn's poorer communities. Ferrin knew Ella had been having some financial difficulties, but he didn't know it had gotten this bad. Worse yet, before he had been captured, she had also taken on the responsibility and guardianship of Old Mother Luka, the oldest, and quite senile, member of the council.

Sylas leaned forward and undid Harlin's ropes, loosening his hands and feet. He even went so far as to pull out a thin scarf and wipe the blood from Harlin's lip before tying the same scarf around Harlin's neck to hide his shiny new collar. Sylas pursed his lips a moment as he sat back to get a good look at Harlin's bruised face. "Perhaps we should have waited to kick him until after our visit. Oh well, not much we can do about it now. It will have to do." He turned and looked at Ferrin. "Not much we can do about those either," he said, glancing down at the shackles. "You'll just have to stand behind us and hope they don't notice."

Sylas waited for the bulradoer to hop down and open the door before stepping out and sucking in a deep breath of air, which had him coughing and wiping a hanky in front of his nose. "This place smells awful."

Ferrin stared at the man. Was this the same person who'd spend hours and hours every day cutting bits and pieces off people until they soiled themselves? A man who lived and worked in the lowest form of sewer you could find? Ferrin felt like he was living a dream where everything was topsy-turvy. It made Sylas even more disturbing, if that was possible.

Harlin was the next out, leaving Ferrin sitting in the carriage.

Sylas turned. "What are you waiting for?"

"I'm not going in there to watch you round up my friends."

"You will if you want to keep me from torturing them while I do. From what Harlin here tells me, it doesn't sound like the old woman would last very long if I did."

Ferrin gritted his teeth and stepped out of the carriage. He trudged slowly behind Sylas and Harlin as they made their way inside the tenement and up the rickety stairs to the third floor, where Sylas knocked, and they waited. The bulradoer stood just behind Ferrin, guarding against any attempted escape.

A rat scurried across Harlin's shoes, and he yelped. Sylas stabbed the rodent with the bottom of his cane and smiled at the squeal it made.

The light patter of footsteps could be heard on the other side of the door before it opened. Ferrin tensed when he saw the young woman standing in the doorway. Ella wore a faded blue-and-yellow dress under a somewhat ratty wool cloak, with what looked like several layers of thick stockings to keep her feet and legs warm. The building was just as cold on the inside as the out.

Ferrin wished he could warn her, shout for her to run, not that there was anywhere she could have gone, but at least then he wouldn't feel so guilty.

"Lord Harlin?" Ella looked befuddled. She coughed a hoarse, raspy cough that had her swallowing whatever had come loose. "Is there something I can help you with?"

Harlin looked at Sylas. Ferrin could see the hesitancy in the man's eyes, but he continued. "Ella, this is Lord Sylas, a friend of mine who would like to help you and Mother Luka, if he may. Might we come in?"

Sylas flashed his deepest, most sincere smile as he removed his hat and bowed from the waist. "It's a pleasure to meet you, my dear."

Ella smiled and stepped aside. "It's a pleasure to meet you, Lord Sylas. Please, come in." Ferrin, who was thankful to be wearing a cloak with a hood, turned his head away so she wouldn't see his face as he followed the others into the very small one-room living quarter. In the back were two cots, one of which was occupied. Mother Luka had her back turned and was presently snoring.

Ella looked around embarrassedly and rushed over to grab two crates that were turned on end around a single-leg table. She carried them over and laid them in front of Harlin and Sylas. "I'm afraid this is all the seating I can offer. I wasn't expecting company."

Ferrin looked around the quaint hovel. Why hadn't she let them know how bad it had gotten? Ferrin would have certainly helped. At the very least, he could have offered them a place with him and Myriah.

"It's quite all right, Ella," Harlin said as he walked across the room to where Mother Luka lay shivering under her blankets. "How is she doing today?"

Ella blew on her hands, then rubbed them together. "Not so well, I'm afraid. We ran out of wood two days ago, and the coal is too expensive this time of year." She put on a brave face. "We are thankful for what you and Lady Myriah have done."

"Oh?" Harlin turned, looking a little puzzled.

"The food has been a blessing," she said. "We wouldn't have made it without your generosity."

Harlin smiled, but he still looked like he had no idea what she was talking about. "Think nothing of it, my dear."

Ferrin shook his head. What sort of generosity was it when he lived on an estate with no less than a dozen bedchambers, and he let an old woman and her young caretaker die from exposure? It wasn't like these were just random people off the street. They were members of the wielder family. They were friends.

Harlin leaned over the old woman's cot as if to inspect her illness. Ferrin heard a metallic click. Old Mother Luka shot up in her bed and screamed. Ferrin was so stunned by the old woman's reaction he stumbled backward, nearly colliding with the bulradoer.

Ella was just as startled as the others, practically freezing in place. Before she could turn or run to help, Sylas snapped a second collar around her neck from behind. She grabbed at the metal ring in a panic, attempting to pull it off, her eyes shifting back and forth like a cornered alley cat looking for a way of escape.

"What is this?" she asked. "Lord Harlin, what are you doing?" Ella ran to the old woman's side and wrapped her arms around her to stop her screams.

"I'm sorry, Ella," Harlin said, backing away. "I didn't have a choice." He pulled down the scarf hiding his own collar.

Ella looked over at Sylas in confusion. "Who are you? Why are you doing this?"

Sylas smiled. "I'll let my friend here explain everything to you as I have a quick word with our Lord Harlin here about the location of our next stop." He turned and leaned over to Ferrin. "Bring them down to the carriage as soon as you're through, and make sure that old hag doesn't open her mouth. If she screams even once, I'll use the key on her, and I'll make it last for hours." Sylas motioned for Harlin to join him, and they left the room, shutting the door as they went. Ferrin could hear the creak of the steps in the hall as they headed down the stairs.

Unfortunately, he left the bulradoer there with them. If Ferrin could subdue the bulradoer, then perhaps he could use his key to release Ella and Mother Luka. Frantically, he glanced around the room for something to use as a weapon. Closest thing he could find was one of the empty crates Ella had turned over for them to use as a makeshift seat. He was going to have to be fast.

He grabbed the crate and spun as fast as he could, hoping to catch the wielder in the head before he had a chance to—

Ferrin was hit by a fist of air that had him sailing overtop their cots and slamming into the wall on the other side, splitting the wood. He landed on his hands and knees.

"Try that again," the bulradoer said, "and I'll cook you alive." He raised his hand, and a ball of flame appeared.

Ferrin crawled back to his feet and pulled back his hood.

Ella's face blanched. "Ferrin? Is that you? How?"

Ferrin helped the two of them up and took a moment to quickly explain how and why he was there, about his capture, and his time in the Tower, finishing with his escape. "Just do what they tell you. Don't give them an excuse to hurt you." He looked at Mother Luka, who was still shaking. "It might be best if we gag her."

Ella's eyes widened. "I'll do no such thing."

"Can you guarantee you can keep her quiet? If she cries out even once, Sylas will use the collar to torture her. And believe me, that's not something you want to see happen. It might not be pleasant, but if you want to keep her alive, then we need to do it."

Ella's hands were shaking. In fact, her whole body was shaking as she finally nodded. With Ferrin's help, they managed to use a piece of thin lace to tie around Mother Luka's mouth. Surprisingly, the old woman didn't argue or put up a fight. She almost seemed to think it was all some sort of game. She even laughed at one point. Ferrin only hoped it stayed that way.

"Hurry up," the bulradoer said, waiting by the door.

With Ella's help, Ferrin managed to get Mother Luka down the stairs and into the awaiting carriage. Ferrin took the seat next to Sylas to keep the two women from having to. With a couple taps of his cane on the ceiling, the carriage started off once again.

"I wasn't sure if you had it in you, smith," Sylas said with a proud grin as he stared at the gag in Mother Luka's mouth. "One more stop to make, and I believe this one will hold some sentimental value. In fact, from what Harlin tells me, you might even want to be the one to collar him yourself."

Ferrin looked at Harlin, unsure as to what Sylas was referring to, but Harlin was too busy staring out the window to bother looking back. "Why? Where are we going?"

"We are going to pay a visit to an old friend of yours. I believe his name is . . . Garreth?"

Garreth was hardly a friend, but even still, Ferrin would have never wished to see him imprisoned by the Tower. "I have no intention of collaring anyone, unless of course you wish to hold your neck out."

Sylas chuckled. "You and your jokes."

The carriage passed through the eastern gates of the city, and they started into the forest between the walls of Rhowynn and the lower foothills of the Northern Heights. Ferrin had no idea where Garreth lived, but given his propensity for all things wood, it made sense that the man would choose to live in a place surrounded by it.

They hadn't ridden too far out of town before the carriage turned off the main road and onto a smaller, rougher lane that had the carriage and those inside bouncing up and down with each new divot the wheels struck. Sylas looked to be growing rather annoyed, while Mother Luka swung her arms about each time she was sent flying from her cushioned seat. Ella, who was seated between Mother Luka and Harlin, was too preoccupied with keeping the old woman from cracking her skull on the roof to show her own feelings, while Harlin kept to his huddled position in the corner, his face looking rather green.

The carriage finally came to a stop outside a small snow-covered cottage.

Ferrin climbed out of the carriage behind Sylas and Harlin and started up the newly shoveled walk toward the front of the house. The bulradoer moved up behind, his black robes contrasting sharply against the fallen snow.

There were several ribbons tied around the front porch posts for Winter's Eve. Ferrin couldn't believe another year had already come and gone. He used to enjoy the Winter's Eve celebrations in town: the beautiful colors and decorations, the lanterns hanging in the windows, the friendly way people you didn't know would wish you well as you strolled down the street. It was the one time of the year when things seemed to find a sense of peace—and here he was spending that time going door to door, helping Sylas round up members of the wielder council for the Tower.

Harlin knocked on the door and took a step back beside Sylas who, once again, put on a cheerful face. A woman came to the door—Garreth's wife. Ferrin had only seen her once or twice during their council banquets, since she generally stayed home to watch their kids. Much like Ella, Garreth's wife looked similarly confused by the visit.

"Lord Harlin? Can I—"

Before she could even finish her sentence, Sylas lunged forward and grabbed the woman by the neck and yanked her out the door.

"What are you doing?" Harlin shouted.

Ferrin dove at the inquisitor but hit another invisible wall from the bulradoer.

Garreth, who was just inside the door, swung a spiked cudgel at Harlin, and Harlin jumped backward. He barely missed getting his head lopped off as he landed in a pile of snow just off the porch. Garreth stepped through the door and laid his hand on the front logs of their home, and spikes, similar to that of his club, tore from the sides of the wood.

"Enough!" Sylas shouted, whipping out a knife from his sleeve and cutting into the soft flesh on the side of Garreth's wife's neck. She squealed, and Garreth released his grip on the logs.

"Stop! Please, don't hurt her!"

"Put down the weapon!" Sylas demanded, and Garreth quickly dropped his club onto the porch and raised his hands.

Ferrin stared beyond him back into the house. He thought he saw movement and prayed that Garreth's kids had enough sense not to show themselves.

Sylas reached into his coat and pulled out a collar and handed it to Ferrin, but Ferrin took a step back. "I want no part of this!"

Garreth moved to try seeing who was behind the hood, but Ferrin kept his head lowered enough that he couldn't.

Sylas tossed the collar to Harlin. "Fine. You do it."

Harlin picked himself up from the snow and walked over and grabbed the collar. He then started toward Garreth, but a single growl from the woodsman, and Harlin backed away.

"Don't make me use the key on you," Sylas said.

"Please, no! I beg you!" Harlin turned and tossed the collar to Garreth. "Put it on."

If Garreth's eyes could kill, Harlin would have been dead a hundred times over. "You flaming coward! Is this what happened to Ferrin? Did you sell him out too?"

Harlin didn't say anything, too afraid to speak.

"Well?" Sylas said, turning to Ferrin. "I believe that answer would be best coming from you, wouldn't it?"

Ferrin raised his hands, making sure Garreth saw that they were shackled, and pulled back his hood.

Garreth's reaction was identical to Ella's, except without the notable gasp. "I don't understand. Are you a part of this?"

"No. I've been a prisoner of the Tower for the last year."

"And we were having such a wonderful time of it too," Sylas said sarcastically. "At least until he stuck a knife in my neck and escaped." He spared a quick glance at Ferrin. "Gave us quite the chase, didn't you? He crossed from one side of Aldor to the other just to rescue his sister, and what does he find? The very man who betrayed him had taken her to wife." Sylas roared with laughter. "I couldn't have hurt him more had he spent every day on the rack for the next six months." Sylas looked at Harlin. "And I thought I was a proficient torturer. You have far surpassed me." He laughed once more.

Garreth looked more confused now than when he had seen Ferrin in the first place. The one thing he didn't look confused by, though, was his hatred for Harlin as he finally snapped the collar around his own neck. "I'm going to kill you, Harlin, and it won't be swift. I'll mount your head to the front of my house. That way every time I step outside, I can spit in your face."

Sylas nearly doubled over, he was laughing so hard. "Quite the friends you have here, my dear nobleman." He smeared his fingers through the blood running down Garreth's wife's neck.

"He's no friend of mine!" Garreth spat. He looked to Sylas. "You have me. Now let my wife go. She can do you no harm. She's not ven'ae."

"Yes, that is what Harlin tells me. However, if there's one thing I've learned when it comes to making people talk, it's that nothing works quite so well as torture, and no torture works quite so well as on those who you care about most." He winked at Ferrin. "As long as I have your wife, I'm assured of your cooperation. And if that isn't enough, I direct your attention to the man standing behind our good smith. He is one of the Tower's bulradoer. I'm sure you know what that means."

Garreth gulped as he glanced past Ferrin to the man in the black robes.

"And if that is not convincing enough, there is always this." Sylas held up the silver key.

"What's that supposed to—"

The silver rod turned blue, and before Ferrin could even prepare himself, another wave of incredible pain tore through him, and he dropped face first into the snow. Harlin squealed as he went down. Garreth managed to get half a shout out before his throat squeezed shut.

Sylas lowered the key, but it took a while for the ache to subside enough to catch their breath. Ferrin was the first back to his feet. He walked over and helped Garreth, leaving Harlin to wallow in the snow, which he had colored with his now-empty bladder.

Sylas turned and pointed back toward the awaited carriage. "Your ride awaits."

To Garreth and his wife's credit, neither so much as glanced over their shoulders toward the house as they were being marched down the walkway. It was clear they wanted to give Sylas no reason to believe that anyone else lived there. Ferrin was surprised that Harlin hadn't mentioned it. Perhaps that was further than even he was willing to go.

Ferrin climbed aboard behind Sylas, who kept Garreth's wife close at hand, and took a seat next to her, leaving only one space open on the other seat, which Garreth took. Ella was whimpering in the corner with her arm around Mother Luka as the others climbed on board, the cloth gag still in place.

"I see we're not the only ones Harlin has betrayed today," Garreth said as he scooted in beside Mother Luka, who waved at him.

Harlin took one look at the seating arrangements, realizing there were no empty places left, and stopped.

"I'll . . . I'll just sit up top with the drivers."

"Get in here, where I can keep an eye on you," Sylas said.

Harlin turned and looked at the woods.

"Don't even think about it."

The bulradoer moved up alongside Harlin and practically shoved him into the only place left for him to go. The floor.

"Well, my dear smith, it appears you might be in luck. Barring no uncertain calamity befalling us, by this time tomorrow you might be sharing a wagon with your sister." Sylas smiled. "I do so look forward to your company on the long ride back to the Tower. What conversations we will have." Sylas struck the carriage roof. "Back to the house!"

With a jolt that had Harlin rolling around on the floor, the carriage took off.

Ferrin looked at the inquisitor, his heart pounding to the beat of the horses' hooves.

By this time tomorrow, one of the two of them would mostly likely be dead.

Chapter 74 | Ty

TY WOKE TO A SPLITTING HEADACHE. "What happened?" He opened his eyes. Everything around him was spinning. He tried sitting up, but a strong hand pushed him back down, which was a good thing considering the dizziness that washed over him nearly had him emptying his stomach. "I don't feel right."

"You took quite the blow to the head."

Ty recognized his brother's voice and smiled. "What happened?"

"We were captured, is what happened."

Ty bolted upright. "Mangora!" The world spun, and he grabbed the bars in front of him and retched over the right side of the wagon, feeling better immediately afterward. He wiped his mouth and turned. "I saw her, Breen. She was there when we first came out of the mirror."

"I know. They were waiting for us. I don't know how, but they knew we were coming."

Ty slumped against the bars. "How is that possible? How could they have even known we were going after the key?" Ty gasped and grabbed for his neck.

"Don't bother," Breen said grimly. "She already took it."

"And she took my gold and jewels," Narendi groused, sounding more upset about that than the fact that they were now prisoners of the White Tower.

Ty raised his hand and felt the lump on the back of his head and winced.

"How long have I been out?"

"You were in and out most of the night."

"What about Kraea?"

Breen pointed to the back of the wagon. "They have her locked in the next one over. She's been whining most the night. At least, I think it's whining. Don't rightly know. Not like I've had much experience with draakars. The bulradoer seemed awful excited by her presence, though."

"There's bulradoer here as well?"

"Apparently, Mangora brought quite the force with her this time. I don't think she intends to go back empty-handed again. Strangely enough, she's been by nearly every hour to check on you. The way she acts, you'd think she was your grandmother." Breen smiled. "Okay, maybe great-great-grandmother."

"Why would she—"

The front of the thick canvas tarp draped over their wagon lifted. "Ah, I see the faeling is finally awake."

The sharp gravelly voice pierced Ty to his very soul, practically incapacitating him as a sudden rush of memories flooded his mind: memories of his mother being eaten alive by spiders, memories of his standoff with the dark witch in front of his home, memories of her in his mind, controlling him, forcing him to kill his family and friends.

"I have so looked forward to our next meeting," Mangora said. "I feel as though we have a special bond, you and I, a unique kinship." She cackled. "I guess this is what it feels like to be joined to another. I never much saw the practicality of sharing one's life with someone else, but after sharing yours, I can see the amusement."

Ty shot to his feet and called on his flames, aiming both palms directly at her.

Mangora leaned back and roared.

Ty looked at his hands. There was no fire, not even a puff of smoke. "What did you do to me?"

Mangora pointed to Ty's neck, her bony finger half hidden by her eerie-looking spider ring with its legs wrapped snuggly around her flesh. Its abdomen was made from a reddish stone that glowed softly in the early morning light. Ty reached for his neck, and his fingers clasped around a cold piece of metal. He turned and looked at Breen and Narendi, surprised by the fact that they, too, were wearing collars and he hadn't even noticed. That must have been the source of the wrongness he was feeling. He thought it was just the sickness.

"Where is the rest of the shorlock?" Mangora demanded. "Where's the bloodstone? You wouldn't have come this far without it. Give it to me!"

"How did you know we were looking for it?"

Mangora smiled. "We have our ways."

"What does that mean?"

"It means the Tower has ears everywhere."

"How did you know where to find us? You couldn't have possibly known where we were."

"True. We had no idea where you were. Didn't even know if you were still alive. The one thing we did know, however, is where you would eventually have to come. And I must admit, you made good time. You almost beat us here. We only just arrived a few short days ago." She chuckled. "Imagine how foolish I would have felt had I shown up a few days later and sat here for weeks or even months, and all for nothing."

Ty laughed. "I guess your luck just ran out after all, 'cause I don't have the missing piece." As upset as Ty was at having left the final piece of the key behind in exchange for Kraea, he had to admit it was almost worth it to see the look on Mangora's face.

Mangora stared up at him through the bars, her crooked yellow teeth bared, clearly trying to determine if he was telling her the truth. Her face suddenly shifted into a sneer. "Then you leave me with little choice. If you won't talk, I guess I will have to find a way to persuade you."

She turned to the Tower guards standing beside her. "We'll give our young friend here a moment to reconsider. If he doesn't, then take those two," she said, pointing at Breen and Narendi, "and I'll see if I can't get one of them to talk. At the very least, my Syglara hasn't been fed today." She turned and wiggled her finger to their left, which was obscured by the tarp hanging partway down. Suddenly the cage shook, and several giant hairy legs poked through the bars where the canvas had been pulled back.

Ty flung himself back against the bars at the back to escape the giant spider's legs, pulling Narendi with him. She actually shrieked when she saw the creature. Breen was there as well, pressing against the back.

The wagon behind theirs began to jostle back and forth as Kraea roared at the giant spider, which turned and hissed in reply.

Mangora look at the draakar and smiled. "The arachnobes and the draakar, what few are left, are natural enemies. It is quite impressive that you have one. Wherever did you find her? As far as I know, their nests have only been seen around the caves of the Caldera. And where's her mother? Most draakar spend their early years learning to hunt. This one doesn't look old enough to have even left the nest."

Kraea growled through the bars, this time at Mangora, but Mangora stared the creature down.

"What did she say? I know you can hear her. Your faerie blood allows it, so don't try hiding the fact."

In reality, Kraea hadn't said anything. Her growl was simply that, a growl. "She says that she has a terrible itch on the side of her neck, and she would be ever so grateful if you were to stick your arm through the bar and scratch it."

Mangora chuckled.

Kraea shot Ty a harsh look. *"I said no such thing."*

"Actually," Ty continued, "she says you are one of the ugliest blood sacks she has ever seen, and as soon as she breaks free, she is going to use your bones to clean her teeth."

"I'm going to chew on you, *you fool, if you don't close your mouth! Are you trying to get me killed?"*

Ty's grin shriveled on his face. *"Sorry. I didn't think about that."* The last thing he needed was someone else's blood on his hands. His connection to the creature was the one thing he could hold on to that Mangora couldn't take from him. At least, he hoped she couldn't take it.

Mangora stared at Kraea's wagon a bit longer. "I've never had a live draakar to study. I look forward to the opportunity." The way she said it sent a chill down Ty's back.

Kraea snarled. *"Thanks for that, faerie."*

"My name is Ty and . . . I'm sorry. I just really hate this woman."

Mangora turned back around. "I will give you some time to consider your options. Hopefully, your friends will be able to persuade you to talk. If not, I brought along an inquisitor who will be more than happy to have a crack at it. There's no one better suited to getting information than an inquisitor." She pointed to the guards, and they cautiously walked forward and pulled the canvas back down over their side of the bars, keeping as far from the arachnobe as possible.

With another loud cackle that sounded like a bag of rocks grinding against each other, Mangora called Syglara back down from their cage, and they walked off together.

Ty tried peeking around the corner of the canvas, but all he could see was snow-covered rock. Their wagon seemed to be sitting inside a narrow pass of some sort. He wondered which mountain chain they had stepped into. "What are we going to do?" he asked, resting against the bars and blowing into his hands, which were already beginning to shake from the cold. "She thinks we have the missing piece."

"I know," Breen said. "She didn't believe me any more than you."

"What if I can't persuade her? She's talking about turning you over to an inquisitor."

Breen tucked his hair back behind his ears. "I've heard rumors about what the inquisitors do. Don't have any desire to find out."

"What is faeling?" Narendi asked. "She called you faeling. What is this?"

Breen looked at Ty with a good-luck-explaining-that expression on his face.

Ty sat down beside the bars. "Remember when I told you that I'm not exactly like other magic wielders because I have more than one gift?" She nodded. "That's because I'm not like other humans either." He paused to judge whether or not he should continue, but other than a cocked eyebrow, she didn't seem too unsettled so far. "I'm only half human. I'm also half faerie."

"What does this mean . . . faerie?"

Ty had tried explaining about the Fae in a very simplistic way while they were staying with the Imbatoo. He told them of their arrival and how it was the Fae who had brought magic into the realm of man in the first place, but this time he went into more detail, a history lesson of everything he and Breen knew about the topic, which admittedly wasn't much. By the time he was done, she was looking at him considerably differently.

"And you are one of these faerie? You don't look like a faerie."

"Oh, you've seen a faerie before, have you?" Ty asked.

"No."

"Then how do you know I don't look like one?" He took his cap off and pointed to the top of his head. "See? I have white hair."

"You say these Fae are evil, and you do not look evil." She leaned forward and rubbed her hand across the top of his head. "I like your hair. Yes, I have chosen well with my vows." She gave him as smug expression as she looked him over— like she had just won the prize stallion at the fair.

Ty gritted his teeth but didn't bother arguing. It seemed no matter what he said, she was going to ignore it and do whatever she wanted.

"How do we make this witch believe?" Narendi asked.

Ty looked at Breen, his shoulders slumping under the weight of the question. He had no idea.

"What I want to know," Breen said, "is how did that trader back at the Live Market end up with the stone in the first place? Did he somehow pass the final test himself?"

Ty stiffened. "If he did, does that mean we left the stone for nothing?"

Breen hesitated. "How else could he have gotten it? Every piece of the key required some form of test that involved one of four traits: faith, wisdom, strength, and compassion."

"You left my mother to die. How is that compassionate?"

Ty turned and stared out the back of their cage at Kraea, where she lay curled on top of the hay they'd thrown inside to give her a little extra warmth. "I didn't leave your mother to die. I promised her I'd take you with me, and I did." He wanted to tell her how much he'd lost in doing so, but having lost his own mother, he couldn't bring himself to do it.

Kraea blew out her lips, sending pieces of straw in all directions.

"What was that about?" Breen asked, both he and Narendi looking at the draakar's wagon.

"Nothing. She's hurting."

"I know her feeling," Narendi said, a little sadness in her own eyes as well.

Ty took a deep breath and shook his head. So many people had given up so much for him to have gotten this far, and now it seemed it was all for nothing. "Perhaps it was a good thing we didn't get the final piece."

Breen started to open his mouth, but then shut it with a nod. "As much as I hate to admit it, you could be right. I can't imagine what would happen if the White Tower were to ever get their hands on this wizarding school. The way Nyalis talks, it would be the downfall of us all."

"I still want to know how they knew we were even looking for the shorlock in the first place."

"I want to know how we tell her we don't have it," Narendi said.

Ty pressed his fists against the sides of his head. "I don't know what to do." He grabbed at the collar and yanked. "Not with this thing on my neck." He pulled until his neck hurt.

"You're wasting your strength," Breen said. "I've already tried. Whatever these things are, they aren't coming off. There's not even a keyhole that I can see."

Sounds of boots crushing fallen snow had them all turning. The canvas parted.

"Time's up," Mangora's irritating voice called out as she rode in on Syglara. A couple of Black Watch guards tied back the rest of the canvas. Mangora climbed down off the great spider's back and walked over to the side of their cage and peered in. "Are you going to tell me where you're hiding the bloodstone, or do I have to cut it out of your companions? And don't tell me you didn't bring it with you. I know better."

Ty wanted to reach through the bars and strangle the life out of her, but Mangora had wisely kept her distance. "I can't give you what I don't have. Here," he said, standing up and spinning in a circle. "Search us! You'll see we don't have it. You saw us come through the mirror. You know we didn't have time to hide anything. We didn't even know you were there."

Mangora's lips tightened. "Fine. Have it your way. Let's start with her," she said, pointing at Narendi. Three of the guards walked around to the back and unlocked the door.

"No!" Ty shouted desperately. "She doesn't have it. I'm telling you, we left it at the Market. We traded it for Kraea."

"What kind of fool do you take me for, boy? No one would trade the Keep of Aero'set for an overgrown lizard, not even someone as gullible as you."

"You'd be surprised," Breen mumbled under his breath as he got to his feet.

Three more guards stood outside the cage with bows lifted, their arrows pointed at Breen and Ty, letting them know that if they interfered, they would regret it. The guards at the back opened the door and stepped inside, cautiously walking toward the front of the wagon where the three were pressed up against the wood.

As soon as they grabbed Narendi, Kraea bellowed out an angry roar, which distracted the two men enough for Narendi to leap on the first, throwing her full body weight around the man and sending him crashing to the floor. Breen grabbed the second and spun him around just as the archers unleashed their arrows. The guard in front of Breen took two to the chest. The third arrow whizzed past Ty's head as he threw himself on the floor to keep from getting shot.

Narendi grabbed a handful of the first guard's hair and his chin and twisted his neck around till it popped. She shoved the dead man off her and tried crawling back to her feet, but not before half a dozen more guards climbed in the back and threw everyone to the ground. They dragged Narendi out, kicking and screaming.

The remaining guards held Ty and Breen to the floor until they had managed to remove their dead. As soon as they were released, Ty and Breen ran for the door, but the guards shut it before they could reach it. A row of archers stood at the back with their bows up.

"Don't shoot the white-haired one!" Mangora shouted at the men, and several bows quickly shifted to Breen.

"Please!" Ty begged as he watched them carry Narendi off. "She doesn't have anything to do with this. She doesn't know anything. Wait! I'll . . . I'll show you where it is! Please, don't hurt her."

"Ty, what are you doing?" Breen hissed. He turned away from the cage, keeping his voice lowered. "We don't have the stone."

"She doesn't know that," he whispered back. "Do you have a better idea?"

Mangora turned and walked back to the wagon, anticipation flashing in her eyes. "What did you say?"

"I said I'll show you where I hid the stone, but you have to promise not to hurt her."

"I promise I most certainly will if you don't."

Ty clenched his teeth so tight his jaw ached. He wanted to kill her so badly he could taste it. "Fine. Let her go, and I'll show you."

Mangora pointed at what appeared to be the captain of this particular regiment, by the patch on his sleeve, similar to that of the one Ty remembered seeing Captain Hatch wear back in Easthaven. "Get him out of there."

"What about the big one?" the captain asked.

Mangora looked at Ty's brother a moment. "Bring all of them just in case."

The captain pointed to a couple of guards, and they rushed over with a set of keys and unlocked the door once again. "You heard her," the captain shouted. "Get out! And don't try anything stupid, or my archers will finish what they started." He addressed Breen, since Mangora had just ordered them not to shoot Ty.

Breen was the first out, Ty right behind. Both stood at the back, waiting to see what the Tower guards would do with Narendi. "Well, are you going to release her?" Ty asked.

"When I see my stone," Mangora answered. "Now where is it?" She looked at him like she expected him to magically pull it out of his pocket.

"Where's the mirror?"

Mangora pointed back down the mountain trail, where the wagons were presently holed up.

Ty turned and walked past the archers, sparing a quick glance at Kraea, who was standing at the edge of her cage watching them walk by. *"If you find a way to escape,"* he said, using their link, *"don't hesitate. And don't worry about us. Find someplace to hide and stay there."*

"I have no intention of worrying about you," she said.

"You don't have to sound so pleased about it." Ty shook his head as he continued on down the narrow crevice in the rock, his boots sinking to the ankles in snow. He kept his ears perked, glancing up toward the higher rock every so often as they made their way deeper into the mountainside.

Behind him, Breen and Narendi were being held by a line of guards plus a couple of those black-robed bulradoer, and between Ty and them was Mangora and her monstrous spider, who, every time he looked its way, began clicking its hideous mandibles. Ty had no doubt had Mangora not been there to control it, Syglara would have been on top of Ty in a heartbeat.

Up ahead, he could hear the echoes of voices coming their way. He wondered if it was part of a patrol sent out to guard the mirror, but the closer the voices came, the less likely it seemed. Sure enough, before Ty had reached the corner of the next bend, a couple of fur-clad trappers stepped out.

Both stopped when they saw Ty and the long line of Black Watch guards behind him. However, one look at Syglara and the two men dropped their gear and pelts and took off running in the opposite direction.

"Get them!" Mangora shouted, and Syglara took off up the side of the rock with Mangora still on her back. How she managed to stay there without falling off,

Ty couldn't guess. They flew by with speeds that seemed altogether unnatural, the great spider's legs clicking against the hard stone as it snagged its footholds. It was truly a terrifying sight. Shouts and screams could be heard ahead as Ty and the rest of the guards ran to catch up. They found the two men lying in their own blood and guts, with Syglara standing over them, pieces of meat hanging from its mouth.

Mangora was searching through the men's clothing. As soon as the Black Watch arrived, she ordered them to do an even more thorough examination of the trappers, which resulted in the guards stripping the two men naked and tossing their bodies to the side for Syglara to feed on. The rest of the clothing was carefully combed through, but no bloodstone, as Mangora had called it, was found.

Mangora climbed back atop Syglara and ordered everyone forward. Syglara didn't seem too happy with leaving her food behind, but whatever Mangora said, she was quick to obey. Ty once again took the lead as they continued farther into the mountain pass. It wasn't much farther before Mangora directed Ty to another even smaller fissure in the rock on the left, which led back to an opening not much larger than the lobby of the East Inn.

Straight ahead, Ty could see part of the mirror's frame jutting out from the side of the rock as though built right into the mountainside itself. If not for the reflection it gave when he moved in for a closer look, it would have been difficult to spot, as the glass reflected the rock surrounding it. The problem was, now that they were there, what was he going to do? He reached for his pocket on instinct, but the little silver compass was no longer there either, not that it mattered. Even if he could remember what the names had been, which he couldn't, where were they going to go? Right back to the Live Market?

"Well?" Mangora said, as she climbed down off Syglara and started forward. "Where's the stone?"

"I, uh . . . it's over here," he said and walked over to the side of the mirror and began digging around in some of the loose rock around the edge. What was he going to do? He hadn't thought that far ahead, he was just trying to keep Mangora from killing Narendi and Breen. In the process, he'd ended up getting two other innocents killed. This was all his fault, and he couldn't think of how to get himself out of it.

"What's going on over there?" the witch hissed. "Where's my stone?"

Ty finally stopped his digging. It was over. He had hoped some chance of an idea would pop into his mind, but there was nothing. He finally stood and turned around. His hands were empty. "I . . . I couldn't find it."

"You what?"

"Someone must have taken it." He pointed back down the way they'd come. "Those trappers must have it."

"They have nothing!"

Ty fumbled for something, anything. "Then they must have hidden it." He turned and started digging through the rock once more, searching for one big enough to throw. "I found it!" He turned and threw the rock as hard as he could.

Mangora flung her arm to the side, and the rock spun to the right and hit the wall on the other side. Her eyes flared, and she flung her arm again, and Ty was struck by something hard, sending him flying backward into the mountainside.

"There's no stone here, is there?" Mangora shouted.

Ty shook his head. "No, I . . ."

Mangora turned and shouted at the men behind her. "Strip them all! I want that stone!"

The guards took Breen and Narendi and threw them up against the rock on either side of Ty, fronts facing the wall, and stripped all three down to their nothings. "There's no stone here, Mistress," the captain said, sounding almost as frustrated as Mangora.

Ty, already too embarrassed and too frozen to do anything else, quickly pulled his clothes back on, Breen and Narendi doing the same. All three turned back around when finished.

"I told you we don't have the stone," Ty said angrily, knowing there was nothing he could do to change their situation. "If you want it, you can find it at the Live Market in the Riverlands. Gave it to a nice fellow by the name of Dalibor in exchange for our freedom. Actually, no," Ty said with a smirk. "I guess you can't ask Dalibor. The last time I saw him, he was flying into the swamp with the bloodstone in his hands and a draakar around his waist."

Mangora hobbled over and looked Ty in the eyes, her face close enough for him to smell her breath. She smelled as though she'd been feeding on Syglara's leftovers. Bile rose in the back of his throat, and he fought to swallow it down. Mangora's lips parted, and for a moment, Ty thought she was going to bite him. "You really don't have it, do you?"

"I told you I didn't."

Mangora lifted her head and released an ear-piercing shriek that had Ty stumbling backward, worried about another avalanche. A chill colder than the snow he was standing in shot straight through him, forcing the hairs on his arms to stand on end. Even the captain and his guards backed away. Only Syglara seemed unaffected.

When the last reverberating echo disappeared into the rock above them, Mangora spun on her heels. "Fine! Then I'll make my own bloodstone!" She hopped aboard Syglara, and the two took off down the narrow corridor back toward camp. "Bring them!" she shouted back over her shoulder just before they disappeared around the corner.

Ty turned and looked at Breen. "You don't think she can make her own bloodstone, do you?"

Breen wiped the sweat from his forehead. "For all our sakes, I hope not."

Chapter 75 | Ty

BY THE TIME THEY MADE it back to their wagon, Mangora and Syglara were nowhere to be seen. Ty did get his first glimpse of the Black Watch encampment, but he stepped out from around the wagon to see what was on the other side before the guards grabbed him and shoved him back toward the door.

Ty only managed to catch a small part of the encampment, but it was enough to know that even without his collar, they didn't stand a prayer's chance of fighting their way free. In addition to an entire regiment of white uniforms, there were several of the black- and even some grey-robed wielders walking around. Ty had never seen the grey robes before. He wondered about their significance to the bulradoer hierarchy. From the few he counted, there seemed to be more of the grey than the black. Regardless, there were far more than what the three of them could deal with, even if Kraea lent her aid, which at this point he wasn't counting on.

Ty climbed in the back and huddled up against the others for warmth, wrapping himself in one of three blankets the guards had left them for their bedding. It was hardly enough to stay warm, but definitely better than nothing. Ty glanced out the back at Kraea's cage. "*I see you decided to stick around.*"

"*If only to watch the witch torture you,*" she shot back with a slight hint of pleasure. Kraea lay curled on one side with her tail wrapped around her body. "*She looked awful angry when she and the eight-legged one rushed by. You're in a lot of trouble,"* she said, barking out a garbled sort of laugh.

Breen drew his blanket tighter around his shoulders, shivering up against the others. "Well, that was a waste of time."

"Kept Mangora from taking you to the inquisitor, didn't it?" Ty said.

"And killed two others in our place."

Ty lowered his head.

"I prefer the inquisitor to being searched again," Narendi said with a mostly straight face. "You two are pretty to look at, but not so pretty."

Ty couldn't tell if she was being serious or trying to be lighthearted. With her, you never knew, as there oftentimes tended to be something missing in the translation.

"At least she believes us that we don't have the stone now," Ty said, his teeth beginning to chatter. "I only hope that—"

Their cage rattled as a sword was dragged down the length of the bars, stopping Ty mid-thought. He turned toward the back to see the Black Watch captain step around the tarp with a set of keys in his hand.

The man peered in. "Mangora has requested that you be brought to her tent to witness . . ." He paused a moment in thought. "To witness the birth of a bloodstone, I think is how she put it." He shrugged. "No matter. You're to come with me."

"All of us?" Breen asked.

"Yes."

Behind the captain stood a row of armed guards waiting with swords drawn as the three slowly made their way out of the back and into the snow. The harsh winter wind whistling through the pass behind them sent prickles up and down Ty's arms. His toes had already begun to numb.

"You don't simply make a bloodstone," Kraea said, rising to her feet to stare out the back of her cage.

Ty turned. *"What do you mean? Are you saying she can't? I hope that's the case, because if she finds a way to create one, then we are all in trouble."*

"Unless she plans on doing it unnaturally."

The guards marched Ty around the front of their wagon and away from Kraea's cage, the encampment stretching out in front of them. *"What do you mean by unnaturally?"* Ty could feel a chill running through his bond with the draakar, and it wasn't from the cold.

Kraea didn't say more, her side of the link going eerily silent.

The captain paraded Ty and the others at sword point through the Black Watch camp, which had been set up in a round basin at the bottom of whatever mountain they were up against. There were far more of them here than had been with Captain Hatch in Easthaven. Those within eyeshot stopped what they were doing to turn and watch. The grey-robed individuals seemed particularly fascinated by them. The black-robed bulradoer didn't seem quite as interested as they slowly sauntered through the camp, performing whatever tasks they had been given.

They made their way through the tents and campfires, finally stopping outside a large black pavilion near the center, easily three times the size of the largest tent they'd passed. The front of the shelter was guarded by more armsmen, their white mantles billowing in the wind. Several of the black-robed bulradoer were hovering around the entrance, while a short line of grey-robed individuals lined up at the side of the opening, looking anxious to be let in.

The captain shoved Ty and the others forward, and the bulradoer moved aside to let them pass. As soon as Ty stepped through the open flap, he felt a shiver run through him, similar to that of stepping through one of the traveling mirrors. He glanced at Breen and Narendi. Both looked around, clearly noticing the change as well. They had just stepped through some sort of invisible wall or barrier. Ty could feel the magic prickling his skin.

It took a moment for Ty's eyes to adjust to the darkness, the only light being provided by a collection of thick candles placed haphazardly around the room, and a stone pit at the center that was presently heating a large cauldron overtop.

Behind them, bulradoer began to file in one by one, slowly filling part of the outside wall, starting from the entrance and spreading out nearly halfway around. Each of the black-robed wielders remained a good arm's length apart. Ty didn't see any of the grey robes. Perhaps they weren't part of the bulradoer after all.

Mangora stood on the other side of the pavilion, her back to them as she bent over a table, laying out jars of who knew what, along with several types of cutting instruments and what could only be described as a large collection of dippers. She placed them in ascending order, each a different size from the next. There was also a mallet, a set of tongs, and a pair of thick gloves similar to those used by Fergus McKesh, one of the more prominent blacksmiths in Easthaven. Most importantly, though, Ty could see the shorlock resting face up on the right side of the table, waiting for its final piece to be locked in place.

Beside the table was a podium with a leather-bound tome resting open on top, its pages old and worn.

Beside the podium, facing toward the front of the tent and the fire, was a large rack, similar to images he'd seen in books describing the favored tools of the Inquisition. Sitting next to the rack on a short stool was a man wearing snow-white robes. The robes bore no decorative symbols or crests or markings of any kind to demonstrate who he was, but he did have quite the collection of runic letters tattooed across the top of his bald head. This must be the inquisitor she had spoken of. Ty guessed they were planning on torturing them after all.

His gut was swimming. Kraea had already planted the seeds of dread in his mind with her mention of unnatural transformations, but one look at this place and Ty was ready to mount an expedition back to the Live Market to find the missing bloodstone just to keep whatever was about to happen from taking place. His skin was crawling, and nothing had even been done or said. He spared a passing glance at Breen and Narendi. Both looked equally as concerned as they stared at the rack and the set of utensils on the table. Ty didn't just have a bad feeling about this—he was terrified.

As soon as the last of the jars and pots and utensils had been placed along the back of the table, Mangora turned around. "A ritual creation such as this hasn't been performed in generations. You are all privileged to bear witness to such an event. Bloodstones are indeed rare. Most were created back during the time of the dragons. Dragon blood was a powerful component used in the creation of many things—one was that of bloodstones. However, we have since learned of another way in which these stones can be produced. That would be through the ritual of *Sola de Blanava*, which is the harvesting of soul blood."

If Ty's skin had been crawling before, it was now ready to peel completely off.

Mangora pointed toward the front of the tent. "Does the silencing spell still hold?"

"No sound will leave this sanctum," a woman in black robes on Ty's right said.

That's a useful trick, Ty thought, then his imagination caught up, and he wondered why they would need to make sure no one outside the tent could hear what was happening inside.

"Bring in the first subject," Mangora ordered in her usual crackly voice.

Subject? Ty didn't like where this was going, and hoped he, Breen, and Narendi didn't end up as subjects themselves.

One of the bulradoer stepped outside, and when they returned, they were followed by one of the grey-robed people waiting out front. By their size, it was clear that the person being let in was a man, or an unusually tall and muscular woman. The bulradoer walked the man across the room and over in front of where Mangora stood. The man in grey bowed deferentially to one knee. Did he have any idea what was about to happen? Had he volunteered for this, whatever *this* was, or were the grey robes completely in the dark?

Mangora took a cup from the table and held it down to the man. "Drink this."

The man obeyed, draining whatever was inside before handing it back to her. She placed the cup back on the table and turned to the man, who was still on his knees. However, instead of having him rise, she just stood there staring at him as if waiting for—

The man started to shake and convulse. He managed a single squeak before he collapsed onto the floor, his body as stiff as the spine from one of Adarra's books. Was he dead? Ty didn't understand. How would poisoning someone create a bloodstone?

Two of the bulradoer left their places on the side and walked over to start undressing the body. They removed his shirt and then lifted him up onto the rack, where the inquisitor went about clamping the shackles on the man's wrists and ankles.

Even from his place near the door, Ty could see that the man's eyes were still open and moving. At one point, the man looked at Ty, and Ty flinched. There was fear. Ty turned and found Mangora watching.

She smiled. "He is not dead, only immobilized."

Ty could feel Narendi's arm quivering beside him, or maybe it was his arm that was quivering.

Mangora turned back to the table and began opening the jars one by one, scooping out their contents with the neatly aligned dippers, all while continuously stopping to inspect the instructions from the open book. After what seemed like a great while, long enough for Ty's legs to stiffen and his back to ache, Mangora finally turned around, holding a stone mixing bowl with three short legs. She then walked over to the man on the rack and nodded to the inquisitor sitting next to him.

The inquisitor stood with not so much as the smallest hint of an expression on his face as he picked up a thin blade with a white handle and walked over to the man on the rack and slowly ran it across the man's right wrist.

Ty couldn't pull his eyes away as he watched the stream of red dripping from the man's arm into Mangora's bowl. The man didn't make a sound, or even open his mouth, but everything Ty needed to know was written right there in those terrified eyes. Ty suddenly wondered why they had a need for a silencing spell when the person was wholly incapable of making a sound after drinking her tonic. Perhaps it was for Ty, Breen, and Narendi. Mangora might have feared them saying something that might have given the others outside pause.

Mangora carried the bowl over to the cauldron hanging from a tri-leg stand over the fire. Behind her, the inquisitor rubbed some kind of paste over the slit in the man's arm, and the blood slowed. Mangora stood over the cauldron and began to chant. It was too muffled for Ty to make out what she was saying. All he could tell was that it wasn't in the Aldoran tongue, most likely an incantation in the ancient Fae tongue.

A strange wind began to swirl around the room as the chanting grew more intense. Without warning, the man on the rack began to thrash about uncontrollably, his mouth opened as if screaming, but no sounds came out. Narendi grabbed Ty's hand and squeezed as Mangora emptied the contents of the bowl into the cauldron, releasing a hiss of smoke. The man on the rack suddenly stiffened and lurched forward, pulling against the manacles to the point Ty worried he would rip his limbs off.

Mangora placed the bowl back on the table, then returned to the cauldron. She leaned over and grabbed what Ty had at first thought was nothing more than a ladle, but what turned out to be one of the most unusual knives he had ever seen. The blade appeared to be cut from a piece of clear crystal, while the handle was clearly fashioned out of the human bone of—judging by its size—a small child. She walked over to the man on the rack and without warning plunged the knife into the man's chest. The man's eyes bulged so wide it appeared he had no lids, both screaming out where his mouth was unable.

Ty shook from head to toe, and yet he couldn't seem to pull his eyes away from the gruesome sight. The blade began to change color. Veins of red spread throughout the inside of the crystal as the blood from the man's heart pumped across it. And then the unspeakable happened. A faint golden light was slowly drawn out of the man, as if it were his very soul, and sucked down into the blade's shard.

The man's skin turned a milky white, the same as what would happen to a corpse if left unburied for too long. He fell back against the rack and went still, his dead eyes staring out across the room.

Mangora pulled out the knife and inspected it a moment, then placed it back within the cauldron, blade down. "What you just witnessed was the removal of a wielder's magic, their source of power. That magic is now stored within the crystal until such time that it is needed."

Ty was too scared to even retch, too scared to even move or breathe. The room began to spin and darken, and he nearly blacked out by the time he realized he wasn't breathing, and hurriedly sucked in a deep gulp. Before he'd managed to pull himself together, three of the bulradoer had already lifted the dead man from the rack, wrapped him back in his robes, and carried him into the next room.

Before Ty knew it, another one of the initiates was being escorted inside.

Ty wanted to grab them and warn them what was about to happen, but he was too frightened to even move. Worse, he didn't want Mangora suddenly deciding to use one of them in their place. Besides, these people had aligned themselves with the White Tower. They got what they deserved. At least, that was what he told himself to try lessening the horror of it all.

Helpless to do anything to stop what was happening, Ty finally lowered his head and stared at the ground. A quick glance to either side showed that Breen and

Narendi both had their heads lowered as well. Narendi actually had her eyes closed, her grip on Ty's hand never wavering.

Three more initiates were marched in, given Mangora's drink, stripped, placed on the rack, and had their wrists slit. Three more times Mangora marched over to the cauldron, chanted, tossed in her mixings, then retrieved the crystal knife and stabbed the helpless victim in the chest. Three more times that victim had had their essence sucked out of them and into the knife. Three more times the bulradoer wrapped the corpse and carried it into the next room.

After the final victim had been hauled away, Mangora held up the blade for all to see. By now, the shard was completely changed, not a speck of transparency anywhere, its insides a deep red. She took the knife over to the table and grabbed a mallet. Holding the blade by its handle, she struck the bottom of the shard hard enough to snap the bone clean off, leaving nothing but the crystal, which didn't seem to have been affected at all. Ty watched as she placed the shard inside a metal tube. Using a pair of tongs, she carried the tube over to the cauldron and lowered it inside.

Once again, she recited another set of incantations, and the fire sparked, shifting from its natural color to a dark green as the cauldron's contents began to bubble up over the sides. The fire burned hotter and brighter than before, filling the room with heat to the point that Ty's face was dripping with perspiration.

Moments later, the fire simmered, and she lifted the steaming tube back out. The shard was no longer sticking out of the top. She walked over to the table where a small cast had been set up—small enough to mirror the size of the empty socket on the shorlock where the bloodstone should have gone—and poured the heated crystal into the mold. Steam shot out from the cast as soon as the heated liquid touched the cool metal.

Mangora laid the tube upright after making sure all the contents had been drained and, taking off her gloves, walked over to the book. After spending a moment reading the page, she headed back to the table and raised her hands over the liquid mold and began to recite another incantation.

Ty couldn't see what was happening from across the tent, but he had a pretty good idea. By the time Ty had managed to slow his breathing enough to not feel so lightheaded, Mangora turned back around with a perfectly formed gem raised above her head.

"A new bloodstone has been born!"

She stepped over to where the shorlock was resting on the right side of the table and picked it up for all to see. Ty noticed that the gem didn't automatically fly into place like the other pieces. Then again, the true bloodstone hadn't done so either. He did notice that the stone in her hand was pulsing, similar to the way the one at the Live Market had inside the jeweler's pocket, also similar to the spider ring's stone around Mangora's finger.

Slowly, Mangora placed the stone inside the shorlock and waited. Nothing really seemed to happen. Ty had almost expected some kind of flash of light or gust of wind, or something. For all the work it had taken to retrieve the pieces and get them back together, this seemed a rather disappointing climax. Even Mangora looked a little uneasy from the lack of oomph, but it didn't slow her long, as she turned to the others.

"We are now one step closer to finally claiming Aero'set for the Tower!"

The surrounding bulradoer cheered.

Mangora turned to the three of them and smiled. "Take them back to their wagon. We have a long day tomorrow."

Ty was the first one out of the tent, shivering as he passed through the magical barrier. Outside, an armed escort was waiting to take them back to their wagon. The return trip didn't seem to take as long as when they had first arrived, Ty's eyes mostly focused on his footsteps in the snow and not looking about the camp as he had the first time. He couldn't get the image of the first man's eyes out of his mind as Mangora plunged the knife in and ripped his magic from him. It was an image he'd never forget.

"I see you found out the hard way what it means to create an unnatural bloodstone," Kraea said. She stood on their approach, watching each as they strode to the back of their wagon and stepped inside.

"It was worse than I could have imagined," Ty said aloud, once the guards had locked the door and marched away.

Both Breen and Narendi looked at Ty, then over at the second wagon where Kraea was staring out the back. Realizing he wasn't talking to them, they walked over to their pile of hay against the back wall and sat down, wrapping their wool blankets around them.

Ty stayed at the door. "Why didn't you tell me what it would be like?"

"I was hoping she wouldn't let you see. Creating unnatural bloodstones is a highly guarded secret among the darker forms of magic. If she wasn't planning on showing you, there was no point in telling you beforehand and getting you even more upset."

"How do you know all of this? You're just a . . ." Ty stared at her a moment. "How old are you?"

She stared back with her deep golden eyes. *"How old are you?"*

"I'm soon to be seventeen years." Ty had almost forgotten he had a birth celebration coming up. He wondered if he'd even be alive to witness it.

Kraea barked out a garbled laugh.

"What's so funny?"

"You look puny for your age."

"And you look . . ." He couldn't think of a good comeback. "Hey, you never told me how old you were."

"I'm fifteen cycles."

"Aha!"

"What?" Breen asked, looking around for possible trouble.

"Oh, sorry. It's nothing. Turns out I'm older than Kraea is."

"Congratulations," Breen said and pulled his blanket tighter around his neck.

"Yeah, well, I'm better looking," Kraea added, spinning in a circle with her long red tail hanging down at her side.

"That's debatable."

She growled, but Ty could feel a sense of playfulness through their link. Her head shot up. *"She's coming."*

Kraea had barely gotten the words out when Ty heard the crunch of boots in the snow drawing closer. "Mangora's coming," Ty said and scooted toward the back corner alongside Breen and Narendi as they waited for the inevitable. Sure enough, the canvas tarp was pulled aside, and Mangora stepped up to the bars. Around her neck hung the shorlock, the bloodstone glowing as though it were filled with some sort of shiny liquid that was in a constant state of motion, slowly swirling and spinning, the magic seemingly wanting to be let out.

Ty couldn't help but cringe at the sight of it. All his hard work to assemble the incredible piece now laid to waste and forever tainted by the blood of those sacrificed for its creation. "Your journey is nearly complete, my young faeling, but our journey is just getting started. When you stand beside me and open the gates to Aero'set and return the keep, you'll finally understand your greater purpose—the reason the master has chosen you."

"Aerodyne didn't choose me any more than I chose myself," Ty spat.

Mangora hissed. "How dare you use the master's name in such a familiar way!"

"He's not *my* master."

Mangora cackled. "How little you know. The master has long foreseen your arrival. Your destinies are intertwined."

"I choose my own destiny."

Mangora shook her head. "Which only shows how ignorant you really are. Just think, by this time tomorrow, we will be standing in the Valley of Needrin with the power of the Wizard's Keep at our fingertips."

Ty sneered. "By this time tomorrow, Kraea will be chewing on your bones."

"Will you quit bringing me into this, you stupid oaf!"

Ty didn't acknowledge Kraea. He'd come so close, and now it was all being ripped away, and he was helpless to do anything about it.

Mangora was still laughing when she turned to leave. It was a familiar laugh, one that brought back memories he wished he could forget, memories of his mother.

He might not have been able to fight back, but there was still one way he knew to get under the witch's skin and possibly throw her off balance at the same time. "I almost forgot," Ty said as he walked over to the bars. "Douina sends her love."

Mangora stopped halfway between steps, her feet locked in place so tight she nearly tripped over them. She spun around, raced back to the wagon, grabbed Ty by the hem of his coat, and yanked him up against the bars. The top of her spider ring pressed against his stomach. "What did you just say?"

Ty could see the dumbfounded shock in the witch's eyes. "I said, Douina sends her love."

"How do you know that name?" She pulled even harder, as though hoping to snatch him clean through the cage. "Answer me!"

Ty smiled, basking in the moment. "I spent a rather lovely evening with her not too long ago. You know, she's quite the cook, not to mention an excellent storyteller."

"Impossible!" Mangora spat, her knuckles white as she clung to the hem of his coat like her life depended on it.

"Not at all, I assure you," Ty said. "Her stories were quite intricate."

Mangora hissed. "Douina's dead! She died over fifty years ago."

Ty pursed his lips. "Then she's quite talkative for a dead woman."

"You lie! Nyalis told you of her."

"Then how would I know that she is your twin? In fact, when I first saw her, I thought she was you. Took some convincing, but after she had me feel her magic, I saw she was right. It wasn't the same. Hers hadn't been tainted by death."

"Where . . . where is she?"

"Exactly where you left her fifty years ago."

"Tricks! This is nothing you couldn't have learned from Nyalis."

"I bet Nyalis doesn't know the real reason you tried to kill her."

Mangora screeched as she raised her hands and sent Ty flying across the wagon. He bounced off the bars at the back and landed on his hands and knees on the wooden bed. He could barely catch his breath, the pain shooting through his back. Both Breen and Narendi rushed to help him up. Ty could taste blood in his mouth from where the wall of air had hit him in the face. He looked up at Mangora, but she was already stomping away in a heated fit.

"What was that about?" Breen asked, helping Ty to the back of the wagon where they sat him down and wrapped a blanket around him.

"The past catching up," Ty said, then spit the blood through the bars.

"Why *did* she try killing her sister?" Narendi asked, seemingly just as curious as Breen.

"Why does anyone try killing their twin? The love of a man."

"Love?" Breen nearly choked on his own tongue as he barked at a sarcastic laugh. "That woman, if indeed she even is one, wouldn't know love if it stabbed her in the neck."

"From what Douina told me, she and Mangora were inseparable. That is, until a man came looking for the shorlock."

"What man?"

Ty looked at him. "Who else do we know who is completely obsessed with finding Aero'set?"

Breen looked taken aback. "No. It couldn't be."

"Could not be who?" Narendi demanded impatiently.

"The archchancellor?"

Ty nodded. "Has to be. Nyalis told me that Valtor had gone in search of the key long ago but had never been able to find it. He said Valtor's been searching for the keep ever since."

"That might answer the question as to how they knew where we'd be," Breen said. "If Valtor has been searching for it for so long, then it stands to reason he at least knew where we'd be going once we found the key."

"Who is this arch . . . arch ancelor?"

"Archchancellor," Ty corrected. "His name is Valtor. He's the head of the White Tower." Ty went on in as brief a way as possible to explain more about the White Tower and its role in Aldor, and Valtor's goal of bringing about some sort of battle between the ven'ae and jun'ri, and ultimately his desire to return the Dark Wizard and his followers back into the world of men by releasing them from Taerin nu'Cyllian, the magical prison found deep inside the Pits of Aran'gal.

Narendi's eyes looked like they had glossed over by the time he'd finished. "So why did she try killing her sister?"

Ty sighed. "After all that, that's all you want to know?" Narendi smiled, and Ty shook his head. "Fine. Where was I?"

"You were telling us of when Valtor showed up looking for the key," Breen said.

"Right. As I was saying, Valtor, or someone we believe was Valtor, came looking for the key, and during his stay he manipulated the sisters. He played them off each other, Mangora falling the hardest. At least, that's how Douina put it. However, every time Valtor attempted to get Abinayu to open up to him, he was turned away. Mangora told Valtor that her sister knew of a way to trick Abinayu into revealing his secrets, but he would have to seduce it out of her."

Breen frowned. "I don't like where this is going."

"According to Douina, that was exactly what Valtor attempted to do, but Douina said that she never gave in, which angered Valtor to the point of leaving. Mangora was so enraged at the thought of Valtor leaving, and the fact that she thought he had shared himself with Douina, that she attacked her sister. She blamed Douina for everything and attempted to kill her by poisoning her food." Ty paused a moment to catch his breath.

"Well?" Narendi asked, growing irritated by the unanswered story. "Tell us what happened."

"She killed her, that's what happened."

Breen and Narendi looked confused. "If she killed her, then how is Douina alive?" Breen asked.

"Because Abinayu managed to revive her, but not until after Mangora had left their home in search of her missing love. Douina has never once since stepped foot outside the marsh."

Breen scooted back against the wooden slats at the front of the wagon and sighed. "What a tragic tale."

"Poisons can be so unreliable," Kraea said unexpectedly. *"Tastier to feast on their flesh."*

Ty grimaced.

"What?" Breen asked.

"Just something Kraea said." When Breen and Narendi pressed, he repeated her sentiments.

Narendi grimaced as well. "Ick."

Kraea chuckled. Sometimes Ty couldn't tell when she was being serious or simply trying to put him on edge. He turned and stared out through the cage bars at the snow-covered rocks outlining the mountain pass. Little as it might have been, he felt he had won that round with Mangora, but he knew the real battle was just around the corner.

Chapter 76 | Ferrin

ARLIN'S CLOSET WAS surprisingly quiet for the number of people locked inside. The only two people from their party not in attendance were Harlin and Sylas. Ferrin had actually been surprised that Sylas didn't place Harlin in with the rest of the prisoners just for sport. It would have been something Sylas would have gotten no end of enjoyment from, but perhaps he still had use for the whimpering nobleman.

Sylas had already been in to wish everyone a pleasant night's sleep, a routine he had initiated their first night inside. From there, he would crawl into bed and have one or two members of the Black Watch tie his arms and legs to the four-corner bedposts before drifting off to sleep. As usual, he had given the durma key over to one of the guards standing watch outside his door, making sure Joren didn't wake in the middle of the night and give it to Lenara.

"So, you're saying that the man out there is actually two different people in the same body?" Garreth asked, having finally calmed down enough to have a rational conversation. As soon as they returned to Harlin's estate, Sylas had ordered Garreth's wife be shipped off to wherever it was they were keeping Ferrin's sister. It was Sylas's way of keeping them in line.

"Yes," Lenara said, answering in Ferrin's place, since she knew more about what was happening than any of them, at least when it came to Joren and Sylas. Ferrin sat with his back propped against a lower shelf while holding Mother Luka's head in his lap from where she had nodded off. Ella had removed the old woman's gag but kept it close just in case she had another one of her fits.

Lenara went on to explain briefly the two's unusual bonding, and Joren's infrequent visits, which were growing few and far between. Ferrin could see by the concern on her face that she feared one of these times would be his last, and Joren would simply cease to exist.

"How is something like that possible?" Garreth asked.

"How do you think?" Elson exclaimed. "Magic."

"There are many secrets hidden away within the walls of the White Tower," Lenara said. "Most would be best left unfound." She went on to explain in detail the events that led up to Sylas being returned through the Tree of Souls. Elson and Ismara looked none too happy with having to listen to it all over again, and Ella and Garreth looked none too happy for having to hear it the first time. Mother Luka was too busy snoring to care one way or the other.

"What's it like in the Tower?" Garreth asked, this time firmly directing the question to Ferrin.

"Nothing but sponge baths and peppermint sticks, I'm sure," Elson said with a grin.

Ferrin gave Elson a sharp look. The man's sarcasm was hardly helping, but it was also one of the reasons Ferrin preferred his company over the others. What you saw was what you got. And now that his mind wasn't quite so clouded with drink, his tongue seemed to hold a much finer edge.

Ferrin took a moment to think about how best to describe his experience inside the Tower. "It's a place where nightmares come true," he started, earning him the response he had hoped for as everyone leaned in a little closer. Everyone, of course, except Lenara. "They keep the prisoners in windowless stone cells, where if the cold and damp doesn't kill you, the rats just might."

"I hate rats," Ella exclaimed, drawing a few eyes.

"And those are the lucky ones," Ferrin said. "The rest of us spent our days being dragged down into the Hall of Inquisition, where they would strap us to metal racks and torture us to the brink of death. Then, just before that final sweet release, they would bring in a healer to rip us back from the edge, so they could do it all over again the next day. And there was no inquisitor better at his job than Sylas."

"That man out there?" Elson asked, pointing toward the bedchamber door. He was seated next to Ismara in the corner, up under one of the lanterns.

"The one inside him, yes," Ferrin said with an affirmative nod.

"Great," Elson said with a shiver. "Something to look forward to on our long trip back to the Tower. No need to worry about a long, dull ride across Aldor. I'm sure we'll all be kept entertained every night by the sounds of each other's screams. Maybe we should start laying wagers now. I'm sure I'll win if there's a stake on who can scream the loudest."

Lenara growled from her spot near the door on the other side of the room, a common reaction she seemed to have whenever Elson spoke.

Ferrin would have laughed if he hadn't known how close Elson was to the truth.

Garreth, on the other hand, wasn't laughing. "At least my children are safe." He looked at Ismara. "You say you have a crew. Any chance we get some help from them? They must be looking for you, correct?"

"It's not whether they will come looking, but if they can find us."

Garreth released a heavy sigh as he rubbed his hands together. "Doesn't mean they won't."

Elson looked like he had something to add, but wisely kept it to himself.

"Tell me about Myriah," Ferrin said to Garreth and Ella. "What happened to her after my imprisonment?" Elson had provided Ferrin with some information, but after Ferrin's disappearance, Elson's attendance at the meetings had supposedly become less frequent, and eventually he had stopped altogether.

"She took your disappearance hard," Garreth said.

"Even tried searching for you," Ella added.

"She spent weeks trying to find some hint of where you'd gone. In fact, Harlin was the one to take charge of that rescue effort." Garreth balled his fists. "I always wondered why he'd been so vocal about it, knowing how little the two of you cared for the other. Now we know. He probably had her running in circles, making sure she never actually figured out where you'd gone."

"With the Black Watch in town," Elson said, "and the state of your house when Myriah returned the next morning, it was pretty clear what had happened."

Garreth nodded. "With you gone, Harlin's attempts at wooing her only increased. To her credit, she held off as long as she could, but eventually she ran out of money and, times as difficult as they were, none of the rest of us had enough to spare. She was determined not to lose your home and smithy, and made Harlin swear that he would keep it if she agreed to a union." Garreth passed a quick look at Elson. "I'm not going to say she's been the happiest I've ever seen her, but Harlin has clearly provided for her." He looked around the room at all the gowns and fancy suits.

Ferrin cringed. "I've heard enough." It was supposed to be his job to provide for his sister, and now he was just hoping to keep her alive. Not wanting to hear more, he bid them all a good night.

Sleep was long in coming, and short-lived once it arrived, as it was plagued with dreams that had him waking in a cold sweat. He was more than ready to be up when the door opened, and dawn's light flooded their room.

Sylas stood in the doorway, a bright, cheerful smile resting on his smug face. "It's going to be a beautiful day, don't you think, smith? I sense a family reunion in the air."

Sylas left the room before Ferrin could think of a witty comeback, his mind too clouded with lack of sleep and thoughts of what lay ahead. Soon enough, a couple of guards arrived with trays of bread, fruit, and a couple of pitchers of watered ale, all of which helped to clear his mind. He was bursting with anticipation at finally being able to see his sister. He wondered if she even knew he was still alive and that all of this was because of him. He wondered if Sylas had said anything to her about him. Knowing the inquisitor, he probably told her that Ferrin had died in the Tower in some horrific way and that she would soon follow.

After their meal, the guards came and escorted them down to the main floor, where they found Sylas and what looked like half a regiment waiting in the main hall. The inquisitor passed a brief smile Ferrin's way and headed out the front door, wearing another one of Harlin's colorful jackets and carrying the same silver-tipped cane he'd carted along with him the previous day. Ferrin and the others filed out the door, flanked on either side by guards, and were marched to the carriage house, where two carriages awaited their approach. Ferrin could see Harlin inside the first, sitting alongside Sylas.

Their party was split in two: Ferrin, Ella, and Mother Luka took the first with Sylas and Harlin, while Ismara, Elson, and Garreth took the second, along with a uniformed officer to make sure they didn't try to escape. Not that they would have gotten far, considering the armed guards on horseback that waited to escort the two carriages to wherever it was they were going.

Ferrin hoped that an armed escort of this size would attract attention, perhaps even give Captain Treygan and his crew a chance of spotting them. Those hopes were quickly dashed, though, when the mounted troops split off from the two carriages as soon as they reached the street.

"Where are they going?" Ferrin asked as he watched the last of the riders head north, while the carriages headed south.

"You don't think me foolish enough to announce my comings and goings with a parade, do you?" Sylas asked with a triumphant grin.

Ferrin bit back his disappointment, focusing his efforts instead on seeing his sister for the first time in nearly a year, imaging what she must look like now, and what her reaction would be to seeing him again. Beyond that, he spent the rest of his time pondering their escape. His hands were quivering with excitement as he stared out the window at the passing snow-covered buildings.

The sun was out and bright, adding a sheen across the top of the white powder that made it sparkle like diamonds, but its beauty meant nothing to him. The buildings and people they passed meant nothing as well, other than a way to judge how close they were getting to the city's gates.

Their carriage passed the millworks on the left, and Ferrin's heart raced. He knew the next thing he'd see was the wall and the watchtowers. Without needing to stop, the carriages passed through the southern gate and headed south on the main road, but quickly diverted to a smaller, less-traveled stretch of road that headed east into the forest toward Tara Springs.

He thought back on the last time he'd been ushered out of the city and the wielders he shared his prison transport with. He could even remember some of their names. He remembered Gillion, the old man who went by Rascal. He remembered Sasha, the shy girl who wouldn't speak to anyone but Rascal. Then there was Narrisa, whose husband had sold her for the gold he could get. Ferrin wondered if she ever made it back after their escape, and if so, what she had done to him when she arrived. There was also Brennon and his wife, and Telsa, who had flirted with one of the guards in order for Ferrin to escape. And finally, Beese and his son Cory.

Ferrin was surprised by how much he remembered. Then again, when you shared an experience like they had, those faces and names tended to get seared into your memory; like etching a crest into the side of a blade, they were there to stay.

He wondered what had become of them all, if they had managed to make it over the Razor Spine. So much had happened over the last year. It was as though he had gone in a great circle, and here he was, right back where he'd started.

The carriage bumped along at a steady pace, slow enough that the drivers could miss the deepest of the holes, but not so much that it would take them the rest of the day to reach their destination, wherever that was. Sure enough, after a good hour and a half out of town, the trees opened into a small clearing, with three wagons sitting end to end in a row on the far-left side, butting up against the tree line.

At the back of the camp, in the far-right corner, a corral had been set up for the Black Watch's horses. It was much larger than expected, their escort having grown considerably. It looked like a second regiment had been waiting here with the other prisoners, while the first had been sent into town to watch them. Men in white uniforms moved about the camp between their bivouacs and cooking fires, giving Ferrin the impression that escape was not going to be an option.

Ferrin peered anxiously out the window at the three wagons on the side as the carriages came to a stop. Unfortunately, they were covered, so he couldn't see much. Guards stood ready to greet the carriages, opening the doors to let those inside out, Sylas being the first through the door. The guards stared rather markedly at his fanciful clothes, some looking twice, just to make sure it was the same man. Ferrin didn't get the impression they were all that happy with him trading in the Black Watch mantle for a colorful coat and silk shirt.

There were a few, however, who didn't seem too bothered, possibly those he'd been traveling with since leaving the Tower. Ferrin was certain they would have realized by now that something was different about the man, especially if they had noticed his mood swings at night. Sylas might have even told them who he really was.

Sylas walked over to Ferrin and raised his hood. "Don't want anyone seeing you just yet and spoiling the surprise." He turned back around. "How are our guests today?" he asked as he headed toward the three wagons on the other side of camp from the carriages. At the back of the group, Harlin stood well away from the other prisoners, especially Ferrin and Garreth, as they made their way between the cook fires.

"They have been very cooperative," one of the ranking officers said as he kept pace with Sylas.

"Glad to hear it." Sylas brought them to a stop just in front of the second of the three transports, and then demanded the canvases be lifted.

Ferrin kept his hood raised to keep his face hidden for the time being, barely able to catch his breath as he watched several guards walk over and lift up the front side coverings with long poles. He didn't recognize the faces in the first wagon on the left, or those in the third on the right. However, the second was filled with members of the Rhowynn wielder council, and Ferrin's eyes quickly scanned the lot, searching for the one face he knew—

Near the back of the wagon, he spotted a tuft of red hair pushing through the others to get a look at who the guards had brought in this time. Ferrin started to cry when he saw the tired, dirty face of his sister peering through the bars. *Myriah!*

"Garreth! I see they caught you as well," a familiar voice called out from the front. It was Doloff, one of the more negative members of the council, earning him the nickname Doldrum.

"Is that Ella and Mother Luka with you?" Ilene called out on the right, pushing her way toward the bars. She, too, was on the council, and had the extraordinary gift of turning chaos into order.

"We're here," Ella said, as if they all couldn't see the two of them standing there plain as day.

"What's that coward doing here?" Doloff shouted, pointing toward the back, where Harlin was conveniently trying to hide behind several of the guards. "Put him in here with us. We'll be more than happy to give him a proper greeting."

Myriah stood at the front with tears in her eyes as she stared at Harlin, looking both humiliated and crushed all at the same time.

Harlin took a step out from the back of the group. "Sylas, you promised me my life and Myriah's if I helped you with . . ." He looked at those in the wagon and decided not to finish. "I expect you to keep your word."

Those in the wagon turned and looked at Myriah as though she had been a part of this from the beginning, as absurd as that was. She merely shook her head. "I know nothing of this."

Sylas pointed at a couple of the guards. "Put him back in the carriage. I'll deal with him later." Three of the guards grabbed Harlin by the arms and half walked, half dragged him back to the first carriage as he shouted out his demands to be released. They tossed him inside and shut the door. For the briefest moment, Ferrin wondered what Sylas had in mind when he said he would deal with Harlin later, but the moment was fleeting, as Ferrin turned and looked at his sister.

"I have a special treat for you today," Sylas said with a wide grin as he motioned for one of the guards standing near the back of the wagon to unlock the door. Sylas looked nearly as excited to tell them who he had captured as Ferrin was to see the look on his sister's face when he did. "I've chased this wielder across half of Aldor, a prize highly sought after by the archchancellor himself. The only man to not only survive the racks but the first to ever escape the White Tower."

Sylas certainly wasn't holding back, capturing the attention of those inside as prisoners pressed to the bars to see who he was talking about. Sylas grabbed Ferrin by the arm and pulled him to the front, pausing just long enough to build the suspense as everyone tried to peer beyond the darkened cowl of his cloak. Sylas was all but quivering with excitement as he finally reached up and yanked back Ferrin's hood.

No one inside moved, no one except Myriah as she grabbed the bars and shouted, "Ferrin!"

Ferrin sprinted for the back of the wagon. The door was already open. The guard with the keys reached for his weapon when he saw him coming, but Ferrin slammed into him so hard the man hit the ground and rolled into the brush behind. Ferrin charged up the steps and straight into Myriah's arms as she had shoved the others out of the way to reach him.

He lifted her up, shackled and all, and swung her around. She buried her head in his neck and bawled. "I thought you were dead. They told me the Tower had taken you. I never thought I'd see you again."

"Not even the Tower could keep me from you," he said as he slowly lowered her back to the wagon bed. She kissed his cheeks and squeezed his neck so tight he nearly blacked out.

It was the most wonderful moment of his life.

Unfortunately, it was soon followed by the worst as a row of guards rushed into the wagon and dragged her out.

"As touching as this little reunion is," Sylas said with a sneer, "I'm afraid I will feel much safer having her with me."

"No!" Ferrin leapt at the guards, their swords already drawn. The first lunged, but Ferrin was too fast. He sidestepped and grabbed the man's arm, snapping it with a loud pop as he flung him to the side. He recovered the guard's sword and deflected the second in line, punching the man in the face and plunging his sword through the man's chest. The guard fell backward out of the wagon, coughing blood the whole way down.

Ferrin flew out of the back at the next three men. Halfway in the air, a jolt of lightning tore through his body, and he landed on his stomach in the snow, writhing until the initial shock wore off. He opened his eyes, surprised to find his sword still gripped between his fingers. He couldn't feel it, nor could he feel his fingers as he tried turning over.

"Now, now, now, my dear smith. We will have none of that. What kind of example are you setting for your sister?"

"Kill them all!" Myriah shouted, trying and failing to pull away from the two guards holding her.

Sylas roared with laughter. "I can see where she gets her fire from. It will be a pleasure to get her on my rack."

It took every ounce of will Ferrin had to push his way up to his knees. By then, Sylas had Myriah by the arm.

Behind them, Harlin came rushing out from behind one of the carriages. "Unhand her, Sylas! You gave me your word!"

Sylas turned. "Get back in that carriage or I'll cut your fingers off and feed them to you."

Whatever look was on Sylas's face had Harlin scrambling back around the side of the carriage and flinging himself inside.

Sylas turned and looked down at Ferrin, the silver key glowing in his hand. "Yes, this reunion has proven most enjoyable. If I had known how fruitful this adventure would have been, I would have released you months ago. Might have saved your sister the heartache of giving herself to the very man who sold her brother to the Black Watch."

Myriah jerked her arm out of Sylas's grip. "What?"

Sylas acted surprised. "You didn't know? How could you not, after seeing what your husband has been willing to do to save his own skin?" Sylas pointed at the second wagon and her friends inside. "Were you never curious what had happened to your brother? Never even for one moment did you not have the smallest inclination, a whisper in the back of your mind as you lay down beside him? I find that hard to believe."

Myriah looked at Ferrin, and he could see the anguish and shame in her eyes. She turned away, Sylas's words doing more damage than his knife ever could.

"It's not your fault," Ferrin said, his own words feeling forced. Even he had a hard time understanding why she would have chosen Harlin.

Sylas nodded to the guards, and they relieved Ferrin of his weapon and dragged their fallen members away, including the man inside, who was cursing Ferrin's entire existence as he clutched a very awkward-looking arm to his chest.

"Put him with the others," Sylas said, then handed Myriah off to the guards. "And please escort this one to my carriage. No, wait. Best not to put her in that one. She might very well spoil my fun by killing her husband. Put her in the second." Sylas chuckled as he watched them haul her back to the carriages. "All this excitement has worked up an appetite." He headed to the last cooking fire on the right, closest to the entrance, and took a seat.

"On your feet," one of the guards said to Ferrin as he lifted Ferrin from the snow and dragged him over to the steps leading into the back of the wagon. Elson and Garreth were there waiting to help him the rest of the way in as the guards shut and locked the door behind them. Ferrin barely made it to the corner before his legs gave out and he slumped down beside the bars.

One of the Black Watch, his hood raised against the cold, held back while the others walked off toward the cook fires. He walked over to the corner of the cage, where Ferrin was resting. "Chin up, my friend. Help is on the way."

Ferrin's head shot up. *That voice.* Ferrin grabbed the bars and pulled himself around as the lone guard looked up at him and winked.

Myron?

Chapter 77 | Ferrin

ERRIN WAS IN SHOCK. Even after having seen his dead friend with his own eyes, he still was having a hard time coming to terms with the fact that he hadn't imagined it. To make matters worse, Myron had left without saying a word, evidently not wanting to look suspicious by hanging around the prison wagon chatting with those inside.

Unfortunately for Ferrin, the members of the wielder council hadn't seen fit to do the same, as they peppered him with an unending string of questions, barely giving him a chance to catch his breath after having suffered the durma's kiss.

It was the most interaction he'd had with most of the council members since his joining.

Lenara and Ismara sat off to the side watching the others, not feeling comfortable enough to join in, though Ismara had no qualms with speaking her mind if she thought the need significant enough to warrant it.

The rest of the council distanced themselves from the two, mainly Lenara. Even with her collar, they knew who or what she was, and the thought of sharing a wagon with one of the Tower's bulradoer had them all extremely jumpy, and they kept a close, distrustful eye on her. There wasn't much known about bulradoer. The vast majority of those living in Aldor had no idea they even existed. The very notion that the White Tower would employ wielders seemed preposterous to all but the wielders they had been sent to hunt down.

"Has anyone seen who is in the other two prison transports?" Ferrin asked. "Are they from Rhowynn as well?"

"I don't believe so," Doloff said. "At least, I didn't recognize any of them. Probably picked up from other towns and villages along the way."

Ferrin nodded. "I wasn't sure if maybe there had been a large increase in the wielder council since I left."

Garreth snorted. "Hardly."

"I still can't believe you're alive," Ilene said, her greying hair resting across her narrow shoulders. She was a short woman with a hooked nose that seemed to work very well for holding spectacles, something she was rarely seen without from what Ferrin could recall. As a highly respected clerk who pored over figures all day, her eyesight wasn't what it once had been, requiring her to rely more and more on the eyepieces to get around.

"I still can't believe he escaped," Garreth added, drawing several grunts from the others. "No one has ever escaped the Tower."

"I didn't do it alone." Ferrin had already told them of his cellmate, Azriel, and of Rae and Suri and his not-so-dead friend Myron, along with a brief explanation of what they had been through to make it back to Rhowynn. "And we can't do this alone, either."

As if hearing his statement, the canvas flap at the back opened, and a white-cloaked mantle moved underneath. "Ferrin?"

"I'm here," Ferrin said, recognizing the voice. The others moved out of the way so he could reach the corner where the guard was standing. His hood was still up, covering his face. Ferrin pressed against the bars and grabbed his friend's arm. "How is this possible? I watched them kill you."

Myron shifted his hood, letting the snow fall off the top as he moved close enough for the others to see his face. "What can I say? I'm too stubborn to die."

Ferrin smiled. "No doubt."

"Actually, it was Rae. She found me."

"Rae? How in the Pits did she find us?"

Myron snorted. "She followed us from the ship."

Ferrin shook his head. For once, her headstrong determination to completely ignore anything he said had worked to their advantage. "Wait, I have her crystal, how did she manage to use her magic?"

"We keep one aboard for emergencies," Ismara said.

"Your father gave it to her before she left," Myron said, turning back to Ferrin. "She was there when the guards carried the bodies out back and managed to get to me just in time."

"What about Lendrick?" Ismara asked. "Does he live?"

Ferrin had never known the young sailor's name who had fought alongside them in Harlin's home. He wished he'd taken the time to have at least asked.

Myron shook his head apologetically. "I'm afraid he was already gone."

Ismara's face tightened. "Where's my father? The crew?"

Myron looked at the next wagon up as if having heard something. He waited a moment, then finally turned around. "They're close. But they needed to know what the situation was like here before charging in blind. And by the looks of it, I'm glad we did. There're a lot more of the Tower's guards than we were expecting, and they have wielders as well."

"I know," Ferrin said. "I killed one of them."

"Apparently, you aren't very good at it. She's sitting right behind you."

Ferrin turned to find Lenara kneeling behind him, the others quickly shifting positions to keep from having to sit so close. "She's with us."

"I doubt that. Do you know who that is? That's Lenara. She's one of the archchancellor's favorites." He sneered at the dark wielder. "A rising name among the bulradoer."

Lenara growled and the council members moved even further away.

"Not anymore," Ferrin said. "Circumstances have changed."

"What circumstances are those? She's bulradoer."

"And you were a captain in the Black Watch," Ferrin reminded him.

Having his former title thrown in his face gave Myron pause. "Fine. But I'd keep an eye on her all the same. I've seen what she can do."

"How many bulradoer did you count?" Lenara asked, ignoring Myron's skepticism. "We've seen very little since they lowered the tarps. We heard riders a while back. Who were they?"

"Just as bossy as a bulradoer too," Myron said with a snort. "More of the Tower's guards. The other half of this regiment, if I were to guess."

"And the bulradoer?"

"Two, I believe," Myron said, "and several of those grey-robed trainees of yours."

"They might be in training, but don't underestimate them. They have been instructed in combat."

Myron bit his lower lip nervously. "Even with the element of surprise, we're going to be heavily outnumbered, and with them having their own wielders, I don't see us coming out of this in very good shape, if at all. Not without help from you. And by *you*, I mean all of you," he said, looking across the inside of the wagon. "If we can't find a way to get those collars off, we won't stand much of a chance."

"I have a plan for that," Ferrin said, "but it's going to require us getting our hands on our crystals. Without them, there's not much we can do."

"Yes," Lenara said, "but at least without the collars, it would allow us to fight without the fear of being incapacitated by one of those keys."

Myron nodded. "She's got a point."

Ferrin looked at Myron. "You've got to find the box with our crystals. It's probably sitting inside one of the carriages."

"Sylas has them pretty well guarded," Myron said, "what with Harlin and your sister being held there. One thing's for sure: The snow's setting in. Could last the night, which might give us an edge." He looked at Ferrin. "Box or no box, tonight's our best chance. We need to catch them unprepared."

Ismara scooted forward. "Tell my father to wait for our signal."

"Oh?" Myron asked. "And what signal will that be?"

"He'll know it when he hears it."

Myron nodded. "If I find the chest with your crystals, I'll do my best to snatch them. If not . . ." His smile faded. "Best of luck to us all." With that, he turned and left.

One hour passed.

No Myron. Those inside the wagon grew restless.

Then two.

Still no Myron. Ferrin was actively pacing back and forth as he tried to think of what they could do without the use of their magic.

"Where's this friend of yours?" Lenara asked. "We need those crystals." The others of the council huddled in the corner, everyone except Elson and Garreth, who were sitting with Ferrin, Ismara, and Lenara, waiting for something to happen.

"He'll be here," Ferrin said, though he was beginning to doubt. After the sun went down and there was still no word from Myron, Ferrin began to grow nervous. "He must not have been able to get to the box."

"Crystals or no crystals," Lenara said, "we need to get these collars off. Give me your key, and I'll relink everyone's collar to it. That way, at least Sylas won't be able to use his own key against us."

"What do you mean relink the key?" Ferrin asked.

"I mean the key is of no use unless it's linked to a specific collar."

Ferrin blanched. He had no idea something like that was needed. His whole plan had stemmed on being able to use his key to unlock their collars. If Lenara hadn't been there, his plan would have been for nothing.

He pulled off his boot, shook out the cylindrical key, and handed it to Lenara. "How does it work?"

Lenara turned to several of the council members. "Go keep watch. We can't have anyone seeing what we're doing here."

Four of the members split off, each moving to one of the four corners of the wagon, where they could try to peek between the edges of the canvas. The best they could do was to listen for footsteps. Lenara grabbed the closest person she could get her hands on, which happened to be Elson, and pulled him over.

"Now watch how this is done." She turned Elson around so his back was to the sliver of light shining in between the canvas. Instead of touching the collar with the tip of the key as Ferrin had seen others do, she laid the key longways on the collar from top to bottom. It snapped into place.

"What next?" Ferrin asked.

She held up her hand. "Wait." The key suddenly began to glow, as did the back of the collar, golden symbols appearing as if from nowhere, and then faded after a moment. Ferrin hoped none of the guards outside had noticed the light. As soon as the symbols had vanished, the key released itself from the collar and fell back into Lenara's palm.

"That's how you link a key to a specific collar. Now only that key will work." She looked at Elson and grinned. "Would you like me to test it out?"

Elson squeaked. "Please don't. I'll take your word for it."

Lenara placed the tip of the key against the center of Elson's collar, and they both began to glow once more, gold symbols appearing just before the collar snapped open. The silver piece of smooth metal split as an unseen hinge opened the collar wide enough for Elson to slide it off his neck, which he did in a hurry. The others stood around in amazement as they waited anxiously to get their own collars off.

"Here," Lenara said, handing Ferrin the key. "Show me you were paying attention." She pulled her frizzy, radish-colored hair out of the way. "Unlock mine."

"Not until you unlock the others."

She turned, her eyes revealing both surprise and hurt. "What, you don't trust me, either?"

"Let's just say I'm a cautious man."

She stared at him a moment, anger flaring in the gold flecks around her raspberry eyes. "Fine." She snatched the key from his hands and spun him around. He couldn't see what was happening, and nothing felt all that different until he heard the snap. Then a flutter rushed through his body, and he could once again feel the metal surrounding him, the bars of the cage, the nails in the wood, the pieces of iron connecting the wheels and braces under the wagon, the swords and buckles of the guards by their fires, even the collars themselves, though they felt different from the rest. He could feel the metal and the way it was formed, but there was something unusual about it.

Unfortunately, as much as his magic would allow him to sense the metal, without his crystal, he was powerless to do anything with it. He snatched the collar off his neck and watched as Lenara went through the other council members one by one, linking the key to their collars so she could unlock them as well, until it was finally her turn. She handed Ferrin the key and pulled back her hair.

Garreth grabbed his arm. "Do you think that wise?"

"I think we don't have much choice."

"Someone's coming," one of the watchers near the front called out.

"Hurry," Lenara said.

Ferrin hoped he didn't end up regretting it. Holding up the key, he did what he'd seen her do a dozen times now and placed it longways across the collar. Just like the others, it snapped into place and began to glow, the same golden symbols appearing and then disappearing before the key released and fell back into his palm. He then started to place the tip end against the smooth metal, but the watcher at the front called back again.

"They're almost here."

Ferrin didn't have time to finish. Quickly, he and Lenara dropped alongside everyone else in the wagon and pretended to be sleeping, doing their best to stay as far from the light as possible to not give away that they were no longer wearing their collars. Ferrin peeked through his lids as he watched the guard and his torch scurry by. He could hear the underbrush parting behind the wagon, and it became obvious what the man was doing when he released a heavy sigh in relief, after which point, he came trotting back, stopping only long enough to peer inside the door before heading back to his fire.

Once past, the watcher crawled back to the corner and peeked through the canvas. "He's gone."

Lenara rolled over and snatched the key out of Ferrin's hand before he had time to argue and pressed it to her collar. The set of symbols appeared around the metal just before he heard the snap. Lenara released a heavy sigh of relief as she snatched the collar off her neck and placed it with the others up under the hay. She then turned and handed Ferrin the key back.

Ferrin looked at Ismara, who was sitting right behind him. "What kind of signal were you going to give to let your father know we were ready?"

She pulled out a small metal tube with a ball attached to the end from one of her long coat sleeves and held it up.

"What's that?"

"A bosun's call."

No one said a word.

"It's a whistle."

"Oh." Ferrin looked at the tiny piece of metal. "Will it be loud enough?"

Ismara smiled and tucked it back in her sleeve.

"What about our crystals?" Elson whispered.

"And weapons," Garreth added. "I watched them place my bludgeon inside one of the carriage seats. I bet you anything that's where our crystals are being kept."

"The problem is that the carriages are located on the opposite side of the camp," Ferrin said. "Which means the only thing standing between us and them is the entire Black Watch contingent."

"Someone needs to get over there before the fighting starts," Ismara said. "I guarantee that will be the place they move to guard first."

Ferrin looked at the back of the wagon. "If I had a way to unlock the door, I could make my way through the woods and over to the carriages without being seen."

"Why you?" Garreth asked. "They have *my* weapon as well."

"They have *my* sister."

Garreth cleared his throat. "Right, sorry."

"The problem is," Ferrin continued, "how do we get out the door? Without Myron, it's not like we can just ask to use the privy."

"I might be able to help with that," Lenara said, turning to look at Elson. "Go watch the back."

Elson scrunched his nose. "Why are you always picking on me?"

She snarled, and he took off for the back. He looked out the door and then waved at the others, letting them know it was clear.

"Stand back," Lenara said, not that she needed much convincing as most tended to move out of her way regardless. She walked over to the back of the wagon and placed her hands between the bars as if measuring the distance between them. Then she mumbled something under her breath, and the bars on either side of her hands started to move.

Everyone, including Ferrin, quickly moved to the opposite side of the wagon as the bulradoer slowly bent the two bars wide enough to fit someone through. When she finished, she held out her hand to the open hole. "Will this work?"

Ferrin took a step forward hesitantly, running his hand through his hair. "How did you . . . I don't understand. You've had a crystal this entire time and you didn't tell us?"

"Yes and no."

"What does that mean? Either you do or you don't."

"I do, but not like you think."

"Then how did you just bend those bars?"

"I created a shield of air and slowly wedged it between them."

"No, I mean . . ." Ferrin was completely confused, but at this point none of it mattered. He held out his hand. "Where's the crystal? I can use it to get to the wagon and—"

"Afraid it will do you little good. I can't give you my crystal."

"Why not?"

"Because . . ." She looked at those standing nearby and sighed. "Because it's inside me."

Ferrin stood with what was sure to be a dumb look on his face, similar to the rest of those gathered around. "What?"

She grabbed the neckline of her black robe and yanked it down to the top of her chest, turning toward the light coming in from the back. There was a small ridge of skin just above her right breast, a scar that had grown over by the look of it.

"Over a thousand years ago," she said, "wizards found a way to get around the cumbersome aspect of carrying a crystal around with them everywhere they went in order for their magic to work. It was a process they went through to ensure they never lost it."

"By cutting a hole in themselves and sticking it inside of them?" Elson asked, having left his post to come stare enthusiastically at the top of her exposed chest.

She lifted her robe back into place. "No, nothing so rudimentary as this. They had a way to infuse their skin with crystal dust. Very painful, but very effective. Not only did it ensure that they would always have their magic, but it tended to give them an even greater use of it. As I'm sure you know, the closer you are to a crystal, the stronger your abilities are, and the farther away you get, the weaker they become. Imagine what you could do if every inch of your skin was permeated with crystal?"

No one said anything, like Ferrin, too enraptured by the thought of having their entire body become its own transferal, something none of them would have ever considered. The wizards of old must have been truly something.

"So why didn't you do that instead of cutting a hole in yourself?" Ismara asked.

"Because that secret died with them."

Ferrin turned and addressed the whole group. "Then this is what we do. Lenara and I will make our way around to the carriages and see if we can find a way to reach the crystals. The rest of you stay here. If another guard passes by, we can't have him seeing an empty wagon. If we can find the crystals, we'll bring them back and sound Ismara's signal."

"And if you don't make it back," Ismara asked, "like Myron hasn't?"

"Then blow your whistle and hope for the best."

"I just hope your crew doesn't mistake me for one of the other bulradoer,"

Lenara said to Ismara.

"If Myron was able to get out of camp and meet with them," Ferrin said. "Then I'm sure he told them who to watch for."

Lenara didn't look too convinced. Honestly, neither was Ferrin.

"And no one touches Sylas," Lenara said. "You do, and you'll answer to me."

Ferrin walked over to the hole in the cage and stuck his head through to make sure it was wide enough. "Let's go before Captain Treygan grows impatient and decides to storm the place, signal or no signal." He looked at Elson, who had walked back to the door to keep watch. "Do you see anyone coming?"

"No. If you're going to go, now's the time. And good luck to you both."

Ferrin squeezed through the bars, barely fitting his broad shoulders between. Once on the ground, he peeked out from under the tarp. Not seeing anyone coming, he lifted Lenara out and lowered her to the ground. Knowing who she was and what she was capable of, Ferrin felt a little awkward handling her in such a way, but she didn't seem that bothered by it, so he tried not to think about it either.

Quietly, they made their way through the snow and into the thicker underbrush behind the wagon. Ferrin hoped he didn't end up walking through the spot where the guards had been relieving themselves, and so took care to stay away from the closest trees. His hands quickly grew numb from the snow as he moved through the brush, moving low-hanging branches out of the way so they could pass. They never went beyond sight of the campfires, in order to make sure they didn't lose their bearing as they circled around.

Up ahead, the sound of snow crunching under boots had Ferrin and Lenara dropping to their bellies. Whoever it was, they were coming right for them. Light from the patroller's torch flared out of the night. Ferrin felt around for a limb thick enough to use as a club, but all he managed to come back with was a handful of snow, which he quickly rolled into a hardened ball. At the very least, he could use it to stun the man.

He felt something touch his arm, and he turned to see Lenara shaking her head. She looked up and muttered something under her breath, and a sudden gust of wind swept up into the trees just above where the guard was heading. The wind struck the upper branches, and they released their snow straight down on the man's head, dousing his torch in the process. A string of curses filled the night as the guard trudged back toward the camp, leaving them free to continue.

They made it about halfway around when a loud, all-too-familiar voice rang out through the trees. "You'll never believe who I just found wandering about the woods!"

Ferrin froze, Lenara right beside him. "Do you think he knows?"

She shrugged, and they quickly crawled through the undergrowth to get a better look. By the time they reached the outer edge of the camp, a couple of the white guards were busy lifting the canvas tarp on their wagon. If Sylas didn't know they were gone, he soon would. Lenara grabbed Ferrin's shoulder and pointed toward the fire at the center of camp, where several guards were standing around Sylas, holding someone in the middle. It looked like another guard.

Ferrin strained to see who it was. "Is that Myron?"

"I guess we know why we haven't heard from him," Lenara said.

Two of the guards that were holding him shifted, giving Ferrin a better view. It was Myron. The hood of his cloak was down, and his robes were torn and bloody. What had they done to him?

"I guess I'm not the only man capable of rising from the dead!" Sylas called out, staring at the wagons on the left. He must have still thought they were inside.

Ferrin looked at the two carriages on the right. There was no way they'd be able to get to them in time. Not before Sylas killed Myron all over again, and this time made sure he stayed dead.

"What do you want to do, smith? Whatever it is, it better be fast."

Their plan was falling apart. There was no way they could get to the carriages now. As soon as the guards realized the wagon was missing two people, the search would begin, and Sylas would order a full watch on the crystals. Worse, Ferrin had just gotten his friend back, and he wasn't going to just sit there and let him die all over again.

He looked at Lenara. "How good is your aim?"

Chapter 78 | Ferrin

DO YOU THINK YOU can hold their attention long enough for me to get to the carriages?"

Lenara looked at Ferrin like he'd forgotten who he was talking to, and then turned and took aim. "Get ready." Her face hardened in concentration as she began to mutter another incantation. She waved her arms in a circle as though running her hands across a large invisible ball, then flung the ball straight for the group at the center of the camp.

A blast of wind—so strong it nearly caused Ferrin to stumble forward as it sucked all the air around him toward it—shot from her hands and flew over the firepits. The entire circle of men standing in front of the middle prison wagon were lifted off their feet and thrown ten or fifteen feet through the air, landing on top of each other in the snow just beyond the final transport wagon.

Ferrin didn't have time to see what happened next. He took off at a dead sprint across the back side of the camp, passing bivouacs and Tower guards as he made a crazed dash straight for the carriages. No one seemed to notice him; all eyes were on the men who had just performed the incredible aerial feat across camp. Ferrin slid to a stop just behind the first carriage and scrambled behind the back wheel, snow covering his arms and legs. The shrill of a high-pitched whistle pierced the night.

Ferrin hoped there was someone out there to answer its call.

He ripped open the door of the first carriage and hopped inside, only to find himself face-to-face with Harlin, who'd been staring out the window. Harlin had barely gotten his mouth open when Ferrin leaped on top of him. He wanted to wring his neck like a chicken, but that would have been too quick a death for what the man deserved. Instead, he resorted to a very satisfying fist to Harlin's face, and then two more. Harlin's head whipped around like a hoot owl, and he dropped unconscious on the floor between the seats.

A loud roll of thunder erupted outside, and the entire carriage shook from the force. Men in white uniforms flew by. Several smacked against the side, one landing on the roof.

Ferrin was running out of time. He snatched the cushions off the seat and lifted the concealed top. He found several small chests, none of which had the collars and crystals. He did the same to the other side and found a cache of weapons, including his two magic-infused swords and Garreth's club. He grabbed all three, along with as many other weapons as he could carry.

Behind him, the door opened, and Ferrin plunged his sword straight through a very surprised man in a white uniform. Thankfully, it wasn't Myron. The man dropped dead, painting the snow with his blood. Ferrin left an unconscious Harlin lying on the floor and hopped out.

The snowstorm outside was heavy enough now that Ferrin was having a hard time seeing from one side of the camp to the other. He was able to make out the prison wagons with the light of the campfires, but only just.

By the time he'd made it to the second carriage, shouts rang out from the far side of the camp, over near the horse pens. Ferrin could see riders pouring out of the trees, but he couldn't see much else. He knew they weren't Black Watch, since they didn't blend in with the snow.

Ferrin reached the second carriage and started to turn the handle when the door snapped open and hit him in the face, knocking him backward. He lost most of the weapons he'd been carrying in the fall. A blurry shape tumbled out of the carriage on top of him. It was one of the Tower's guards. The man had a very strange look on his face, no doubt due to the bloody slit across his throat. Ferrin shoved the corpse aside and started to his feet when he was hit from behind and sent face first into a pile of snow.

He turned and grabbed his assailant, barely stopping them from plunging a small belt knife in his chest. "Myriah? It's me!"

"Ferrin?" She crawled off of him, and they both climbed back inside the carriage. "What's going on?"

"No time to explain, but we're getting out of here."

"The camp's under attack," she said, staring out the window.

Ferrin could hear the familiar sound of steel against steel, of men screaming and dying as bolts of thunder and balls of fire and wind flooded the camp. The entire glen was in utter chaos.

"I know! They're with me." He moved her to the side and ripped off the cushions on the right seat.

"What are you doing?" she asked. "You can spoil his carriage some other time."

"I'm not trying to spoil his carriage," he said, lifting the hidden compartment underneath. "I'm looking for the chest that holds our crystals. It's the same one those flaming durma collars are being stored in."

"I haven't seen them." She turned and pulled off the cushion on the opposite seat, but before she got the chance to open the storage lid underneath, the door to the carriage swung open. Three guards stood just outside.

Ferrin didn't hesitate. "Keep looking!" he shouted as he grabbed the nearest weapons he could get his hands on—a dagger and Garreth's club—and dove out the door on top of the men.

He slashed the first man's throat with the dagger before they hit the snow, and then plunged that same dagger into the chest of the second. Rolling to the side, he was back on his feet and facing the third, who had his sword drawn and was swinging for Ferrin's head. Ferrin raised Garreth's club, and the sword bounced off. He then spun and caught the man in the back of the head with the full weight of the bludgeon. There was a dull thud like the cracking of a week-old melon, and the guard hit the snow. The spikes had penetrated deep enough that Ferrin had to stand on the guard's head just to pull the club free.

"I think I found it," Myriah said, looking rather pale after seeing what was left of the guard's head.

Ferrin climbed back inside the wagon, and Myriah pointed to a chest at the back, almost too large to even fit inside the seat. The lid was open, and Ferrin could see the durmas inside, the light from the lantern behind them reflecting off their silver sheen. Beside the pile of collars lay a bag of jewelry, each with a crystal conveniently placed in a specific setting as a way to hide what it was. Ferrin could feel his magic coming to life as he dug around inside the bag. He found Rae's crystal and strung the necklace over his head, then handed Myriah the bag. "Guard that with your life."

He snatched the weapons off the floor and started to turn for the door when his eye caught something he hadn't expected to find. He reached down beside the durma chest and grabbed two silver rods.

He'd seen them before. Fought against them, in fact. He tucked them into his trousers, and they both scurried out the door and into the snow.

"What are those?" Myriah asked, staring at the bulge in Ferrin's waistline.

"Something very powerful." He didn't have time to try explaining. In truth, he didn't know what they were, just what they could do. They circled around to the front of the carriage and crouched behind the wheel so Ferrin could get a good look at the battle and determine how they were going to get to the other side of camp. "We need to get to the prison wagons," he said, pointing straight ahead.

"Are you crazy?" Myriah said, staring at the chaos between them and the tree line on the other side. "How are we going to get through that?"

Captain Treygan and the crew of the *Wind Binder* were locked sword to sword against the might of the Black Watch. What the Tower's guards made up for in numbers, the rivermen made up for with pure resolve and determination as they fought their way down the center of camp, swords clashing, blood spewing, as men in white uniforms dropped around them.

Balls of fire volleyed back and forth near the last of the cooking fires on the left, the ground shaking from the force of the concussive blasts of air being used between the wielders. Several trees had been knocked down, those unlucky enough to have been in the way of one of the wielder's discharges.

Ferrin was having a hard time spotting Lenara through the snow and the gusts of wind that whipped the white powder into the air around them, but what he could see was that she was alone, standing against two of her fellow bulradoer and their recruits. She deflected their attacks as fast as she could with some sort of invisible shield, lobbing her own balls of fire and pockets of air back in return.

Two of the grey-robed wielders were already down. One looked as though they'd been twisted nearly in half. The other was still smoldering. Both of the Tower's bulradoer carried flaming weapons, and with each new volley they seemed to gain more ground. Ferrin had to find a way to get Lenara her own magical weapons before it was too late.

Quickly, he scanned the camp for Sylas, but the inquisitor was nowhere to be seen. Knowing him, he was somewhere in the woods hiding, waiting to see the final outcome before showing his face. There was also no sign of Myron. Ferrin wondered what had happened to him after Lenara had sent them all flying. Hopefully, he'd been able to escape before Captain Treygan and his men arrived.

Ferrin dropped his armful of weapons in the snow, all but his two swords and Garreth's club.

"What are you doing?" his sister asked.

"They're just going to slow me down." He motioned them back, and they made their way around the backside of the carriages, following in his own footprints.

"Where are you going? I thought we needed to get to the wagons?"

"We do, but I need to help a friend first."

"What about these?" she asked, holding up the bag of crystals.

"They aren't going to do us much good if the person I'm trying to help dies. The wielder council hasn't been trained to fight. Even with their crystals, they wouldn't stand a chance against battle-trained wielders like the bulradoer."

They stopped at the back of the first carriage. Ferrin didn't hear movement inside, leading him to believe Harlin was still unconscious, or at least pretending to be.

"Where are we going?" Myriah asked, peeking out from behind Ferrin's shoulder.

Ferrin pointed to the flashes of light ahead.

She groaned. "I was afraid you were going to say that."

Ferrin would have left her in the carriage if he didn't think that Sylas would try to get his hands on her and use her for leverage. He tightened his grip on his swords, the same black blades he'd created during their stay in Iraseth. He could all but taste the metal as his magic flowed out of him and into the weapons. "Stay behind me."

They left the protection of the carriages and ran at an angle across the back of the camp, their eyes glued to the battle ahead. They stopped behind the first set of tents that weren't on fire and crouched in the snow, waiting for the right moment. A ball of fire bounced off one of the bulradoer's shields and flew directly at them. Myriah squealed as Ferrin dove on top of her. The flames struck the tent beside them and set it ablaze.

He quickly pulled her back to her feet, and they ran for the protection of the trees, working their way over several large trunks that had been snapped in half during the fight. His heart was racing as they made their way through the back of the underbrush, staying as low to the ground as possible to keep from getting struck by a stray ball of fire or gust of hardened air.

"Wait here," he said, placing Myriah behind one of the larger trees. "I've got to get closer."

She nodded. "Be careful."

With a deep breath to steady his nerves, he started through the underbrush. He could see Lenara just ahead, the Tower's wielders nearly on top of her. The two in black wielded swords of gold-and-green flame as the remaining grey-robed wielders hammered her shields with balls of conjured fire. As fast as he could, he crawled through the piles of debris and burnt rubble, trying to reach her without being spotted. He figured the safest place to be was directly behind her, so he worked his way toward her back.

Another ball of flames was sent darting off her shield, and he rolled through the snow to keep from getting hit, putting him directly at her rear and exactly where he wanted to be. With swords in hand, he crawled on his belly through the snow. His hands and face and feet were freezing, his fingers going numb. He was now close enough to toss the two rods to her, so he slowly pushed his way up to one knee. About the time he'd pulled back his cloak to grab the weapons, an unexpected gust struck her shield, and she was flung backward, landing directly on top of him.

Ferrin wasn't sure who was more surprised, him or her. "Brought you something," was about all he had time to say as he opened his cloak.

Her face lit up when she saw what lay beneath.

She grabbed the two rods, but before she could turn, one of the bulradoer charged and swung for her head. Ferrin barely had time to respond as he shoved her to the side and raised his swords. The wielder's weapon slammed into his blades and stopped, sparks shooting in all directions as the weapons hissed.

The bulradoer's eyes bulged. "What?"

Ferrin kicked the confused man backward far enough for Lenara to hit him with a pocket of air that sent him flying into his fellow wielders.

"Get back!" she shouted, then raised the two rods out to the side. "*Cryora!*"

Ferrin scrambled to his feet and ran as the two long strips of red flame stretched out from the top of her rods and fell across the snow, melting everything they touched. Just ahead, he could see Myriah running in his direction, no doubt having seen him go down. Ferrin made it about ten feet when he was hit by a blast of air that sent him and Myriah cartwheeling into the trees behind them.

Ferrin hit a large pine and landed in a pile of snow at the bottom. He crawled to his knees, the forest spinning. He could hear his sister calling his name, her voice seemingly getting louder. Next thing he knew, she was under his arm and pulling him to his feet.

"Are you hurt?" she asked.

Ferrin couldn't answer. He was still waiting for the wind that had been knocked out of him to return. A moment later, he finally managed to find his air. His back hurt, his chest hurt, his left arm hurt, but apparently there didn't seem to be anything broken. He looked down at his hands, rather shocked to find that he was still clutching his swords and Garreth's club. "Are you all right?" he asked.

She nodded. "I landed on a pile of brush, but . . ." She held up her hands. "I lost the crystals."

"*What?* Where?"

"I don't know. I landed over there."

They ran over to where she had hit the brush and scoured the ground, but as dark as it was, and with the heavy snowfall, they couldn't find it.

"What are we going to do?" she asked.

"Leave them. We need to get those people out of the wagons. They're open targets. I still have my crystal, which means I won't need a key."

They both turned to make a run for it, but a deadening crack spun them around. Ferrin froze, mouth gaping, as he watched Lenara's whips cut through the night like flashes of red lightning, sparking against the bulradoers' weapons, cutting through their defenses. The bulradoers' swords swung left and right, fighting to keep up with her, doing everything they could to keep from getting cut down. She broke through one of the shields, and her whip hit a recruit. The flaming brand went right through him, splitting him completely in two.

Myriah nearly retched, and Ferrin grabbed her by the shoulders, and they took off running while the Tower's wielders were preoccupied. They passed the first wagon and stopped at the second, only to find it empty.

"Where'd everyone go?" He turned and scanned the trees behind them, but it was too dark to see much past the first two or three. There wasn't much he could do for them now, so he turned, and they ran back to the first wagon. "Come on."

He reached the first the wagon and pulled back the canvas tarp. The people inside screamed and ran for the other side of the cage.

"Stop!" he said. "We're here to get you out." He stuck his swords into the snow at his feet and grabbed hold of the bars. His magic pulsed into the metal, and they easily bent outward, leaving a large hole for the prisoners to escape.

He and Myriah helped them out, and they gathered around him at the back. "Keep quiet and stay low." He peeked out from behind the first wagon at the battle being fought on the other side, then quickly ran for the next, the group following him as they made their way toward the third and final prison transport.

A shriek behind him had Ferrin turning.

A couple of white guards were attacking those at the rear, cutting down the defenseless people as they tried to scatter. "Move!" Ferrin shouted as he barreled through the wielders, swords in the air. Three of their people were already down and bleeding in the snow.

Ferrin's rage took over, his magic flowing through his own blades and into those of the guards. Their swords bent backward as soon as they touched his, leaving the men just as helpless as the unarmed wielders. He killed them both with swift thrusts to the chest.

Bending down, he lifted the one wielder who was still breathing and handed her to a couple of the others. "Stay here while I free those in the front wagon." They huddled in a circle in back of the middle wagon and waited while Ferrin headed to the next one up.

Like the first, he found a cage full of scared men, women, and children. After he pulled the bars apart, he quickly helped them out and led them back to the second transport where the rest of the prisoners were waiting. A loud boom had them all dropping to their knees. Ferrin peered around the wagon to see if he could get a better idea of what had caused it, but he couldn't see much through the snow and the clash of fighters in the center of camp.

Ferrin hoped Lenara was all right. He turned to Myriah. "I want you to take these people into the woods and find somewhere to keep them hidden."

"What about you?"

"Those are my friends out there fighting for our lives. I've got to help them, but I can't do that if I'm having to worry about you and the rest of these defenseless people."

She hugged him. "You better come back to me."

"I always do." He kissed her cheek. "Now go while you have the chance." He watched the group melt into the surrounding woods, saying a small prayer for their safety, something he was doing more often than not of late. Azriel would have been proud.

Quickly, he made his way to the front wagon chain and peered around the edge. The front of the camp was empty, nothing but a couple of supply wagons and horse pens, which had been cut and the animals released. He worked his way around to the front of the wagon and stopped at the corner to get his bearings.

Ahead, through the campfires, he could see Captain Treygan and his men fighting as hard as they could to hold the Black Watch troops off. They didn't appear to be winning. The ground they had gained looked to be slipping. They were now somewhere between the middle wagon and the one he was hiding behind.

Ferrin spotted Ismara near the front alongside her father, which meant Myron might be in there as well. Quickly, he turned and scanned the rest of the camp. There was still no sign of Sylas. The inquisitor was probably halfway back to the city by now. Ferrin would have to worry about him later. Right now, he had a battle to join.

With swords raised, Ferrin charged out from behind the wagon and straight for the fight ahead.

Chapter 79 | Ferrin

ERRIN PUSHED HIS WAY to the front. "Glad to see you're still alive," he shouted at Ismara and stuck his blade through the first white cloak he saw.

"Where've you been?" she shouted back angrily, her cutlass doing most of the talking as it hacked and stabbed and sliced away at the Tower's guards. "We need those wielders."

"Afraid I'm all you got."

"What?" Captain Treygan bellowed on Ferrin's right as he tore into two men at once, cutlass in one hand, his bone-handle knife in the other. What he lacked in finesse, he made up for in power and speed. "Where are they?"

Beside the captain, Bones, his tall first mate, spun a set of hand kamas about like Ferrin had never seen, carving through men like a sculptor with a block of wood, the white paint on his dark skin making him all the more intimidating.

"We don't have no help coming?" a familiar voice grumbled out somewhere on the other side of Bones. It was hard to mistake Kettle's natural whiny tone, as he always seemed in a constant state of complaining, reminding Ferrin a little of Doloff.

"We don't have the crystals," Ferrin said as he plunged his sword into another member of the Watch, then yanked it free. "Without magic, most of the prisoners will just get in the way." He blocked a swing for his head and kicked the man backward while his sword was in the air. "Has anyone seen Myron?"

"I'm over here!" a voice rang out just left of Ismara. Myron was wearing a wool coat overtop his uniform, no doubt to keep Treygan's men from accidentally mistaking him for the enemy.

"Where's Sylas?" Ferrin shouted as he kept his swords moving, deflecting those coming at him, while pushing his magic through the metal of his own blades into those they touched, bending them back on themselves.

"After we were hit by the freakish gust of wind, he took off into the woods."

Both Garreth and Elson were there as well, fighting between other members of the crew to keep their left flank from getting overrun. Most of the help came from Whitey, who was quite frankly one of the biggest men Ferrin had ever seen, and for a smith of Ferrin's stature, that was saying something. The riverman was every bit as tall as Bones, with a tree trunk for a back. His wide-brim hat still sat atop his head despite the frosty breeze blowing in with the storm.

Ferrin helped divert another drive from those in front, cutting one man's legs out from under him while dismantling another's sword, his magic coursing through him and into his blades. The magic warmed him against the cold. The first break he got, he grabbed Garreth's bludgeon out from under his cloak and held it up. "I have something of yours, Garreth!"

Garreth swung like a madman at one of the guards trying to break through their line. He got a hold of the man and started punching him in the face with the crossguard of his sword. When the man finally went down, his face bloody beyond recognition, Garreth turned. His eyes widened when he saw the bludgeon. "Throw it!"

Ferrin tossed the spiked club to him, and Garreth snatched it out of the air, then turned and clubbed the first guard close enough to reach, sending even more blood and viscera up into the air as the spikes connected with the man's head.

Elson howled on Garreth's left and went down, disappearing from view. Garreth jumped into the middle to dam up the hole that had been created by the loss, using his sword to block and parry, while piercing arms and shoulders and heads with his spiked club. But no matter how hard he tried, Ferrin could see he wasn't going to be able to hold the line for long.

Ferrin tried pulling away from his spot to help, but two more of the Watch managed to push their way past Treygan. Ferrin blocked the first blade, but the second caught his arm, and he lost one of his swords. The cut was deep, but desperation forced him to fight through the pain as he stabbed the second man straight through the thigh and then kicked him to the side for Treygan to finish off. Spinning, he diverted the first guard's swing, then grabbed the man's sword with his bare hand and snapped off the blade. The guard's jaw dropped, and he quickly melted back into the Watch's dwindling ranks.

Pulling back, Ferrin pushed his way through their own fighters to reach his friend. He grabbed Elson by the arms and dragged him out of the fight and over near one of the cook fires so he could better see the wound. Elson gritted his teeth as his hand clutched a bloodstained hole in his jacket. Ferrin pulled back the coat. The shirt underneath was already soaked.

"You wouldn't happen to be carrying a flask on you by chance, now would you?" Elson asked, blood in his mouth as he coughed. "I'd hate to go out without a stiff drink. Always thought I'd die with a bottle in my hand."

There was nothing Ferrin could do except try to wad the bottom of Elson's shirt and hold it over the wound. He didn't even have time to stand by his friend's side as he died. If he didn't get back to the line, they were all going to die.

Elson seemed to understand. "Go!" He pushed Ferrin back with what little strength he still had. "I'll be fine." He smiled bravely as Ferrin stood. Ferrin nodded, offering a smile that said he wished there was something more he could do. "Better here than in the Tower," he said.

Unable to wait longer, Ferrin turned and ran for the back of the rivermen's ranks. The Tower's guards might have been going down, but not fast enough. If they didn't find a way to turn the tide, they were going to be overrun.

He barely made it three strides when something smashed into his side and sent him rolling, something heavy and full of fur. By the time he realized what it was, the wolf had Ferrin's arm between his teeth, the same arm that had been wounded during the fight. He cried out as the pain seared him like a piece of steel hot off the coals. Out of the woods on Ferrin's right, a pack of dark-grey wolves closed in on the back of their ranks.

Ferrin shouted at the crew in warning as he spun on his back in a circle to keep the wolf from reaching his neck. He pounded the creature in the face with his fist, hard enough to knock it off his arm, then kicked it backward into the snow. The wolf shot back to its feet, opened its jaws, and charged. Ferrin reached for his sword, getting it over just in time to catch the creature in full lunge. It dropped beside him.

With his arm completely numb from the elbow down, he pushed his way to his feet, his legs shaking. There was only one person who could have sent a pack of frenzied animals to attack them. Ferrin quickly scanned the tree line, but there was no sign of the inquisitor anywhere. Another boom shook the glen, originating from the far side, where Ferrin could still see flashes of green and red and gold sparking in the distance, along with short trails of lightning and smoke. The sound was loud enough that even the wolves stopped to see what had happened before continuing their attack.

Bones, along with a couple of the crew, spotted the wolves and pulled back to meet them. The pack charged, and the tall dark-skinned man barely managed a single swing of his kamas when an enormous shape tore out of the trees and plowed straight through the entire pack, carrying one of the wolves away in its jaws. Ferrin almost shouted when Nola flung the now-dead animal and turned to face the others, teeth bared. A shape detached itself from the top of the great white wolf and ran straight for him.

Rae nearly knocked Ferrin off his feet as she wrapped her arms around him and buried her head in his chest. He cried out at the sudden onslaught of pain that ripped through his body at her embrace, and she quickly released him. Without taking the time to tell her how happy he was to see her, he lifted her off her feet with his one good arm and sprinted back toward the cookfire, where he set her down beside Elson's body.

"Help him, please." Elson's eyes where shut, and he wasn't moving. "Save him if you can."

Rae grabbed the crystal still hanging from Ferrin's neck and put her hands over the wound, and they began to glow a soft purple, the magic seeping down into Elson's skin, something Ferrin was all too familiar with.

There was a loud barking growl behind him, and Ferrin spun, sword in hand. One of the wolves had broken free of the pack and was bounding through the snow straight for them. Ferrin's magic tore through the sword, and the blade extended, giving him a longer reach as he rushed the creature, his one good arm up, howling just as loud as the wolf. With a well-placed swing, he hit the animal across the front of its chest, but not deep enough to stop him.

The wolf leaped, and Ferrin dove to the side, his sword reshaping into a long dagger, with the extra metal forming a basket guard over Ferrin's hand like the guard of a cutlass. He turned and slashed at the creature as it attacked from the side. The wolf howled and spun, snapping at him, but only catching the protective metal over Ferrin's hand. Ferrin's left arm hung limp at his side, numb from blood loss and cold.

They circled each other a moment, then the wolf spotted Rae and Elson. Realizing they were much easier prey, it turned and sprinted in their direction.

"Rae! Watch out!"

Rae turned and shrieked, throwing her arms in the air.

The wolf dove, but Elson suddenly sat up, grabbed his sword from off the ground, and stuck it through the creature's neck. The dead animal barreled into them, knocking Rae into the snow and landing on top of Elson.

Elson pushed the creature off his chest and shot to his feet. "Wow! That was a rush! I feel like a brand-new man." He raised his sword and ran toward the battle, shouting at the top of his lungs the entire way.

Ferrin was about to do the same when Rae grabbed his arm and pulled him around. He felt her magic flood through him as soon as she touched her crystal. The ice slithered in through his shoulder and down his arm, and the pain faded. He leaned down and kissed her, then took off running back toward the fight, leaving her standing there a little doe-eyed.

He passed Nola on the way. She had the wolves on the run, half their pack lying dead at her feet. Apparently, Sylas only had so much control over them before instinct and common sense took over. Nola's white fur was stained red, blood dripping from her mouth. She looked positively terrifying. Ferrin smiled at the big creature on the way by. She bared her teeth, and he cringed, but he stopped long enough to point back toward the fire. "Go protect Rae!" Nola seemed to understand and trotted over to the short healer and stood protectively beside her.

Knowing Rae had someone, or something, there to keep her safe, Ferrin turned and fought his way back to the front line, where he found Garreth swinging his club wildly at anything in front of him. Blood covered half his face, most of it his.

Ferrin pulled the man back from the front. "Go have the healer look at that." He shoved Garreth in the general direction and quickly took his place, cutting back the white guards as fast as he could. He grabbed a spare sword off the ground, leaving his newly shaped long dagger with the protective guard just as it was, and began hacking away at the Tower's front ranks.

He had a renewed strength, courtesy of Rae's magic, and he couldn't let it go to waste. On his right, Ismara took a knife to her arm and nearly went down, but Ferrin managed to chop the guard's arm off at the elbow as he lunged for the final kill. "Rae's here! Go see to your wound!"

"Go see to your own flaming wounds!" she shouted and stabbed the next man in the throat with her own long dagger.

Ferrin stepped back from the front to catch his breath and nearly tripped over Rae, who was busy moving through the back of their ranks, healing those in the worst shape and offering a small dose of renewed strength to the rest. Nola was right there beside her, keeping watch with her large golden eyes.

Ferrin started to reprimand her for getting so close, but another loud boom shook the glen, diverting his attention as streams of lightning poured down from the sky, so bright everyone was forced to stop to cover their eyes. All the hair on Ferrin's body seemed to be standing on end. By the time the streaks of light had faded and the smoke cleared, there was nothing left of the bulradoer and their grey recruits but a pile of charred flesh and smoldering cloth.

A single black-robed figure stood amidst the smoke, two flaming red whips stretched out beside her. Lenara turned and looked at what was left of the Black Watch. One look at those fiery red strands and what remained of their own wielders, and they threw down their weapons and surrendered.

Treygan and his men, those not being healed by Rae, marched the Tower's guards over to the prison wagons and used a key they'd collected from one of the guards to lock them in. With Myron's help, Ferrin scoured the section of the camp where he'd lost his second sword during the fight. They found it sticking halfway out from under one of the fallen guards. Ferrin cleaned off the blood and handed it to Myron, so they each had one to carry.

With the Tower's soldiers out of the way, Ferrin and Myron took off into the woods in search of Myriah and the other wielders. The falling snow made it more difficult to track them, as their trail had been mostly covered.

They eventually split up to cover more ground, both shouting at the top of their lungs as they pressed forward. How far had they gone? Ferrin wondered as he trudged through the snow, nearly knee-deep in some places. The trees all looked the same. It would be easy to get lost out here in the daytime, let alone after dark and in the middle of a snowstorm.

"Over here!" Myron shouted on his right. Ferrin raced through the undergrowth to find the large group holed up under a couple of downed trees. They had dug out a small shelter with their hands, using tree limbs to try keeping the snow off as best they could. There were at least two dozen men, women, and children, all huddled with their hoods up against the snow.

Ferrin spotted his sister after she had lowered her hood, and he snatched her up in his arms. She was shivering. "It's over. You're safe." He turned to Myron. "We need to get them back to the fires." With his arm around his sister, they led the shivering group of wielders back toward camp, where they were met by rivermen who helped them over to the cooking fires.

"You need to rest," Ferrin said, pulling her aside and sitting her down on a stump near the central pit. There were dark circles under her eyes and her legs were trembling. It was a wonder she could even stand on her own.

Rae walked over and joined them by the fire. Noticing Rae's attention wasn't on him but the redheaded woman standing at his side, Ferrin quickly introduced her to his sister, then left them to get better acquainted as he walked over to where Lenara was slowly picking through the pile of burnt bodies on the far side of the camp.

"Glad you're on our side," he said as he stopped beside one of the smoldering corpses.

"I'm not on anyone's side," she said and knelt down and lifted a hilt out from under some charred cloth.

"Is that one of those fire weapons?"

Lenara nodded. "They need to be protected. Don't want them falling into the wrong hands."

"And what hands would that be, as you say you don't have a side?"

Lenara rolled her shoulders. "They will be safe with me." She turned and looked at Ferrin. "I see you found your sister. Did you find Joren?"

Ferrin shook his head. "Myron was the last to see him. He said as soon as you hit them with that gust of wind, Sylas took off running into the woods."

"Curse him!" She stood and looked at the tree line.

"It'll do little good to go wandering through there in the dark," he said. "We'll wait till daybreak and use Nola to track him down."

"Who?"

Ferrin pointed back toward the fires where the great white wolf was standing beside Rae. "That's Nola."

Lenara spotted the wolf, and her brows rose slightly. "You have a frost wolf?"

"A what?"

Lenara left the pile of bodies and walked with Ferrin back across the camp to get a better look. She lowered her hood on approach, especially when Nola's lips parted and released a deep-throated growl. Treygan's crew moved aside as the bulradoer stepped over to examine the wolf. Ferrin wasn't sure if they were moving for Lenara's sake or for Nola's.

"She's beautiful," Lenara said, slowly circling the enormous animal. "I never thought to actually see one." Lenara was careful not to touch Nola, but it didn't stop her from getting close enough to if she wanted. "It is said that the frostborn wolves were used in the making of hor'hounds. Looking at her, I can see why."

Ferrin looked at Nola as though seeing her for the first time. "She's a hor'hound?"

"No. But they were created from her kind."

"What is this frostborn you speak of?"

Lenara gave him a curious look. "The frostborn. Those born in the Northlands."

"The Frozen North?"

She nodded. "Those that live beyond the Gates of Bel'Taag are considered frostborn. That is where she is from." Lenara turned and looked at Nola. "How she found her way through is quite the mystery."

"Look at her," Ferrin said. "I'm sure it wasn't too hard to make it across the mountains."

Lenara stared at the wolf, but her mind was somewhere else. "Let's hope that's not the case."

"What do you mean?"

Lenara turned and looked at him. "Because that would mean the shroud is weakening."

"The shroud?"

"After the fall of . . . of the first wizard, and his imprisonment in the Pits of Aran'gal, the Gates of Bel'Taag were closed, sealing off Aldor from the rest of the North, making sure to keep any of his remaining followers from reaching Taerin nu'Cyllian in an attempt to set him free. To keep any from finding their way in or out of the Frozen North, a barrier was put in place throughout the mountains. A shroud of mist said to be impenetrable." She looked at Nola. "If she is truly frostborn, then that could mean the barrier is weakening."

Ferrin felt queasy. That was a history lesson he would rather not have known right now. The thought that containment in and out of Aerodyne's prison might be weakening was about the last thing he wanted to hear. Those gathered around to listen looked just as disturbed.

"Where did you find her?" Lenara asked.

"I . . . I don't know. She found us."

"Interesting. Who has she bonded with?" Lenara looked at Rae. "With you?"

"She is closest to Suri," Ferrin said. "Rae's daughter." He was curious what she meant by bonding.

"My daughter talks to her," Rae added defensively, her hand going to her belt knife as she glared at Lenara. She walked over to stand beside Ferrin. "Why is she here? Do you not know who she is?"

"Yes, I know who she is, or was. She will not harm you."

Rae sneered. "She's with Sylas."

"Not anymore."

Lenara turned her back on Nola and walked over to Rae. "You have nothing to fear from me, I—"

A small ruckus on the left had everyone turning as one of the wielders suddenly grabbed Myriah and dragged her away from the fire and back toward the prison wagons.

Ferrin drew his sword and started for them but stopped when he saw the glimmer of a blade at her throat. "What do you think you're—"

The wielder threw back his hood, and Ferrin's heart nearly stopped.

Sylas!

Chapter 80 | Ferrin

SYLAS MUST HAVE DISGUISED himself as one of the prisoners while in the woods and simply walked into camp with the rest of them.

Ferrin tightened his grip on his long dagger as he slowly inched his way forward. "Sylas, you so much as look at her wrong and you'll be begging me for the wiggler."

"No!" Lenara rushed forward and grabbed Ferrin's arm, pulling him to a stop. "You promised me."

Ferrin looked at Sylas, then back at Lenara. "If he hurts her, there's no promise in Aldor that will stop me from mounting his head on a pike."

Sylas continued to back slowly toward the wagons, where the Black Watch guards stood watching. "Unlock the cages."

Treygan and his crew drew their weapons and started forward, but Ferrin quickly held out his hand. "Don't anyone move."

They stopped but kept their weapons at the ready.

Ferrin looked at Sylas. "You should have kept running while you had the chance."

Sylas sneered. "And let you go? Ha! I'll see us both dead before I—"

Sylas froze for a split moment, his eyes staring straight ahead but looking at nothing.

"—let that happen," he continued. Sylas looked around as though he wasn't quite sure what had just happened. Concern on his face, he whistled over his shoulder, and several horses trotted out of the woods. No doubt some of those that the *Wind Binder*'s crew had set free during their raid. Sylas smiled triumphantly at Ferrin. "Now open the—"

Sylas's face went rigid once again. "No! I forbid it! How are you—"

Sylas turned and looked at the bulradoer standing beside Ferrin. "Lenara?"

The knife pressing against Myriah's throat lowered slightly.

"Joren?" Lenara started for him, but Ferrin grabbed her just as the knife lifted once more.

"No, you don't!" Sylas shouted, talking to nobody in particular. "You don't think I can feel you dying inside me?"

"What in the flaming Pits is going on?" Treygan demanded, his crew now pressing up behind Ferrin and Lenara, just waiting for the word to attack. Ferrin could hear Ismara behind him, trying to explain to her father what was happening.

"The key!" Sylas demanded. "Now!" He turned and looked back over his shoulder at the tree line. "Bring me the collars."

Ferrin wondered who he was talking to, then a figure stepped out from behind one of the trees and started forward between the wagons. Ferrin bit down, his teeth grinding as he squeezed the hilt of his swords.

Harlin trembled as he made his way over to Sylas, carrying a set of silver collars in his hands. A darkened area about the size of Ferrin's fist colored the side of his face. He looked at Sylas and the blade pressed against Myriah's throat. "You promised me you'd keep her alive."

"Do what I tell you and I just might." He nodded toward Ferrin. "Now collar him." He looked at Lenara. "Collar them both."

A flash of red on Lenara's right caught Ferrin's eye, and everyone behind her backed away. Ferrin didn't need to look to know she'd just ignited one of her whips.

Harlin stopped a few steps out, his eyes glued to the flaming weapon.

Ferrin reached over and put his hand on Lenara's arm. "Don't. Not while he has a knife to Myriah's throat." The thought of having that piece of silver back around his neck was crippling, but nothing was more important to him than his sister.

Harlin turned and looked at Sylas for instruction.

"Go on! What are you waiting for?"

Harlin cautiously walked over and placed the collar around Ferrin's neck. Ferrin took a deep breath as it snapped shut and his magic vanished.

Harlin turned to Lenara, and she raised her whip. "You take another step closer and I'll cut you in half. No one is going to put a collar on me ever again."

Ferrin was growing nervous. It was clear Lenara had no qualms with seeing Myriah killed as long as it meant not being imprisoned again.

Sylas glared at Lenara. "I can't wait to get you back under—"

Sylas's eyes went blank once more, the knife lowering.

Ferrin wasn't waiting a third time. He backhanded Harlin so hard it sent him cartwheeling into the snow, then made a dash for Sylas. He was going to put an end to the man once and for all. An invisible force hit him in the side and sent him careening to the left, where he landed just in front of the next wagon over. He was back on his feet before he came to a complete stop and raced for Sylas again, only to slam headfirst into one of Lenara's shields.

"What do you think you're doing?" he shouted at Lenara as he pounded on the invisible barrier. She didn't answer, her eyes on the battle in front of her, a battle between two men for possession of a single body.

"No!" Sylas shouted and raised his blade, forcing Lenara to stop a few feet away.

Sylas's face softened, and Joren's knife lowered. "Lenara. I can't hold him back!" Joren was fighting with everything he had to remain in control. Ferrin wasn't sure how he was doing it, since apparently the only time the young guard was able to maneuver his own body was when Sylas was in a deep sleep. Perhaps desperation was the driving force.

"She's mine!" Sylas shouted, the fire in his eyes returning. "You will not—"

Joren grabbed Myriah and shoved her straight at Lenara. Lenara grabbed her and heaved her in Ferrin's direction, his shield suddenly disappearing. "Take her!" She turned to Joren. "Hold on!" She ran for him, but he held out his hand.

"Stop!"

The fire in his eyes returned. "What do you think you're doing?" Sylas demanded. "You've lost! Now be a good little . . ." His eyes widened, nothing but fear inside. "No!"

Joren's head lifted. "I am no longer yours to control!" He looked at Lenara. "Forgive me," he said, and plunged the dagger into his chest.

Lenara screamed and ran to him, catching him before he hit the ground, cradling his head to her chest. "Why? We could have found a way."

Joren smiled, blood dripping from the corners of this mouth. "It was too late, and we both know it." His breathing grew rigid. "It took everything I had left to give."

"Bring me the healer, quick!" she demanded.

Rae pushed through the crowd of onlookers and knelt down beside them in the snow. She reached out with her hand, but Joren slapped it away and shook his head. "No." He looked at Lenara, his breaths staggered. "This is the only way I can keep you safe." His words were weak as he fought to hold on. "Healing me will only bring him back." He tried smiling, barely able to catch one more gulp of air. "I love you."

She leaned down and kissed him, and when she lifted her head, he was gone.

Rae stood and backed away slowly, joining the others as they moved to give Lenara room. Ferrin stood as well, staring at the dead man with a mix of emotions. He certainly wasn't going to shed a tear for Cheeks, but at the same time, he wished for Lenara's sake that there had been a way to save her young guard. The man had saved Ferrin's sister at the cost of his own life. Ferrin was tempted to walk over and try consoling the bulradoer, but the way she was crying, he thought it best not to. Instead, he directed his sister over to one of the cooking fires where he found Myron, Rae, and Elson standing alongside Ismara and Treygan.

"Where is Suri?" Ferrin asked.

"I left her on the ship with Needle," Rae said.

Myron walked over and placed a blanket around Myriah's shoulders. "Thought you might need this."

Ferrin's head shot up. "Harlin." He turned and scanned the ground over near where he'd last seen the pompous lord, but there was no sign of him. "Where'd that son of a coward go!"

"Last I saw of him," Garreth said, his arm protectively around his wife, "he was running in that direction." Garreth pointed to the trees on the left side of the camp, just beyond the burnt remains of the Tower's wielders. "I doubt anyone will be seeing him anytime soon, or at all." He started to chuckle but received a swift elbow to the side from his wife, who nodded toward Myriah.

Several of the others on the council looked at Myriah as well, seemingly unsure how to respond, as he was her husband.

Myriah lowered her head. "I'm sorry. If I had known—"

"None of us knew," Elson was quick to pipe in. "There's nothing to be sorry for. The man was a good-for-nothing snake who was willing to sell us all out to save his own skin."

"What about our crystals?" someone asked. It was a man from one of the other prison wagons that Ferrin had set free, wielders the Tower had collected before reaching Rhowynn.

"We'll have to search for them in the morning," Ferrin said. "They were lost during the battle, but I know the general location of where they ought to be. We shouldn't have any problem once the sun comes up."

The man didn't look all that happy as he turned and walked back over to join his friends around the next fire over.

"What do we do now?" Doloff asked.

Ferrin hadn't even noticed the council's pessimist standing there. He was busy helping Ella wrap Old Mother Luka in a spare blanket they'd procured from one of the nearby bivouacs.

"We go home," Garreth said.

Ferrin was sure Garreth and his wife were anxious to leave, knowing their children were still at home, having no idea what had happened to them.

"But is it safe?" Ilene asked. Ilene had a very structured way of looking at things, which was what made her such a sought-after clerk. "The Tower knows where we are. They know now where to look."

A rustling of brush behind, and Nola trotted out of the woods with something in her mouth. She stopped beside the first firepit and dropped it into the snow. Whatever it was, it was still alive.

Myron took a couple of steps toward forward. "Is that?"

"It is," Ferrin said and took off through the blood-soaked snow toward the squirming ball of whimpering flesh.

Harlin turned over and actually cried when he saw Ferrin. "Please don't—"

Ferrin grabbed Harlin by the front of his shirt and yanked him off the ground. There were gash marks and blood on both sides of his body from where Nola had carried him. Ferrin drew his long dagger and pressed it to Harlin's neck. He'd been waiting for this moment for nearly a year. The only two things that had kept him going through it all were the chance of rescuing his sister and his desire to get his revenge on Harlin.

But now that he was face-to-face with the man, for some reason he couldn't bring himself to do it. Harlin was all but whimpering, tears running down his cheeks, snot dripping from his nose. He was a shell of himself. A man who had sold out everyone he had ever known. His life was over, and he knew it, and in that moment, Ferrin just couldn't find the pleasure he had hoped for in plunging in his knife.

A hand gripped his arm and Ferrin turned. It was Myriah. She was crying as well, looking at her husband. She looked at Ferrin, and the compassion in her eyes had him lowering his blade. Instead of killing him, Ferrin marched him over to the wagon holding the remaining members of the Black Watch and tossed him inside. After locking the door behind him, Ferrin stopped beside Lenara on his way back to the fire, as she was in the process of trying to lift Joren by herself. "Here, let me help."

Lenara shoved his arm away. "Stay back. No one touches him but me."

Ferrin stood to the side respectfully and watched as she hefted Joren's body up over her shoulder and carried him into the woods. He wanted to help, knowing how badly she must be hurting, but with Lenara it was best not to press. He watched her disappear into the trees before joining the others around the fire.

Elson looked at Ferrin, then back toward the woods. "Should we . . ."

Ferrin shook his head. "Best we leave her alone." He turned and looked at Ilene. "You are correct. The Tower knows we are here. It's going to get even more dangerous for those of you who plan on staying."

Elson put his hand on Ferrin's shoulder. "Are you saying you're not?"

Ferrin looked at the others gathered round, most of which were members of the wielder council, and a few from the *Wind Binder*'s crew, those who hadn't been sent to scour the campsite for supplies. "My only reason for coming back was my sister," he said, putting his arm around Myriah and hugging her close. "The inquisitors had planned on capturing her to get to me. My intention was to sneak in, grab her, and have the two of us sneak back out without anyone the wiser. That way, the Tower wouldn't have known about the rest of you."

"Clearly, that plan didn't work out as intended," Elson said, producing a stoppered jug of ale he must have procured from one of the other fires. He took a quick swig and gritted his teeth. "That's got bite."

Ferrin sighed. "Obviously things didn't go to plan."

Ismara grunted. "As we are all painfully aware."

Ferrin gave her a harsh look, and she shrugged. "Just saying."

He stared at the frightened faces around the warm blaze as the snow continued to fall. "I suggest you think about leaving Rhowynn. If you have family living elsewhere, this might be a good time to consider joining them."

"But we've killed or captured everyone who knows about us," Garreth said, him and his wife looking rather troubled at the idea of leaving their home. "Why should *we* be forced to leave?"

"And how do you know that this was all of them?" Ferrin asked. "This might not have been the entire regiment. They could have very well left others behind. They could have sent some back to the Tower even as we speak. And even if by chance this was all of them, there is still the corax."

Elson lowered his jug, halfway through another swallow. "The what?"

"The White Tower's winged watchers. They've been tracking us since we left the Tower months ago."

Everyone turned and looked up, not that they could have seen anything through the snowfall.

"The point is," Ferrin said, "that we really don't know how safe we would be if we stayed. In a city the size of Rhowynn, you could simply move and that might be enough. For those of us who have noted vocations like my smithy, hiding will be a lot more difficult. I can't tell you what is best for you and your family, but for me and mine, we are going to push on."

"Where do you plan to go?" Doloff asked. As one of the city's poulters, his occupation might have been one not as easily hidden. "A mite cold to be wandering around Aldor this time of year."

Ferrin started to tell him his plan of heading east to the capital of Sidara, then thought better of it. "Perhaps it might be safest for all of us if we didn't share that sort of information with each other. We've already seen how dangerous that can be in the wrong hands." All of the council members turned at the same time and looked back at the prison transport, where Harlin sat curled in the back and as far from the Tower's guards as possible.

"Do that, though," Ella said, one arm around Mother Luka, "and I feel as though they have won. They've managed to frighten us into silence, no longer willing to even be seen together, to socialize. We are a far greater threat to them together than apart."

Ferrin hated to admit it, but the soft-spoken young woman had a point. She didn't even need to use her gift with emotions to persuade them. At least he didn't think she was. "What she says isn't wrong."

"And I, for one, agree," Garreth chimed in rather quickly, receiving an approving nod from his wife. "We plan on staying. Our home is located outside the city, and less open to incursion, so if it will make you feel safer, we can continue our meetings there. Our doors are always open."

The others looked almost relieved with the offer, clearly not wanting to move their entire lives.

"In truth, though," Ferrin said, "for those of you who intend to stay, please give heed to my suggestion of at least moving to a different part of the city. For those of you interested in leaving, however, you are always welcome to join us. Captain Treygan and his crew, I'm sure, will be more than happy to carry you as far south as . . ." He turned and looked at Treygan.

"We can assure you safe passage as far as Hedgemont," Treygan said. "Or, if you prefer traveling beyond the Razor Spine, we could take you all the way to Aramoor, but I'll be honest, the royal city isn't what it used to be. Dakaran isn't his father. Taxes are up, trade is down, and it seems the Tower's guards are everywhere. You can't throw a rock in Aramoor and not hit a member of the Black Watch. Not to mention, the city is being heavily overrun by Cylmarans. The splendor that was Aramoor is quickly losing its luster."

"I don't believe we are in any immediate danger," Ferrin said, "as I'm sure it will take a while for the Tower to reassign another regiment to the city, but for those of you who plan on moving, I'd consider looking sooner rather than later. I'll be putting my smithy up for auction as soon as I get back."

"Don't take too long," Captain Treygan said. "I have a business to run as well.

I can't sit around spinning my thumbs. If my ship isn't toting cargo, me and my men don't get paid."

Ferrin smiled. "I'm sure we can find a way to make it worth your while."

"I am wife to a Rhowynn lord," Myriah said. "I have no doubt I can see to you and your crew's needs, Captain."

Ferrin looked at her, a little surprised.

Myriah shrugged. "What? At least I can salvage something out of my poorly chosen marriage."

"Speaking of," Myron said, gesturing back over his shoulder toward the wagons. "What do we do with all of them? It's not like we can just turn them over to the city patrollers."

"I say we kill 'em and be done with it," Ismara said, getting a hardy "Aye" from the *Wind Binder*'s crew.

"I don't know," Ilene said. "Killing defenseless people like that seems like something the other side would do."

"Exactly," Elson said, helping himself to another chug of ale. "It's precisely what they had planned for all of us. Actually, after hearing Ferrin's story, what they had planned was a whole lot worse. Killing them would be a mercy."

Doloff rubbed the top of his head nervously. "Ilene is right, it just doesn't feel right."

"Then what do you suggest we do with them," Elson asked. "Should we turn them over to the city patroller, who will no doubt release them before we make it out of the office?"

A shrill cry of rage and grief rose from the woods behind them as Lenara broke through the underbrush, her hands in the air. Many of those around the fire dropped to the ground as several strands of blinding green light shot from the sky and struck the prison wagon. It was like reliving Ferrin's first arrival at the White Tower all over again as the bodies inside the cage exploded, many with their parts blowing through the bars to cover the ground outside the wagon.

Even Nola ran behind the carriages to hide.

As soon as the lightning was over and the last of the blood and viscera had landed, those around the fire cautiously crawled back to their feet and watched the short bulradoer storm across the camp toward the carriages. Nola howled when she saw the wielder coming and quickly padded across the snow and over to where Rae and Ferrin were standing, causing several of the wielders to back away. Nothing like a horse-sized wolf with bloody fangs to give a person reason to move.

"I guess that answers that question," Elson said with a gulp, his face as pale as the others.

Ferrin looked at Myriah. Her eyes bulged in shock as she stared at the bloody meat wagon. He put his arm around her and turned her away. "Don't look." He hated that she had just witnessed something like that. Harlin was a pig and had it coming, but even Ferrin was feeling a twinge of guilt at what had just taken place. "I'm sorry."

Myriah didn't say anything, her body trembling as she stared at the fire.

Ferrin looked out across the camp, the part not covered in blood and guts, then up at the sky. "Best we sleep here tonight. The storm's too strong to try riding back into Rhowynn. We'll wait for first light and start back in the morning." He turned to Garreth. "Will your children be safe enough at home without you?"

Garreth nodded. "Our oldest is thirteen. She can keep the others in line for tonight."

"What do we do about that?" Myron asked, pointing back toward the wagons and the gruesomeness inside.

"We'll burn it," Ferrin said. "Burn it all. Get rid of the evidence." He looked at Treygan. "Best we start with salvaging what we can of the soldiers' tents."

"Already ahead of ya, lad." He nodded toward the northernmost firepit closest to the supply wagons. The crew had already begun setting up tents around the fire. Kettle was standing just beside, stirring a large pot with an apron over his clothes.

After what they'd just witnessed, Ferrin doubted anyone was up to eating.

Everyone scurried about, trying to help as best they could, though no one was willing to go near the carriages for fear of disturbing Lenara. Ferrin unfortunately didn't have a choice. She was the one person who knew how to get his collar off, and the rest of the collars and keys were still sitting inside the second carriage.

The rest of the evening passed rather quietly as everyone huddled near the fires with blankets over their heads to keep off the snow as they sipped on the hot soup Kettle had prepared. No one complained. Of course, that might have had more to do with the bloody butcher knife hanging from Kettle's waist than the quality of the cooking.

Ferrin sat in silence, pondering over everything he'd been through, every obstacle he'd faced to get him to this point. He stared out over the fire at the members of the Rhowynn wielder council and wondered where his journey would lead him next. He wondered if he'd ever see any of them again. For a group of wielders that he'd never really felt connected to while living in Rhowynn, he now shared a close-knit bond with them, and found he'd actually miss them.

He couldn't believe how far he'd come, the friends he'd made, some as close to him now as family. With his sister and Myron on one side and Rae huddled up close on the other, he couldn't help but smile. With this leg of his journey finally coming to an end, he wondered where the next would lead and what would be waiting for him when he got there.

Chapter 81 | Ayrion

YRION WATCHED QUIETLY AS Ozlin Beartooth stroked his thick red beard from his bone-antler seat in front of the hearth. "I can take you if you want to go," Ozlin said. "I just don't know why you'd want to after your last visit." He pulled the pipe from his mouth and pointed it at Ayrion. "Reckon I've not seen the oracle that upset in some time. She might not have any wish to see you." Ozlin filled his cheeks, then released the smoke up over his head, where it floated evenly across the ceiling of the magistrate's stone dwelling.

It had been several days since they'd first set foot in the oracle's lair, and it had left Ayrion shaken. He'd spent every night since tossing and turning, dreaming of himself back inside the enormous stone chamber with all its decoratively carved scenes depicting Aldoran history. The stone doors on the far side of the cavern would open, only for him to find death waiting on the other side. Sometimes it was the Black Watch and their sniffers, other times it was Argon and the vulraak. But every time the doors opened, they brought death. Worse were the dreams of him plunging one of his dragon-hilt blades through the old woman's chest as she declared that he needed to do it. It was destiny.

Destiny be hanged! He couldn't wait any longer. He needed answers.

Ayrion leaned forward in his seat. "When a woman, whom your people hold in complete veneration, tells me that I'm going to be the harbinger of her death, then I need to know more. Perhaps there's a way to stop it."

Tameel and Zynora, who were enjoying the sway of their rockers as they quietly carried on their own conversation with Ozlin's wife, Hanani, turned to listen in. Hanani gently ran her hands through her long fiery hair. She watched Ayrion with sharp eyes. She might speak softly, but there was a spark in her eyes that said if you ever crossed her, she'd pull an axe out of her woolen undergarments and show you how it was used. Ayrion was still cautious how he talked to her, considering their first introduction had her reaching for her meat knife.

Bek and Nell sat on the smaller sofa by themselves. Kuwa, the magistrate's tall assistant, had taken Taylis and Marissa out to look at the bluff.

"You think that might be possible?" Ozlin asked.

Ayrion shrugged. "I don't know. Have you ever known one of her predictions to not come true?"

Ozlin looked over at Hanani, and they both shook their heads.

"She didn't actually say that you would be her death," Zynora pointed out. "She said that your fates are intertwined, which meant she was nearing her end."

"Yes, exactly. She said that our fates are intertwined, which must mean I have something to do with her death."

Tameel decided to put in his thoughts. "She could just mean that you're going to be around when she dies, not that you are going to be the one to kill her."

Ayrion pressed his thumbs to his temples. "Which is why I need to see her again. I want to find out more. Maybe there is a way to stop it." Just as much as he wanted to know if there was a way around the old woman's death, he also wanted her to look once more into whether there was a way for him to regain his memories. He was tired of living what felt like two lives.

Ozlin didn't say anything, as he continued to puff on his pipe. After a moment, he pulled it from his mouth. "It seems you don't leave me much choice. If there's a chance she can find a way around this prediction, then I'll take you."

"I'll be fine going alone," Ayrion said. "There's no need to waste your time. I'm sure you have plenty of other things to do." Truth was, Ayrion wanted to see if the oracle would be more willing to open up if it was just the two of them. He also wanted to see more of the great pictorial history that had been carved into the walls of the Hall of Records, not to mention have more time examining the Doors of Light, which the people of Upper Wellhollow called Harok Laos.

"Nonsense," Ozlin said, pulling the pipe from his mouth. "I'll be happy to go." Of course, they both knew that was a lie. Ozlin had already made it clear that he didn't like going in to see the old blind oracle. "Besides, you won't get past the guards without my presence." Ozlin looked at his wife almost as though seeking approval, but she was too preoccupied with her conversation with Zynora to notice, so he turned back to Ayrion. "As soon as you feel ready."

"Now, if you're up to it."

Ozlin grunted and stood from his seat, Ayrion following him up. The other conversations halted as the two men walked toward the door. "I'm taking Ayrion to see the oracle."

"Why would you do that?" Hanani asked, parroting her husband's initial sentiments.

"Trust me, I tried talking him out of it. I doubt she even lets him in." He shrugged. "But the Upakan has his mind set, so what am I to do?"

"It's your time to waste," she said. "But don't be upset if you come back to find we've eaten the rest of the plum tartlets. I'd planned on getting them out when Kuwa made it back with the children."

Ozlin's face tightened, or what you could see through his beard. "That's not fair, my love. You know they're my favorite." He patted his swollen midriff.

"I'll see if I can manage to save a few, but I make no promises."

Ozlin walked over and kissed his wife on the cheek. "You're very good to me."

"I know," she said with a sly grin. "Now be off with you. I'm sure that cook is throwing the pies in the oven as we speak."

Ozlin left a trail of smoke out the door and down the hall as he briskly made his way to the front entrance, stopping only long enough to grab his bear coat on the way out. Ayrion was right on his heels, slipping on his wool coat and shutting the door behind them. He didn't bother with his gloves, but he did stuff his hands as deep into his pockets as he could to protect them against the frigid gusts swirling in and around the mountain peaks.

They headed across the bluff, passing several dugout homes and storefronts as they went. Ayrion couldn't help but admire the ingenuity it took to create Upper Wellhollow, as the entire town had been built right into the side of the mountain. Even the narrow walkways they called streets rising up the sides of the peak had been completely carved out of solid stone. It was quite a remarkable place.

Once they reached the tunnel at the back, they disarmed and started in. The torchlight was more than enough for Ayrion to see what lay ahead. In fact, he had to do his best not to stare directly into the light, as it tended to blur his vision once his eyes had adapted to the darkness. They walked for some distance, the tunnel winding its way deeper and deeper into the mountain. Their steps and the flicker of the torch were the only sounds heard.

Ahead, Ayrion could hear the slight echo from their steps reverberating in a way that let him know they were nearing their destination. The echoes grew more hollow as they reached the first of the two caverns, the time between each repeat lengthening. Ozlin stopped before entering, holding out his torch to see if he could find Angioma. After a single pass with the light and not seeing anyone, he finally spoke.

"Oracle? Are you there?" There was no response, other than the chorus of echoes bounding off the walls. "Perhaps she's in the Hall of Records."

Ayrion nodded, and they followed the rugs on the floor straight ahead, where they ended at the beginning of another tunnel.

They made their way through the passage toward the other side. Ayrion could hear muffled sounds coming from ahead, but the way forward was shrouded in darkness. Ayrion wondered how it was the old woman, blind or not, could spend her life so far removed from everyone and everything. It had to be a lonely existence.

Ozlin stopped just outside the entrance and held up his torch, but Ayrion could tell by the way he continued to move the light around that he couldn't quite make out where the seer was. Ayrion, however, could see her kneeling in front of the great doors on the other side of the cavern. She seemed to be carrying on a conversation with them, but her voice was too muffled to make out what she was saying.

Ozlin waited until she was finished, or at least until the first long break, before daring to speak, and when he did, his voice cracked. "Oracle?"

Angioma released a heavy sigh as if not appreciating the disturbance. "Yes, I know. You may leave us, Ozlin."

"But . . ." Ozlin cleared his throat, clearly torn between his desire to not be there and not wanting to leave Ayrion with her alone. "But, Oracle, I would prefer—"

"I will be perfectly safe, Magistrate. I assure you. You may leave us, but before you go, please light the troughs."

Ozlin gave his beard a displeased tug, but he did eventually walk over to the left side of the tunnel entrance, where a long thin furrow ran nearly the entire perimeter of the room, and stuck his torch inside. The narrow trench burst to life, the flames racing down the entire length of the trough as they quickly worked their way around the side of the cavern, bringing the room and its artwork to life. He then proceeded to do the same to the trough on the other side.

Still not wanting to leave, Ozlin held back a moment longer, as if hoping the oracle would change her mind, but she never did. Instead, she remained where she was on her knees in front of Harok Laos. With one last firm tug, Ozlin grunted. "Have it your way." He stepped into the tunnel and left the two alone.

Ayrion listened as the magistrate's steps slowly faded into the distance.

"I did not think to see you again so soon," Angioma said, remaining where she was. "Most who come to see me and receive news such as yours would be hard-pressed to want to return. But, as we've already established . . ." She turned her head and looked back at him with her glazed eyes, not quite seeing, but yet somehow knowing where to look. ". . . you're not like most, are you?"

"I have come to see what more I can learn. I feel . . ."

"Lost?"

Ayrion lifted his head. "Yes. How did you . . . never mind."

Angioma smiled and turned back to Harok Laos.

He wanted to ask her outright whether she thought her death would be at his hand, but he decided instead to work his way around to it, unsure if the topic would cause her to grow upset and leave before he could ask anything else.

"I feel as though I'm two different people," Ayrion said, hoping to find the correct words, "never knowing which is the real me. I need my memories to tell me who I am and what my place is in this world."

Angioma laughed, the echoes reverberating off the stone tomb surrounding them, seeming to add an unsettling sort of deeper significance behind the gesture, as if there was a secret that only she knew, a secret that Ayrion wasn't sure he wanted to know.

"Isn't that what we all seek? To believe we serve a greater purpose, that our lives will make a difference, and yet at the same time demand that our lives are our own and balk at the notion that we are not in complete control. Quite the paradox." She turned around to face him, still sitting cross-legged. "Do you believe that with these memories you will somehow discover something new about yourself that you didn't already know? What makes you . . . you? Do you believe that if those memories are restored, you will suddenly change?"

"I don't know. And that's what frightens me."

"Are your memories what make you who you are, or is it the character inside you? What if you don't like what you see? Are you willing to take that chance?"

Once again, Ayrion was without an answer, at least not one worth voicing.

"If your memories are restored, will you become who you were, or who you are now?" She paused to let a little of what she was saying sink in. "Perhaps this is a gift, or perhaps it is the will of the Creator."

"How could it be the Creator's will to strip me of who I am?"

Angioma shrugged. "Who am I to know the Creator's will? But let me ask you this. If you still had your memories, would you be standing here right now? If you still had your memories, what do you think would have happened when Argon and the vulraak were set loose? Would you have been there to stop them?"

"How did you know . . ." He had to keep reminding himself she was a seer. She was also right. "If I had retained my memories, there would have been no need for me to remain with Tameel and Zynora. I would have no doubt returned to Aramoor."

She nodded. "And Argon would have continued to spread beyond anyone's containing. Half the world might have been under his control by now."

Ayrion's mind swam with the ambush of logic he was being accosted with by this old woman. The answers he thought were so clear just a moment ago were now slipping from his grasp. If he did find a way to regain those memories, would he like who he was? Would having those memories change him? For once, he wasn't sure. He raised his hands and looked at them, staring at the branded "X" on his open wrist, thinking back on all the hours he'd spent staring at that mark, wondering where it had come from and why. Who he was at that moment felt right, but yet, there was still that growing concern that he was missing something, something he needed, something important.

"Are you saying that everything I've been through is part of some larger plan?"

"That is not for me to say, but for you to decide."

He put his hands to his temples and pressed. For the first time, he wasn't completely sure he wanted his memories back. And that scared him most of all.

Angioma stood, a kind, almost grandmotherly smile appearing on her face as she did. "As I said, quite the paradox." She looked up at the walls of the cavern and the ancient depictions carved thereon. "They are beautiful, are they not?"

Ayrion looked up. "They are."

"But no matter how well you describe them to me, it will never be the same as seeing them with my own eyes."

Ayrion stared at one of the upper scenes depicting two opposing forces. There were soldiers on both sides. A great battle, but not like anything he'd seen before. Instead of armies of horsemen, there were ships that sailed across the land, and instead of arrows and spears, robed men and women fought with maelstroms and flame. Some even rode enormous winged beasts. Ayrion shook his head. How could he explain what he was seeing in a way that Angioma could grasp when he himself didn't understand it. "I see your point."

She nodded. "What I do is no different. I can see glimpses, fragments of futures that I cannot explain because I have no context. I could tell you that you will be buried beneath an avalanche, but I cannot tell you when, or how, or where it will take place. In hearing that, you could then decide to leave Wellhollow as quickly as possible and in doing so cause that very avalanche to take place in your hurried escape down the mountain. Then the question becomes, if I had never told you, would it still have happened?"

Ayrion started to answer, then stopped, wondering if perhaps he hadn't fully understood the question. It seemed too simple. Finally, unable to come up with any other logical explanation, he answered. "Yes, of course it would have happened. You saw it."

She pursed her lips. "Yes, but it might not have happened when it did. Perhaps it would have taken years for it to come to pass. Perhaps, in your fear of being caught under the snow, you would decide to stay in Wellhollow and never leave, and in doing so, never fulfill your true purpose." She pinched her lips. "Not my finest example, I admit, but you get my meaning."

"I think I do."

"Don't focus so much on what has already happened, or what is yet to come. If you do, you will fail to see what is right in front of you."

"See," Ayrion said, "now why couldn't you have just said that in the first place?"

Angioma chuckled and reached out her arm for his assistance, and he guided her over to a boulder on the left side of the entrance, flat enough for her to sit on. He helped her down and took a step back, finding himself once again captivated by the amulet she wore around her neck. It was a clear crystal set inside what appeared to be a golden eye.

"What is it you wished to ask?" she asked. "Your silence is screaming in my ears."

"Sorry. I was just admiring your amulet. Is it a transferal?"

She raised her hand and stroked the clear stone inside its gold setting. "No. A seer needs no transferal." She chuckled. "I was about to ask why you had never been taught this, but I guess that would be a foolish question given what we just discussed about your memories. An oracle's gift does not come from the Fae. Seers were around long before the faeries broke into our realm. Our sight is a gift from the Creator himself. Unlike normal magic, we cannot manipulate our surroundings or control the natural elements. In fact," she said with what sounded like a healthy dose of resentment, "we have no control over anything, including what we see."

She grabbed the eye and held it up. "This is a symbol of who I am. It has been passed down through my family for generations. Never has there been a generation that did not have at least one member with the gift of sight. Each of us have worn the mantle proudly, waiting for the day when our family's legacy would be fulfilled." She stood from her seat and held out her hand. "I am the last. And I believe that day is upon us."

This was the moment Ayrion had been waiting for. "You said our paths are linked and that . . . that your time was nearing its end. What did you mean? Are you saying . . ." He was almost afraid to ask. "Do you believe I will be the cause of your death?"

Angioma lowered her head and closed her eyes. "That is an answer I cannot give, for I do not know. I do know that your arrival in Wellhollow has been seen by many of the previous oracles. It is the one vision we all share, but it's also the one vision that has most eluded us. No additional visions have been given concerning this time other than your arrival and the knowledge that it will herald something even greater. I am the only oracle who has been given more." She hmphed. "And trust me, I would have preferred not knowing." She lifted her head. "Our lives are indeed intertwined, but how far that thread goes, I cannot tell you. I'm sorry. I know it's not what you seek, but it's all I have to give."

Ayrion sat down beside her on the stone, feeling more than a little overwhelmed. He couldn't imagine what Angioma must be feeling, knowing that the man who signaled the possible end of her life was sitting beside her, a man she had been having visions about since she was a child.

They sat there in silence for some time as Ayrion stared at the incredible depictions on the walls, wondering if some of them might be future predictions. He started to ask, but the sounds of booted feet hurrying down the tunnel on their left had him standing. Ayrion grabbed one of the knives he had hidden inside his coat and moved in front of Angioma. Two lights suddenly flared out of the entrance. It was the sentries who'd been standing watch outside.

"Oracle!" the shorter man on the right said, completely out of breath, having just run the length of the mountainside to reach her. "The white riders are coming. They're almost through the pass. We need to get you to safety."

Angioma straightened her amulet and turned to Ayrion. "It appears that time we spoke of has just arrived."

Chapter 82 | Ayrion

AYRION LEFT ANGIOMA INSIDE the cavern and raced through the tunnel. He needed to get to his weapons before the Black Watch reached the plateau.

With torch in hand—one he'd confiscated from the guards—he tore through the winding passageway, picking up speed as he went, hoping against hope he was able to reach the wagons ahead of the white riders. After his initial run-in with the Black Watch in Lower Wellhollow, he'd kept his dragon swords hidden.

A faint light signaled he was nearing the entrance, so he doused the torch, not wanting to draw attention to himself in case he'd arrived too late.

The plateau was bathed in moonlight. Apparently, his time spent with the oracle had been longer than he thought, as the sun had set while he was inside. Men and women were scurrying about like jackrabbits, all in furs, all carrying weapons. Above him, archers lined the upper walkways around the three sides of the plateau.

Ozlin stood at the bluff on the right, shouting out orders, his greataxe resting just over his back as he directed his people, though they didn't seem to need that much instruction. The mountainfolk of Upper Wellhollow looked more than ready, as though they'd been preparing for this moment their entire lives. Unlike the lower township at the foot of the mountain, these people looked ready for war.

"Ayrion!"

Ayrion turned to see Tameel, Zynora, and Bek rushing over, a wrapped bundle in Tameel's arms. Tameel and Zynora were each wearing their colorful tinker cloaks, the ones with the fur around the collars. The wind whipped them apart far enough for him to notice a set of long daggers at their sides. Behind them, Bek looked much like the rest of the mountainfolk, with furs and leathers and even his zabatas. His two long hatchets bounced against the sides of his legs, each with an axe on one side and spike on the other.

"We were just coming to find you," Zynora said. "The Black Watch have been spotted in the passes. They'll be here any moment."

Ayrion nodded. "The oracle's sentries let me know." He looked at the bundle in Tameel's arms. "My swords?"

Tameel handed them over. "I fetched them. Figured you might need them." He looked around at the hustle of people rushing from one side of the bluff to the other. "I think perhaps we should stay inside and out of sight. I'm sure the Tower is here looking for wielders. Ozlin says they have places here in the mountain where those with abilities can remain hidden. If they search and don't find any, then perhaps they'll leave."

Ayrion studied the determined faces of the townsfolk as he hooked his swords around his back. He didn't see them letting the Tower's guards step a single foot on their bluff without a fight. "Where are Nell and the children?"

"They went with Hanani and the others to the crags," Bek said. "They should be well hidden there." He glanced up at the archers lining the streets above. "I don't see this ending well. From what I gather, this is the first time the Tower has sent riders this far north. I don't see these people letting the Black Watch walk off with anyone, let alone take the time to search."

Ayrion nodded. "My thoughts exactly."

The sound of boots on stone from the tunnel behind them had Ayrion and the others spinning around. Angioma and the two sentries stepped out of the cavern entrance and into the pale light of the very large moon, which sat just off the bluff, lending its brilliance to those in need. And right now, Wellhollow was in desperate need.

"Where are you taking her?" Ayrion asked.

"To the crags with the rest of those who wish to remain hidden."

"No." The oracle grabbed the guard's arm. "My place is here."

"But, Oracle, we need to get you to safety. If they find you, they'll take you for sure."

"No," she stated adamantly. "My job is to protect Harok Laos, and I cannot do that while huddled away in some dank hole with the children and the feeble."

"You also can't do that by just standing here either," Ayrion said. He turned to the sentries. "Move her into the tunnel where it's out of the way. Can you spare some extra men?"

One of the sentries nodded and took off running across the plateau to where Ozlin was still barking out orders on the other side. A few moments later, he returned with six additional fur-clad fighters.

"What should we do?" Tameel asked.

"Pray," Bek said, and not in a joking way as he laid his hands on the top of his hatchets.

The plateau opposite the entrance leading to the passes below was covered in armed bodies. Men and women with swords and knives and axes stood ready in a very rough-looking formation, waiting for a signal. Ayrion almost felt sorry for the Black Watch. They had no idea what they were walking into. Ozlin crossed the plateau in front of the fighters and headed straight for the tunnel and the four of them.

"What do you think, Upaka? We could use someone with your skills to lead the charge. Every last man and woman here will lay down their lives if necessary."

Ayrion shook his head. "I'm not the right man for this. They trust *you*. You're the one they will follow. Half these people are still too nervous to get within arm's reach of me. We will do what we can, but the best option for all of us at this point is to see if there is a peaceful way to work through this. If those with gifts are hidden, then perhaps they will leave of their own accord when their search comes up empty."

Bek grunted his doubt.

Ozlin hefted his battle-axe. "Those Tower pigs won't be searching anything. Let them come. We'll bring the mountain down on them."

Ayrion looked up toward the peaks, suddenly remembering the oracle's example of an avalanche raining down on his head, and started to wonder if it had actually been a vision. "Actually, that could work to our advantage." Ayrion turned to Zynora. "What do you think? Any chance you could use a little of that power to bring the snow down on them?"

"I don't know. I need to see it first."

Ozlin led the group over to the edge of the pass leading down through the mountainside. Ayrion remembered how difficult it had been to bring the wagons up such a steep climb, which was the perfect vantage point for an ambush. Above them on either side, the rock sloped inward, both sides holding a thick layer of white powder, certainly enough to do the job.

Ayrion turned to Ozlin. "Do your people have enough provisions to last the rest of the winter?"

Ozlin thought a moment, but eventually nodded, if hesitantly. "I believe we could make it through. Why?"

"Then I say we bring down the snow and seal the pass. That will keep them from reaching the town and stave off any possible battle."

"But for how long? They will be back, will they not? Best we show them why they should never return now, rather than to wait until spring when we are too hungry and weak to fight."

Ozlin raised a good point.

"They will be back, but having that extra time would help you build a better defense for Wellhollow. This is your home. It's your choice."

Ozlin looked down the pass at the glow of torches just coming into view on the other side. "I say we stand and fight."

"Then how about a compromise?" Ayrion added. "That pass and the snow is a powerful weapon at your disposal. Use it. Not so much to block the pass, but to wait until the majority of their force makes it in, then bring it down on their heads. That way you'll seal the pass and take out your enemy all at the same time."

Ozlin gave his long beard a firm tug. "We will need to pull our archers out first, then," he said, pointing up the slope, where a line of men could be seen waiting just inside the pass with arrows nocked.

Ayrion nodded, and Ozlin ordered a runner to direct the bowmen and bowwomen back to the plateau. They returned about the time the first of the Black Watch started into the main pass leading up to the plateau. The horses slowed, and the entire company came to a stop, at least the front part that they could see from the top of the bluff. They were sure to have more around the bend that couldn't be seen.

"They aren't stupid," Bek said. "They can see the potential for an ambush."

"Then we need to send them an invitation," Ayrion said.

Ozlin turned. "What kind of invitation?"

"A small welcome party that can go down to greet them and bring them up."

"But wouldn't that be an unnecessary risk?" Zynora asked. "What if they get trapped under the snow with the rest?"

"There's no such thing as a risk-free battle," Ayrion said. "Having said that, we wouldn't want to unleash the snow until those guiding the Tower's guards up have returned, because it will no doubt take that long to make sure the majority of their force is well inside the final pass."

"I'll go," Ozlin said.

Ayrion shook his head. "No. Your people need you here. Can't take a chance of anything happening to you and leave them without a leader in case something goes wrong." He looked at those gathered. "Bek can go." When the others looked at him, he added, "I'm too important to risk losing as well."

Ayrion held his face for as long as he could, but the look of stunned shock on the others' faces was more than he could handle, and he burst out laughing. Bek reared back and slugged him in the shoulder. Ayrion had seen it coming but figured he'd earned it, so he didn't move. "Sorry, but there are times when you need a little humor before a battle. Helps cut the fear."

"I didn't find it too funny," Bek said, a faint smile creeping across his face. The others chuckled.

Ayrion turned and looked down at the men on the other side of the pass below. "I'll go with Bek, and we'll bring them up." He turned to Zynora. "What do you think? Is a snowslide within your capability?"

Zynora tucked her arms back under her cloak and grabbed the handles of her two daggers. "Have I ever given you reason to doubt it?"

Ayrion smiled. He removed his swords and their carrier from his back and handed them to Tameel. "Probably best I don't walk down there wearing those as a way to greet our guests. He looked at Bek. "Ready?"

"I'm ready to see them buried under a mountain of snow."

"Good enough."

"Be careful, you two," Zynora said. "Don't do anything foolish." She shook her head. "What am I saying? I'm talking to the two of you."

"We'll do our best," Ayrion said.

Bek looked at Zynora. "If something does happen, tell Nell . . ."

Zynora put her hand on his arm. "I'll tell her."

Ozlin walked over and grabbed one of the torches lining the perimeter wall. He handed it to Bek, then Bek and Ayrion started into the pass and down the steep slope leading to the horsemen below. The moon was bright, but it wasn't quite high enough in the sky to reach clear to the bottom of the pass, which meant the way ahead was covered in shadow. The two men kept to the sides of the pass as they made their way down, using the rock to stabilize their feet and to keep them from slipping. The snow was fairly deep, halfway up Ayrion's shins in places, but it gave them a surer footing than simply sliding down icy rock.

They reached the bottom and slowly started through the towering sides of stone. Torches flickered in the distance as the Black Watch waited patiently on the other side. Ayrion looked up only once, the temptation to see what was over his head too great. He did his best not to look after that, or let Bek look, in case they gave away what they were intending to do.

"Not too late to turn back," Bek said.

"I think it was too late the moment we stepped off the plateau."

Bek grunted. "I should have stayed in Belvin. You know, they were wanting to make me magistrate?"

"Yeah, I was there when Abiah told us."

"Oh. Well, can you imagine me running a city?"

"Perish the thought."

"Hey, I would have made a splendid magistrate. After we rebuilt, I could have had my pick of homes for me and Nell and the children. Lap of luxury, my friend, lap of luxury."

"And you would have hated every minute of it. Stuck in an office day after day, poring over papers, resolving disputes, laying down the law, dictating policy—"

"Fine. You're right. It would have been a nightmare. Then again, I wouldn't have found myself walking through a deathtrap in the middle of the night to meet with an army of Black Watch troops in hopes of leading them into an avalanche that I pray doesn't land on my own head." He paused a moment. "I wonder what Abiah's up to right about now. Probably sitting in front of a cozy fire, warming his throat with a stout ale. Right about now, I'm thinking he might have made the right decision."

Ayrion smiled but didn't respond. They were close enough to be heard, close enough to see the faces of the men in the front line, none of which looked particularly happy to be there. "Welcome to Upper Wellhollow," Ayrion said in as jovial a voice as he could muster. "It's kind of late for a social call, don't you think?" He drew his fur-lined coat up tighter around his shoulders and at the same time let the guards see he carried no sword. As warm as the new jacket was, he was really missing his black leathers, and more importantly, his swords, but he couldn't take the chance of anyone recognizing him, especially not when he couldn't recognize himself. "If you had let us know you were coming, we would have put on the boar."

Bek looked at him like he'd lost his mind. Ayrion was simply trying to seem friendly and inviting. Banter wasn't exactly his strong suit; then again, it wasn't Bek's either. Thankfully, whoever the officer in front was, he wasn't one of those they had met on their way through Lower Wellhollow. If so, it would have looked rather awkward being greeted by a group of traveling tinkers than the actual townsfolk. Ayrion hadn't even considered that possibility when he had volunteered them.

The officer shifted in his saddle. "We are here on Tower business and require your full cooperation."

"And you shall have it," Ayrion said. "Still." He glanced down the long row of horsemen, unable to see any farther back than the next bend in the trail. "It seems an odd time to travel, what with it being the middle of the night. Most of the townsfolk are making ready for bed."

The officer in front frowned, his long brown hair cupping the sides of his face, giving him the appearance of a very unhappy individual. "I couldn't agree more, but we have our orders." He looked beyond them and up toward the higher peaks, leading to the bluff above. "How safe is it to travel through?"

"Safe enough," Bek said, holding up his torch as he and Ayrion turned to have a look behind them. "Any later and you might take the chance on the odd slide here or there, but we had a late coming winter this year, which left the snow more packed."

The officer nodded but kept his eyes on the upper slopes.

"Still," Ayrion added with an encouraging smile, "I would make sure to keep as quiet as possible going through. No need to take any unnecessary risks."

The officer finally pulled his gaze away from the rising stone. "Aye." He twisted in his saddle and looked at the men behind him. "Pass it back. Anyone so much as coughs, I'll run them through with their own blade."

They waited until the officer felt enough time had passed for his message to have made it all the way down the line. With a simple wave of his arm, he motioned them forward. "Lead on."

Ayrion looked at Bek, and they started back the way they'd come, following their footsteps all the way through the pass toward the final slope, leading up to the plateau. They kept the pace slow to make sure as many of the Tower's guards as possible made it into the pass. Ayrion kept his eyes fixed on the upper slopes and his ears open for any sign of movement from above.

As they reached the final slope and started up, Ayrion could hear the creaking sound of wheels and turned to see a couple of supply wagons edging around the corner. He hoped they didn't trigger a slide before he and Bek managed to get to the top.

The torchlights of Wellhollow rose out of the night above them as they continued to climb. The Black Watch weren't far behind, the front ranks already starting up the hill. Ayrion could just make out a couple of figures at the very top, looking down at them. One of them was Zynora. Ayrion turned to Bek. "Keep going. I'll be right back."

Ayrion scooted back down the slope toward the front of the line where the officer they'd spoken with was off his horse and leading it up the incline. He slid to a stop in front of the man. "We'll run ahead and get some men to help you with your wagons."

"We already have plenty of men."

"Yes, but without a proper pulley system in place they'll never make it to the top. We tried it with a couple of tinker wagons. Nearly lost both."

The captain nodded. "Fine. I'll have the wagons wait."

Ayrion didn't give the man a chance to change his mind and quickly headed up the slope. He managed to catch up with Bek about the time they reached the bluff, winded from having sprinted the entire second half.

Ayrion turned to Ozlin, who was standing next to Zynora and Tameel. "I told them I would run ahead and gather some men to help with their wagons."

Ozlin gave Ayrion a suspicious look. "And they believed you?"

"I told them the slope was very slick and they'd need rope for the wagons if they intended to get them up."

Ozlin looked down the pass. "Should we get ready?"

Zynora stepped toward the edge of the bluff.

"Not yet," Ayrion said. "We need to wait until we know the majority of them are inside the pass." He could see the torch light below snaking all the way through the pass and beyond. Whatever was going on, this wasn't just some simple extraction.

The Black Watch officer and the front line of the ranks were just reaching the top, and Ayrion went to greet them and bowed. "We are getting the pulley set up now. It will be ready by the time they reach the slope, I assure you." Ayrion quickly directed the officer to the left and away from the front, hoping to draw his attention away from the armed men and women standing on the other side of the bluff. "Let me introduce you to the town's magistrate." Ayrion practically grabbed the man's arm and dragged him over to Ozlin as more of the white-clad guards crested the plateau. "This is Ozlin Beartooth, official magistrate of Upper Wellhollow. Our doors are open to the Tower."

Ozlin held out his hand hesitantly as Ayrion turned back around. The line of torches continued on, but by now at least a dozen men had reached the bluff. They were out of time. He turned to Zynora. "Now!"

"Now what?" the officer asked. "What's going on?" He spun and reached for his sword but didn't get a chance to draw it before Ozlin stuck a knife through his neck, and he dropped into the snow. The other soldiers fumbled for their swords as well, but the archers on the street above them finished them off before they got a chance to even draw.

Shouts rang out from those still trying to breach the top, shouts of warning that would fall on deaf ears as Zynora raised her hands and released one of her pulse blasts into the side of the mountain.

The entire plateau shook, and Ozlin stumbled forward, trying to regain his balance as he stared up at the moonlit peaks above. "Yep. I'd say that'll just about do it."

Chapter 83 | Ty

HAT WAS THAT?" Ty asked as he grabbed the bars at the back of the cage and tried peering out. He could hear shouting near the front of the caravan and a loud rumble as though the mountain was about to shake itself apart.

"I don't know," Breen said, standing just to the left of Ty as he and Narendi attempted to get a glimpse of something other than rock and white uniforms. "Whatever it is, I'm getting that sinking feeling in my gut."

The wagon jerked to a sudden stop, sending all three careening onto their backs. Ty hopped to his feet and ran to the front and banged on the wood between them and the driver's seat. "What's going on out there?"

The man in front suddenly began to scream like he knew his life was about to end. His screaming continued as he jumped off the wagon and ran past, disappearing into the line of fleeing men behind them. Where were they going?

"It's an avalanche!" Kraea shouted from the wagon behind them, panic in her voice. *"I can hear it!"*

Ty spun around. "Kraea says it's an avalanche!"

"What is avalanche?" Narendi asked.

"Death," Breen answered.

Outside, the Tower's guards were running past the wagon in stampede formation. Those that fell in the rush were buried under the others' boots.

Breen ran to the front of their wagon and jerked back the canvas as far as he could so they could see what was going on. The pass ahead and up the slope was filled with torches and men in white uniforms, most either trying to scramble up the hill or run back toward them. Their wagon was dead center of the chaos.

"Look!" Ty exclaimed, pointing up toward the top of the cliffs. Already a waterfall of snow was washing down the side, entombing those closest to the wall. "We've got to get out of here or it's going to bury us too!"

Breen let go of the tarp and grabbed at the boards blocking them from the seat in front and started to heave. "Help me!"

Ty and Narendi jumped up beside him and grabbed hold. Two of the boards had a large enough crack between that they were able to fit their fingers through.

"Harder!" Breen shouted, the veins bulging on the side of his head as he strained against the nails. Ty yelled as he pulled with everything he had, desperation fueling his arms. Without warning the board gave way, and they all flew backward into the straw.

Ty couldn't believe that worked.

They hopped to their feet, and Breen all but shoved Ty and Narendi through the open slats before crawling through himself and out onto the front. Ty could see a gathering of black and grey robes partway up the slope. He couldn't tell if any of them were Mangora. There was no sign of her spider. Behind their wagon, the first of the heavy snow began to cascade down into the back of the pass, covering those trying to escape out the south entrance.

"*Hurry!*" Kraea cried out. Her wagon was next. The driver was still sitting on the seat, too scared to know what to do.

"I'm coming!" Ty shouted and grabbed Breen's arm. "We've got to save Kraea." They climbed down off the seat on the right side of the wagon—the only side not pouring snow on top of them—and crawled up underneath to keep from being seen by the soldiers running by as Ty, Breen, and Narendi made their way to the back. So far, no one was looking at the wagons.

By the time they reached the back, the driver on Kraea's wagon was nowhere to be seen. He must have taken off with everyone else. "Let's go." The three hustled out from under the wagon and around the next set of horses, leaping up under the second wagon just as another line of guards came rushing past.

"Who are you?" Ty spun to find himself face-to-face with who Ty assumed was the wagon's driver, since he wasn't wearing a uniform. It was too dark for the man to see their faces, and Ty reared back to punch him, but his brother leaped on top of the man before Ty could, pinning him to the ground with an arm behind his back.

"Do you carry keys for the cages?" Breen asked. When the man didn't answer right away, Breen bent his arm even further, and the man screamed.

"Yes! I have them!"

"Good. Hand them over."

The man fumbled into his robe with his free arm and brought out a ring with three keys. "Here!" he said, tossing them at Ty. "Take them! Doesn't matter. We're all going to die anyway."

Breen punched the man in the jaw, and his head flopped to the side. He looked at Ty. "Go!"

Ty rolled out the back of the wagon and climbed the stairs. "I'm here, Kraea." He fumbled the first key into the lock, but it wouldn't budge. The sound of the snow was growing. "Blazes!" He tried the second, and it didn't move either. Quickly, he thrust in the third, and it turned. He flipped back the latch, and Kraea nearly knocked him over as she scrambled to get out.

She looked up. "Here it comes!"

Breen and Narendi barely made it out from under the wagon when the stars above them disappeared. The sound of snow plummeting down through the rock was deafening. They had nowhere to run and no magic to save them. Narendi grabbed his hand as Ty closed his eyes and waited for the end.

"Look!" Breen shouted.

Ty opened his eyes, and his breath caught in his throat. The entire mountain of snow was now sliding over their heads as though being funneled through the pass by an invisible furrow. Ty turned. The black- and grey-robed wielders were all standing there with their arms raised toward the snow. Ty couldn't help but admire the power.

"Hurry." Breen grabbed Ty's arm, and they ran for the next wagon behind Kraea's, which was one of the supply wagons used to tote the gear. "We need to find some weapons."

The driver of the wagon, like all the others, had already run off in the chaos and was probably buried under the first pile of snow farther back in the pass. They raced to the back of the wagon, and Breen jumped inside. Ty was too distracted by the incredible sight of the massive snowdrift overhead as it continued to flow down through the pass in the direction they'd just come from. Any of the soldiers who had fled were about to get a rude awakening.

Breen grabbed Ty's arm, and he jumped. "Our bags are still here!" his brother shouted over the din of the snow plowing through the pass.

Ty glanced over the side. Sure enough, he could see Breen's bow and arrows. Ty had thought Mangora would have kept them close with her, seeing as how they had come from her shop in the first place.

"Where are they?" Narendi demanded. She jumped into the back alongside

Breen and dug frantically through the sacks and crates, looking for her own bag. "Where are my gold and jewels?"

It took Ty a little longer, but he did finally manage to find his own bag stuffed under what looked like a sack of potatoes. Yanking it free, he reached inside and felt around until finally coming out with his pipes. He was excited to see they were still there, and unbroken. He tucked them inside his coat for safekeeping, then reached for his sword. Unfortunately, neither the shorlock nor his compass were there; not that he had really expected them to be.

"What do you think you're doing?" someone behind them called out.

Ty barely had time to turn, when he was suddenly lifted off his feet, along with Breen and Narendi, and sent hurling against the side of the mountain behind them. Sharp pain flooded his body, and he fell into the snow. He reached for his sword, but it was nowhere to be seen. He turned to find one of the bulradoer standing behind the wagon. Before he could even open his mouth, he was suddenly lifted into the air and slammed against the stone once again, the wall of hardened air pressing so hard Ty thought his ribs would crack.

"Mangora sent me to make sure you were still alive. Imagine my surprise when I looked inside your cage." The man lifted a small silver rod from beneath his robes that had been hanging around his neck.

Ty's eyes widened when he recognized what it was, and he held out his hand. "No! Wait!" Pain erupted inside, and he screamed, his agony blending in with Breen's and Narendi's.

Suddenly a third voice was added to the mix as the bulradoer himself shrieked. Ty dropped into the snow, the pain gone. He opened his tear-filled eyes to find the bulradoer's right arm clutched between Kraea's jaws. Ty could sense her hunger through their link as she bit down.

"Get the key!" she shouted as she jerked the bulradoer to the ground. The man raised his hand to attempt a spell, but she clamped down on his neck before he could get any words out. He didn't move after that.

Ty crawled over to the bleeding corpse and unhooked the key from his neck, then looked up at Kraea and smiled. "Thanks."

"Get his crystal as well," Breen said, working to help Narendi to her feet.

"I didn't even think of that," Ty said and began searching the dead man for another necklace or bracelet or anything that would have held a crystal, but after a thorough examination, he came away empty. "He doesn't have one. Maybe he's like us and doesn't need a crystal."

Breen shrugged, and Kraea dragged the bulradoer's body under the wagon and began to feed. Ty's stomach nearly emptied at the enjoyment she was getting out of it, and the way it funneled back to him through their link.

He pushed the thought aside and looked at the key. He'd seen it used enough on Breen and Narendi to have a basic idea of what needed to be done, so he crawled back over and placed the tip against the back of Breen's collar. The same golden symbols appeared that he'd seen before, and the collar snapped open.

He handed the key to Breen, and Breen did the same for Ty and Narendi. "What do you think we should do with these?" Breen asked, holding the durmas as he hung the key around his neck and tucked it under his tunic.

"Keep them. Might come in handy if we run into more bulradoer." He looked at the wagon, and more importantly what was under it. Even with a cloudless sky, the pass was barely light enough to see. Other than the sound of flesh being stripped from bone, if it wasn't for Kraea's golden eyes, he wouldn't have even noticed her there. He shook his head. "Idiot. *Ru'kasha Kor.*" The night brightened, and Ty was suddenly able to see farther than just the few feet in front of his face.

Breen looked at him and smiled. "I completely forgot about that. *Ru'kasha Kor.*"

Narendi looked at the two of them, confusion on her face. "I don't understand your words."

Ty was going to give her the incantation but then remembered it wouldn't have done any good. "It's just a little bit of magic to help you see better in the dark, but without a crystal, you won't be able to use it."

"Oh." She looked disappointed as she turned and gathered up her spear and strung it over her back.

By the time they had collected their bags, the last of the snow overhead was slithering away, and the stars were once again reappearing in the sky. They huddled near the back of the wagon. Most of the Black Watch soldiers had already rushed back toward the slope, having seen that the pass behind them was completely blocked off with snow.

Ahead, Ty could hear the clash of steel and the shouts of men and women dying. He peeked out from behind the wagon. The black- and grey-robed wielders were just cresting the bluff, sending out flames in all directions.

"We've got to help those people before they're slaughtered," Breen said.

"We've got to stop Mangora before she gets to Aero'set," Ty added. "She can't be allowed to use that key."

Beside them, Narendi had pulled out her Mzwati headwrap and tied it on, her spear hanging over her back, her curved sword already at her waist. She looked a little silly wearing the baka over her tunic and cloak, but it was more symbolic than anything. Ty strapped on his short sword, but he didn't see himself using it. His magic was finally back and flooding through him. It warmed him from the inside out.

Breen started forward, but Ty grabbed his arm and pulled him short. "I need to go first. I'm the one with the shields."

Breen paused as if to consider arguing the fact, since he had always been the one to insist on going first to protect Ty. He finally nodded. "Fine."

Ty conjured one of his shields. "Let's go!" He looked under the wagon. "You coming, Kraea? Or are you just going to stay here and eat all night?"

"Stay here and eat."

"Fine. Then I guess there'll be no one there to stop the arachnobe as it feasts on all the flesh up on that bluff."

Kraea's head shot up so fast she bumped her horns against the undercarriage. *"I'm coming!"*

The four of them scurried their way around the wagons and over piles of snow and fallen bodies toward the slope and the battle ahead. The last of the Black Watch troops had already made it to the top, so Ty and the others didn't need to worry about being seen. They rushed up the rocky gradient, keeping to the left wall, which made for a sturdier climb, as it allowed them to use their hands to pull themselves up along the stone. It also kept them hidden within the deeper shadows and out of sight.

Ty slowed when they reached the crest, and the four of them huddled against the side of the mountain, behind a rather tall pile of fallen rocks. Ty wondered if it had come down during the earlier quake that had nearly drowned them all under a mountain of snow. He dropped his satchel down beside the pile. "I can't see anything from here. We need to get up there for a better look."

"I'll give you a hand," Breen said, laying his own bag beside Ty's. With his help, the three of them crawled on top of the pile, keeping flat against the largest of the boulders as they stared out at the battle ahead. Kraea remained below, since there wasn't enough room for all four of them.

Numerous bodies lined the front of the entrance, many of them charred, and most covered in fur like great two-legged mountain wolves or very short bears. They had clearly been standing ready for the attack, but instead of facing men with swords, they had been hit by the White Tower's wielders.

Most of the Tower's wielders seemed to be focusing their efforts on the right side of the bluff, where archers were raining down arrows as fast as they could draw. The archers hid behind short walls that stood at the front of what looked like the town's streets that ran up and around the entire side of the mountain.

On the left, the Black Watch had taken up formation and were locked in battle with what was left of the fur-clad mountainfolk, who were slowly being forced toward the edge of the bluff.

At the center of that conflict, Ty could see three men who seemed to be repelling all comers. The leader of the three was a man in a rather colorful wool coat with black hair and two black swords that moved in a way that left Ty completely captivated, swift and direct, never missing their marks. No one seemed to be able to reach him. On either side of the man were two others who looked more animal than human, one even wearing the head of a bear as he swung a greataxe, cutting down anyone who got in the way. The much taller one on the left wielded two smaller axes like they were mere extensions of his own arms. Whoever came near those three weren't long for this world.

As good as they were, their numbers were far fewer than those of the Black Watch.

Ty wondered why the mountainfolk had taken up the weaker, more dangerous, position against the edge of the bluff, but then he saw it. Every time one of the wielders tried to work their way around to reach the townsfolks' ranks, one of the men in the middle would call for them to shift, and the entire company slowly turned, keeping the Black Watch between them and the bulradoer. It was actually kind of smart.

"I don't see Mangora anywhere," Breen said, casting about as he scanned the upper mountainside. "Do you?"

Ty shook his head. He'd already been looking, but with so many wielders clumped together in their black and grey robes, he wasn't sure who anyone was. And there'd been no sign of the arachnobe. He looked at the wielders on the right. They were managing to keep the archers from firing, as they pounded the upper walkways with balls of fire and fists of hardened air.

A few of the wielders broke off from the bunch and started for the battle on the other side. If they managed to break through the Watch's ranks, the townsfolk wouldn't stand a chance, possibly ending up over the side of the cliff. Breen must have had the same thought, as he had already nocked his first arrow and looked ready to stand and draw.

"I'm hungry," Kraea said, anxiously waiting down below, peeking out from behind the same pile of rocks as she danced from paw to paw.

Ty ignored her and kept his eyes on the wielders. There were two in black robes and three in grey. "See if you can hit one of the black ones," Ty said.

Breen stood slowly and drew to his cheek. He released, and the string thrummed, but the arrow ricocheted to the right. "Blazes! They're holding shields."

The wielders turned, and Ty tried to pull Breen back down, but they'd already spotted him. One of the recruits raised his hands and sent a flaming ball of death straight at them. Narendi shrieked as Ty raised his shield and sent the fireball careening over their heads. The recruit looked stunned.

"They don't recognize us," Ty said.

"They will now." Breen grabbed another arrow from the quiver, this time a black one, and pulled. He released, and the arrow drove straight through the wielder's shield and buried itself into the side of the closest bulradoer. The man screamed, grabbing at the shaft as he went down. The three recruits, as well as the other bulradoer, looked down at the man in shock, and then at each other, no doubt wondering whose shield had failed.

Before Breen could grab another arrow, all four wielders turned and unleashed a wall of fire directly at them. Narendi leaped off the pile as Ty raised his shield and braced for the impact. The flames were powerful when they hit, driving him backward to the point that Breen had to grab him before he tipped off the back of the rock. The fire ripped at his shield, the heat so intense he had to turn his face.

Kraea tore around the shield without hesitation and raced across the bluff, straight at the wielders. Ty could feel the anxious hunger inside her as she imagined getting her jaws around one of them.

Two of the grey robes tried hitting her with their flames, but she was quick, dodging each before leaping straight at the one in black. The bulradoer hit Kraea with a pocket of air that sent her flying into the side of one of the stone buildings behind them, rock and wood and glass exploding on impact. She slowly crawled back to her feet, dazed, and tried shaking it off, but the bulradoer hit her full on with her flames, burying her under an orange inferno.

"Kraea!" Ty screamed and leaped to the front of the rockpile, sending his own blue fire hurling against the side of their shields. He forced the wielders back, but there was nothing he could do for the draakar from the other side of the bluff. Breen grabbed another of his black arrows, but before he got the chance to nock, Kraea suddenly shot out of the flames without so much as a singed scale and dove straight for the wielder.

The bulradoer extinguished her flames and hit Kraea with another hardened fist of air, sending her flying once more, this time directly into the back of the Black Watch troops. She rolled to a stop and grabbed a leg she found before the guard had time to even process what had hit him. He went down screaming. The others attacked, and she quickly retreated.

Ty charged out from behind the pile of rocks and onto the bluff, leaving his satchel behind. "We've got to get to the townsfolk," he said, deflecting multiple balls of fire being thrown from the three grey robes as Breen and Narendi followed him out. The fire came in waves as the wielders tried to conserve their magic. Releasing a single stream of fire for an extended period of time could suck the strength right out of you, as Ty well knew after his standoff with Mangora.

The one remaining bulradoer in their group turned back to help, now that the draakar was no longer her concern but the Watch's.

Breen nocked his next black arrow but held it.

"Why are you not shooting?" Narendi asked. "Kill her!"

Breen looked at Ty. "Can I shoot through your shield? I don't want this thing bouncing back at us."

Ty smacked away another ball of fire from the recruits. "I guess. I don't know. It went through their shields."

"I better make sure." Breen grabbed the arrow and stabbed at Ty's shield, or where he thought it was.

Ty could feel the vibration in his magic as soon as the arrow punctured the barrier. "I felt it. It went through."

Breen nodded, re-nocked the arrow, and lifted the bow, but not before the bulradoer had sent a battering ram of hardened air into the side of the mountain just over their heads. It was like hitting the rock with a giant sledgehammer. The stone crumbled, releasing several large boulders down on top of them.

"Look out!" Ty conjured a second shield to keep them from getting buried alive, and they all dove to the left as the rocks smashed against the side of the mountain where they'd been standing. One of the boulders hit the edge of Ty's shield, and he was thrown sideways into the ground, the wind knocked completely out of him, losing both shields in the process.

"Ty!" Narendi screamed.

Ty turned over to see another round of fire heading straight for them. He didn't even have time to catch his breath as he quickly called up his magic and conjured enough of a shield to counter the next round as Breen and Narendi dove down beside him to keep from getting struck.

Somewhere in the distance, Ty heard Kraea roar. He couldn't see her because of the white-robed guards, but he could sense her anger and desperation through their link.

"Are you all right?" Breen snatched him off the ground.

Ty nodded, still trying to catch his breath. "The shields might stop fire and arrows, but when it comes to getting hit by something that heavy, they're not that much different from carrying a wooden shield."

With fire in his eyes, Breen spun, drew on the remaining black-robed wielder, and released, but the bulradoer was ready this time.

"*Dorfang!*" A blade of golden fire sparked to life, and she batted the arrow away.

"Flaming magical weapons!" Breen shouted in anger.

By this time, the Tower's wielders had reached the back of the Black Watch troops, and the bulradoer ordered those at the back to attack.

A dozen men broke off and charged their position.

"Finally!" Narendi shouted and raised her scarf up over her mouth and nose, hiding everything but her eyes. "I'm Mzwati. Come meet my spear!" Before Ty could grab her, she ran out from behind the shield and straight at the oncoming soldiers, screaming the entire way. A couple of those in front actually hesitated when they saw her coming, and she gutted the first two before releasing the shaft and drawing her curved blade to cut down two more.

"What does she think she's doing?" Breen said as he stuffed the black arrow back into his quiver and grabbed a regular one.

"Trying to get herself killed, apparently."

Ty blocked another volley of fireballs, one right after the other. The Tower's wielders sent them in continuous intervals, attempting to overpower him, making sure not to give him a chance to fight back. "Protect Narendi," Ty shouted, and Breen spun and fired on the guards, then he drew and released four more in quick succession.

Five men went down under his gifted aim, but it still wasn't enough. Narendi was cutting men down as fast as she could, at least half a dozen and counting, but even with her skill, she wasn't cutting them down fast enough, and more were on the way. Breen took down three from the second wave as others moved in behind her. "Ty, we've got to get to her!"

"I'm trying." All of Ty's concentration was on the wielders, who had now changed their minds about going after the townsfolk and were now coming straight for them. The bulradoer was at the back with her blade of gold fire, while the recruits were busy in front, keeping Ty's arms moving as he blocked their continuous volleys. The bulradoer raised her hand and sent another blast of hardened air against Ty's shield. It was like getting hit by one of Fraya's father's prize bulls.

Ty was thrown backward, where he collided with Breen, and they both hit the mountain behind them. Breen was the first up, and he quickly helped Ty, who was busy doing everything he could to keep his shield in place.

Behind the wielders, Ty caught his first glimpse of Kraea dancing between a group of armed guards, all trying to pin her in place long enough to get their swords in and finish her off.

"*Get out of there, Kraea!*" he shouted. He had no way of getting to her. He could sense her desperation and fear, as it was strong enough to almost overwhelm him. He forced it aside. There wasn't anything he could do, and Narendi needed their help. She was still close enough to reach.

"Look out!" Breen said as the bulradoer raised her hands once more.

Ty braced for the hit. The last one had stunned him enough that he'd nearly lost his shield. He couldn't let that happen again.

This time, when she unleashed the battering ram of hardened air, he angled the shield instead of catching it full-on like the last time. The hammer struck, and he was still shoved slightly to the side, but not like the first time. The ball of air ricocheted and struck the pile of rock back near the entrance, sending a quarter of it scattering down the slope.

Ty drew his own ram of air and sent it at the wielders, but they angled their shields and sent it careening behind them, clearly having had more experience using them than he did.

"I'm gonna make a run for it," Breen said as he unleashed one more arrow into the chest of a man who was working his way around Narendi's right side. Narendi was now backed up almost to the mountain itself, with nowhere to go. Ty could see cuts and blood on the sleeves of her shirt. It was a miracle the Imbatoo princess had lasted this long.

Ty angled the shield and tried extending it a bit to give his brother a chance, but as soon as Breen stepped out from behind the shield's protection, the bulradoer and the recruits sent a barrage of flames straight at him. Breen dove back behind the shield just before getting hit. The fire struck the mountain instead, scattering pieces of stone everywhere, many of which flew behind Ty's shield, hitting the two of them. A shard sliced the side of Ty's face, and he could feel warm blood running down his cheek.

Narendi was about to be overrun. If he didn't do something fast, she would die right in front of him. Desperation taking over, Ty turned to send his own flames into the Black Watch, hoping he didn't scorch Narendi in the process, but before he got his hand up, he heard Kraea roar. The draakar suddenly burst through the Tower's guards and attacked the four wielders coming for Ty and Breen, forcing them to halt their attack.

Ty looked at Breen. "Go!"

Breen dashed out from behind the shield and straight for Narendi just as Kraea slammed into the wielders' shields from behind, momentarily diverting their attention. It gave Ty another chance to go on the offensive.

Holding his shield in place with his right hand, he ignited flames in his left. Ty could almost hear the magic crying to be released as he sent a huge wave of blue fire against their shields. Searing pain tore through Ty's left arm, letting him know he was once again expending enough magic to grow his markings.

The magic coursing through his body was glorious and powerful. All it took was a single grey-robed recruit who didn't have the training or the strength to stand against magic that strong, and Ty's flames plowed through the opening, igniting all three recruits, and even the bulradoer. They went down screaming.

Kraea leaped onto the pile of smoldering bodies, snapping at the blue flames as if trying to catch them in her mouth. Ty could sense her enjoyment through the link. It was intoxicating.

Ty was surprised he didn't feel all that much weaker after expending such a large burst. His body must have been growing stronger with its use of the magic. On his left, Breen released another barrage of arrows, dropping several more guards as they tried to flank the two.

Ty sent his own fist of air into a group of white guards on Narendi's right, and they went flying. He raised his hand to burn them to ash but caught a bright flash out of the corner of his eye and spun around. A ball of flame from behind him hit high on his shield, and he managed to deflect it up over his head.

Several more of the Tower's wielders, who had been dealing with the archers, had spotted him, and were now heading in his direction. Three carried wizard weapons, *ter'aks* Nyalis called them: two swords—one green and one blue—and a red battle-axe.

Ty turned to the draakar. "*Kraea! Help Narendi and Breen!*"

Kraea turned, spotting the two, and roared as she charged the back of the Tower's guards.

Ty moved to face the oncoming group of wielders, searching for Mangora, but not finding her. He didn't like the fact that she was nowhere to be seen. For all he knew, she could be using the shorlock right then.

With his shield in place, Ty moved away from the side of the mountain and out toward the middle of the bluff, just behind the Black Watch, drawing this new batch of bulradoer and their recruits to him and away from his brother and Narendi. Wave after wave of fire and air came at him, overwhelming him to the point of not being able to fight back.

The only consolation he could take was that from where he was standing, the balls of flame and fists of air were doing more damage to their own ranks, as he deflected them toward the Tower's guards as they continued to fight against the fur-clad townsfolk.

Pretty soon, the Black Watch were shifting position once again, trying to keep out of reach, which looked to be giving the townsfolk a small advantage, as they were no longer being forced toward the bluff's edge.

However, for every new attack Ty thwarted, the wielders gained more ground. Pretty soon, they were going to have him backed all the way into the white mantles of the Tower's guards.

Chapter 84 | Ayrion

HAT IN THE FLAMING stones was that?" Ozlin Beartooth shouted at Ayrion.

Ayrion, who had somehow ended up at the front of the charge after Ozlin ordered the initial attack, tried his best to see where the strange blue fire had come from, but there were too many of the white cloaks standing between them. The only reason they had seen the initial attack was because the ranks had split momentarily to get out of the way. It looked like the attack had come from somewhere over near the entrance to the pass.

"That wasn't our tinker friends, was it?" Ozlin shouted as he buried his axe in a guard's shoulder and kicked the man out of the way.

"No!" Ayrion shouted back. "It wasn't one of us." Ayrion cut down several more guards as the fighting pressed the Wellhollow ranks back against the edge of the bluff. If they didn't do something fast, they were all going over the side.

"We've got to turn the ranks!" Bek shouted on Ayrion's left, his hatchets swinging in all directions, sending streams of blood out across the tops of those standing nearby. "Quit holding back!"

Ayrion ignored his friend's comment and severed a man's arm as it swung a sword for his head. "We need to reach the right wall and whoever it is that's fighting those wielders. I'll take my chances with them any day." About the time he said it, several balls of orange flame struck the back left of the Tower's lines, and the entire company shifted once more, forcing the Wellhollow fighters straight for the side of the mountain and away from the edge of the bluff.

Ayrion moved with the formation and cut his way toward the right. In the back of his mind, though, Bek's question pricked at his conscience. He knew he was holding back, but he also remembered what it had been like when he turned himself fully over to the magic. It was like he was no longer in control. He also didn't like the way it made him feel. The rush of power. *Son of the night*, the oracle had called him. He feared what he became under the magic and whether one day it would simply not release its control once he turned himself over to it. But right now, just as with the vulraak, he didn't have a choice, and memories or not, if he didn't turn the tide, they were going to be swept away.

"Ayrion, on your left!" Bek shouted.

Ayrion deflected the guard's swing, kicked him in the leg, and stuck his left sword through his neck as he fell. He looked around. Their numbers were dwindling. If those wielders on the other side ever made it around, then they'd be pinned for sure. Ayrion's swords might have been magic-wrought, at least from what he could tell, but they weren't going to stop a bulradoer's fire.

"Fight for the mountain!" Ozlin shouted once more, drawing his remaining men and women to him. "We need to reach the caverns. Protect the oracle!"

In the initial conflict after the snow and avalanche had failed them, it was the wielders who had first reached the plateau. Ayrion and the others had not expected so many and with such power. Their flames had killed at least a third of their fighters before the archers were able to force their attention away long enough for the rest to retreat. Unfortunately, the only direction the wielders gave them was toward the bluff. They had tried to reach the caves, but those in the black and grey robes had cut them down fairly quickly, leaving them only one other option as the white uniforms poured out of the pass and onto the plateau.

It was Ayrion who had ordered the retreat, and his idea to use the Tower's guards as a barricade between them and the wielders. But now, they had no choice. Ayrion only hoped that whoever was fighting back against the Tower's wielders was there to help. At this point, what other option did they have?

He could hear strange roars from some kind of creature on the other side of the bluff, and saw the occasional flash of blue and orange flame toward the middle. A flash of memory struck, and Ayrion was suddenly pulled from the fight and standing on the edge of a bluff overlooking a great battle. He watched as a troop of mounted riders tore into the side of an oncoming force of giant wolflike creatures, slowing their momentum.

". . . Ayrion! Ayrion!" Something struck his shoulder and the vision vanished. "Wake up!" Bek shouted as he cut down two men on Ayrion's left. "Terrible time to be daydreaming."

Ayrion cut down two more men. Ozlin shouted and went down for a moment, then was back up, blood on the side of his face. They were about to be overrun. Ayrion had to do something. Diving deep inside himself, he released the magic and then turned himself over to it. He let the heat of it consume him, the chaos and noise suddenly growing dim as everything came into focus.

"On me!" he shouted and unleashed his blades, his arms moving in perfect harmony between offense and defense as he struck and blocked, deflected and thrust. One sword to protect, the other to kill. He fought his way forward, straight through the center of the Black Watch formation. Behind, he could hear Ozlin shouting for his fighters to follow.

Ayrion's entire body moved as only it could with magic, the visions coming so fast he could hardly keep up as he ducked and dodged and wove his way around the oncoming blades. Nothing touched him, bodies dropping in his wake as he passed, his swords claiming the lives of all that came within reach. The rush was thrilling. The power of life and death in his hands. He was something more than human. He was—

A blast of air struck the back of the Black Watch ranks just as he broke through the lines, and it sent him flying like a rag doll over the top of his own fighters to land somewhere in the middle. He staggered back to his feet with the help of some very surprised Wellhollow townsfolk he had landed on top of. Nothing like a punch to the gut to remind him of his place and keep him humble. Quickly, he rushed back to the front.

"You all right?" Bek asked.

"I've never seen any man fight like that before," Ozlin said. "It was incredible. Of course, I've never seen a man fly before either." He laughed.

"Who is that?" Bek asked, pointing to a young man in front of them, standing off against the Tower's wielders. The young man swiped his hand in the air, and several balls of fire from the robed wielders went sailing to the right, where they impacted against a group of men in white uniforms, setting them ablaze and sending the rest running for cover.

The young man turned for a split second and caught Ayrion's eyes. He was younger than Ayrion had thought, just a teenager. He had the brightest blue eyes Ayrion had ever seen, or at least remembered seeing. "I'll try to hold them back," the boy shouted, then turned to fight back another barrage of fire, sending one or two blasts of his own blue flames in return.

"I don't know who he is," Ayrion said, "but it seems the safest place to be is right behind him. Get our fighters in line. We'll stand our ground here and protect his flank." He spotted two others fighting over near the right side of the mountain. "Take some men and see if you can help those two over there." About the time he said it, something roared and leaped into the air between several of the guards who were currently engaging the fighters.

"What in the flaming Pits is that?" Ozlin shouted, his eyes bulging.

It was about the size of a large wolf, but without the fur, and it looked to have wings, if you could call them wings. They were too short and stumpy to be used for flying.

"Whatever it is," Bek said. "I hope it's on our side." Quickly, he ordered a section of fighters on him as they rushed from the center of the plateau toward the right side, where the small battle was being fought.

Ayrion turned around to face the main battle behind them just as the last of their people moved out from the split in the Tower's ranks. By the time he pushed his way to the front, it had already closed, but the job was done. They were now the ones at the front, pushing the Tower's troops toward the edge of the bluff. Ayrion hoped the young man behind them could hold back the wielders' flames long enough to allow them to press their advantage. Up until now, it had all been about keeping away from the wielders.

Now, it was their turn.

Chapter 85 | Ty

TY RAISED HIS SHIELD, waiting for the next blast, angling it just enough to make sure not to hit the mountainfolk behind him. He hoped they were smart enough to stay behind him. Their leader seemed to be. The man in the brightly colored wool coat with those incredible black swords looked even more scary up close, blood covering his face and eyes as dead as a three-day corpse. Whoever he was, Ty hoped he remained on his side.

Ty deflected another assault and sent his own blast of air right between two of the grey wielders, hitting them with enough force that they both went flying, their shields collapsing as they hit the ground. He tried to burn them, but the three bulradoer behind them extended their shields before he got the chance.

Ty was pelted with another blast of air, and he stumbled backward over the smoldering pile of dead wielders behind him. A metallic scrape caught his attention, and he looked down, spotting the silver hilt of a bulradoer's wizard sword. Maybe he could use it to break through their shields. He snatched it up between volleys and pushed his magic into it, but nothing happened. No flaming blade appeared, just the hilt. There were runes on the side. They looked like letters, but he couldn't read them.

Come on! Work! The Tower's wielders were about to be on him, and he needed a weapon to fight with in close combat. He started to push another wave of magic into the blade, but then he remembered hearing the bulradoer shout something before she had swatted back Breen's arrow.

Blazes! What was it? "*Dorang! Dulnang!*" He batted back several more fireballs and nearly went down with a particularly large blast of air. He barely managed to get his shield up in time, and the strike sent him sideways, scattering several lines of men behind him on the left, mostly Black Watch, but some were fur clad. He had to be more careful. He repositioned himself and sent another burst of blue flame at the oncoming wielders, who were now only about twenty feet away and still gaining.

He kept a tight grip on the hilt of his new fire sword and tried again. "*Dorene! Fornang!*"

"*Dorfang, you imbecile!*" Kraea shouted at him. "*The black one said Dorfang!*"

Ty held up the hilt. "*Dorfang!*" Flames shot from the crossguard to form a long golden blade, much longer than the shortsword he'd been carrying at his waist, but yet the weight didn't seem anything at all. His shield was struck with another pocket of hardened air, but he'd been too focused on the sword to get the shield into the correct position, and the ball of air sent him careening backward, cartwheeling toward the back lines of the battle behind him.

He rolled to a stop, pain shooting through his left arm, the same arm he was using to hold his shield. The pain was excruciating. He hoped it wasn't broken. Gritting his teeth, he looked down and realized that he was no longer holding the wizard sword. Where was it? He looked up and saw the hilt back near where he'd been standing. The blast must have knocked it from his fingers, the golden flames extinguished.

The oncoming wielders saw the sword as well and ran for it. Ty climbed to his feet and hit them with a wave of fire as he, too, made a desperate dash for the fallen weapon. He deflected another blast of air, which nearly ripped his arm back from having angled his shield too much, then hit them with one in return, but instead of directing it at their shields, he hit the ground in front, cracking the stone and sending a wave of debris up across the front of their ranks, slowing them just enough to dive for the sword and wrap his hand around the hilt.

"*Dorfang!*" he shouted and rolled back to his feet, colliding with the first of the wielders. A female in grey just stood there in stunned silence staring at him. The others behind her pulled to a stop. It took Ty a moment to realize the golden blade was sticking out the back of her robes. He hadn't even felt the weapon go in. There'd been no resistance at all.

He slid it free and raised his shield in time to keep from getting his own head whacked off as two more of the fiery weapons swung for his shoulders. He could feel the heat as they bounced off his shield. The one remaining recruit, who didn't possess a weapon, quickly moved to the back, giving the three bulradoer plenty of room as they attacked from one side to the other, trying to find an opening.

It became clear that the weapons didn't penetrate their shields as he had thought they might, which turned out to be a good thing for him. If they had, he would have been dead already. It took everything Ty had just to keep his shield up and sword moving fast enough to not get cut in half. He dove to the right, deflecting both the green and blue swords as he did, then rolled back to his feet, swinging his own golden weapon at the first set of black robes he saw, forcing the man to counter and move.

Ty's first thought, other than being grateful to be alive, was that he wished Lyessa were there. There was no telling what she could have done with one of these blades. He swung to the left and blocked the red battle-axe, surprised by the minimal impact, given the force of his swing, then raised his shield and jumped back as the blue sword flew past and cut a hole straight into the stone under his feet.

These weapons were incredibly powerful. Ty's arms were tiring as they whipped about, doing everything they could to keep the flaming weapons from hitting him, but he couldn't keep it up. He wasn't a swordsman. The fact that he'd been able to stave off their advances this long was due to sheer luck and desperation. He swung left to block the bulradoer with the green sword, his shield stopping the blue, but it left him open on the right to the red axe.

Ty realized his mistake as soon as his blade sparked against the green. But there was nothing he could do. The battle-axe was in the air, and it was as though the world suddenly slowed. He was being forced to watch his own death, while knowing that no matter what he did, he could never move fast enough to stop it.

The axe swung downward, lighting the bulradoer's face beneath his cowl with a sinister red glow, giving him the look of a sadistic faerie, or at least what Ty imagined a sadistic faerie looked like. The blade was going to enter through top of Ty's neck and slice downward, probably exiting somewhere around his waist on the opposite side, cutting him completely in two. Somewhere in the distance, he thought he could hear his brother screaming, but it might have just been his imagination. Either way, he hoped Breen didn't have to witness his death, or more importantly the aftermath of what was left.

Ty's blade was still sparking against the green as the axe plunged downward. He wanted to close his eyes, but he couldn't. He doubted it was bravery, most likely not enough time.

Suddenly the axe stopped in midair, its red flames burning the side of his face. He turned to find a sword, black as a starless night, holding the weapon in place. Red sparks flew into the air, and the bulradoer barely had time to look surprised before a second blade removed his head. Ty had never seen eyes quite as astonished as the bulradoer's. They stared at him as the head flew by.

Suddenly, everything seemed to speed up at once. He dropped his shield and hammered the remaining two bulradoer with a heavy fist of air, sending them both flying backward as he turned to see the man in the colorful wool coat standing beside him. The man looked calm—too calm for a situation like this. He didn't even seem to be breathing all that hard.

The bulradoer rolled back on their feet and released a torrent of flame at the man with the black blades.

"Watch out!" Ty shouted and swung his shield around to counter the attack just before his unexpected protector was roasted alive. The man held his arms up to cover his face as the flames ricocheted back in the direction of the pass.

"Thanks, kid."

Kid? Ty clenched his teeth.

The two remaining wielders began to circle them. Ty wondered if they were simply curious or actually afraid. They seemed more interested in the dragon-hilted swords than they were the one holding them.

Ty spared a passing glance over at the man with the dead eyes. "Who are you?"

"Someone who's always in the wrong place at the wrong time."

Ty hmphed. "I know the feeling. This your home?"

"Nope. As I said . . . wrong place, wrong time." The man looked at Ty, his grey eyes sending chill bumps down Ty's arms. "I'll take the one on the left."

Before Ty could even nod, the man was already rushing straight at the two wielders. He had to be crazy. Ty sent a quick blast of air at the black wielders to force them to raise their shields and not resort to their flames, then he charged. But by the time he reached the fight, the man with the black blades had already engaged both wielders at once. Had he lost his mind? Didn't he realize who it was he was fighting?

Ty couldn't even get close enough to swing. Every time he did, the man would shift positions and get in Ty's way. The man moved between the bulradoers' blades with agility that didn't seem possible. It was like he could anticipate every move. Every swing was a miss, every thrust was nothing but air. Even their shields were doing little to stop him and his swords as they worked their way in between the bulradoers' guard.

Within moments, one of the bulradoer went down, their green blade vanishing. The second dove backward and sent a ball of flame at him, but Ty managed to throw his own shield in front of the man, which until that moment, he didn't know he could do, and sent the flames veering to the right.

The swordsman rolled to his feet and threw one of his blades.

The last bulradoer didn't stand a chance. His shield was out of position in order to throw his flames. Ty had seen his father and brother throw a brace of knives with pinpoint accuracy, but never an entire sword. The blade buried in the man's chest, and the blue flames of his sword flashed out of existence.

The swordsman recovered his unique weapon about the time that the rest of the Tower's wielders had given up their attack on the archers. They turned to see where they were needed most, finding Ty and the swordsman standing there, surrounded by dead bulradoer.

Behind Ty, the battle seemed to be winding down, and as luck would have it, the mountainfolk were coming out ahead, as those of the Black Watch were in a full retreat back toward the pass. One look at the state of things, not to mention the fallen number of wielders, and the remaining bulradoer and recruits decided to join their brethren and edge their way toward the pass as well.

Ty worked his way over to the swordsman to protect him in case the wielders attempted to unleash one last volley. He could have tried attacking the wielders, but he had no desire to go chasing them all the way back down the mountainside. They'd been beaten. He doubted they'd be back anytime soon. The wielders reached the entrance and turned, but instead of looking at Ty or the swordsman, or the rest of the mountainfolk, they looked up at the surrounding cliffs, and Ty could see it in their eyes.

"They're going to seal us in."

"Do something," the swordsman shouted.

Ty raised his hands frantically, not really knowing what to do. He started to pull the air to him when a loud crack filled the night, and a blast of energy shook the ground, throwing him and the swordsman on their faces. Ty looked up to see the Tower's wielders suddenly disappearing over the slope.

"What happened?" he asked. It was like the wielders were there one moment and gone the next, thrown so far back they simply disappeared into the darkness of the pass.

The swordsman was on his feet before Ty had made it to his knees. Ty winced as the man grabbed his injured arm to help him up.

"She happened," the swordsman said, nodding toward the buildings behind them, where an old woman in a very colorful tinker's dress and cloak stood watching. An old man was standing next to her, holding her up. "Those are friends of mine. Come, I'll introduce you. I'm Ayrion."

"Ty." Ty turned to see where his brother and Narendi and Kraea were, but before he managed to get halfway, the swordsman grabbed his injured arm once again and spun him around.

"What is that?"

Ty turned, half expecting to find Kraea standing there with someone's arm hanging from her mouth, but the swordsman wasn't looking over at the bluff. He was looking directly up at the mountainside. A dark shadow worked its way down the cliff face and into a cavern on the backside of the bluff.

"Mangora." Ty started to run for the tunnel, but the swordsman grabbed him and spun him around.

"Who's Mangora? Tell me, quickly! The oracle's in there!"

"She's a witch. She—"

"What's going on?" Breen asked almost defensively as he and Narendi rushed over, along with the two fur-clad mountain men Ty had seen fighting alongside the swordsman.

"Mangora just went in there," Ty said, pointing at the hole in the rock. "The arachnobe is with her."

Ayrion ran for the tunnel. "The oracle's in danger!"

The bear man with the red beard nearly knocked Ty over as he sprinted after Ayrion, his large battle-axe bouncing on his back.

Ty turned and ran after them, knowing they had no idea who they were dealing with. Breen and Narendi were hot on his heels. Ty didn't have time to ask how either was doing. Clearly, they were alive, and that was all that mattered. He didn't see Kraea. She was probably curled up somewhere with a couple of corpses.

Ty reached the entrance and found several dead mountainfolk. Ayrion and the bear man were busy inspecting the dead, those within the moonlight's reach.

"Here." Ty raised his hand, and it ignited in blue flame, chasing the shadows further into the cavern and giving the men light enough to see by.

"She's not here," the bear man said, and he and Ayrion took off running down the tunnels.

"Did I hear someone say something about an arachnobe?" a woman's voice said behind them.

Ty turned to find the old man and old woman, who had somehow dispensed of the wielders a moment ago, hobbling over. The old man grabbed the last remaining torch from the wall.

"Yes," Ty said. "Syglara. She's Mangora's arachnobe." He pointed down the dark passageway ahead, where Ayrion and the two fur-clad mountain men had just run. "What's this about an oracle?"

The older couple's eyes bulged. "The oracle is in there?" They took off running as well.

Ty looked at Breen and Narendi, and they chased after them, passing the older couple on the way. Ty kept his blue fire in the air to light their way. Their younger, faster legs managed to catch up with the three men as they raced through the winding tunnel ahead.

"You need to slow down," Ty tried telling them. "You have no idea who you're messing with here. She's more powerful than all those wielders out there combined."

Neither of the men slowed.

They ran for what felt like forever, following the tunnel's twists and turns through the mountainside. Without warning, they suddenly emerged into a large open cavern. There was a cooking fire on the right and what looked like living quarters on the left. The floor was crisscrossed with rugs that led all over the place. Ty raised his hand and quickly scanned the walls and ceiling. He didn't want to use his magic to find them for fear of alerting Syglara.

A loud barking roar and several hissing screeches echoed out of another tunnel on the other side of the cavern. Ty didn't need to be told who it was. He could feel her. "Kraea! She's fighting the arachnobe."

This time it was Ty who took off running, but the others were right behind. They reached the end of the tunnel and collided with an invisible barrier. Ty, Ayrion, and Breen went down first, the others nearly tripping on them as they did. Ty released his flames to keep from accidentally setting the others on fire as Narendi helped him up. Her spear was on her back, and she carried her satchel over her shoulder, the same satchel that held the jewels she had confiscated from the trader back in the Live Market.

Ayrion beat his fists against the barrier, even tried one of his swords, but it didn't budge.

Beyond the wall was another cavern, fire rising from some kind of trough that ran along most of the perimeter. On the other side, Mangora was standing in front of a set of enormous stone doors. The walls of the cavern seemed to be covered in ornately sculpted images.

"Angioma!" Ayrion shouted and continued beating against the shield.

To the left of the entrance, just beyond the barrier, lay an old woman even older than the one who had gotten rid of the wielders outside. Ty would have thought she was dead, if not for the occasional flinching of one of her arms. Had the arachnobe gotten her?

Kraea, too, was inside the barrier, growling and snapping at the enormous spider. The arachnobe was much bigger than she was, but Kraea was fast, and her scales, though not fully formed, helped defend against most of the spider's strikes. Kraea got her teeth around one of the creature's legs, and the arachnobe hissed. Syglara struck Kraea on the head, hard enough to loosen her grip, and then crawled up the side of the wall.

"Kraea! Protect the woman."

Kraea hissed. *Get in here and help me, faerie!*

Ty pressed against the barrier. "I'm trying!"

"Oracle?" The bear man with the red beard pushed Ty and the others out of the way to get a better view. One look at the old woman and he unhooked his axe and began beating against the side of the shield.

"Move!" Breen said. "Let me through." Breen was the biggest man there, but not by much when compared to the fur-clad huntsman with the two hatchets. Still, the others didn't seem to want to let him pass.

"Move!" Ty finally shouted at them, spinning around with fire bursting from his hands. "Let him through." He lowered his voice as the others quickly backed away. "My brother has the only weapon that can pierce a wielder's shield."

Ayrion looked at Breen, then turned and grabbed the man with the bear's head and pulled him back out of the way so Breen could move into position.

Breen raised his bow, a black arrow already nocked, and pulled the string to his cheek. He released, and the arrow shot through the barrier, but Mangora spun and waved her hand, and the arrow veered to the left, clanging off the wall.

"Did you think to hurt me with my own weapon?"

The others looked at Breen, and he shrugged. "I used it to stop her before." He looked at Ty. "These aren't going to do any good."

"They will against the arachnobe."

Breen smiled. "Good point." He nocked another arrow, pulling the string to his cheek, but Syglara had already skittered up across the ceiling and out of sight. "Blazes!" Breen shook his head. "Where'd she go?" Without a shot, he stepped aside to let Ayrion and the bear man back to the front, where they continued pounding against the shield.

Hearing approaching footsteps from the tunnel, they turned to see the old man and woman finally catching up. Ayrion left the invisible wall and walked over to the old woman. "Zynora, is there something you can do?"

She looked nearly ready to topple over. "Afraid not. I don't have anything left in me, and even if I did, all I'd likely manage to do is bring the mountain down on our heads."

Ayrion looked at Ty. "What about you? You seem to know who this witch is. What does she want?"

"I don't . . ." Ty looked across the chamber at Mangora. She was still standing in the same place, but with her hands out in front. Ty looked at her hands, and his heart nearly stopped. "It's the shorlock."

"What?" Breen and Narendi pushed their way to the front. "She's using it here?" Breen asked. "This is Aero'set?"

Ty shook his head, still in shock. "I don't know."

"Shorlock? Aero'set?" Ayrion stared at the three, desperation on his face.

"What the flaming hailstones are you talking about?"

Ty stared at Mangora as she held the key toward the stone doors. Nothing seemed to be happening. "It's kind of a long story," he said, not sure how much he should reveal. He glanced over at Kraea, who was now sitting in front of the old woman, just outside the entrance. Every now and then the draakar would look up toward the ceiling and growl, no doubt at the arachnobe. "Stay where you are," Ty said. "Don't attack the black one," which was what Kraea called the bulradoer.

"If you're going to do something," Kraea said, *"you better do it fast. This old one doesn't look too good. She smells of death."*

Ty clenched his fists in frustration. "I know. I'm working on it."

"Working on what?" the bear man asked, staring down at the injured lady in the chamber.

Ty turned. "Sorry, I was talking to Kraea." He pointed at the draakar but didn't offer an explanation. Instead, he turned to those gathered, still unsure as to what to say, but since they seemed to have been caught up in the middle of this, much like Narendi, he guessed he owed them at least some of the truth. "My name is Ty." He pointed beside him to his brother. "That's Breen, and that's Narendi. She's of the Imbatoo." Narendi was still wearing her baka over her head but had removed the scarf from around her face. "That woman out there is Mangora. She's an Ahvari witch who works for the White Tower."

He decided not to go into the details of who he was, as far as being half faerie, or the previous battles he'd had with Mangora, but sticking strictly with what had brought them to where they were right then, wherever that was. "Where exactly are we?"

The others shared a confused look. "You're in Upper Wellhollow," the man with the bear on his head said, tugging vigorously on his long red beard. "My name is Ozlin Beartooth. I'm the magistrate. How do you not know where you are?"

Ty looked at Breen and blew out his lips. "That's another long story."

"Starting to see a pattern here," Ayrion said.

"Then make it short," Ozlin pushed, periodically glancing back over his shoulder toward the old woman on the other side of the barrier. "Will the oracle be safe with whatever that thing is?"

"That thing is a draakar," Ty said. "Her name is Kraea. And yes, she'll be safe with her. As I was saying, Mangora is here for me. She was waiting for us when we arrived."

"Why?" Ayrion asked. "If you don't even know where you are, why would she be here waiting?"

Ty released a frustrated sigh, and without thinking, pulled off his black cap to rub the top of his head. The others looked startled. "Oh, sorry. I keep forgetting about that." He put the cap back on. "I'll see if I can make this short. A wizard named Nyalis sent me on a quest to recover the shorlock."

"And what is that?" the big man with the hatchets asked. He quickly introduced himself, as well as the old couple behind them. "I take it you've already met Ayrion."

Ozlin looked at Ayrion. "I thought your name was Jair?"

Ayrion gave Bek a harsh look, then turned to Ozlin. "We can talk about it later." He looked at Ty. "You were saying."

"The shorlock is a magical key that was split into four parts over a thousand years ago and hidden."

"And you've managed to recover it?" Ayrion asked.

Ty nodded.

"What does it do?" Bek asked.

"It's supposed to bring back the Keep of Aero'set."

Zynora gasped. "The wizard's keep?"

Ty nodded once more, surprised the old woman recognized the name.

Her eyes sparked with excitement. "The wizard's keep was said to have been the last stand against the Defiler during the Wizard Wars. Can you imagine what we might be able to accomplish if we were to get our hands on it?"

"Can you imagine what the *Tower* will accomplish if they do instead?" Breen added.

"There is much more at stake than what we see here," Ty said, echoing Nyalis's earlier sentiments. "The rise or fall of all Aldor could depend on what is happening inside that room. We've got to stop her."

The stone beneath their feet began to shake, and Ty, along with the others, scurried over to the barrier. Mangora was still holding out the key with both hands, aiming straight at the doors. Ty could hear her chanting. Whatever she was saying, it seemed to be working, as the mountain quaked under its use.

Ty had to get in there before she managed to open those doors. He grabbed hold of Ozlin and Ayrion and pulled them away from the barrier. The time for caution was long past. "Stand back." He hit Mangora's shield as hard as he could with a heavy fist of air, but all he managed to do was put a crack in the side of the wall beside the entrance, which had the others scampering backward and out of the way in case he caused a collapse.

Ty shouted in frustration. How was he going to get in there?

Kraea must have been able to feel his desperation through their link, for the next thing Ty knew, she was charging across the room and straight for Mangora.

"Kraea, no!"

A loud hiss rang out from somewhere on the ceiling, and Mangora spun, a dagger appearing in her hand as if by magic.

Kraea roared and leaped, her jaws open wide, hungry for the kill.

Mangora swept to the side with a speed that didn't match her age and plunged the dagger into Kraea's softer underbelly, then hit her with a huge burst of air that sent the draakar flying across the cavern. She landed in a heap, nearly on top of the old woman, moaned, and went still.

Ty grabbed his brother and pushed him toward the entrance. "Kill that spider if it shows its face." He could see the knife still sticking from Kraea's belly. *"Hold on, Kraea. I'm coming."*

Breen pressed against the invisible wall as he raised his black Sol Ghati bow, arrow nocked, waiting for any sign of the spider coming down to feast on Kraea or the old woman. Without warning, Mangora's shield disappeared, and Breen tumbled inside.

Ty dove for the opening, as did Ayrion, but the wall was back up before either could get through. Ty leaped back to his feet and peered inside.

"Breen!"

Chapter 86 | Ty, Ayrion

Y BEAT HIS HANDS against the barrier, but other than producing a dull thud, it made little difference. What he knew of magic wasn't enough to fill his cap. What good was being a faeling and having all this supposed power if he couldn't even get past a single barrier? How was Mangora maintaining it? Ty couldn't even keep a shield in place without constant thought. The smallest distraction or lack of concentration would cause him to lose it.

On the other side of the wall, Breen was quickly checking on the old woman and Kraea. Both seemed to be breathing, but neither doing well. He kept his eyes on Mangora, who was back to holding up the key and chanting. Breen knelt beside Kraea and looked at the knife. "Should I pull it out?"

"No," Zynora said, pushing her way forward with a little help from Tameel and Bek. "She will bleed to death if you do. You will need to seal the wound."

"With what?"

"Something very hot."

A clicking noise had Breen spinning and raising the bow up toward the ceiling. "Got you now."

Mangora spun and raised her hand, and Breen was suddenly lifted off his feet and thrown against the back wall, the impact knocking the bow from his hands. She kept her hand raised, and Breen's face tightened, a slight wheezing coming out of his mouth. He was being pressed against the stone, the same as she had done to them the previous day. Breen's face was turning red.

"Let him go!" Ty shouted as he beat against the barrier, pushing with everything he had to break through. Both his hands ignited in flame, and he smashed them against the wall. The others moved back to get out of his way as he pounded against it, shaking the stone around them, but nothing happened. The wall held.

Mangora made some kind of waving motion with her hand and mumbled something under her breath, then turned back to the doors.

Ty looked at Breen. He was still held firmly against the wall, but at least he seemed to be able to breathe now. Whatever she had done must have been similar to the barrier, something that locked into place.

Mangora lifted the key once again and began to chant. The bloodstone glowed and the room began to shake. After a long moment of not knowing whether she was about to bring the mountain down on their heads or open the doors, Mangora dropped her arms and released an ear-piercing screech.

"Why isn't this working?" She spun around. "If you want to keep your brother alive, then help me. Get this key to work, and I'll spare him." She turned and raised one arm in Breen's direction. "Don't, and I'll make you watch as I slowly keep squeezing."

Breen looked like a fresh-caught fish out of water as she slowly tightened the invisible wall pressing against him. His mouth opened and closed, trying to gasp for air.

"Fine," Ty said. "I agree. Just don't hurt him."

Ayrion grabbed Ty by the shoulder and pulled him around. "What are you doing, lad? You just said that the future of Aldor hinges on the Tower not getting their hands on this keep. You said nothing was more important. I know he's your brother, and I'm sorry for it, but there are scores of men and women outside who just gave their lives tonight to defend this place. You can't just throw their sacrifice away."

"I'm not," Ty said, keeping his voice lowered enough so Mangora couldn't hear, "but as long as we are standing on this side of the barrier, there's little any of us can do. At least on the other side, I have a chance to try stopping her."

Ayrion held his gaze, those grey eyes making Ty's skin crawl. "Fine." The swordsman released Ty's arm and stepped back.

Ty turned to Mangora. "Release him first."

Mangora stared at him a moment, then raised her hand once more and mumbled an incantation, and Breen was lowered back to the cavern floor. He sucked in a mouthful of air, but when he tried to take a step toward Ty, he hit a barrier.

Ty looked at Mangora. "You said you would release him."

"No. I said I would let him live, as long as you get the shorlock working. For now, he stays where he is." She looked up at the cavern's ceiling. "Keep an eye on him, Syglara."

The arachnobe skittered down the side of the wall just above where Breen was being held, and swept all the way to the floor, standing directly in front of him. She was enormous, close to the size of a full-grown draakar. She raised one of her great hairy legs to get at Breen, but the invisible shield barred her way. She hissed and skittered over to Kraea, whose chest was rising intermittently, blood pooling on the stone beneath her.

"Keep that thing away from her," Ty demanded, "or you'll get nothing from me."

Mangora smiled and looked at the arachnobe. "Not now, my sweet. Maybe later." Syglara clicked her mandibles in response, then skittered back over to Breen.

"Get in there, son, and help the oracle," Ozlin said, all but pushing Ty toward the invisible wall, his voice trembling as he stared at the old woman.

Ty stood at the barrier and waited.

"Tell the others to back away," Mangora said.

Ty looked at the rest of the group and nodded, and they scooted back a few feet.

"Farther!" she hissed. "I don't want to see a single face but yours when I lower it."

The others turned and headed further down the tunnel, far enough to make Mangora feel safe enough to lower her barrier. "Well, what are you waiting for? Get in here."

Ty held out his hand. The barrier was down. He stepped out of the tunnel's entrance, and the wall went back up. He could feel it just behind him, a small tingling sensation across his skin. He looked at Breen, and his brother shook his head. "Don't you let her through those doors. Don't you—" Breen was suddenly unable to speak, or Ty was unable to hear him. Breen's mouth was moving but nothing was coming out.

"Much better," Mangora said.

Ty spun around. "What did you do to him?"

"I've done nothing to him. A simple silencing spell. I believe you are familiar with it," she added with a smile.

Kraea growled softly, and Ty rushed to help her. He needed to get that knife out of her chest and seal the wound before she bled to death. Three steps away, and he hit a wall himself. He spun. "I need to help her!"

"No! You need to get this key to work." Mangora held out the shorlock. "The longer you wait, the more you risk her life. Is that what you want?"

Ty clenched his teeth till they hurt. He had to do something, but what? If he attacked her outright, there was the chance he could win. He was stronger now than he was when they'd first fought. But he doubted he could defeat her before she killed Breen. How did she always manage to do this to him? Why was she always one step ahead?

The whole reason he wanted to bring this magic school back was so he could finally learn about who he was and how to control his magic. Now the flaming witch was about to take it all from him. Worse, he was about to serve it to her on a gold platter like a blasted chamberlain.

"Zwaneri a Wakale."

Ty turned to see Narendi staring at him from the other side of the wall.

"Remember—"

Mangora conjured another silencing spell over the tunnel, and whatever it was that Narendi was trying to say after that was cut off. *Remember Zwaneri a Wakale? Remember what?* What did the ancient desert temple have to do with anything?

"Take the key!" Mangora hissed.

Ty turned his back on the tunnel and his friends and started across the room. *Zwaneri a Wakale. What was she trying to tell him?* The temple was a mirage. Unfortunately, Mangora wasn't. Neither was Kraea as she lay dying with a knife in her chest.

His time was running out. Ayrion was right. He couldn't allow himself to be used to bring back Aero'set for the Tower. Ty kept his steps slow as he tried to prolong the inevitable as best he could, his mind racing to think of a way out of this. Perhaps he could fake it, make it look as though the key wouldn't work for him either? Was that possibly what Narendi was saying? No, that didn't make sense. Either the key worked, or it didn't. And acting like it didn't wasn't exactly a solution. Mangora would just kill them all out of spite. Maybe he was looking at this wrong. Perhaps what she was trying to say was to make Mangora think he had been successful? No, that didn't make sense either. It wasn't like he could somehow make her believe the doors had opened. Or could he? He brushed his arm against the front of his coat, reassuring himself the flute was still there.

Unfortunately, he was out of time, and so were Kraea and the old woman if he didn't do something. Was he really going to be forced to choose between all their lives and this mythical keep? All he had was an old wizard's word that it was worth protecting, but did he believe it enough to risk all their lives? The Tower would just send others, wouldn't they?

He stopped in front of her and reached out and took the key. The stone at the center swirled and glowed much in the same way the one on Mangora's spider ring did, but something about it felt off, like looking at an image where you know something is out of place, but you can't quite put your finger on what. There was a wrongness to the stone that was off-putting. He could feel the pulse of the bloodstone as it worked its way through the pieces of the shorlock and into him. It made his skin crawl. He wasn't sure if it was the key itself doing it, or the thought of what had been done in order to create it.

"Well? What are you waiting for? Open the doors."

Ty had no idea how to open the doors. Nyalis had never given him any instructions on what to do with the key once he got it. He didn't even know there would be doors to open. All he was told was to collect the pieces and bring back the keep. Absolutely ridiculous instructions, if he said so himself. Perhaps the keep was just beyond the doors. Either way, it didn't matter. He was trying to prevent them from opening, which meant he had to find a way to make it look like it wasn't going to work.

He held out the key and cleared his throat, doing his best to look as official as possible as Mangora watched with nervous excitement, waiting for something to happen. He closed his eyes, concentrating on keeping his magic at bay, making sure not to accidentally release it and cause the key to suddenly flare to life. It took most of his concentration just to keep his stomach from turning over at the touch of the bloodstone and the death he could feel just inside. It left a bad taste in his mouth, nausea washing over him.

He waited a moment with his hands in the air and the key aimed toward the doors, but nothing happened.

"Are you trying to get your friends killed?" Mangora said behind him. "Quit wasting time and make that key work."

"I'm trying, but it doesn't seem to be working."

"Then try harder!"

"Maybe the key needs to be touching the stone," Ty said and walked toward the doors, his hands out of Mangora's eyesight. He placed the key against the stone with his left hand, the same side that Mangora was presently watching from, and with his right, he slowly slid his hand inside his jacket pocket, his fingers slipping around his pipes. He started to pull it out when Mangora, finally growing too impatient, walked over.

"Is it working?"

Ty released the pipes and quickly grabbed the other side of the key. "I think so," he lied, not knowing what else to say. "Let me try again." He closed his eyes and pretended to mumble something under his breath, loud enough for her to hear the noise, but not enough for her to hear him talking in gibberish.

"Why isn't it working?"

"Maybe you used the wrong kind of blood. Why don't you slit your own throat and try that."

She snarled, then suddenly looked like she had a thought. "Why didn't I think of that?" She grabbed Ty's hand, and before he could stop her, she whipped out another knife and cut a deep slice across the top of his palm and placed the key back in his hand, smearing his blood across the top.

The pieces of the key suddenly began to spin, and Ty took a step back, nearly dropping the artifact in the process. What was happening? He tried fighting back against the key, but his magic wouldn't respond. It was being ripped from him, and there was nothing he could do to stop it. The three stones on the outside of the key lit up as well. He fought to hold his magic at bay, but it wasn't listening. A wind from out of nowhere whipped around the cavern. He wondered if this was what it felt like for the dead wielders Mangora had pulled their magic from. Was this what was happening to him?

"Hold it up!" Mangora shouted over the growing tempest. "Hold it up, or your brother dies!"

Ty was afraid he'd waited too long. The key had just come to life and there was nothing he could do to stop it.

Mangora grabbed his hand and held it up to the doors. Large symbols that weren't visible before suddenly flared to life in bright gold around the edge of the stone. The entire room was shaking now. The magic inside the bloodstone twisted Ty's gut to the point he could hardly think straight, the sickness inside so strong that he nearly retched.

Mangora's robes billowed under the force of the wind. Ty could tell she was having a difficult time keeping to her feet, but the fervor in her eyes said there was no going back. The key began to glow even brighter, the symbols around the door doing the same. This was it. Ty could feel it. Whatever was about to happen, it was going—

Suddenly the bloodstone exploded in a blinding flash of light that threw Ty and Mangora backward and sent them rolling across the floor. For a brief moment, the shields went down, but she had them back up before the others had even realized.

Ty could see those inside the tunnel were on the ground as well. Whatever energy had just been released must have hit them when the barrier went down. Ayrion was back up and beating against the wall with his swords with no success. Ty made it back to his feet and turned on Mangora. He drew his magic and raised his hands, but she was already prepared, and Breen was suddenly thrown back against the wall.

Ty quickly lowered his hands. "Stop!" He released his magic. "Let him go!"

She lowered her hand, and his brother dropped. She then stumbled over and grabbed the key from him and looked at the doors. The symbols had vanished, and both still remained closed. "No. No!" she screamed. "This can't be!" She ran over to the doors and thrust the key against the stone in desperation. "This should have worked!"

Ty snatched his flute out from his jacket while her back was turned. This was his last chance, and he had to make it count. He needed something strong enough to break her concentration. And there was only one person he could think of who could do that.

As soon as his lips touched the holes at the top, the room folded in on itself. The stone walls disappeared, and the doors vanished, replaced with a wall of long, tangled vines that surrounded a peaceful glen. On the right was a hill with a familiar cabin on top. Smoke poured from the brick stack, its plume rising up into Abinayu's overreaching branches as they spread out across the quaint little paradise within Reed Marsh.

Ty concentrated on the music. Those in the trance never seemed to really hear it, as their eyes showed them things that weren't really there.

Mangora spun around. "What have you done?" Her eyes searched the surrounding area, but it was clear she could no longer see Ty. She turned and raised her hands, but as soon as she did, a familiar voice called her name.

"Hello, Mangora. I've been waiting a long time."

Mangora turned, and the breath caught in her throat. Douina was there, a warm smile on her face.

The melody shifted, filling the room with a sense of longing and regret, of something lost that needed to be found, of home.

Ty could feel the barrier go down behind him. He couldn't see it, being swept up in the vision himself as he concentrated on the music. He didn't know if the others were seeing the same thing he and Mangora were. He didn't see them anywhere inside the marsh witch's garden. He also had no idea what was happening with the arachnobe, but he didn't have time to look. All of his concentration was being poured into the music.

Mangora took a single step toward her sister. A metallic snap broke through the music, and she shrilled. Ty released the pipes, and Douina and the marsh paradise vanished as the walls of the cavern suddenly spun back into view.

Narendi was standing behind Mangora, having just placed her own durma collar around the witch's neck. Mangora dropped the shorlock and screamed.

"Watch out!" Ty shouted and dove at Narendi, pulling her out of the way just as Syglara dropped down where she'd been standing. Mangora leaped onto the spider's back, and they made a dash for the door.

Ty flung a ball of fire, but the spider was too quick, and it missed. Ayrion drew one of his swords, but instead of being able to swing at the creature, he was forced to jerk the old tinker couple out of the way as the great spider tore through the tunnel.

Ayrion rolled over from where he had snatched Zynora and Tameel out of the creature's way and tried swiping at the creature with his swords, but the spider was already out of reach.

The young wielder's brother grabbed his bow and arrow off the ground and pulled, but the witch was already inside the tunnel and disappearing around the corner. Behind him, the bald, dark-skinned girl had her spear out and was racing for the tunnel herself, but Ty called her back.

"Let her go! You won't catch her now."

Ayrion helped Zynora and Tameel back to their feet and rushed over to where Ozlin was already cradling the oracle in his lap. "How is she?"

Ozlin shook his head. "Not good."

"How did you do that, boy?" Tameel asked as he and Zynora hobbled over to see if they could be of any help. "One minute the witch was screaming at the doors, and the next she seemed to go eerily calm. We couldn't hear anything from inside the tunnel, but we could see you playing those pipes." He pointed at Ty's hand. "What sort of talisman is that?"

"I'll tell you about it later," Ty said and stuffed the pipes back in his jacket pocket. "Is there anything you can do for Kraea?"

"The oracle is in bad shape," Zynora said. "I need to see to her first. The best you can do for the creature is to pull the blade and seal the wound with something hot enough to melt the flesh." Zynora turned and placed her hand just under Angioma's nose, then she placed her ear against her chest and listened to her heart. She looked up at Ozlin. "She is very weak." She felt along the back of the seer's head, her hands coming away covered in the oracle's blood. "Give me something to wrap her head, quick."

The Imbatoo girl dug around in her bag, the same bag she had produced one of those magical collars from, and pulled out a blanket. She cut it into several long strips and handed them to Zynora, along with a jar of white cream.

"What is this?" Zynora asked.

"It is to help with pain," the girl said, then walked back over to where the young wielder and his brother were busy trying to help the creature.

Ozlin held the oracle as Zynora attempted to apply some of the paste, but not until after she had smelled it and rubbed it around on her fingers first. Once satisfied, she spread it on the back of Angioma's head and then tied off several of the thick strips.

"Will she make it?" Ozlin asked, nearly in tears.

Zynora looked up at Ayrion, and he could see the answer in her eyes. She didn't believe the oracle would survive. But that was exactly what Angioma had predicted. She knew this was her end, and she'd wanted to be here in this chamber for it. Ayrion lifted the old woman's pendant out from underneath the top of her neckline and placed it out for all to see, a symbol of who she was. A seer. An oracle.

Angioma's eyes flittered open.

"Oracle?" A bright grin spread across Ozlin's face, showing even through his thick red whiskers. "Oracle, you're alive. The Creator be praised."

She raised her head and smiled, even went so far as to give his beard a slight tug that had him chuckling. "Your people will need you now more than ever," she said, her voice weak. "Everything will change." Ozlin's smile grew pensive as Angioma then turned. "Is the Upakan here?"

Ayrion laid his hand on hers. "I'm here."

She grabbed her amulet and released a slow, almost sorrowful sigh as she pulled it off and handed it to him. "Give this to the white-haired boy. You'll know him when you see him. He will know what to do with it."

"What are you saying, Oracle?" Ozlin asked, realizing perhaps for the first time what the tenor in her voice meant. "This is the symbol of the oracle. It is for you and the one after you." He looked over at where the young wielder and his friends knelt beside their draakar. "Are you saying he will be our next oracle?"

Angioma raised her hand and laid it across his cheek, coughing as she did. "I'm saying you no longer need an oracle." Blood ran from the corner of her mouth, and she turned to Ayrion. "It is our time, Upakan. Sit me up, please."

Ozlin, with Ayrion and Bek's help, carried the oracle over to the side and placed her up against the cavern wall, facing the great doors on the other side. "I'm afraid I will never get the chance to find out what is beyond Harok Laos. I regret that most of all."

"Don't say that, Oracle," Ozlin said, crying openly now. "You will heal, you'll see."

She coughed, blood on her lips. "I'm afraid I am beyond healing, but I have been gifted with one last vision. Something I didn't know was even possible." She raised her hand. "Upakan. Come closer." Ayrion moved forward, letting her place her hands on his face. "I have been waiting for this day my entire life, never truly understanding my role in it until now." She smiled up at him. "My gift I leave with you. The gift of sight. Not of what is to come, but of what has been. Protect them," she said, and her eyes went milky white.

Ayrion screamed. He felt as though the inside of his head had been set on fire. Hundreds, thousands, millions of images flooded into his mind, every moment of every day of his life suddenly bursting into view. His memories, all of them, suddenly restored at once, and he found himself lying on the ground, rain-soaked mud under his hands, thunder and lightning flashing around him. Rhydan lay beside him, his eyes empty, blood pouring from his mouth. Ayrion looked up to see the archchancellor standing over the king's body with a blood-soaked sword, then the vision vanished.

Ayrion couldn't breathe, his chest feeling as though it had taken a direct bolt of lightning. Not even when Argon had ripped his soul from his body had he felt this much pain. He tried to scream once more as the memories flooded in, but he couldn't bring his mouth to open.

Eventually the pain subsided and the trembling ceased. He opened his eyes to find Angioma slumped to the side, Ozlin cradling her head in his arms and weeping. He felt a hand on his shoulder and turned to find Zynora, Tameel, and Bek standing behind him with anxious expressions on their faces, anxious but cautious as well.

He looked up at them. "I remember everything."

Chapter 87 | Ty

Y'S CONCENTRATION WAS momentarily jarred by whatever was happening with the swordsman and the old seer, but he couldn't let it stop him as he turned back to the draakar. If he didn't do something fast, Kraea was going to be joining her.

"Are you ready?" Breen asked.

Ty nodded and grabbed hold of Mangora's dagger, which had somehow struck just between Kraea's scales. Say this for the old witch, she'd proved herself to be just as efficient with a blade as with her magic.

"What are you going to do to stop the bleeding?"

"This," Ty said and raised his other hand, and it ignited in blue flame. With a deep breath and a quick prayer, he pulled the blade out. Kraea released a sad cry, then went still. By the lack of name-calling, she was clearly unconscious. With the blade free, blood poured from the wound. "Hold on, Kraea," he said, and placed his hand over the hole. Her scales were cold to the touch, except for where the blood was flowing. Those scales were quite warm.

He pressed his fire against her flesh, not sure how long he should keep it there or how much he should allow. The flesh wasn't sealing. Blood pumped between his fingers with each new weakened beat of her heart. "Why isn't this working?" Perhaps he needed more. Hotter. He closed his eyes and let the magic escape through his fingers, not just around the surface, but inside the wound as well.

Sure enough, the skin and scales began to mold, but instead of simply melting together, the skin seemed to be growing back, new scales forming where the other had been cut away.

Ty gasped in shock, barely able to keep the flames alive. Was this some new latent gift? Was he becoming a healer like Fraya?

Kraea jerked awake and roared, startling everyone, even those still huddled around the oracle. The draakar's eyes sparked for just a brief moment with what looked like a blue similar to Ty's flames. Then again, it could have just been the reflection of his hand in her eyes.

The draakar climbed to her feet and shook herself. She actually looked taller, if that was possible. She looked down at the wound. *What did you do to me?*

Ty moved to get a better look. "I don't know." He released his magic, and the flames died. "I pulled the knife free and then used the fire to help seal the wound to keep you from bleeding to death."

Both Breen and Narendi were there as well, studying the place where the dagger had been. "That's the best job of sealing I've ever seen," Breen said. "I can't even find where the wound was."

Ty looked at her. "How do you feel?"

She stood on her hind legs and even stretched out her sad little wings, which for some reason looked less pitiful than usual, the skin between the bones thicker, not quite so see-through. *"Stronger,"* she said, then looked around the cavern. *"Strong enough to get my teeth into that spider. Where'd it go?"*

"Afraid you're too late for that. The arachnobe is gone. So is Mangora."

"What?" Kraea snorted disapprovingly. *"I was looking forward to feasting on her flesh."*

"Afraid you'll have to wait until next time."

Someone behind them cleared their throat. "We seem to be getting only half the conversation," Bek said, and Ty stood.

"Don't feel bad," Breen added. "You get used to it."

"Really?"

Breen shook his head. "No."

Bek laughed. "I take it you are talking to the . . ." He pointed at Kraea.

"The draakar?" Ty smiled. "Yes." He would have offered introductions, but the others were still gathered quietly around the oracle's body, so he and Breen and Narendi walked over. "Is she . . ."

"Afraid so," Zynora said.

Ty sighed. "Maybe if I'd been quicker, I could have—"

"There's nothing you could have done."

"She's right," Ayrion said as he stood and turned to look at Ty. "She had foreseen this day since she was a child."

"She was a blessed one?" Narendi asked, rubbing her hand across the top of her bald head after removing her baka.

"She was a seer, if that is what you mean."

"What did she do to you?" Ty asked. "We heard you . . ." He didn't want to say scream, in case the swordsman took offense, but he didn't know how else to characterize it.

"She was returning something to me that had been lost."

Ty had no idea what he was talking about, and before he could ask, Ayrion walked over and held out the oracle's amulet.

"What's this?" The amulet was shaped like a great eye. Oddly appropriate for a seer, Ty thought.

"She said it was to be given to you."

"To me?" Ty took the necklace and stared at it a moment. "Why?"

The swordsman shrugged. "She didn't say, only that it was to be given to the white-haired boy, and that I would know who that was when I saw him. And since you are the only boy I've ever met with white hair, I would say she meant it for you. And trust me, for once, that is an actual fact I can remember."

Again, Ty had no idea what the man was talking about. He seemed to be speaking in riddles. Ty held up the amulet once more, admiring the way the crystal at its center made the eye sparkle. The hairs on his arms suddenly leaped to attention. "It can't be. You don't think?"

"It can't be what?" Breen asked, leaning forward to get a better look for himself.

Ty ran across the room to where Mangora had dropped the shorlock on the ground and picked it up. He looked at the eye, then at the key, then back at the eye, his heart pounding in his chest.

"What is it?" Breen asked, everyone rushing over to see what had gotten Ty so worked up. Even Ozlin, who had carefully laid the oracle down against the wall, joined the others in conference around Ty.

"Look!" Ty said and held up the shorlock and the amulet. "Notice anything?" The group stood there staring in silence. "I'll give you a hint. Look at the crystal." Still, no one said anything. "It's the same size and shape as the socket on the key."

Breen rubbed his hand back through his hair. "Yes, but if it's escaped your attention, that's not a bloodstone. Remember the jeweler's stone we left at the Live Market? It was red." He pointed at the oracle's amulet. "That's just a crystal. And unless you plan on killing a bunch of wielders and ripping out their magic, then I don't see how that is going to help us."

Ty drew his belt knife and carefully dug the crystal out of the eye.

Ozlin leaped forward, attempting to snatch the eye from Ty. "What do you think you're doing?"

Ayrion and Bek held him back. "The seer gave it to him for a reason," Ayrion said, restraining the gruff man until he calmed down.

Ty carefully removed the crystal and turned to place it in the key when it shot from his hand and snapped into place at the center of the shorlock.

Breen's face brightened. "Neither of the other two stones did that."

Ty smiled. "I can feel it."

"Don't just sit there," Breen said. "Try it out."

Ty handed what remained of the oracle's eye back to Ozlin. "It needs to stay with your people." Ozlin took the amulet with a grateful but forlorn nod, then followed Ty and the others over to the great stone doors at the back.

This is it, Ty mused. Everything he and Breen had been through culminated at this very moment. His heart was racing as he raised the key toward the doors and closed his eyes.

The key felt different this time. It didn't give him that sinking feeling in the pit of his gut, like something was about to go horribly wrong. With Mangora's bloodstone, the key had felt diseased, twisted, and dark. This time he felt none of that. However, unlike the last time, nothing seemed to be happening. The room didn't shake, the crystal didn't glow, the doors didn't light up with symbols. Something was wrong. He was missing something. What had he done differently the last time? Oh, wait.

He squeezed his fist where Mangora had cut him earlier and let the blood pool in his palm. "They don't call it a bloodstone for nothing." He turned his hand over and let the blood drip across the top of the crystal. As impossible as it might have been, the blood seeped into the stone, its insides shifting to a faint red as it did. This was it. It was finally working. He held up the key once more and closed his eyes.

Nothing happened.

The needles didn't turn. The stones didn't light up. The wind didn't howl. There wasn't so much as the smallest tremor under his feet. He lowered the key. "I don't understand. It was working before. What am I missing?"

"I am what you're missing," Kraea said from the other side of the room with an irritated growl.

Ty turned. "What do you mean, you're what I'm missing?"

Kraea sighed. *"It's a highly kept secret among the draakar that our blood is used in the creation of many such spells and artifacts. We have been hunted by the White Tower's wielders for centuries, which is why there are so few of us left."*

Ty relayed what Kraea had said to the rest of the group. "Then why didn't

Mangora use your blood for her bloodstone?"

"She did. She collected several vials of my blood while the three of you were still unconscious in the back of your wagon, after we first came through the mirror."

Ty didn't remember Mangora using any other blood specifically during her ceremony. Perhaps it had been in the cauldron she had used for her shard blade. Regardless, Ty relayed her words to the others again, then walked over to where Kraea had been lying earlier and reached down to the pool of blood that had collected in one of the stone depressions and dipped his finger in, but before he could place any of it on the crystal, Breen spoke up.

"If this works, you know what that means, don't you?"

Ty turned.

"It means we didn't fail the last test. It means we were never meant to find the bloodstone in the first place. We were meant to find Kraea. Think about it. The final test was compassion, which we wouldn't have had if we had simply taken the stone and run. And if we had taken the stone and left Kraea behind, who's to say the key would have ever worked."

"If that were the case," Ty said. "Then how would the wizards have known there would be a stone at the Live Market, or that there would have been a draakar there for auction, or that it would have required using compassion to make the pieces fall into place for us to be willing to leave that stone behind? For that matter, how would they have known the Live Market would have been taking place during the very week we showed up? To top it off, how would they have known the oracle would have had the perfect-shaped crystal to fit the shorlock?"

Breen thought a moment. "I guess the same way the oracle knew to give the crystal to you. She was a seer. I'm sure the wizards had seers as well, which allowed them to set this whole thing up."

"Angioma told me that the amulet had been passed down through her family for many generations," Ayrion said, "from one seer to the next. Their job was to guard it and this hall. But she never knew why. If what you say is true, then it would only make sense that these wizards you speak of would have hidden the final piece here, waiting on the day when the right person came to claim it."

Ty pressed his thumbs to the side of his head. He hated prophecies and foretellings. "Still, it all depends on whether this works or not." He leaned over and pressed his finger once more into Kraea's blood, then rubbed it across the stone. Like his, her blood immediately soaked into the key. The three stones lit up, and the three needles began to spin. "I think it's working."

A strong wind filled the cavern, swirling about their heads as he made his way back over to the stone doors, this time with Kraea at his side. Ty held up the key, and the symbols on the two enormous chunks of carved stone flared to life around the outer edges. The crystal at the center of the key was glowing and swirling, his blood intermingling with Kraea's, turning it a deep red.

The mountain began to shake, and the trough of fire surrounding the room suddenly extinguished as the great doors opened outward and light poured through from the other side.

It was the breaking of a new dawn.

Ty and Breen released their night sight as they stepped through the back side of the mountain to find themselves on a shelf overlooking a great open valley below, covered in snow. This had to be the Valley of Needrin that Mangora had mentioned the previous day.

On the far northeastern side, Ty thought he recognized several of the cliff faces, each with a set of falls cascading down to form the start of a small river that flowed south across the valley, disappearing into the trees on the other side, leading into the southernmost peaks.

"It's beautiful," Zynora said.

"It is," Ty agreed, but there was something odd about the mountains, something missing. "Where's the wizard's keep? It should be right there." He pointed to the distant rise where great portions of the mountainside had been dug out, flat open shelves that lay bare. "I remember seeing this place in a vision Nyalis showed me, but there were great constructs and towers all through the mountainside. They're gone."

"Perhaps it was torn down during the Wizard Wars," Tameel said.

Ayrion shook his head. "If that were the case, we would see rubble, but there's nothing there at all."

"Only one way to find out." Breen started for what looked like a set of stairs on the right side of the small bluff, leading down to a small forest below that bordered most of the surrounding mountains.

Ty followed his brother down, Kraea flanking his left while Narendi, having wrapped her baka back around her head, took up a protective position on the right. Two new women in Ty's life, and he didn't know what to do with either one, other than to tread carefully, as both seemed quite opinionated and each as strong-willed as the other.

They reached the bottom of the stairs and waited for the others. Zynora and Tameel needed the most help, but Ayrion and Bek were there to lend a hand. Ozlin brought up the rear, the oracle's amulet hanging from his neck as he gently stroked the outer gold casing with his fingers.

Cautiously, the nine started through the trees, everyone keeping their eyes and ears open for any sign of danger, but other than the howl of the wind through the bare limbs, there didn't appear to be any other signs of life. The entire valley seemed as though it were in a deep slumber, waiting to be woken.

Leaving the forest, they carefully started across the valley floor, weapons in hand, eyes darting about as they kept in tight formation. It took a good part of the day to make it across the valley, mostly because of the slower pace they maintained for the old tinker couple and out of an abundance of caution. If there was one thing Ty had learned through this experience, it was to trust nothing and to be ready for anything.

They reached the far side and stopped at a road that ran from the trees on their right along the riverbank, all the way to the mountains just ahead. It was very obvious from this distance that the formation of the mountains on this side were quite different from the rest. Their shape was not a natural formation, and they were certainly missing whatever they had been cut away for. Beautiful waterfalls lined the back of the cliffs, dropping onto various shelves that pooled and formed dozens of smaller falls that eventually worked their way to the bottom of the valley, where they joined to create the river that ran south along the road they were presently standing on. Some of the slower-moving falls had ice forming around the outer edges that, when the sun's rays hit just right, lit up most of the valley.

It was breathtaking.

"What now?" Ayrion asked, keeping an eye on the valley behind them.

Breen looked at Ty. "Try the key."

Ty was already in the process of fishing it out from under his tunic. "Stand back." The others quickly moved behind him, all but Kraea, who didn't seem all that interested in following his orders. Ty held up the key and waited for something to happen.

As expected, nothing.

"I do not think it worked," Narendi said.

The insides of the bloodstone were still swirling, so the magic must have still been there. "Perhaps it's not meant for this."

Breen hmphed. "I doubt very highly the wizards would have gone to so much trouble just to open a set of doors. Didn't Nyalis tell you what to do when you got here?"

Ty wrinkled his nose. "What do you think?"

Breen shook his head. "Yeah, that's what I thought. A lot of good he is. If all the wizards acted as he did, it's no wonder they went extinct."

"In his defense, he did tell me that he didn't know much about how the key worked. Apparently, he wasn't exactly on the best terms with the wizard council at the time."

Breen chuckled. "No surprise there."

Ty stared at the shorlock. His brother was right about one thing. As much work and forethought and planning that had gone into hiding the pieces of this key and setting up the tests, he doubted it had been done just to get him to the finish line with no way to cross over. Lifting the key with both hands, he closed his eyes. Instead of letting it do all the work, this time he pushed a little of his own magic into the artifact, the same web of feelers he'd used in the underground lake and again in the desert.

The key was strange to the touch. It almost felt . . . alive. He pushed a little harder, letting his magic flow more freely, unhindered by self-doubt and self-preservation, openly giving himself over to it. He could feel something waiting just below the surface, waiting to be released.

"What are you?" He could feel Kraea in the back of his mind turning to look at him, but he hadn't been talking to her. He was talking to the key. *"Tell me what to do."*

"You already know what to do," something replied. At first, he thought it might have been Kraea, but it wasn't her voice. This voice was deep, ageless.

It called to him in such a way he couldn't refuse. It was all-consuming. It wanted him. No. It wanted to bond with him. Ty didn't even pause to consider who or what was reaching out to him, or whether or not the voice could be trusted. He knew it could be. It was instinctual.

Ty wanted to bond with it. He needed to. It was like a piece of him had been missing all along, a piece he hadn't even known existed, but now that he knew it was there, he couldn't live without it. It drew him in like moth to flame, and he couldn't stop it. He didn't want to stop it. With a deep breath, he turned himself over to it, and not knowing why, he released his fire into the key.

The shorlock flared to life, and Ty could feel himself being drawn in, swimming through a stream of his own magic, everything and everyone seemingly disappearing around him. The stone at the center brightened, blinding everything as it engulfed the mountainside in a light so powerful it overtook the sun.

He could hear his mind screaming as the magic coursed through him. Searing pain ravaged both arms as the markings stretched all the way down. He'd never unleashed this much magic before, not even during his battle with Mangora. It felt as though his entire life's essence was being given in exchange, and for a brief moment he hesitated, afraid that the reason Nyalis had not told him everything was because he knew it was going to require Ty's life in the process.

Ty could feel himself dying. His legs buckled, and in the back of his mind he could hear Kraea shouting for him to stop, but he couldn't. He no longer had control. He couldn't release the key even if he had wanted to, which he didn't. It was now a part of him. All across the mountainside, buildings began to materialize, much in the same way things appeared or disappeared when he played his flute.

One moment he'd be standing in the common room at the East Inn, then, next, the walls and floors and ceiling would be transformed into trees and grass and open sky.

The mountain shelves filled with towers and bridges, buildings and courtyards. White stone spires and domes rose into the sky, the water moving throughout the entire construct, revealing a beautiful type of symmetry, as though the buildings had been there all along, but just out of sight. The light continued to pour down the mountainside, reaching the river and continuing even farther as more buildings popped up on either side of the road, several forming around a large holding yard to the north with strange-looking ships that appeared to be docked on dry land.

Ty didn't know how much longer he could hold out as his fingers clutched the sides of the key, white knuckles completely numb from the strain. What little bit of life he clung to was nearly gone. Just as the last few remaining drops of his magic began to dissipate, the light faded, once again returning to the key and winking from existence, leaving him kneeling in the snow, barely able to catch his next breath.

Breen caught him as he tipped, and the key slipped from his fingers. Breen picked it up and hung it back around Ty's neck.

"Here, eat this," the old tinker woman said and stuffed something in Ty's mouth. He chewed slowly and then swallowed. Whatever it lacked in taste, it made up for in effect, since he could once again feel his own limbs. Breen let him lie there for a while before helping him to his feet. They joined the others in speechless awe, gazing upon the most wonderous spectacle any of them had probably ever seen.

In fact, they were so preoccupied with trying to take it all in that they didn't notice they weren't alone.

"*Who's that?*" Kraea asked.

"What?" Ty followed her gaze and spotted a robed individual heading through a gateway on the other side of the river. By the time the others had spotted the person, he was halfway across the bridge. Ayrion moved to the front, his deadly blades already in hand. Bek and Ozlin were quick to follow, weapons out and at the ready. Even Narendi felt it necessary to move forward, her spear in hand as she raised the scarf of her baka.

"Wait!" Ty said, recognizing the long white beard hanging down the front of the man's robes. "It's Nyalis." Breen helped Ty to the front, and they both started for the bridge, the others moving up behind.

Nyalis pulled back the hood of his robe and raised his arms with a bright smile. "Well, my boy, it seems my faith in you has not gone unrewarded. I knew you had it in you." Nyalis stopped at the edge of the bridge and waited, leaning against his large staff to steady his feet. "Welcome to the Valley of Needrin and the Wizarding Keep of Aero'set." He looked at the weary group of travelers behind him, studying each in turn as they stopped a few feet away. "I see you have acquired some new friends," he said as he walked over and placed a hand on Ty's shoulder.

An abrupt jolt flooded Ty's body, and the exhaustion vanished. It was followed closely by a distinct chill that ran down his injured arm, and as soon as it stopped, the pain was gone as well. In fact, he felt strong enough to take Mangora on all over again.

Nyalis smiled, his face looking rather gaunt and weary. "And I see our young Master Breen here ignored my advice and joined you on your quest after all. But who are the rest of your companions?" He turned to the others, starting first with the swordsman. "Ah, no need for introductions here. Even hidden underneath the garb of a tinker I would recognize that bearing. Am I right, Ayrion, son of the Upaka, Guardian Protector of Elondria? You are a long way from Aramoor and your king, are you not?"

"*The* Guardian Protector?" Breen asked, turning to look at the swordsman. Even Ozlin appeared shocked. The two tinkers and the trapper didn't seem quite so taken aback by the revelation.

"How do you know me?"

Nyalis chuckled. "I am Nyalis, First Wizard of Aldor. Do you not think that I keep up with the comings and goings of those in power? We have actually met on several occasions, not that you would remember. I've had my eye on you for some years now, but we can discuss that at a later time." He looked at Narendi. "And I see we even have royalty with us today. Is that not right, Princess Narendi Unsala?"

The others all turned to look at Narendi, and she quickly removed her baka. She looked as taken aback as Ayrion had. "How do you know of me?"

Nyalis smiled. "The Imbatoo are a very hospitable people. I visit when I get the chance. Do you not recognize me?"

Narendi took a step forward, and her eyes widened. "Iridanus?"

Nyalis smiled. "One and the same. It appears my lessons weren't for naught."

Narendi turned to Ty, excited. "I told you of a man who taught me the language of your people in exchange for food and shelter. This was that man."

Ty looked at Nyalis, dumbfounded, but Nyalis simply smiled and turned to Ozlin. More importantly, he looked at the amulet around his neck. "I am sorry for your loss. The people of your village have a very respected history, watching over the oracles and keeping the stone safe. You have served the wizards well and will be rewarded for that service."

"I am Ozlin Beartooth, magistrate of Upper Wellhollow. My people have suffered greatly at the hands of the White Tower, and I look for no reward other than to keep them safe."

Nyalis nodded. "Your sacrifice has been great indeed, as has many others. If it is protection you seek, you will have it, and not only for yourselves, but for all those across Aldor who find themselves at odds with the Tower. Aero'set is a place of refuge, a stronghold against the coming darkness."

"And what is this coming darkness you speak of?" Zynora asked, diverting Nyalis's attention away from Ozlin.

Nyalis smiled. "The fires of the Rhivanni have always been open to the wayward traveler, one of the few peoples still willing to accept those of the ven'ae, and none so much as the Dar clan," he said, staring intently at the copper bracelets on their wrists.

Ty noted that Nyalis didn't answer the woman's question.

"I am Tameel," the older man said, his arm still around his wife for her support, "and this is my wife, Zynora. We are honored to stand in the presence of the First Wizard."

"It is I who am honored. The foretelling of your arrival was recorded centuries ago."

"Our arrival?" Zynora looked at her husband as if not quite sure she had heard Nyalis correctly. "Are you saying the wizards who built this place knew that one day the two of us would be here?"

Nyalis smiled. "All of you, in fact. But best we save that for another time as well." He turned to Bek, and the trapper actually bowed.

"My name is Bek, sir. I am but a humble trapper from Belvin."

"Yes, I heard of the events that took place in your city recently. Nasty business, Argon. One of the remnants of the old guard that should never have been allowed to awaken. The Tower is toying with things they do not understand."

Ty had no idea what they were all talking about, but before he could ask who Argon was, Nyalis turned to Kraea.

"And who do we have here?"

Kraea trotted over to stand in front of the wizard and bowed her head. *"I'm Laansilvic'kraeatori'dulfeyn, daughter of Wuntara'solniici'ruvaraak."*

"Her name is Kraea," Ty said.

"So I heard."

"You can hear her too?"

"I'm a wizard, Ty. Of course I can hear her." He looked at Kraea. "You have a noble heritage, my dear. It is a pleasure to meet you." He pursed his lips. "You are quite young, though, to be on your own."

Ty could feel Kraea's sorrow through their link.

"I recently lost my mother."

"I'm sorry to hear that." Nyalis walked over and inspected her horns, then placed a hand on top of her head and closed his eyes.

"What's he doing?" she asked Ty.

Nyalis smiled and removed his hand from her head. "I see you have already linked with the boy. Good."

Ty shared a confused look with Kraea as she stepped back to stand beside him.

Nyalis turned and addressed the entire group. "I'm sure you have many, many questions to ask, and I assure you those questions will be answered in good time, but I believe the first place to start would be to explain what has just taken place here."

"It was in Y'tarra, wasn't it?" Ty asked.

"Or something close to it," Nyalis said with a proud grin. "Very good."

"Y'tarra?" Ayrion, along with most of the others, looked confused. "I've never heard of it."

"And why would you?" Nyalis said. "It is a place that is neither here nor there."

Ty looked at his brother, and they both rolled their eyes. The others simply exchanged confused looks until someone was finally brave enough to ask. That someone was Narendi.

"I do not understand your words."

Ty jumped in before Nyalis confused them further. "The word Y'tarra means *the In-Between*. It is a place that exists between the realm of man and the realm of the Fae."

"How is something like that possible?" Ayrion asked.

Nyalis chuckled. "With magic, of course. How else?" The wizard then went on to expound what he had already revealed to Ty concerning the wizard's keep and how it had been hidden away through the use of the shorlock, and the decision to divide the key into four parts and hide them across Aldor, until such time as it was needed.

He also clarified how it was actually the faeries who had first built the keep, giving aid to the wizards in its creation, during the time of the Faerie Wars. And it was faerie blood that was needed in order to get the shorlock to work.

Everyone looked at Ty, several of the group going so far as to take a few steps back. Bek pointed at Ty with one of his hatchets. "Are you saying that he's a faerie?" He looked Ty over. "Huh, I thought they would look different." The swordsman seemed the only one brave enough to stand his ground, though he did keep a keen eye on Ty.

"He is half faerie," Nyalis said. "A faeling."

Ty was growing very uncomfortable with all the sudden attention.

"And what's to keep this place from suddenly disappearing as soon as we step inside?" Ozlin asked, looking warily across the river at the first of the towers.

"That key," Nyalis said, pointing to the artifact hanging from Ty's neck. "Which reminds me. We will need to place it in the lower vault for safekeeping." He stared at the key a moment longer, then turned to the group and smiled. "Exciting times ahead, my friends, exciting times indeed." He turned and started over the bridge. "Come, I have much to show you. You will be the first non-wizards to walk these halls in a thousand years." He glanced back over his shoulder at Ty. "I look forward to beginning your training."

That thought, more than any other, had Ty's heart racing.

While the others anxiously followed the old wizard across the bridge, Ty walked about halfway and stopped. Breen, Narendi, and Kraea joined him at the rail and stared out over the water as it coursed through and around the Aero'set compound. Ty finally turned and looked at Breen, unable to hide his excitement any longer, tears burning the corner of his eyes.

"We did it. It almost seems like a dream, doesn't it? Everything we've been through to get us to right here. Reed Marsh and Douina. Tirana and Karpaath. The maze and the maze monster."

"The wall of fire," Breen added. "And the underground lake."

"The monster in the lake," Ty interjected. "The desert. Being saved by the Imbatoo. The orms."

"Wearing my bracelet," Narendi made sure to point out. "Also, Zwaneri a Wakale."

Ty nodded. "The ancient ruins that weren't ruins."

"The Riverlands," Breen continued, "with the great trees and the Live Market."

Narendi hugged her satchel to her chest. "My jewels."

"Me saving your life," Kraea piped in.

"That's not how I remember it," Ty said, and Kraea hmphed.

Breen frowned. "Being captured by Mangora and the making of the bloodstone."

Ty shivered. "Don't remind me."

"The avalanche, and our escape from the cages," Narendi said.

"The dark wielder I ate under the cages," Kraea added with a gruff chuckle.

Ty reached for the shorlock hanging from his neck and looked at each of them in turn. He couldn't believe how much they had been through and survived. "I couldn't have done any of it without you," he said, tears in his eyes. There weren't words enough to express his gratitude for what they had done for him. "Look what we've accomplished."

All four turned and gazed beyond the archway on the far side of the bridge at the wonders that lay beyond. Nyalis was right. There were exciting days ahead.

The End of: *The Four-Part Key*

Book Three of
The Aldoran Chronicles

Dear Reader,

I HOPE YOU enjoyed this third book in the Aldoran Chronicles series. If you found the story entertaining and would like to see more, then please consider helping me reach that goal by leaving a quick review on **Amazon**.

Reviews are very important. They help encourage other readers to try the book while at the same time showing Amazon that the book is worth promoting. Reviews don't need to be long or involved, just a sentence or two that tells people what you liked about the book in order to help readers know why they might like it too.

Thank you in advance!

Want to be notified when the next book comes out? If so, go to this address: *www.michaelwisehart.com/join-the-wielder-council*

Author Note

OVE FANTASY MUSIC? Stop by the SHOP and take a listen. Over 30 minutes of original fantasy score, inspired by The Aldoran Chronicles. You can also grab the digital hi-resolution images for each of the maps, as well as the character art.

« *www.michaelwisehart.com/shop* »

For the Latest News
« *www.michaelwisehart.com* »
« *facebook.com/MichaelWisehart.author* »

Acknowledgments

I THANK GOD for the doors and windows He has allowed to open in order for me to reach this point.

I want to thank my parents, *Mickey and Julie Wisehart*, for their unending loyalty, encouragement, and support over the years. None of this would be possible without you. Love you both.

I want to thank my Author Team, whose endless talent, time, and dedication have made this project possible:

AUTHOR TEAM

I want to thank my cover illustrator and sister, whose imagination and talent have given us our first glimpse of the famed shorlock of Aero'set—*Janelle Wisehart*

I want to thank my cartographer, who patiently worked with me and my continual need to tweak things, and still managed to produce one incredible map for the capital city of Easthaven—*Elwira Pawlikowska*

I want to thank my cartographer, who managed to take a maze of jumbled ideas and turn them into the capital city of Aramoor—*RenflowerGrapx*

I want to thank my content editor, who has spent countless hours advising me on the proper structure of my thoughts—*Nathan Hall*

I want to thank my line editor, who managed to take a floundering script and turn it into something readable—*Danae Smith*

I want to thank my copy editor, whose careful eyes have made my book shine—*Crystal Watanabe*

I want to thank my *Beta Team*, who took precious time out of their busy schedule to suffer through the first draft in order to leave such valuable feedback as to help me make this book worth reading.

About the Author

ICHAEL WISEHART graduated with a bachelor's degree in business before going back to school for film and starting his own production company. As much as he enjoyed his work with film, the call of writing a novel got the better of him, and on April 14, 2014, he started typing the first words of what would become two epic fantasy series: The Aldoran Chronicles and the Street Rats of Aramoor.

He currently lives and writes in North Georgia.

Glossary of Terms

Months of the Year

1. **Aèl** [*ay-el*] First month of the year.
2. **Sòl** [*soul*] Second month of the year.
3. **Nùwen** [*noo-win*] Third month of the year.
4. **Manù** [*mah-noo*] Fourth month of the year.
5. **Toff** [*toff*] Fifth month of the year.
6. **Kwàn** [*quon*] Sixth month of the year.
7. **Nor** [*nor*] Seventh month of the year.
8. **Èldwin** [*el-dwin*] Eighth month of the year.
9. **Kùma** [*koo-muh*] Ninth month of the year.
10. **Akòsi** [*uh-kah-see*] Tenth month of the year.
11. **Èshan** [*ee-shon*] Eleventh month of the year.
12. **Zùl** [*zool*] Twelfth month of the year.

New Character Glossary

Introductory characters not mentioned in prior books

Aaban [*aye-bun*] One of Lord Endric's guards, keeping watch over the stables.

Abinayu [*ă-bin-ah-yoo*] The great tree and guardian of Reed Marsh. A former faerie.

Angioma [*an-jee-o-muh*] Blind oracle to the mountain folk of Wellhollow.

Atiena [*ah-tee-in-uh*] One of the Imbatoo Wazeri who records their histories and prophecies. One of the two who did not attack Ty. Took over as the head of the Wazeri after Mshindu's death.

Aylin [*ay-lin*] Husband of Misha. Owns a chandlery in the town of Minotha.

Baudry [*bod-dree*] An old, sickly woman in Easthaven with no hair.

Bella [*bell-uh*] One of Tomos's hounds sent to track Ferrin and his friends.

Dalibor [*dal-i-bor*] Head of the Live Market. Tall and thick in the chest. Wears all green, including his wide-brim hat.

Delise Cantanil [*duh-leese/can-tuh-nill*] Avid shopper at Aylin and Misha's chandlery in Minotha. Always the first to show up on Fifthday.

Diawandy Unsala [*dee-uh-won-dee / oon-sah-lah*] King of the Imbatoo, a tribe of nomads living in the Wengoby Desert. Father of Narendi Unsala.

Douina [*doo-ee-nuh*] The Marsh Witch who protects one of the traveling mirrors. Mangora's twin sister.

Dunya [*dune-yuh*] Daughter of Lenka, a clothing merchant inside the Riverlands.

Eljin [*el-jin*] Bulradoer who fought Ferrin in Lord Harlin's bedchamber.

Endric Talmanes [*en-drick / tal-mainz*] Lord Talmanes's son. In charge of Minotha while his father is away. Exacts a levy.

Finnly [*finn-ly*] Jailer stationed outside the Sidaran Barracks' cells. Holds the rank of sergeant.

Fowlin [*foul-in*] Weaponsmith in Woodvale.

Garmon [*gar-min*] A carpenter in Minotha.

Hanani [*huh-nah-nee*] Wife of Ozlin Beartooth.

Hanley [*han-lee*] A seamstress in Storyl.

Hussen [*hoo/sen*] One of Lord Endric's guards, keeping watch over the stables.

Iridanus [*ear-ruh-dah-nus*] The name Nyalis took when visiting with the Imbatoo while teaching Narendi how to speak in the Aldoran tongue.

Isha [*ee-shuh*] Old Imbatoo healer. Known for her healing cream.

Josiah Respuel [*jo-si-uh / res-pyool*] Father of Barthol Respuel. Former ship's bosun in the king's navy.

Kovian [*ko-vee-un*] Cobbler in the Riverlands.

Kuwa [*koo-wuh*] Serves the seat of the magistrate in Upper Wellhollow.

Leflin [*lef-lin*] Son of Tomos the blacksmith.

Lendrick [*len-drick*] Young sailor from the *Wind Binder* who went with Ferrin and Ismara into Rhowynn.

Lenka [*leen-kuh*] Shopkeeper of fine clothing in the Riverlands.

Madam Moira [*moy-ruh*] The owner of a noted brothel in Rhowynn.

Marzell [*mar-zell*] Female tavernkeeper in Minotha. Goes by Marz. Flirts with Ayrion. She wears a patch over her left eye.

Maskima [*muh-skee-muh*] King Diawandy Unsala's third wife.

Merrill Treehorn [*may-vun*] Made-up name by Myron to sign in with at the White Pheasant in Storyl.

Misha [*mee-shuh*] Wife of Aylin. Owns a chandlery in the town of Minotha.

Mshindu [*muh-shin-doo*] Head of the Wazeri, keepers of the scrolls, and recorder of the Imbatoo histories.

Myrtle [*mer-tle*] A woman who is part of the cleaning staff at the Beetle Bark Inn.

Narendi Unsala [*nuh-ren-dee / oon-sah-lah*] Princess of the Imbatoo, a tribe of nomads living in the Wengoby Desert. Daughter of King Diawandy Unsala. She is a water diviner, also known as a voda.

Nishka [*nish-kuh*] Elderly innkeeper at the Beetle Bark Inn in the Riverlands.

Noklis [*nah-cliss*] Captain of the Easthaven patrollers.

Nola [*no-luh*] Enormous she-wolf that travels with Ferrin, Rae, Suri, and Myron. Her name means Moon Dancer. She is even bigger than a hor'hound. Born in the Frozen North. Frostborn.

Nyota [*nee-oh-tuh*] King Diawandy Unsala's first wife. Mother of Narendi.

Orlis [*or-liss*] Old guard standing watch outside Sidaran Barracks' main building.

Ozlin Beartooth [*oz-lin*] Patriarch of the original Wellhollow. Protector of the Unwalked Path. Magistrate. Wears a ceremonial bearskin.

Paran [*puh-ron*] One of the Upakans contracted to guard Lord Endric Talmanes.

Pinfagan Tulick [*pin-fay-gun / too-lick* Pin for short. A young stableboy who works at the White Pheasant in Storyl.

Rinson [*rin-son*] Owner of a field that Ty's mother used to pick wildflowers from.

Safiri [*suh-fear-ee*] Daughter of King Diawandy Unsala, by his third wife, Maskima. Half sister to Narendi. She is also a water diviner like Narendi.

Sarren Tulick [*sare-en / too-lick*] Sister of Pinfagan and keeper of the books at the White Pheasant inn in Storyl.

Siranu [*sir-on-oo* One of the Upakans contracted to guard lord Endric Talmanes.

Taggert [*tag-ert* First apprentice to Bulradoer Rukar. Captured Ferrin in Storyl.

Talmanes [*tal-mainz* Minor Sidaran Lord on the Sidaran Assembly. Owns the land Minotha is built on.

Taturov [*tă-tur-ah-v*] A wealthy buyer at the Live Market in the Riverlands.

Tiernan [*tee-air-nun*] Commander of the Sidaran Lancers. Stationed in Easthaven.

Tippi [*tip-ee*] The name Suri gave her pinecone.

Tirana [*ter-ah-nuh*] Leader of Karpaath, a cursed village outside the Maze. Been alive for centuries and waiting for someone to claim the shorlock so they can die.

Tofflin [*toe-fluh*] Ferryman outside of Wellhollow.

Tomos [*toe-muss*] Blacksmith in Woodvale.

Torshuga [*tor-shoo-guh*] An old name ascribed to Aylin during his younger years when he fought back the Cylmaran brigades that had come to drive the Rhivanni from Aldor. It means *the man who wouldn't stop.*

Trick [*trik*] Friend of Pin in Storyl who helps keep watch on those coming and going within the city.

Tulicks [*too-licks*] Owners of the White Pheasant inn in Storyl.

Waseme [*wah-see-me*] King Diawandy Unsala's second wife. Tallest of the three.

Witler [*wit-ler*] Dakaran's royal dresser. An older man with bent back and spectacles that has been dressing Dakaran since he was a child.

Stop by and visit:
« www.michaelwisehart.com »

Printed in Great Britain
by Amazon

30118295R00456